Encyclopedia of Scientific Quantities and Units of Measurement

VOLUME 1

DICTIONARY OF SCIENTIFIC QUANTITIES

Including Dimensionless Quantities with Summary tables

And Tables of Physical and Mathematical Constants

D.S.Dawoud

A.G.Batte

Dedication

To my grandkids:

Adam, Bahya, Louisa

Susana and Gabriel

Dawoud

This volume is dedicated in all sincerity

All my family members

Arthur Godfrey Batte

About this book

The book in the hands of the reader represents the first volume of "Encyclopedia of Scientific Quantities and Units of Measurements". The encyclopedia consists of three volumes representing together the most comprehensive encyclopedia of Physical quantities and units of measurement. The three volumes of the encyclopedia are:

Volume I-Dictionary of Scientific Quantities.

- Consists of more than 1000 Entries
- Each entry consists of:
    o Name of quantity
    o Symbol
    o Definition
    o Units
    o Dimensions
    o Cross-reference

Volume II - Dictionary of Scientific Units of Measurements:

Consists of 2400 entries

Volume III: Tables of Conversion

More than 400 conversion tables arranged:

- Alphabetically
- By Category

Volume I and Volume II are dictionaries that give definitions for the entities that form the dictionary. Some rules are considered while arranging the entities. The reader must be aware of the rules to be able to use the dictionary easily. We are going to start this general introduction by presenting such rules.

About the authors

Bio: Professor Dawoud Shenouda Dawoud

Prof. Dawoud Shenouda Dawoud has a BSc (1965) and MSc (1969) from Cairo University in Communication Engineering. He completed his Ph.D. in Russia in 1973 in the field of Computer hardware, where he succeeded in owning 3 Patents in the field of designing new types of memory, which was the beginning of the FPGAs. In 1984, he was promoted to full Professor at the Egyptian Academy of Science and Technology, National Electronic Research Institute. During the period from 1973 to 1990, he supervised more than 5 PhDs and 15 MSc degrees, all of them focused in the fields of computer and embedded system designs. During the period from 1990-1999, he established the Faculty of Engineering at the University of Botswana. During this period, he supervised 3 PhDs and 7 MSc degrees. In the year 2000, he became Professor of Computer Engineering and Head of the Computer Engineering Department at the University of KwaZulu Natal, Durban, South Africa. For 10 years, he supervised research in the field of Security of Mobile Ad hoc Networks. He supervised 2 PhDs and many MSc degrees in this field and published more than 30 papers. During the same period, he was visiting the National University of Rwanda to run an MSc programme in Communication. He supervised about 15 MSc students during these 4 years before moving to the National University of Rwanda in 2010 to become the Dean of the Faculty of Engineering.

In 2011 he moved to Uganda, where he became the Dean of the Faculty of Engineering at the International University of East Africa (IUEA), where he currently remains. During this time, he also served as the Vice Chancellor of IUEA for a period of 3 years.

Across his career, he has published over 200 Journal and Conference papers, as well as books in the fields of computer engineering, microcontroller system design, embedded system design and

Security of Mobil Ad hoc Networks.

Bio of: Dr. A.G. Batte

Arthur Godfrey Batte, originally from Kampala, Uganda, began his educational journey by graduating from Makerere College School in 1998. He continued his academic pursuits by enrolling at Makerere University in 1999, where he successfully earned a B.Sc. in Geology in 2003, followed by an M.Sc. in Geology in 2006.

In 2007, he expanded his knowledge base by obtaining a Master's degree in Geoinformation Science and Earth Observations from the International Institute for Geoinformation Science and Earth Observations I.T.C. in the Netherlands. His quest for knowledge continued, leading him to complete a Ph.D. in Natural Sciences from the University of Frankfurt, Frankfurt am Main, Germany, in 2012.

Arthur Godfrey Batte embarked on a career in academia and research when he joined the Department of Geology and Petroleum Studies at Makerere University in 2008. Over the years, he has been actively involved in teaching various courses in Petroleum Geophysics, Reservoir Geophysics, Remote Sensing, and G.I.S., both at the undergraduate and postgraduate levels. His dedication and expertise in the field led to his progression from a lecturer and researcher at Makerere University from 2012 to 2018 to his current position as a Senior Lecturer and the Head of the Department.

Throughout his career, he has played a significant role in mentoring and supervising graduate students in the fields of geology, petroleum, and geophysics. Arthur Godfrey Batte has made substantial contributions to the scientific community, with a focus on Seismology and Hydrogeology. His research has primarily revolved around using seismic data to gain insights into the Earth's dynamics and internal structure. Additionally, he has actively participated in the review process for numerous peer-reviewed scientific journals and has been engaged in national university curriculum reviews.

Table of Contents

General

G.1 Quantities and Units

In like manner, there were natural measures of quantity, such as fathoms, cubits, and inches, taken from the proportion of the human body, that were once in use with every nation. But by a little observation, they found that one man's arm was longer or shorter than another's and that one was not to be compared with the other, and therefore wise men who attended to these things would endeavor to fix upon some more accurate measure, that equal quantities might be of equal values. Their method became absolutely necessary when people came to deal in many commodities and in great quantities of them.

(Adam Smith – 1763)

Adam Smith is talking about the cultural origin of the traditional units, which were more organic and less logical than the life needed. He talked upon the need for modern units as SI units.

To investigate any physical phenomena, we must make measurements, communicate them to others, and record them in a way that will be understandable in the future. To do so, a system of quantities and units is required. Measurement is a comparison process in which the value of a quantity is expressed as the product of a value and a unit; that is,

$$\{quantity\} = \{numerical\ value\} \times \{unit\}$$

where the unit is an agreed-upon value of a quantity of the same type. The concept of a quantity such as a length is independent of the associated unit; the length is the same whether it is measured in feet or Meters. A standard is a physical realization of the definition, with an agreed-upon value to be used as a reference.

(Jeff Flowers-2004)

G.1.1   Meaning of Quantity

In English, the word "quantity" means the amount or number of something, especially that can be measured (Cambridge Dictionary). A quantity, in the general sense, is a property ascribed to phenomena, bodies, or substances that can be quantified for or assigned to a particular phenomenon, body, or substance. Examples are mass and electric charge.

A **quantity, in a particular sense,** is a quantifiable or assignable property ascribed to a particular phenomenon, body, or substance. Examples are the mass of the moon and the electric charge of the proton.

A **physical quantity** is a physical property of a material or system that can be quantified by measurement. A physical quantity can be expressed as a *value*, which is the algebraic multiplication of a ' Numerical value ' and a ' Unit '. For example, the physical quantity of mass can be quantified as '32.3 kg ', where '32.3' is the numerical value and 'kg' is the unit. A **physical quantity**, accordingly, can be used in the mathematical equations of science and technology.

A physical quantity, as mentioned by Jeff Flowers, possesses at least two characteristics in common.

- Numerical magnitude.
- Units

A **unit** is a particular physical quantity defined and adopted by convention, with which other particular quantities of the same kind are compared to express their value.

The **value of a physical quantity** is the quantitative expression of a particular physical quantity as the product of a number and a unit, the number being its numerical value. Thus, the numerical value of a particular physical quantity depends on the unit in which it is expressed.

For example, the value of the height h_W of the Washington Monument is $h_W = 169$ m $= 555$ ft. Here h_W is the physical quantity, its value expressed in the unit "Meter," unit symbol m, is 169 m, and its numerical value when expressed in Meters is 169. However, the value of h_W expressed in the unit "foot," symbol ft, is 555 ft, and its numerical value, when expressed in feet, is 555.

G.1.1.1   Symbols and Nomenclature of Physical Quantities

Each physical quantity has a name and symbol. International recommendations for the use of symbols for quantities are set out in ISO/IEC 80000, the IUPAP red book and the IUPAC green book. For example, the recommended symbol for the physical quantity *mass* is m, and the recommended symbol for the quantity *electric charge* is Q.

Tables given in the next section give the symbol of some of the physical quantities.

G.1.1.2   Use of Subscripts and Indices with the Symbols

Sometimes the symbol of the quantity has a subscript. Subscripts are used for two reasons, to simply attach a name to the quantity or associate it with another quantity or index a specific component (e.g., row or column).

Name reference:

The quantity has a subscripted or superscripted single letter, group of letters, or complete word, to label what concept or entity they refer to, often to distinguish it from other quantities with the same main symbol. These subscripts or superscripts tend to be written in upright roman typeface rather than italics, while the main symbol representing the quantity is in italics. For instance, E_k or $E_{kinetic}$ is usually used to denote kinetic energy and E_p or $E_{potential}$ is usually used to denote potential energy.

Quantity reference:

The quantity has a subscripted or superscripted single letter, group of letters, or complete word, to paraMeterize what measurement/s they refer to. These subscripts or superscripts tend to be written in italic rather than upright roman typeface; the main symbol representing the quantity is in italics. For example, c_p or $c_{pressure}$ is heat capacity at the pressure given by the quantity in the subscript.

The type of subscript is expressed by its typeface: 'k' and 'p' are abbreviations of the words *kinetic* and *potential*, whereas p (italic) is the symbol for the physical quantity *pressure* rather than an abbreviation of the word.

Indices: The use of indices is for mathematical formalism using index notation.

G.1.1.3.   Size

Physical quantities can have different "sizes", such as a scalar, a vector, or a tensor. (Ref. Wikipedia)

Scalars

A scalar is a physical quantity that has magnitude but no direction. Symbols for physical quantities are usually chosen to be a single letter of the Latin or Greek alphabet and are printed in italic type.

Vectors

Vectors are physical quantities that possess both magnitude and direction and whose operations obey the axioms of a vector space. Symbols for physical quantities that are vectors are in bold type, underlined or with an arrow above. For example, if u is the speed of a particle, then the straightforward notations for its velocity are $\mathbf{u}$, $\underline{u}$, or $\vec{u}$

Tensors

Scalars and vectors are the simplest tensors, which can be used to describe more general physical quantities. For example, the Cauchy stress tensor possesses magnitude, direction, and orientation qualities.

G.1.2   Meaning of Measurement

Performing a measurement means comparing an unknown physical (or chemical or engineering) quantity with a quantity of the same type taken as a reference using an instrument.

A measurement necessarily involves a reference frame and, therefore, units. Hundreds of years back, there were numerous number of units that had little in common with each other. The first coherent system of units only appeared with the French Revolution: the metric system. This system was internationally ratified by the Meter Convention on May 20, 1875, a diplomatic treaty that set up the Bureau International des Poids et Mesures (BIPM).

In 1960, during the eleventh Conférence Générale des Poids et Mesures (CGPM), the International System of Units, the SI, was developed. It now includes two classes of units:

- **Base unites**;
- **Derived units**.

We must not believe, however, that once set up, this system is fixed. Progress made in science, technology, and the new requirements from society and, therefore, the needs in terms of increased accuracy will lead the LNE and all national metrology institutes to continuously improve the practical realization of all SI units. And this concern involves the references as well as the means for transfer to the users to allow matching, at best, these new needs. Definitions of units sometimes need to be changed and new definitions added.

G.1.3   Dimensions, Units, Conversion Factors, and Significant Digits

G.1.3.1   Dimensions and Units

- **Differences between Dimensions and Units**

  o There is a difference between dimensions and units. A ***dimension*** is a measure of a physical variable (without numerical values), while a ***unit*** is a way to assign a number or measurement to that dimension.

  o For example, length is a *dimension*, but it is measured in *units* of feet (ft) or Meters (m).

  o There are three primary unit systems in use today:

    - the ***International System of Units*** (SI units, from *Le Systeme International d'Unites*, more commonly simply called ***metric units***)
    - the ***English Engineering System of Units*** (commonly called English units)
    - the ***British Gravitational System of Units*** (BG).

  o The latter two are similar, except for the choice of primary mass unit and use of the degree symbol, as discussed below.

  o Note: Besides the three primary units of systems, which will be discussed in detail throughout this book, many others will be introduced, e.g., the Gaussian system and others.

- **Primary dimensions and units**

  o In total, there are seven ***primary dimensions***. Primary (sometimes called *basic*) dimensions are defined as independent or fundamental dimensions from which other dimensions can be obtained.

  o The primary dimensions are mass, length, time, temperature, electric current, amount of light, and amount of matter. For most mechanical and thermal science analyses, however, only the first four of these are required. The others will not be of concern to most mechanical engineering analyses.

  o In order to assign *numbers* to these primary dimensions, ***primary units*** must be assigned. These are listed in Table- G1.1 below for the three unit systems:

DICTIONARY OF SCIENTIFIC QUANTITIES

Table- G1.1   Primary dimensions and unis

Primary Dimension	Symbol	SI unit	BG unit	English unit
Mass	m (sometimes M)	kg (kilo Gramme)	Slug	lbm (pound-mass)
Length	L (sometimes l)	m (Meter)	ft (foot)	ft (foot)
Time	t (sometimes T)	s (second)	s (second)	s (second)
Temperature	T (sometimes Θ)	K (Kelvin)	oR (degree Rankine)	R (Rankine)
electric current	I (sometimes i)	A (ampere)	A (ampere)	A (ampere)
amount of light (luminous intensity)	C (sometimes I)	c (candela)	c (candela)	c (candela)
amount of matter	n or N (sometimes μ)	mol (mole)	mol (mole)	mol (mole)

All other dimensions can be derived as combinations of these seven primary dimensions. These are called *secondary dimensions*, with their corresponding *secondary units*. A few examples are given in Table-G1.2:

Table – G1.2   Secondary Dimensions and Units

Secondary Dimension	Symbol	SI unit	BG unit	English unit
Force	F (sometimes f)	N (Newton = kg· m/s^2)	lbf (pound-force)	lbf (pound-force)
Acceleration	A	m/s^2	ft/s^2	ft/s^2
Pressure	p or P	N/m^2, i.e. Pa (Pascal)	lbf/ft^2 (psf)	lbf/in^2 (psi) (note: 1 ft = 12 in)

Energy	E (sometimes e)	J (Joule = N· m)	ft· lbf (foot-pound)	ft· lbf (foot pound)
Power	P	W (watt = J/s)	ft· lbf/s	ft· lbf/s

o   Note that there are many other units, both metric and English, in use today. For example, power is often expressed in units of Btu/hr, Btu/s, cal/s, ergs/s, or horsepower, in addition to the standard units of watt and ft. lbf/s. There are **conversion factors** listed in many textbooks to enable conversion from any of these units to any other.

Note: The secondary dimensions and units will be given in detail latter

G.1.3.2   Gravitational conversion constant, gc

o   Some authors define a gravitational conversion constant, g_c, which is inserted into Newton's second law of motion. I.e., instead of $\mathbf{F} = m\cdot \mathbf{a}$, they write $\mathbf{F} = m\cdot \mathbf{a}/g_c$, where g_c is defined in the English Engineering System of Units as

$$g_c = 32.174 \frac{\text{lbm} \cdot \text{ft}}{\text{lbf} \cdot \text{s}^2}$$

and in SI units as

$$g_c = 1 \frac{\text{kg} \cdot \text{m}}{\text{N} \cdot \text{s}^2}$$

o   The present author discourages the use of this constant since it leads to much confusion. Instead, Newton's law should remain in the fundamental form in which it was created, without an artificial constant thrown into the equation, simply for the unit's sake.

o   There has been much confusion (and numerical error!) because of the differences between lbf, LBM, and slug. The use of g_c has complicated and further confused the issue, in this author's opinion. The following is an attempt to clarify some of this confusion:

•   **The relationship between force and mass units**

- o The relationship between force, mass, and acceleration can be clearly understood with Newton's second law. The following is provided to avoid confusion, especially with English units.
- o **Case 1: SI units**:

Relationship	Newton's second law, $\mathbf{F} = m\,\mathbf{a}$. [Note: Bold notation indicates a vector.] By definition of the fundamental units, this yields $1\ \text{N} = 1\ \text{kg} \cdot \text{m/s}^2$.
Conversion	$$\left(\frac{\text{N} \cdot \text{s}^2}{\text{kg} \cdot \text{m}} \right)$$
Discussion	The above expression is dimensionless and has a value of 1. Thus it is the conversion factor with which to multiply or divide any equation to simplify the units.
Example	How much force (in Newtons) is required to accelerate a mass of 13.3 kg at a constant acceleration of 1.20 m/s²? Solution: $$F_x = m \cdot a_x = (13.3\ \text{kg})\left(1.20\ \frac{\text{m}}{\text{s}^2} \right)\left(\frac{\text{N} \cdot \text{s}^2}{\text{kg} \cdot \text{m}} \right) = 16.0\ \text{N}$$ to the right, since F_x is the x-component of vector $\mathbf{F}$, and a_x is the x-component of acceleration vector $\mathbf{a}$.
Terminology	It is *not* proper to say that 1.00 kg *equals* 9.81 N, but it *is* proper to say that 1.00 kg *weighs* 9.81 N under standard earth gravity. This is obtained by utilizing Newton's second law with gravitational acceleration, i.e. $$W = m \cdot g = (1.00\ \text{kg})\left(9.81\ \frac{\text{m}}{\text{s}^2} \right)\left(\frac{\text{N} \cdot \text{s}^2}{\text{kg} \cdot \text{m}} \right) = 9.81\ \text{N}$$

- o **English units**:

Relationship	Newton's second law, $\mathbf{F} = m\,\mathbf{a}$. [Note: Bold notation indicates a vector.] By definition of the fundamental units, this yields $1\ \text{lbf} = 1\ \text{slug} \cdot \text{ft/s}^2$, or $1\ \text{lbf} = 32.174\ \text{lbm} \cdot \text{ft/s}^2$.

Conversion	$\left(\dfrac{lbf \cdot s^2}{slug \cdot ft}\right)_{or} \left(\dfrac{lbf \cdot s^2}{32.174\ lbm \cdot ft}\right)_{or} \left(\dfrac{slug}{32.174\ lbm}\right)$
Discussion	The above expressions are dimensionless, and each has a value of 1. Thus any of them can be considered a conversion factor with which to multiply or divide any equation to simplify the units.
Example	How much force (in lbf) is required to accelerate a mass of 13.3 lbm at a constant acceleration of 1.20 ft/s²? $F \longrightarrow \boxed{} \longrightarrow a$ **mass, m** Solution: $$F_x = m \cdot a_x = \left(13.3\ lbm\right)\left(1.20\ \frac{ft}{s^2}\right)\left(\frac{lbf \cdot s^2}{32.174\ lbm \cdot ft}\right) = 0.496\ lbf$$ to the right, since F_x is the x-component of vector **F**, and a_x is the x-component of acceleration vector **a**.
Terminology	It is *not* proper to say that one lbm *equals* one lbf, but it *is* proper to say that one lbm *weighs* one lbf under standard earth gravity. This is obtained by utilizing Newton's second law with gravitational acceleration, i.e. $$W = m \cdot g = \left(1.00\ lbm\right)\left(32.174\ \frac{ft}{s^2}\right)\left(\frac{lbf \cdot s^2}{32.174\ lbm \cdot ft}\right) = 1.00\ lbf$$

G.1.3.3   The Principle of Dimensional Homogeneity

- In any equation, each additive term *must* have the same dimensions. In simple terms, you cannot add apples and oranges.

- Example - The area of a rectangle is the product of its width and its height, $A = W\,H$. The dimensions of both terms in this equation are {length²}. The equation $A = H$ is clearly wrong, i.e., it is dimensionally inconsistent since the dimensions of the left term are {length²} while those of the right term are {length}.

- The Principle of Dimensional Homogeneity is sometimes useful when checking the algebra of a problem solution. Namely, dimensional inconsistency in an equation is a sure sign of an algebraic error!

- The Principle of Dimensional Homogeneity also extends to *units*. The best way to avoid unit errors is to list the units along with any numbers supplied to an equation. Also, it is best to introduce conversion factors in the form of ratios. In the above example, suppose the width W of the rectangle is 48.0 inches, and the Height H is 2.0 feet. The area A is desired in square feet and is calculated correctly as follows:

$$A = W\,H = (48.0\text{ in})\,(2.0\text{ ft})\,(1\text{ ft} / 12\text{ in}) = 8.0\text{ ft}^2.$$

G.3.1.4   Significant Digits

Since the proliferation of calculators in the 1970s, the concept of significant digits has been largely ignored. As a result, many students and practicing engineers today present answers to five, six, or more digits, even when only two or three digits are significant. Many students, for example, will write out every digit (perhaps eight or ten) that is displayed on their calculators, never even thinking about how many of those digits are actually meaningful. The present author encourages all students and engineers to consider significant digits in all written forms of communication - reports, papers, homework, exams, etc. Below is a discussion of the meaning and application of significant digits in engineering.

- o By default, an integer has an *infinite* number of significant digits. For example, the number 43 implies *exactly* 43, as when counting the number of students in a classroom. Unfortunately, many authors do not follow this convention, and it is unclear to the reader how many significant digits there really are, especially when there are trailing zeroes.
- o The number of significant digits is determined by the overall accuracy of a measurement. For example, suppose the diameter of a pipe is measured to be 2.53 mm. By convention, the measurement is only good to the least significant digit; here, the micrometer is accurate to 0.01 mm, but the exact diameter may lie anywhere between 2.525 and 2.535 mm. In this example, the reading is good to three significant digits.
- o When considering the number of significant digits, leading zeroes for numbers below unity do not count, but zeroes within a value do count. For example, 0.367 has three significant digits - the leading zero does not count. Note that this same value can be written in exponential notation as 3.67×10^{-1}, where the number of significant digits is more obvious. Consider the value 34.05. The zero here *does* count, so the value has four significant digits.
- o Trailing zeroes are a little more tricky, especially when not using exponential notation. For example, suppose a pressure reading of 101,300 Pascals is given. It is not obvious how many (if any) of the trailing zeroes are significant. Most likely, the pressure gauge is only accurate to a hundred Pascals, so it is more appropriate to write this measurement as 101.3 kPa, avoiding the

trailing zeroes altogether. The number of significant digits, in this case, is four. A reading of 101.30 kPa implies that the trailing zero *is* significant and the total number of significant digits is five.

o If trailing zeroes are significant, there are two ways to indicate this: First, use exponential notation, which clearly indicates the accuracy. For example, if a reading of 1000 is accurate to all four digits, one would write it as 1.000×10^3. Second, one can write "1000." as the numerical value. The decimal point at the end of the number indicates that all three zeroes are significant. It is understood, then, that "1000." represents four significant digits of accuracy. In this same example, if only three digits are significant, one would write the value as 1.00×10^3. If the exponential notation is not desired, but one still wishes to indicate the number of digits, one can write "1000 to three significant digits".

o Here is an important rule to remember: ***When performing calculations or manipulations of several paraMeters, the final result is only as accurate as the least accurate parameter in the problem.*** For example, suppose A and B are multiplied to obtain C. If A = 2.3601 (five significant digits), and B = 0.34 (two significant digits), then C = 0.80 (only two digits are significant in the final result). Note that most students are tempted to write C = 0.802434, with six significant digits, since that is what is displayed on a calculator after multiplying these two numbers. Let's analyze this simple example carefully. Suppose the exact value of B is 0.33501, which is read by the instrument as 0.34. Also, suppose A is exactly 2.3601, as measured by a more accurate instrument. In this case, C = A times B = 0.79066 to five significant digits. Note that our first answer, C = 0.80, is off by one digit in the second decimal place. Likewise, if B is 0.34499, read by the instrument as 0.34, the product of A and B would be 0.81421 to five significant digits. Our original answer of 0.80 is again off by one digit in the second decimal place. The main point here is that 0.80 (to two significant digits) is the best we can expect from this multiplication since, to begin with, one of the values had only two significant digits. Another way of looking at this is to say that beyond the first two digits in the answer, the rest of the digits are meaningless or not significant. For example, if one reports what his calculator displays, i.e., 2.3601 times 0.34 equals 0.802434, the last four digits are meaningless. As shown above, the final result may lie between 0.79 and 0.81 - any digits beyond the two significant digits are not only meaningless but *misleading* since it implies more accuracy to the reader than is really there.

o Most electronic instruments are good to only three significant digits. When in doubt, for most engineering analyses, three digits are usually the maximum that can be expected.

o   When writing out intermediate results in a calculation, it is okay to record more digits than the number which is significant, as this can avoid round-off errors in subsequent calculations. However, when displaying the final answer, the number of significant digits should be taken into consideration.

G.4 About this book

This book consists of three volumes:

1. Dictionary of Scientific and Engineering Quantities
2. Dictionary of Scientific Units of Measurements
3. Tables of conversions

VOLUME I QUANTITIES:

Dictionary of Scientific (Physical and Engineering) Quantities

In this dictionary, we followed the following while defining the quantities:

1. Name of the quantity

1.1   Quantities, the names of which consist of more than one word, are entered with the most important word first. This is usually (but not always) the only substantive in the name.

1.2 Some names are given to more than one quantity. The names are separated by numbering the usages.

1.3   Some quantities have more than one name and are entered under each.

A note draws attention to the other names and is so worded that the preferred name is indicated.

2 Symbol

2.1   If there is only one symbol, it is placed immediately after the name of the quantity. If there are two or more symbols, they are entered under a special subheading, and an order of preference is indicated.

2.2   An unqualified symbol conforms to a Recommendation of the ISO. (BS) following the symbol means that it is recommended by the relevant British Standard but does not appear in an ISO Recommendation. (O) following the symbol means that it is in common use but has not received formal recognition.

2.3   Alternative symbols are sometimes required because otherwise, two quantities with the same symbol might occur in the same equation.

3   Definition

A verbal definition is given, followed by a defining equation. Sometimes an alternative verbal definition and defining equation are also given.

4   Unit of measurement

This is entered first under the subheading 'unit'. For dimensional quantities, only the SI unit is given, except where its use has not been approved; then, the commonly-used unit is given for dimensionless quantities which possess units, and the recommended unit is given, sometimes with an alternative. A full explanation of the unit will be found under the appropriate entry in Part II (Units).

5   Dimensional forms

These are entered directly after the unit. The systems employed are discussed next.

6   Notes

6.1   These are numbered and enteredunder the final subheading.

6.2   In the case of an electrical quantity in which the rationalized and unrationalised sizes are not equal, a special note, marked (U/R), is included. In it, the first equation gives the connection between the two quantities; the second equation gives the definition of the unrationalised quantity (which is distinguished by carrying a star) that corresponds to the formal definition of the rationalized quantity given previously. The absence of such a note automatically implies that the rationalized and unrationalized quantities are identical

7   Cross references

7.1   Quantities mentioned in the notes to other quantitiesare also entered in their correct alphabetical positions:

7.2   Quantities with names that consist of two or more words are only entered under one word of the name and not under each word.

VOLUME II: SCIENTIFIC UNITS OF MEASUREMENTS

8. Name of the unit

8.1 Units, the names of which consist of more than one word, are entered with the most important word first. This is usually (but not always) the only substantive in the name.

8.2 Where the name of a unit can be spelled in more than one way, the commonest or preferred spelling is used. A note draws attention to the alternatives.

8.3 Some names are given to more than one unit. The names are separated either by a distinguishing comment in parentheses immediately following the name [e.g., second (of arc), second (of time)] or by numbering the usages.

8.4 Some units have more than one name and are entered under each. A note draws attention to the other names, and it is so worded that the preferred name is indicated.

8.5 Uppercase is used to write the names of the units. Foreign units (Asian, Russian, Latin American, Middle East, China, etc.) are written in lowercase and pronounced as in the related country.

9. Unit symbol

9.1 If there is only one unit symbol, it is placed immediately after the name of the unit. If there are two or more unit symbols, they are entered under a special subheading, and an order of preference is indicated.

9.2 An unqualified unit symbol conforms to a Recommendation of the International Organisation for Standardisation (ISO). (BS) following the unit symbol means that it is recommended by the relevant British Standard but does not appear in an ISO Recommendation. (O) following the unit symbol means that it is in common use but has not received formal recognition.

9.3 Alternative unit symbols are sometimes required because otherwise, two units with the same symbol may be used together.

10. Quantity measured by the unit.

10.1   This is entered under its own subheading. In those rare cases where the quantity is not included in Volume I (Dictionary of Quantities), it is explained.

10.2   If the quantity measured can have several different names, the basic name used as an entry in Volume I (Dictionary of Quantities) is given: the other names are listed under this entry.

10.3   It should be noted that the term 'volume' normally refers to a length cubed [e.g., cubic meter, cubic foot], and 'capacity' to other measures [e.g., litre, gallon].

11. System to which the unit belongs

11.1   This is mentioned directly after the quantity measured by the unit. The systems are summarized in Volume I and detailed in Volume II.

11.2   Some units are characterised by the following descriptions:

(a) Metric: derived from the SI and CGS systems by a power of ten;

(b) metric-derived: metric, but derived by a value that is not a power of ten;

(c) Imperial: derived from the FPS (or a similar) system;

(d) all

(e) arbitrary

(f) traditional

(g) none

12. Definition

12.1 A verbal definition is given in every case except where the unit is a multiple or submultiple of a basic metric or imperial unit.

12.2 A defining equation is given in every case except where the verbal definition does not allow it.

12.3 The object of the defining equation of a metric or metric-derived unit is the unit size in terms of the corresponding SI (International System of Units) unit. In the former case, it is an exact conversion; in the second case, it may or may not be.

12.4 Most other defining equations have more than one object. The first is the unit size in terms of the basic unit of the same system and is, therefore, exact. It should be regarded as the formal definition. The last object is the unit size in terms of the corresponding SI unit and may or may not be an exact conversion.

12.5 The defining equation is immediately followed by a reciprocal defining equation, which gives the size of the corresponding SI unit in terms of the unit concerned. In many cases, this is not an exact conversion.

12.6 More definitions and equations are given in next.

12.7 The rule for the number of significant figures is as follows:

(a) When the conversion is exact (i.e., it may be expressed by a terminating decimal), all the significant figures are included.

(b) When the conversion is inexact (i.e., the decimal value involved is nonterminating), six significant figures are given.

(c) When the value is based on a quantity experimentally determined to x significant figures, the conversion value is also given to x significant figures.

12.8 British Standards often provide full conversion tables [e.g., meter to an inch, foot, mile, etc.; and reciprocal values]. Since the exclusive use of SI units is becoming very common in both scientific and non-scientific measurements, it has been felt necessary to give conversion values to and from the SI only.

12.9 Extensive table of unit relationships for the more common quantities are given in Volume II and Volume III [e.g. 1 acre = 100 are = 10 square chain = 160 square rod = 0.4047 hectares; etc.],

12.10 Extensive tables of unit relationships based on the physical phenomenon are given; Tables 3.2 to Table 3.138 in Volume III.

12.11 If the size of a unit as used in the United Kingdom (UK) differs from the size of the corresponding unit used in the United States (US), the name and unit symbols are modified by the addition of the letters UK and US.

12.12 Units of temperature and related temperature scales are included in the dictionary of units at the same time given in more detail in Volume III

Units of paper sizes (A-size, B-size and C-size) have entries in the dictionary. Section 3.5 discusses the subjects in more detail.

13.Notes

13.1 These are numbered and entered under the final subheading.

13.2 The comment 'popularly' means that the usage is common, although it is not found in specialised or scientific works.

13.3 The comment that a unit 'has been called' by another name suggests that the alternative name is no longer used.

14.Cross references

14.1 Units mentioned in the notes to other units are also entered in their correct alphabetical position.

14.2 Units with names that consist of two or more words are only entered under one word of the name (see 1.1) and not under each word

15   US variations

Although formerly, the sizes of many imperial units were given definitions different in the United States from those employed in the United Kingdom, these differences have now been eliminated in all cases except the following:

(a)   Units of capacity. In the UK, the gallon is defined somewhat arbitrarily by the 1963 Weights and Measures Act. In the US, the gallon is defined in terms of the cubic inch.

(b)   The hundredweight and the ton have different formal definitions. Where these variations exist, they are clearly pointed out.

VOLUME III: TABLES OF CONVERSION

This part gives the relation between the different units of measurement. It consists of hundreds of tables: Conversion between units arranged in alphabetic order and arranged according to the physical phenomenon are given.

Physics Symbols List and Their Names

In physics, there are a large number of physical quantities we include while performing calculations. To make it more convenient for users and easier to use and remember, we often use notations/symbols to represent these physical quantities. The notations/symbols we use to represent physical quantities when solving problems related to them or for other purposes are symbols.

The symbols used for physical quantities are vastly different. Sometimes, the symbol may be the first letter of the physical quantities they represent, like, which stands for distance. Other times, they may be completely unrelated to the name of the physical quantities, like c, which stands for the speed of light. They may also be in the form of Greek characters, like λ, which stands for wavelength.

Below are some symbols used commonly in physics with their names, the type of quantities and their SI units.

Symbols used to denote physical quantities related to space and time:

Symbol	Quantity/ Coefficients	S.I Unit	Physical Quantity (Scalar/Vector)
r	Radius, the radius of curvature	Meter	Functions as both scalar and vector

S	Displacement	Meter	Vector
D	Distance	Radian	Scalar
θ, φ	Angular displacement, angular separation, the rotational angle	Meter	Functions as both scalar and vector
x, y, z	Cartesian coordinates	Unitless	Scalar
$\hat{\imath}, \hat{\jmath}, \hat{k}$	Cartesian unit vectors	Unitless	Vector
r, θ, φ	Spherical coordinates	Meter/Radian	Scalar
$\hat{r}, \hat{\theta}, \hat{\varphi}$	Spherical unit vectors	Unitless	Vector
r, θ, z	Cylindrical coordinates	Meter/Radian	Scalar
$\hat{r}, \hat{\theta}, \hat{z}$	Cylindrical unit vectors	Unitless	Vector
$\hat{n}$	Normal unit vector	Unitless	Vector
$\hat{t}$	Tangential unit vector	Unitless	Vector
H	Height, depth	Meter	Scalar
ℓ, L	Length	Meter	Scalar
T	Time	Second	Scalar
D	DiaMeter	Meter	Scalar
C	Circumference	Meter	Scalar
A, A	Area	Square Meter	Functions as both scalar and vector
V	Volume	Cubic Meter	Scalar
T	Time, duration	Second	Scalar
T	Periodic time	Second	Scalar

T	Time Constant	Second	Scalar
F	Frequency	Hertz	Scalar
Ω	Angular frequency	Radian per second	Scalar

Symbols used to denote physical quantities related to Mechanics:

Symbol	Quantity/ Coefficients	S.I Unit	Physical Quantity (Scalar/Vector)
V	Velocity, speed	Meter per second	Functions as vector
A	Acceleration	Meter per second squared	Functions as and vector
a_c	Centripetal/Centrifugal acceleration	Meter per second squared	Functions as vector
G	Acceleration due to gravity	Meter per second squared	Functions vector
M	Mass	KiloGramme	Scalar
F	Force	Newton	Functions as vector
F_g /W	Force due to gravity/Weight	Newton	Functions as vector
F_n, N	Normal force, normal	Newton	Functions as vector
F_f	Force of friction	Newton	Functions as vector
µ	Coefficient of friction	Unitless	Scalar
P	Momentum	KiloGramme Meter per	Functions as vector

		second	
J	Impulse	Newton second	Functions as vector
E	Energy	Joule	Scalar
K	Kinetic energy	Joule	Scalar
U	Potential energy	Joule	Scalar
V_g	Gravitational potential	Joule per kiloGramme	Scalar
H	Efficiency	Unitless	Scalar
P	Power	Watt	Scalar
Ω	Rotational speed, rotational velocity	Radian per second	Functions as vector
A	Rotational acceleration	Radian per second squared	Functions as vector
T	Torque	Newton Meter	Functions as vector
I	Moment of inertia	KiloGramme Meter squared	Scalar
L	Angular momentum	KiloGramme Meter squared per second	Functions as vector
H	Angular impulse	Newton Meter second	Functions as vector
K	Spring constant	Newton per Meter	Scalar
P	Pressure	Pascal	Scalar
Σ	Stress	Pascal	Scalar

T	Shear stress	Pascal	Scalar
P	Density, volume mass density	KiloGramme per cubic Meter	Scalar
Σ	Area mass density	KiloGramme per square Meter	Scalar
Λ	Linear mass density	KiloGramme per Meter	Scalar
F_B, B	Buoyancy	Newton	Functions as vector
q_m	Mass flow rate	KiloGramme per second	Scalar
q_v	Volume flow rate	Cubic Meter per second	Scalar
F_D, R	Drag or air resistance	Newton	Functions as vector
C_D	Drag coefficient	Unitless	Scalar
H	Viscosi	Pascal-second	Scalar
N	Kinematic viscosity	Square Meter per second	Scalar
Ma	Mach number	Unitless	Scalar
Re	Reynolds number	Unitless	Scalar
Fr	Froude number	Unitless	Scalar
E	Young's modulus of elasticity	Pascal	Scalar
G	Shear modulus of rigidity	Pascal	Scalar
K	Bulk modulus of compression	Pascal	Scalar

E	Linear strain	Unitless	Scalar
Γ	Shear strain	Unitless	Scalar
Θ	Volume strain	Unitless	Scalar
Γ	Surface tension	Newton per Meter	Scalar

Symbols used to denote physical quantities related to thermal physics:

Symbol	Quantity/Coefficients	S.I Unit	Physical Quantity (Scalar/Vector)
COP	Coefficient of performance	Unitless	Scalar
W	Ways, number of identical microstates	Unitless	Scalar
S	Entropy	Joule per kelvin	Scalar
U	Internal energy	Joule	Scalar
E	Emissivity	Unitless	Scalar
K	Thermal conductivity	Watt per Meter Kelvin	Scalar
P	Heat flow rate	Watt	Scalar
N	Number of particles	Unitless	Scalar
N	Amount of substance	Mole	Scalar
L	Latent heat/specific latent heat	Joule per kiloGramme	Scalar
C	Specific heat capacity	Joule per	Scalar

		kiloGramme Kelvin	
Q	Heat	Joule	Scalar
B	Volume expansivity, coefficient of volume thermal expansion	Inverse kelvin	Scalar
A	Linear expansivity, coefficient of thermal expansion	Inverse kelvin	Scalar
T	Temperature	Kelvin	Scalar

Symbols used to denote physical quantities related to Waves and Optics:

Symbol	Quantity/Coefficients	S.I Unit	Physical Quantity (Scalar/Vector)
M	Magnification	Unitless	Scalar
F	Focal length	Meter	Scalar
N	Index of refraction	Unitless	Scalar
L	Level	Decibel, decineper	Scalar
I	Intensity	Watt per square Meter	Scalar
v, c	Wave speed	Meter per second	Scalar
Λ	Wavelength	Meter	Scalar
P	Power of a lens	Dioptre	Scalar

Symbols used to denote physical quantities related to Electricity and Magnetism:

Symbol	Quantity/Coefficients	S.I Unit	Physical Quantity (Scalar/Vector)
S	Poynting vector, intensity	Watt per square Meter	Functions as vector
H	Energy density	Joule per cubic Meter	Scalar
N	Turns per unit length	Inverse Meter	Scalar
N	Number of turns	Unitless	Scalar
Φ_B	Magnetic flux	Weber	Vector
B	Magnetic field	Tesla	Functions as vector
F_B	Magnetic force	Newton	Functions as vector
Σ	Conductivity	Siemens per Meter	Scalar
G	Conductance	Siemens	Scalar
P	Resistivity	Ohm-Meter	Scalar
R, r	Electric resistance/internal resistance	Ohm	Scalar
I	Electric current	Ampere	Scalar
ϵ	Dielectric constant	Unitless	Scalar
C	Capacitance	Farad	Scalar
$\mathcal{E}$	Electromotive force (emf)	Volt	Scalar
V	voltage, electric potential	Volt	Scalar
U_E	Electric potential energy	Joule	Scalar
Φ_E	Electric flux	Newton Meter squared per	Functions as vector

		coulomb	
E	Electric field	Newton per coulomb/volt per Meter	Functions as vector
F_E	Electrostatic force	Newton	Functions as vector
Λ	Linear charge density	Kilogramme per Meter	Scalar
Σ	Area charge density	Kilogramme per square Meter	Scalar
P	Volume charge density	Kilogramme per cubic Meter	Scalar
q, Q	Electric charge	Coulomb	Scalar

Symbols used in modern physics:

Symbol	Quantity/Coefficients	S.I Unit	Physical Quantity (Scalar/Vector)
D	Dose/ dose absorbed	gray	Scalar
	Half-life	Second	Scalar
$\psi(r,t)$, $\psi(r)\varphi(t)$	Wave function	Unitless	Functions as vector
Φ	Work function	Joule	Scalar
H	Effective dose	Sievert	Scalar
Γ	Lorentz factor/Lorentz gamma	Unitless	Scalar

Dictionary of Scientific (Physical and Engineering) Quantities

A

ABBE NUMBER

Symbol: V

Definition: In optics and lens design, the **Abbe number**, also known as the **V-number** or **constringence** of a transparent material, is an approximate measure of the material's dispersion (change of refractive index versus wavelength), with high values of V indicating low dispersion.

It is named after Ernst Abbe (1840–1905), the German physicist who defined it. The term V-number should not be confused with the normalized frequency in fibers.

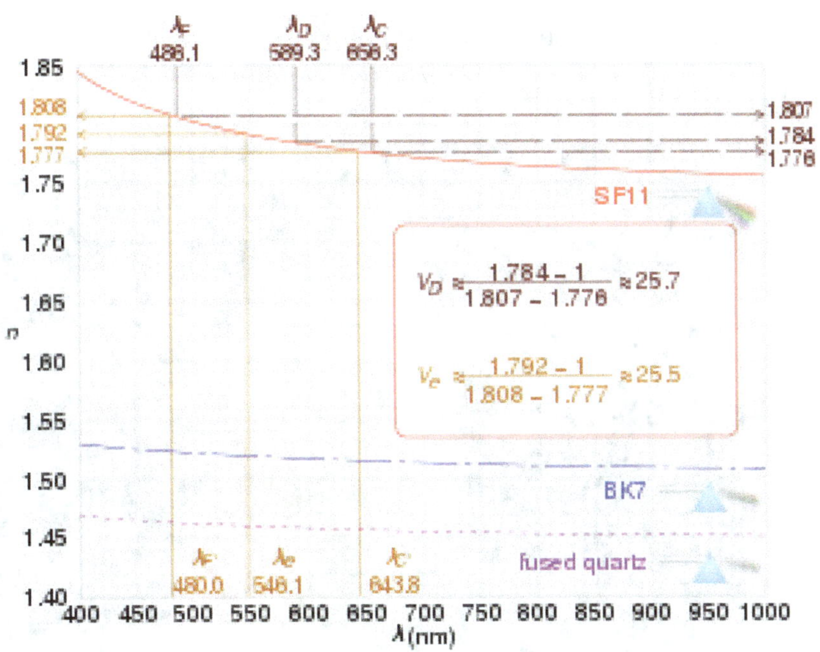

The above graph gives the refractive index variation for SF11 flint glass, BK7 borosilicate crown glass, and fused quartz and the calculation for two Abbe numbers for SF11.

The Abbe number, V_D, of a material is defined as

$$V_D = \frac{n_D - 1}{n_F - n_C},$$

Where n_C, n_D and n_F are the refractive indices of the material at the wavelengths of the Fraunhofer C, D_1, and F spectral lines (656.3 nm, 589.3 nm, and 486.1 nm, respectively). This formulation only applies to the visible spectrum. Outside this range requires the use of different spectral lines. For non-visible spectral lines, the term V-number is more commonly used. The more general formulation is defined as,

$$V = \frac{n_{center} - 1}{n_{short} - n_{long}};$$

where n_{short}, n_{center} and n_{long} are the refractive indices of the material at three different wavelengths. The shortest wavelength index is n_{short}, and the longest is n_{long}.

Abbe numbers are used to classify glass and other optical materials in terms of their chromaticity. For example, the higher dispersion flint glasses have $V < 55$, whereas the lower dispersion crown glasses have larger Abbe numbers. Values of V range from below 25 for very dense flint glasses, around 34 for polycarbonate plastics, up to 65 for common crown glasses, and 75 to 85 for some fluorite and phosphate crown glasses.

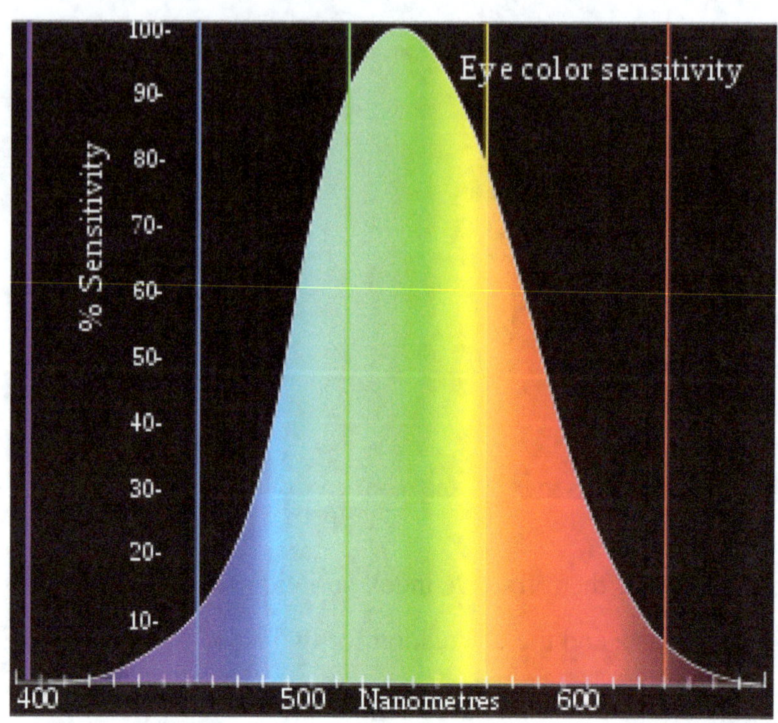

Most of the human eye's wavelength sensitivity curve, shown here, is bracketed by the Abbe number reference wavelengths of 486.1 nm (blue) and 656.3 nm (red)

Abbe numbers are used in the design of achromatic lenses, as their *reciprocal* is proportional to dispersion (slope of refractive index versus wavelength) in the wavelength region where the human eye is most sensitive (see the above graph). For different wavelength regions or for higher precision in characterizing a system's chromaticity (such as in the design of apochromatic), the full dispersion relation (refractive index as a function of wavelength) is used.

***Unit*: It has no units or dimensions**

(Ref.: Encyclopedia Science and Computing)

ABSEMENT (or ABSITION)

Symbol: A

Definition: In kinematics, absement (or absition) is a measure of the sustained displacement of an object from its initial position, i.e., a measure of how far away and for how long. In other words, it is a measure of sustained displacement and is given by the first integral with respect to the time of displacement.

Note 1: The word absement is a portmanteau of the word's absence and displacement. Similarly, absition is a portmanteau of the words absence and position.

Note 2: As the displacement can be seen as a mechanical analogue of electric charge, the absement can be seen as a mechanical analogue of the time-integrated charge, a quantity useful for modeling some types of memory elements.

Note 3: Applications: In addition to modeling fluid flow and for Lagrangian modeling of electric circuits, absement is used in physical fitness and kinesiology to model muscle bandwidth and as a new form of physical fitness training. In this context, it gives rise to a new quantity called "actergy", which is to energy as energy is to power. Actergy has the same units as action (joule-seconds) but is the time-integral of total energy (time-integral of the Hamiltonian rather than time-integral of the Lagrangian).

Unit: m.s

Dimensions: L.T

ABSEMENT, STRAIN

Definition: Strain absement is the time-integral of strain and is used extensively in mechanical systems and memsprings: a quantity called absement which allows mem-spring models to display hysteretic response in great abundance

Note:

Absement, as mentioned above, is the first integral with respect to time of displacement. Just as displacement and its derivatives form kinematics, so do displacement and its integrals form "integral kinematics" (Janzen *et al.* 2014), giving rise to the ordered list of *n*-th derivatives of displacement:

(the negative sign in derivatives means integration)

*n*th derivative	Name	Units of measure
-12	Abset	$m \cdot s^{12}$
-11	Absut	$m \cdot s^{11}$
-10	Abshot	$m \cdot s^{10}$
-9	Absrop	$m \cdot s^{9}$
−8	Absock	$m \cdot s^{8}$
−7	Absop	$m \cdot s^{7}$
−6	Absackle	$m \cdot s^{6}$
−5	Absnap	$m \cdot s^{5}$
−4	Abserk	$m \cdot s^{4}$
−3	abseleration	$m \cdot s^{3}$
−2	Absity	$m \cdot s^{2}$
−1	**absement**	$m \cdot s$ ($m \cdot s^{1}$)
0	displacement	m ($m \cdot s^{\pm 0}$)
1	Velocity	$m \cdot s^{-1}$
2	acceleration	$m \cdot s^{-2}$
3	jerk; jolt	$m \cdot s^{-3}$

4	snap; jounce	$m \cdot s^{-4}$
5	crackle; flounce	$m \cdot s^{-5}$
6	pop; pounce	$m \cdot s^{-6}$
7	Lock	$m \cdot s^{-7}$
8	Drop	$m \cdot s^{-8}$
9	Shot	$m \cdot s^{-9}$
10	Put	$m \cdot s^{-10}$
11	Get	$m \cdot s^{-11}$

ABSORBANCE

Symbol: A

Definition: Absorbance corresponds to loss of energy absorbed in a given medium in comparison with loss in reference. Quantitatively, it is defined as the logarithm to base 10 of the ratio of the intensity of radiation passing through reference l_o and through investigated sample l.

$$A = log_{10} \left(\frac{l_o}{l} \right)$$

Unit: There are no units or dimensions.

Note: 1. It is assumed that losses for reflection, solvent absorption, and refraction are compensated and that there is no interaction due to scattered radiation.

2. It is also known as "absorbency" and "optical density."

See *"internal transmission density."*

ABSORBANCY

See "absorbance"

ABSORBED DOSE

Symbol: D

Definition: Amount of energy imported to matter by ionizing participles per unit mass of irradiant material at a place of interest,

Unit: Gray (Gy) also, *J. kg⁻¹*

Other units: Rad, Erg

Dimension: $L^2 T^{-2}$

Notes: 1.   Absorbed dose is used in the calculation of dose uptake in living tissue in both radiation protection (reduction of harmful effects) and radiology (potential beneficial effects, for example, in cancer treatment).

2.   It is also used to directly compare the effect of radiation on inanimate matter.

3.   The older, non-SI CGS unit "*rad*" is sometimes also used, predominantly in the USA.

See "*dose*"

ABSORBED DOSE RATE

Definition: Absorbed dose received per unit of time

Unit: Gray per second (Gy/s)

Dimension: $L^2 T^{-3}$

ABSORPTANCE

Symbol: α

Definition: A measurement of the ability of a body or substance to absorb radiation as expressed by the fraction of incident that is absorbed by the body. For radiant heat, the absorptance of a body, measured against a vacuum, depends on the thermodynamic temperature T of the body receiving the radiation and on the wavelength.

The absorptance of a body was formally known as its "absorptivity". It is equal to its "*emissivity.*" It is equal to 1 (unity) minus the *transmittance*.

Unit: There are no units or dimensions.

Note: 1. The absorptance is usually expressed as a percentage. Typical values are given below.

2. The absorptance at a fixed frequency is called the "*spectral absorptance.*"

3. This should not be confused with absorbance and absorption coefficient.

See "*absorptivity*" and "*transmittance.*"

Absorptance (%) for mental film boundaries

Wavelength (nm)	Silver	Aluminum	Gold
450	10	13	67
600	7	11	16
700	5	13	8
800	3	15	5
4000	2	6	3

ABSORPTANCE INTERNAL

Symbol: α_i

Definition: A measure of the ability of an object to absorb radiation equal to the ratio of the absorbed radiant flux to the incident flux Φ_a/Φ_i. For a layer of material, the ratio of the flux absorbed between the entry and exit surfaces of the layer to the flux leaving the entry surface is the internal absorptance.

Unit: There are no units or dimension

Note: 1.   Internal absorptance does not apply to loss of intensity by scattering or to a reflection of radiation at the surface of the substance.

2.   The internal absorptance is related to the internal transmittance by the relation: $\Phi_i + \tau_i = 1$

See *"absorptance" and "transmittance, internal."*

ABSORPTION

Definition: 1. The process in which a gas or liquid is taken up by another substance, usually a solid. Thus, the absorbed material permeates into the bulk of the solid, as opposed to adsorption, which involves the accumulation of material at a surface.

Definition 2- Reduction in the flux of electromagnetic radiation or other ionizing radiation on passage through matter.

Definition 3- Reduction in the intensity of sound on passage through matter.

Definition *4-* The property of a dielectric in a capacitor that causes a small charging current to flow after the plates have been short-circuited, allowed to stand for a few minutes, and short-circuited again. Also known as a ***dielectric soak***.

Definition *5-* In physiological: The transformation of nonliving into living matter, i.e., food to protoplasm.

See: *"adsorption", "absorption", "coefficient",* and *"absorbitivity."*

ABSORPTION AREA, EQUIVALENT

Symbol: *E*

Definition: That area of perfectly absorbing surface (surface having a reverberation absorption coefficientα *of unity*) of which would absorb sound energy at the same rate as the room or object in the room under the same conditions.

$$E = \alpha\ A$$

Where A = surface area of the room or object

Unit: 1. The equivalent absorption area depends on the frequency of the sound.

2. The *"Sabin"* is also in use as an acoustic unit of equivalent absorption.

ABSORPTION COEFFICIENT

Symbol: α, sometimes α_a

Definition: A measure of the ability of a body or substance to absorb radiation as expressed by the energy E_a absorbed by a surface divided by that incident on it E_o under identical conditions, $\alpha = E_a/E_o$

Unit: There are no units or dimensions.

Note: 1. The quantity is also called the "absorption factor" and also "absorptance."

2. The absorption coefficient is generally expressed as a percentage.

3. The absorption coefficient is the sum of scattering coefficient δ and transmission coefficient τ, i. e., $\alpha = \delta + \tau$

4. For radiant heat, the absorptance of a body, measured against a vacuum, depends on the

thermodynamic temperature T of the body receiving the relation and the frequency.

5. For sound: The absorption coefficient depends on the frequency of the sound and the material. Some typical values of the absorption coefficient (expressed as a percentage) are shown below.

f(Hz)	Carpet pile	Concrete	3 plywood
250	14	1	28
500	37	2	26
1000	43	2	9
2000	27	2	12
4000	25	3	11

When the incident sound is distributed completely at random, the quantity is termed the reverberation absorption coefficient.

A perfect absorber, for which the coefficient is l, is often called an ***"open window,"*** and the ***"open window unit"*** has been used as a unit of absorption coefficient, being the area of an open window having the same degree of absorption as the whole area of the boundary under consideration.

ABSORPTION COEFFICIENT, LINEAR

Symbol: α; also μ_a

Definition: For a parallel beam of monochromatic radiation passing through a uniform medium, the absorption coefficient is the factor α in the expression.

$$\frac{\emptyset_x}{\emptyset_o} = e^{-ax}$$

Where, $\emptyset_o$ is the initial flux and $\emptyset_x$ the flux after a distance x (the remaining unabsorbed flux)

Unit: Per meter

Dimension: L^{-1}

Note: 1. The above equation is known as *Bouguer's law* or *Lambert's law* of absorption. It only applies in practice if factors such as reflection and scattering are negligible or can be corrected.

2. The absorption coefficient is less than the attenuation coefficient since it does not include that part of the energy which escapes in the form of secondary radiation.

ABSORPTION COEFFICIENT, MASS

Definition: It is the factor corresponding to the linear absorption coefficient α in the case of X-ray. In this case, it is more convenient to consider the mass per unit area rather than the thickness of the absorbing radiation.

Mass absorption coefficient = a/density of the material.

Unit: Meter squared per kilo Grammeme

Dimension: $M^{-1}L^2$

See *"absorption coefficient, linear."*

ABSORPTION COEFFICIENT, MOLAR

Symbol:ε

Definition: Is the linear absorption coefficient divided by the molar density of the material c.

$\varepsilon = a/c$

Unit: Meter squared per mole.

Dimension: $L^2 N^{-1}$

See *"absorption coefficient, linear."*

ABSORPTION CROSS-SECTION

Definition: Cross-section of a nucleus of atom for absorption of bombarding particles.

Unit: meter square

Dimension: L^2

See *"cross-section."*

ABSORPTION INDEX

Symbol: k

Definition: Is the absorption coefficient divided by the wavenumber in vacuum v times 4π.

$k = a/4\pi v$

Unit: There are no units or dimensions.

See *"absorption coefficient, linear"* and *"complex refractive index."*

ABSORPTIVITY

Definition: 1. A measure of the ability of a substance to absorb radiation as expressed by the internal absorptance (absorption coefficient) of a layer of the substance of unit thickness under conditions in which the boundary of the material has no influence.

2. Formerly the fraction of radiant energy, an incident from a vacuum on a body at temperature T that is absorbed by the body. This term has now been replaced by "absorptance".

3. The constant "a" in Beer's law relation $A = abc$, where A is the absorptance, b is the path length, and c is the concentration of solution.

Also known as *"absorptive power"*. Formerly known as *"absorptancy index,"* *"absorption constant,"* and *"extinction coefficient."*

Unit: There are no units or dimensions.

ABSORPTIVE, MOLAR

Symbol: ε

Definition: Absorbance of solution of unit molar concentration (unit molarity) and unit path length. Its numerical value is usually calculated from the Lambert-Beer law applied to measurement results for diluted solution.

Unit: There are no units or dimensions.

Note: It is also called the "molar absorbency index."

See also *"absorptivity"* and *"molarity."*

ACCELERATION

Symbol: *a*. the symbol *f,* formerly used, is no longer preferred.

Definition: Rate of change of velocity *v* with respect to time *t*.

$a = dv/dt$

Unit: Meter per second squared *(m. s^{-2})*.

Dimensions: LT^{-2} (vector)

Note: 1.   The symbol g is used for the value of the local acceleration of free fall. The standard value g_n is given by $g_n = 9.806\ 65$ meters per second squared.

2. Acceleration is a vector quantity (they have magnitude and direction) and add according to the parallelogramme law. The vector of the net force acting on a body has the same direction as the vector of the body's acceleration, and its magnitude is proportional to the magnitude of the acceleration, with the object's mass (a scalar quantity) as proportionality constant.

ACCELERATION, ANGULAR

Symbol: ϕ; sometimes α.

Definition: Rate of change of angular velocity with respect to time *t*.

$\phi = d\omega/dt$

Unit: Radian per second squared, degree per second squared, hertz, squared.

Dimension: T^2 (vector).

ACCELERATION, CENTRIPETAL

Definition: The radial component of the acceleration of a particle or object moving around a circle, which can be shown to be directed toward the center of the circle.

Unit: Meter per second squared.

Dimension: LT^{-2}

ACOUSTIC IMPEDANCE

Definition: **Acoustic impedance** and **specific acoustic impedance** are measures of the opposition that a system presents to the acoustic flow resulting from an acoustic pressure applied to the system.

Unit*:* Pascal second per cubic meter (Pa·s/m^3) or the rayl per square meter (rayl/m^2),

For specific acoustic impedance is the pascal second per meter (Pa·s/m) or the rayl.

Dimension:

Note: 1. Here, the symbol rayl denotes the MKS rayl.

2.   It has a close analogy with electrical impedance, which measures the opposition that a system presents to the electrical flow resulting from an electrical voltage applied to the system.

ACTION

Symbol*: L*

Definition*:* 1. For a conservative dynamical system: It is the space integral of the total momentum of the system,

$$L = \int_{p1}^{p2} \sum_i m_i \frac{dr_i}{dt} . dr_i$$

Where m_i is the mass and r_1 *is* the position vector of the i_{th} particle, *t* is the time, and the system is assumed to pass from configuration p$_1$ to p$_2$.

This expression reduces to twice the integral of the total energy E with respect to time t.

$$L = 2 \int E \, dt.$$

2. In Hamiltonian mechanics, the action is the product of a component of momentum$p$1, and the change in the corresponding position coordinate, q_1, more precisely:

$$L = \int p_i \, dq_i$$

Unit*:* Joule second

Dimension*:* ML^2 T^{-1} (scalar)

Note: The integral $\int p \, dq$ over a cycle of a dynamic system is called *"action variable"* and also known as *"action integral"*.

ACTIVE CURRENT

Definition: The component of an alternating current that is in phase with the voltage, the current and voltage being regarded as vectors.

Unit: Ampere

Dimension: I

ACTIVE VOLTAGE

Definition: The component of an alternating voltage that is in phase with the current, the voltage and current being regarded as vectors.

Unit: Volt.

Dimension: $L^2\,M\,T^{-3}\,I^{-1}$

ACTIVE VOLT-AMPERE

Definition: The product of the current and the active voltage or the product of the voltage and the active current.

Unit: Watt.

Dimension: $L^2\,M\,T^{-3}$

ACTIVITY

1. In Radioactivity:

    Symbol: A

    Definition: The number N of disintegration taking place in a radioactive specimen divided by the time t. Activity $= N/t$.

    More precisely, Activity $= -Dn/dt$

    Unit: Curie, Rutherford

    Dimensions: T^{-1}

    Note: The quantity is also termed the *"radioactive disintegration rate"*.

2.   In chemical Thermodynamics:

    Definition: A thermodynamic function that correlates change in the chemical potential with change in experimentally measurable quantities, such as concentrations or potential pressures, though relations were formally equivalent to those for ideal systems.

an **Absolute activity (λ):** is defined as:

$\lambda = exp(\mu/RT),$

where μ = chemical potential of the substance,

R = the molar gas constant, and

T= thermodynamic temperature.

b.   The relative activity (a) is given by:

$a = \lambda/\lambda$

Where λ is the absolute activity of the pure substance at the same temperature and pressure as the mixture.

The law of mass action is valid if concentrations are replaced by activities.

Unit: There are no units or dimensions.

3. In optics

Definition: The ability of certain solutions and crystals to rotate the plane of polarization plane-polarised light in proportion to the length of substance traversed and the concentration case of solution. It may arise from the asymmetric arrangement of atoms in a molecule. When looking towards the conco light, if the rotation is clockwise, the optional activity is called right-handed (dextrorotatory); if rotation is anticlockwise, it is called left-handed (laevorotatory).

Note: The "*angle of optical rotation*": is the angle through which the plane is rotated.

Unit: Radians

ACTIVITY COEFFICIENT

Symbol: f_b

Definition: Measure of deviation of thermodynamic properties of a constituent in a given solution from its properties in an ideal solution. It is defined by the relation:

$$f = \frac{\alpha}{\aleph}$$

where: α = activity of solution constituent,

$\aleph$ = molar fraction of the condtituent

Activity coefficient depends on pressure, temperature, and other components of solution.

Unit: There are no units or dimensions.

ADMITTANCE

Symbol: Y

Definition: An admittance of a linear constant-paraMeter system is the ratio of the phase equivalent of the steady-state sine-wave current (*I*) or current-like quantity (response) to the phasor equivalent of the corresponding voltage-like quantity (driving force) (*V*).

Y=I/V

Unit: Siemens (Symbol S)

Dimension: $M^{-1}L^{-2}T^3I^2$

Note: 1. The simple definition of the admittance is the reciprocal of the electrical impedance

Y=1/Z

2. Y = G + i B (G = conductance, B = susceptance)

$Y = |Y|.\, e^{i\phi}$ (*ϕ=phase displacement); hence |Y| = (G^2 + B^2)^{1/2}* The term admittance is sometimes given to the modulus |Y| being termed the complex admittance.

3.   The older, synonymous of the admittance unit is mho, and its symbol is ℧ (an upside-down uppercase omega Ω).

4.   Oliver Heaviside coined the term *admittance* in December 1887.

ADMITTANCE (THERMAL)

Definition: The property of building materials and the spaces they enclose, which determines their response to sinusoidal variation in external temperature.

Unit: Watt per meter squared kelvin

Dimension: $ML^{-2}\,T^{-1}$ (Scalar)

ADSORPTION

Definition: It can be defined as the formation of a layer of a foreign substance, usually a gas, on an impermeable surface. Equally, it can be defied as the removal of one or more components of a gas mixture or the removal of a dissolved substance from an aqueous solution by contact with a solid surface.

The absorbed components are held on the surface of the solid by one of two ways: chemisorption, in which the gas molecules or atoms are held by covalent bonds, and physisorption, in which they are held by the weaker van der Waals forces. In chemisorption, a single layer of absorbed molecules is formed; physisorption may involve the production of several layers.

Note: The adsorption is distinguished from absorption, in which the gas permeates into the material.

See "*absorption*"

ADSORPTION COEFFICIENT

Symbol: K

Definition: Constant in Langmuir equation equal to the ratio of adsorption rate constant to corresponding desorption rate constant and which depends on the kind of system and on temperature.

Unit: There are no units or dimensions

ADSORPTIVITY

Definition: The ability of a given adsorbent to adsorb a certain substance. It represents the concentrating power of adsorbent.

AFFINITY

Symbol: A

Definition: The tendency of an atom or compound to react or combine with atoms or compounds of different chemical constitutions. Quantitatively, the chemical affinity is measured by the free energy decrease. If v_B is the stoichiometric coefficient of reagent B (positive for products, negative for substances) and μ_B is the chemical potential of the reagent B, and the affinity of the chemical reaction is the summation:

$$A = \sum_{B} v_B \mu_B$$

AFFINITY CONSTANT

Definition: The intrinsic tendency of substance, a, F_a, divided by the tendency of substance b to combine F_b.

Affinity constant = F_a / F_b

Unit: There are no units or dimensions.

AGGREGATE MODULUS

Symbol: Ha

Definition: In relation to biomechanics, the **aggregate modulus** (Ha) is a measurement of the stiffness of a material at equilibrium when the fluid has ceased flowing through it.

The aggregate modulus can be calculated from Young's modulus (E) and the Poisson ratio (v).

$$Ha = E(1 - v)/[(1 + v)(1 - 2v)]$$

The aggregate modulus of a similar specimen is determined from a unidirectional *deformational* testing configuration, i.e., the only non-zero strain component is E_{11}, as opposed to Young's modulus, which is determined from a unidirectional *loading* testing configuration, i.e., the only non-zero stress component is, say, in the $\mathbf{e}_1$ direction. In this test, the only non-zero component of the stress tensor is T_{11}.

ALBEDO

Symbol: α

Definition: Is the measure of the diffuse reflection of solar radiation out of the total solar radiation and measured on a scale from 0, corresponding to a black body that absorbs all incident radiation, to 1, corresponding to a body that reflects all incident radiation.

Surface albedo is defined as the ratio of "radiosity J_e" to the "irradiance E_e" (flux per unit area) received by a surface. The proportion reflected is not only determined by properties of the surface itself but also by the spectral and angular distribution of solar radiation reaching the Earth's surface. These factors vary with atmospheric composition, geographic location and time. While bi-hemispherical reflectance is calculated for a single angle of incidence (i.e., for a given position of the Sun), albedo is the directional integration of reflectance over all solar angles in a given period. The temporal resolution may range from seconds (as obtained from flux measurements) to daily, monthly, or annual averages.

Unless given for a specific wavelength (spectral albedo), albedo refers to the entire spectrum of solar radiation. Due to measurement constraints, it is often given for the spectrum in which most solar energy reaches the surface (between 0.3 and 3 µm). This spectrum includes visible light (0.4–0.7 µm), which explains why surfaces with a low albedo appear dark (e.g., trees absorb most radiation), whereas surfaces with a high albedo appear bright (e.g., snow reflects most radiation).

Albedo is an important concept in climatology, astronomy, and environmental management (e.g., as part of the Leadership in Energy and Environmental Design (LEED) proGramme for sustainable rating of buildings). The average albedo of the Earth from the upper atmosphere, its *planetary albedo*, is 30–35% because of cloud cover but widely varies locally across the surface because of different geological and environmental features.

Unit: There are no units or dimensions.

(Ref. Encyclopedia of Science and Computing)

ALTITUDE

Definition: 1. Height above sea level. It influences atmospheric pressure and barometric pressure since, at whatever height above or below sea level datum these pressure are taken, they will become progressively low as height, i.e., altitude increases or progressively lower as depth increases. Pressure gauge readings therefore are on the high side on mountains and on the low side in deep mines.

2. One of a pair of coordinates, the other being azimuth, giving the position of a star. It is the angular elevation of the star above the plane of the horizon, measured on the great circle passing perpendicular to that plane through the star in question and the zenith.

3. In mathematics, it is the perpendicular distance from the base to the top (a vertex or parallel line) of a geometric figure such as a triangle or paralleloGramme.

Unit: meter

Dimension: L

AMOUNT CONCENTRATION

Symbol: c

Definition: Amount of substance n divided by volume V.

$c = n/V$

Unit: Mole per cubic meter

Dimension: $N.L^{-3}$

Note: 1. It is the reciprocal of "*molar volume.*"

      2. N is used as the dimensional symbol of the molar value

See *"molar volume"* and *"amount of substance."*

AMOUNT OF SUBSTANCE

Symbol: n

Definition: The number of moles present. It is proportional to the number N of specified particles of a substance. The specified particle being an atom, molecule, ion, electron, photon, etc, or any specified group of any of these particles. The proportionality constant is the reciprocal "Avogadro constant (or number) L" and is the same for all substances.

$$n = N/L$$

Unit: mole

Dimension: N

Note: 1. It is also called "Molar value"

      2. N is used as the dimensional symbol of the molar value.

See *"Avogadro constant"*

AMPERAGE

Symbol: Amp, 1

Definition: The amount of electric current in amperes

Unit: Ampere

Dimension: I

See *"current (electric)"*

AMPHORA

Measurement unit of volume/capacity

Definition: An ancient Roman unit of capacity for grain and liquid products. Quantitatively equals to 48 *sextarii* and equivalent to about 27.84 litres (7.36 U.S. gallons).

Unit: The SI unit is liter

Dimension: L^3

Note: The term *amphora* was borrowed from the Greeks, who used it to designate a measure equal to about 34 liters (9 U.S. gallons).

Note: sextarii is a historic Roman unit of liquid. It is the volume of 5/3 Roman pound of wine

AMPLITUDE

Definition: The peak value of an alternating quantity in either the positive or negative direction. This term is applied particularly to the case of sinusoidal vibration.

It is x in the expression $x = x\ sin(\omega t + \vartheta)$

Unit: Depends on the physical quantity.

Dimension: Depends on the physical quantity.

Note: 1.   The **amplitude** of a periodic variable is a measure of its change over a single period (such as time or spatial period).

2.   There are various definitions of amplitude, which are all functions of the magnitude of the difference between the variable's extreme values. In older texts, the phase is sometimes called the amplitude.

AMPLITUDE LEVEL

Symbol: N

Definition: The natural logarithm of the ratio of two amplitudes a_1, a_2 each measured in the same units.

$N = \ln (a_2/a_1)$

Unit: Neper

Dimension: There are no dimensions

Note: The name and symbol given are commonly used for this quantity, but neither is standard.

See *"level"*.

ANGLE (ONE)

Symbol: Many of lowercase letters of the Greek alphabet are used as symbols. The most common are: $\vartheta, \propto, \beta, \phi$

Definition: The angle is that geometric figure, arithmetic quantity or algebraic signed quantity determined by two rays emanating from a common point or by two planes emanating from a common line.

The value of the angle is the ratio between the arc length s cut out on a circle and the radius r of the circle.

$$\vartheta = s/r$$

Unit: Radian, degree

Dimension: There are no dimensions (scalar, although a direction, e.g., clockwise or anticlockwise, can, if necessary, be associated with the angle)

Note: 1 The phase angle (phase displacement, phase difference) is the constant ϑ in the equation for a variable x which alters with time t, $x = x \sin(\omega t + \vartheta)$, ω being another constant.

ANGLE CONTACT

Symbol: Θ

Definition: In a system of coexisting liquid-solid gas phases, the angle between the flat surface of a solid body and tangent to the liquid surface at a common point of three interfaces in an equilibrium state, it is given by:

$$cos\Theta = \frac{\delta_{sg} - \delta_{sl}}{\delta_{lg}},$$

Where δ_{sg} = solid-gas surface tension,

δ_{sl} = solid-liquid surface tension, and

δ_{lg} = liquid-gas surface tension.

Unit: radian

Note: Also known as "wetting angle"

ANGLE, LOSS

Symbol: δ

Definition: Phase shift angle between the current vector and its capacity component in dielectric placed in alternating electric field.

Unit: Radian

Dimensions: There are no dimensions.

Note: also known as *"loss factor"*

ANGLE, SOLID

Symbol: ω Sometimes Ω

Definition: An area is said to be subtended in three dimensions, a solid angle at an outside point in an analogous manner to the subtends by a line at a non-collinear.

The solid angle that an object subtends at a point is a measure of how big that object appears to an observer at that point. For instance, a small object nearby could subtend the same solid angle as a large object far away.

The solid angle is measured by the area subtended (by projection) on a sphere of the unit radius or the ratio of the area A cut out a spherical surface divided by the square of the radius r of the sphere.

$$\omega = A/r^2$$

Unit: Steradian. There are no dimensions (scalar)

Note: 1. The quantity defined as above was formerly more correctly called analytical solid angle and possessed no units. The size of an analytical solid angle was made equal to the size of the corresponding geometrical solid angle, the last named being as the region cut out in space by an arbitrary cone and measured in steradians.

2. The solid angle completely surrounding a point is 4π units of solid angles, steradian if a small area (dA) is at a distance r from a point and its normal makes an angle∂ with a line drawn to the point, the solid angle formed by the area and point is $dA\cos\vartheta/r^2$

3. Practical applications: The solid angle is used in:

- Defining luminous intensity and luminance
- Calculating spherical excess E of a spherical triangle
- The calculation of potentials by using the Boundary Element Method (BEM)

ANGLE OF REPOSE

Definition: 1. Less common name for the "angle of friction." See "friction, angle of"

2. The maximum angle of a heap of loose material, such as sand, when in equilibrium under gravity.

Unit: Radian

Dimension: There are no dimensions.

ANGULAR DISPLACEMENT

Definition: The angle through which a point, line, or body is rotated, in specific and about a specific axis.

Unit: Radian

Dimension: There are no dimensions.

ANGULAR DIAMETER DISTANCE

Symbol: d_A

Definition: The **angular diameter distance** is a distance measure used in astronomy. It is defined in terms of an object's physical size, x, and θ the angular size of the object as viewed from earth.

$$d_A = \frac{x}{\theta}$$

The angular diameter distance depends on the assumed cosmology of the universe. The angular diameter distance to an object at redshift, z, is expressed in terms of the comoving distance, r, as:

$$d_A = \frac{S_k(r)}{1 + z}$$

Where $S_k(r)$ is the FLRW coordinate defined as:

$$S_k(r) = \begin{cases} \sin\left(\sqrt{-\Omega_k}H_0 r\right) / \left(H_0\sqrt{|\Omega_k|}\right) & \Omega_k < 0 \\ r & \Omega_k = 0 \\ \sinh\left(\sqrt{\Omega_k}H_0 r\right) / \left(H_0\sqrt{|\Omega_k|}\right) & \Omega_k > 0 \end{cases}$$

Where Ω_k is the curvature density and H_0 is the value of the Hubble parameter today.

In the currently favoured geometric model of our Universe, the "angular diameter distance" of an object is a good approximation to the "real distance", i.e., the proper distance when the light left the object. Note that beyond a certain redshift, the angular diameter distance gets smaller with increasing redshift. In other words, an object "behind" another of the same size, beyond a certain redshift (roughly z=1.5), appears larger on the sky and would therefore have a *smaller* "angular diameter distance".

Units: meter (SI units)

Dimensions: L

ANGULAR DISTANCE

Definition: The apparent distance between two celestial bodies, measured in terms of the angle subtended by the bodies at the point of observation.

APERPTURE CONDUCTIVITY

Symbol: α

Definition: The ratio of the density of *a* medium to the acoustic mass ma at an aperture

$$\alpha = \rho/m_a$$

Unit: Kilogramme per Pascal second squared.

Dimension: L.

API gravity

Definition: The American Petroleum Institute gravity, or **API gravity**, is a measure of how heavy or light a petroleum liquid is compared to water: if its API gravity is greater than 10, it is lighter and floats on water; if less than 10, it is heavier and sinks.

API gravity is thus an inverse measure of a petroleum liquid's density relative to that of water (also known as specific gravity).

Unit: No units

Dimension: No dimension (see notes 2 and 3)

Note: 1. It is used to compare the densities of petroleum liquids. For example, if one petroleum liquid is less dense than another, it has a greater API gravity.

2. Although API gravity is mathematically a dimensionless quantity, it is referred to as being in 'degrees'. API gravity is graduated in degrees on a hydroMeter instrument. API gravity values of most petroleum liquids fall between 10 and 70 degrees.

3. In 1916, the U.S. National Bureau of Standards accepted the Baumé scale, which had been developed in France in 1768, as the U.S. standard for measuring the specific gravity of liquids less dense than water. Investigation by the U.S. National Academy of Sciences found major errors in salinity and temperature controls that had caused serious variations in published values. Hydrometers in the U.S. had been manufactured and distributed widely with a modulus of 141.5 instead of the Baumé scale modulus of 140. The scale was so firmly established that, by 1921, the remedy implemented by the American Petroleum Institute was to create the API gravity scale, recognizing the scale that was actually being used.

ARCHIMENDES NUMBER

Symbol: **Ar**

Definition: In viscous fluid dynamics, the **Archimedes number** (**Ar**) is a dimensionless number used to determine the motion of fluids due to density differences, named after the ancient Greek scientist and mathematician Archimedes.

It is the ratio of gravitational forces to viscous forces and has the form:

$$\mathrm{Ar} = \frac{gL^3 \frac{\rho - \rho_\ell}{\rho_\ell}}{\nu^2}$$

$$= \frac{gL^3 \rho_\ell (\rho - \rho_\ell)}{\mu^2}$$

where:

- g is the local external field (for example gravitational acceleration), $\mathrm{m/s^2}$,
- L is the characteristic length of body, m.
- $\dfrac{\rho - \rho_\ell}{\rho_\ell}$ is the Submerged specific gravity,
- ρ_ℓ is the density of the fluid, $\mathrm{kg/m^3}$,
- ρ is the density of the body, $\mathrm{kg/m^3}$,
- $\nu = \dfrac{\mu}{\rho_\ell}$ is the kinematic viscosity, $\mathrm{m^2/s}$,
- μ is the dynamic viscosity, $\mathrm{Pa \cdot s}$,

Field of application: fluid mechanics (motion of fluids due to density differences)

Units: It has no units or dimensions

AREA

Symbol: A; sometimes S.

Definition: A measure of the size of a two-dimensional surface or a region on the surface contained by a closed curve. The size of the area will be expressed by a formula, the nature of which depends on the shape of the surface or that of the region.

Unit: Meter squared.

Dimension: $\mathrm{L^2}$.

Note: Surface area refers to the region that separates a solid from its surroundings.

AREA DENSITY

Symbol: ρ_A

Definition: Mass per unit area

Unit: Kilogram per square Meter, $\mathrm{kg \cdot m^{-2}}$

Dimension: $\mathrm{M\,L^{-2}}$

AREA, MOMENT, MAGNETIC

See *"moment, electromagnetic."*

AREA, SPECIFIC

Symbol: a.

Definition: Area A per unit mass m.

A = A/m

Unit: Meter squared per kilogramme

Dimension: $M^{-1} L^2$

See "specific", "area density."

AREAL VELOCITY

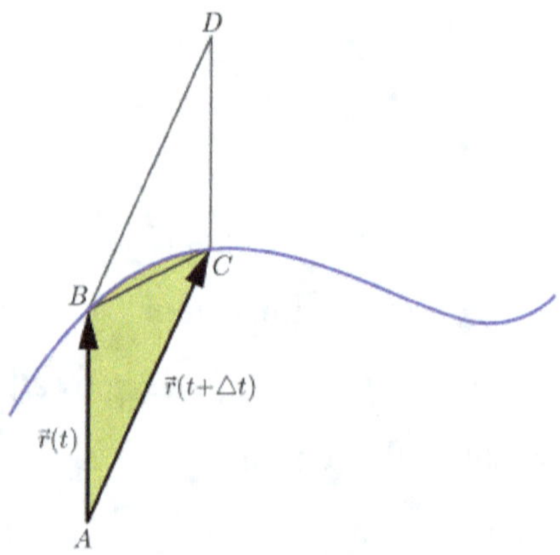

Definition:　In classical mechanics, **areal velocity** (also called **sector velocity** or **sectorial velocity**) is the rate at which an area is swept out by a particle as it moves along a curve.

In the adjoining figure, suppose that a particle moves along the blue curve. At a certain time, t, the particle is located at point B, and a short while later, at time $t + \Delta t$, the particle has moved to point C. The area swept out by the particle is the green area in the figure, bounded by the line segments AB and AC and the curve along which the particle moves. The areal velocity equals this area divided by the time interval Δt in the limit that Δt becomes vanishingly small. It is an example of a pseudo vector (also called an **axial vector**), pointing normal to the plane containing the position and velocity vectors of the particle.

Note: The concept of areal velocity is closely linked historically with the concept of angular momentum. Kepler's second law states that the areal velocity of a planet, with the sun taken as its origin, is constant. Isaac Newton was the first scientist to recognize the dynamical significance of Kepler's second law. With the aid of his laws of motion, he proved in 1684 that any planet that is attracted to a fixed center sweeps out equal areas in equal intervals of time. By the middle of the 18th century, the principle of angular momentum was discovered gradually by Daniel Bernoulli and Leonard Euler and Patrick d'Arcy; d'Arcy's version of the principle was phrased in terms of swept area. For this reason, the principle of angular momentum was often referred to in the older literature in mechanics as "the principle of equal areas." Since the concept of angular momentum includes more than just geometry, the designation "principle of equal areas" has been dropped in modern works.

ATOMIC POLARIZATION

Symbol: PA

Definition: The atomic polarization is defined as:

$$P_A = \frac{1}{3\varepsilon_0} N_A \alpha_A$$

Where N_A = Avogadro number.

α_A = atomic polarizability,

ε_0 = permittivity of free space

Note: The atomic polarizability is the dielectric polarization (per molecule) arising in a unit local field due to the shift of atomic nuclei.

See also *"molar polarization."*

ATOMIC WEIGHT (or Relative Atomic Mass)

Symbol: A_r

Definition: Ratio of the mean atomic mass of a given element and 1/12 of the mass of ^{12}C nuclide. The mean atomic mass is calculated as an average of the natural abundance of a nuclide, e.g., A_r (CI) = 35.453

Unit: There are no units or dimensions.

Note: 1. it is also called "relative atomic mass".

2. Concept of relative atomic mass can be extended to any mixture of nuclides. However, a natural mixture is assumed if not stated otherwise.

ATTENUATION

Definition: the reduction of a radiation quantity, such as intensity, particle, flux density, or energy flux density, upon the passage of the radiation through matter. It may result from any type of interaction with the matter, such as absorption, scattering, etc.

In an electric circuit, it is the reduction in current, voltage or power along a path of energy flow.

See *"attenuation constant", "attenuation coefficient," and "linear attenuation coefficient."*

ATTENUATION COEFFICIENT (1)

Symbol: α; Sometimes a

Definition: For a parallel beam of radiation passing through a uniform medium, the attenuation coefficient is the factor α *in the expression.*

$$e^{-\alpha x} \; cos\,\beta(x\text{-}x_o)$$

for the fraction remaining attenuated after passing through a layer x. β (or b) is the phase coefficient. The propagation coefficient γ (or p) is defined by $\alpha + i\beta$.

Unit: *1. if x is in meter see no*te (1) and *"Linear attenuation coefficient":*

(Neper) per meter.

Dimension: L^{-1}

2. Mass attenuation coefficient (x in kilogrammes per meter squared):

Meter squared per kilogram.

Dimension: $M^{-1} \; L^2$

3. Molar attenuation coefficient (x in moles per meter squared)

Meter squared per mole.

Dimension: $L^2 \; N^{-1}$

Note: 1. if x is in meter, the coefficient is called the *"Linear attenuation coefficient"*. An alternative definition can be used. (See *"linear attenuation coefficient"*.

2. The attenuation coefficient is greater than the absorption coefficient since it takes into account of secondary radiation. See *"linear attenuation coefficient" and also "attenuation coefficient (2)"*.

ATTENUATION COEFFICIENT (2)

Definition: The attenuation coefficient is the sum of the scattering coefficient δ and the absorptivity (absorb coefficient) α

Attenuation coefficient = $\delta + \alpha$

Unit: there are no units or dimensions (scalar)

Note: the quantity is also termed the attenuation factor.

See *"linear attenuation coefficient."*

ATTENUATION COEFFICIENT, LINEAR

Symbol: μ

Definition: a measure of the ability of a medium to diffuse and absorb radiation. If a collimated beam of radiation passes through the medium, it loses intensity due to absorption and scattering. The linear attenuation coefficient is defined by the equation::

$$\mu = \frac{1}{\varnothing} \frac{d\varnothing}{dl}$$

Where $d\varnothing$ is the decrease in luminous or radiant flux $\varnothing$

Passing through a section dl of the material perpendicular to its face.

The linear attenuation coefficient is more general than the absorption coefficient, which only applies to an absorbing medium. The part of the linear attenuation coefficient not due to absorption is sometimes called the *"scattering coefficient"*.

Unit: per meter.

Dimension: L^{-1}

ATTENUATION CONSTANT

Symbol: α

Definition: for a plane progressive wave at a given frequency, the attenuation constant is the rate of exponential decrease in amplitude of voltage, current, or field-component in the direction of propagation of the wave. For example;

$$J_2 = I_1 e^{-\alpha x}$$

Where l_2 and l_1 are current at two points a distance x apart (l_1 being nearer the source of the wave)

Unit: Neper or decibel.

ATWOOD NUMBER

Symbol: A

Definition: The Atwood number (A) is a dimensionless number in fluid dynamics used in the study of hydrodynamic instabilities in density-stratified flows. It is a dimensionless density ratio defined as:

$$A = \frac{\rho_1 - \rho_2}{\rho_1 + \rho_2}$$

where

ρ_1 = density of heavier fluid

ρ_2 = density of lighter fluid

Field of Application: fluid mechanics (onset of instabilities in fluid mixtures due to density differences)

Units: No units or dimensions

AVOGADRO CONSTANT (NUMBER)

Symbol: L or N_A

Definition: the number of molecules contained in one mole of any substance. Amount of substance is proportional to the number of specified entities of that substance, the Avogadro constant being the proportionality factor. It is the same for all substances, and its value is $6.022169 \times 10^{23}\,mol^{-1}$

Unit: reciprocal mole (mol^{-1})

Dimension: N^{-1}.

Note: N is used as a dimensional symbol of the molar value.

See also, *"Lischmidt's number"*

AZIMUTH

Definition:

1.   One of a pair of coordinates, the other being altitude, gives a star's position. It is

the angular distance of a celestial object and the observer's zenith from the south point of the observer's horizon. The azimuth is measured westward from the south point, which is taken as 0o.

2. In relation to elliptically polarized light, the direction of the vibration plan of the light if the phase difference corresponding to ellipticity is reduced to zero without altering the amplitude of the components.

3. In general, azimuth is a bearing or similar angle measured in a horizontal plane.

Unit: Radians

Dimension: There are no dimensions.

B

BAGNOLD NUMBER

Symbol: Ba

Definition: The Bagnold number (Ba) is the ratio of grain collision stresses to viscous fluid stresses in a granular flow with interstitial Newtonian fluid, first identified by Ralph Alger Bagnold. The Bagnold number is defined by

$$Ba = \frac{\rho d^2 \lambda^{1/2} \dot{\gamma}}{\mu}$$

Where ρ is the particle density, d is the grain diameter, $\dot{\gamma}$ is the shear rate, and μ is the dynamic viscosity of the interstitial fluid. The parameter λ is known as the linear concentration and is given by:

$$\lambda = \frac{1}{(\phi_0/\phi)^{\frac{1}{3}} - 1}$$

Where ϕ is the solids fraction, and ϕ_0 is the maximum possible concentration (see random close packing).

In flows with small Bagnold numbers (Ba < 40), viscous fluid stresses dominate grain collision stresses, and the flow is said to be in the 'macro-viscous' regime. Grain collision stresses dominate at large Bagnold number (Ba > 450), which is known as the 'grain-inertia' regime. A transitional regime falls between these two values.

Unit: No units or dimension

(Ref: Bagnold, R. A. (1954). "Experiments on a Gravity-Free Dispersion of Large Solid Spheres in a Newtonian Fluid under Shear". *Proc. R. Soc. Lond. A* 225 (1160): 49–63.)

BANDWIDTH

Definition: bandwidth is a measure of frequency range and is typically measured in Hetz.

Unit: Hertz

Dimension: T^{-1}

Notes:

1. Bandwidth is a central concept in many fields, including information theory, radio communications, signal processing, and spectroscopy.

2. Bandwidth is related to channel capacity for information transmission and is often confused with it. In particular, in common usage, "bandwidth" also refers to data (information) transmission rates when communicating over certain media or devices.

BASIC REPRODUCTION NUMBER

Symbol: R_0

In epidemiology, the basic reproduction number, or basic reproductive number (sometimes called basic reproduction ratio or incorrectly basic reproductive rate), denoted R0 (pronounced *R nought* or *R zero*), of an infection, is the expected number of cases directly generated by one case in a population where all individuals are susceptible to infection. The definition assumes that no other individuals are infected or immunized (naturally or through vaccination). Some definitions, such as that of the Australian Department of Health, add the absence of "any deliberate intervention in disease transmission". The basic reproduction number is not necessarily the same as the effective reproduction number R (usually written Rt [*t* for a time], sometimes Re), which is the number of cases generated in the current state of a population, which does not have to be the uninfected state. R0 is a dimensionless number (persons infected per person infecting) and not a time rate, which would have units of $time^{-1}$ or units of time like doubling time.

R0 is not a biological constant for a pathogen as it is also affected by other factors, such as environmental conditions and the behavior of the infected population. R0 values are usually estimated from mathematical models, and the estimated values are dependent on the model used and the values of other parameters. Thus values given in the literature only make sense in the given context, and it is recommended not to use obsolete values or compare values based on different models. R_0 does not by itself give an estimate of how fast an infection spreads in the population.

The most important uses of R_0 are determining if an emerging infectious disease can spread in a population and determining what proportion of the population should be immunized through vaccination to eradicate a disease. In commonly used infection models, when R0>1, the infection will be able to start spreading in a population, but not if $R_0<1$. Generally, the larger the value of R_0, the harder it is to control the epidemic. For simple models, the proportion of the population that needs to be effectively immunized (meaning not susceptible to infection) to prevent the sustained spread of the infection has to be larger than $1-1/R_0$. Conversely, the proportion of the population that remains susceptible to infection in the endemic equilibrium is $1/R_0$.

The basic reproduction number is affected by several factors, including the duration of infectivity of affected people, the infectiousness of the microorganism, and the number of susceptible people in the population that the infected people contact.

Unit: Has no units or dimensions

(Ref. Encyclopedia Science and Computing)

BAT

Alternative Titles: baht, bath, ephah

Definition: **Bat is an** ancient Hebrew unit of liquid and dry capacity. Estimated at 37 liters (about 6.5 gallons) and approximately equivalent to the Greek *metrētēs*.

The bat contained 10 *omers*, 1 *omer* being the quantity (based on tradition) of manna allotted to each Israelite for every <u>day</u> of the 40-year sojourn in the desert recorded in the Bible.

Unit: The SI unit is Littre

Dimension: L^3

See also: *"metrētēs", "litre", "omer."*

BEJAN NUMBER

Symbol: Be

Definition: Two different Bejan numbers (Be) are used in the scientific domains of thermodynamics and fluid mechanics. Bejan numbers are named after Adrian Bejan.

Definition 1: Thermodynamics:

In the field of thermodynamics, the Bejan number is the ratio of heat transfer irreversibility to total irreversibility due to heat transfer and fluid friction:

$$Be = \frac{\dot{S}'_{gen,\,\Delta T}}{\dot{S}'_{gen,\,\Delta T} + \dot{S}'_{gen,\,\Delta p}}$$

Where

$\dot{S}'_{gen,\,\Delta T}$ is the entropy generation contributed by heat transfer

$\dot{S}'_{gen,\,\Delta p}$ is the entropy generation contributed by fluid friction.

Schiubba has also achieved the relation between Bejan number Be and Brinkmann number Br.

$$Be = \frac{\dot{S}'_{gen,\,\Delta T}}{\dot{S}'_{gen,\,\Delta T} + \dot{S}'_{gen,\,\Delta p}} = \frac{1}{1 + Br}$$

Definition 2: Fluid Mechanics

In the field of fluid mechanics, the Bejan number is identical to the one defined in heat transfer problems, being the dimensionless pressure drop along the fluid path length L in both external flows and internal flows:

$$Be_L = \frac{\Delta p\, L^2}{\mu \nu}$$

where

μ is the dynamic viscosity

ν is the momentum diffusivity (or Kinematic viscosity).

Field of application: fluid mechanics (dimensionless pressure drop along a channel)

Unit: No units or dimension

BINGHAM NUMBER

Symbol: Bi (or Bm)

Definition: Bingham number, abbreviated as Bm, a dimensionless number, is the ratio of yield stress to viscous stress. It describes the extent to which the controllable yield stress can exceed the viscous stress (typically Bi $\gg$ 1) and is an essential descriptor of Bingham plastic behavior.

It is used in momentum transfer in general and flow of Bingham plastics calculations in particular. It is normally defined in the following form:

The relation gives Bingham the number:

$$Bm = \frac{\tau_y\, l}{\mu\, v}$$

Where:

l: characteristic length *(m)*

μ: dynamic viscosity *(Pa s)*

v: velocity (m/s)

τ_y :   yield stress (Pa)

Note: Magnetorheological (MR) fluids are described using two dimensionless numbers, the Bingham and Mason numbers. The Mason number is the ratio of particle magnetic forces to viscous forces and describes the behavior of MR fluids at the microscopic, particle level scale. At the macroscopic continuum scale, Bingham number is the ratio of yield stress to viscous stress, describing the fluid's bulk motion. If these two nondimensional numbers can be related, then microscopic models can be directly compared to macroscopic results. We show that if microscopic and macroscopic forces are linearly related, then Bingham and Mason numbers are inversely related, or, alternatively, that the product of the Bingham number and the Mason number is a constant. This relationship is experimentally validated based on measurements of apparent viscosity on a high shear rate, $\gamma' \approx -\ 10\ 000\ \text{s}^{-1}$, Searle cell rheometer. This relationship between Mason and Bingham numbers is then used to analyze a Mason number-based result and inform the MR fluid device design process.

Field of application: fluid mechanics, rheology (ratio of yield stress to viscous stress)

Unit: Dimensionless

BIOT NUMBER

Symbol: B_i

Definition: The Biot number (Bi) is a dimensionless quantity used in heat transfer calculations. It is named after the eighteenth-century French physicist Jean-Baptiste Biot (1774–1862) and gives a simple index of the ratio of the thermal resistances *inside of* a body and *at the surface* of a body. This ratio determines whether or not the temperatures inside a body will vary significantly in space while the body heats or cools over time from a thermal gradient applied to its surface.

The Biot number is defined as:

$$\mathrm{Bi} = \frac{h}{k} L$$

where:

- k is the thermal conductivity of the body [W/(m·K)]
- h is a convective heat transfer coefficient [W/(m²·K)]
- L is a characteristic length [m] of the geometry considered.

The characteristic length in most relevant problems becomes the heat characteristic length, i.e., the ratio between the body volume and the body's heated (or cooled) surface: $L = V/A_Q$.

Here, Q for *heat* is used to denote that the surface to be considered is only the portion of the total surface through which the heat Q passes. The physical significance of the Biot number can be understood by imagining the heat flow from a small hot metal sphere suddenly immersed in a pool to the surrounding fluid. The heat flow experiences two resistances: the first within the solid metal (which is influenced by both the size and composition of the sphere) and the second at the surface of the sphere. If the thermal resistance of the fluid/sphere interface exceeds the thermal resistance offered by the interior of the metal sphere, the Biot number will be less than one. For systems where it is much less than one, the interior of the sphere may be presumed to be a uniform temperature, although this temperature may change as heat passes into the sphere from the surface. The equation to describe this change in (relatively uniform) temperature inside the object is a simple exponential one described in Newton's law of cooling.

In contrast, the metal sphere may be large, causing the characteristic length to increase to the point that the Biot number is larger than one. Now, thermal gradients within the sphere become important, even though the sphere material is a good conductor. If the sphere is made of a thermally insulating (poorly conductive) material, such as wood or styrofoam, the interior resistance to heat flow will exceed that of the fluid/sphere boundary, even with a much smaller sphere. In this case, the Biot number will again be greater than one..

Field of application: heat transfer (surface vs. volume conductivity of solids)

Unit: Has no units or dimension

(Ref. Encyclopedia Science and Computing)

BIOT NUMBER, MASS TRANSFER

Symbol: Bi_m

Definition: An analogous version of the Biot number (usually called the "mass transfer Biot number" or (Bi_m) is also used in mass diffusion processes:

$$Bi_m = \frac{k_c}{D} L$$

where:

- K_c: convective mass transfer coefficient (analogous to the h of the heat transfer problem)
- D: mass diffusivity (analogous to the k of heat transfer problem)
- L: characteristic length

Units: Dimensionless

BITRATE

(Sometimes written bit rate, data rate or as a variable R_{bit})

Definition: is the number of bits that are conveyed or processed per unit of time.

Bit rate is often used as a synonym for the terms connection speed, transfer rate, channel capacity, maximum throughput and digital bandwidth capacity of a communication system.

Unit: 'bit per second' (bid/s or bps),

Note: 1. The unit bit/s is often comes in Onjunction with a SI prefix such as kilo (Kbit/s or kbps), mega (Mbit/s or Mbps), Giga (Gbit/s or Gbps) or Tera (Tbit/s or Tbps).

1,000 bit/s = 1 Kbits/s (one kilobit or one thousand bits per second)

1,000,000 bit/s = Mbits/s (one megabit or one million bits per second)

1,000,000,000 bit/s = 1 Gbit/s (one gigabit or one billion bits per second)

2.   while often referred to as "speed", bitrate does not measure distance /time but quantity /time and thus should be distinguished from the "propagation speed" (which depends on the transmission medium and has the usual physical meaning).

3.   gross bitrate or raw bitrate is the total number of physically transferred bits per second, including both useful payload data and protocol overhead.

4.   the net bitrate or useful bit rate is measured at some reference point above the physical layer and excludes lower layer protocol overhead, for example, redundant channel coding (forwarded error correction).

BITRATE, AVERAGE

Definition: average bit rate refers to the average amount of data transferred per second.

Unit: bit per second

Notes: 1. Average bitrate is commonly referred to for digital music or video. An mps file, for example, has an average bit rate of 128 kbit/s transfers, on average 128,000 bits every second. It can have a higher bit rate and lower bit rate parts, and the average bit rate is obtained by dividing the sum of the bit rate of each sample by the number of samples.

2. Bit rate is not fully reliable as a measure of audio/video quality, as some formats, such as wma and vorbis, produce higher sound quality than the standard mps format at the same bit rate.

3. average bit rate can also refer to a form of variable bitrate encoding where the encoder will try to average the use of data for high and low complexity areas so that the bitrate of every audio segment averaged yields a specified bitrate.

BLAKE NUMBER

Symbol: B

Definition: The Blake number in fluid mechanics is a nondimensional number showing the ratio of inertial force to viscous force. It is used in momentum transfer in general and in particular for the flow of a fluid through beds of solids. It is a generalization of the Reynolds number for flow through porous media.

Expressed mathematically, the Blake number B is:

$$B = \frac{u\rho D_h}{\mu(1 - \epsilon)}$$

where

E = void fraction

M = dynamic viscosity

P = fluid density

D_h = hydraulic diameter

U = flow velocity

Field of application: geology, fluid mechanics, porous media (inertial over viscous forces in fluid flow through porous media)

Unit: Has no units or dimension

BODENSTEIN NUMBER

Symbol: B_0

Definition: The Bodenstein number (abbreviated *Bo*, named after Max Bodenstein) is a dimensionless parameter in chemical reaction engineering, which describes the ratio of the amount of substance introduced by convection to that introduced by diffusion. Hence, it characterizes the back mixing in a system and allows statements of whether and how much volume elements or substances within a chemical reactor mix due to the prevalent currents.

It is defined as the ration of the convection current to the dispersion current. The Bodenstein number is an element of the *dispersion model of residence times* and is also called the *dimensionless dispersion coefficient.*

The equation calculates the Bodenstein number:

$$Bo = \frac{u \cdot L}{D_{ax}}$$

where

- u : flow velocity
- L: length of the reactor
- D_{ax}: axial dispersion coefficient

Mathematically, two idealized extreme cases exist for the Bodenstein number. These, however, cannot be fully reached in practice:

- B_0=0 corresponds to full back mixing, which is the ideal state to be reached in a continuous stirred-tank reactor.
- B_0=∞ corresponds to no back mixing but a continuous through-flow as in an ideal flow channel.

Control of the flow velocity within a reactor allows adjusting the Bodenstein number to a pre-calculated desired value so that the desired degree of back mixing of the substances in the reactor can be reached.

Unit: Has no units or dimension

BOHR MAGNETON NUMBER

Symbol: n_0

Definition: The magnetic moment per atom expressed in Bohr magneton.

Unit' Bohr magneton

Dimension: $ML^3 T^{-2} I^{-1}$

See "Bohr magneton"

BOHR RADIUS

Symbols: $\alpha_{o.}$

Definition: Radius of lowest energy Bohr orbit of hydrogen atom (1s). For a hydrogen atom in Is state distance of maximum electron density is:

$$a_o = \frac{\hbar^2}{2me^2} = 0.529167 \times 10^{-10} \text{ m}$$

where: m = electron mass, e = electron charge,

$\hbar$ = Planck constant / 2π.

Unit: meter

Dimension: L

BOLLARD PULL

Bollard pull is a conventional measure of the pulling (or towing) power of a watercraft.

Definition: Bollard pull is the force exerted by the towboat running full ahead while secured by a long line to a stationary bollard.

It is defined as the force (in tons or kilonewtons (kN)) exerted by a vessel under full power on a shore-mounted bollard through a tow-line, commonly measured in a practical test (but sometimes simulated) under test conditions that include calm water, no tide, level trim, and sufficient depth and side clearance for a free propeller stream. Like a car's horsepower or mileage rating, it is a convenient but idealized number that must be adjusted for operating conditions that differ from the test.

The bollard pull of a vessel may be reported as two numbers, the *static* or *maximum* bollard pull - the highest force measured - and the *steady* or *continuous* bollard pull, the average of measurements over an interval of, for example, 10 minutes. An equivalent measurement on land is known as drawbar pull or tractive force, which is used to measure the total horizontal force generated by a locomotive, a piece of heavy machinery such as a tractor, or a truck (specifically a ballast tractor), which is utilized to move a load.

Bollard pull is primarily (but not only) used for measuring the strength of tugboats, with the largest commercial harbour tugboats in the 2000-the 2010s having around 60 to 65 short tons-force (530–580 kN) of bollard pull, which is described as 15 short tons-force (130 kN) above "normal" tugboats. Far Samson of Farstad Shipping is the world's strongest tug, with a bollard pull of 423 metric tons.

Units: tons or kilonewtons

Dimensions: M L T^{-2}

BOLTZMANN CONSTANT

Symbol: k

Definition: the quotient of universal gas constant R and Avogadro number N_A.

$k = R/N_A = 1.38054 \times 10^{-23}$

Unit: Joule per kelvin.

Dimension: $ML^2 T^{-3}$.

BOND NUMBER (B_0),

also known as the EÖTVÖS NUMBER (EO)

Symbol: B_0

Definition: In fluid mechanics, the Bond number Bo, also known as Eötvös Number (Eo), is a dimensionless number that describes the ratio of gravitational to capillary forces; in other words, it describes the ratio of body forces (often gravitational) to surface tension forces. It is given by the equation:

$$\mathrm{Eo} = \mathrm{Bo} = \frac{\Delta \rho \, g \, L^2}{\gamma}.$$

$\Delta \rho$: difference in density of the two phases (SI units: kg/m^3)

- g: gravitational acceleration, (SI units: m/s^2)
- L: characteristic length, (SI units: m) (for example, the radii of curvature for a drop)
- γ : surface tension, (SI units: N/m)

The Bond number can also be written as

$$\mathrm{Bo} = \left(\frac{L}{\lambda_c}\right)^2$$

where $\lambda_c = \sqrt{\gamma/\rho g}$ is the capillary length

Sometimes the density scale used is the difference in density between the two phases, $\Delta\rho$.

The Bond number is a measure of the importance of surface tension forces compared to body forces. A high Bond number indicates that the system is relatively unaffected by surface tension effects; a low number (typically less than one is the requirement) indicates that surface tension dominates. Intermediate numbers indicate a non-trivial balance between the two effects.

Note: A high value of the Eötvös or Bond number indicates that the system is relatively unaffected by surface tension effects, a low value (typically less than one) indicates that surface tension dominates. Intermediate numbers indicate a non-trivial balance between the two effects. It may be derived in a number of ways, such as scaling the pressure of a drop of liquid on a solid surface.

Field of application: geology, fluid mechanics, porous media

Units: Dimensionless

BREADTH

See *"length"*.

BRIGHTNESS,

APPARENT (or SUBJECTIVE)

Definition: The amount of light that appears to be emitted by a body

Unit: Nit

Dimension: MT^{-3}

Note: This is the deprecated name of *"luminance'*

See *"luminance"*

BRIGHTNESS TEMPERATURE

Definition: The brightness temperature of a black – body radiator that has the same photometric luminance as the radiating body at a specific wavelength. The brightness temperature is always lower than the true temperature.

Unit: Kelvin

Note: it is also called "illuminance temperature".

BRILLIANCE, POINT

Definition: The illumination produced by a source on a plane at the observer's eye normal to the incident flux

Dimension: $M\ T^{-3}$

Note: The quality refers to a source so distant that it's apparent diameter is insignificant.

BRINKMAN NUMBER

Symbol: B_r

Definition: The Brinkman number (Br) is a dimensionless number related to heat conduction from a wall to a flowing viscous fluid, commonly used in polymer processing. It is named after the Dutch mathematician and physicist Henri Brinkman. There are several definitions; one is:

$$Br = \frac{\mu u^2}{\kappa(T_w - T_0)} = \Pr Ec$$

where

- μ is the dynamic viscosity;
- u is the flow velocity;
- κ is the thermal conductivity;
- T_0 is the bulk fluid temperature;
- T_w is the wall temperature;
- Pr is the Prandtl number
- Ec is the Eckert number

It is the ratio between heat produced by viscous dissipation and heat transported by molecular conduction. i.e., the ratio of viscous heat generation to external heating. The higher its value, the slower the conduction of heat produced by viscous dissipation and hence the larger the temperature rise.

In, for example, a screw extruder, the energy supplied to the polymer melt comes primarily from two sources:

- viscous heat generated by shear between elements of the flowing liquid moving at different velocities;
- direct heat conduction from the wall of the extruder.

The former is supplied by the motor turning the screw, the latter by heaters. The Brinkman number is a measure of the ratio of the two.

Field of application: heat transfer, fluid mechanics (conduction from a wall to a viscous fluid)

Unit: has no units or dimension

BULK MODULUS

Symbol: K or B

Definition: The bulk modulus of a substance is a measure of how resistant to compression that substance is. It is defined as the ratio of the infinitesimal pressure increase to the resulting relative decrease of the volume.

The bulk modulus is a constant that describes how resistant a substance is to compression. It is defined as the ratio between pressure increase and the resulting decrease in a material's volume. Together with Young's modulus, the shear modulus, and Hooke's law, the bulk modulus describes a material's response to stress or strain.

Usually, the bulk modulus is indicated by K or B in equations and tables. While it applies to uniform compression of any substance, it is most often used to describe the behavior of fluids. It can be used to predict compression, calculate density, and indirectly indicate the types of chemical bonding within a substance. The bulk modulus is considered a descriptor of elastic properties because a compressed material returns to its original volume once the pressure is released.

Bulk modulus may be calculated using the formula:

Bulk Modulus (K) = Volumetric stress / Volumetric strain

This is the same as saying it equals the change in pressure divided by the change in volume divided by initial volume:

Bulk Modulus (K) = ($p_1 - p_0$) / [($V_1 - V_0$) / V_0]

P_0 and V_0 are the initial pressure and volume, respectively, and p_1 and $V1$ are the pressure and volume measured upon compression.

Bulk modulus elasticity may also be expressed in terms of pressure and density:

$K = (p_1 - p_0) / [(\rho_1 - \rho_0) / \rho_0]$

Here, ρ_0 and ρ_1 are the initial and final density values.

Units: Pascals (Pa) or newtons per square meter (N/m^2) in the metric system, or pounds per square inch (PSI) in the English system.

Dimensions: $M\ L^{-1}\ T^{-2}$

(Source:

- *De Jong, Maarten; Chen, Wei (2015). "Charting the complete elastic properties of inorganic crystalline compounds". Scientific Data. 2: 150009. doi:10.1038/sdata.2015.9*
- *Gilman, J.J. (1969). Micromechanics of Flow in Solids. New York: McGraw-Hill.)*

BULK MODULUS, FLUID (K)

There are bulk modulus values for solids (e.g., 160 GPa for steel; 443 GPa for diamond; 50 MPa for solid helium) and gases (e.g., 101 kPa for air at constant temperature), but the most common tables list values for liquids.

Next is a table for the bulk modulus of some fluids. The values are given both in English and metric units:

	English Units *(10^5 PSI)*	SI Units *(10^9 Pa)*
Acetone	1.34	0.92
Benzene	1.5	1.05
Carbon Tetrachloride	1.91	1.32
Ethyl Alcohol	1.54	1.06

Gasoline	1.9	1.3
Glycerin	6.31	4.35
ISO 32 Mineral Oil	2.6	1.8
Kerosene	1.9	1.3
Mercury	41.4	28.5
Paraffin Oil	2.41	1.66
Petrol	1.55 - 2.16	1.07 - 1.49
Phosphate Ester	4.4	3
SAE 30 Oil	2.2	1.5
Seawater	3.39	2.34
Sulfuric Acid	4.3	3.0
Water	3.12	2.15
Water – Glycol	5	3.4
Water - Oil Emulsion	3.3	2.3

The K value varies depending on the state of matter of a sample, and in some cases, on the temperature. In liquids, the amount of dissolved gas greatly impacts the value. A high value of K indicates a material resists compression, while a low value indicates volume appreciably decreases under uniform pressure. The reciprocal of the bulk modulus is compressibility, so a substance with a low bulk modulus has high compressibility.

Note: from the table, it is easy to notice that the liquid metal mercury is very nearly incompressible. This reflects the large atomic radius of mercury atoms compared with atoms in organic compounds and the atoms' packing. Because of hydrogen bonding, water also resists compression.

(Source:

- *De Jong, Maarten; Chen, Wei (2015). "Charting the complete elastic properties of inorganic crystalline compounds". Scientific Data. 2: 150009. doi:10.1038/sdata.2015.9*
- *Gilman, J.J. (1969). Micromechanics of Flow in Solids. New York: McGraw-Hill.)*

C

CALORIFIC VALUE

Definition: The amount of heat liberated by the complete combustion of a unit mass of fuel under standard conditions. Two values are recognized.

1. The Gross (or Higher) Calorific Value (GCV): is the amount of heat evolved in a bomb calorimeter when the products of combustion are cooled to ambient conditions (25^0C) and water vapour formed during combustion (and any water originally present) has condensed, evolving its latent heat. It may be referred to either as constant volume or constant pressure.

2. The Net (lower) Calorific Value: it is the GCV after deducting the latent heat of condensing water. In other words, it is the calorific value when the water formed during combustion (and any water originally present) has condensed, evolving its latent heat. It may be referred to either as constant volume or constant pressure.

   The net calorific value reflects more accurately the heat evolved under operating conditions. However, it will be only an estimate unless the concentration of water vapour in the chimney gases is known accurately.

   Unit: joule per Kilogram

   Dimension: $L^2\ T^{-2}$

CALORIFIC VALUE, VOLUME BASIS.

Symbol: C

Definition: Heat energy Q divided by volume V.

$C = Q/V$

Unit: Joule per meter cubed

Dimension: $ML^{-1}\ T^{-2}$

CANDLE POWER.

Symbol: cp

Definition: Candlepower is luminous intensity expressed in candela's

Unit: Candela

Dimension: $ML^2\,T^{-3}$

Note; Candlepower is the deprecated name of "luminous intensity"

See " *intensity, luminous.* "

CAPACITANCE

Symbol: C

Definition: Capacitance is the property of a system of conductors and dielectrics which permits the storage of electrically separated charges when potential differences exist between the conductors./ it value is expressed as the ratio of an electric charge (Q) to a potential difference (V):

$C = Q/V$

For a given conductor, the capacitance is independent of Q and depends on the size and shape of the conductor. Two conductors together from a capacitor (condenser) and the capacitance C is defined as the ratio of charge on either conductor to the potential difference between them.

Unit: Farad.

Dimension: $M^{-1}\,L^{-2}\,T^4\,I^2$

CAPACITANCE, ACOUSTIC

Symbol: c

Definition: the imaginary part of acoustic impedance due to the stiffness or elasticity *(k)* of the medium. It is given by: $C = S^2/k$, where S is the area in vibration.

In the case of resonators, e.g., Helmholtz resonators, the elasticity is seated in the air of the cavity. In this case, the capacitance (C) is given by:

$\partial v/, \partial p$ where ∂v is the change of volume of air in the cavity caused by an increase of pressure ϑp

For an adiabatic change $\dfrac{\vartheta v}{\vartheta p} = \dfrac{v}{\gamma p} = \dfrac{v}{c^2 \rho}$

Where: c is the velocity of sound,

$\qquad \gamma$ is the ratio of specific heat capacity, and

ρ is the mean density of the medium.

The capacitance is then a function of the volume of the vessel of the resonator.

CAPACITANCE MUTUAL.

Definition: the extent to which two capacitance can affect each other, expressed in terms of the ratio of the amount of charge transferred to one to the corresponding potential difference of the other.

Unit: farad

Dimension: $M^{-1} L^{-2} T^4 I^2$

CAPACITANCE, SPECIFIC INDUCTIVE

See "permittivity, relative".

CAPACITANCE THERMAL

Definition: Entropy S added to a body divided by the resulting temperature difference ϑ.

Thermal capacitance = S/ϑ

Unit: thermal farad = joule per kelvin squared.

Dimension: $ML^{-2} T^2$

Note: The former definition was the quantity of heat that is taken by or lost by a given body or mass of a substance in changing its temperature by one degree of a specific temperature scale.

Thermal capacitance = Q/ϑ

CAPACITIVITY

See *"permittivity, absolute."*

CAPACITOR

Definition:

1. Former name of capacitance.

2. Any system or component possessing appreciable capacitance.

See *"capacitance"*

CAPACITY

See *"volume "*.

CAPACITY, AMPERE-HOUR

Definition: The charge measured in ampere-hours that can be delivered by a storage battery or cell under specified working condition up to the limit to which the battery may be safely discharged.

Unit: Ampere-hour.

Dimension: T I

CAPILLARY NUMBER

Symbol: Ca

Definition: In fluid dynamics, the capillary number (Ca) is a dimensionless quantity representing the relative effect of viscous drag forces versus surface tension forces acting across an interface between a liquid and a gas or between two immiscible liquids. For example, an air bubble in a liquid flow tends to be deformed by the friction of the liquid flow due to viscosity effects, but the surface tension forces tend to minimize the surface area. The capillary number is defined as:

$$Ca = \frac{\mu V}{\sigma}$$

where μ is the dynamic viscosity of the liquid, V is a characteristic velocity, and σ is the surface tension or interfacial tension between the two fluid phases.

Being a dimensionless quantity, the capillary number's value does not depend on the system of units.

Note: In the petroleum industry, the capillary number is denoted Nc instead of Ca.

For low capillary numbers (a rule of thumb says less than 10^{-5}), flow in porous media is dominated by capillary forces, whereas for high capillary numbers, the capillary forces are negligible compared to the viscous forces. Flow through the pores in an oil field reservoir have capillary number on the order of 10^{-6}, whereas flow of oil through an oil well drill pipe has a capillary number on the order of 1.

The capillary number plays a role in the dynamics of capillary flow; in particular, it governs the dynamic contact angle of a flowing droplet at an interface.

Field of application: porous media, fluid mechanics (viscous forces versus surface tension)

Unit: Dimensionless

CATALYTIC ACTIVITY CONCENTRATION

Definition: Change in reaction rate due to the presence of a catalyst per unit volume of the system

Units: $kat \cdot m^{-3}$

Dimension: $L^{-3} T^{-1} N$

CHANDRASEKHAR NUMBER

Symbol: Q

Definition: The Chandrasekhar number is a dimensionless quantity used in magnetic convection to represent a ratio of the Lorentz force to the viscosity. It is named after the Indian astrophysicist Subrahmanya Chandrasekhar. The number's main function is as a measure of the magnetic field, being proportional to the square of a characteristic magnetic field in a system.

The Chandrasekhar number is usually denoted by the letter Q and is motivated by a dimensionless form of the Navier-Stokes equation in the presence of a magnetic force in the equations of magnetohydrodynamics:

$$\frac{1}{\sigma}\left(\frac{\partial \mathbf{u}}{\partial t} + (\mathbf{u} \cdot \nabla)\mathbf{u}\right) = -\nabla p + \nabla^2\mathbf{u} + \frac{\sigma}{\zeta}Q\,(\nabla \wedge \mathbf{B}) \wedge \mathbf{B}$$

Where σ is the Prandtl number, and ζ is the magnetic Prandtl number.

The Chandrasekhar number is thus defined as:

$$Q = \frac{B_0{}^2 d^2}{\mu_0 \rho \nu \lambda}$$

where μ_0 is the magnetic permeability, ρ is the density of the fluid, ν is the kinematic viscosity, and λ is the magnetic diffusivity. B_0 and d are a characteristic magnetic field and a length scale of the system respectively.

It is related to the Hartmann number, Ha, by the relation:

$$Q = Ha^2$$

Field of application: hydromagnetics (Lorentz force versus viscosity)

Unit: Has no units or dimensions

[Ref. Encyclopedia Science and Computing]

CHARACTERISTIC TEMPERATURE

Symbol: Θ

Definition: Temperature at which energy ($k\Theta$) is equal to the energy of the elastic wave in crystal with frequency maximum ω_D at a given temperature.

$$k\Theta = h\omega_D$$

where, k = Boltzmann constant, and h = Planck constant.

Unit: Kelvin.

Dimension $L^2\,T^{-2}$

CHARACTERISTIC (WEISS) TEMPERATURE

Symbol: θ or θ_w

Definition: It is the temperature o in the Curie- Weiss law:

$X = C/ (T- \theta)$

Where X is the susceptibility, and T is the thermodynamic temperature.

Unit: Kelvin.

Note: The value θ in the Curie- Weiss law can be thought of as a correction of the Curie's reflecting the extent to which the magnetic dipoles interact with each other.

In materials exhibiting antiferromagnetism, the temperature θ corresponds to the temperature.

See "Curie temperature" and "Neel temperature ".

CHARGE

Definition*:* The word "Charge" has the following meaning:

1. See "Charge, electric".
2. To convert electrical energy to chemical energy in a secondary battery.
3. To feed electrical energy to a capacitor or other device that can store it.
4. An amount of fuel is fed from time to time to a furnace, e.g., the fissionable fuel placed in a reactor to produce a chain reaction.

CHARGE, ELECTRIC

Symbol*: Q*

Definition*:* Electric charge is a fundamentally assumed concept required by the existence of forces measurable experimentally. It has two forms, known as positive and negative.

1. The electric charge in (or on) a body is the quantity of unbalanced electricity in the body, i.e., the excess or deficiency of electrons which gives the body negative or positive electrification, respectively.
2. The integral of current I with respect to time t.

$$Q = \int I dt$$

Unit*:* Coulomb.

Dimension*:* T I

Note: The quantity is sometimes inadequately termed the quantity of electricity.

CHARGE DENSITY

Symbol*: ρ*; sometimes η:

Definition*:* Charge per unit volume, i.e., charge Q divided by volume V $\quad \rho = Q/V$

Unit*:* Coulomb per meter cubed.

Note: The quantity is better termed the volume density of charge.

CHARGE DENSITY, SURFACE

Symbol: σ

Definition: Charge per unit area, i.e., charge Q divided by surface area A

$$\sigma = Q/A$$

Unit: Coulomb per meter squared.

Dimension: $L^{-2} T I$

CHARGE, SPECIFIC

Symbol: q

Definition: Charge per unit mass, i.e., charge Q divided by mass m

$$q = Q/m$$

Unit: Coulomb per kilogramme

Dimension: $M^{-1} T I$

See "Specific"

CHARGE, THERMAL

See "entropy"

CIRCULAR DICHROISM (CD)

Symbol: CD

Definition: Circular Dichroism (CD) is an absorption spectroscopy method based on the differential absorption of left and right circularly polarized light. Optically active chiral molecules will preferentially absorb one direction of the circularly polarized light.

COEFFICIENT OF DETERMINATION

Symbol: R^2 or r^2

Definition: In statistics, the coefficient of determination, denoted R^2 or r^2 and pronounced "R squared", is the proportion of the variation in the dependent variable that is predictable from the independent variable(s).

It is a statistic used in the context of statistical models whose main purpose is either the prediction of future outcomes or the testing of hypotheses on the basis of other related information. It provides a measure of how well-observed outcomes are replicated by the model based on the proportion of total variation of outcomes explained by the model.

There are several definitions of R^2 that are sometimes equivalent. One class of such cases includes that of simple linear regression where r^2 is used instead of R^2. When an intercept is included, then r^2 is simply the square of the sample correlation coefficient (i.e., r) between the observed outcomes and the observe d predictor values. If additional regressors are included, R^2 is the square of the coefficient of multiple correlation. In both such cases, the coefficient of determination normally ranges from 0 to 1.

In some cases, the computational definition of R^2 can yield negative values, depending on the definition used. This can arise when the predictions that are being compared to the corresponding outcomes have not been derived from a model-fitting procedure using those data. Even if a model-fitting procedure has been used, R^2 may still be negative, for example, when linear regression is conducted without including an intercept or when a nonlinear function is used to fit the data. In cases where negative values arise, the mean of the data provides a better fit to the outcomes than the fitted function values, according to this particular criteria.

Unit: Dimensionless

COEFFICIENT OF FRICTION (μ)

Symbol: μ also C_f

Definition: **coefficient of friction is the** ratio of the frictional force F resisting the motion of two surfaces in contact to the normal force N pressing the two surfaces together. It is usually symbolized by the Greek letter mu (μ).

$$F < \mu_s N \quad \text{static (no slip)}$$

$$F = \mu_s N \quad \text{static, impending slip}$$

$$F = \mu_k N \quad \text{sliding (slip between surfaces)}$$

Where μ_s is the coefficient of static friction, and μ_k is the coefficient of kinetic friction. The value of μ_s is generally higher than the value of μ_k for a given combination of materials.

Mathematically, $\mu = F/N$, where F is the frictional force, and N is the normal force.

The coefficient of friction has different values for static friction and kinetic friction. In static friction, the frictional force resists the force that is applied to an object, and the object remains at rest until the force of static friction is overcome. In kinetic friction, the frictional force resists the motion of an object. For the case of a brick sliding on a clean wooden table, the coefficient of kinetic friction is about 0.5, which implies that a force equal to half the weight of the bricks is required just to overcome friction in keeping the bricks moving along at a constant speed, and the coefficient of static friction is about 0.6. The frictional force itself is directed oppositely to the motion of the object.

Coefficients of friction between materials are best determined through testing. However, it is possible to find tables in the literature for friction coefficients between various materials. Examples of the table are given next.

Unit: Dimensionless

(Note: The table below is from Barrett, "Fastener Design Manual," NASA Reference Publication 1228, 1990):

Coefficients of Static and Sliding Friction				
Materials	Static		Sliding	
	Dry	Greasy	Dry	Greasy
Hard steel on hard steel	0.78	0.11 (a)	0.42	0.029 (k)
	---	0.23 (b)	---	0.081 (e)

	---	0.15 (c)	---	0.080 (i)
	---	0.11 (d)	---	0.058 (j)
	---	0.0075 (p)	---	0.084 (d)
	---	0.0052 (h)	---	0.105 (k)
	---	---	---	0.096 (l)
	---	---	---	0.108 (m)
	---	---	---	0.12 (a)
Mild steel on mild steel	0.74	---	0.57	0.09 (a)
	---	---	---	0.19 (u)
Hard steel on graphite	0.21	0.09 (a)	---	---
Hard steel on babbitt (ASTM No. 1)	0.70	0.23 (b)	0.33	0.16 (b)
	---	0.15 (c)	---	0.06 (c)
	---	0.08 (d)	---	0.11 (d)
	---	0.085 (e)	---	---
Hard steel on babbitt (ASTM No. 8)	0.42	0.17 (b)	0.35	0.14 (b)
	---	0.11 (c)	---	0.065 (c)
	---	0.09 (d)	---	0.07 (d)
	---	0.08 (e)	---	0.08 (h)
Hard steel on babbitt (ASTM No. 10)	---	0.25 (b)	---	0.13 (b)
	---	0.12 (c)	---	0.06 (c)
	---	0.10 (d)	---	0.055 (d)
	---	0.11 (e)	---	---
Mild steel on cadmium silver	---	---	---	0.097 (f)
Mild steel on phosphor bronze	---	---	0.34	0.173 (f)
Mild steel on copper lead	---	---	---	0.145 (f)
Mild steel on cast iron	---	0.183 (c)	0.23	0.133 (f)
Mild steel on lead	0.95	0.5 (f)	0.95	0.3 (f)
Nickel on mild steel	---	---	0.64	0.178 (x)
Aluminum on mild steel	0.61	---	0.47	---
Magnesium on mild steel	---	---	0.42	---

Magnesium on magnesium	0.6	0.08 (y)	---	---
Teflon on Teflon	0.04	---	---	0.04 (f)
Teflon on steel	0.04	---	---	0.04 (f)
Tungsten carbide on tungsten carbide	0.2	0.12 (a)	---	---
Tungsten carbide on steel	0.5	0.08 (a)	---	---
Tungsten carbide on copper	0.35	---	---	---
Tungsten carbide on iron	0.8	---	---	---
Bonded carbide on copper	0.35	---	---	---
Bonded carbide on iron	0.8	---	---	---
Cadmium on mild steel	---	---	0.46	---
Copper on mild steel	0.53	---	0.36	0.18 (a)
Nickel on nickel	1.10	---	0.53	0.12 (w)
Brass on mild steel	0.51	---	0.44	---
Brass on cast iron	---	---	0.30	---
Zinc on cast iron	0.85	---	0.21	---
Magnesium on cast iron	---	---	0.25	---
Copper on cast iron	1.05	---	0.29	---
Tin on cast iron	---	---	0.32	---
Lead on cast iron.	---	---	0.43	---
Aluminum on aluminum	1.05	---	1.4	---
Glass on glass	0.94	0.01 (p)	0.40	0.09 (a)
	---	0.005 (q)	---	0.116 (v)
Carbon on glass	---	---	0.18	---
Garnet on mild steel	---	---	0.39	---
Glass on nickel	0.78	---	0.56	---
Copper on glass	0.68	---	0.53	---
Cast iron on cast iron	1.10	---	0.15	0.070 (d)
	---	---	---	0.064 (n)
Bronze on cast iron	---	---	0.22	0.77 (n)
Oak on oak (parallel to grain)	0.62	---	0.48	0.164 (r)

	---	---	---	0.067 (s)
Oak on oak (perpendicular)	0.54	---	0.32	0.072 (s)
Leather on oak (parallel)	0.61	---	0.52	---
Cast iron on oak.	---	---	0.49	0.075 (n)
Leather on cast iron	---	---	0.56	0.36 (t)
	---	---	---	0.13 (n)
Laminated plastic on steel	---	---	0.35	0.05 (f)
Fluted rubber bearing on steel	---	---	---	0.05 (t)

(a) Oleic acid; (b) Atlantic spindle oil (light mineral); (c) castor oil; (d) lard oil; (e) Atlantic spindle oil plus 2 percent oleic acid; (f) medium mineral oil; (g) medium mineral oil plus ½ percent oleic acid; (h) stearic acid; (i) grease (zinc oxide base); (j) graphite; (k) turbine oil plus 1 percent graphite; (l) turbine oil plus 1 percent stearic acid; (m) turbine oil (medium mineral); (n) olive oil; (p) palmitic acid; (q) ricinoleic acid; (r) dry soap; (s) lard; (t) water; (u) rape oil; (v) 3-in-1 oil; (w) octyl alcohol; (x) triolein; (y) 1 percent lauric acid in paraffin oil.

The table below is from MIL-HDBK-60, "Threaded Fasteners - Tightening to Proper Tension," 1990:

Table II. Examples of coefficients of friction.		
Bolt/Nut Material (See Note)	Lubricant	Coefficient of Friction, μ, ±20%
Steel	Graphite in Petrolatum or Oil	0.07
Steel	Molybdenum disulphide grease	0.11
Steel, Cadmium plated	None added	0.12
Steel, Zinc plated	None added	0.17
Steel	Machine oil	0.15
Steel/Bronze	None added	0.15

Corrosion-resistant steel or nickel base alloys/silver-plated materials	None added	0.14
Titanium/Steel	Graphite in petrolatum	0.08
Titanium	Molybdenum disulphide grease	0.10

COEFFICIENT OF PERFORMANCE

Symbol: COP

Definition: A measure of the efficiency of heat pumps and refrigerators. It is defined as the ratio of useful heat delivered in a heat pump or removed in a refrigerator to the energy required to operate the mechanism. The useful heat is greater than the energy required to power the devices, and so the COP is usually considerably greater than one. If the higher temperature is T_A and the cooler temperature is T_B for the heat pump or refrigerator source and sink, then, by treating the system as reversed Carnot cycles, the theoretical maximum COP for a heat pump is:

$$T_A/(T_A - T_B)$$

And for the refrigerator:

$$T_B/(T_A - T_B)$$

Note, therefore, that COP varies with the operating temperature and definition used. Values of COP of about 3 in practical devices are common.

Unit: Dimensionless

COEFFICIENT OF VARIATION (CV)

Definition: In probability theory and statistics, the coefficient of variation (CV), also known as relative standard deviation (RSD), is a standardized measure of dispersion of a probability distribution or frequency distribution. It is often expressed as a percentage and is defined as the ratio of the standard deviation σ to the mean μ (or its absolute value, $|\mu|$).

$$c_v = \frac{\sigma}{\mu}.$$

The CV or RSD is widely used in analytical chemistry to express the precision and repeatability of an assay. It is also commonly used in fields such as engineering or physics when doing quality assurance studies and ANOVA gauge R&R. Furthermore, CV is used by economists and investors in economic models.

Unit: Dimensionless

COERCIVITY

Symbol: H_C

Definition: The value of the coercive force of a substance that has been initially magnetized to saturation.

Unit: Ampere per meter L^{-1} I

COHESION (or cohesive attraction or cohesive force)

Has more than one definition based on the field:

Definition 1: In Chemistry:

It is the intermolecular attraction between like molecules:

Cohesion (from Latin *cohaesiō*, "cling" or "unity") or cohesive attraction or cohesive force is the action or property of like molecules sticking together, being mutually attractive. It is an intrinsic property of a substance that is caused by the shape and structure of its molecules, which makes the distribution of surrounding electrons irregular when molecules get close to one another, creating an electrical attraction that can maintain a microscopic structure such as a water drop. In other words, cohesion allows for surface tension, creating a "solid-like" state upon which light-weight or low-density materials can be placed.

Units: Newton

Dimensions: M L T^{-2}

Definition 2: Computer Science

In computer science, cohesion is a measure of how well the lines of source code within a module work together:

In *computer programming*, cohesion refers to the *degree to which the elements inside a module belong together*. In one sense, it is a measure of the strength of the relationship between the methods and data of a class and some unifying purpose or concept served by that class. It is also defined as a measure of the strength of relationship between the class's methods and data themselves.

Units: Cohesion is an ordinal type of measurement and is usually described as "high cohesion" or "low cohesion". Modules with high cohesion tend to be preferable because high cohesion is associated with several desirable traits of software, including robustness, reliability, reusability, and understandability. In contrast, low cohesion is associated with undesirable traits such as being difficult to maintain, test, reuse, or even understand.

Cohesion is often contrasted with coupling, a different concept. High cohesion often correlates with loose coupling and vice versa.

The software metrics of coupling and cohesion were invented by Larry Constantine in the late 1960s as part of Structured Design based on characteristics of "good" programming practices that reduced maintenance and modification costs. Structured Design, cohesion and coupling were published in the article by Stevens, Myers and Constantine (1974) and the book Yourdon and Constantine (1979); the latter two subsequently became standard terms in software engineering.

Definition 3: **In Geology**

In geology, cohesion is the part of shear strength that is independent of the normal effective stress in mass movements. In other words: Cohesion is the component of shear strength of a rock or soil that is independent of interparticle friction.

In soils, true cohesion is caused by the following:

1. Electrostatic forces in stiff overconsolidated clays (which may be lost through weathering)
2. Cementing by Fe_2O_3, $CaCO_3$, $NaCl$, etc.

There can also be apparent cohesion. This is caused by:

1. Negative capillary pressure (which is lost upon wetting)
2. Pore pressure response during undrained loading (which is lost through time)

3. Root cohesion (which may be lost through logging or fire of the contributing plants or through the solution)

Note: Other meanings for cohesion are:

- Cohesion (linguistics), the linguistic elements that make a discourse semantically coherent
- Cohesion (Social policy) the bonds between members of a community or society and life
- Cohesion (album), the fourth studio album by Australian band Gyroscope
- Cohesion (band), a musical group from Surrey, England

COLLISION NUMBER

Symbol: z also Z_{AB} or Z_{AA}

Definition: Average number of two-molecular collisions in a unit time interval that tale place in a unit volume of rarefied gas in equilibrium conditions.

$$\bar{z} = n^2 \frac{\pi}{4} \left(\frac{m}{mkT}\right)^{3/2} \int_0^\infty \delta v^3 exp\left[-\frac{mv^2}{4kT}\right] dv$$

Where k = Boltzmann constant,

T = Thermodynamic temperature,

n = molecule density

v = relative velocity of pair of molecules,

δ = cross-section for two-molecular collision

In the hard-sphere core model δ is constant, and then:

$$\bar{z} = 2n^2 d^2 \left(\frac{\pi kT}{m}\right)^{1/2}$$

Unit: per meter cubed second.

Dimension: M^{-3} T^{-1}

COLOUR TEMPERATURE

Definition: Temperature at which the black body radiation spectrum is identical to the radiation spectrum of the grey body at a given temperature.

Unit: Kelvin

COMPLEX REFRACTION INDEX

Symbol: $\hat{n}$

Definition: For refractive index n and absorption index k, the complex refractive index is:

$\hat{n} = n + ik$

Unit: There are no units or dimensions.

See "*refractive index*" and "*absorption index.*"

COMPLIANCE ACOUSTICAL

Symbol C_a

Definition The reciprocal of the acoustical stiffness S_a

$Ca = I/S_a$

Unit: Meter cubed per pascal

Dimension $M^{-1} L^4 T^2$

Note: The acoustic compliance can be calculated equally by the equation

$C_a = 2\pi$ x (frequency of vibration) x (reciprocal of acoustic reactance associated with the potential energy of the medium or its boundaries).

COMPLIANCE (MECHANICAL)

Symbol: C

Definition: The reciprocal of the mechanical stiffness s, i.e., the extension on displacement under unit load

$C = 1/s$

Unit: meters per newton.

Dimension: $M^{-1} T^2$

Note: The electric analogue of compliance is the capacitane, where the analogue of force is voltage, of velocity is current, and displacement is a charge.

COMPLIANCE CONSTANT

Definition: Any on of the coefficients of the relations in the generalized Hook's law used to express strain components as linear functions of the stress components. Also known as *"elastic constant."*

COMPRESSIBILITY (BULK)

Symbol: X sometimes k

Definition: The property of a substance capable of being reduced in volume by application of pressure; qualitatively, it is the reciprocal of the bulk modulus of elasticity (or volume elasticity) K

$X = 1/K$

Alternatively, compressibility can be defined as the ratio of the volume strain to the pressure change (stress) dp. Suppose a body of isotropic material of volume v and under pressure p is subject to a change of pressure dp a change in volume of the body dv, with constant temperature. In that case, the volume strain is the ratio dv/v, and the numerical value of the compressibility is:

$X = (1/v) . (dv/dp)$

Unit: Per pascal = meter squared per newton

Dimension: $M^{-1} L T^2$

Note: 1: the quantity as defined above is isothermal compressibility. It is called isentropic compressibility if the changes occur with constant entrop*y*.

2. The quantity is more correctly termed the *"coefficient of compressibility.*

3. The compressibility of liquids is small, and liquids are usually considered incompressible except in the case of sudden starting and stopping of flow. Gases are highly compressible fluids, although compressibility is only important in the motion of air as the velocity of flow approaches the velocity of sound.

4. Compressibility is also related to Young's modulus E and Poisson's ratio ∞ by the ration:

$$X = 3\left(\frac{1-2\sigma}{E}\right)$$

COMPRESSIBILITY FACTORS

Symbols: z

Definition: an Empirical coefficient depending on the nature of substance, pressure p and thermodynamic temperature T, applied in the description of properties of real gas by an equation of state in the form

$Z = pV_m/RT,$

Where: V_m = molar volume of real gas, and R= universal gas constant

Unit: There are no units or dimensions

Note: also called *"compression factor"*

COMPRESSION, MODULUS OF

See "bulk modulus of elasticity" and "elastic modulus."

COMOVING AND PROPER DISTANCES

Definition: In standard cosmology, comoving distance and proper distance are two closely related distance measures used by cosmologists to define distances between objects.

Proper distance roughly corresponds to where a distant object would be at a specific moment of cosmological time, which can change over time due to the expansion of the universe.

Comoving distance factors out the expansion of the universe, giving a distance that does not change in time due to the expansion of space (though this may change due to other local factors, such as the motion of a galaxy within a cluster). Comoving distance and proper distance are defined to be equal at the present time; therefore, the ratio of proper distance to comoving distance now is 1. At other times, the scale factor differs from 1. The universe's expansion results in the proper distance changing, while the comoving distance is unchanged by this expansion because it is the proper distance divided by that scale factor.

Units: meter

Dimension: L

CONCENTRATION

See "density"

Note: The term "Concentration" may be used to give the amount of solute present in a given volume of substance and is usually expressed in moles per meter cubed. It is better in such cases to use *"molality" and "molarity."*

See *"molality" and "molarity."*

CONCENTRATION MOLAR

Also called molarity

See *" molarity"*

CONCENTRATION, CATALYTIC ACTIVITY

Definition: Change in reaction rate due to the presence of a catalyst per unit volume of the system

Units: $kat \cdot m^{-3}$

Dimension: $L^{-3} T^{-1} N$

CONDUCTANCE

Symbol: G

Definition: The conductance of an element, device, branch, or system is the factor by which the mean- square voltage must be multiplied to give the corresponding power lost by dissipation as heat per as other permanent radiation or loss of electromagnetic energy from the circuit

1. For conductors
   a) Conductance to a Direct Current

      Definition: The reciprocal of the electrical resistance R.G=1/R
   b) Conduction to an alternating current

      Definition: The real part of admittance Y.Y= G+I B

      (B= susceptance)
2. For dielectric:

   Definition: The quotient of the conduction current I_c by the applied voltage V.

   $$G = 1 = I/V$$

   Unit: Siemens

   Dimension: $M^{-1}L^{-2}T^{3}I^{2}$

CONDUCTANCE QUANTUM

Symbol: G_0

Definition: The conductance quantum, G_0, is the quantized unit of electrical conductance. It is defined by the elementary charge e and Planck constant h as:

$$G_0 = 2\ e^2\ h = 7.748091729...\times 10^{-5}\ S.$$

It appears when measuring the conductance of a quantum point contact and, more generally, is a key component of the Ladauer formula, which relates the electrical conductance of a quantum conductor to its quantum properties. It is twice the reciprocal of the von Klitzing constant ($2/R_K$).

Note that the conductance quantum does not mean that the conductance of any system must be an integer multiple of G_0. Instead, it describes the conductance of two quantum channels (one channel for spin up and the other channel for spin down) if the probability for transmitting an electron that enters the channel is unity, i.e. if the transport through the channel is ballistic. If the transmission probability is less than unity, then the conductance of the channel is less than G_0. The total conductance of a system is equal to the sum of the conductances of all the parallel quantum channels that make up the system.

Units: S, Semen

Dimensions: $M^{-1}L^{-2}T^3I^2$

CONDUCTANCE, SPECIFIC

See" conductivity, electrical."

CONDUCTANCE, THERMAL

Symbol: h sometimes K or U (K is preferred for surface thermal conductance.)

Definition: the amount of heat transmitted by a material divided by the difference in temperature of the surface of the material. In general, it is the heat flow rate density q divided by temperature difference ϑ

$$h = q/\vartheta$$

Unit: Watt per meter squared kelvin

Dimension: $ML^{-2}T^{-1}$

Note: The quantity is also termed the "heat transfer coefficient" or "thermal transmittance".

CONDUCTIVITY, ELECTRICAL

Symbol: Y

Definition: it is the ability of a substance to conduct electricity. It equals to the conduction current density J divided by the electric field strength E in the material.

$$y = -(dq/dt)/A)/(dV/dx) = J/E$$

Where: q= charge, T= time, A= area through which current flows, dv= potential difference in the direction x of current flow

Conductivity is also defined as the reciprocal of the resistivity (ρ)

$$y = 1/\rho$$

The first definition is often more useful when considering solutions; it is then known as *"electrolytic conductivity."*

Unit: Siemens per meter .

Dimensions: $M^{-1}L^{-3}T^3I^2$

Note: 1. the quantity is also termed the *"specific conductance"*

Electric conductivity ranges from 10^8 to 10^6 for metals, 10^6 to 10^{-6} for semiconductors, and 10^{-6} to 10^{-14} for insulators. Among the elements in the solid state, Ag has the highest conductivity ($0.6 \times 10^8 S.m^{-1}$ at 20^0C), yellow sulphur the lowest $5x\ 10^{-14}S.M^{-1}$ at 20^0C)

CONDUCTIVITY, IONIC

Symbol:σ

Definition: The product of Faraday constant F and the electric mobility u of the ion. $\gamma = \frac{\overline{z}}{F}/u$

Where /z/ is the charge number of an ion.

Unit: Siemens meter squared per mole.

Note: Also called *"Molar conductivity of an ion"*

CONDUCTIVITY, MOLAR

Symbol: J_m

Definition: The conductivity of an electrolyte solution γ divided by the concentration ρ of electrolyte present measured in moles per cubic meter.

$$J_M = \gamma/\rho$$

Unit: siemens meter squared per mole

Dimension: $M^{-1}\ T^3\ I^2\ mol^{-1}$

Note: The word molar in this definition means "divided by concentration" and not "divided by amount of substance"

See "*molar*"

CONDUCTIVITY THERMAL

Symbol: γ ; sometimes k

Definition: it is that property of the material which determines, in association with the area of flow and the temperature gradient, the actual rate of conductive heat flow; it is calculated as the quantity of head conducted under steady flow conditions in unit time through a unit area of a homogenous material of unit thickness when a unit temperature difference exists between the two faces of the material and heat flow is normal to it.

In general, if the quantity of heat Ω flowing in time t normally between two areas A a distance x apart and differing in temperature by ϑ when the system is a steady state, the; $\left(\frac{d\Omega}{dt}\right) = \gamma A\left(\frac{d\vartheta}{dx}\right)$

(The minus sign is accoutered for by defining γ as positive; $d\vartheta/dx$ is negative for $(d\Omega/dt)$ positive)

Unit: Watt per meter kelvin

Dimension: $ML^{-1}T^{-1}$

Note: 1: The equivalent thermal conductivity of a body (such as a wall made up of slabs of thickness x_1, x_2…….. and thermal conductivities v_1, v_2…….. is given by $\gamma e = \sum x,/\sum x1/y1$

2. The thermal conductivity varies with the density of the material and temperature level

3. The thermal conductivity of a gas, on the kinetic theory, is given by: $\gamma = \frac{1}{3}pc\,LC_V$

So that the conductivity is independent of the pressure, this is true for moderate pressure, but at very low pressure, the conductivity becomes proportional to the pressure.

4. It is also referred to as "conductivity", "conductivity coefficient", "K- Factor," and "K- factor."

See "*conduction*"

5. Diamond has the highest thermal conductivity of 2320 $Wm^{-1}K^{-1}$ Other examples are; Ag=429, Cu=401, Si=149, Ge=2 $Wm^{-1}K^{-1}$ (lowest)

6. The thermal conductivity of a solid metal is related to the electric conductivity by the Wiedemann- Franz- Lorenz Law

CONDUCTION

Definition: The transmission of electric, thermal, or acoustic energy via a medium without movement of the medium as such.

Thermal conduction is to be distinguished from convection, and electrical conduction from the transmission of electromagnetic radiation.

See "conduction, thermal", "and conductivity, thermal".

CONDUCTION, THERMAL

Definition: The mode of heat transfer in a solid material accessioned by a temperature difference between different parts of the material. Conduction also occurs in liquids and gases but is generally associated with convection and, possibly, in case of gases, radiation. Conduction within a solid is a transfer of internal energy, i.e, the energy of motion of the consistent molecules, atoms and particles of which the material consists.

Each material has, then, a property known as" thermal conductivity," which determines the actual rate of conductive head flow in association with the area of flow and the temperature gradient.

See "Conductivity, *thermal.*"

CONSTANT, DIELECTRIC

See "permittivity, *relative.*"

CONSTANT, ELECTRIC

Symbol: εo

Definition: The scalar which relates the electric flux density (the displacement), D, in vacuum to the electric field strength E

$D = \varepsilon o E$

It is also the scalar that relates the mechanical force F between two charges in a vacuum to their magnitudes (and Q_2) separation r

$F = Q_1 Q_2 / 4\pi\varepsilon_0 r^2$

Unit: Farad per meter

Dimension: $M^{-1}\ L^{-3}\ T^{-4}\ I^{2}$

Note: It is also called "permittivity of Vacuum"

See "permittivity, *absolute.*"

CONSTANT, MAGNETIC

Symbol: μ_0

Definition: The scalar which relates the magnetic flux density B, in vacuum to the magnetic field strength H,

$B = \mu_0 H$

It is also the scalar which relates the mechanical force F between two currents in a vacuum to their magnitudes and the geometrical configuration.

The force F on a length *I* of two parallel straight conductors of infinite length and negligible circular cross-section, carrying constant current I_1 and I_2 and separated by a distance r in a vacuum, is: $\mu_0\ I_1 I_2 /\ 2\pi r$

Unit: Henry per meter

Dimension: $M\ L\ T^{-2}\ I^{-2}$

See "moment"

CORRELATION

Definition: In statistics, correlation or dependence is any statistical relationship, whether causal or not, between two random variables or bivariate data. In the broadest sense, correlation is any statistical association, though it commonly refers to the degree to which a pair of variables are linearly related. Familiar examples of dependent phenomena include the correlation between the height of parents and their offspring and the correlation between the price of a good and the quantity the consumers are willing to purchase, as depicted in the demand curve.

Correlations are useful because they can indicate a predictive relationship that can be exploited in practice. For example, an electrical utility may produce less power on a mild day based on the correlation between electricity demand and weather. In this example, there is a causal relationship because extreme weather causes people to use more electricity for heating or cooling. However, in general, the presence of a correlation is not sufficient to infer the presence of a causal relationship (i.e., correlation does not imply causation).

Formally, random variables are *dependent* if they do not satisfy a mathematical property of probabilistic independence. In informal parlance, *correlation* is synonymous with *dependence*. However, when used in a technical sense, correlation refers to any of several specific types of mathematical operations between the tested variables and their respective expected values. Essentially, correlation is the measure of how two or more variables are related to one another. Several correlation coefficients, often denoted ρ or r, measure the degree of correlation. The most common of these is the *Pearson correlation coefficient*, which is sensitive only to a linear relationship between two variables (which may be present even when one variable is a nonlinear function of the other). Other correlation coefficients – such as *Spearman's rank correlation* – have been developed to be more robust than Pearson's, that is, more sensitive to nonlinear relationships. Mutual information can also be applied to measure the dependence between two variables.

Unit: Dimensionless

(Ref. HandWiki)

COUPLING COEFFICIENT

Symbol: k

Definition: It is the ratio of the mutual impedance M of the coupling to the square root of the product of the self- impedances of similar elements in the two circuit loops considered. Unless otherwise specified, the coefficient of coupling refers to inductive coupling; in this case, the coupling coefficient equals the mutual inductance M divided by the geometrical mean of the self-inductances, i.e.

$$k = M/(L_1 L_2)^{1/2}$$

Where: L_1 is the self-inductance of one loop, and L_2 is the self-inductance of other

Unit: There are no units or dimensions

Note: 1. The leakage coefficient is one minus the square of the coupling coefficient

3. The coupling coefficient may be defined as the ratio of an electron's maximum charge in energy traversing an interaction space to the product of the peak alternating gap voltage and the electronic charge.

CRACKLE

Symbol: $c \rightarrow$ (vector)

Definition: Change of jounce per unit time: the fifth time derivative of position

Units: m/s^5

Dimension: $L\,T^{-5}$

See: "jounce", "derivatives," and "abasement strain."

$$r \quad \text{Position}$$

$$\frac{d\mathbf{r}}{dt} = \dot{\mathbf{r}} \quad \text{Velocity (speed)}$$

$$\frac{d^2\mathbf{r}}{dt^2} = \ddot{\mathbf{r}} \quad \text{Acceleration}$$

$$\frac{d^3\mathbf{r}}{dt^3} = \dddot{\mathbf{r}} \quad \text{Jerk}$$

$$\frac{d^4\mathbf{r}}{dt^4} = \ddddot{\mathbf{r}} \quad \text{Snap (jounce)}$$

$$\frac{d^5\mathbf{r}}{dt^5} = \dddddot{\mathbf{r}} \quad \text{Crackle}$$

$$\frac{d^6\mathbf{r}}{dt^6} = \ddddddot{\mathbf{r}} \quad \text{Pop}$$

Time-derivatives of position

In physics, the fourth, fifth and sixth derivatives of position are defined as derivatives of the position vector with respect to time – with the first, second, and third derivatives.

CROSS-SECTION (nuclear physics)

Symbol σ

Definition: in nuclear physics, the term cross-section connotes the strength of the interaction between nuclear particles. If a beam of nuclear particles is incident on a target made up of the same or other nuclei, the following relation generally defines the cross-section:

σ = (number of interactions per unit target nuclei per unit time) / (beam particles per unit volume of an incident beam) x (beam particles velocity)

If the incident beam particles are considered points, and the target nuclei act as hard-sphere scatterers of radius a, then the above definition takes form.

$\sigma = 4\pi a^2$

Unit: Meter squared

Dimension: L^2

CRYSTALLINITY

Definition: Crystallinity refers to the degree of structural order in a solid. In a crystal, the atoms or molecules are arranged in a regular, periodic manner. The degree of crystallinity greatly influences hardness, density, transparency and diffusion. In a gas, the relative positions of the atoms or molecules are completely random. Amorphous materials, such as liquids and glasses, represent an intermediate case, having order over short distances (a few atomic or molecular spacings) but not over longer distances.

Many materials, such as glass ceramics and some polymers, can be prepared in such a way as to produce a mixture of crystalline and amorphous regions. In such cases, crystallinity is usually specified as a percentage of the volume of the material that is crystalline . Even within materials that are completely crystalline, however, the degree of structural perfection can vary. For instance, most metallic alloys are crystalline, but they usually comprise many independent crystalline regions (grains or crystallites) in various orientations separated by grain boundaries; furthermore, they contain other crystallographic defects (notably dislocations) that reduce the degree of structural perfection. The most highly perfect crystals are silicon boules produced for semiconductor electronics; these are large single crystals (so they have no grain boundaries), are nearly free of dislocations, and have precisely controlled concentrations of defect atoms.

Crystallinity can be measured using X-ray crystallography, but calorimetric techniques are also commonly used.

Note: Rock crystallinity

Geologists describe four qualitative levels of crystallinity:

- holocrystalline rocks are completely crystalline;
- hypocrystalline rocks are partially crystalline, with crystals embedded in an amorphous or glassy matrix;
- hypohyaline rocks are partially glassy;
- holohyaline rocks (such as obsidian) are completely glassy.

(References: Oxford Dictionary of Science, 1999, ISBN 0-19-280098-1.)

CURE FACTORS (ENERGY PATTERN FACTORS)

A number used to relate wind speed to the power in the wind. This power, P (energy passing per unit time), is proportional to the cube of the wind, v, i.e.

$P = av^3$

Where a is a constant. However, wind speeds fluctuate greatly even over short periods, so the average power in the wind is given by:

$P = a(\underline{v^3})$

Where (v^3) is the average of the cubed speed. (v^3) is not equal to $(v)^3$, the average speed cubed their ratio:

$(v^3)/(v)^3$ is called the cube factor or energy pattern factor. Commonly the value is nearly two

CURIE- TEMPERATURE

Symbol: Tc

Definition: Critical temperature at which ferro and ferrimagnets lose their spontaneous magnetization and become paramagnets. Alternatively, the critical temperature at which ferroelectrics lose their spontaneous polarization.

Unit: Kelvin.

See also "characteristic temperature."

CURRENT

Symbol: I

Definition: There is no formal definition of current, but the word "current" is used as a generic term when there is no danger of ambiguity to refer either to conduction current or displacement current. For example, in the expression "the current in a simple series circuit", the word current refers to the conduction current in the wire of the inductor and to the displacement current between the plates of the capacitor.

Unit: Ampere

Dimension: $M^{1/2}L^{1/2}T^{-1}\varphi^{1/2}$

Note: Engineers sometimes term the quantity "amperage"

See "amperage"

CURRENT, CONDUCTION

Definition: The conduction current through any surface is the integral of the normal component of the conduction current density over that surface.

Unit: Ampere

Dimension: $M^{1/2}L^{1/2}T^{-1}\varphi^{1/2}$

CURRENT, DISPLACEMENT

Definition: The displacement current through any surface is the integral of the normal component of the displacement current density over the surface.

It is due to a change in the electric flux density in a dielectric, e.g., the current through a capacitor when connected in series with alternating potential difference. When a capacitor is charged, the conduction current flowing into it is considered to be continued through the dielectric as a displacement current so that the current is, in effect, flowing in a closed circuit. Displacement current does not involve the motion of the current carriers (as in conductors) but rather the formation of an electric dipole (a phenomenon known as electric polarization), thus setting up the electric stress. The recognition of Maxwell that a displacement current in a dielectric gives rise to his electromagnetic theory of light.

Unit: *Ampere*

Dimension : $M^{1/2}L^{1/2}T^{-1}\varphi^{1/2}$

CURRENT DENSITY

Symbol: J; Occasionally S

Definition: Current density is a generic term used when there is no danger of ambiguity to refer to conduction current density or to, displacement current density, or both. In general, it is the ratio of the current to the cross-sectional area of the current carrying medium. The medium may be a conductor or a beam of charged particles. The ration may be specified as a " mean current density" or as " density at a point".

Unit: Ampere per meter squared.

Dimension: L^{-2} I; $M^{1/2}L^{3/2}T^{-1}\varphi^{-1/2}$

CURRENT DENSITY, CONDUCTION

Definition:

The electric conduction current density at any point at which there is a motion of the electric charge is a vector quantity whose direction is that of the flow of positive charge at this point and whose magnitude is the limit of the time rate of flow of net(positive) charge across a small plane area perpendicular to the motion, divided by this area. The flow of charge may result from the movement of free electrons or ions but is not in general, except in microscopic studies, taken to include motion of charges resulting from the polarization of the dielectric.

Unit: Ampere per meter squared

Dimension: I L^{-2}

CURRENT DENSITY, DISPLACEMENT

Definition: the displacement current density at any point in an electric field is (in the international system) the time rate of change of the electric-flux density vector at that point.

Unit: Ampere per meter squared

Dimension: $I\,L^{-2}$

CURRENT DENSITY, LINEAR

Symbol: A; sometime α

Definition: current I divided by breath b of the conductor

$A=I/b$

Unit: Ampere per meter

Dimension: $I\,L^{-1}$

CURRENT, THERMAL

Definition: The rate of flow of entropy S with respect to time t

Thermal current $=ds/dt$

Unit: thermal Ampere = per meter kelvin: MT^{-1}

Note: the former definition was the rate of flow of heat energy Q with respect to time. Thermal current $=dQ/dt$

CURVATURE

Symbols: **C**

Definition the reciprocal of the radius of curvature r (the radius of the circle which most nearly approximates a curve at a given point)

$C=I/r$

It is also the rate of change of the unit tangent vector to a curve with respect to the arc length of the curve. In Cartesian coordinates,

$C= (d^2y/dx^2)/ (1 + (dy /dx)^2)^{3/2}$

Unit: Meter to the power of minus one

Dimension: L^{-1}

Note:

1. The unit of curvature is also called a " diopter."
2. The curvature is applied to mirrors and lens surfaced and wavefronts
3. The sign of curvature depends on the convention

CUSEC

Definition: **Cusec** is a measure of flow rate and is an informal shorthand for "cubic feet per second" (28.317 litres per second). In the United States, it is generally applied to water flow, particularly in rivers and canals. Other informal synonyms are *cfs* and *second-feet*.

- $1\ ft^3 s^{-1} = 0.028316847 m^3 s^{-1}$, $1\ ft^3 s^{-1} = 1$ cusec
- $1\ ft^3 s^{-1} = 28.316847$ litre s^{-1}, 1 cubic foot per minute = 1 cufm

- 1 cusec = 1.699 m^3min^{-1}, 1 cusec = 1699 litres min^{-1}
- 1 gallon per minute = 0.07577 litre s^{-1}, 1 gallon per minute = 7.577x10-5 m^3s^{-1}

(These are UK, not US gallons: 1 imperial gallon = 1.201 US gallons)

- 1 cusec = 1.699 m^3min^{-1}, 1 cusec = 1699 litres min^{-1}

(These are UK, not US gallons: 1 imperial gallon = 1.201 US gallons)

D

Damköhler numbers

Symbol: Da

Definition: The **Damköhler numbers (Da)** are dimensionless numbers used in chemical engineering to relate the chemical reaction timescale (reaction rate) to the transport phenomena rate occurring in a system. It is named after German chemist Gerhard Damköhler. The **Karlovitz number (Ka)** is related to the Damköhler number by $Da = 1/Ka$.

In its most commonly used form, the Damköhler number relates the reaction timescale to the convection time scale and volumetric flow rate through the reactor for continuous (plug flow or stirred tank) or semi-batch chemical processes:

$$Da = \frac{\text{reaction rate}}{\text{convective mass transport rate}}$$

In reacting systems that include interphase mass transport, the **second Damköhler number (Da_{II})** is defined as the ratio of the chemical reaction rate to the mass transfer rate.

$$Da = \frac{\text{flow time scale}}{\text{chemical time scale}}$$

It is also defined as the ratio of the characteristic fluidic and chemical time scales:

$$Da = \frac{\text{flow time scale}}{\text{chemical time scale}}$$

Since the reaction timescale is determined by the reaction rate, the exact formula for the Damköhler number varies according to the rate law equation. For a general chemical reaction $A \rightarrow B$ following the Power law kinetics of n-th order, the Damköhler number for a convective flow system is defined as:

$$Da = kC_0^{n-1}\tau$$

Where:

- k = kinetics reaction rate constant
- C_0 = initial concentration
- n = reaction order
- tau = mean residence time or **space-time**

On the other hand, the second Damköhler number is defined as:

$$\mathrm{Da_{II}} = \frac{kC_0^{m-1}}{k_g a}$$

where

- k_g is the global mass transport coefficient
- a is the interfacial area

The value of Da provides a quick estimate of the degree of conversion that can be achieved. As a rule of thumb, when Da is less than 0.1, a conversion of less than 10% is achieved, and when Da is greater than 10, a conversion of more than 90% is expected. The limit $\mathrm{Da} \to \infty$ is called the Burke–Schumann limit.

Field of application: chemistry (reaction time scales vs. residence time)

Unit: Dimensionless

DAMPING COEFFICIENT

Symbol: δ occasionally Δ

Definition: If F is a function of time given by:

$$F(t) = Ae^{-\delta t} \sin \frac{2\pi t - t_o}{T}$$ then δ is the damping coefficient.

Unit: (Neper) per second.

Dimension: T^{-1}

Note:

1. The quantity is also termed "decay coefficient" or "decay factor".

2. Damping coefficient has to be differentiated from the "damping ratio", which is the ratio of the actual resistance in damped harmonic motion to that necessary to produce critical damping.

DAMPING RATIO

Definition: **Damping** is an influence within or upon an oscillatory system that has the effect of reducing, restricting or preventing its oscillations. In physical systems, damping is produced by processes that dissipate the energy stored in the oscillation Examples include viscous drag in mechanical systems, resistance in electronic oscillators, and absorption and scattering of light in optical oscillators. Damping not based on energy loss can be important in other oscillating systems, such as those that occur in biological systems and bikes.

The **damping ratio** is a dimensionless measure describing how oscillations in a system decay after a disturbance. Many systems exhibit oscillatory behavior when they are disturbed from their position of static equilibrium. A mass suspended from a spring, for example, might, if pulled and released, bounce up and down. On each bounce, the system tends to return to its equilibrium position but overshoots it. Sometimes losses (e.g. frictional) damp the system and can cause the oscillations to gradually decay in amplitude towards zero or attenuate. The damping ratio is a measure describing how rapidly the oscillations decay from one bounce to the next.

The damping ratio is a system parameter, denoted by ζ (zeta), that can vary from **undamped** ($\zeta = 0$), **underdamped** ($\zeta < 1$) through **critically damped** ($\zeta = 1$) to **overdamped** ($\zeta > 1$).

The behaviour of oscillating systems is often of interest in a diverse range of disciplines that, include control engineering, chemical engineering, mechanical engineering, structural engineering, and electrical engineering. The physical quantity that is oscillating varies greatly and could be the swaying of a tall building in the wind or the speed of an electric motor, but a normalized or non-dimensionalized approach can be convenient in describing common aspects of behavior.

Unit: **Dimensionless**

[Ref. HandWiki]

DARCY NUMBER

Symbol: **Da**

Definition: In fluid dynamics through porous media, the **Darcy number (Da)** represents the relative effect of the permeability of the medium versus its cross-sectional area—commonly the diameter squared. The number is named after Henry Darcy and is found from nondimensionalizing the differential form of Darcy's Law. This number should not be confused with the Darcy friction factor, which applies to pressure drop in a pipe. It is defined as

$$Da = \frac{K}{d^2}$$

where

- K is the permeability of the medium (SI units: m2);
- d is the characteristic length, e.g. the diameter of the particle (SI units: m).

Note: Alternative forms of this number do exist depending on the approach by which Darcy's Law is made dimensionless and the geometry of the system.

The Darcy number is commonly used in heat transfer through porous media.

Unit: Dimensionless

DEAN NUMBER

Symbol: De

Definition: The **Dean number** (*De*) is a dimensionless group in fluid mechanics, which occurs in the study of flow in curved pipes and channels. It is named after the British scientist W. R. Dean, who was the first to provide a theoretical solution of the fluid motion through curved pipes for laminar flow by using a perturbation procedure from a Poiseuille flow in a straight pipe to a flow in a pipe with very small curvature.

The Dean number is typically denoted by *De* (or *Dn*). For a flow in a pipe or tube, it is defined as:

$$De = \frac{\sqrt{\frac{1}{2}\,(\text{inertial forces})(\text{centripetal forces})}}{\text{viscous forces}} = \frac{\sqrt{\frac{1}{2}\,(\rho\,D^2\,R_c\,\frac{v^2}{D})(\rho\,D^2\,R_c\,\frac{v^2}{R_c})}}{\mu\,\frac{v}{D}\,D\,R_c}$$

$$= \frac{\rho\,D\,v}{\mu}\sqrt{\frac{D}{2\,R_c}} = Re\,\sqrt{\frac{D}{2\,R_c}}$$

where

- ρ is the density of the fluid
- μ is the dynamic viscosity
- v is the axial velocity scale
- D is the diameter (for non-circular geometry, an equivalent diameter is used; see Reynolds number)
- Rc is the radius of curvature of the path of the channel.
- Re is the Reynolds number.

The Dean number is, therefore, the product of the Reynolds number (based on axial flow v through a pipe of diameter D) and the square root of the curvature ratio.

Field of application: turbulent flow (vortices in curved ducts)

Unit: **Dimensionless**

[Ref. HandWiki]

DEBORAH NUMBER

Symbol: **De**

Definition: The **Deborah number (De)** is a dimensionless number often used in rheology to characterize the fluidity of materials under specific flow conditions. It quantifies the observation that, given enough time, even a solidlike material might flow, or a fluid-like material can act solid when it is deformed rapidly enough. Materials that have low relaxation times flow easily and, as such, show relatively rapid stress decay.

The Deborah number is the ratio of fundamentally different characteristic times. Formally, the Deborah number is defined as the ratio of the time it takes for a material to adjust to applied stresses or deformations and the characteristic time scale of an experiment (or a computer simulation) probing the response of the material:

$$De = \frac{t_c}{t_p}$$

Where t_c stands for the relaxation time and t_p for the "time of observation", typically taken to be the time scale of the process.

The numerator, relaxation time, is the time needed for a reference amount of deformation to occur under a suddenly applied reference load (a more fluid-like material will therefore require less time to flow, giving a lower Deborah number relative to a solid subjected to the same loading rate).

The denominator, material time, is the amount of time required to reach a given reference strain (a faster loading rate will therefore reach the reference strain sooner, giving a higher Deborah number).

Equivalently, the relaxation time is the time required for the stress induced by a suddenly applied reference strain to reduce by a certain reference amount. The relaxation time is actually based on the rate of relaxation that exists at the moment of the suddenly applied load.

This incorporates both the elasticity and viscosity of the material. At lower Deborah numbers, the material behaves in a more fluid-like manner, with an associated Newtonian viscous flow. At higher Deborah numbers, the material behavior enters the non-Newtonian regime, increasingly dominated by elasticity and demonstrating solidlike behavior.

Field of application: rheology (viscoelastic fluids)

Unit: Dimensionless

[Ref. HandWiki]

DECAY

Definition:

1. The transformation of a radioactive nuclide, the parent, into its daughter product by disintegration, resulting in the gradual decrease in the activity of the parent.
2. The gradual decline of the brightness of an excited phosphor.
3. Vibration that decreases in amplitude with time. The decay is due to the resistance of the medium to the vibration.

DECAY COEFFICIENT

See "damping coefficient".

DECAY CONSTANT

Symbol: λ

Definition: The activity A (A = -dN/dt) divided by the number N of the undecayed nuclei present at time t:

$$\lambda = A/N = (-dN/dt). (1/N)$$

Unit: per second

Dimension: T^{-1}

Note: 1. Decay constant represents the probability per unit time of the radioactive of an unstable nucleus.

2. The exponential decrease with time t of the activity of a radionuclide in there are N_0 nuclei at $t = 0$ is found from the relation: $N = N_o\, e^{-\lambda t}$. The time for half the original number of nuclei to decay ($N = 1/2\ N_0$) is the "*half-life*", $T^1{}_{/2}$, by: $T^1{}_{/2} = 0.69315/\lambda$

3. The reciprocal of the decay constant is the "*mean life*".

4. Decay constant is also called "***disintegration constant.***"

See "Activity" and "half-life, radioactive."

DECIBEL

Symbol: **dB**

Definition: The **decibel** (symbol: **dB**) is a relative unit of measurement equal to one-tenth of a **bel (B)**. It expresses the ratio of two values of a power or root-power quantity on a logarithmic scale. Two signals whose levels differ by one decibel have a power ratio of $10^{1/10}$ (approximately 1.26) or root-power ratio of $10^{1/20}$ (approximately 1.12).

The unit expresses a change in value (e.g., +1 dB or −1 dB) or an absolute value. In the latter case, the numeric value expresses the ratio of a value to a fixed reference value; when used in this way, the unit symbol is often suffixed with letter codes that indicate the reference value. For example, for the reference value of 1 volt, a common suffix is "V" (e.g., "20 dBV").

Two principal types of scaling of the decibel are in common use. When expressing a power ratio, it is defined as ten times the logarithm in base 10. That is, a change in *power* by a factor of 10 corresponds to a 10 dB change in level. When expressing root-power quantities, a change in *amplitude* by a factor of 10 corresponds to a 20 dB change in level. The decibel scales differ by a factor of two so that the related power and root-power levels change by the same value in linear systems, where power is proportional to the square of the amplitude.

The definition of the decibel originated in the measurement of transmission loss and power in telephony of the early 20th century in the Bell System in the United States. The **bel** was named in honor of Alexander Graham Bell, but the bel is seldom used. Instead, the decibel is used for a wide variety of measurements in science and engineering, most prominently in acoustics, electronics, and control theory. In electronics, the gains of amplifiers, attenuation of signals, and signal-to-noise ratios are often expressed in decibels.

DELTA-v

Symbol: Δv (scalar)

Definition: **Delta-v** (literally "change in velocity") is a measure of the impulse per unit of spacecraft mass that is needed to perform a maneuver such as a launch from or landing on a planet or moon or in-space orbital maneuver. It is a scalar that has the units of speed.

Delta-*v* is produced by reaction engines, such as rocket engines, and is proportional to the thrust per unit mass and the burn time.

$$\Delta v = \int_{t_0}^{t_1} \frac{|T(t)|}{m(t)}\, dt$$

where

T(t) is the instantaneous thrust at a time, t.

m(t) is the instantaneous mass at time, t.

As a simple example, take a conventional rocket which achieves thrust by burning fuel. Delta-v is the change in velocity that can be achieved by burning that rocket's entire fuel load.

Delta-v is used to determine the mass of propellant required for the given maneuver through the Tsiolkovsky rocket equation.

Units: It is a scalar that has the units of speed, i.e. meter per second

Dimensions: L T^{-1}

DENSITY

Symbol: ρ_A ; sometimes ρ_z

Definition: The intrinsic property of the substance that measures the amount of substance that occupies a given amount of space. Precisely defined, density is the mass of a substance per unit volume, i.e. it is the mass m of the given substance divided by its volume V.

P = m/v

Unit: Kilogramme per meter cubed

Dimension: L^{-3} M

Note:

1. The quantity is more properly called mass density. It is called concentration when it refers to the mass of one substance dissolved in a volume of a second substance.

2. Density, in general, is used to express the closeness of any linear, superficial, or space distribution, e.g. "electron density" means the number of electrons per unit volume.

3. Density is an intrinsic property of an object, i.e., it will not vary from one part of a homogeneous object to another, but it does depend upon the volume of the object. Hence, density is a function of those variables that can change the volume of the object. In general, the volume of an object is a function of both temperature and pressure. This functional dependence of volume on temperature and pressure is most striking for gaseous materials, but temperature is also an important consideration for all three states of matter. It is the custom, specially for gases, to give density values at the standard temperature and pressure (STP) values of $0^{o}C$ and 1 atmosphere.

4. In the case of gases, if the density is measured under any arbitrary condition, it can be converted to the STP values by using the following equation (assuming ideal gas):
    $$p = m/V = m\,P_o\,[1 + 0.003366\,(T - T_o)\,/PV$$
    Where M is the mass of the gas, V is the volume of the gas at pressure P and temperature T (K), and P_o and T_o are the standard values of pressure and temperature.

5. Since density is an intrinsic property of a substance and is, in general, a unique value for each substance, density can be used as a way to distinguish one substance from another. In systems where the force on objects is proportional to mass, as in a gravitational field, differences among the densities of fluids can be used to separate fluids from one another.

TABLE OF TYPICAL DENSITIES

Substance	Density (Kg/M^3)
Smooth density of galactic material throughout the universe	2×10^{-28}
Mean density of	3×10^{-21}

interstellar gas	
Mean density of the moon	3.3×10^3
Typical densities of some materials	1.293
Air	0.58×10^3
Teak wood	0.80×10^3
Alcohol	0.917×10^3
Ice (0^0C)	0.999841×10^3
Water (0^0C)	0.999973×10^3
Water (4^0C)	0.998203×10^3
Water (20^0C)	2.70×10^3
Aluminum	8.96×10^3
Copper	10.5×10^3
Silver	13.6×10^3
Mercury	19.3×10^3
Gold	21.5×10^3
Platinum	
Substance	**Density (Kg/M^3)**

Mean plant densities	
Saturn	0.70×10^3
Jupiter	1.33×10^3
Mars	3.93×10^3
Venus	5.24×10^3
Earth	5.515×10^3
Densities of stars	
The sun	1.41×10^3
White dwarf	1×10^9
Neutron star	2×10^{17}
Density of nuclear matter (using solid sphere model)	2×10^{17}
Mean densities of atoms (using solid sphere model)	
Hydrogen	4.4×10
Oxygen	2.0×10^3
Uranium	1.7×10^5

DENSITY, AREA

Symbol: ρ_A; sometimes ρ_s

Definition: Mass m divided by area A.

Area density $= m / A$

Unit: Kilogramme per meter squared.

Dimension: $L^{-2} M$

Note: Also known as "*surface density*"

DENSITY, LINE

Symbol: ρ'

Definition: Mass m divided by length l:

$\rho' = m/l$

Alternatively, for a body of uniform cross-section, the line density is the product of its density ρ and cross-sectional area A

$\rho' = \rho A.$

Unit: Kilogramme per meter

Dimension: $L^{-1}M$

DENSITY, OPTICAL

Symbol : D

Definition: It gives the degree of opacity of a translucent medium and is expressed as:

$D = \log\ (l_o / l)$

Where l_o is the intensity of the incident ray and l is the intensity of the transmitted ray. Alternatively, it is the logarithm to base 10 of the reciprocal of transmittance, i.e. $D = \log\ (1/\tau)$

Unit: There are no units or dimensions.

Note: 1. Also called" Transmission density".

2. The definition given to "*absorbance*" is also used as a definition for optical density.

See "*opacity* ", "*transmittance*", "transmission coefficient", and also "*absorbance* ",

DENSITY, REFLECTION

Symbol: D

Definition: The logarithm to base 10 of the reciprocal of the *"reflectance"* ρ, i. e. $D = -\log \rho$

Unit: There are no units or dimensions,

DENSITY, RELATIVE

Symbol: d

Definition: Density ρ_1 of a substance divided by the density ρ_2 of a reference substance under conditions specified for both substances (normally equal temperatures and pressures).

$d = \rho_1 / \rho_2$

Unit: There are no units or dimensions.

Note: I. This quantity was formerly called ***"specific gravity"*** when the reference substance is water. This name is now deprecated because of the special meaning given to the word "specific".

2. The specified temperatures are often the temperature at which the water has a maximum of 1000 kilogrammes per meter cubed, and thus the specific gravity of a substance is numerically equal to one-thousandth of its density.

DENSITY, VAPOUR

Symbol: d

Definition. The density ρ of a gas vapour divided by the density ρ_o, of hydrogen, both being at STP (standard temperature and pressure)

$d = \rho / \rho_o$

Unit: There are no units or dimensions.

DEPOSITION POTENTIAL

Symbol: ε_w

Definition: Electrical potential which should be exceeded to observe the effective course of a given electrode process;

$$\varepsilon_w = \varepsilon + \eta$$

where ε = reversible electrode potential,

η = overvoltage of tested electrode process Unit: Volt

Dimension: $L^2 M T^3 I^{-1}$

DERIVATIVES: FOURTH, FIFTH, AND SIXTH DERIVATIVES OF POSITION

In physics, the **fourth, fifth and sixth derivatives of position** are defined as derivatives of the position vector with respect to time – with the first, second, and third derivatives being velocity, acceleration, and jerk, respectively. Unlike the first three derivatives, the higher-order derivatives are less common,[1] thus their names are not as standardized, though the concept of a minimum snap trajectory has been used in robotics and is implemented in MATLAB.

The fourth derivative is often referred to as **snap** or **jounce**. The name "snap" for the fourth derivative led to **crackle** and **pop** for the fifth and sixth derivatives, respectively, inspired by the Rice Krispies mascots Snap, Crackle, and Pop. These terms are occasionally used, though "sometimes somewhat facetiously".

The following table gives the names of the first six derivatives of the position.

$$r \quad \text{Position}$$

$$\frac{d\mathbf{r}}{dt} = \dot{\mathbf{r}} \quad \text{Velocity (speed)}$$

$$\frac{d^2\mathbf{r}}{dt^2} = \ddot{\mathbf{r}} \quad \text{Acceleration}$$

$$\frac{d^3\mathbf{r}}{dt^3} = \dddot{\mathbf{r}} \quad \text{Jerk}$$

$$\frac{d^4\mathbf{r}}{dt^4} = \ddddot{\mathbf{r}} \quad \text{Snap (jounce)}$$

$$\frac{d^5\mathbf{r}}{dt^5} = \ddddot{\dot{\mathbf{r}}} \quad \text{Crackle}$$

$$\frac{d^6\mathbf{r}}{dt^6} = \ddddot{\ddot{\mathbf{r}}} \quad \text{Pop}$$

Time-derivatives of position

DIELECTRIC LOSSES

Symbol: ε'

Definition: The imaginary part of the complex permittivity.

$\varepsilon' = \varepsilon \tan \delta$

where: δ = loss factor, ε = permittivity.

Unit: Farad per meter

Dimension: $L^{-3} M^{-I} T^4 I^2$

DIELECTRIC RELAXATION TIME

Definition. Time interval after the electric field is switched off in which dielectric polarization decreases to lie its original value.

Unit: Second

Dimension: T

DIFFUSION

Definition. : Diffusion, in a microscopic sense, is a universal process that leads to the eliminating of a partial gradient of certain physical quantities such as concentration, thermal energy, or momentum in a one-phrase Solid, liquid or gaseous. At the molecular level, it arises because atoms or molecules undergo small, random displacive movements as a result of their thermal energy. Diffusion is one of the four properties of matter "viscosity ", "diffusion", "thermal energy", "conductivity ", and (in electrically conducting media) "electrical conductivity ". Each of these properties measures the flux of some quantity in a gradient. Diffusion measures the flow of mass in a concentration gradient.

The term diffusion is also used in other fields; accordingly, the following definitions are given.

A. IN PHYSICS:

The process by which fluids and solids mix intimately with one another due to kinetic motions of particles (atoms, molecules, groups of molecules). Mixing occurs completely unless one set of particles is much heavier than the other, in which case dynamic equilibrium between diffusion and sedimentation under gravity occurs. Interdiffusion of solids (e.g. gold into load) also occurs.

B. IN OPTICS

Diffuse reflection: The scattering of a beam reflected from a rough surface do not obey the laws of reflection but is scattered in many directions.

Diffuse transmission. Light transmitted by certain materials does not obey the laws of refraction and is scattered in the medium.

C. IN ACOUSTICS

The degree to which the directions of propagation of sound waves vary over the volume of a reverberant sound field

D. IN ELECTRONICS:

A method of producing a junction into a semiconductor at a high temperature

E. IN SOLID STATE:

The actual transport of mass, in the form of discrete atoms, through the lattice of a crystalline solid

The movement of carriers in a semiconductor

DIFFUSION COEFFICIENT

Symbol: D

Definition: If mass m of substance transported in time t across and area A when there is a concentration gradient dc/dz across this area, then the diffusion coefficient is D in the relation:

$Dm/dt = DA \ (dz/dc)$

Unit: Meter squared per second.

Dimension: $L^2 T^{-1}$

Note:

1. When the above equation refers to the diffusion of a solute through a solution, it is known as Frick's first law.

2. The diffusion coefficient, according to the above definition, is a measure of the average rate with which the displacement of the particle occurs.

3. The diffusion coefficient depends on the temperature. The studies lead to the following empirical relationship:

$$D = D^o \, exp \, [-QIRT)]$$

Where R is the displacement, D_o and Q are experimental parameters that are essentially temperature independent and characterize the diffusion process in the system at hand.

DIFFUSION LENGTH

Symbol: *L.*

Definition: The square root of the product of the diffusion coefficient *D* and the relaxation time τ.

$$L = \sqrt{D\tau}$$

Unit: Meter.

Dimension: *L.*

See "diffusion coefficient" and 'relaxation time".

DIFFUSIVITY, MAGNETIC

Symbol: η

Definition: A measure of the tendency of a magnetic field to diffuse through a conducting medium at rest; it is equal to the partial derivative of the magnetic field strength with respect to time divided by the Laplacian of the magnetic field or to the reciprocal of $4\pi\mu\sigma$,

Where μ is the magnetic permeability and σ is the conductivity in electromagnetic units.

DIFFUSIVITY, THERMAL

Symbol: *a*

Definition: A measure of the rate at which heat diffuses through a substance. It is defined as the thermal conductivity λ divided by the product of the density ρ and the specific heat capacity at constant pressure.

$^c\rho.$

$$a = \lambda / \rho c_\rho$$

Unit: Meter squared per second.

Dimension: $L^2 \, T^{-1}$

DIPOLE

Definition: A system of two equal and opposite charges placed at a very short distance apart. The distance between the two charges is known as the *dipole moment.*

A small magnet constitutes a magnetic dipole.

Also known as a *"doublef"*

DIPOLE MOMENT, ELECTRIC

Symbol: p; occasionally p_e

Definition: The dipole moment of an electric dipole is the product of the charge Q on one element of the dipole and the distance between the charges d.

$$p = Qd$$

The vector product of the dipole moment p and the electric field strength E is equal to the moment of the force M.

$$P \times E = M$$

Unit: Coulomb meter.

Dimension: L T 1.

Note: The electric dipole moment per unit volume of a dielectric material is the polarization vector.

See "polarization, electric".

DIPOLE MOMENT, MAGNETIC

Symbol: j

Definition: A vector associated with a magnet, current loop, particle, or such, whose vector product with the magnetic field strength H is equal to the moment of the force M exerted on the system by the field.

$$j \times H = M$$

Unit: Weber meter.

Dimension: $M L^3 T^{-2} I^{-1}$

Note: 1. The quantity was formerly termed the "magnetic moment", a name now as an alternative for the electromagnetic moment.

2. For an unrationalized system: $j* x H* = M$

DIRAC CONSTANT

Symbol: $\hbar$

Plank constant h divided by 2π

$\hbar = h/2\pi$

Unit: Joule second

Dimension: $L^2 M\ T^{-1}$

See "Plank constant".

DISINTEGRATION

Definition: Any process in which a nucleus emits one or more particles, such as beta Alpha particles and gamma rays, either spontaneously or following a collision.

See "Activity" and "decay constant".

DISINTEGRATION CONSTANT

See "Decay constant".

DISINTEGRATION RATE, RADIOACTIVE

See "activity ",

DISPLACEMENT

A. MECHANICAL:

Definition: 1. See *"length"*

Displacement of a particle is its change of position and is a vector quantity. If point A is the position of a particle at a time t_1 and B is its position at a later time t_2, its displacement in the time interval t_1-t_2 is the vector **AB,** no matter whether the path is straight or curved.

The distance of an oscillating particle from its equilibrium position

Unit: meter.

Dimension: L

B. CHEMISTRY:

Definition: 1. The replacement of one kind of atom, molecule or radical by another. It can be represented by the scheme-

$$A X + B \; ----> \; B X + A$$

An ionic change in which two elements exchange charges either by oxidation or reduction.

C. FLUID MECHANICS:

Definition: 1. The weight of fluid which is displaced by a floating body equals the weight of the body and its contents.

Unit: Kilogramme

Dimension: M

Note: The displacement of a ship is measured, normally, in long tons (1 long ton = 2240 pounds) The volume of fluid which is displaced by a floating body.

Unit: meter cubed

Dimension: L^3

See also *" displacement, electric "*.

DISPLACEMENT, EINSTEIN

Definition: The displacement of a ray of light from a star when passing to the sun's limb as seen by an observer on the Earth. It is predicted by a general theory of relativity.

DISPLACEMENT, ELECTRIC

Symbol: D

Definition: The electric displacement (also called electric flux density) is a quantity related to the charge displaced within a dielectric by the application of an electric field. Electric flux density at any point in an isotropic dielectric is a vector which has the same direction as the electric field strength and a magnitude equal to the product of the electric field strength and the permittivity ε

$$D = \varepsilon \; \mathbf{E}.$$

In a nonisotropic medium, ε may be represented by a tensor, and D is not parallel to E.

Unit: Coulomb per meter squared

Dimension: $L^{-2} T 1$

Note: 1. The divergence of the displacement **D** equals the charge surface density

2. The quantity is also termed the "*electric flux density* ".

3. The unrationalised displacement D* is also termed the "*electric induction*" defined as: $\Delta.D^* = 4\pi\sigma$, i.e. $D^* = 4\pi D$.

DISSIPATION COEFFICIENT

See "scattering coefficient."

DISTANCE

See "length"

DISTANCE MODULUS

The **distance modulus** is a way of expressing distances that is often used in astronomy. It describes distances on a logarithmic scale based on the astronomical magnitude system.

Definition: The distance modulus $\mu = m - M$ is the difference between the apparent magnitude m (ideally, corrected from the effects of interstellar absorption) and the absolute magnitude M of an astronomical object. It is related to the distance d in parsecs by:

$$\log_{10}(d) = 1 + \frac{\mu}{5}$$
$$\mu = 5\log_{10}(d) - 5$$

This definition is convenient because the observed brightness of a light source is related to its distance by the inverse square law (a source twice as far away appears one quarter as bright) and because brightness's are usually expressed not directly but in magnitudes.

Units: meter

Dimensions: L

DISTRIBUTION COEFFICIENT

Symbol: D_g

Definition: Ratio of the equilibrium concentration of a substance in the stationary and mobile phase, respectively.

Unit: There are no units or dimensions.

DOSE

A quantity of radiation or absorbed energy.

1. **ABSORBED DOSE:**

   Symbol: D

   Definition: Amount of energy imported to matter by ionizing particles per unit mass of irradiated material at a place of interest.

   Unit: Gray or rad (radiation absorbed dose)

   Dimension: $L^2 T^2$

2. **EXPOSURE DOSE:**

   Definition: It is a measure of X- or gamma-radiation to which a body is exposed. It is expressed by the total charge collected on ions of one sign produced in a unit mass of dry air by all secondary electrons liberated in a volume element by incident photons stopped in the element.

   Unit: Roentgen

3. **EQUIVALENT DOSE**

   Definition: Is used for protection purposes and is defined as:

   1 rem = I rad x Q.F.

   where: rem is the unit of the equivalent dose, and QF is the "quality factor" for a particular type of radiation and is a means of relating absorbed doses of different radiation to give the same biological effect.

   Some typical quality factors (QF) are:

Radiation	QF.
X-rays, Gamma-rays and high-energy Beta-rays	1
Lower energy Beta-rays	1.8
Neutrons	10

DRAG COEFFICIENT

Symbol: c_d, c_x or c_w

Definition: In fluid dynamics, the **drag coefficient** (commonly denoted as c_d, c_x or c_w) is a dimensionless quantity that is used to quantify the drag or resistance of an object in a fluid environment, such as air or water. It is used in the drag equation in which a lower drag coefficient indicates the object will have less aerodynamic or hydrodynamic drag. The drag coefficient is always associated with a particular surface area.

The drag coefficient of any object comprises the effects of the two basic contributors to fluid dynamic drag: skin friction and form drag. The drag coefficient of a lifting airfoil or hydrofoil also includes the effects of lift-induced drag. The drag coefficient of a complete structure such as an aircraft also includes the effects of interference drag.

The drag coefficient cd is defined as

$$c_d = \frac{2F_d}{\rho u^2 A}$$

Where:

F_d is the drag force, which is, by definition, the force component in the direction of the flow velocity,

ρ is the mass density of the fluid,

u is the flow speed of the object relative to the fluid,

A is the reference area.

The reference area depends on what type of drag coefficient is being measured. For automobiles and many other objects, the reference area is the projected frontal area of the vehicle. This may not necessarily be the cross-sectional area of the vehicle, depending on where the cross-section is taken. For example, for a sphere , $A=\pi r^2$ (note this is not the surface area $= 4\pi r^2$).

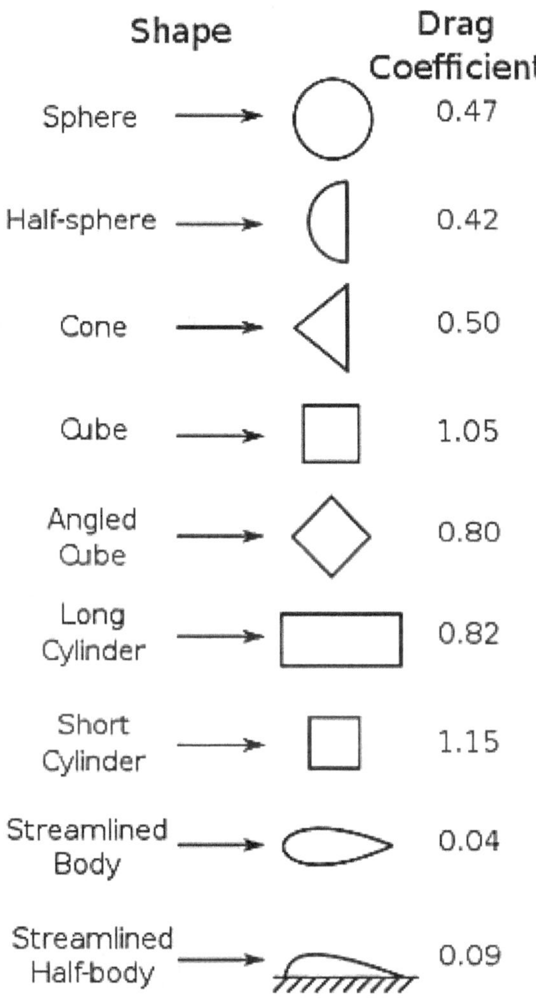

Measured Drag Coefficients

Drag coefficients in fluids with Reynolds number approximately 10^4

Field of application: aeronautics, fluid dynamics (resistance to fluid motion)

Unit: **Dimensionless**

[Ref. HandWiki]

DUKHIN NUMBER

Symbol: **Du**

Definition: The **Dukhin number (Du)** is a dimensionless quantity that characterizes the contribution of surface conductivity to various electrokinetic and electroacoustic effects, as well as to electrical conductivity and permittivity of fluid heterogeneous systems. The number was named after Stanislav and Andrei Dukhin.

It was introduced by Lyklema in "Fundamentals of Interface and Colloid Science" A recent IUPAC Technical Report used this term explicitly and detailed several means of measurement in physical systems.

The Dukhin number is a ratio of the surface conductivity κ^σ to the fluid bulk electrical conductivity K_m multiplied by particle size a:

$$Du = \frac{\kappa^\sigma}{K_m a}$$

There is another expression of this number that is valid when the surface conductivity is associated only with ions motion above the slipping plane in the double layer. In this case, the value of the surface conductivity depends on ζ-potential, which leads to the following expression for the Dukhin number for a symmetrical electrolyte with equal ions diffusion coefficient:

$$Du = \frac{2(1 + 3m/z^2)}{\kappa a}\left(\cosh\frac{zF\zeta}{2RT} - 1\right)$$

where the parameter m characterizes the contribution of electro-osmosis into the motion of ions within the double layer

$$m = \frac{2\varepsilon_0\varepsilon_m R^2 T^2}{3\eta F^2 D}$$

- F is Faraday constant
- T is an absolute temperature
- R is gas constant
- C is ions concentration in bulk
- z is ion valency
- ζ is electrokinetic potential
- ε_0 is vacuum dielectric permittivity
- ε_m is fluid dielectric permittivity
- η is dynamic viscosity

- *D* is the diffusion coefficient

***Unit*:** Dimensionless

[Ref. HandWiki]

DYNAMIC MODULUS

Dynamic modulus (sometimes **complex modulus**) is the ratio of stress to strain under *vibratory conditions* (calculated from data obtained from either free or forced vibration tests in shear, compression, or elongation). It is a property of viscoelastic materials.

E

ECKERT NUMBER

Symbol: **Ec**

Definition: The **Eckert number** (**Ec**) is a dimensionless number used in continuum mechanics. It expresses the relationship between a flow's kinetic energy and the boundary layer enthalpy difference and is used to characterize heat transfer dissipation. It is named after Ernst R. G. Eckert.

It is defined as

$$Ec = \frac{u^2}{c_p \Delta T} = \frac{\text{Advective Transport}}{\text{Heat Dissipation Potential}}$$

where

- u is the local flow velocity of the continuum,
- c_p is the constant-pressure local specific heat of the continuum,
- ΔT is the difference between wall temperature and local temperature.

Field of application: convective heat transfer (characterizes dissipation of energy; a ratio of kinetic energy to enthalpy)

Units: Dimensionless

EFFECTIVE ATOMIC NUMBER (EAN)

Symbol: Z_{eff}.

Definition: Total number of electrons surrounding the central atom of metal in a metal complex. This number is equal to an atomic number of the nearest noble gas.

Unit: There are no units or dimensions.

Note: Effective Atomic Number is composed of the metal atom's electrons and the bonding electrons from the surrounding electron-donating atoms and molecules. Thus, for example, the effective atomic number of the cobalt atom in the complex $[Co(NH_3)_6]^{3+}$ is 36, the sum of the number of electrons in the trivalent cobalt ion (24) and the number of bonding electrons from six surrounding ammonia molecules, each of which contributes an electron pair ($2 \times 6 = 12$).

See "Atomic number."

EFFECTIVE NUMBER OF BOHR MAGNETONS

Symbol: μ_{ef}

Definition: Magnetic moment of atom, ion or molecule determined from experimentally measured magnetic susceptibility according to an assumption of its temperature dependence given either by Curie law or by Curie- Weiss law:

$$\mu_{ef} = 2.83\sqrt{C_M}\ \mu_B = 2.83\sqrt{\aleph_M(T - \Theta)}\ \mu_B$$

Where: $\aleph_M$ = Molar magnetic susceptibility

μ_B = Bohr Magneton

C_M = Molar Curie constant

Θ = Paramagnetic Curie Temperature

"See Bohr magneton."

EFFICIENCY

Symbol: η

1. For a machine

    Definition: The work done by the machine divided by the work done on it. For steady operation, this is equal to the power output. P_i

    $$\eta = P_o/P_i$$

2. For heat Engine:

    Definition: The work done by the engine divided by the heat input. For an ideal reversible engine in which all heat input is at the temperature T_1 and all waste heat is discharged at a lower temperature T_2

$$\eta = (T_1 - T_2)/T_1$$

The temperature being thermodynamic temperature.

Unit: There are no units or dimensions.

Note: 1. Efficiency is usually expressed as a percentage

2. In nuclear physics, efficiency means the probability that a count will be produced in a counter tube by a specified particle or quantum incident.

3. In statistics: An estimator is more efficient than another if it has a smaller variance. Also, an experimental design is more efficient than another if the same level of precision can be obtained in less time or less cost.

EFFICIENCY, AMPERE-HOUR

Definition: The ratio of the quantity of electricity available during discharge to the quantity of electricity used to charge the cell.

Unit: There are no units or dimensions.

Note: It is usually used with accumulators.

EFFICIENCY, LUMINOUS

Symbol: V

Definition: A dimensionless quantity defined by the ratio between the luminous efficacy K to the maximum spectral luminous efficacy K_m

$V = K/K_m$

Unit: There are no dimensions or units.

Note: 1. The term was formerly applied to what is now called *"luminous efficacy"*. The term efficacy is now more properly left for dimensionless ratios.

2. If monochromatic radiation is considered, the property is called the *"spectral luminous efficiency"* or *"relative luminous efficiency"*.

See also *"efficiency, luminous, relative", and "luminous efficacy."*

EFFICIENCY, RADIANT

Symbol: η also η_e

Definition: The ratio of the radiant flux Φ emitted by a source of radiation to the power consumed P.

$$\eta = \Phi/P$$

It is the radiant equivalent of the photometric quantity luminous efficacy.

Unit: There are no units or dimensions.

See *"luminous efficacy."*

EFFICIENCY, RELATIVE LUMINOUS

Symbol: V_λ

Definition: Relative luminous efficiency is Luminous efficiency K_λ divided by maximum luminous efficiency K_m

$$V_\lambda = K_\lambda/K_m$$

Alternatively, the relative luminous efficiency is the radiant flux at a given wavelength divided by that at the wavelength, which produces equally intense luminous sensations under specified photometric conditions, the maximum value of the ratio being made equal to unity.

Unit: There are no units or dimensions.

Note: 1. It is also known as spectral luminous efficiency

EFFICIENCY, SPECTRAL LUMINOUS

(of a monochromatic radiation of wavelength λ)

Symbols: V(λ) for photopic vision. V'(λ) for scotopic vision

Definition: Ratio of the radiant flux at wavelength λ_m to that at wavelength λ such that both radiations produce equally intense luminous sensations under specified photometric conditions, and λ_m is chosen so that the maximum value of this ratio is equal to one.

. *Note*: unless otherwise indicated, the values used for the spectral luminous efficiency in **photopic vision** are the values agreed upon internationally in 1931 by the CIE and adopted in 1933 by the International Committee on Weights and Measures. For **scotopic vision,** the CIE in 1951 provisionally adopted new values for young observers (CIE)

CIE in 1951 provisionally adopted new values for young observers (CIE). See. luminosity curve.

(Ref. The Free Dictionary)

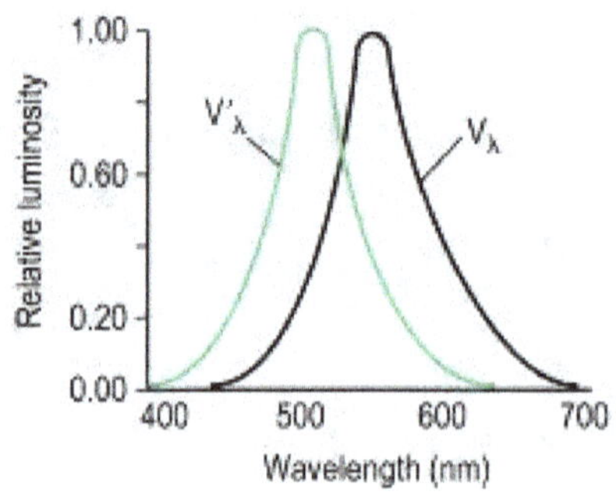

Fig. E1 Relative luminous efficiency curves for photopic V_λ and scotopic V'_λ levels of adaptation for an equi-energy spectrum. These data represent the sensitivity (i.e

Table: Photopic and scotopic relative luminous efficiency factors. The data are based on an average from a large number of individuals agreed by the CIE in 1931 for the photopic factor V_λ and in 1951 for the scotopic factor V'_λ

wavelength (in nm)	V_λ	V'_λ
380	0.000 0	0.000 589
400	0.000 4	0.009 292
420	0.004 0	0.096 61
440	0.023 0	0.328 1
460	0.060 0	0.567 2
480	0.139 0	0.793 0
500	0.323 0	0.981 8
507	-	1.000 0
520	0.710 0	0.935 2
540	0.954 0	0.649 7
555	1.000 0	-
580	0.870 0	0.121 2

600	0.631 0	0.033 15
620	0.381 0	0.007 374
640	0.175 0	0.001 497
660	0.061 0	0.000 312 9
680	0.017 0	0.000 071 55
700	0.004 1	0.000 017 80
720	0.001 05	0.000 004 78
740	0.000 25	0.000 001 379
760	0.000 06	0.000 000 425
780	0.000 00	0.000 000 139

EFFORT

Definition: That comparatively small force which is used in a machine to overcome a large force (e.g. the weight lifted by a system of pulleys) called the load.

Unit: Newton

Dimension: LMT^{-2}

Note: The principle of work states that:

Work done by effort = work done on load + work lost in friction.

The efficiency = (work done on load) / (work done by effort)

The efficiency is necessarily less than 1.

See *"mechanical advantage"* and *"velocity ratio."*

EKMAN NUMBER

Symbol: Ek

Definition: The Ekman number (Ek) is a dimensionless number used in fluid dynamics to describe the ratio of viscous forces to Coriolis forces. It is frequently used in describing geophysical phenomena in the oceans and atmosphere in order to characterize the ratio of viscous forces to the Coriolis forces arising from planetary rotation. It is named after the Swedish oceanographer Vagn Walfrid Ekman. When the Ekman number is small, disturbances are able to propagate before decaying owing to low frictional effects. The Ekman number also describes the order of magnitude for the thickness of an Ekman layer, a boundary layer in which viscous diffusion is balanced by Coriolis effects rather than the usual convective inertia.

It is defined as:

$$Ek = \frac{\nu}{2D^2\Omega \sin \varphi}$$

where

D is a characteristic (usually vertical) length scale of a phenomenon; ν, the kinematic eddy viscosity;

Ω, the angular velocity of planetary rotation; and φ, the latitude.

The term $2\,\Omega \sin \varphi$ is the Coriolis frequency. It is given in terms of the kinematic viscosity, ν; the angular velocity, Ω; and a characteristic length scale, L.

Unit: Dimensionless

ELASTANCE, Electrical

Symbol: S

Definition: The reciprocal of the capacitance C.

Elastance $S = 1/C$

Unit: Per farad (daraf)

Dimension: $L^2MT^{-4}I^{-2}$

Notes: 1.   The concept of elastance is not widely used by electrical and electronic engineers. The value of capacitors is invariably specified in units of capacitance rather than inverse capacitance. However, it is used in theoretical work in network analysis and has some niche applications at microwave frequencies.

2.   The term *elastance* was coined by Oliver Heaviside through the analogy of a capacitor as

a spring.

3.   In Mechanical: The term is also used for analogous quantities in some other energy domains. It maps to stiffness in the mechanical domain and is the inverse of compliance in the fluid flow domain, especially in physiology. It is also the name of the generalized quantity in bond-graph analysis and other schemes analyzing systems across multiple domains.

In mechanical:

$$\text{Elastance} = 1/\text{Compliance} = \text{Pressure change} / \text{Volume change}$$

4.   In Medicine: A measurement of the tendency of the lung, urinary bladder, gallbladder or other cavity to recoil inwards. Opposite of compliance.

ELASTIC MODULUS

Definition: The ratio of stress to strain for a body obeying Hooke's law. There are several moduli corresponding to various types of strain.

(1) YOUNG'S MODULUS

Symbol: E

Definition: Normal stress σ (i.e. the applied load per unit area of cross-section) divided by tensile strain e, i.e. (increase in length per unit length).

$$E = \sigma/e$$

Note: Young's modulus applies to tensional stress when the sides of the rod or bar concerned are not constrained.

(2) RIGIDITY MODULUS

Symbol: G

Definition: Shear stress τ divided by shear strain γ.

$$E= \tau/ \gamma$$

Note: *The quantity is also termed the shear modulus.*

(3) BULK MODULUS

Symbol: K

Definition: Bulk stress p divided by bulk strain θ.

$$K = p/\theta$$

Note: 1. This modulus applies to compression or dilation, e.g., when a body is subject to changes in hydrostatic pressure.   Fluids, as well as solids, have bulk moduli.

2. The quantity is also termed the hydrostatic modulus, modulus of compression or volume elasticity.

(4) AXIAL MODULUS

Definition: Is defined in the same way as Young's modulus with the proviso that the sides of the specimen are restricted so that there is no lateral change.

Note: The quantity is also termed modulus of simple longitudinal extension.

Unit: Pascal

Dimension: $L^{-1}MT^{-2}$.

Note: If stress is not proportional to strain, as in the case of cast metal, marble, concrete, and wood, the moduli have to be defined as the ratio of a small change in stress to a small change in strain at a particular value of the stress.

ELASTICITY (economics)

Definition: In economics, **elasticity** measures the percentage change of one economic variable in response to a change in another. If a good's price elasticity of demand is -2, a 10% increase in price causes the quantity demanded to fall 20%.

Unit: Dimensionless

ELECTRIC CONSTANT

Symbol: ε_0

Definition: The electric constant pertinent to any system of units is the scalar which in that system relates the electric flux density D, in a vacuum, to the electric field strength E: ($D = \varepsilon_o E$).

It also relates the mechanical force between two charges in a vacuum to their magnitudes and their separation. Thus in the equation:

$$F = \varepsilon_r Q_1 Q_2 / 4\pi\varepsilon_0 r^2$$

For the force F between charges Q_1 and Q_2 separated by a distance r, ε_0 is a dimensionless factor which is unity in a rationalized system, and 4π in an unrationalized system.

Note: 1.　　In the cgs electrostatic system ε_0 is assigned measure unity and the dimension "numeric."

2.　　In the cgs electromagnetic system, the measure of ε_0 is that of $1/c^2$ and the dimension is: $L^{-2}T^2$.

3.　　In the SI system, the measure of ε_0 is $10^7/4\pi c^2$ and the dimension is $[L^{-3}M^{-1}T^4I^2]$. Here c is the speed of light in the appropriate system of units.

4. Electric constant $\varepsilon_0 = 8.854187817...\times10^{-12}$ F·m^{-1} (farads per meter), i.e.

$[m^{-3} kg^{-1} s^4 A^2]$

5. The electric constant is commonly called: physical constant ε_0　the **vacuum permittivity**, **permittivity of free space** or the **distributed capacitance of the vacuum**,

See also *"Permittivity, absolute and relative."*

ELECTRIZATION

Symbol: E_i Sometimes K_i

Definition: Electric polarization P divided by the electric constant ε_0

$E_i = P/\varepsilon_0 = P*/\varepsilon o*$

Unit: Volt per meter = newton coulomb.

Dimension: $LMT^{-3} I^{-1}$

Note: The equation defining polarization P, i.e.

$D = \varepsilon_0 E + P.$

can be rewritten in terms of electrization as:

$D = \varepsilon_0 (E + E_i)$

Note: Electrization, as a noun, means: The action or process of electrifying something, electrification; specifically the application of electricity to the body for therapeutic purposes

ELECTROMOTIVE FORCE

Symbol: E and sometimes V

Definition 1: Work done in taking a charge completely around a circuit, i.e. The circular integral of the electric field strength K

$$E = \oint K.\, dx \; (x = \text{distance})$$

Unit: Volt.

Dimension: $L^2MT^{-3}I^{-1}$

Definition 2: The force or electric pressure that causes or tends to cause a current to flow in a circuit, equivalent to the potential difference between the terminals and commonly measured in volts: abbrev. *E*, *EMF*, or *emf*

Note: 1. In definition 1, the work may be done by electromagnetic induction, thermoelectric effects, or chemical reaction. This work is reversible, i.e. if the process is driven in reverse, the circuit does work upon the source of electromotive force.

2. Electromotive force (e.m.f), which is not a force in the normal sense but a measure of how much work would be done by moving an electric charge, must be distinguished from potential difference. In a circuit, the latter is the rate of energy dissipation divided by current and is inherently irreversible.

3. If a battery of e.m.f. E and resistance r maintains a current I in an external resistance, R, the rate of doing work is IE, which equals the rate of dissipation $(R+r).\, I^2$.

The potential drop between the terminals is $V = IR$. If R tends to infinity, the value E tends to that of V, so the e.m.f. is equal to the potential drop between the terminals on the open circuit, although its nature is different.

See also *"induction, motional."*

ELECTRON AFFINITY

Definition: Energy ensuing from electron capture by atom or molecule resulting in formation of negative ion.

Also can be defined as The energy released when an electron is attached to an atom or molecule, used as a measure of its ability to form an anion.

ELECTRONIC LEPTON NUMBER

Symbol: L_e

Definition: Number attributed to elementary particles, for electron and electronic neutrino, $L_e = 1$, for their antiparticles, $L_e = -1$. Other particles and antiparticles have $L_e = 0$.

Electronic lepton number is conserved in all interactions.

Unit: There are no units or dimensions.

ELECTRONIC POLARIZABILITY

Symbol: α_E

Definition: Dielectric polarization (per molecule) arising in a unit local field due to deformation of electron density.

Definition (electricity)

Polarization arises from the displacement of electrons with respect to the nuclei with which they are associated upon application of an external electric field.

ELONGATION, FRACTIONAL (or RELATIVE)

See "*strain (1).*"

EMISSIVITY, TOTAL

Symbol: ε

Definition: The ratio of the power per unit area radiated from a surface to the radiated from a black body at the same temperature.

Alternatively, it can be defined as The total emissivity of an element of the surface of a temperature radiator is the ratio of its radiant flux density (radiant exitance) M_e to that of a blackbody at the same temperature M^o_e

$$\varepsilon = \frac{M_e}{M_e^o},$$

Unit: There are no units or dimensions.

Note: 1.   The **emissivity** of the surface of a material is its effectiveness in emitting energy as thermal radiation. Thermal radiation is electromagnetic radiation, and it may include both visible radiation (light) and infrared radiation, which is not visible to human eyes.

2.   The emissivity, accordingly, is restricted to radiation produced by thermal agitation of atoms, molecules, etc.

3. Sometimes called *"Total Hemispherical emissivity."*

See *"radiant, exitance, heat transfer coefficient"* and also compare with "absorptivity."

Total emissivity of some material

Material	Emissivity
Aluminum foil	0.03
Aluminum, anodized	0.9
Asphalt	0.88
Brick	0.90
Concrete, rough	0.91
Copper, polished	0.04
Copper oxidized	0.87
Glass, smooth (uncoated)	0.95
Ice	0.97
Limestone	0.92
Marble (polished)	0.89 to 0.92
Paint (including white)	0.9
Paper, roofing or white	0.88 to 0.86
Plaster, rough	0.89

Material	Emissivity
Silver, polished	0.02
Silver, oxidized	0.04
Snow	0.8 to 0.9
Transition metal Disilicides (e.g. $MoSi_2$ or WSi_2)	0.86 to 0.93
Water, pure	0.96

EMISSIVITY in FREQUENCY, SPECTRAL

Symbol: ε_ν

Definition: The spectral emissivity of an element of a surface of a temperature radiator at any frequency is the ratio of its spectral radiant exitance in frequency of that surface ($M_{e,\nu}$) to the spectral radiant existence in frequency of a black body at the same temperature as that surface ($M_{e,\nu}$)

$$\varepsilon_\nu = \frac{M_{e,\nu}}{M_{e,\nu}^\circ},$$

Unit: There are no units or dimensions.

EMISSIVITY in WAVELENGTH, SPECTRAL

Symbol: ε_λ

Definition: The spectral emissivity of an element of a surface of a temperature radiator at any wavelength is the ratio of its radiant flux density per unit wavelength interval (spectral radiant exitance) at that wavelength to that of a blackbody at the same temperature.

$$\varepsilon_\lambda = \frac{M_{e,\lambda}}{M_{e,\lambda}^\circ},$$

Unit: There are no units or dimensions.

EMISSIVITY, DIRECTIONAL

Symbol: ε_Ω,

Definition:

$$\varepsilon_\Omega = \frac{L_{e,\Omega}}{L_{e,\Omega}^\circ},$$

where

- $L_{e,\,\Omega}$ is the radiance of that surface;
- $L_{e,\Omega}^0$ is the radiance of a black body at the same temperature as that surface.

Unit: There are no units or dimensions.

EMISSIVITY, SPECTRAL DIRECTIONAL EMISSIVITY: in frequency and in wavelength

Symbol: $\varepsilon_{v,\Omega}$ and $\varepsilon_{\lambda,\Omega}$ respectively

Definition: Spectral directional emissivity in frequency and spectral directional emissivity in wavelength of a surface, denoted $\varepsilon_{v,\Omega}$ and $\varepsilon_{\lambda,\Omega}$ respectively, are defined as:

$$\varepsilon_{\nu,\Omega} = \frac{L_{e,\Omega,\nu}}{L_{e,\Omega,\nu}^\circ},$$

$$\varepsilon_{\lambda,\Omega} = \frac{L_{e,\Omega,\lambda}}{L_{e,\Omega,\lambda}^\circ},$$

Where:

- $L_{e,\Omega,\nu}$ is the spectral radiance in frequency of that surface;
- $L_{e,\Omega,\nu}^0$ is the spectral radiance in frequency of a black body at the same temperature as that surface;
- $L_{e,\Omega,\lambda}$ is the spectral radiance in wavelength of that surface;
- $L_{e,\Omega,\lambda}^0$ is the spectral radiance in wavelength of a black body at the same temperature as that surface.

Unit: There are no units or dimensions

EMISSIVITY, SPECTRAL

Symbol: $\varepsilon(\lambda)$

Definition: The spectral emissivity of an element of a surface of a temperature radiator at any wavelength is the ratio of its radiant flux density per unit wavelength interval (spectral radiant exitance) at that wavelength to that of a blackbody at the same temperature.

Unit: There are no units or dimensions.

EMITTANCE, LUMINOUS

Symbol: M; occasionally M_v

Definition: At a point on a surface, luminous flux Φ emergent from an infinitesimal element of surface containing the point whose radiant emittance is to be determined, divided by the area A of the element.

$$M = d\Phi/dA$$

Unit: Lux

Dimension: M T^{-3}

Note: The quantity is also termed the *"luminous exitance"*

See, "exitance, radiant"

EMITTANCE, RADIANT

Symbol: *M,* sometimes M_e

Definition: At a point on a surface, Radiant flux Φ emergent from an infinitesimal element of surface containing the point whose radiant emittance is to be determined, divided by the area A of the element.

$$M = d\Phi/dA$$

Unit: Watt per meter squared.

Dimension: M T^{-3}

Note: The quantity is also termed the *"radiant exitance"* and also *"emitted radiant flux"*. According to Stefan's law, it is proportional in size to the fourth power of the absolute temperature T of the emitter in the case of black body.

$$M = \sigma T^4$$

where σ is Stefan's constant.

It has also been termed the *"radiant flux density"* and the *"radiancy.*

ENERGY

Symbol: E

Definition: The quantity that is the measure of the capacity of a body or a system for doing work. It follows the principle of conservation of energy. According to this principle, when a body does a work W, its energy decreases by an amount equal to W. The energy of the body upon which it does work increases by exactly the same amount so that the total energy of the system does not change.

Energy, in its wide sense, is defined mathematically as the product of force F and the distance s moved in the direction of the force.

$$E = F\, s$$

Unit: Joule

Dimension: $L^2\, M\, T^{-2}$

Note: There are several special types of energy:

1. KINETIC ENERGY

    Symbol: T or E_k

    Definition: The energy possessed because of motion and is equal to the work that a body would do if brought to rest with respect to a certain observer. For a particle of mass m with speed v, the translation kinetic energy is

    $$T = \left(\tfrac{1}{2}\right) m\, v^2,$$

    A rotating body with a moment of inertia l about its axis of rotation and angular velocity ω has rotational kinetic energy.

    $$T = \frac{1}{2} l\omega^2$$

2. **POTENTIAL ENERGY**

    Symbol: U; sometimes V, E_p

    Definition: The energy possessed by a system because of the position of a body with respect to the standard. For a body of mass m raised to a height h above the ground, the potential energy is:

$$U = m\,g\,h$$

Where g is the acceleration of free fall.

Unit: Joule

Note: 1. In general, it is defined as the work done in changing a system from some standard configuration to its present state.

2. If the work done is independent of the way in which the change is made, the system is said to be conservative. If there is friction, the system is nonconservative.

3. If a conservative system is in equilibrium, the change in potential energy in any infinitesimal displacement is zero.

4. Definition as per Britannica: Energy, in physics, is the capacity for doing work. It may exist in potential, kinetic, thermal, electrical, chemical, nuclear, or other various forms. There are, moreover, heat and work—i.e., energy in the process of transfer from one body to another. After it has been transferred, energy is always designated according to its nature. Hence, heat transferred may become thermal energy, while work done may manifest itself in the form of mechanical energy.

All forms of energy are associated with motion. For example, any given body has kinetic energy if it is in motion. A tensioned device such as a bow or spring, though at rest, has the potential for creating motion; it contains potential energy because of its configuration. Similarly, nuclear energy is potential energy because it results from the configuration of subatomic particles in the nucleus of an atom.

3.   INTERNAL ENERGY

Symbol: U; sometimes, E

Definition: The sum of the potential energies of the molecular interactions and the kinetic energies of the molecular motions within a body.

Note: 1. It is important to differentiate between internal energy U and heat energy Q. The internal energy of a body may be changed by both of the processes of work W or heat:

$$dU = W + Q$$

Where dU is the change in the internal energy of the system due to the heat received Q by the system and the work done W on it.

Thus it is not correct to use the term *"heat energy"* for U since it is not uniquely related to heat. Moreover, it is possible to transfer internal energy from a colder to a hotter body by doing work.

2. The equation of note (1) can be used to define internal energy.

Definition: The internal energy is a thermodynamic function of a system that changes by an amount dU equal to the algebraic sum of the heat received by the system Q and the work done on it W.

$$dQ = Q + W$$

3. The internal energy is never absolutely determined, only changes in its value are important. Sometimes a conventional standard state is considered to have U equal to zero, and other states have a value of U equal to the change in internal energy in moving to this state from the standard state.

4. For a particle in a potential, the sum of the particle's kinetic energy and potential energy is called *"particle energy."*

4. CHEMICAL ENERGY:

Definition: The energy required to break the chemical bonds in a substance. It is a property of the system as a whole; it is not a property of either constituent by itself. Strictly, the energy change depends on the change of *"Gibbs function."*

5. NUCLEAR ENERGY

Definition: The energy released during nuclear reactions due to forming new bonds that are stronger than those that must be broken.

6. Thermodynamics (Ref. Britannica)

Definition: **Internal energy** in thermodynamics is the property or state function that defines the energy of a substance in the absence of effects due to capillarity and external electric, magnetic, and other fields. Like any other state function, the value of the energy depends upon the state of the substance and not upon the nature of the processes by which it attained that state. In accordance with the first law of thermodynamics, when a system undergoes a change of state as a result of a process in which only work is involved, the work is equal to the change in internal energy. The law also implies that if both heat and work are involved in the change of state of a system, then the change in internal energy is equal to the heat supplied to the system minus the work done by the system.

7. See also *"energy, particle", "electric energy", "enthalpy", "Gibbs function," "energy luminous", and "energy, radiant". See the next table summarizing the types of energy.*

8. All the above-mentioned types of energy have specific forms, defined as energy divided by mass, their symbols are the lowercase equivalents of the symbols tabulated.
See *"specific"* and *"energy specific."*

Some forms of energy (that an object or system can have as a measurable property)	
Type of energy	**Description**
Mechanical	the sum of macroscopic translational and rotational kinetic and potential energies
Electrical	potential energy due to or stored in electric fields
Magnetic	potential energy due to or stored in magnetic fields
Gravitational	potential energy due to or stored in gravitational fields
Chemical	potential energy due to chemical bonds
Ionization	potential energy that binds an electron to its atom or molecule
Nuclear	the potential energy that binds nucleon to form the atomic nucleus (and nuclear reactions)
Chromodynamic	potential energy that binds quarks to form hadrons
Elastic	potential energy due to the deformation of a material (or its container) exhibiting a restorative force
Mechanical Wave	the kinetic and potential energy in an elastic material due to a propagated deformational wave
Sound wave	the kinetic and potential energy in a fluid due to a sound-propagated wave (a particular form of mechanical wave)
Radiant	Potential energy stored in the fields of propagated by electromagnetic radiation, including light
Rest	potential energy due to an object's rest mass

Thermal	kinetic energy of the microscopic motion of particles, a form of disordered equivalent of mechanical energy

ENERGY DENSITY

Symbol: w; E in acoustics; u for radiant energy density

Definition: Energy E divided by volume V at a point.

$w = E/V$

Unit: Joule per meter cubed.

Dimension: $L^{-1} M T^{-2}$.

ENERGY, FREE

Symbol: F

In physics and physical chemistry, free energy refers to the amount of internal energy of a thermodynamic system that is available to perform work. There are different forms of thermodynamic free energy:

1. Gebbs free energy

Definition: Gibbs free energy, the energy that may be converted into work in a system that is at constant temperature and pressure. The equation for Gibbs free energy is:

$G = H - TS$

where G is Gibbs free energy, H is enthalpy, T is temperature, and S is entropy.

Unit: Joule

Dimension: $L^2 M T^{-2}$

2. Helmholtz free energy:

Definition: **Helmholtz free energy** is energy that may be converted into work at constant temperature and volume. The equation for Helmholtz free energy is:

$A = U - TS$

where A is the Helmholtz free energy, U is the internal energy of the system, T is the absolute temperature (Kelvin), and S is the entropy of the system.

3. *Landau free energy*

Definition: **Landau-free energy** describes the energy of an open system in which particles and energy may be exchanged with the surroundings. The equation for Landau free energy is:

$$\Omega = A - \mu N = U - TS - \mu N$$

where N is the number of particles and μ is chemical potential.

4. *Variational Free Energy*

In information theory, variational free energy is a construct used in variational Bayesian methods. Such methods are used to approximate intractable integrals for statistics and machine learning.

5. *Other Definitions*

In environmental science and economics, the phrase "free energy" is sometimes used to refer to renewable resources or any energy that does not require monetary payment.

Note: Free energy may also refer to the energy that powers a hypothetical perpetual motion machine. Such a device violates the laws of thermodynamics, so this definition presently refers to pseudoscience rather than hard science.

Sources

- *Baierlein, Ralph (2003). Thermal Physics. Cambridge University Press. ISBN 0-521-65838-1.*

See *"Gibbs function."*

ENERGY, LUMINOUS

Symbol: Q occasionally Q_v

Definition: The total radiant energy emitted by a source, evaluated according to the capacity to produce visual sensation and expressed as the integral of the luminous flux Φ with respect to time t.

$$Q = \int \Phi dt$$

Unit: Talbot or lumen second (or lumber).

Dimension: $L^2 M T^{-2}$.

Note: 1. Luminous energy is not the same as radiant energy, the corresponding objective physical quantity. This is because the human eye can only see light in the visible spectrum and has different sensitivities to light of different wavelengths within the spectrum. When adapted for bright conditions (photopic vision), the eye is most sensitive to light at a wavelength of 555 nm. Light with a given amount of radiant energy will have more luminous energy if the wavelength is 555 nm than if the wavelength is longer or shorter. Light whose wavelength is well outside the visible spectrum has a luminous energy of zero, regardless of the amount of radiant energy present.

2. The name Talbot is in honor of William Henry Fox Talbot.

ENERGY, MOLAR

Definition: Energy E divided by molar value n.

Molar energy $= E/n$

Unit: Joule per mole

Dimension: $L^2 M T^{-2} N^{-1}$

Note: N is used as the dimensional symbol of molar value.

ENERGY, PARTICLE

Definition: For a relativistic particle, the sum of the particle's potential energy, kinetic energy, and the rest energy, the later is equal to the product of the particle's rest mass m_o and the squared of the speed of light c.

Unit: Joule

Dimension: $L^2 M T^{-2}$

Note: 1. In the case of nonrelativistic particles, the particle energy is the sum of the potential energy and the kinetic energy of the particle. (See *energy/note 4 of internal energy*.)

2. Nonrelativistic particle means a particle whose velocity is small with respect to that of light.

ENERGY, RADIANT

Symbol: Q; sometimes W, Q_e or U

Definition: Energy in the form of radiation. The integral of the radiant flux Φ, with respect to time t.

$$Q = \int \Phi_e \, dt$$

Unit: Joule

Dimension: $L^2 \, M \, T^{-2}$

ENERGY, REST

Definition: The energy equivalent to the rest mass m_o of a particle or body.

Rest Energy $= m_o \, c^2$

Where c is the speed of light

Unit: Often expressed in electron volt

Dimension: $L^2 \, M \, T^{-2}$

ENERGY, SPECIFIC

Symbol: e

Definition: Energy E divided by mass m

$e = E/m$

Unit: Joule per kilogramme.

Dimension: $L^2 \, T^{-2}$

Note: All the types of energy given under energy (note) have specific forms, defined as above, their symbols are the lowercase equivalent of the symbols tabulated.

ENERGY, SPECTRAL RADIANT

Symbol: U_λ

Definition: Rate of variation of radiant energy U with wavelength λ

$U_\lambda = dU \, / \, d\lambda$

Unit: Joule per meter

Dimension: L M T^{-2}

ENTHALPY

Symbol: H Sometimes *l*

Definition: The sum of internal energy U of a system plus the product of the system's volume V multiplied by the pressure P exerted on the system by its surroundings.

$$H = U + PV$$

Unit: Joule

Dimension: L^{2}MT^{-2}

Note: 1. Also known as *"heat content,"* *"sensible heat"*, *"total heat"*, and "enthalpy function."

2. For a reversible change at constant pressure, the work done by the system is equal to the product of the pressure times the change of volume. The heat absorbed in such a process is thus equal to the increase of enthalpy of the system.

3. For a reversible change, the "heat capacity" C_p of a system at constant pressure is given by:

$$C_p = \left(\frac{\partial H}{\partial T}\right)_p$$

4. The joule-Kelvin effect is a nonreversible flow process in which the initial and final states have the same enthalpy.

5. Enthalpy is usually expressed as the change in enthalpy (ΔH) for a process between initial and final states:

$$\Delta H = \Delta U + \Delta PV$$

If temperature and pressure remain constant through the process and the work is limited to pressure-volume work, then the enthalpy change is given by the equation:

$$\Delta H = \Delta U + P\Delta V$$

Also, at constant pressure, the heat flow (q) for the process is equal to the change in enthalpy defined by the equation:

$$\Delta H = q$$

ENTHALPY, MOLAR

Symbol: H_m

Definition: Enthalpy H divided by molar value n.

$H_m = H/n$

Unit: Joule per mole

Dimension: $L^2MT^{-2}N^{-1}$

Note: N is used as the dimensional symbol of molar value.

ENTROPY

Symbol: S, formerly Φ

1.   THERMODYNAMICS

Definition: A property of a system that changes, when the system undergoes a reversible change, by an amount dS equal to the energy dQ absorbed by the system divided by the thermodynamic temperature T

$dS = dQ/T$

Entropy depends on the state of the system and not on the path by which that state is reached.

Unit: Joule per Kelvin.

Dimension: $L^2 M T^{-3}$

Note: 1. The entropy is a quantity with an arbitrary zero, with only changes in its value being of significance.

2. The entropy of a system is a measure of the unavailability of its internal energy to do work in a cyclic process. Thus if two bodies at unequal temperatures have the same internal energy, that at the higher temperature has lower entropy.

3. The quantity is also termed the "thermal charge"; the unit is then termed the thermal coulomb.

2.   MATHEMATICS

Definition: In a mathematical context, this concept is attached to dynamical systems, transformations between measure spaces, or systems of events with probabilities, it expresses the amount of disorder inherent or produced.

3.   STATISTICAL MECHANICS

Definition: Measure of disorder of a system, equal to the Boltzmann constant times the natural logarithm of the number of microscope states corresponding to the thermodynamic state of the system. This statistical-mechanical definition can be shown to be equivalent to the thermodynamic definition.

$$S = k_B \log \Omega$$

Where Ω is the number of microstates, and k_B is Boltzmann constant, and S is the entropy

ENTROPY, DENSITY

Symbol: S_v

Definition: Entropy per unit volume.

$S_v = S/V$

where S = entropy and V = volume of a macroscopic element of system.

Unit: Joule per Kelvin cubic meter

ENTROPY FACTOR

Definition: In absolute reaction-rate theory, the entropy factor is given by:

Entropy factor = $\exp(\Delta S^{\neq}/R)$,

where $S^{\neq}$ = entropy of activation, R = universal gas constant.

Unit: There are no units or dimensions.

Note: Entropy factor is a counterpart to the steric factor P in the collision theory.

See *"Steric factor."*

ENTROPY, MOLAR

Definition: Entropy S divided by molar value *n*.

Molar entropy = S/n

Unit: Joule per mole Kelvin

Dimension: M N^{-1}

Note: N is used as the dimensional symbol of molar value.

ENTROPY, SPECIFIC

Symbol: s

Definition: Entropy S divided by mass m.

$s = S/m$

Unit: Joule per kilogramme Kelvin.

Dimension: No mechanical units.

EÖTVÖS NUMBER

Symbol: Eo

Definition: In fluid dynamics, the **Eötvös number** (**Eo**), also called the **Bond number** (**Bo**), is a dimensionless number measuring the importance of gravitational forces compared to surface tension forces and is used (together with Morton number) to characterize the shape of bubbles or drops moving in a surrounding fluid. The two names commemorate the Hungarian physicist Loránd Eötvös (1848–1919) and the English physicist Wilfrid Noel Bond (1897–1937), respectively. The term Eötvös number is more frequently used in Europe, while Bond number is commonly used in other parts of the world.

Describing the ratio of gravitational to capillary forces, the Eötvös or Bond number is given by the equation:

$$\mathrm{Eo} = \mathrm{Bo} = \frac{\Delta \rho\, g\, L^2}{\gamma}.$$

- $\Delta\rho$: difference in density of the two phases (SI units: kg/m^3)
- g: gravitational acceleration, (SI units: m/s^2)
- L: characteristic length, (SI units: m) (for example, the radii of curvature for a drop)
- γ: surface tension, (SI units: N/m)

The Bond number can also be written as

$$\mathrm{Bo} = \left(\frac{L}{\lambda_c}\right)^2,$$

Where

$$\lambda_c = \sqrt{\gamma/\rho g}$$

Is the capillary length.

A high value of the Eötvös or Bond number indicates that the system is relatively unaffected by surface tension effects; a low value (typically less than one) indicates that surface tension dominates. Intermediate numbers indicate a non-trivial balance between the two effects. It may be derived in a number of ways, such as scaling the pressure of a drop of liquid on a solid surface. It is usually important, however, to find the right length scale specific to a problem by doing a ground-up scale analysis. Other similar dimensionless numbers are:

$$Bo = Eo = 2\,Go^2 = 2\,De^2$$

where Go, and De are the Goucher and Deryagin numbers, which are identical: the Goucher number arises in wire coating problems and hence uses a radius as a typical length scale, while the Deryagin number arises in plate film thickness problems and hence uses a Cartesian length.

Field of application: fluid mechanics (shape of bubbles or drops)

Unit: Dimensionless

[Ref. HandWiki]

EQUIVALENT CONDUCTIVITY

Symbol: A_c

Definition: Conductivity of one gramme equivalent of electrolyte in solution with a given concentration. For a solution of specific conductance $\aleph$ and concentration c gramme equivalent per cubic decimeter:

$$A_c = (1000\aleph)/c$$

ERICKSEN NUMBER

Symbol: E_r

Definition: In the study of liquid crystals, the **Ericksen number (Er)** is a dimensionless number used to describe the deformation of the director field underflow. It is defined as the ratio of the viscous to elastic forces. In the limit of a low Ericksen number, the elastic forces will exceed the viscous forces, and so the director field will not be strongly affected by the flow field. The Ericksen number is named after United States mathematics professor Jerald Ericksen of the University of Minnesota. The number is defined as:

$$Er = \frac{\mu v L}{K}$$

where

- μ is the fluid's dynamic viscosity,

- v is a characteristic scale for the fluid's velocity,
- L is a characteristic scale length for the fluid flow,
- K is an elasticity force, for example, the elasticity modulus times an area.

Field of application: fluid dynamics (liquid crystal flow behavior; viscous over elastic forces)

Unit: Dimensionless

[Ref. Larson, R.; Mead, D. (1993), "The Ericksen number and Deborah number cascades in sheared polymeric nematics", *Liquid Crystals* **15** (2): 151–169,]

EULER NUMBER

Symbol: **Eu**

Definition: The Euler number (Eu) is a dimensionless number used in fluid flow calculations. It expresses the relationship between a local pressure drop caused by a restriction and the kinetic energy per volume of the flow and is used to characterize energy losses in the flow, where a perfect frictionless flow corresponds to an Euler number of 0. The inverse of the Euler number is referred to as the Ruark Number with the symbol Ru.

The Euler number is defined as

$$\text{Eu} = \frac{\text{pressure forces}}{\text{inertial forces}} = \frac{(\text{pressure})(\text{area})}{(\text{mass})(\text{acceleration})} = \frac{(p_u - p_d)\,L^2}{(\rho L^3)(v^2/L)} = \frac{p_u - p_d}{\rho v^2}$$

where

- ρ is the density of the fluid.
- p_u is the upstream pressure.
- p_d is the downstream pressure.
- v is a characteristic velocity of the flow.

Field of application: hydrodynamics (stream pressure versus inertia forces)

Unit: dimensionless

EXERGY

See energy (note)

EXITANCE, LUMINOUS

See *"emittance luminous."*

EXITANCE, RADIANT

See *"emittance radiant."*

EXPANSION COEFFICIENT

1. LINEAR EXPANSION COEFFICIENT

Symbol:α; occasionally λ.

Definition: Fractional increase in length l divided by the increase in temperature T under specified conditions.

$$\alpha = \frac{\Delta l}{l\Delta T} \approx \frac{l}{l} \cdot \frac{dl}{dT}$$

2. AREAL EXPANSION COEFFICIENT

Symbol: β

Definition: Fractional increase in area A divided by the increase in temperature T under specified conditions.

$$\beta = \frac{\Delta A}{A\Delta T} \approx \frac{1}{A} \cdot \frac{dA}{dT}$$

Note: the quantity is also termed the superficial expansion coefficient.

3. CUBICAL EXPANSION COEFFICIENT

Symbol: γ; occasionally $\propto$ *or* β

Definition: Fractional increase in volume V divided by the increase in temperature T under specified conditions.

$$\gamma = \frac{\Delta V}{V\Delta T} \approx \frac{1}{V} \cdot \frac{dV}{dT}$$

Note: The quantity is also the volume expansion coefficient or the expansivity.

Unit: Per Kelvin

Dimension: $L^{-2} T^2$

Note: The condition specified is generally standard pressure. Because the expansion coefficient varies with temperature, the quantity is usually quoted at a given temperature (e.g., 15^0C) or as a mean value over a given temperature range (e.g., O^0C to 100^0c).

See: "coefficient of thermal expansion."

EXPANSIVITY

Also called the *"cubical expansion coefficient."*

See "expansion coefficient (3)."

EXPOSURE

Symbol: *H*

Definition: The product of the illuminance E, or the irradiance, and the time Δt for which the material in question is illuminated or irradiated.

$$H = E.\Delta t$$

Unit: Lux second or Watt per meter second.

Dimension: $M T^{-2}$

Note: 1. The quantity Δt in the above expression is the "exposure time" and should not be confused with the term "exposure"

2. Exposure in case of nuclear physics has the following definitions:

 i. The total quantity of radiation at a given point, measured in air.

 ii. The cumulative amount of radiation exposure to which nuclear fuel has been subjected in a nuclear reactor, usually expressed in terms of thermal energy produced by the reactor per ton of fuel initially present, as megawatt days per ton.

3. Light exposure can be defined as the surface density of the total quantity of light received by a material.

See also *"irradiance"* and *"illuminance."*

EXTINCTION

Definition: 1. [OPTICS] Phenomenon in which plane polarized light is almost completely absorbed by a polarizer whose axis is perpendicular to the plane of polarization.

2. PHYSICS, CHEMISTRY] See *"absorbance."*

EXTINCTION COEFFICIENT

Symbol: e

Definition: The natural logarithm of the reciprocal of transmisivity *t*.

e= ln(1/t)

Unit: There are no units or dimensions.

Notes: Extinction coefficient, in general, refers to several different measures of the absorption of light in a medium:

- Attenuation coefficient sometimes called the "extinction coefficient" in meteorology or climatology
  - Mass extinction coefficient, how strongly a substance absorbs light at a given wavelength, per mass density
  - Molar extinction coefficient, how strongly a substance absorbs light at a given wavelength, per molar concentration
- Imaginary part of the complex index of refraction in physics

Note: See also "absorptivity"

EXTINCTION COEFFICIENT, MOLAR

Symbol: ε

Definition: The term molar extinction coefficient (ε) is a measure of how strongly a chemical species or substance absorbs light at a particular wavelength. It is an intrinsic property of chemical species that is dependent upon their chemical composition and structure.

Units: The SI units of ε are m^2/mol, but in practice, they are usually taken as $M^{-1}cm^{-1}$.

Notes: 1.   The molar extinction coefficient is frequently used in spectroscopy to measure the concentration of a chemical in a solution.

2.   It is possible to use the Beer-Lambert Law to calculate a chemical species' ε:

$$A = \varepsilon L c$$

Where:

- a is the amount of light absorbed by the sample for a particular wavelength
- ε is the molar extinction coefficient
- L is the distance that the light travels through the solution
- c is the concentration of the absorbing species per unit volume

Rearrange the Beer-Lambert equation in order to solve for the molar extinction coefficient:

$$\varepsilon = A/Lc$$

F

FANNAING FRICTION FACTOR

Symbol: f

Definition: *The* **Fanning friction factor**, named after John Thomas Fanning, is a dimensionless number used as a local parameter in continuum mechanics calculations. It is defined as the ratio between the local shear stress and the local flow kinetic energy density:

$$f = \frac{\tau}{\rho \frac{u^2}{2}}$$

where:

- f is the local Fanning friction factor (dimensionless)
- τ is the local shear stress (unit in $\frac{lb_m}{ft \cdot s^2}$ or $\frac{kg}{m \cdot s^2}$ or Pa)
- u is the bulk flow velocity (unit in $\frac{ft}{s}$ or $\frac{m}{s}$)
- ρ is the density of the fluid (unit in $\frac{lb_m}{ft^3}$ or $\frac{kg}{m^3}$)

In particular, the shear stress at the wall can, in turn, be related to the pressure loss by multiplying the wall shear stress by the wall area ($2\pi RL$ for a pipe with circular cross-section) and dividing by the cross-sectional flow area (πR^2 for a pipe with circular cross-section). Thus

$$\Delta P = f \frac{L}{R} \rho u^2$$

Unit: Dimensionless

FARADAY CONSTANT

Symbol: F

Definition: The quantity of electricity equivalent to one -mole electrons, i.e., the product of Avogadro constant L and the charge on an electron e in coulombs.

$F = e\,L$

It is, therefore, the quantity of electricity required to liberate or deposit 1 mole of a univalent ion, its value is:

$F = 9.648533289(59) \times 10^4$

Unit: Coulomb per mole.

Note: ***2019 definition***: With the 2019 redefinition of SI base units and the exact definitions of the elementary charge and the Avogadro constant, the Faraday constant will be exactly $(1.602176634 \times 10^{-19}\ \text{C}) \times (6.02214076 \times 10^{23}\ \text{mol}^{-1}) = 96485.3321233100184\ \text{C/mol}$.

FARADAY EFFICIENCY

Faraday efficiency (also called ***faradaic efficiency***, ***faradaic yield***, ***coulombic efficiency*** or ***current efficiency***) describes the efficiency with which charge (electrons) is transferred in a system facilitating an electrochemical reaction.

Note: The word "faraday" in this term has two interrelated aspects. First, the historic unit for a charge is the Faraday, but it has since been replaced by the coulomb. Secondly, the related Faraday's constant correlates charge with moles of matter and electrons (amount of substance). This phenomenon was originally understood through Michael Faraday's work and expressed in his laws of electrolysis.

FEIGENBAUM CONSTANTS

Definition: *In* mathematics, specifically bifurcation theory, the **Feigenbaum constants** are two mathematical constants which both express ratios in a bifurcation diagram for a non-linear map. They are named after the physicist Mitchell J. Feigenbaum (1944-2019).

First Constant:

The first Feigenbaum constant δ is the limiting ratio of each bifurcation interval to the next between every period doubling of a one-parameter map.

$$x_{i+1} = f(x_i)$$

Where $f(x)$ is a function parameterized by the bifurcation parameter a.

It is given by the limit.

$$\delta = \lim_{n \to \infty} \frac{a_{n-1} - a_{n-2}}{a_n - a_{n-1}} = 4.669\,201\,609 \ldots ,$$

Where a_n are discrete values of a at the nth period doubling.

Note: 1 The first constant takes the following names:

- Feigenbaum bifurcation velocity
- delta

2. Some possible values are:

- 30 decimal places: $\delta = 4.66920160910299067185320382046\ldots$
- (SequenceA006890 in the OEIS)
- A simple rational approximation is 621/133, which is correct to 5 significant values (when rounding). For more precision, use 1228/263, which is correct to 7 significant values.
- Is approximately equal to $10(1/\pi - 1)$, with an error of 0.0015%

Second Constant:

The second Feigenbaum constant or Feigenbaum's alpha constant (sequence A006891 in the OEIS),

$$\alpha = 2.502907875095892822283902873218\ldots,$$

Is the ratio between the width of a tine and the width of one of its two subtines (except the tine closest to the fold). A negative sign is applied to α when the ratio between the lower subtine and the width of the tine is measured.

These numbers apply to a large class of dynamical systems (for example, dripping faucets to population growth).

A simple rational approximation is $13/11 \times 17/11 \times 37/27 = 8177/3267$.

Unit: *Dimensionless*

[Ref. handWiki]

FIELD

Definition: A region under the influence of some physical agency. Typical examples are electric, magnetic and gravitational fields that result from the presence of charge, magnetic dipole, and mass, respectively. A field can be pictorially represented by a set of curves, often referred to as lines of flux (or lines of force); the density of these lines at any given point represents the strength of the field at that point, and their direction represents the direction conventionally associated with the agency. Thus, electric fields run from positive to negative, magnetic fields from north-seeking to south-seeking and gravitational fields from lighter to heavier.

A field is also used to describe the region inhabited by nucleons in which exchange forces are set up. In addition, it has been used in connection with scalar quantities to describe distributions of temperature, electric potential, etc.

FIELD STRENGTH, ELECTRIC

Symbol: E, K is also used, especially when E is required for electromotive force.

Definition: The electric field strength at a given point in an electric field is the vector limit of the quotient of the force that a small stationary charge at that point will experience, by virtue of its charge, to the charge as the charge approaches zero.

$E = F/Q = - grad\ V$

Where F is the force exerted by the electric field on the electric charge Q.

Unit: Volt per meter = Newton per coulomb.

Dimension: $LMT^{-3}I^{-1}$

Note: The quantity is also termed as *"electric field intensity"*

FIELD STRENGTH, GRAVITATIONAL

Symbol: R

Definition: The gravitational force F acting on a mass m at a particular point in the gravitational field divided by that mass.

$R = F/m$

Unit: Newton per kilogramme.

Dimension: $L\,T^{-2}$

FIELD STRENGTH, MAGNETIC

Symbol: H

Definition: The ratio between flux density B and the permeability of the medium μ

$H = B/\mu$

Alternatively, the curl of the magnetic field strength is equal to the sum of the current density J and the rate of change of displacement D with respect to time t.

$$\nabla x H = J + \frac{\partial D}{\partial}$$

(Maxwell's equation)

Unit: Ampere per meter.

Dimension: $L^{-1}\,I$

Note: 1. The magnitude of the magnetic field strength of the magnetic field at a point in the direction of the line of force at that point.

2. The integral of the magnetic field strength along a closed line is equal to the magnetomotive force. (See "*magnetomotive force*")

3. Magnetic field strength, formerly called "*magnetic intensity*".

4. When referring to the magnetic field strength of the earth's field, the symbols used are H_o for the horizontal component, V for the vertical component, and R for the resultant.

FINE-STRUCTURE CONSTANT

Symbol: α

Definition: In physics, the **fine-structure constant**, also known as **Sommerfeld's constant**, commonly denoted by α (the Greek letter *alpha*), is a fundamental physical constant which quantifies the strength of the electromagnetic interaction between elementary charged particles. It is a dimensionless quantity related to the elementary charge e, which denotes the strength of the coupling of an elementary charged particle with the electromagnetic field, by the formula $4\pi\varepsilon_0\hbar c\alpha = e^2$. As a dimensionless quantity, its numerical value, approximately 1/137, is independent of the system of units used.

While there are multiple physical interpretations for α, it received its name from Arnold Sommerfeld, who introduced it in 1916 when extending the Bohr model of the atom. α quantifies the gap in the fine-structure of the spectral lines of the hydrogen atom, which had been measured precisely by Michelson and Morley in 1887.

Unit: Dimensionless

FLUID

Definition: A collective term embracing liquids and gases. A perfect fluid offers no resistance to change of shape, i.e., has zero viscosity.

FLUIDITY

Symbol: ϕ

Definition: The reciprocal of the (dynamic) viscosity η

$$\phi = 1/\eta$$

Unit: Meter squared per Newton second.

Dimension: $M^{-1} LT$.

FLUIDITY, THERMAL

See *"resistivity, thermal."*

FLUX

Symbol: ϕ

Definition: Refers to the flow of physical entities such as energy, charge, radiation, or atomic particles across or through a given surface. A particular flux will be defined by its units according to the physical quantities involved.

In the case of nuclear physics, a flux of neutrons (or gamma photons) is a measure of their number, density and speed, being proportional to both these quantities. If a parallel beam of neutrons (or photons), all of the same energy, is considered, then the flux ϕ is equal to the number of neutrons (photons) per unit volume n multiplied by their speed v.

$$\phi = n.$$

More generally, where neutrons (or protons) have a spectrum of speed (or energies) and are moving in different directions, the flux is equal to the total track length per second of all neutrons (or protons) in a unit volume of the material through which they are passing.

Unit: Depends on the quantities.

Note: The word "Flux" is also used as a chemical that will combine with a substance of high melting point (generally an oxide), forming a new, readily fusible substance. It is used in smelting, soldering, brazing and welding of material.

FLUX, ELECTRIC

Symbol: ψ

Definition: The electric flux through a surface in an electrostatic field is the surface integral of the normal component of the electric flux density over the surface. It represents the quantity of electricity displaced across the surface and normal to it. It can also be defined as the scalar product of the displacement D and the area A.

$$\psi = D.A$$

Unit: Electrical flux has SI units of voltmeters ($V\, m$), or, equivalently, Newton meters squared per coulomb ($N\, m^2\, C^{-1}$)

SI base units of electric flux are $kg{\cdot}m^3{\cdot}s^{-3}{\cdot}A^{-1}$

Dimension: $L^3 MT^{-3} I^{-1}$

Note: Also known as the *"flux of displacement"*

FLUX, FLUID

Definition: The flow of fluid across a surface and normal to it. It is usually expressed as the volume of fluid flowing in unit time.

The flux through a surface is the amount of fluid that crosses the surface in a flow per unit of time at any one instant. If the velocity field is $v(x)$, and the surface is S, it is the integral over the surface.

$$\int_S v.n$$

where n is the normal to the surface. This is the general definition of a flux of a vector field applied to the special case of the velocity field.

Unit: Meter cubic per second.

Dimensions: $L^3 T^{-1}$

FLUX, HEAT

Symbol: ϕ

Definition: A measure of the heat energy per unit of time flowing normally to the direction of the flux is propagating.

Unit: Watt per square meter

Dimension: $M T^{-3}$

FLUX, LUMINOUS

Symbol: Φ Sometimes, F

Definition: The rate of flow of luminous energy, i.e., the luminous power. It is the quantity characteristic of a radiant flux that expresses its capacity to produce for the light-adapted eye (adopted by the Commission Internationale de l'Eclairage.)

Unit: Lumen.

Dimension: $M L^2 T^{-3}$

Note: 1. The luminous flux emitted by a source is equal to the mean luminous intensity of the source in all directions in space, multiplied by 4π.

2. The adaptation of the radiant flux to get the luminous flux takes place as follows: Consider a source of monochromatic radiation of wavelength λ and with radiant flux Φ. The luminous flux is then proportional to $\Phi_e V(\lambda)$, where $V(\lambda)$ is the spectral luminous efficiency. This factor weighs the radiant flux according to the sensitivity of a standard observer to radiation of wavelength. (λ). Specifically, the luminous flux is given by:

$$\Phi_v = K_m \Phi_e V(\lambda)$$

Where K_m is a constant relating the units of luminous flux to those of radiant flux. For polychromatic radiation, the radiant flux will generally vary with wavelength and luminous flux can be defined by:

$$\Phi_v = K_m \int (d\Phi_e/d\lambda)V(\lambda)d\lambda$$

Where $(d\Phi_e/d\lambda)V(\lambda)d\lambda$ is the radiant flux of light with wavelengths in the range λ to $\lambda + d\lambda$.

The constant K_m is the maximum spectral luminous efficacy and can be obtained by applying the above formula to a black body at the temperature of freezing platinum and has the value of 680 lumens per Watt for photopic vision.

FLUX, MAGNETIC

Symbol: Φ

Definition: The magnetic flux through a closed figure (e.g., a circular or rectangular loop) is the surface integral of the normal component of the magnetic flux density over the surface.

$$\phi = \int B.dA$$

In the case of constant flux, it is the scalar product of the magnetic flux density B and the area A

$$\phi = B.A$$

Unit: Weber (in SI base units: $kg.m^2\ s^{-2}\ A^{-1}$)

Dimension: $L^2MT^{-2}I^{-1}$

FLUX, NEUTRON

Definition: The product of the number of free neutrons per unit volume n and their mean speed v.

Neutron flux $= n.v$

Unit: Per square meter per second.

Dimension: $L^{-2} T^{-1}$

Note: The neutron flux in a power reactor lies in the range 10^{16}-10^{18} per square meter per second.

FLUX, RADIANT

Symbol: ϕ

Definition: The total power emitted or received by a body in the form of radiation. It is the rate of flow of radiant energy U with respect to time t.

$\phi = dU/dt$

Unit: Watt.

Dimension: $M L^2 T^{-3}$ (In SI base units: kg. m^2. S^{-3})

Note: 1 The term radiant flux is usually applied to the transfer of energy in the form of electromagnetic radiation as opposed to particles, but it is not usually applied to radio waves.

2. The quantity has also been termed the *"radiance."*

FLUX, SOUND

Symbol: P or ϕ; sometimes N or W.

Definition: The mean rate of flow of sound energy E with respect to time t through an area normal to the direction of flow, i.e., acoustical power.

$P= dE/dt$

For a plane or spherical progressive wave with a velocity of propagation c in an isotropic medium of density ρ, the sound flux through an area A at a point where the root-mean-square sound pressure is p reduces to:

$P=p^2A/\rho c$

Unit: Watt (In SI base units: kg. m^2. S^{-3})

Dimension: M L^2 T^{-3}

FLUX DENSITY, ELECTRIC

Symbol: D

Definition: The electric flux per unit area.

Unit: Coulomb per square meter (in SI base units m^{-2}. s. A)

Dimension: $L^{-2}T$ I

Note: This quantity is also called the *"displacement, electric"*

See *"displacement, electric."*

FLUX DENSITY, MAGNETIC

Symbol: B

Definition: It may be defined as the magnetic flux per unit area at right angle to the flux or as the product of the magnetic intensity and permeability. The vector product of the magnetic flux density and the current I is equal to the force F per unit length s.

B x I = *F/s* (note: x means vector product)

Unit: Tesla. (In SI base units: kg.s^{-2}. A^{-1})

Dimensions: M T^{-2} I^{-1}

Note: 1. The quantity is also termed the *"magnetic induction"*

    2. The concept of flux density is extended to a point inside a solid body by defining the flux density at such a point as that which would be measured in a thin disk-shaped cavity in the body centred at that point, the axis of the cavity being in the direction of the flux density.

3. The flux density indicates the strength of the magnetic field, often in terms of the effects of the field. For example, the vector product of the magnetic flux density and the current in a conductor gives the force per unit length of the conductor.

FLUX DENSITY, MAGNETIC INTRINSIC

See "*polarization magnetic.*"

FLUX DENSITY, RADIANT

Definition: The radiant flux per unit area. Also known as "irradiance or irradiancy."

See "emittance, radiant."

Unit: Watt per square meter. (in SI base units: kg. s^{-3})

Dimensions: M T^{-3}

Note: See "*irradiance*"

FLUX, ENERGY

Definition: The energy passing through or incident upon a given area of surface measured in terms of energy per unit area per unit time;

Unit: Watt per square meter. (in SI base units: kg. s^{-3})

Dimensions: M T^{-3}

Note: See "power"

f-Number

Definition: In optics, the **f-number** of an optical system, such as a camera lens, is the ratio of the system's focal length to the diameter of the entrance pupil ("clear aperture"). It is also known as the **focal ratio**, **f-ratio**, or **f-stop** and is very important in photography. It is a dimensionless number that is a quantitative measure of lens speed; increasing the f-number is referred to as *stopping down*. The f-number is commonly indicated using a lower-case hooked f with the format f/N, where N is the f-number.

The f-number is the reciprocal of the **relative aperture** (the aperture diameter divided by focal length).

Unit: Dimensionless

FORCE

Symbol: F; sometimes P.

Definition: The influence on a body that causes it to accelerate. Quantitatively, it is the rate of change of momentum p with respect to time t.

$F=dp/dt.$

When the mass m is constant, force is the product of mass and acceleration a.

$F = m\,a$

Unit: Newton **(In SI base units: kg.m.s^{-2})**

Dimension: M L T^{-2}.

Note: 1. The quantity is also termed tension or thrusts.

2. Weight (W; occasionally G or P) is the vertical force acting on a body as a result of the existence of gravity. It is that force which, when applied to the body, gives it an acceleration equal to the local acceleration of free fall. The local acceleration of free fall includes both the gravitational and centrifugal components but excludes the effect of atmospheric buoyance.

FORCE, CENTRIFUGAL

Symbol: F_c

Definition: Inertial force that appears to act on all objects when viewed in a rotating frame of reference

Units: Newton. radian- N·rad (In SI base units: kg·m·rad·s^{-2})

Dimensions L M T^{-2}

FOURIER NUMBER

Symbol: F_o

Definition: A dimensionless quantity used in the study of heat transfer. It is defined by the function:

$F_o = a\,t\,/l^2$

- a is the thermal diffusivity (m^2/s)
- t is the characteristic timescale (s)
- l is the length scale of interest (m), it is a characteristic length

Unit: There are no units or dimensions.

Note:

1. The general Fourier number is the ratio of the diffusive or conductive transport rate to the quantity storage rate, where the quantity may be either heat (thermal energy) or matter (particles).

$$Fo = \frac{\text{diffusive transport rate}}{\text{storage rate}}$$

2. The number is named after the French scientist J.B Fourier (1768-1830), who put the theory of heat in a firm mathematical basis.

FOURIER NUMBER FOR MASS TRANSFER

Symbol: $F_o{}^*$

Definition: A dimensionless number used in mass transfer. It is given by:

$$F_o{}^* = D\, t/l^2$$

Where D is the diffusion coefficient, t represents time, and l is the characteristic length.

Unit: There are no units or dimensions.

FREQUENCY

Symbol: f; the symbol v, formerly widely used, is no longer preferred.

Definition: The number of cycles completed by a periodic quantity in a unit of time.

Accordingly, it is the reciprocal of periodic time T.

$$F = 1/T$$

Unit: Hertz

Dimension: T^{-1}

Note: 1. The frequency f is related to the angular frequency ω, by the relation:

$$\omega = 2\pi f$$

2. In the case of alternating current, the frequency is defined as the number of times the current passes through its zero value in the same direction in unit time.

3. In statistics, frequency means the number of times an event or item falls into or is expected to fall into a certain class or category.

4. The term pitch is used as a measure of musical awareness of frequency.

For example, the pitch of note A in the treble stave is a frequency of 440 hertz. (See also *"pitch"*)

5. Frequency is also referred to as **temporal** *frequency*, which emphasizes the contrast between spatial frequency and angular frequency

See: Spatial frequency, angular frequency and circular frequency

FREQUENCY, ANGULAR (OR CIRCULAR)

Symbol: ω

Definition: The frequency of a periodic quantity expressed as the product of the frequency f in hertz and the factor 2π

$$\omega = 2\pi f$$

It is also defined as the rate of change of angular displacement, θ, (during rotation), or the rate of change of the phase of a sinusoidal waveform (notably in oscillations and waves), or as the rate of change of the argument to the sine function:

$$y(t) = \sin(\theta(t)) = \sin(\omega t) = \sin(2\pi f t)$$
$$\frac{d\theta}{dt} = \omega = 2\pi f$$

Unit: Radian per second

See also *"velocity, angular."*

FREQUENCY, ROTATIONAL

Symbol: n

Definition: Number of revolutions N divided by time t.

$n = N/t$

Unit: Hertz

Dimension: T^{-1}

Note: The quantity, also termed rotational speed, must be distinguished from angular velocity.

FREQUENCY, SPATIAL

Definition: Spatial frequency is analogous to temporal frequency, but the time axis is replaced by one or more spatial displacement axes. e.g.:

$$y(t) = \sin(\theta(t, x)) = \sin(\omega t + kx)$$
$$\frac{d\theta}{dx} = k$$

Wavenumber, k, is the spatial frequency analogue of angular temporal frequency and is measured in radians per meter. In the case of more than one spatial dimension, the wavenumber is a vector quantity.

In mathematics, physics, and engineering, **spatial frequency** is a characteristic of any structure that is periodic across positions in space. The spatial frequency is a measure of how often sinusoidal components (as determined by the Fourier transform) of the structure repeat per unit of distance.

Unit: The SI unit of spatial frequency is cycles per meter.

Dimensions: $T^{-1} L^{-1}$

FRICTION, ANGLE OF

Definition: The angle whose tangent is the coefficient of friction. In measuring the coefficient of friction, a body is placed on a plane, and the latter is tilted until the body will just slide down when gently tapped. The angle of the plane to the horizontal is then the angle of the Radian.

Unit: Radian

Note: This angle has the less common name *"angle of repose"*

See also *"angle of repose."*

FRICTION COEFFICIENT

1) Static friction coefficient

   Symbol: μ; rarely f.

   Definition: Limiting statistical frictional force F divided by normal reaction R.

   $$\mu = F/R$$

2) Dynamic friction coefficient

Symbol: μ'

Definition: Limiting dynamical frictional force F' divided by normal reaction R

$$\mu = F'/R$$

Note: The quantity is also termed the kinematic friction coefficient

Unit: The quantity is also called a factor of friction. The value of the static coefficient between two surfaces exceeds the value of the dynamic coefficient between the same two surfaces.

Dimensions: Dimensionless

FRICTION FACTOR (F)

Symbol: f

Definition: Friction factor (f) is a dimensionless number used to determine the pressure loss or flow rate through the pipe. knowledge of the friction between the fluid and the pipe is required.

Pressure loss in piping without any size changes or fittings occurs due to friction between the fluid and the pipe walls. There have been a number of methods developed to describe this relationship; generally, a friction factor is used to determine the pressure loss.

The key influences on the pressure drop as a fluid moves through a pipe are the Reynolds Number of the fluid and the roughness of the pipe.

Friction Factors: Fanning and Darcy

There are two common friction factors in use, the Darcy and Fanning friction factors. The Darcy friction factor is also known as the Darcy–Weisbach friction factor or the Moody friction factor. It is important to understand which friction factor is being described in an equation or chart to prevent errors in pressure loss or fluid flow calculation results.

The difference between the two friction factors is that the value of the Darcy friction factor is 4 times that of the Fanning friction factor. In all other aspects, they are identical, and by applying the conversion factor of 4, the friction factors may be used interchangeably.

$$f = 4f_F$$

Head Loss and Pressure Loss – Darcy Friction Factor

Head Loss:

$$h_f = f \frac{L}{D} \frac{V^2}{2g}$$

Pressure Drop:

$$\Delta p = f \frac{L}{D} \frac{\rho V^2}{2}$$

$$\text{Darcy Friction Factor} = \frac{\Delta p}{h_f}$$

Where:

h_f : Head loss due to friction

p: pressure

L : length of Pipe

V: Average Velocity

D: Pipe diameter

g: Gravity

ρ: Density

FROUDE NUMBER

Symbol: Fr

Definition: A dimensionless parameter used in fluid dynamics and appears during the study of the relative motion of a floating body (e.g., a ship) and a fluid. It is defined by the relationship:

$$Fr = v/(gl)^{1/2}$$

Where v is the velocity of the liquid, g is the acceleration of free fall, and l is the characteristic length. The numerical value of Fr depends upon the units in which v, g and l are measured.

Field of application: fluid mechanics (wave and surface behavior; a ratio of a body's inertia to gravitational forces)

Unit: There are no units or dimensions.

Note: The number is named after W. Froude (1810-1879), who derived it in 1869.

FUEL CONSUMPTION

See *"traffic factor."*

G

GAIN (electronics)

Definition: In electronics, the **gain** is a measure of the ability of a two-port circuit (often an amplifier) to increase the power or amplitude of a signal from the input to the output port by adding energy converted from some power supply to the signal. It is usually defined as the mean ratio of the signal amplitude or power at the output port to the amplitude or power at the input port. It is often expressed using the logarithmic decibel (dB) units ("dB gain"). A gain greater than one (greater than zero dB), that is, amplification, is the defining property of an active component or circuit, while a passive circuit will have a gain of less than one.

The term *gain* alone is ambiguous and can refer to the ratio of output to input voltage (*voltage gain*), current (*current gain*) or electric power (*power gain*). In the field of audio and general - purpose amplifiers, especially operational amplifiers, the term usually refers to voltage gain, but in radio frequency amplifiers, it usually refers to power gain. Furthermore, the term gain is also applied in systems such as sensors where the input and output have different units; in such cases, the gain units must be specified, as in "5 microvolts per photon" for the responsivity of a photosensor. The "gain" of a bipolar transistor normally refers to the forward current transfer ratio, either h_{FE} ("beta", the static ratio of I_c divided by I_b at some operating point) or sometimes h_e (the small-signal current gain, the slope of the graph of I_c against I_b at a point).

The gain of an electronic device or circuit generally varies with the frequency of the applied signal. Unless otherwise stated, the term refers to the gain for frequencies in the passband, the intended operating frequency range of the equipment. The term *gain* has a different meaning in antenna design; antenna gain is the ratio of radiation intensity from a directional antenna to $P_{in}/4\pi$ (mean radiation intensity from a lossless antenna).

1. **Power gain**

Power gain, in decibels (dB), is defined as follows:

$$\text{gain-db} = 10 \log_{10}\left(\frac{P_{out}}{P_{in}}\right) \text{ dB}.$$

Where P_{in} is the power applied to the input, P_{out} is the power from the output.

A similar calculation can be done using a natural logarithm instead of a decimal logarithm, resulting in nepers instead of decibels:

$$\text{gain-np} = \frac{1}{2}\ln\left(\frac{P_{out}}{P_{in}}\right) \text{ Np}.$$

2. Voltage gain

The power gain can be calculated using voltage instead of power using Joule's first law $P=V^2/R$; the formula is:

$$\text{gain-db} = 10 \log \frac{\frac{V_{out}^2}{R_{out}}}{\frac{V_{in}^2}{R_{in}}} \text{ dB}.$$

In many cases, the input impedance R_{in} and output impedance R_{out} are equal, so the above equation can be simplified to:

$$\text{gain-db} = 10 \log \left(\frac{V_{out}}{V_{in}}\right)^2 \text{ dB},$$

$$\text{gain-db} = 20 \log \left(\frac{V_{out}}{V_{in}}\right) \text{ dB}.$$

This simplified formula, the 20 log rule, is used to calculate a **voltage gain** in decibels and is equivalent to a power gain if and only if the impedances at input and output are equal.

3. Current gain

In the same way, when power gain is calculated using current instead of power, making the substitution $P=I^2R$, the formula is:

$$\text{gain-db} = 10 \log \left(\frac{I_{out}^2 R_{out}}{I_{in}^2 R_{in}}\right) \text{ dB}.$$

In many cases, the input and output impedances are equal, so the above equation can be simplified to:

$$\text{gain-db} = 10 \log \left(\frac{I_{\text{out}}}{I_{\text{in}}} \right)^2 \text{dB},$$

$$\text{gain-db} = 20 \log \left(\frac{I_{\text{out}}}{I_{\text{in}}} \right) \text{dB}.$$

This simplified formula is used to calculate a **current gain** in decibels and is equivalent to the power gain if and only if the impedances at input and output are equal.

GALILEI NUMBER

Symbol: Ga

Definition: In fluid dynamics, the Galilei number (Ga), sometimes also referred to as Galileo number, is a dimensionless number named after Italian scientist Galileo Galilei (1564-1642). It may be regarded as proportional to gravity forces divided by viscous forces. The Galilei number is used in viscous flow and thermal expansion calculations, for example, to describe fluid film flow over walls. These flows apply to condensers or chemical columns.

$$\text{Ga} = \text{Re}^2 \text{Ri} = \frac{g L^3}{\nu^2}$$

- g: gravitational acceleration, (SI units: m/s^2)
- L: characteristic length, (SI units: m)
- v: characteristic kinematic viscosity (SI units: m^2/s)
- R_e: the Reynolds number
- R_i: the Richardson number

Field of application: fluid mechanics (gravitational over viscous forces)

Unit: Dimensionless

GIBBS FUNCTION

Symbol: G

Definition: A thermodynamic function of a system given by its enthalpy H minus the product of its entropy S and its thermodynamic temperature T.

$G = H\text{-}TS$

Unit: Joule (In SI base units: kg m^2 s^{-2})

Dimension: $M L^2 T^{-2}$

Note: In a reversible change occurring at constant temperature and pressure, the change in the Gibbs function of a system is equal to the work done on it. If a system is considered at constant pressure and temperature and the only work done is that caused by changes in volume, the system will be in equilibrium when G has a minimum value. In a chemical reaction, the change in G is zero when equilibrium has been attained.

The Gibbs function is often used in chemical reactions because these take place at constant pressure. Helmoholtz function (free energy) is used with reaction at constant volume.

See *"energy, free"* and *"potential, thermodynamic."*

GÖRTLER VORTICES

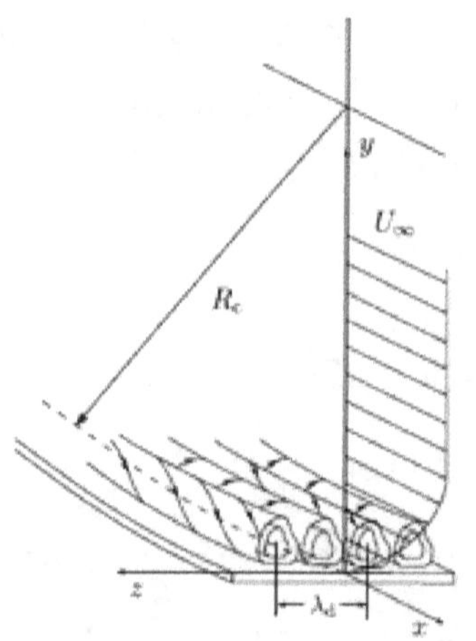

Görtler vortices in a boundary layer

Symbol: G

Definition: In fluid dynamics, **Görtler vortices** are secondary flows that appear in a boundary layer flow along a concave wall. If the boundary layer is thin compared to the radius of curvature of the wall, the pressure remains constant across the boundary layer. On the other hand, if the boundary layer thickness is comparable to the radius of curvature, the centrifugal action creates a pressure variation across the boundary layer. This leads to the centrifugal instability (Görtler instability) of the boundary layer and the consequent formation of Görtler vortices.

The onset of Görtler vortices can be predicted using the dimensionless number called **Görtler number (G)**. It is the ratio of centrifugal effects to the viscous effects in the boundary layer and is defined as

$$G = \frac{U_e \theta}{\nu} \left(\frac{\theta}{R} \right)^{1/2}$$

where

U_e = external velocity

Θ = momentum thickness

v = kinematic viscosity

R = radius of curvature of the wall

Görtler instability occurs when G exceeds about 0.3.

Note: A similar phenomenon arising from the same centrifugal action is sometimes observed in rotational flows which do not follow a curved wall, such as the rib vortices seen in the wakes of cylinders and generated behind moving structures.

Field of application: fluid dynamics (boundary layer flow along a concave wall)

Unit: Dimensionless

(**Reference:** *Williamson, C. H. K. (1996). "Vortex dynamics in the cylinder wake". Annual Review of Fluid Mechanics. 28: 477–539. Bibcode:1996AnRFM..28..477W. doi:10.1146/annurev.fl.28.010196.002401)*

GRAETZ NUMBER

Symbol: **Gz**

Definition: In fluid dynamics, the **Graetz number (Gz)** is a dimensionless number that characterizes laminar flow in a conduit. The number is defined as:

$$Gz = \frac{D_H}{L} \mathrm{Re}\, \mathrm{Pr}$$

where

D_H is the diameter in round tubes or hydraulic diameter in arbitrary cross-section ducts.

L is the length

Re is the Reynolds number and

Pr is the Prandtl number.

This number is useful in determining the thermally developing flow entrance length in ducts. A Graetz number of approximately 1000 or less is the point at which flow would be considered thermally fully developed.

When used in connection with mass transfer, the Prandtl number is replaced by the Schmidt number, Sc, which expresses the ratio of the momentum diffusivity to the mass diffusivity.

$$\mathrm{Gz} = \frac{D_H}{L}\mathrm{Re}\,\mathrm{Sc}$$

Note: The quantity is named after the physicist Leo Graetz.

Field of application: heat transfer, fluid mechanics (laminar flow through a conduit; also used in mass transfer)

Unit: Dimensionless

GRASH OF NUMBER

Symbol: Gr

Definition: A dimensionless parameter used in dimension analysis of convection in fluid due to the presence of a hot body. It approximates the ratio of the buoyancy to viscous force acting on a fluid. It is given by:

$$Gr = l^3 g\alpha\Delta T\rho^2/\eta^2$$

OR

$$\mathrm{Gr}_L = \frac{g\beta(T_s - T_\infty)L^3}{\nu^2}$$

Where l is a typical dimension of the body, g is the acceleration of free fall, α is the cubic expansion coefficient, η is the viscocity of the fluid, ρ is the density of the fluid, and ΔT is the temperature difference between the hot body and the fluid.

Notes: 1. Two convection flows are dynamically similar if their respective Grashof and Prandtl numbers are equal.

2. The number is named after the German scientist F. Grashof (1826-1893), who was an authority on heat.

Field of application: heat transfer, natural convection (ratio of the buoyancy to viscous force)

Unit: Dimensionless

GRASHOF NUMBER FOR MASS TRANSFER

Symbol: Gr*

Definition: A dimensionless number used in mass transfer problems is given by:

$$\mathrm{Gr}* = l^3 g \left(\frac{\partial \rho}{\partial x}\right) T . P \frac{\Delta x \rho}{\eta}$$

Where: g is the acceleration of free fall, l is characteristic length, ρ is the density at a point of coordinate x, and η is viscosity.

Note: 1.   In the case of mass transfer, natural convection is caused by concentration gradients rather than temperature gradients.

The following equation can be used:

$$\mathrm{Gr}_c = \frac{g \beta^* (C_{a,s} - C_{a,a}) L^3}{\nu^2}$$

where:

$$\beta^* = -\frac{1}{\rho}\left(\frac{\partial \rho}{\partial C_a}\right)_{T,p}$$

and:

g is the acceleration due to the Earth's gravity

$C_{a,s}$ is the concentration of species a at surface

$C_{a,a}$ is the concentration of species a in the ambient medium

L is the characteristic length

ν is the kinematic viscosity

ρ is the fluid density

C_a is the concentration of species a

T is the temperature (constant)

p is the pressure (constant).

Unit: There are no units or dimensions.

HAGEN NUMBER

Symbol: **Hg**

Definition: The **Hagen number (Hg)** is a dimensionless number used in forced flow calculations. It is the forced flow equivalent of the Grashof number and was named after the German hydraulic engineer G. H. L. Hagen.

It is defined as:

$$\text{Hg} = -\frac{1}{\rho}\frac{\mathrm{d}p}{\mathrm{d}x}\frac{L^3}{\nu^2}$$

Where:

- dp/dx is the pressure gradient
- L is a characteristic length
- ρ is the fluid density
- ν is the kinematic viscosity

For natural convection

$$\frac{\mathrm{d}p}{\mathrm{d}x} = \rho g \beta \Delta T.$$

Consequently, the Hagen number then coincides with the Grashof number.

Field of application: heat transfer (ratio of the buoyancy to viscous force in forced convection)

Unit: Dimensionless

See: Grashof number

HALF-LIFE, BIOLOGICAL

Definition: It is the time in which a living tissue organ or individual eliminates, through biological processes, one-half of a given amount of substance which has been introduced into it, and when the rate of elimination is approximately exponential.

Effective Half-Life is a term usually applied to a radioactive substance in or biological organism.

The effective Half-life = [Radioactivity Half-Life x (Biological Half-Life)]/

[(Radioactive Half-Life) + (Biological Half-Life)

Unit: Second

Dimension: T

See *"Half-Life, radioactive."*

HALF-LIFE, RADIOACTIVE

Symbol: $T_{1/2}$, $t_{1/2}$

Definition: The time in which the amount of a radioactive nuclide decays to half its original value.

Statistically, the rate of disintegration of radioactive nuclei is proportional to the number of nuclei present at any instant. Accordingly, if any radioactive sample started with N_o nuclei, the number of nuclei remaining N falls exponentially with time t,

$$N = N_o e^{-\lambda t}$$

Where λ is the radioactive decay constant.

The half-life $T_{1/2}$ is the time taken for half the nuclei to disintegrate (i.e., when $N = 1/2\, N_o$)

$$T_{1/2} = \lambda^{-1} log2 = (0.69315)\, \lambda^{-1}$$

Unit: Second

Dimension: T

Note: 1. The half-life varies over the range of 10^{-9} seconds to 10^{10} years for different nuclei.

2. The half-life is related to the mean life τ by $T_{1/2} = 0369315\, \tau$

See *"mean life"* and *"decay constant."*

HARDNESS

There are a number of arbitrarily defined meanings for this quantity. See the Appendix.

HARDNESS [ELECTROMAGNETIC]

Definition: That quantity which determines the penetrating ability of X-ray; the shorter the wavelength, the harder and more penetrating the rays.

HARDNESS, MAGNETIC

Definition: Magnetic hardness of a ferromagnetic material is a qualitative term expressing the size of the magnetic field required to produce saturation. The greater this field, the harder the material.

HARTMANN NUMBER

Symbol: $\quad$ Ha

Definition: The **Hartmann number** (**Ha**) is the ratio of electromagnetic force to the viscous force, first introduced by Julius Hartmann (1881 – 1951) of Denmark. It is frequently encountered in fluid flows through magnetic fields. It is defined by:

$$\mathrm{Ha} = BL\sqrt{\frac{\sigma}{\mu}}$$

where

- B is the magnetic field intensity
- L is the characteristic length scale
- σ is the electrical conductivity
- μ is the dynamic viscosity

Field of application: magnetohydrodynamics (ratio of Lorentz to viscous forces)

Unit: **Dimensionless**

HATTA NUMBER

Symbol: **Ha**

Definition: The **Hatta number** (**Ha**) was developed by Shirôji Hatta, who taught at Tohoku University. It is a dimensionless parameter that compares the rate of reaction in a liquid film to the rate of diffusion through the film. For a second-order reaction ($r_A = k_2 C_B C_A$), the maximum rate of reaction assumes that the liquid film is saturated with gas at the interfacial concentration ($C_{A,i}$); thus, the maximum rate of reaction is $k_2 C_{B,bulk} C_{A,i} \delta_L$.

$$Ha^2 = \frac{k_2 C_{A,i} C_{B,bulk} \delta_L}{\frac{D_A}{\delta_L} C_{A,i}} = \frac{k_2 C_{B,bulk} D_A}{(\frac{D_A}{\delta_L})^2} = \frac{k_2 C_{B,bulk} D_A}{k_L^2}$$

For a reaction m^{th} order in A and n^{th} order in B:

$$Ha = \frac{\sqrt{\frac{2}{m+1} k_{m,n} C_{A,i}^{m-1} C_{B,bulk}^n D_A}}{k_L}$$

It is an important parameter used in Chemical Reaction Engineering.

Unit: **Dimensionless**

HEAT

Symbol: Q

Definition: A form of energy associated with the motion of individual atoms or molecules of a body. It is to be distinguished from temperature, which is a measure of the degree of hotness.

In thermodynamics, it is energy in transit due to a temperature difference between the source from which the energy is coming and a sink toward which the energy is going.

Other types of energy in transit are called work.

Note: 1. Radiation can generally be regarded as heat or work. Radiation is regarded as heat when the spontaneous emission from a hotter body is absorbed by one at a lower temperature. Radiation can also transfer energy by doing work, for example, a transmitter does work on a radio receiver, the temperatures being irrelevant.

2. Although absorption of heat generally produces a rise of temperature in the absorbing substance, it may produce instead a change of state (fusion, vaporization, sublimation) at a temperature dependent upon the pressure under which the change occurs. The temperature of the system does not change until the change of state is complete. The change of state in the opposite sense is accompanied by the liberation of heat.

HEAT CAPACITY

Symbol: c; sometimes C.

Definition: The rate of increase of heat energy Q with temperature θ under specified conditions.

$$c = dQ/d\theta$$

Unit: Joule per Kelvin. (In SI base units: $kg.m^2.s^{-2}K^{-1}$)

Dimensions: M

Note: 1. The former name of heat capacity was thermal capacity

2. The heat capacity under constant pressure $c_p = (dq/d\theta)_p$ and that under constant volume $c_v = (dq/d\theta)_v$

3. The heat capacity per unit mass of a substance is the "*specific heat*" of that substance, and that of a unit mole of a substance is its "*molar heat capacity.*"

See "*heat capacity molar*" and "*heat capacity molal.*"

HEAT CAPACITY, MOLAL

Symbol: C

Definition: The elementary heat δQ received isochronally or isobarically by one mole of a substance divided by the corresponding temperature change δT caused by this process.

$$C = \frac{\delta Q}{\delta T}$$

Unit: Joule per Kelvin per mole

Dimension: $L^2 M T^{-3} N$

See also *"molal heat capacity at constant pressure"* and *"molal heat capacity at constant volume."*

HEAT CAPACITY, MOLAR

Symbol: C_m

Definition: The heat capacity of a unit amount of substance of an element, compound, or material. Quantitatively, it is the heat capacity c divided by the molar value n.

$$C_m = c/n$$

Unit: Joule per Kelvin per mole (In SI base units: $kg.m^2.s^{-2}.K^{-1}.mol^{-1}$)

Dimension: $M\,L^2\,T^{-3}\,N$

HEAT FLOW RATE

Symbol: Φ or q

Definition: Heat is thought of as energy E transferred from one substance to another in a unit of time t.

$$q = E/t$$

Unit: Watt (In SI base units: $kg.m^2.s^{-3}$)

Dimension: $M\,L^2\,T^{-3}$

Note: The name *"specific rate of heat flow"* was formerly used. It is deprecated because of the meaning of *"specific"*.

HEAT FLOW RATE DENSITY

Symbol: ϕ or u

Definition: Heat flow rate Φ divided by area A.

$$u = \Phi/A$$

Unit: Watt per meter squared. (In SI base units: $kg.s^{-3}$)

Dimension: $L^{-2}\,T^{-1}\,Q$.

Note: 1. The quantity is also called heat flow rate intensity.

2. The thermal conductivity is the heat flow rate density divided by the temperature

gradient.

HEAT, LATENT

Symbol: L

Definition: The quantity of heat Q absorbed or released in an isothermal transformation of phase. The quantity of heat released or absorbed per unit mass is called specific latent heat, and that absorbed or released per unit amount of substance (mole) is called molar latent heat.

See "*latent heat, speficic*", "*specific latent heat of fusion*", "*specific latent heat of vaporisation,*" and "*specific latent heat of sublimation.*"

HEAT OF FUSION

Definition: The increase of enthalpy accompanying the conversion of 1 mole, or a unit of mass, of a solid to a liquid at its melting point at constant pressure and temperature.

Unit: Joule per kilogramme or joule per mole. (In SI base units: $m^2.s^{-2}$)

Dimension: $L^2 T^{-2}$

HEAT RELEASE

Symbol: H.

Definition: Quantity of heat Q released (in furnaces, etc.) divided by the product of volume V and time t.

$H = Q/Vt$.

Unit: Watt per meter cubed. (In SI base units: $kg.m^{-1}.s^{-3}$)

Dimension: $L^{-3} T^{-1} Q$.

HEAT TRANSFER COEFFICIENT

Symbol: h

Definition: In thermodynamics, the **heat transfer coefficient** or **film coefficient**, or **film effectiveness**, is the proportionality constant between the heat flux and the thermodynamic driving force for the flow of heat (i.e., the temperature difference, ΔT). It is used in calculating heat transfer, typically by convection or phase transition between a fluid and a solid. The heat transfer coefficient has SI units in watts per square meter Kelvin ($W/m^2/K$).

The overall heat transfer rate for combined modes is usually expressed in terms of an overall conductance or heat transfer coefficient, U. In that case, the heat transfer rate is:

$$\dot{Q} = hA(T_2 - T_1)$$

Where (in SI units):

- A: surface area where the heat transfer takes place (m^2)
- T_2: temperature of the surrounding fluid (K)
- T_1: temperature of the solid surface (K)

The general definition of the heat transfer coefficient is:

$$h = \frac{q}{\Delta T}$$

where:

- q: heat flux (W/m^2); i.e., thermal power per unit area,
- ΔT: difference in temperature between the solid surface and surrounding fluid area (K)

The heat transfer coefficient is the reciprocal of thermal insulance. This is used for building materials (R-value) and for clothing insulation.

There are numerous methods for calculating the heat transfer coefficient in different heat transfer modes, different fluids, flow regimes, and under different thermohydraulic conditions. Often it can be estimated by dividing the thermal conductivity of the convection fluid by a length scale. The heat transfer coefficient is often calculated from the Nusselt number (a dimensionless number). There are also online calculators available specifically for Heat transfer fluid applications. Experimental assessment of the heat transfer coefficient poses some challenges, especially when small fluxes are to be measured (e.g., < 0.2 W/cm^2)

Units: watts per square meter Kelvin (W/m^2/K)

See: "Nussel Number"

HUMIODITY

Definition: The presence of water vapour in the atmosphere.

Several means of specifying the humidity of the atmosphere are in current use.

See "*humidity, absolute,*" "*humidity mixing rate*", "*humidity, relative*", "*humidity specific,*" and "*saturation ratio.*"

HUMIDITY, ABSOLUTE

Symbol: d_v

Definition: The mass m of water vapour present in a sample of moist air divided by the volume V of moist air.

$d_v = m/V$

Unit: Kilogramme per meter cubed. (In SI base units: $kg.m^{-3}$)

Dimension: $M\,L^{-3}$

Note: 1. The quantity is also termed the "*vapor concentration*"

2. The absolute humidity is proportional to the ratio of the actual vapour pressure to the thermodynamic temperature. Because this is strongly dependent on temperature, the use of "*relative humidity*" is more useful to measure the humidity.

HUMIDITY MIXING RATIO

Symbol: r; sometimes q.

Definition: The mass of water vapour per unit mass of dry constituents of the atmosphere. It is the ratio of the mass of water vapour m to the mass of dry air m_o that contains it.

$r = m/m_o$

Unit: There are no units or dimensions.

Note: This is more frequently employed to measure humidity than specific humidity.

See "*humidity, specific.*"

HUMIDITY, RELATIVE

Symbol: ϕ_p ; sometimes U.

Definition: Actual partial water vapour pressure p in the atmosphere divided by the saturation vapour pressure p_o at the same temperature.

$$\phi_p = p/p_o$$

Unit: There are no units or dimensions.

Note: 1. It is the much more commonly employed measure for the sensation of wetness or dryness of the air, and it is usually expressed as a percentage.

2. The relative humidity and the saturation ratio differ only slightly at temperatures below about 40^0C.

3. Since the amount of water vapour the atmosphere can hold increases with temperature, the relative humidity may vary appreciably, even with absolute humidity remaining sensibly constant.

4. The single word "humidity" is normally used to the relative humidity.

See *"saturation ratio."*

HUMIDITY, SPECIFIC

Symbol: x; sometimes q.

Definition: Mass m of water vapour present in a sample of moist air divided by mass m_o of moist air.

$x = m/mo$

Unit: There are no units or dimensions.

Note: A more frequently employed measure is the humidity mixing rate.

See *"humidity mixing rate."*

HYDROSTATIC MODULES

See *"elastic modulus."*

I

ILUMINANCE

Definition: Another name for "illumination."

See *"illumination, the intensity of."*

ILLUMINATION

Definition: It is an applied science subject; its object is the provision of light of a suitable amount and suitable quantity at the place where illumination, the entity, is required. It may be required for the purpose of facilitating a visual task or from a purely aesthetic point of view.

ILLUMINATIONS (INTENSITY OF)

Symbol: E; occasionally E_v

Definition: The illumination at a point of a surface is the luminous flux Φ incident on an infinitesimal element of a surface containing the point under consideration divided by the area A of the element.

$E = d\Phi/dA$

Unit: Lux (lx) (In SI base units: cd.sr.m^{-2})

Dimension: M T^{-3}

Note: 1. The quantity is also termed the *"illuminance"*

2. Illumination defines the extent to which a surface is illuminated or the application of visible radiation to a surface. The brightness of an object depends on its illuminance and its reflectance. Many properties of vision, such as visual city, depend on illumination.

IMPEDANCE

Symbol: Z

Definition: In general, the impedance of a linear constant-parameter system is the ratio of the phasor equivalent of a steady-state sine-wave voltage or voltage-like quantity (driving force) to the phasor equivalent of a steady-state sine wave current or current-like quantity (response).

In electromagnetic radiation, electric field strength is considered the driving force and magnetic field strength is the response. In mechanical systems, mechanical force is always considered as a driving force and velocity as a response.

Unit: In a general sense, the units (and dimensions) of impedance depend on the field of application. It results from the ratio of the units (dimensions) of the quantity chosen as the driving force to the unit (dimensions) of the quantity chosen as the driving force to the unit (dimension) of the quantity chosen as the response.

IMPEDANCE, ACOUSTICAL

Symbol: Z_o; occasionally, Z

Definition: Complex ratio of the alternating sound pressure p to the strength U of the sound (the rate of volume displacement of the surface that is vibrating to produce the sound)

$Z_o = p/U$

Unit: Pascal second per meter cubed. (In SI base units: kg. $m^{-4}.s^{-1}$)

Dimension: $M L^{-4} T^{-1}$

Note: 1. The acoustical impedance is defined for a surface producing a simple sinusoidal source of sound.

2. $Z_a = R_a + i X_a$, where R_a – acoustical impedance and X_a = acoustical reactance.

IMPEDANCE, ELECTRICAL

Symbol: Z

Definition: The total virtual resistance of an electric circuit to alternating current arising from the resistance and reactance of the conductor. It is the complex representation of potential difference V divided by the complex representation of current I.

$Z = V/I$

Unit: Ohm.

Dimension: $M L^2 T^{-3} I^{-2}$ (In SI base units: $kg.m^2.s^{-3}.A^{-2}$)

Note: 1. $Z = R + iX$ where R = Resistance, X = Reactance

2. The term impedance is sometimes given to the modulus (amplitude) $|Z| = (R^2 + X^2)^{1/2}$. The polar form of the impedance is $Z = |Z|e^{i\emptyset}$, where ϕ is the phase.

IMPEDANCE, MECHANICAL

Symbol: Z_m; occasionally w

Definition: The mechanical impedance of a vibrating system is the complex ratio of the force F acting in the direction of motion at a point or surface to the velocity v at that point or surface.

$Z_m = F/v$

Unit: Newton second per meter.

Dimension: $M T^{-1}$

Note: The mechanical impedance is meant to act as the mechanical analogue of electric impedance and acoustic impedance. The concept has been further extended by writing.

$Z_m = R_m + i X_m$

where R_m = mechanical resistance and X_m = mechanical reactance.

IMPEDANCE, MUTUAL

Definition: Mutual impedance between two loops (meshes) is the factor by which the phasor equivalent of the steady-state sinewave current in one loop must be multiplied to give the phasor equivalent of the steady-state sinewave voltage in the other loop caused by the current in the first loop.

Unit: Ohm. (In SI base units: $kg.m^2.s^{-3}.A^{-2}$)

Dimension: $M L^2 T^{-3} I^{-2}$

IMPEDENCE, SELF

Definition: The self-impedance of a loop (mesh) is the impedance of a passive loop with all other loops of the network open-circuited.

Unit: Ohm. (In SI base units: $kg.m^2.s^{-3}.A^{-2}$)

Dimension: M L^2 T^{-3} I^{-2}

IMPEDANCE, TRANSFER

Definition: A transfer impedance is the impedance obtained when the response is determined at a point other than that at which the driving force is applied. In electric circuits, the response may be determined in any branch except that which contains the driving force.

Unit: Ohm. (In SI base units: kg.m^2.s^{-3}.A^{-2})

Dimension: M L^2 T^{-3} I^{-2}

IMPEDANCE, SPECIFIC ACOUSTICAL

Symbol: Z_s; sometimes W

Definition: Complex ratio of the sound pressure p to the sound particle velocity v.

$Z_s = p/v$

Alternatively, the specific acoustical impedance is the product of the acoustical impedance Z_a and the area A.

$Z_s = Za\ A$

Unit: Pascal second per meter. (In SI base units: kg.m^{-2}.s^{-1})

Dimension: M L^{-2} T^{-1} .

Note: 1. The quantity was formerly called the unit-area acoustical impedance.

2. The specific acoustical impedance refers to a point in a medium in which sound waves are propagated.

3. $Z_s = R_s + iX_s$, where R_s = specific acoustical resistance and X_s, = specific acoustical reactance.

IMPULSE

Symbol: I

Definition: The integral of force F with respect to time t.

I = $\int F dt$

In the case of constant force F, the impulse is:

$I = F\,t,$

Where t is time for which the force acts.

Unit: Newton second (In SI base units: kg.m.s^{-1})

Dimension: M L T^{-1}

Note: 1. The impulse of force equals the change of momentum produced by it.

2. An impulsive force is one that is very large but acts only for a very short time; it can be represented by a Dirace function.

INDUCTANCE

Definition: A property of an electric circuit that results from the magnetic field set up when a current flows. It is the property that gives rise to the phenomenon of electromagnetic induction. Inductance relates the magnetic flux through the circuit to the current flowing in the circuit-self-inductance or in a nearly circuit-mutual inductance. Alternatively, it is a quantitative measure of this given by the e.m.f. produced per unit rate of change of current.

Unit: Henry (In SI base units: kg.m^2.s^{-2}.A^{-2})

Dimension: M L^2 T^{-2} I^{-2}

See "*inductance, mutual* and "*inductance, self.*"

INDUCTANCE, MUTUAL

Symbol: M or L_{12}

Definition: The mutual inductance between two loops (meshes) in a circuit is the quotient of the flux linkage $\emptyset$ produced in one loop divided by the current I in another loop, which induces the flux linkage.

$M = \emptyset/I$

Unit: Henry (In SI base units: kg.m^2.s^{-2}.A^{-2})

Dimension: M L^2 T^{-2} I^{-2}

INDUCTANCE, SELF

Symbol: L

Definition: 1. Magnetic flux $\emptyset$ through a loop caused by a current I in the loop, divided by the current

$L = \emptyset/I$

If a voltage v is induced in the circuit, then $v = d\ (LI)/dt$.

2. Is the factor L in the expression $1/2\ L\ I^2$ which gives the energy stored in the magnetic field as a result of the current I.

Unit: Henry (In SI base units: $kg.m^2.s^{-2}.A^{-2}$)

Dimension: $M\ L^2\ T^{-2}\ I^{-2}$

Note: 1. The two definitions are not equivalent except when L is constant. In all other cases, the definition being used must be specified.

2. The two definitions are restricted to relative slow changes in I, that is, to low frequencies, but by analogy with the definitions, equivalent inductances may often be evolved in high-frequency applications such as resonators and wavelength "circuits". Such "inductances," when used, must be specified.

3. The two definitions are restricted to cases in which the branches are small in physical size compared with a wavelength, whatever the frequency. Thus in the case of a uniform 2-wire transmission line, it may be necessary, even at low frequencies, to consider the parameters as "distributed" rather than to have one inductance for the entire line.

INDUCTANCE, THERMAL

Definition: The product of the temperature difference θ and time t, divided by the mean rate of flow of entropy S with respect to time.

Thermal inductance $= (\theta\ t)\ /(\frac{ds}{dt})$

Unit: Thermal henry $=$ kelvin squared second per watt.

Dimension: $M^{-1}\ L^2$

Note: The former definition was: the product of the temperature difference and the time divided by the rate of flow of heat energy Q with respect to time.

Thermal inductance = $(\theta\ t)/(dQ/dt)$

INDUCTION, ELECTRIC

Definition: Alternative name for electric displacement.

See "*displacement, electric.*"

INDUCTION, MAGNETIC

Definition: Alternative name for magnetic flux density.

See "*flux density, magnetic.*"

INDUCTION, MOTIONAL

Symbol: E_m

Definition: The electromotive force produced in a circuit (e.g., a loop of conducting wire) when the circuit changes its position in a non-varying with time (fixed) magnetic field. It is proportional to the rate of decrease of flux due to the motion of the circuit as a whole, or to its deformation or to a combination of both. For a circuit that exists in a constant field or flux density B, v being the velocity of an infinitesimal line element dl of the circuit,

$$E_m = \int (v\ x\ B)\ dl$$

Unit: Volt (In SI base units: $kg.m^2.s^{-3}.A^{-1}$)

Dimension: $ML^2\ T^{-3}\ I^{-1}$

Note: 1. If the circuit is stationary, but the magnetic field is changing, the electromotive force E induced in the circuit will be:

$$E = -\int \frac{\partial B}{\partial t} ds$$

Where B is the flux density, and the surface integral is over any surface bounded by the circuit.

2. If, simultaneously, the circuit is moving and the magnetic field is varying, the induced electromotive force is:

Total induced electromotive force $= E + E_m$

See also *"electromotive force."*

INERTIA

Definition: 1. The property of a body by virtue of which it tends to persist in a state of rest or uniform motion in a straight line, i.e., it is the resistance offered by a body to acceleration.

In other words, Inertia is the resistance of any physical object to any change in its velocity. This includes changes to the object's speed or direction of motion. An aspect of this property is the tendency of objects to keep moving in a straight line at a constant speed when no forces act upon them.

2. In photographic work, the optical density of an exposed and processed negative varies linearly with the logarithm of the exposure over the usual working portion of the range. The inertia is the exposure that would just being to affect the density of the linearly held at such small exposure.

INTENSITY

Definition: A measure of the concentration of some factors, such as sound or light, usually over a given area or volume.

Unit: Depends on the factor under consideration.

Note: The term *"illuminance"* is replacing *"intensity of illumination"*, and the terms *"magnetic and electric field strength"* have replaced *"magnetic and electric intensity"*.

See *"field strength, magnetic"*, *"intensity, luminous"*, *"intensity, radiant"*, *"intensity, sound"*, and *"illuminance"*.

INTENSITY LEVEL

Symbol: N

Definition: The common logarithm of the ratio of two intensities, I_1, I_2 or two powers P_1, P_2 or two energies, E_1, E_2, each expressed in the same units.

$$N = log(I_2/I_2) = log(P_2/P_1) = log(E_2/E_1)$$

Unit: Bel; in practice, the decibel is always used.

Dimension: There are no dimensions.

Note: 1. The symbols L_p, L_n and L_w are also used for power level.

2. In acoustics, the conventional reference levels are the rounded values of the threshold level of aural sensation: $I_l = 10^{-12}$ watts per meter squared, $P_l = 10^{-12}$ watts, $E_l = 10^{-12}$ joules.

3. Intensity level is also equivalent to (sound) pressure level (L_p *or* L), defined as the common logarithm of the ratio of two pressure p_1, p_2 each expressed in the same units.

$$N = log(p_2/p_1).$$

The conventional reference levels are $p_1 = 2\ x\ 10^{-5}$ Pascals in air and $p_1 = 0.1$ Pascal in water

See "*pressure level-sound.*"

INTENSITY, LUMINOUS

Symbol: I: occasionally, I_v

Definition: The luminous intensity in a given direction is the luminous flux Φ emitted by a point source in an infinitesimal cone containing the direction divided by the solid angle ω of the cone.

$$I = d\Phi/d\omega$$

In other words, it is the luminous flux emitted per unit solid angle by a point source in a given direction.

Unit: Candela

Dimension: $M\ L^2\ T^{-3}$

Note: 1. The quantity has also been given the deprecated name candle power.

2. The standard source is a full (i.e., planckian) radiation at the temperature of the solidification of platinum (2 045K)

3. The source may radiate unequally in different directions, and the direction has to be specified. If the luminous intensity is averaged over all the directions, it is called "*mean spherical intensity*".

4. For extended sources the luminous intensity per unit area or "*luminance*" is used.

5. The luminous intensity of a source can be compared to that of a standard tungsten

filament lamp to an accuracy (at the National Physical Laboratory) of one part in 5 000.

INTENSITY, RADIANT

Symbol: l; symbol l_e

Definition: The radiant intensity in a given direction is the radiant flux Φ emitted by a point source in an infinitesimal cone containing the direction divided by the solid angle ω of the cone.

$$l = d\Phi/d\omega$$

Unit: Watt per steradian.

Dimension: $M\, L^2\, T^{-3}$

INTENSITY, SOUND

Symbol: I; occasionally J or L.

Definition: Mean rate flow of sound energy E through a unit area A normal to the direction of propagation of the sound wave.

$$I = \frac{1}{A} \cdot \frac{dE}{dt} \, (t = time)$$

For a plane or spherical progressive wave with a velocity of propagation c in an isotropic medium of density ρ, the sound intensity at a point is related to the root-mean-square sound pressure p by:

$$I = p^2/\rho\, c$$

Unit: Watt per meter squared.

Dimension: $M\, T^{-3}$

INTERNAL TRANSMISSION DENSITY

Symbol: D_i

Definition: a measure of the ability of a body to absorb radiation as expressed by the logarithm to base ten of the reciprocal of the internal transittance (τ_i)

$D_i = log_{10}(1/\tau_i)$

Unit: it has no units or dimensions

Note: It is also called absorbance

See also *"absorbance"* and *"transmittance internal."*

INTERVAL

Symbol: I

Definition: The relation between the two pitches measured wither as the ratio of the frequencies f_1, f_2 of corresponding pure tones (i.e., standard sinusoidal plane progressive tones of equal pitches) or in terms of the logarithm of their ratio. The ratio is generally expressed as a fraction greater than unity.

$I = f_1 / f_2$ *or*

$I = k \log (f_1 / f_2)$

Where k depends on the units used

Units: For I as a ratio, there are no units

For I expressed in terms of the logarithm of a ratio, the units are:

Octave, in this case, $k = 1/\log 2$

Cent, in this case $k = 1200/\log 2$

Savart, in this case $k = 1000$

Modified savart, in this case, $k = 300/\log 2$

Dimension: there are no dimensions

Note:

1. The quantity is also termed the pitch (or frequency) interval.
2. Although the octave is associated with metric measurements, the cent is in more common use because of the convenient sizes of intervals in the scale of equal *"temperament"*.
3. The advantage of expressing intervals logarithmically is that they are combined by addition. Intervals expressed as ratios must be combined by multiplication
4. The musical scales have been developed gradually and sometimes without any mathematical approach. Modern scales being associated, among other things, with musical instruments of fixed design and operation, having intervals designated sizes, although the

ear is capable of accepting and expects – variations from the standards values. The more important are the scales of just temperament and the scales of equal temperament.

Diatonic scales of just temperament contain seven intervals of three different kinds. The largest intervals are tones; the larger whole tone (T_1) is an interval of 9/8 = 170 millioctaves = 204 cents, and the lesser whole tone (T_2) is an interval of 10/9=152 millioctaves = 182 cents. The smallest intervals are semitones (S) of size 16/15=93

In the major scale, the order of interval is:

$$T_1 T_2 S T_1 T_2 T_1 S$$

Chromatic scales of just temperament contain twelve intervals and are derived from the corresponding diatonic scales by dividing the whole tones into two semitones. Each larger chromatic semitone of size 135/128 =77 millioctaves = 92 cents. Similarly, each lesser whole tone is divided into a diatonic semitone and a smaller chromatic of size 25/24 =59 millioctaves =71 cents.

In scales of equal temperament, all the semitones have the same size, $2^{1/12}$ =83 milioctaves = 100 cents (exactly). Each whole tone equals two semitones. The sizes of various named intervals as ratios are given in Tables 1 and 2

Table – 1   **Intervals of Just Temperament**

Unison	1/1
Major second	9/8
Major third	5/4
Perfect fourth	4/3
Perfect fifth	3/2
Major sixth	5/3
Major seventh	15/8
Octave	2/1

Table -2   **Interval of Equal Temperament**

Unison	2^0	=	1.00
Major second	$2^{2/12}$	=	1.12
Major third	$2^{4/12}$	=	1.26
Perfect fourth	$2^{5/12}$	=	1.33
Perfect fifth	$2^{7/12}$	=	1.50
Major sixth	$2^{9/12}$	=	1.68
Major seventh	$2^{11/12}$	=	1.89
Octave	$2^{12/12}$	=	2.0

5. The term interval is used also for the separation of two events in a four- dimensional continuum.

IONIC STRENGTH

Symbol: μ

Definition: The ionic strength is a measure of the intensity of the electrical field existing in a solution. It is defined as half the sum of the products of ion molalities and the square of the ion valencies. For a univalent electrolyte with one bivalent ion and one univalent ion, the ionic strength is three times the molality.

Units: mol per cubic meter. m^{-3}.mol

IRIBARREN NUMBER

Symbol: Ir or ξ

Definition: In fluid dynamics, the **Iribarren number** or **Iribarren parameter** – also known as the **surf similarity parameter and breaker parameter** – is a dimensionless parameter used to model several effects of (breaking) surface gravity waves on beaches and coastal structures. The parameter is named after the Spanish engineer Ramón Iribarren Cavanillas (1900–1967), who introduced it to describe the occurrence of wave breaking on sloping beaches.

 For instance, the Iribarren number is used to describe breaking wave types on beaches; or wave run-up on – and reflection by – beaches, breakwaters and dikes.

The Iribarren number, which is often denoted as Ir or $\xi -$, is defined as:

$$\xi = \frac{\tan \alpha}{\sqrt{H/L_0}}, \qquad \text{with} \qquad L_0 = \frac{g}{2\pi} T^2,$$

Where ξ is the Iribarren number, α is the angle of the seaward slope of a structure, H is the wave height, L0 is the deep-water wavelength, T is the period, and g is the gravitational acceleration. Depending on the application, different definitions of H and T are used, for example: for periodic waves, the wave height H0 at deep water or the breaking wave height Hb at the edge of the surf zone. Or, for random waves, the significant wave height is Hs at a certain location.

Field of application: wave mechanics (breaking surface gravity waves on a slope)

Unit: Dimensionless

IRRADIANCE

Symbols: *E;* sometime E_e

Definition: In radiometry, the irradiance at a point surface is the radiant flux Φ incident on an infinitesimal element of surface containing the point divided by the are A of the element.

$$E_e = \frac{\partial \Phi_e}{\partial A}$$

where

- ∂ is the partial derivative symbol;
- Φ_e is the radiant flux received;
- A is the area.

Irradiance is often called intensity, but this term is avoided in radiometry, where such usage leads to confusion with radiant intensity. In astrophysics, irradiance is called *radiant flux*.

Units: Watt per meter squared W/m^2) (SI unit)

erg per square centimeter per second (erg·cm−2·s−1) (CGS unit)

Note: The CGS unit is often used in astronomy

Dimension: M T^3

Note: the quantity has also been termed the irradiancy

See also "spectral irradiance"

J

JAKOB NUMBER (phase-change number, *Ja*)

Symbol: Ja

Definition: Jakob number is a dimensionless number that represents the ratio of sensible heat to latent heat absorbed (or released) during the phase change process.

$$Ja = \frac{c_{p,f}(T_w - T_{sat})}{h_{fg}}$$

Where:

C_p: specific heat at constant pressure (Pa)

T_{sat}: saturation temperature (K)

T_w: wall temperature (total stagnation temperature) (K)

h_{fg}: latent heat condensation (evaporation enthalpy change) (kJkg)

Field of application: heat transfer (ratio of sensible heat to latent heat during phase changes)

Unit: Dimensionless

JERK

Symbol: ***J*** (vector)

Definition: Change of acceleration at the unit time: the third time derivative of position

Units: Meter per second cubic (In SI base units: m/s^3)

Dimension: $L\ T^{-3}$

Note: Jerk refers to many meanings depends on the field in which it is defined

See *"Derivatives"*

Joule–Thomson (Kelvin) coefficient

Symbol: μ

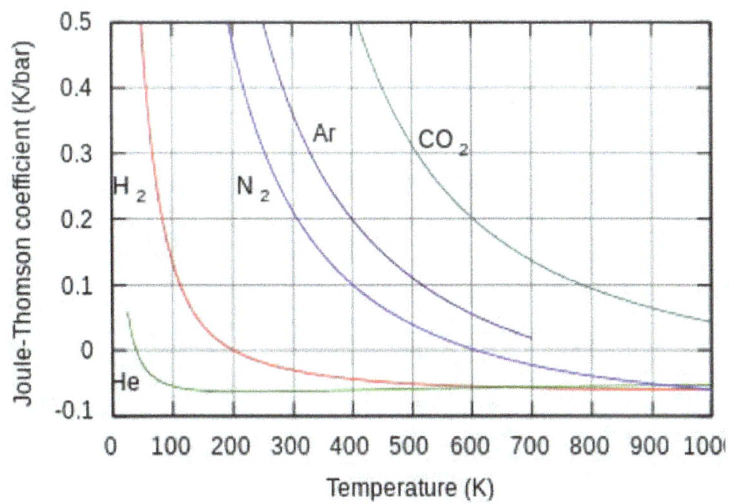

Fig. Joule–Thomson coefficients for various gases at atmospheric pressure

The rate of change of temperature T with respect to pressure P in a Joule–Thomson process (that is, at constant enthalpy H) is the *Joule–Thomson (Kelvin) coefficient* μ_{JT} . This coefficient can be expressed in terms of the gas's volume V, its heat capacity at constant pressure C_p , and its coefficient of thermal expansion μ as:

$$\mu_{\mathrm{JT}} = \left(\frac{\partial T}{\partial P}\right)_H = \frac{V}{C_\mathrm{p}}(\alpha T - 1)$$

Units: kelvin per Pascal (In SI base units: $kg^{-1}.m.\ s^2.K$

Dimensions: $M^{-1}L\ T^2\theta$

(θ is temperature)

JOUNCE (or snap)

Symbol: s (vector)

Definition: In physics, jounce, also known as snap, is the fourth derivative of the position vector with respect to time, or the rate of change of jerk with respect to time. Equivalently, it is the second derivative of acceleration or the third derivative of velocity.

Units: meters per fourth power of time ("meters per second to the fourth")(m/t^4)

Dimension: $L\ T^{-4}$

Note: Jounce and the fifth and sixth derivatives of position as a function of time are "sometimes somewhat facetiously" referred to as snap, crackle, and pop, respectively. However, time derivatives of positions of higher order than four appear rarely.

See "*Derivatives*"

K

KAPITZA NUMBER

Symbol: Ka

Definition: The **Kapitza number** (**Ka**) is a dimensionless number named after the prominent Russian physicist Pyotr Kapitsa (Peter Kapitza). He provided the first extensive study of the ways in which a thin film of liquid flows down inclined surfaces. Expressed as the ratio of surface tension forces to inertial forces, the Kapitza number acts as an indicator of the hydrodynamic wave regime in falling liquid films. Liquid film behavior represents a subset of the more general class of free boundary problems. And is important in a wide range of engineering and technological applications such as evaporators, heat exchangers, absorbers, microreactors, small-scale electronics/microprocessor cooling schemes, air conditioning and gas turbine blade cooling.

Unlike most dimensionless numbers used in the study of fluid mechanics, the Kapitza number represents a material property, as it is formed by combining powers of the surface tension, density, gravitational acceleration and kinematic viscosity.

$$Ka = \frac{\sigma}{\rho(g\sin\beta)^{1/3}\nu^{4/3}}$$

Where

σ: is the surface tension (SI units: N/m),

g: is the gravitational acceleration (m/s^2),

ρ: is density (kg/m^3),

β: is inclination angle (rad), and ν is kinematic viscosity (m^2/s).

Field of application: fluid mechanics (a thin film of liquid flows down inclined surfaces)

Unit: Dimensionless

(**References**: *Kalliadasis, Serafim; Christian Ruyer-Quil; Benoit Scheid; Manuel García*

Velarde (2011). Falling Liquid Films (Volume 176 of Applied Mathematical Sciences). Springer. ISBN 978-1-84882-367-9.)

KARLOVITZ NUMBER

Symbol: K_a

Definition: In combustion, the **Karlovitz number** is defined as the ratio of chemical time scale t_F to Kolmogorov time scale t_η, named after Béla Karlovitz. The number reads as

$$Ka = \frac{t_F}{t_\eta}$$

In premixed turbulent combustion, the chemical time scale can be defined as:

$$t_F = D_T/S_{L'}^2$$

Where D_T is the thermal diffusivity, and S_L is the laminar flame speed, and the flame thickness is given by $\delta_L = D_T/S_L$, in which case,

$$Ka = \frac{\delta_L^2}{\eta^2}$$

where η is the Kolmogorov scale. The Karlovitz number is related to the Damköhler number as

$$Ka = 1/Da$$

if the Damköhler number is defined with the Kolmogorov scale. If $Ka<1$, the premixed turbulent flame falls into the category of corrugated flamelets and wrinkled flamelets, otherwise into the thin reaction zone or broken reaction zone flames.

Field of application: turbulent combustion (characteristic flow time times flame stretch rate)

Unit: Dimensionless

[Ref. Peters, N. (2000). Turbulent combustion. Cambridge university press.]

KERMA (KINETIC ENERGY RELEASED IN MATTER)

Symbol: K

Definition: The sum of the initial kinetic energies of all charged particles produced by the indirect effect of ionizing radiation in a small volume of a given substance divided by the mass of the substance in that volume.

Unit: Gray (In IS base units: $m^2.s^{-2}$)

Dimension: L^2T^{-2}

See "energy specific.'

KEULEGAN–CARPENTER NUMBER

Symbol: K_C

Definition: In fluid dynamics, the **Keulegan–Carpenter number**, also called the **period number**, is a dimensionless quantity describing the relative importance of the drag forces over inertia forces for bluff objects in an oscillatory fluid flow. Or similarly, for objects that oscillate in a fluid at rest. For small Keulegan–Carpenter number, inertia dominates, while for large numbers, the (turbulence) drag forces are important.

The Keulegan–Carpenter number K_C is defined as:

$$K_C = \frac{V\,T}{L}$$

Where:

- V is the amplitude of the flow velocity oscillation (or the amplitude of the object's velocity, in case of an oscillating object),
- T is the period of the oscillation, and
- L is a characteristic length scale of the object, for instance, the diameter for a cylinder under wave loading.

The Keulegan–Carpenter number is named after Garbis H. Keulegan (1890–1989) and Lloyd H. Carpenter.

A closely related parameter, also often used for sediment transport under water waves, is the **displacement parameter** δ:

$$\delta = \frac{A}{L}$$

with A the excursion amplitude of fluid particles in oscillatory flow and L a characteristic diameter of the sediment material. For the sinusoidal motion of the fluid, A is related to V and T as $A = VT/(2\pi)$, and:

$$K_C = 2\pi\delta.$$

The Keulegan–Carpenter number can be directly related to the Navier–Stokes equations by looking at characteristic scales for the acceleration terms:

- Convective acceleration:

$$(\mathbf{u} \cdot \nabla)\mathbf{u} \sim \frac{V^2}{L}$$

- Local acceleration:

$$\frac{\partial \mathbf{u}}{\partial t} \sim \frac{V}{T}.$$

Dividing these two acceleration scales gives the Keulegan–Carpenter number.

A somewhat similar parameter is the Strouhal number, in form equal to the reciprocal of the Keulegan–Carpenter number. The Strouhal number gives the vortex shedding frequency resulting from placing an object in a steady flow, so it describes the flow unsteadiness as a result of an instability of the flow downstream of the object. Conversely, the Keulegan–Carpenter number is related to the oscillation frequency of an unsteady flow into which the object is placed.

Field of application: fluid dynamics (ratio of drag force to inertia for a bluff object in oscillatory fluid flow)

Unit: Dimensionless

[Ref. Keulegan, G. H.; Carpenter, L. H. (1958), "Forces on cylinders and plates in an oscillating fluid", *Journal of Research of the National Bureau of Standards* **60** (5): 423–440]

KNUDSEN NUMBER

Symbol: K_n

Definition: The **Knudsen number (Kn)** is a dimensionless number defined as the ratio of the molecular mean free path length to a representative physical length scale. This length scale could be, for example, the radius of a body in a fluid. The number is named after *Denmark* physicist Martin Knudsen (1871–1949).

The Knudsen number is a dimensionless number defined as

$$\text{Kn} = \frac{\lambda}{L}$$

where

λ = mean free path [L^1],

L = representative physical length scale [L^1].

The Knudsen number helps determine whether statistical mechanics or the continuum mechanics formulation of fluid dynamics should be used to model a situation. If the Knudsen number is near or greater than one, the mean free path of a molecule is comparable to the length scale of the problem, and the continuum assumption of fluid mechanics is no longer a good approximation. In such cases, statistical methods should be used.

Relationship to Mach and Reynolds numbers in gases

The Knudsen number can be related to the Mach number and the Reynolds number.

Using the dynamic viscosity

$$\mu = \frac{1}{2}\rho\bar{c}\lambda,$$

with the average molecule speed (from Maxwell–Boltzmann distribution)

$$\bar{c} = \sqrt{\frac{8k_{\mathrm{B}}T}{\pi m}}$$

The mean free path is determined as follows:

$$\lambda = \frac{\mu}{\rho} \sqrt{\frac{\pi m}{2k_{\mathrm{B}}T}}$$

Dividing through by L (some characteristic length), the Knudsen number is obtained:

$$\mathrm{Kn} = \frac{\lambda}{L} = \frac{\mu}{\rho L} \sqrt{\frac{\pi m}{2k_{\mathrm{B}}T}}.$$

where

$\bar{c}$ is the average molecular speed from the Maxwell–Boltzmann distribution [$L^1\,T^{-1}$],

T is the thermodynamic temperature [θ^1],

μ is the dynamic viscosity [$M^1\,L^{-1}\,T^{-1}$],

m is the molecular mass [M^1],

k_B is the Boltzmann constant [$M^1\,L^2\,T^{-2}\,\theta^{-1}$],

ρ is the density [$M^1\,L^{-3}$].

The dimensionless Mach number can be written as

$$\mathrm{Ma} = \frac{U_\infty}{c_{\mathrm{s}}},$$

where the speed of sound is given by

$$c_{\mathrm{s}} = \sqrt{\frac{\gamma RT}{M}} = \sqrt{\frac{\gamma k_{\mathrm{B}}T}{m}},$$

Where

U_∞ is the freestream speed [$L^1\,T^{-1}$],

R is the Universal gas constant (in SI, 8.314 47215 J K^{-1} mol^{-1}) [$M^1\,L^2\,T^{-2}\,\theta^{-1}\,\mathrm{mol}^{-1}$],

M is the molar mass [$M^1\,\mathrm{mol}^{-1}$],

γ is the ratio of specific heat [1].

The dimensionless Reynolds number can be written as

$$\mathrm{Re} = \frac{\rho U_\infty L}{\mu}.$$

Dividing the Mach number by the Reynolds number:

$$\frac{\mathrm{Ma}}{\mathrm{Re}} = \frac{U_\infty/c_{\mathrm{s}}}{\rho U_\infty L/\mu} = \frac{\mu}{\rho L c_{\mathrm{s}}} = \frac{\mu}{\rho L \sqrt{\frac{\gamma k_{\mathrm{B}} T}{m}}} = \frac{\mu}{\rho L}\sqrt{\frac{m}{\gamma k_{\mathrm{B}} T}}$$

and by multiplying by $\sqrt{\dfrac{\gamma\pi}{2}}$ yields the Knudsen number:

$$\frac{\mu}{\rho L}\sqrt{\frac{m}{\gamma k_{\mathrm{B}} T}}\sqrt{\frac{\gamma\pi}{2}} = \frac{\mu}{\rho L}\sqrt{\frac{\pi m}{2 k_{\mathrm{B}} T}} = \mathrm{Kn}.$$

The Mach, Reynolds and Knudsen numbers are therefore related by

$$\mathrm{Kn} = \frac{\mathrm{Ma}}{\mathrm{Re}}\sqrt{\frac{\gamma\pi}{2}}$$

Field of application: gas dynamics (ratio of the molecular mean free path length to a representative physical length scale)

Unit: Dimensionless

[Ref. HandWiki]

K-space or k-space / Reciprocal space position

Definition: The K-space can refer to:

- Another name for the spatial frequency domain of a spatial Fourier transform
    - Reciprocal space, containing the reciprocal lattice of a spatial lattice
    - Momentum space, or wavevector space, the vector space of possible values of momentum for a particle
    - K-space ((magnetic resonance)
- Another name for a compacity generated space in topology
- K-space (functional analysis) is an F-space such that every twisted sum by the real line splits
- K-space (band), a British-Siberian music ensemble

Units: per meter

Dimensions: $\mathrm{L^{-1}}$

KUTATELADZE NUMBER

Symbol: Ku

Definition: Dimensionless number used in fluid mechanics and given by the relation:

$$Ku = \frac{U_h \rho_g^{1/2}}{(\sigma g(\rho_l - \rho_g))^{1/4}}$$

Field of application: fluid mechanics (counter-current two-phase flow)

Unit: Dimensionless

L

LAPLACE NUMBER

Symbol: La

Definition: The Laplace number (La), also known as the Suratman number (Su), is a dimensionless number used in the characterization of free surface fluid dynamics. It represents a ratio of surface tension to the momentum-transport (especially dissipation) inside a fluid.

It is defined as follows:

$$La = Su = \frac{\sigma \rho L}{\mu^2}$$

Where:

- σ = surface tension
- ρ = density
- L = length
- μ = liquid viscosity

$$La = \frac{Re^2}{We}$$

Laplace number is related to the Reynolds number (Re) and Weber number (We) in the following way:

Field of application: fluid dynamics (free convection within immiscible fluids; ratio of surface tension to momentum-transport)

Unit: Dimensionless

LATENT HEAT, SPECIFIC

Symbol: l

Definition: quantity of heat energy Q absorbed or released in an isothermal transformation of phase, divided by mass m

$l = Q/m$

Unit: Joule per kilogramme

Dimension: L^2T^{-2}

Note: The quantity is often erroneously referred to by its former name, latent heat

See " heat latent."

LATITUDE

Symbol: θ

Definition:

1. **GEOGRAPHICAL LATITUDE:** of a place is the angle between the normal to the earth's surface and the plane of the equator. It is the latitude found from astronomical observation.

2. **GEOMETRIC LATITUDE:** Is the angle between a line joining the place to the earth's center and the plane of equator. It differs from the geographical latitude because the earth is an oblate spheroid, and the maximum difference (at latitude 45^0) is equal to 11'36'

3. **CELESTIAL LATITUDE**
   See " altitude'

Unit: Radian degree

Dimension: there are no dimension

LEAKAGE

Definition: 1. The flow of an electric current, due to imperfect insulation, in a path other than intended

2.   A net loss of particles from a region or across a boundary in a nuclear reactor

3.   See " *leakage , magnetic.* "

LEAKAGE COEFFICIENT

Symbol: σ

Definition: it is one minus the square of the coupling coefficient

$$\sigma = 1 - k^2$$

Unit: There are no units or dimensions

See: *"coupling coefficient."*

LEAKAGE COEFFICIENT, MAGNETIC

Symbol: σ

Definition: The total magnetic flux divided by the effective (or useful) magnetic flux. It exceeds, usually unity on account of magnetic leakage.

$$\sigma = (total\ magnetic\ flux) / (effective\ magnetic\ flux)$$

$$= (\text{Effective flux} + \text{leakage flux}) / (\text{Effective flux})$$

$$= 1 + (\text{Leakage flux} / \text{effective flux})$$

Unit: there are no units or dimensions

LEWIS NUMBER

Symbol: Le

Definition: The Lewis number (Le) is a dimensionless number defined as the ratio of thermal diffusivity to mass diffusivity. It is used to characterize fluid flows where there is simultaneous heat and mass transfer. The Lewis number puts the thickness of the thermal boundary layer in relation to the concentration boundary layer. The Lewis number is defined as

$$Le = \frac{\alpha}{D} = \frac{\lambda}{\rho D_{im} c_p}$$

where α is the thermal diffusivity and D the mass diffusivity, λ the thermal conductivity, ρ the density, D_{im} the mixture-averaged diffusion coefficient, and c_p is the specific heat capacity at constant pressure.

The Lewis number can also be expressed in terms of the Prandtl number P_r and the Schmidt number S_c :

$$Le = \frac{Sc}{Pr}$$

It is named after Warren K. Lewis (1882–1975), who was the first head of the Chemical Engineering Department at MIT. Some workers in the field of combustion assume (incorrectly) that the Lewis number was named for Bernard Lewis (1899–1993), who for many years was a major figure in the field of combustion research.

Field of application: heat and mass transfer (ratio of thermal to mass diffusivity)

Unit: Dimensionless

LIFT COEFFICIENT

Symbol: C_L

Definition: The lift coefficient (CL) is a dimensionless coefficient that relates the lift generated by a lifting body to the fluid density around the body, the fluid velocity and an associated reference area. A lifting body is a foil or a complete foil-bearing body, such as a fixed-wing aircraft. CL is a function of the angle of the body to the flow, its Reynolds number and its Mach number. The section lift coefficient cl refers to the dynamic lift characteristics of a two-dimensional foil section, with the reference area replaced by the foil chord.

The lift coefficient C_L is defined by

$$C_L \equiv \frac{L}{qS} = \frac{L}{\frac{1}{2}\rho u^2 S} = \frac{2L}{\rho u^2 S}$$

where L is the lift force, S is the relevant surface area, and q is the fluid dynamic pressure, in turn, linked to the fluid density ρ and to the flow speed u.

Field of application: aerodynamics (lift available from an airfoil at a given angle of attack)

Unit: Dimensionless

LIGHT

Definition: Electromagnetic radiation with wavelengths capable of causing the sensation of vision.

It is ranging approximately from 400 nanometers (extreme violet) to 770 nanometers (extreme red)

More generally, it is defined as the electromagnetic radiation of any wavelength.

Note: 1.   Following the first definition, light is known also as " light radiation" or "visible radiation"

2.   The infrared and ultraviolet radiation are covered by the second definition

3.   When light frequencies are multiplied by the Planck constant $h(h=6.636 \times 10^{34}$ joule second)

LINKAGE OF MAGNETIC FLUX

Definition: Linkage of magnetic flux is a measure of the flux and the number of turns of the coil or circuit with which it links. Quantitatively, it is the product of the number of lines of magnetic flux and the number of turns of the coil or circuit through which they pass.

Linkage of magnetic flux = number of magnetic lines x number of turns

Units: Line turn or Maxwell turn

LOAD

Definition: 1. A Device or material in which electrical signal power is dissipated or received, i.e., a device that absorbs power from a source of electrical signal. Examples include loudspeakers, TV and radio receivers and logic circuits.

2.   The power delivered by a machine, generator, transducer, or electronic circuit or device.

3.   The mechanical force applied to a body

4.   The weight supported by a structure

See also *"effort"* and *"mechanical advantage."*

LOCKHART–MARTINELLI PARAMETER

Symbol: χ

The **Lockhart–Martinelli parameter** (χ) is a dimensionless number used in internal two-phase flow calculations. It expresses the liquid fraction of a flowing fluid. Its main application is in two-phase pressure drop and boiling/condensing heat transfer calculations. It is defined as:

$$\chi = \frac{m_\ell}{m_g}\sqrt{\frac{\rho_g}{\rho_\ell}};$$

where

- **m_ℓ is the liquid phase mass flowrate;**
- **m_g** is the gas phase mass flowrate;
- **ρ_g** is the gas density;
- **ρ_ℓ** is the liquid density.

Field of application: two-phase flow (flow of wet gases; liquid fraction)

Unit: Dimensionless

LOGARITHMIC DECREMENT

Symbol:λ

Definition: If a system be set to execute oscillations in the presence of frictional forces, the amplitude of the resulting oscillation will diminish. If no external forces are applied to maintain the oscillation, the successive amplitude of oscillation a_1, a_2, ..., a_n are going to follow the relation $a_1/a_2 = a_2/a_3 = a_{n-1}/a_n = \exp(\lambda)$ where is known as the logarithmic decrement. The logarithm decrement is, then, the natural logarithm of the amplitude of one oscillation to that of the next when no external forces are applied to maintain the oscillation.

$$\lambda = \log_e (a_1/a_2) = \log_e (a_1\text{-}a_n)/(n\text{-}1)$$

Alternatively, it is defined as the product of the periodic time T of the oscillation and the damping coefficient δ,

$$\lambda = \delta T$$

Unit: Neper

Dimension: There are no dimensions

Note: The ration π/λ is called the Q- factor

See *"dumping coefficient."*

LONGITUDE

Definition: The terrestrial longitude of a place is the angle between the terrestrial meridian through that place and the meridian through Greenwich; it is measured eastwards or westwards from Greenwich from 0^0- 180^0.

Unit: Degree

LOSCHMIDT's NUMBER

Definition: The number of molecules present in one cubic centimeter of an ideal gas at Standard Temperature and Pressure (S.T.P.). It has a value of 2. 68719 $x10^{19}cm^3$

Unit: per cubic centimeter

Dimension: L^{-3}

See also "*Avogadro constant.*"

LOSS ANGLE

See " *angle, loss.*"

LOSS FACTOR

See " *angle, loss.*"

LOUDNESS

Symbol: S or N

Definition: An observer's auditory impression of the volume of a sound referred to a sound of a given equivalent loudness P. When the loudness is measured as one sone, the given equivalent loudness is 40 phons: in general, the loudness is given by:

$$S = 2^{(P-40)/10}$$

Unit: Sone

Dimension: There are no dimensions

LOUDNESS, LEVEL

Symbol: *P* or *LN*

Definition: A quantity measured by the sound pressure level in decibles, relative to 0.0002 microbars, of a standard pure tone of given frequency coming from directly in front of the observer, subjectively judged to be of equal loudness by an ontologically normal ear. (The mean, or rather the modal value of a series of readings, should be taken). The standard pure tone of a given frequency is a sinusoidal plane progressive wave of frequency 1000 hertz.

Unit: Phon

Dimension: There are no dimensions

Note: The quantity is also termed the loudness equivalent

LOVE NUMBERS

Symbol: *h*, *k*, and *l*

Definition

The Love numbers h, k, and l are dimensionless parameters that measure the rigidity of a planetary body and the susceptibility of its shape to change in response to a tidal potential. In 1909 Augustus Edward Hough Love introduced the values h and k, which characterize the overall elastic response of the earth to the tides. Later, in 1912, T. Shida of Japan added a third Love number, l, which was needed to obtain a complete overall description of the solid earth's response to the tides.

The Love number h is defined as the ratio of the body tide to the height of the static equilibrium tide; also defined as the vertical (radial) displacement or variation of the planet's elastic properties. In terms of the tide generating potential $V(\theta,\phi)/g$, the displacement is $hV(\theta,\phi)/g$ where θ is latitude, ϕ is east longitude, and g is the acceleration due to gravity. For a hypothetical solid Earth, h=0. For a liquid Earth, one would expect h=1. However, the deformation of the sphere causes the potential field to change and thereby deform the sphere even more. The theoretical maximum is h=2.5. For the real earth, h lies between these values.

The Love number k is defined as the cubical dilation or the ratio of the additional potential (self-reactive force) produced by the deformation of the deforming potential. It can be represented as

$kV(\theta,\phi)/g$, where $k=0$ for a rigid body.

The Love number l represents the ratio of the horizontal (transverse) displacement of an element of mass of the planet's crust to that of the corresponding static ocean tide.[2] In potential notation, the transverse displacement is $l\nabla(V(\theta,\phi))/g$, where ∇ is the horizontal gradient operator as with h and k, $l=0$ for a rigid body.

Unit: Dimensionless

LUMINANCE

Symbol: L; Occasionally L_v

Definition: That property by virtue of which a surface emits more or less light in the direction of view. For sources of light, it is defined as the luminous intensity *I* per unit projected area.

$$L = dt/dA. \cos \vartheta$$

Where *A* is the area, and ϑ is the angle between the surface and the specified direction

For illuminated surfaces, it is defined as the illuminance E per unit solid angle.

$L = dE/d\Omega$

The illuminance is taken over an area perpendicular to the direction of the incident radiation.

An alternative definition, used by engineers (but deprecated), is the luminance, whatever the direction from which it is viewed.

$L = \rho l$ (where ρ is the reflexion coefficient)

Unit: Nit (candela per square meter $cd.m^{-2}$)

Dimension: MT^{-3}

Note: The quantity has also been given the deprecated name brightness.

LUMINANCE, ADAPTATION

Definition: The average luminance, or brightness, of objects and surfaces in the immediate vicinity of an observer estimating the visual range.

Also known as *"adaptation brightness"*, *"adaptation illuminance,"* *"adaptation level,"* *"field brightness,"* and *"field luminance."*

LUMINANCE EQUIVALENT

Definition: The luminance of light at a colour temperature of a full (i.e., planckian) radiator at the temperature of solidification of platinum, which specified conditions has a luminosity equal to that of the light considered.

Unit: Nit

Dimension: L^{-2} F

Note: 1. The quantity equivalent luminance is required for coloured lights at low luminance because of the Purkinje effect: a comparison of the luminosities of differently coloured sources depends on the luminance level of the sources, particularly below about 10 nits.

2. The temperature of solidification of platinum = 2045K

LUMINANCE FACTOR

Definition: The luminance of a body when illuminated and observed under certain conditions divided by that of a perfect diffuser under identical conditions.

Unit: There are no units or dimensions

Note: The luminance factor depends on the angle of incidence, mode illumination and spectral composition of the incident light.

LUMINESCENCE

Definition: Light emission that cannot be attributed merely to the temperature of the emitting body but results from such causes as chemical reactions at ordinary temperatures, electron bombardment, electromagnetic radiation, and electric field.

LUMINOSITY

1. Definition

The attributes of visual perception are such that an area appears to emit more or less light. The luminosity depends on the power emitted by the source, i.e., on the radiant flux, but also on the fact that the sensitivity of the eye varies for different wavelengths. Radiant quantities are pure physical quantities based on absolute energy measurements, whereas luminous quantities depend on some judgment of brightness by an observer and, thus, on the spectral sensitivity of the eye. By using methods of hetechromatic photometry, it is possible to compare the radiant flux of light at one wavelength with that at a different wavelength to get the one which produces the same luminous sensation.

2. *Symbol*: L

Definition: The intrinsic or absolute brightness of a star or other celestial body. It is the total energy radiated per second from the body for a body of radius R and effective temperature T_e.

$$L = 4\,\pi\,R^2\,\sigma\,T_e^4$$

Where σ is Stefan- Boltzmann constant

Note: 1. The effective temperature of the surface is the temperature of a black body having the same radius and radiating the same total energy per unit area per second as the body.

Unit: Nit

Dimension: $L^{-2}F$

LUMINOUS

Definition: a qualifying adjective denoting physical quantities used in photometry in which energies of light are evaluated by an observer. They are distinguished, usually from their corresponding radiant quantities, by adding a subscript *v* (for visual) to their symbols.

LUMINOUS EFFICACY

A property relating luminous flux for radiation or for a source

1. **For Radiation**

   Symbol: K

   Definition: The ratio of the luminous flux Φ_v of radiation to its radiant flux Φ_e:

   $$K = \Phi_v/\,\Phi_e$$

   Note: see "*luminous efficacy spectral*" for monochromatic radiation

2. **For a source**

   Symbol: η

   Definition: The ratio of the luminous Φ emitted by a source to the power P consumed by the source

   $$= \Phi/P$$

Unit: Lumen per watt (lm/W) (In IS base units: $cd.sr.kg^{-1}.m^{-1}.s^3$)

Dimension: $M^{-1}L^{-2}T^3F$

LUMINOUS EFFICACY, SPECIAL

Symbol: K_λ

Definition: it is the luminous efficacy if monochromatic radiation is considered. It is defined as the ration of the luminous flux at a given wavelength. $\Phi_{v,\lambda}$ of radiation to its corresponding radiant flux $\Phi_{e,\lambda}$:

$$K_\lambda = \Phi_{v,\lambda} / \Phi_{e,\lambda}$$

Unit: Lumen per watt (lm/W) (In IS base units: cd.sr.kg^{-1}.m^{-1}.s^3)

Dimension: M^{-1}L^{-1}T^3 F

Note: the quantity can be measured for the complete visual wavelength range

LUNDQUIST NUMBER

Symbol: S

Definition: In plasma physics, the Lundquist number (denoted by S) is a dimensionless ratio that compares the timescale of an Alfvén wave crossing to the timescale of resistive diffusion. It is a special case of the magnetic Reynolds number when the Alfvén velocity is the typical velocity scale of the system and is given by

$$S = \frac{L v_A}{\eta}$$

Where L is the typical length scale of the system, η is the magnetic diffusivity , and vA is the Alfvén velocity of the plasma.

High Lundquist numbers indicate highly conducting plasmas, while low Lundquist numbers indicate more resistive plasmas. Laboratory plasma experiments typically have Lundquist numbers between 102−108, while in astrophysical situations, the Lundquist number can be greater than 1020. Considerations of Lundquist number are especially important in magnetic reconnection.

Unit: Dimensionless

M

MACH NUMBER

Symbol: Ma: sometimes N_{ma}

Definition: a dimensionless number being the ratio of the relative velocity of a body in a fluid, v, to the local speed of sound v_s in the fluid.

$$Ma = v/v_s$$

Alternatively, it is defined, in aerodynamics, as the ration of the speed of an object compared with the speed of sound in the same medium.

Unit: There are no units or dimensions

Note: 1. The name of the number is after the Austrian scientist E. Mach (1838-1916), who used it for the first time in 1887.

   2. A Mach number in excess of 1 indicates a supersonic velocity; in excess of 5, it is said to be hypersonic.

3. The Mach number appears in all problems of flow in which compressibility is importance. The resistance to motion of a body moving at high speed in a fluid of small viscosity is, in general, a function of both Mach and Reynolds numbers. The latter is of higher value, and compressibility is of more importance than viscosity.

Field of application: gas dynamics (compressible flow; dimensionless velocity)

Unit: Dimensionless

See also "Alfven number."

MACH NUMBER, MAGNETIC

Symbol: M_{ma}

Definition: a dimensionless number equal to the ratio of the velocity of fluid v to the velocity of Alfven waves v_a in fluid

$$M_{ma} = v / v_a$$

Unit: There are no units or dimensions

Note: Alfven wave is a hydromagnetic shear wave which moves along magnetic field lines, a major accelerative mechanism of charged particles in plasma physics and astrophysics. For fluid of density ρ and magnetic field strength B_v, the Alfven speed v_a is:

$v_a = B_v / \sqrt{\rho\mu}$, where μ is the magnetic permeability

MAGNETIC REYNOLDS NUMBER

Symbol: R_m

Definition: The **magnetic Reynolds number** (R_m) is the magnetic analogue of the Reynolds number, a fundamental dimensionless group that occurs in magneto hydrodynamics. It gives an estimate of the relative effects of the advection or induction of a magnetic field by the motion of a conducting medium, often a fluid, to magnetic diffusion. It is typically defined by:

$$R_m = \frac{UL}{\eta} \sim \frac{\text{induction}}{\text{diffusion}}$$

where

- U is a typical velocity scale of the flow
- L is a typical length scale of the flow
- η is the magnetic diffusivity

The mechanism by which the motion of a conducting fluid generates a magnetic field is the subject of dynamo theory. When the magnetic Reynolds number is very large, however, diffusion and the dynamo are less of a concern, and in this case, focus instead often rests on the influence of the magnetic field on the flow.

Unit: Dimensionless

MAGNETISATION

Symbols: M; Occasionally H_i

Definition: The magnetic polarization J divided by the magnetic constant μ_0.

$$M = B/\mu_o - H$$

i.e., it is the difference between the ratio of the magnetic density B/μ_o and the magnetic field strength H

Unit: Ampere per meter

Dimension: $L^{-1}I$

Note: in case of an unrationalised system

$$M^* = 4\,\mu_o M; \qquad M^* = (B/\mu_o^*) - H^*$$

MAGNETOMOTIVE FORCE

Symbols: F; sometimes F_m

Definition: The magnetomotive force acting in any closed path in a magnetic field is the line integral of the magnetic field strength H around the path

$$F = \oint H\,dx \quad (\,x = \text{distance})$$

Unit: Ampere- turn

Dimension: 1

MANNING ROUGHNESS COEFFICIENT (also GAUCKLER–MANNING COEFFICIENT)

Symbol: ***n***

Definition: The **Manning formula** or **Manning's equation** is an empirical formula estimating the average velocity of a liquid flowing in a conduit that does not completely enclose the liquid, i.e., open channel flow. However, this equation is also used for calculation of flow variables in case of flow in partially full conduits, as they also possess a free surface like that of open channel flow. All flow in so-called open channels is driven by gravity.

It was first presented by the French engineer Philippe Gaspard Gauckler in 1867 and later re-developed by the Irish engineer Robert Manning in 1890. Thus, the formula is also known in Europe as the Gauckler–Manning formula or Gauckler–Manning–Strickler formula (after Albert Strickler).

The Gauckler–Manning formula is used to estimate the average velocity of water flowing in an open channel in locations where it is not practical to construct a weir or flume to measure flow with greater accuracy. Manning's equation is also commonly used as part of a numerical step method, such as the standard step method, for delineating the free surface profile of water flowing in an open channel.

The Gauckler–Manning formula states:

$$V = \frac{k}{n} R_h{}^{2/3}\, S^{1/2}$$

Where:

- V is the cross-sectional average velocity (L/T; ft/s, m/s);
- n is the **Gauckler–Manning coefficient**. Units of n are often omitted; however n is not dimensionless, having units of: ($T/[L^{1/3}]$; $s/[ft^{1/3}]$; $s/[m^{1/3}]$).
- R_h is the **hydraulic radius** (L; ft, m);
- S is the stream slope or hydraulic gradient, the linear hydraulic head loss (L/L); it is the same as the channel bed slope when the water depth is constant. ($S = h_f / L$).
- k is a conversion factor between SI and English units. It can be left off as long as you make sure to note and correct the units in the n term. If you leave n in the traditional SI units, k is just the dimensional analysis to convert to English. $k = 1$ for SI units, and $k = 1.49$ for English units. (Note: $(1\ m)^{1/3}/s = (3.2808399\ ft)^{1/3}/s = 1.4859\ ft^{1/3}/s$)

Field of application: open channel flow (flow driven by gravity)

Unit: Units of n are often omitted. However, n is not dimensionless, having units of: ($T/[L^{1/3}]$; $s/[ft^{1/3}]$; $s/[m^{1/3}]$).

MARANGONI NUMBER

Symbol: Ma

Definition: The **Marangoni number** (**Ma**) is, as usually defined, the dimensionless number that compares the rate of transport due to Marangoni flows with the rate of transport of diffusion. The Marangoni effect is flow of a liquid due to gradients in the surface tension of the liquid. Diffusion is of whatever is creating the gradient in the surface tension. Thus as the Marangoni number compares flow and diffusion timescales, it is a type of Péclet number. The Marangoni number is defined as:

A common example is surface tension gradients caused by temperature gradients. Then the relevant diffusion process is that of thermal energy (heat). Another is surface gradients

$$Ma = \frac{\text{advective transport rate, due to surface tension gradient}}{\text{diffusive transport rate, of source of gradient}}$$

caused by variations in the concentration of surfactants, where the diffusion is now that of surfactant molecules.

The number is named after Italian scientist Carlo Marangoni, although its use dates from the 1950s, and it was neither discovered nor used by Carlo Marangoni.

The Marangoni number for a simple liquid of viscosity μ with a surface tension change $\Delta\gamma$ over a distance L parallel to the surface can be estimated by the equation:

$$Ma = \frac{uL}{D} = \frac{\Delta\gamma L}{\mu D}$$

Or

$$Mg = -\frac{d\sigma}{dT}\frac{L\Delta T}{\eta\alpha}$$

Note that we assume that L is the only length scale in the problem, which in practice implies that the liquid be at least L deep. The transport rate is usually estimated using the equations of Stokes flow, where the fluid velocity is obtained by equating the stress gradient to the viscous dissipation. A surface tension is a force per unit length, so the resulting stress must scale as $\Delta\gamma/L$, while the viscous stress scales as $\mu u/L$, for u the speed of the Marangoni flow. Equating the two, we have a flow speed $u=\Delta\gamma/\mu$. As Ma is a type of Péclet number, it is a velocity times a length, divided by a diffusion constant, D. Here this is the diffusion constant of whatever is causing the surface tension difference.

Field of application: fluid mechanics (Marangoni flow; thermal surface tension forces over viscous forces)

Unit: Dimensionless

MARKSTEIN NUMBER

Symbol: M

Definition: In combustion engineering   and   explosion   studies,   the **Markstein number** characterizes the effect of local heat release of a propagating flame on variations in the surface topology along the flame and the associated local flame front curvature. The dimensionless Markstein number is defined as:

$$\mathcal{M} = \frac{\mathcal{L}}{\delta_L}$$

Where $\mathcal{L}$ is the Markstein length, and δ_L is the characteristic laminar flame thickness. The larger the Markstein length, the greater the effect of curvature on localised burning velocity.

It is named after George H. Markstein (1911—2011), who showed that thermal diffusion stabilized the curved flame front and proposed a relation between the critical wavelength for the stability of the flame front, called the Markstein length, and the thermal thickness of the flame. Phenomenological Markstein numbers with respect to the combustion products are obtained by means of the comparison between the measurements of the flame radii as a function of time and the results of the analytical integration of the linear relation between the flame speed and either flame stretch rate or flame curvature. The burning velocity is obtained at zero stretch, and a Markstein length expresses the effect of the flame stretch acting upon it. Because both flame curvature and aerodynamic strain contribute to the flame stretch rate, there is a Markstein number associated with each of these components.

Field of application: turbulence, combustion (Markstein length to laminar flame thickness)

Unit: Dimensionless

MASS FRACTION

Symbol: *w_i or x*

Definition: In chemistry, the **mass fraction** of a substance within a mixture is the *ratio* w_i (alternatively denoted Y_i) of the *mass m_i* of that substance to the total mass m_{tot} of the mixture. Expressed as a formula, the mass fraction is:

$$w_i = \frac{m_i}{m_{\text{tot}}}.$$

Units: Kilogramme per Kilogramme

Dimension: 1

MASS, MOLAR

See "molar mass."

MASS, REDUCED

Symbol: *m*

Definition: For a system of two particles with masses m_1 and m_2 exerting equal and opposite forces on each other and subject to no external forces, the reduced mass is the mass *m* such that the motion of either particle, with respect to the other as origin, is the same as the motion with respect to a fixed origin of a single particle with mass *m* acted on by the same force. It is given by

$$m = (m_1 . m_2) / (m_1 + m_2)$$

Unit: kilogramme

Dimension: M

MASS, REST

Symbol: *m_o*

Definition: The mass of a particle in a Lorentz reference frame in which it is at rest

Unit: Kilogramme

Dimension: M

MASS EXCESS

Symbol: Δ

Definition: The **mass excess** of a nuclide is the difference between its actual mass m_a, and its mass number A in (unified) atomic mass units m_u.

$$\Delta = m_a - A\, m_u$$

Unit: kilogramme

Dimension: M

See "*atomic mass*," "*mass number*," and "*atomic mass, unified.*"

MASS NUMBER

Symbol: A

Definition: The number of nucleons in the nucleus of a particular atom. It is the number nearest to the atomic mass m_a of a nuclide.

The difference ($m_a - A\, m_u$) is the mass excess, where m_u is the unified atomic mass unit.

Unit: There are no units or dimensions

Note: also known as " nucleon number."

See "*atomic mass unit*, unified" and " *mass excess.* "

MEAN LIFE

Symbol: τ

Definition: 1. The average time for which the unstable nuclei of a radionuclide exist before decaying. It is equal to the decay constant.

$$\tau = T_{1/2}/\, 0.69315$$

Where $T_{1/2}$ is the half-life

2. The average time of survival for elementary particles, ions, etc., in a given medium or a charge in a semiconductor.

Unit: second

Dimension: T

See" *decay constant*" and "*half- life.*"

MECHANICAL ADVANTAGES

Symbol: M

Definition: the load (output force) F_1 moved by a machine during the application of a certain effort (input force) divided by the effort F_2

$$M = F_1/F_2$$

Unit: There are no units or dimensions

See" *effort*"

MIXING RATIO

See "*humidity mixing ratio.*"

MOLAL CONCENTRATION

Is called "molality."

See "*molarity*"

MOLALITY

Symbol: m

Definition: Molar value n of solute divided by mass M of solvent

$$m = n/M$$

Unit: Mole per kilogramme (In SI base units: $kg^{-1}.mol$)

Dimension: $M^{-1}N$

Note: 1. N is used as the dimensional symbol of molar value

2. Also known as "*molal concentration.*"

MOLAL HEAT CAPACITY

See "*heat capacity, molal.*"

MOLAL HEAT CAPACITY, APPARENT

Symbol: Φ_s

Definition: Intensive quantity which expresses excess of heat capacity of the solution above that of pure solvent alone, calculated for one mole of particular solute;

$$\Phi_s = (C_p - n_{solve}.\ C^o_{p.solv})\ /n_s$$

Where: C_P = heat capacity of pure solution,

$\quad C^o_{p,solv}$ = molal heat capacity of pure solvent

$\quad n_{solve}$ = number of moles of solvent

$\quad n_s$ = number of moles of solute.

Unit: Joule per kelvin per mole

Dimension: $L^2MT^{-3}N$

See also *"Heat capacity, molal."*

MOLAL HEAT CAPACITY AT CONSTANT PRESSURE

Symbol: C_P

Definition: The rate of change of molal enthalpy H_m with temperature T under constant pressure p

$$C_p = \left(\frac{\partial Hm}{\partial T}\right)_p$$

Unit: joule per mole degree kelvin

Dimension: $L^2M^3\ T^{-3}\ N^{-1}$

MOLAL HEAT CAPACITY AT CONSTANT VOLUME

Symbol: C_v

Definition: Rate of change of molal internal energy U_m with temperature T under constant volume v

$$C_v = \left(\frac{\partial Um}{\partial T}\right)_v$$

Unit: joule per mole degree kelvin

Definition: $L^2 M T^{-3} N^{-1}$

MOLAR

Definition: a term now restricted in its meaning to "divide by amount of substance". In practice, this means "per mole," e.g., molar volume is the volume per mole.

MOLAR CONCENTRATION

Symbol: C

Definition: **Molar concentration** (also called **molarity, amount concentration** or **substance concentration**) is a measure of the concentration of a chemical species, in particular of a solute in a solution, in terms of the amount of substance per unit volume of solution, i.e., it is the amount of substance per unit volume. In chemistry, the most commonly used unit for molarity is the number of moles per liter, having the unit symbol mol/L.

A solution with a concentration of 1 mol/L is said to be 1 molar, commonly designated as 1 M.

Units: mol per cubic meter

Dimension: $L^{-3} N$

Note: 1. In the SI system, the base unit for molar concentration is mol/m^3. However, this is impractical for most laboratory purposes, and most chemical literature traditionally uses mol/dm^3, which is the same as mol/L.

2. The reciprocal quantity of molar concentration represents the dilution (volume) which can appear in Ostwald's law of dilution.

MOLARITY

Symbol: c

Definition: Molar value n of solute divided by volume V of solvent

$$c = n/V$$

Unit: mole per meter cubed (more general, moles per liter : m^{-3}.mol

Dimension: $L^{-3} N$

Note: N is used as the dimensional symbol of molar value

MOLAR MASS

Symbol: M

Definition: Mass of one mole of given type of particles, i.e., atom, molecules, ion, free radicals, elementary particles, or atomic group. Numerically molar mass is equal to the corresponding relative atomic or molecular mass.

Units: kilogramme per mol

MOLAR POLARIZATION

Symbol: P_m

Definition: a measure of dipole moment inducted by an electric field of unit strength in 1 mole of a substance. It is defined by:

$$P_m = \frac{1}{3\,\varepsilon_o} \cdot N_A \left(\alpha_1 + \alpha_o\right)$$

Where, N_A = Avogadro constant,

α_1 = induced polarizability, α_o = orientation polarizability, ε_0 = permittivity of space

Note: also called "*molecular polarization*"

MOLAR REFRACTION

Symbol: R_m

Definition: Constant characteristic for a given substance and defined by

$$R_m = [(n^2 - 1)/(n^2 + 2)] \, V_m$$

Where: n is the refractive index, and V_m is the molar volume

Unit: Cubic meter per mole (In IS base units: $m^3 \cdot mol^{-1}$)

Dimension: $L^3 N^{-1}$

Note: N is used as the dimensional symbol of molar value

MOLAR VALUE

Symbol: n

Definition: Is the amount of substance and equals to the number of moles present

Unit: Mole

Dimension: A convenient dimensional symbol is N

MOLAR ROTATION

Definition: Quantity equal to the product of specific rotation and 1/100 of molar mass of a given compound.

MOLAR VOLUME

Symbol: V_m

Definition: Volume of substance V divided by amount of substance n

$$V_m = V/n$$

Unit: Cubic meter per mole ($m^3 \cdot mol^{-1}$)

Dimension: $L^3 N^{-1}$

Note: 1. N is used as the dimensional symbol of molar value

2. According to Avogadro's hypothesis, all ideal gases have the same molar volume at the same pressure and temperature. The value at STP (Standard Temperature and Pressure) is $2.241387 \ 10^{-2} \ m^3 mol^{-1}$

3. Molar volume is the reciprocal of molarity

See: "*molarity*"

MOLAR GAS CONSTANT

Symbol: R

Definition: The constant occurring in the equation of state for 1 mole of an ideal gas, namely;

$$pV = RT$$

Where p is the pressure exerted by the gas, V is the molar volume, and T is the temperature.

Unit: Joule per kelvin per mole

Dimension: $ML^2T^{-3}N$

Note: 1. The molar gas constant is related to Boltzmann constant k by the relation:

$$k=R/L$$

Where L is the number of molecules present in one mole of the gas (i.e., the Avogadro constant)

2. The molar gas constant is a universal constant for all gases and equals to:

$$R=8.314510 \ JK^{-1}mol^{-1}$$

3. The molar gas constant equals to two- thirds of the total translational energy of the molecules in 1 mole of a gas at a temperature of 1 kelvin.

MOMENT

Symbol: *M,* sometimes *T* or *N*

Definition: The moment of a force *F* about a point is the vector product of the radius vector *r* from the point to any point on the line of action of the force and the force (i.e., it is the product of the force and its perpendicular distance from the point)

Unit: Newton meter (never joule) (In SI base units: $kg.m^2.s^{-2}$)

Dimension: ML^2T^{-2}

Note:

1. The quantity is more correctly termed the *"moment of a force"*. It is also termed the *"moment of a couple"* or, more loosely, couple, also *"torque"*. The *bending moment* is a particular kind of moment.

2. The moment of a system of coplanar forces about an axis perpendicular to the plane containing them is the algebraic sum of the moments of the separate forces about that axis (anticlockwise moments are taken conventionally to be positive and clockwise ones negative)

3. The sum of the moments of a number of vectors with a common origin, about a line, is equal to the moment of their resultant, with the same origin, about that line. The above theorem is called *"Varignon's Theorem."*

4. The term *"moment"* is also used in statistics. The *nth* moment of a distribution *f(x)* about a point x_o is the expected value of $(x\text{-}x_0)^n$, that is, the integral of *$(x\text{-}x_o)^n df(x)$*, where *df(x)* is the probability of some quantity's occurrence. The first moment ($n = 1$) is the mean of the distribution, while the variance may be found in terms of the first and second moments.

MOMENT, ELECTROMAGNETIC

Symbol: m

Definition: a vector associated with a magnet, current loop, particles, or such, whose product with the magnetic flux density *B* is equal to the moment of the force *M* exerted on the system by the field.

$$m \: x \: B = M$$

It is a property possessed by a permanent magnet or current – carrying coil and is used as a measure of magnetic strength. It is the torque experienced when the magnet or coil is set with its axis at right angles to a magnetic field of unit size.

Unit: Ampere meter squared

Dimension: $L\,I$

Note: The quantity is also termed the magnetic moment or the magnetic area moment; it should not be confused with the magnetic dipole moment in which the magnetic field strength *H* is used to calculate the torque.

See *"dipole moment, magnetic."*

MOMENT, MAGNETIC

Definition: 1. The former name of magnetic dipole moment and an alternative name for electromagnetic moment.

See *"dipole moment, magnetic"* and *"moment electromagnetic."*

2. Of a particle

Symbol: μ

Definition: A property of a particle arising from its spin. The electron magnetic moment μ_e is very nearly equal to Bohr magneto μ_B. It has a value 9.284770×10^{-24}

In a system of particles, such as an atom, a particle also has a magnetic moment associated with its orbital motion in the system.

The magnetic moment of an orbital electron of orbital quantum number $l = l$. μ_B

Unit: Ampere meter squared or Joule per second (In SI base units: m^2.A or $J.s^{-1}$)

Dimension: $L^2 I$

MOMENT OF INERTIA (DYNAMIC)

Symbol: I; occasionally, J

Definition: The moment of inertia of a body about an axis is the sum of the products of its elements m_i, and the squares of their distances r_i form the axis:

$$I = \sum m.r_i^2$$

Unit: Kilogramme meter squared

Dimension: ML^2

Note: 1. In the case of continuous body, the summation in the above expression is replaced by integration

2.   The kinetic energy of a body of moment of inertia I rotating about that axis with angular velocity w is $\frac{1}{2} I w^2$, which corresponds to $\frac{1}{2} mv^2$ for the kinetic energy of a body of mass m translated with velocity v

MOMENT, SECOND

(1) SECOND MOMENT OF AREA

Symbol: I or I_a

Definition: The second moment of area of a plane area about an axis in its plane is the sum of the products of its elements of area and the squares of their distances from the axis.

$$I = \sum A_l r_i^2$$

Note: an alternative definition is: The moment of inertia of an imaginary sheet of matter whose mass/unit area is unity and which coincides with and has the same boundaries as the surface considered. Accordingly, it is known as the geometrical moment of inertia.

(2) SECOND POLAR MOMENT OF AREA

Symbol: I_P or J

Definition: the second polar moment of area of a plane area about a point in its plane is the sum of the product of its elements of area A_i and the squares of their distances r_i from the point.

$$I_p = \sum A_I r_i^2$$

Unit: Meter to the fourth power

Dimension: L^4

MOMENTUM, ANGULAR

Symbol: b

1. OF A PARTICLE

Definition: The angular momentum of a particle about a point is the vector product of the radius vector r from the point to the particle and the momentum p of the particle

$$b = r \, x \, p$$

Alternatively, angular momentum is the product of moment of inertia I and angular velocity

$$b = I \, w$$

2. OF A RIGID BODY OR SYSTEM OF PARTICLES

Definition: The algebraic sum of the angular momentum of the individual particles of the body about the same axis

Unit: Kilogramme meter squared per second

Dimension: $M \, L^2 \, T^{-1}$

Note: the quantity is also termed the *"moment of momentum"*

MOMENTUM, KINETIC

Definition: The kinetic momentum of a charged particle of charge e in an electromagnetic field A is the vector given by

$$\text{Kinetic momentum} = p - (e/c) \, A$$

Where p is the momentum, and c is the speed of light

Unit: Kilogramme meter per second

Dimension: M L T^{-1}

MOMENTUM (TRANSLATIONAL or LINEAR)

Symbol: p

Definition: The linear momentum of a particle is the product of mass m and velocity v of the particle.

$$p = mv$$

The linear momentum of a body or of a system of particles is the vector sum of the linear momenta of the individual particles. If a body of mass M is translated with a velocity $\mathbf{V}$, its momentum is:

$$p = M\,V$$

Where M is assumed to be at the centre of gravity of the body

Unit: Kilogramme meter per second

Dimension: $M\,L\,T^{-1}$

Note: The above definition of linear momentum is for nonrelatives particles (or a system of particles). For a single relativistic particle of rest mass m of velocity v, the momentum is

$$p = m\,v\,(1 - v^2/c^2)^{1/2}$$

Where c is the speed of light.

MORTON NUMBER

Symbol: Mo

Definition: In fluid dynamics, the Morton number (Mo) is a dimensionless number used together with the Eötvös number or Bond number to characterize the shape of bubbles or drops moving in a surrounding fluid or continuous phase, c. It is named after Rose Morton, who described it with W. L. Haberman in 1953.

The Morton number is defined as

$$Mo = \frac{g\mu_c^4\,\Delta\rho}{\rho_c^2\sigma^3}$$

where g is the acceleration of gravity, μ_c is the viscosity of the surrounding fluid, ρ_c the density of the surrounding fluid, $\Delta\rho$ the difference in density of the phases, and σ is the surface tension coefficient. For the case of a bubble with a negligible inner density, the Morton number can be simplified to

$$\mathrm{Mo} = \frac{g\mu_c^4}{\rho_c\sigma^3}$$

Field of application: fluid dynamics (determination of bubble/drop shape)

Unit: Dimensionless

MOTION

Definition: Motion of a particle with respect to other particles or objects is its state of continual changing of position with respect to them.

MOTION, RELATIVE

Definition: The displacement, velocity and acceleration of a body with respect to a fixed point on the earth are called *absolute* displacement, velocity and acceleration, respectively. The displacement, velocity and acceleration with respect to the earth are called *relative* displacement, velocity and acceleration, respectively.

Note: 1.   The laws of physics which apply when you are at rest on the earth also apply when you are in any reference frame which is moving at a constant velocity with respect to the earth. For example, you can toss and catch a ball in a moving bus if the motion is in a straight line at a constant speed.

2.   The motion may have a different appearance as viewed from a different reference frame, but this can be explained by including the relative velocity of the reference frame in the description of the motion

MOTION, RECTILINEAR

Definition: Motion along a straight path

MOTION, CURVILINEAR

Definition: Motion along a curved path.

N

NEEL TEMPERATURE

Symbol: T_N.

Definition: Temperature of maximum magnetic susceptibility of antiferromagnetic related to loss of its magnetic ordering.

Unit: Kelvin.

Dimension: There are no dimensions.

Note: Also known as *"Neel point"*, *antiferromagnetic* curie point".

See also *"characteristic temperature"*.

NOISE FACTOR

Definition: The ratio of the total noise power per unit bandwidth at the output of a system N_o, to the portion of the noise power that is due to the input termination N_i, at the standard noise temperature of 290K.

Noise factor = N_o / N_i.

Unit: There are no units or dimensions.

Note: Also known as *"noise figure"*.

NOISE LEVEL

Definition: The intensity of unwanted sound or the magnitude of unwanted current or voltage, averaged over a specified frequency range and time interval and weighted with frequency in a specified manner.

Unit: Decibels relative to a specified reference.

NOISE LEVEL, PERCEIVED

Definition: A quantity measured by the sound pressure level of a reference sound subjectively judged by a listener to be equally noisy. The reference sound consists of a band of random noise of width one-third to one octave centered on a frequency of one thousand hertz.

Unit: Perceived noise decibel.

Dimensions: There are no dimensions.

NORMALITY

Symbol: N

Definition: The number of gramme equivalent of solute divided by the volume of solvent in liters.

Unit: Gramme equivalent per liter.

NUMBER, ATOMIC

Symbol: Z

Definition: The number of protons in the nucleus of an atom or the number of electrons revolving around the nucleus.

Unit: There are no units or dimensions.

Note: 1. The atomic number determines the element's position in the periodic table and its chemical properties.

2. All the isotopes of an element have the same atomic number, although different isotopes have different mass numbers.

See "number, *mass*".

NUMBER DENSITY

Symbol: n

Definition: The number of particles, atoms, molecules, etc., per unit volume.

NUMBER, MAGNETIC

Symbol: $R_M.$

Definition: A dimensionless number used in magneto fluid dynamics, equal to the square root of the magnetic force parameter.

Unit: There are no units or dimensions.

NUMBER, MASS

Symbol: A.

Definition: The number of nucleons in the nucleus of a particular atom. It is the number nearest to the atomic mass, m_a, of a nuclide. The difference $(m_a\text{-}Am_u)$ is the "mass excess", where m_u is the unified atomic mass unit.

Unit: There are no units or dimensions.

NUMBER, NEUTRON

Symbol: N.

Definition: The number of neutrons present in the nucleus of an atom. The neutron number is obtained by subtracting the atomic number Z from the mass number A.

$$N = A - Z$$

Unit: There are no units or dimensions.

NUSSELT NUMBER

Symbol: Nu.

Definition: This is a dimensionless coefficient used in fluid dynamics to describe the heat transfer between a moving fluid and a solid surface, given by;

The Nusselt number is the ratio of convective to conductive heat transfer across a boundary. The convection and conduction heat flows are parallel to each other and to the surface normal of the boundary surface and are all perpendicular to the mean fluid flow in the simple case.

$$Nu_L = \frac{\text{Convective heat transfer}}{\text{Conductive heat transfer}} = \frac{h}{k/L} = \frac{hL}{k}$$

Where h is the convective heat transfer coefficient of the flow, L is the characteristic length, and k is the thermal conductivity of the fluid.

- Selection of the characteristic length should be in the direction of growth (or thickness) of the boundary layer; some examples of characteristic length are the outer diameter of a cylinder in (external) cross-flow (perpendicular to the cylinder axis), the length of a vertical plate undergoing natural convection, or the diameter of a sphere. For complex shapes, the length may be defined as the volume of the fluid body divided by the surface area.

- The thermal conductivity of the fluid is typically (but not always) evaluated at the film temperature, which for engineering purposes may be calculated as the mean-average of the bulk fluid temperature and wall surface temperature.

In contrast to the definition given above, known as the *average Nusselt number*, the local Nusselt number is defined by taking the length to be the distance from the surface boundary to the local point of interest.

$$\mathrm{Nu}_x = \frac{h_x x}{k}$$

The *mean*, or *average*, number is obtained by integrating the expression over the range of interest, such as:

$$\overline{\mathrm{Nu}} = \frac{\frac{1}{L}\int_0^L h_x\, dx\, L}{k} = \frac{\bar{h}L}{k}$$

Unit: There are no units or dimensions.

Note: 1. The number is called also **Biot number** after J.B.Biot (1774-1864), the first scientist to express slaws of conviction in a mathematical form.

2. In 1933, the number was named after the German Engineer W. Nusselt, who derived it in 1905.

See also "Nusselt number for mass floow".

NUSSELT NUMBER FOR MASS FLOW

Symbol: Nu*

Definition: A dimensionless number used in mass transfer problems is given by:

$$Nu^* = ml/t\,A\,\rho\,D,$$

Where: m is the mass transferred across an area A in time t, ρ is the diffusion coefficient, and l is a typical dimension of the body.

Unit: there are no units or dimensions.

See also *"Nusselt number"*.

O

OCTANE NUMBER

Definition: A number used in automobile engineering to describe the "anti-knock" properties of spark ignition engine fuel and is based on the percentage of "anti-knock" components in a standard fuel. It is defined as the percentage by volume of trimethypentane *(Iso-Octane)*, which must be blended with *n* heptane to give the mixture the same "anti-knock" characteristics as the petrol (gasoline) under test.

Units*: There are no units or dimensions.

Note: 1.   The octane number was proposed in 1927 and was defined by the American Society for Testing Materials (ASTM) in 1934.

2. In 1956, a suggestion was made and approved by the ASTM to extend the scale to octane numbers above 100 by adding tetra –ethyl-lead to the *iso*-octane.

3. High-compression spark ignition engines need petrol with an octane number of 85 or more for efficient performance.

4. The **cetane number** is used with compression ignition (diesel) engines.

See also ***"cetane number"***.

OHNESORGE NUMBER

Symbol: Oh

Definition: The **Ohnesorge number (Oh)** is a dimensionless number that relates the viscous forces to inertial and surface tension forces. The number was defined by Wolfgang von Ohnesorge in his 1936 doctoral thesis.

It is defined as:

$$Oh = \frac{\mu}{\sqrt{\rho \sigma L}} = \frac{\sqrt{We}}{Re} \sim \frac{\text{viscous forces}}{\sqrt{\text{inertia} \cdot \text{surface tension}}}$$

Where

- μ is the dynamic viscosity of the liquid
- ρ is the density of the liquid
- σ is the surface tension
- L is the characteristic length scale (typically drop diameter)
- Re is the Reynolds number
- We is the Weber number

Field of application: fluid dynamics (atomization of liquids, Marangoni flow)

Unit: Dimensionless

OPACITY

Definition: The light flux incident upon a medium E_0, divided by the light flux transmitted by the medium E_1. It is the reciprocal of the transmission coefficient τ.

$$\text{Opacity} = E_0 / E_1 = 1/\tau$$

Unit: There are no units or dimensions.

Note: Opacity is a measure of the ability of a solid, liquid, or gaseous body to absorb radiation.

OPTICAL ACTIVITY

See *"activity"*

P

PACKING DENSITY

1. Electronics:

- The number of elements within a given area of an integrated circuit.

- The amount of information a given storage medium, such as a tape or magnetic drum, can hold.

2. Computer programming:

The number of bits or storage cells per unit length, area, or volume on a storage medium; for example, the number of characters per track on a magnetic disk.

PACKING FRACTION

Symbol*: f*

Definition: A measure of the stability of an atomic nucleus, given by the ratio of the mass defect to the atomic number. If M_i is the isotopic weight and A is the atomic number:

$$\text{Packing fraction} = (M_i - A)\,/A$$

Unit: There are no units or dimensions.

PARTIAL PRESSURE (of Substance B)

Symbol*: PB*

Definition: The pressure of an individual gas B that additively contributes to the total pressure in a gas mixture.

Unit: Pascal

Dimension: $L^{-1} MT^{-2}$

PÉCLET NUMBER

Symbol: *Pe*

Definition 1: In continuum mechanics

In continuum mechanics, the **Péclet number** (**Pe**, after Jean Claude Eugène Péclet) is a class of dimensionless numbers relevant in the study of transport phenomena in a continuum. It is defined to be the ratio of the rate of advection of a physical quantity by the flow to the rate of diffusion of the same quantity driven by an appropriate gradient.

Definition 2: In the context of species or mass transfer, the Péclet number is the product of the Reynolds number and the Schmidt number

$$Pe = (Re \times Sc).$$

Definition 3: In the context of the thermal fluids, the thermal Péclet number is equivalent to the product of the Reynolds number and the Prandtl number

$$Pe = (Re \times Pr).$$

The Péclet number is defined as:

$$Pe = \frac{\text{advective transport rate}}{\text{diffusive transport rate}}$$

For mass transfer, it is defined as:

$$Pe_L = \frac{Lu}{D} = Re_L\, Sc$$

Such ratio can also be re-written in terms of times as a ratio between the characteristic temporal intervals of the system:

$$Pe_L = \frac{u/L}{D/L^2} = \frac{L^2/D}{L/u} = \frac{\text{diffusion time}}{\text{convection time}}$$

For $Pe_L \gg 1$ diffusion happens in a much longer time compared to convection, and therefore, the latter of the two phenomena predominates in mass transport.

For heat transfer, the Péclet number is defined as:

$$Pe_L = \frac{Lu}{\alpha} = Re_L\, Pr.$$

Where L is the characteristic length, u the local flow velocity, D the mass diffusion coefficient, Re is the Reynolds number, Sc is the Schmidt number, Pr is the Prandtl number, and α is the thermal diffusivity, $\alpha = \dfrac{k}{\rho c_p}$

where k is the thermal conductivity, ρ the density, and c_p is the specific heat capacity.

Notes:

1. In engineering applications, the Péclet number is often very large. In such situations, the dependency of the flow upon *downstream* locations is diminished, and variables in the flow tend to become 'one-way' properties. Thus, when modeling certain situations with high Péclet numbers, simpler computational models can be adopted.

2. A flow will often have different Péclet numbers for heat and mass. This can lead to the phenomenon of double-diffusive convection.

3. In the context of particulate motion, the Péclet number has also been called **Brenner number**, with symbol **Br**, in honor of Howard Brenner.

4. The Péclet number also finds applications beyond transport phenomena as a general measure for the relative importance of the random fluctuations and of the systematic average behavior in mesoscopic systems

Note: 1. Also known as ***"diffusion number"***.

2. The name is after J.C.Peclet (1793-1857), who was the first to apply Fourier's ideas of thermal conductivity to engineering problems.

Field of application: fluid mechanics (ratio of advective transport rate over molecular diffusive transport rate), heat transfer (ratio of advective transport rate over thermal diffusive transport rate)

Unit: Dimensionless

See also *"Diffusion number"*, *"Reynolds number,"* and *"Schmidt number*

PÉCLET NUMBER OF MASS TRANSFER

Symbol*: Pe**

Definition*: The product of "Reynolds number *Re* and Schmidt number *Sc*.

$Pe^* = Re.Sc$

Alternatively, it is defined as the ratio of velocity *v* times a length dimension *l* divided by diffusion coefficient D.

$Pe^* = v\, l\, /\, D$

Note: This number is used in mass transfer problems.

Unit: There are no units or dimensions.

PELTIER COEFFICIENT

Symbol: α_ρ

Definition: Heat energy E liberated or absorbed at a thermoelectric junction (junction of two metals in the Peltier effect) divided by the charge Q flowing through the junction.

$$\alpha_\rho = E/Q$$

Unit: Joule per coulomb: volt. (In SI base units: $kg.m^2.s^{-3}.A^{-1}$)

Dimension: $L^2 \, M \, T^{-3} \, I^{-1}$

Note: Peltier effect: heat is liberated or absorbed at the junction of two dissimilar metals carrying a small current, depending upon the direction of the current.

PERIOD

Definition: A distinct and identifiable length of time; specific uses include:

1. **In physics**:

Symbol: T

Definition: the duration of a single repetition of a cyclic phenomenon. It is related to the frequency f by the relation:

$$T = 1/f.$$

2. **In mathematics**:

Definition: A number T such that $f(x+T) = f(x)$ for all values of x, where $f(x)$ is a specified function of a real or complex variable.

Also, the period of an element α of a group G is the smallest positive integral n such that α^n is the identity element. If there is no such integral, α is said to be an infinity period.

3. **In nuclear physics:**

Definition: The time required for exponentially rising or falling neutron flux in a nuclear reactor to change by a factor of e (2.71828).

4. **In Astronomy**:

a. The interval of time between two phases of a periodic event.

b. The interval between successive times of maximum brightness or minimum brightness of a variable star.

Note: In chemistry, the period is not related to time but is defined as a series of elements that form a horizontal row across the periodic table in order of increasing atomic number, beginning with alkali metal and exhibiting α steady trend toward the last element, a noble gas.

PERMEABILITY

1. **In Electromagnetic**:

   Definition: is a general term used to express various relationships between magnetic flux density and magnetic field strength. These relationships are either *"absolute permeability"* or *"relative permeability."*

   See *"permeability, absolute," "permeability, relative," and "magnetic constant."*

2. **In fluid mechanics**:

   The ability of a membrane or other material to permit a substance to pass through. Quantitatively, the amount of substance that passes through the material under a given condition. See *"permeability coefficient."*

PERMEABILITY, ABSOLUTE

Symbol: μ

Definition: Magnetic flux density B divided by magnetic field strength H.

$\mu = B/H$

Unit: Henry per meter (In SI base unit: $kg.m.s^{-2}A^{-2}$)

Dimension: $L\ M\ T^{-2}\ I^{-2}$

Note: 1. The absolute permeability of free space (vacuum) is known as *"magnetic constant"* and is given the symbol μ_o

2. For unrationalized system: $\mu^* = B/H^*$

See *"magnetic constant."*

PERMEABILITY, RELATIVE

Symbol: μ_r

Definition: Absolute permeability divided by the magnetic constant.

$\mu_r = \mu/\mu_o$

Unit: There are no units or dimensions.

Note: For most substances, the relative permeability has a constant value. If it is less than unity, the material is diamagnetic; if it exceeds unity, the material is paramagnetic. Ferromagnetic materials have high permeabilities, which are not constant but vary with the field strength.

PERMEABILITY COEFFICIENT

Definition: [Fluid mechanics] The rate of water flow in gallons per day through a cross-section of 1 square foot under a unit hydraulic gradient at the prevailing temperature or at 60^0F (16^0C).

Unit: Gallon per day per square foot.

Dimension: L T^{-1}

Note: Also known as *"coefficient of permeability," "hydraulic conductivity,"* and *" Meinzer unit"*

PERMEANCE

Symbol: P; Sometimes P_m

Definition: The reciprocal of reluctance R

$$P = 1/R$$

Unit: Henry (In SI base units: $kg.m^2.s^{-2}.A^{-2}$)

Dimension: $L^2 MT^{-2}I^{-2}$

Note: Fore unrationalized system: $P^* = 1/R^*$

PERMITTIVITY, ABSOLUTE

Symbol: ε

Definition: Electric displacement **D** in a dielectric medium divided by the applied electric field strength **E**

$$\varepsilon = D/E$$

Unit: Farad per meter (In SI base units: $kg^{-1}.m^{-3}.s^4.A^2$)

Dimension: $L^{-3} M^{-1} T^4 I^2$

Note: 1.   The permittivity indicates the degree to which the medium can resist the flow of electric charge.

2.   The absolute permittivity of free space (vacuum) is called *"electric constant"* and is given the symbol ε_o. Its value is 8.84187817 x 10^{-12} Fm^{-1}

3.   For unrationalized system $\varepsilon^* = D^*/E$

4.   The quantity is also occasionally termed the *"capacitivity."*

PERMITTIVITY, COMPLEX

Symbol: ε^*

Definition: For the material of permittivity ε and dielectric loss ε', the complex permittivity is defined by:

$$\varepsilon^* = \varepsilon - i\,\varepsilon'$$

Where $i = \sqrt{-1}$

PERMITTIVITY, RELATIVE

Symbol: ε_r

Definition: The relative permittivity of any homogeneous isotropic material is the ratio of the capacitance of a given configuration of the electrodes with the material as a dielectric to the capacitance of the same electrode configuration with a vacuum as the dielectric. It is equal to the absolute permeability ε divided by the magnetic constant. ε_o

$$\varepsilon_r = \varepsilon/\varepsilon_{o.}$$

Unit: There are no units or dimensions.

Note:

1. The quantity is known as *"relative capacity"*, *"dielectric constant,"* and *"specific inductive capacitance."*

2. The value of the relative permittivity varies from unity for vacuum to over 4000 for ferroelectric materials but normally does not exceed 10.

pH VALUE

Definition: A logarithmic measure of the hydrogen ion (or hydroxonium, H_3O^+) concentration of a solution. It is the negative logarithm (base 10) of the hydrogen ion (or hydroxonium ion, H_3O^+) concentration in gram-ions (moles) per liter.

Unit: There are no units or dimensions.

Note: If the pH is greater than 7, the solution is alkaline, and if it is less, the solution is acid.

$$pH = log_{10}\{H^+\}$$

$\{H^*\}$	1	10^{-1}	10^{-2}	....	10^{-7}	....	10^{-12}	10^{-13}	10^{-14}
pH	0	1	2	...	7	..	12	13	14
		Acid			Neutral		Alkaline		

PHASE

1. CASE OF PERIODIC SYSTEM

Definition: The fraction of the whole period that has elapsed, measured from some fixed datum.

Note:

a.   A quantity that varies sinusoidally may be represented by a rotating vector, whose amplitude is proportional to the peak value of the quantity, and it rotates through 360^0 about the origin during one period T.

b.   For two quantities that have the same frequency, the angle between the two rotating vectors representing them is called the phase angle.

c.   Periodic quantities having the same frequency and the same waveform are said to be in phase if they reach corresponding values simultaneously (zero phase angle); otherwise they are said to be out of phase. If the waveforms are not alike but have the same fundamental frequency, these terms are used in connection with the fundamental components of the waveforms.

2. POLYPHASE SYSTEMS

Definition: One of the separate circuits or windings of a polyphase system, machine, or other apparatus.

Also, it refers to one of the lines or terminals of a polyphase system.

3. GENERAL PHYSICS

Definition: Any homogenous and physically distinct part of a system that is separated by definite bounding surfaces from other parts of the system; e.g., the various crystalline forms of ice, water, and water vapor are phases of the water system.

See also *"phase difference"* and *"phase angle"*

PHASE ANGLE

Symbol: $\emptyset$

Definition: The angle between the two vectors that represent two sinusoidal alternating quantities having the same frequency. The term may be used in connection with periodic quantities that are not sinusoidal but that have the same fundamental frequency, and it is then the angle between the vectors representing their fundamental components.

Units: Radian or degree.

Note: In astronomy, the phase angle is the angle formed by the earth and sun when viewed from the moon or another object.

See also *"phase"* and *"phase difference"*.

PHASE COEFFICIENT

See *"attenuation coefficient."*

PHASE DIFFERENCE

Symbol: ϕ

Definition: The difference of phase between two sinusoidal quantities that have the same frequency.

Unit: It may be expressed as a time (second) or an angle (radian or degree)

Note: If the phase difference is expressed in terms of angle, it is called *"phase angle."*

See also "Loss angle" and "phase angle"

PHASE DISPLACEMENT

See *"angle"* (note 2)

Pi

Symbol: π

Definition: The ratio of the length of the circumference of a circle to its diameter

Unit: There are no units or dimensions

Note: 1. The symbol π was first used in this sense by the English writer William Jones in 1706

2. Ancient approximations to π include

3	Old Testament
25/8	Babylonian
256/81	Egyptian
22/7	Greek
355/113	Chinese, and
$\sqrt{10}$	Indian

3. In 1429, the Arabian mathematician Al-Kashi calculated a value of π correct up to 16 decimal places

4. Pi was proved to be irrational by Lambert in 1767 and transcendental by Lindemann in 1882.

PITCH

1. **Acoustics**

Definition: That psychological property of sound characterized by highness or lowness, depending primarily upon the frequency of the sound stimulus but also upon its sound pressure and waveform. *(see also " frequency")*

2. **Mechanics**

Definition: The angular displacement of a body about a transverse horizontal axis parallel to the lateral axis of the body.

i)   The pitch of an aerospace vehicle is the angular displacement about an axis parallel to the lateral axis of the vehicle.

ii)   Also, it is the rising and falling motion of the bow of a ship or the tail of an aero plane as the craft oscillates about a transverse axis.

iii)   Also, it is the distance apart of successive threads or of successive teeth of a gear wheel.

3. **In engineering**

Definition: It is the inclination or degree of slope of an object or structure

Also, the distance between successive elements arranged similarly between two points on a surface or part, such as the grooves that separate tracks of a disk recording or the threads of a screw.

Also: the pitch of a helix is the amount by which a point on the helix is displaced, in a direction parallel to the axis, in making one revolution about the axis.

4. **In Robotics**

Definition: The vertical wrist movement in a robotic arm.

5. **In Graphic Arts**

Definition: The pitch on a typewriter or in a given printing font is a unit of width expressing the number of characters that will fit in one-inch space.

PLANCK CONSTANT

Symbol: h

Definition: A universal constant having the value 6.626076×10^{-34}

Units: joule second (In SI base units: $kg.m^2.s^{-1}$)

Dimension: $L^2 M T^{-1}$

PLANCK CONSTANT, RATIONALIZED

Symbol: $\hbar$ (called "crossed h")

Definition: $\hbar = h/2\pi$. It has a value of 1.054573×10^{-34}

Unit: Joule second

Dimension: $L^2 M T^{-1}$

Note: also called "*Dirac constant*"

PLANCK FUNCTION

Symbol: Y

Definition: The negative of the Gibbs function G divided by the thermodynamic temperature T :

$$Y = - G/T$$

Unit: joule per kelvin

Dimension: $L^2 M T^{-3}$

See *"Gibbs function."*

PLANCK LENGTH

Definition: The distance over which quantum fluctuations are theorized to become significant and is given by:

$$\text{Planck length} = (G \hbar/c^3)^{1/2}$$

Where $\hbar$ *is the rationalised* Planck constant, G is the gravitational constant and c is the speed of light. It arises in theories relating quantum theory to gravitation and equals to 1.61599×10^{-35}

Unit: Meter

Dimension: L

PLANCK MASS

Definition: The mass of a particle having reduced Compton wavelength that is equal to the Planck length. It is defined as:

$$\text{Planck length} = (c \hbar/G)^{1/2}$$

Where $\hbar$ is the rationalized Planck constant, G is the gravitational constant, and c is the speed of light. It arises in theories relating quantum theory to gravitation and equals to 2.17684×10^{-8}

Unit: Kilogram.

Dimension: M

See *"Planck length"*,

POISSON'S RATIO

Symbol: μ or v

Definition: The ratio of the transverse contracting strain, $\Delta d / d_o$ (i.e., fractional decrease in diameter Δd from the diameter d_o in a specified reference state) to the tensile strain e, when a rod is stretched by forces which are applied at its ends and which are parallel to the rod's axis

$$\mu = \Delta d / d_o e$$

Unit: There are no units or dimensions.

Note: 1. The quantity is also termed "*Poisson's number*"; it was originally defined (by Poisson) as the reciprocal of the present definition.

2. If the volume of the rod does not change under stretching, Poisson's ratio = 0.5, but the value is often less in practice, being typically 0.3 for a metal.

POLARIZATION, DIELECTRIC

Symbol: ***P***; occasionally ***D***;

Definition: Stress set up in a dielectric due to the existence of an electric field, as a result of which each element of the dielectric functions as an electric dipole. The electric dipole moment per unit volume of a dielectric material is the electric polarization. It is measured through its effect on the flux present in the dielectric. The polarization increases the flux present in the dielectric due to the presence of the latter and is defined as the product of the electric constant ε_0 and the electrization or as the vector quantity defined by the equation:

$$\boldsymbol{P} = (\boldsymbol{D} - \varepsilon_o \boldsymbol{E})$$

where ***D*** is the electric flux density, and ***E*** is the electric field strength.

In the case of an unrationalized system, the relation takes the form: $\boldsymbol{P} = (\boldsymbol{D} - \varepsilon_o \boldsymbol{E})/4\pi$

Unit: Coulomb per meter squared.

Dimension: $L^{-2} T I$

Note: 1. The magnitude of the electric polarization represents the charge density bound at the electrodes by a polarized dielectric.

2. Also known as *"electric polarization,"* and it is important to differentiate it from *"electrical polarization"*.

See "polarization, electrical,"

POLARIZATION ELECTRICAL

Definition*:* Phenomena occur in simple electrolytic cells and cause the fall of the obtained current because of the formation of a gas layer on one of the plates of the cell. Consider a simple cell consisting of two plates in an electrolyte, such as Zn and Cu in dilute H_2SO_4. The copper plate will collect hydrogen bubbles, resulting in the formation of a layer of hydrogen. The gas layer on the plate increases the internal resistance of the cell and also sets up an e.m.f. of opposite direction to the cell. As a result, the current obtained soon falls considerably. To make cells effective for longer periods, some means must be adopted to prevent gas deposition.

POLARIZATION, ELECTRONIC

Symbol*:* P_E

Definition: Measure of electronic polarization defined by:

$$P_E = (1/3\ \varepsilon_o).\ N_A\ \alpha_E$$

where: N_A = Avogadro constant,

α_E = Electronic polarizability, and

ε_o = Permittivity of free space.

POLARIZATION, MAGNETIC

Symbol*:* J; occasionally B_i

Definition*:* The product of the magnetization M and the electric constant μ_o

$$J = \mu_O\ M\ = (B - \mu_O\ H)$$

Unit: Tesla. (In SI base units: $kg.s^{-2}.A^{-1}$)

Dimension: $M\ T^{-2}\ 1^{-1}$

Note: 1. The quantity is also termed the *"intrinsic magnetic flux density, "*

2. For an unrationalized system of units:

$$J* = J / 4\pi; \quad J* = \mu_o * M* / 4\pi$$

POLARIZATION, MOLECULAR

Definition: When a molecule is subjected to an electric field, there is a small displacement of electrical centers that induces a dipole in the molecule. If $m = \alpha E$, where m is the electric dipole moment induced by held strength E, then the constant α is called the *polarizability* of the molecule.

POLE STRENGTH, MAGNETIC

Symbol: m

Definition: It represents the magnitude of a (fictional) magnetic pole and is defined as the force F exerted on the pole, divided by magnetic field strength H

$$m = F/H$$

Unit: Newton meter per ampere. (In SI base units: $kg.m^2.s^{-2}.A^{-1}$)

Dimension: $L^2 M T^{-2} I^{-1}$

Note: 1. For unrationalized units: $m* = F/H*$

2. This quantity is now regarded as associated with an imaginary concept and is no longer employed.

3. Also known as *"Pole Strength"*

POP

Definition: In physics, **pop** is the sixth derivative of the position vector with respect to time, with the first, second, third, fourth, and fifth derivatives being velocity, acceleration, jerk, snap or (jounce), and crackle, respectively; pop is thus the rate of change of the crackle with respect to time.

Unite: meter per sixth power of second ($m.s^{-6}$)

Dimension: $L T^{-6}$

POROSITY

Definition: ***Porosity*** or **void fraction** is a measure of the void (i.e., "empty") spaces in a material and is a fraction of the volume of voids over the total volume, between 0 and 1, or as a percentage between 0% and 100%. Strictly speaking, some tests measure the "accessible void," the total amount of void space accessible from the surface (cf. closed-cell foam).

There are many ways to test porosity in a substance or part, such as industrial CT scanning.

The term porosity is used in multiple fields, including pharmaceutics, ceramics, metallurgy, materials, manufacturing, petrophysics, hydrology, earth sciences, soil mechanics, and engineering.

POTENTIAL

Symbol: Usually $\varphi(r)$.

Definition: The potential at a point in a conservative field, say gravitational or electrostatic field, is the work done in bringing unit mass or unit charge to this point from a point infinitely distance from the cause of the field. Since the fields are conservative, the potential is a function only of the position of a particular point. It varies in magnitude from point to point and, hence a scalar function of position.

Note: The word potential is a Latin word meaning "having power."

See "Potential, gravitational' and "Potential energy."

POTENTIAL, CHEMICAL

Symbol: μ

Definition: Energy per unit change in amount of substance

Unit: J/mol (In SI base units: $kg.m^2.s^{-2}mol^{-1}$)

Dimension: $L^2\,M\,T^{-2}\,N^{-1}$

POTENTIAL, ELECTRIC

Symbol: V

Definition: With a reversed sign, the electric field strength E is given by the rate of change of electric potential with respect to distance x.

$$E = -dV/dx$$

Alternatively, the electric potential is the work W done against an electric field in bringing a charge Q from infinity to its position in the field.

$$V = W/Q$$

Unit: volt (In SI base units: $kg.m^2.s^{-3}.A^{-1}$)

Dimension: $L^2 \, M \, T^{-3} \, I^{-1}$

POTENTIAL, GRAVITATIONAL

Symbol: Ω

Definition: The work done by a gravitational field to bring a unit mass from infinity to its position in the field. In general, if the work W is done to bring mass m from infinity to the point in the field:

$$\Omega = W/m$$

Alternatively, with a reversed sign, the gravitational field strength R is given by the rate of change of gravitational potential with respect to distance x.

$$R = -d\Omega/dx$$

Unit: Joule per kilogram.

Dimensions: $L^2 \, T^{-2}$

Note:

1. The first definition may also be used to define electrostatic and magnetostatic potentials at a point in the field: The work done in bringing the unit positive charge or unit positive pole, respectively, from infinity to the point.

Gravitational potential is always negative, but electrostatic and magnetostatic potentials may be positive or negative.

2. Since these are conservative fields, the gravitational, electrostatic, and magnetostatic potentials are a function only of the position of the point.

3. The difference in potential between two points in the field is the work done in taking the unit

object from one point to the other.

POTENTIAL, INNER ELECTRIC

Symbol: $\emptyset$

Definition: Electrical potential between point in phase and point at infinity

POTENTIAL, KINETIC

Symbol: L.

Definition: An expression for the total minus the potential energy in a conservative system:

$$L = T\,(q_1, q_1') - V\,(q_1, q_1')$$

where q_1 are the generalized coordinates.

Note: Also known as *"Lagarangian function" and "Lagarangian "*.

POTENTIAL, MAGNETIC

Symbol: U

Definition: With a reversed sign, the magnetic field strength H is given by the rate of change of magnetic potential with respect to distance x.

$$H = -\,dU/dx.$$

Unit: Ampere (-turn)

Note: It is the former name of the magnetomotive force.

For unrationalized units: $H^* = -\,dU^*/dx$

POTENTIAL, THERMODYNAMIC

Definition: A measure of the energy level of a system that represents the amount of work obtainable when the system undergoes a change. The main types are: *"Internal energy",* *"Helmholtz function, "Enthalpy," and "Gibbs function".*

See" energy, internal", "Helmholtz function", "Enthalpy," and "Gibbs function",

POTENTIAL, VELOCITY

Symbol: $\emptyset$

Definition: For irrotational motion, it is a scalar function its partial derivatives in the Cartesian coordinates give the velocity components of a fluid.

$$u = \partial\phi/\partial x \quad v = -\partial\phi/\partial y \qquad w = -\partial\phi/\partial z$$

where $u,\ v,\ w$ are the velocity components of the fluid at point $(x,\ y,\ z)$.

Unit: Meter squared per second. $(m^2.s^{-1})$

Dimension: L^2T^{-1}

Note: The negative sign in the definition is conventional and is sometimes omitted.

POTENTIAL DIFFERENCE, ELECTRIC

Symbol: V; sometimes U.

Definition: The potential difference between two points 1 2 in an electric field of strength E is the scalar-product line integral of the electric field strength along any path from 1 to 2

$$V = \int_1^2 E\,dx \qquad (x = \text{distance})$$

Alternatively: The work done W against an electric field when a charge Q moves from one to the other of two points (by any path) divided by the charge.

$$V = W/Q.$$

Unit: Volt. (in SI base units: $kg.m^2.s^{-3}.A^{-1}$)

Dimension: $L^2M\ T^{-3}\ I^{-1}$

Note: 1. The quantity is also termed the voltage or the electric tension.

2. The potential difference between any given point and an agreed-upon reference point, usually the point at infinity, is called the *"electrostatic potential"* of the given point.

POTENTIAL DIFFERENCE: MAGNETIC

Symbol: U_m; sometimes U

Definition: The difference between the magnetic states of two points, 1 and 2, in a magnetic field. It equals the line integral of the magnetic field strength H between the two points.

$$U = \int_{H1}^{H2} H\,dx$$

Where x is a distance.

Unit: Ampere (-turn)

Dimension: I

Note: 1. In the presence of electric current, the line integral is many-valued, and the concept of magnetic potential difference is invalid. It is, however, applicable to regions having boundaries that make it possible for any closed path to link an electric current.

2. For unrationalized units: $U^* = 4\pi U$

POTENTIAL DIFFERENCE, THERMAL

See *"temperature"* (note 3)

POTENTIAL ENERGY

Symbol: V

Definition: Energy is possessed by virtue of position and can be defined only in the conservative field of force. It is the negative value of the work done by a conservative force in displacing a particle from its standard position to any other position. The Zero potential energy is usually the potential energy at a point infinitely distant from the cause of the field. In the case of bodies situated above the earth's surface, the surface is usually taken as the zero of potential energy; for a small object of mass m at an altitude h, the potential energy is:

$$V = m\,g\,h,$$

where g is the acceleration of free fall.

In an isolated system, the total energy T (potential V plus kinetic L) is conserved. In moving from point A to point B, potential energy might be acquired at the expense of kinetic energy. This potential energy is released on returning to A, with an equivalent gain in kinetic energy.

Unit: Newton meter

Dimension: $L^2\,M\,T^{-2}$

See "Potential, Kinetic"

POWER

Symbol: P

Definition: The rate at which energy transferred, or work is done. If energy E transferred in a certain time t:

$$P = E/t$$

Unit: Watt. (In SI base units: $kg.m^2.s^{-3}$)

Dimension: $L^2M\ T^{-3}$

Note: 1. The quantity is also termed (energy) *flux*; it has also been termed *activity*.

2. The thermal equivalent is also termed *"heat flow rate"*. The radiation equivalent is also termed (radian) flux. The photometric equivalent is also termed (luminous) flux. The acoustical equivalent is also termed (sound).

3. In an alternating current circuit where, the potential difference and the current are given by:

$$v = \tilde{V}\cos\omega t, \qquad i = \hat{\imath}\cos(\omega t - \emptyset)$$

Where v and i are the values of the potential difference and current at time t, $\tilde{V}$ and $\hat{\imath}$ are their maximum values, ω is a constant and $\emptyset$ is the phase angle between the current and the voltage.

The following types of power occur:

i.   APPARENT POWER:

Symbol: S or P_s,

Definition: $S = IV$

where I and V are the rms (effective) values of the current and potential difference, respectively.

Unit: Voltampere

ii.   ACTIVE POWER

Symbol: P

Definition: $P = I\,V\cos\emptyset$

Unit: Watt

Dimension: $\mathbf{L^2\ M\ T^{-3}}$

iii. REACTIVE POWER

Symbol: Q or P_p.

Definition: $Q = V I \sin \emptyset$

Unit: var

The three types are related by the equation:

$$S^2 = P^2 + Q^2$$

and the ratio P/S = cos $\emptyset$ is termed the power factor (See "*power factor* ").

4. The term "power" is used in optics, normally called optical power, and has the following meaning:

Definition: The power of a lens, or minor, is the reciprocal of the focal length in meters.

It is generally positive if converging and most commonly applied to the dioptric power of a lens. For mirrors, the term catoptric power is sometimes used. (See "Power, Optical)

POWER, OPTICAL

Symbol: P

Definition: Measure of the effective curvature of a lens or curved mirror; inverse of focal length

Unit: diopter (dpt = m^{-1})

Dimension: L^{-1}

POWER FACTOR

Symbol: F_p

Definition: The ratio of the active power P to the apparent power S

$$F_p = P/S$$

Unit: There are no units or dimensions.

Note: 1. If the voltage and current are sinusoidal, the power factor is equal to the cosine of the phase angle θ between the voltage and current vectors, $F_p = \cos \theta$

2. The power factor is also defined as the ratio of the total watts to the root-mean-square (RMS) volt-amperes of an AC circuit.

See also 'power ".

POWER LEVEL

1.   In Electrical Engineering: See "intensity level"

2.   In Nuclear physics:

Definition: The power production of a nuclear reactor. Unit: Watt

Dimension: $L^2 M T^{-3}$

POWER, THERMOELECTRIC

Symbol: P

Definition: Electromotive force E developed in a thermocouple divided by the difference in temperature ΔT between the junctions.

$$P = E/\Delta T$$

Unit: Volt per kelvin

Dimension: $L^2 M T^{-3} I^{-1}$

POYNTING VECTOR

Symbol: S

Definition: A vector giving the direction and magnitude of energy flow in an electromagnetic field. It is equal to the vector product of the electric field strength E and the magnetic field strength H.

$$S = E \, x \, H$$

At a given point and time, the magnitude of the vector is proportion to the power per unit area, and the direction of the vector indicates the direction of the energy flow at the given point and time.

Unit: Watt per meter squared.

Dimension: $M T^3$.

Note: If the unrationalized magnetic field strength H* is used.

$$S = (E \, x \, H^*)/ \, 4\pi$$

PRANDTL NUMBER

Symbol: *Pr*

Definition: The ratio of the viscosity η of a fluid divided by the density ρ of the fluid times the thermal diffusivity *a*.

$Pr = \eta / \rho \alpha$

The Prandtl number can be defined as the ratio of the molecular diffusivity of momentum to the molecular diffusivity of heat. It may be calculated as follows:

$$Pr = \frac{\text{viscous diffusion rate}}{\text{thermal diffusion rate}} = \frac{\mu C_p}{k}$$

Where:

C_p: Specific heat (J/kg.K)

K: Thermal conductivity of the fluid (W/m.K)

Pr: Prandtl number

μ: Dynamic viscosity of the fluid (kg/m.s)

Small values of the Prandtl number (less than 1) in a given fluid indicate that thermal diffusion occurs at a greater rate than momentum diffusion, and therefore, heat conduction is more effective than convection. Conversely, if the Prandtl number is large (greater than 1), momentum diffuses at a greater rate than heat and convection is more effective than conduction.

The tables below contain some typical Prandtl numbers for air, water and R32gas.

AIR AT 1 BAR

Temperature (K)	Prandtl Number
200	0.738
240	0.724
280	0.710
300	0.705

WATER AT 1 BAR

Temperature (K)	Prandtl Number
280	10.3
300	5.69
320	3.65
340	2.60
380	1.59

DIFLUOROMETHANE (R32) GAS AT 1 BAR

Temperature (K)	Prandtl Number
250	0.908
280	0.860
300	0.842
320	0.836
350	0.831

Field of application: heat transfer (ratio of viscous diffusion rate over thermal diffusion rate)

Unit: There are no units or dimensions.

Note: 1. The number appears in the dimensional analysis of convection in a fluid due to the presence of a hot body.

2. The unit was deduced by Nusselt in 1910 but has been named after L. Prandtl (1875-1953).

3. At 20 °C the Prandtl number lies between 0.67 and 1.0 for gases: for water, it is 6.7, and

it is of the order of thousands for every viscous liquid.

PRESSURE

Symbol: P or p

Definition: Fundamentally intrinsic molecular activity of any substance in either its solid, liquid or vapor state, but principally the latter two. In liquid and vapor it derives from the heat content of the substance since the greater this is, the more pronounced will be a molecular impact on the sides of the vessel containing the substance. Pressure is a uniformly distributed force F acting on the unit area of the surface of any barrier opposing such force and can manifest in potential energy or kinetic energy form. In general, it is the force F divided by the area A over which the force acts uniformly.

$$P = F/A$$

Unit: Pascal (In SI base units: $kg.m^{-1}.s^{-2}$)

Dimension: $L^{-1} M T^{-2}$

Note: 1. The quantity is also termed the stress or, more properly, normal stress; it is then often represented by f. In cases where twisting takes place, the quantity involved is the shear stress q. In the case of the fluids, it is often termed *hydrostatic stress* (or pressure) or bulk stress. The somewhat inappropriate term mechanical tension has also been used.

2. In a liquid, the pressure increases uniformly with depth, h, according to the formula:

$$P = \rho\, g\, h,$$

where ρ is the density of the liquid, and g is the acceleration of free fall.

3. In a gas under isothermal conditions, the pressure decreases exponentially with height h, according to the formula;

$$P_h = P_o\, e^{-\left(\frac{\mu g}{RT}\right)h}$$

Where μ is the relative molecular mass, R is the molar gas constant, and T is the thermodynamic temperature.

PRESSURE, SOUND

Symbol: p.

Definition: The instantaneous value of the periodic portion of the pressure at a particular point in a medium that is transmitting sound. It is that part of the pressure that is due to the propagation of sound in the medium and has an average value of zero over a period of time. The root-mean-square value of the pressure level is often used.

Unit: Pascal.

Dimension: $L^{-1} M T^{-2}$

Note: When referring to the whole range of acoustic waves, the term *"acoustic pressure"* is used instead of sound pressure.

PRESSURE COEFFICIENT

Symbol: β

1.   In Thermodynamics:

Definition: Fractional increase in pressure p of a gas divided by the change in temperature θ under specified conditions.

$$\beta = \frac{\Delta p}{p \Delta \theta} = \frac{1}{p}\frac{dp}{d\theta}$$

Unit: Per kelvin

Dimension: $L^{-2} T^{2}$.

Note: The condition specified is generally constant volume

See also "pressure coefficient, relative. "

2.   In fluid mechanics:

Is the dimensionless quantity defined by:

Pressure coefficient $= (p - p')/ (1/2\ p'\ v'^{2})$

where p is the pressure at a specified point in the flow of fluid around a body, p', ρ', v' are the pressure, density, and fluid velocity far from the body,

Unit: There are no units or dimensions.

Note: It is important to differentiate between the pressure coefficient and pressure loss coefficient.

Field of application:

Aerodynamics, hydrodynamics (pressure experienced at a point on an airfoil; dimensionless pressure variable)

See "pressure loss coefficient."

PRESSURE LEVEL, SOUND

Symbol: L_p

Definition. A dimensionless quantity equals to the natural logarithm of the ratio of the sound pressure, p, to a reference sound pressure, p_o.

$$L_p = \log_e(p/p_0) = \log_e(10) \times \log_{10}(p/p_0)$$

The reference pressure p_o is either stated or taken to be 2×10^{-5} pascals in air or 0.1 pascals in water.

Unit: Decibel or neper

Dimension: There are no dimensions.

Note: 1. If the pressure levels p and p_o are given as root-mean-square values, the definition will be twice the natural logarithm of the ratio of the root-mean-square pressures p and p_o.

2. $Lp = 1\ dB$ when $20 \log_{10}(p/p_o) = 1$

See also. *"intensity level (note 3) "*

PRESSURE LOSS COEFICIENT

Definition: For fluid of density p flowing in a pipe of diameter d with average velocity $\bar{u}$, if the pressure loss over the length l of the pipe is ΔP, then the dimensionless quantity

$d.\ \Delta p / (\frac{1}{2} pu^{-2})\, l$

represents the pressure loss coefficient.

Unit: There are no units or dimensions.

PRINCIPAL SPECIFIC HEAT CAPACITIES RATIO

Symbol: γ.

Definition: Specific heat capacity at constant pressure c_p divided by specific heat capacity at constant volume c_v.

$$\gamma = c_p/c_v$$

Unit: There are no units or dimensions.

PROPAGATION COEFFICIENT

Symbol: γ

Definition: A complex quantity that measures the properties of propagation for a given medium or transmission line at a specific frequency. The real part "α" is the attenuation coefficient (neper per meter), and the imaginary part β is the phase coefficient (radians per meter);

$$\gamma = \alpha + i\beta$$

Note: It is also called ***Propagation Constant.***

See "attenuation coefficient."

PULSITNCE

Symbol: ω

Definition: Angular velocity in radians, equal to $2\pi f$, where f is the frequency in hertz.

See" velocity, angular ".

Q

Q-FACTOR

See "logarithmic decrement" and also "quality factor"

QUALITY FACTOR

Symbol: Q

Definition: 1. is that measure of the quality of a component, network, system, or medium considered as an energy storage unit in the steady state with a sinusoidal driving force, which is given by:

$$Q = \frac{2\pi \text{ (maximum energy in storage)}}{\text{Energy dissipated per cycle of driving force}}$$

2. For single components, such as inductors and capacitors, the quality factor is the ratio of the equivalent series reactance X to the resistance R;

$$Q = |X|/R$$

Unit: There are no units or dimensions.

Note: 1. For networks that contain several elements and for distributed parameter systems, the Q is generally evaluated at a frequency of resonance.

2. For a resonant system such as a cavity resonator, for which values of R, C, and L cannot be specified, the first definition is to be used for getting its quality factor.

3. The *"nonleaded Q"* of a system is the value of Q obtained when only the incidental dissipation of the system elements is present. The *"loaded Q"* of a system is the value of Q obtained when the system is coupled to a device that dissipates energy.

4. The quality factor is also known as the *"storage factor"*, *"Q-factor"*, and *"Q"*

QUANTITY OF ELECTRICITY

Symbol: Q

Definition: The time integral of the electric current I

$$Q = \int I dt$$

It is equivalent to the electric charge.

Unit: Coulomb (Ampere second)

Dimension: T I

QUANTITY OF LIGHT

Symbol: Q.

Definition: The time integral of the luminous flux Φ.

$$Q = \int \Phi dt$$

Unit: Talbot (or lumberg)

Dimension: T F

Note: Called also *"luminous energy "*.

See "energy, luminous ".

R

RADIANCE

(SI radiometry units)

Symbol: L; sometimes L_e, also $L_{e\Omega}$

Definition: The radiance at a point surface in a given direction is the radiant intensity I in the given direction of an infinitesimal element of surface containing the point divided by the orthogonally projected area A of the element in a plane normal to the given direction.

$L = dI/dA$

Also, Radiant flux emitted, reflected, transmitted or received by a *surface*, per unit solid angle per unit projected area.

Unit: watt per steradian per square meter,$(\mathbf{W \cdot sr^{-1} \cdot m^{-2}})$

Dimension $L^{-2}\,T^{-1}\,Q$ or $M.T^{-3}$

Note: 1. The quantity was formerly termed the *steradiancy.*

2. This is sometimes also confusingly called "intensity."

RADIANCE, SPECTRAL: (SI radiometry units)

Symbol*: $L_{e,\Omega,\nu}$ or $L_{e,\Omega,\lambda}$*

Definition: Radiance of a *surface* per unit frequency or wavelength. The latter is commonly measured in $\mathbf{W \cdot sr^{-1} \cdot m^{-2} \cdot nm^{-1}}$.

Notes:

1. This is a *directional* quantity.

2. This is sometimes also confusingly called "spectral intensity".

Units: watt per steradian per square meter per hertz- $W \cdot sr^{-1} \cdot m^{-2} \cdot Hz^{-1}$ *or* watt per steradian per square meter, per meter- $W \cdot sr^{-1} \cdot m^{-3}$

Dimensions: $M \cdot T^{-2}$ *or* $M \cdot L^{-1} \cdot T^{-3}$

RADIANCY

See *"emittance, radiant "*.

RADIANT ENERGY: (SI radiometry units)

Symbol: Q_e

Definition: Energy of electromagnetic radiation.

In physics, and in particular, as measured by radiometry, **radiant energy** is the energy of electromagnetic and gravitational radiation.

Notes: 1. The quantity of radiant energy may be calculated by integrating radiant flux (or power) with respect to time.

2. In branches of physics other than radiometry, electromagnetic energy is referred to using E or W.

3. The term is used particularly when electromagnetic radiation is emitted by a source into the surrounding environment.

4. This radiation may be visible or invisible to the human eye.

 Unit: joule, J (In SI base units: $kg.m^2.s^{-2}$)

Dimensions: $M \cdot L^2 \cdot T^{-2}$

RADIANT ENERGY DENSITY (SI radiometry unit)

Symbol: w_e

Definition: Radiant energy per unit volume.

Units: joule per cubic meter; J/m^3

Dimensions: $M \cdot L^{-1} \cdot T^{-2}$

RADIANT EXITANCE

Symbol: M_e

Definition: Radiant flux *emitted* by a *surface* per unit area. This is the emitted component of radiosity. "Radiant emittance" is an old term for this quantity. This is sometimes also confusingly called "intensity."

Radiant exitance of a *surface* is defined as

$$M_e = \frac{\partial \Phi_e}{\partial A}$$

where

- ∂ is the partial derivative symbol;
- Φ_e is the radiant flux *emitted*;
- A is the area.

Note: The letter "e" in the symbol M_e is for "energetic" to avoid confusion with photometric quantities)

Unit: watt per square meter (W/m^2)

Dimension: M·T^{-3}

RADIANT EXPOSURE

Symbol: H_e

Definition: Radiant energy received by a *surface* per unit area, or equivalently irradiance of a *surface* integrated over time of irradiation. This is sometimes also called "radiant fluence".

Radiant exposure of a *surface*, denoted H_e ("e" for "energetic" to avoid confusion with photometric quantities), is defined as

$$H_e = \frac{\partial Q_e}{\partial A} = \int_0^T E_e(t)\,dt,$$

where

- ∂ is the partial derivative symbol;
- Q_e is the radiant energy;
- A is the area;
- T is the duration of irradiation;
- E_e is the irradiance.

Unit: joule per square meter (J/m^2)

Dimension: **M·T^{-2}**

See: "spectral exposure"

RADIANT FLUX: (SI radiometry units)

Symbol: Φ_e

Definition: In radiometry, **radiant flux** or **radiant power** is the radiant energy emitted, reflected, transmitted, or received per unit time,

This is sometimes also called "radiant power".

Units: watt; W= J/s

Dimensions: **M·L²·T⁻³**

See: "Radiant Intensity", "Spectral flux."

RADIANT INTENSITY (SI radiometry units)

Symbol: $I_{e,\Omega}$

Definition: Radiant flux emitted, reflected, transmitted or received per unit solid angle. This is a *directional* quantity.

Radiant intensity, denoted $I_{e,\Omega}$ ("e" for "energetic" to avoid confusion with photometric quantities, and "Ω" to indicate this is a *directional* quantity), is defined as

$$I_{e,\Omega} = \frac{\partial \Phi_e}{\partial \Omega}$$

where

- ∂ is the partial derivative symbol;
- Φ_e is the radiant flux emitted, reflected, transmitted or received;
- Ω is the solid angle.

In general, $I_{e,\Omega}$ is a function of viewing angle θ and potentially azimuth angle. For the special case of a Lambertian surface, $I_{e,\Omega}$ follows Lambert's cosine law $I_{e,\Omega} = I_0 \cos\theta$.

Note: 1.   Radiant intensity is distinct from irradiance and radiant exitance, which are often called *intensity* in branches of physics other than radiometry.

2. In radio-frequency engineering, radiant intensity is sometimes called **radiation intensity**.

Units: watt per steradian, W/sr

Dimensions: $\mathbf{M \cdot L^2 \cdot T^{-3}}$

RADIANT EXITANCE (SI radiometry units)

Symbol: M_e

Definition: Radiant flux *emitted* by a *surface* per unit area. This is the emitted component of radiosity. "Radiant emittance" is an old term for this quantity. This is sometimes also confusingly called "intensity."

Units: watt per square meter - W/m^2

Dimensions: $\mathbf{M \cdot T^{-3}}$

RADIANT EXPOSURE: (SI radiometry units)

Symbol: H_e

Definition: Radiant energy received by a *surface* per unit area, or equivalently irradiance of a *surface* integrated over time of irradiation. This is sometimes also called "radiant fluence".

Units: joule per square meter - J/m^2

Dimensions: $\mathbf{M \cdot T^{-2}}$

RADIOSITY: (SI radiometry units)

Symbol: J_e

Definition: Radiant flux *leaving* (emitted, reflected and transmitted by) a *surface* per unit area. This is sometimes also confusingly called "intensity."

Units: watt per square meter; W/m^2

Dimensions: $\mathbf{M \cdot T^{-3}}$

RADIOSITY, SPECTRAL: (SI radiometry units)

Symbol: $J_{e,\nu}$ *or* $J_{e,\lambda}$

Definition: Radiosity of a *surface* per unit frequency or wavelength. The latter is commonly measured in $W \cdot m^{-2} \cdot nm^{-1}$. This is sometimes also confusingly called "spectral intensity."

Units: watt per square meter per hertz - $W \cdot m^{-2} \cdot Hz^{-1}$

  or

  watt per square meter, per meter - W/m^3

Dimensions: $M \cdot T^{-2}$ *or* $M \cdot L^{-1} \cdot T^{-3}$

RATIO OF HEAT CAPACITIES

Symbol: γ

Definition: The heat capacity at constant pressure c_p divided by the heat capacity at constant volume C_v.

$$\gamma = c_p/c_v.$$

Unit: There are no units or dimensions.

See *"Heat capacity."*

RAYLEIGH NUMBER

Symbol: Ra

Definition: The **Rayleigh number** is a dimensionless number named after Lord Rayleigh. The **Rayleigh number** is closely related to the Grashof number, and both numbers are used to describe natural convection (Gr) and heat transfer by natural convection (Ra). It describes the ratio of thermal transport via diffusion vs thermal transport via convection.

The **Rayleigh number** is simply defined as the product of the <u>Grashof number</u>, which describes the relationship between buoyancy and viscosity within a fluid, and the <u>Prandtl number</u>, which describes the relationship between momentum diffusivity and thermal diffusivity.

$$Ra_x = Gr_x. Pr$$

The **Grashof number** is defined as the ratio of the buoyant to a viscous force acting on a fluid in the velocity boundary layer. Its role in natural convection is much like that of the Reynolds number in forced convection. Natural convection occurs if this motion and mixing are caused by density variations resulting from temperature differences within the fluid. Usually, the density decreases due to increased temperature and causes the fluid to rise. This motion is caused by the buoyant force. The major force that resists the motion is the viscous force. The Grashof number is a way to quantify the opposing forces.

The **Rayleigh number** is used to express heat transfer in natural convection. The magnitude of the Rayleigh number is a good indication of whether the natural convection boundary layer is laminar or turbulent.

The **Rayleigh number** is defined as:

$$Ra_L = Gr_L . Pr = \frac{g\beta(T_{wall} - T_\infty)L^3}{v . \alpha}$$

$$Ra_x = \frac{g\beta}{v\alpha}(T_s - T_\infty)x^3$$

Where:

g is the acceleration due to Earth's gravity

β is the coefficient of thermal expansion

T_{wall} is the wall temperature

T_∞ is the bulk temperature

L is the vertical length

α is the thermal diffusivity

v is the kinematic viscosity.

For gases $\beta = 1/T$ where the temperature is in K. For liquids, β can be calculated if the variation of density with the temperature at constant pressure is known. For a vertical flat plate, the flow turns turbulent for the value of:

$Ra_x = Gr_x . Pr > 10^9$

As in forced convection, the microscopic nature of flow and convection correlations are distinctly different in the laminar and turbulent regions.

Field of application: heat transfer (buoyancy versus viscous forces in free convection)

Units: There are no units or dimensions

REACTANCE, ACOUSTICAL

Symbol: Xa.

Definition: The magnitude of the imaginary part of the acoustical impedance Z_a.

$Z_a = Ra + i\, Xa$ (Ra = acoustic resistance).

Unit: Pascal second per meter cubed.

Dimension: $L^{-4}\,M\,T^{-1}$.

Note: If the reactance is solely due to inertia, it is termed the acoustical mass reactance; if it is solely due to stiffness, it is termed the acoustical stiffness reactance.

See also *"reactance, specific acoustical "*.

REACTANCE, ELECTRICAL

Symbol: X

Definition: The magnitude of the imaginary part of the complex impedance Z.

$$Z = R + i\,X\ (R = resistance)$$

Unit: Ohm.

Dimension: $L^2\,M\,T^{-3}\,I^{-2}$

Note: Reactance due to pure inductance $X_L = \omega L$ (L = inductance) and is called inductive reactance; reactance due to pure capacitance $X_C = 1/\,\omega C$ (C = capacitance) and is called capacitive reactance.

REACTANCE, MECHANICAL

Symbol: X_m

Definition: The magnitude of the imaginary part of the mechanical impedance Z_m

$$Z_m = R_m + i\,X_m\ \ (R_m = \text{mechanical resistance}).$$

Unit: Newton second per meter.

Dimension: $M\,T^{-1}$

Note: If the reactance is caused by inertia, it is termed the mechanical mass reactance; if it is solely due to stiffness, it is termed the mechanical stiffness reactance.

REACTANCE, SPECIFIC ACOUSTICAL

Symbol: X_S.

Definition: The magnitude of the imaginary part of the specific acoustical impedance Z_S,

$$Z_{S,} = R_{S,} + i\,X_{S,}\ (R_S = \text{specific acoustical resistance}).$$

Unit: Pascal second per meter.

Dimension: $L^{-2}\,M\,T^{-1}$

Note: 1. The quantity was formerly termed the *unit-area acoustical reactance*.

2. If the reactance is caused by inertia, it is termed the specific acoustical mass reactance; if it is due to stiffness, it is termed the specific acoustical stiffness reactance.

See also "*reactance, acoustical*".

REACTIVE CURRENT

Definition: The component of an alternating current that is in quadrature with the voltage, the current and voltage being regarded as vector quantities.

Unit: Ampere

Dimension: I

Note: Also called: "reactive component of current," "wattless component of' current," "quadrature component of the current," and "idle component of the current."

REACTIVE VOLTAGE

Definition: The component of an alternating voltage that is in quadrature with the current, the voltage and current being regarded as vector quantities.

Unit: Volt.

Dimension $L^2\,M\,T^{-3}\,I^{-1}$

Note: Also called: "reactive component of voltage," "wattless component of the voltage, ". "quadrature component of the voltage," and "idle component of the voltage. "

REACTIVITY

Definition: An indication of the departure of a nuclear reactor from the condition in which the reaction can just take place (*the critical reaction*). It is related to the effective multiplication constant k (the ratio of the number of neutrons produced in a generation to the total number absorbed or lost) by the relation:

$$\text{Reactivity} = (1 - 1/k)$$

In short, reactivity indicates the extent to which a nuclear reactor deviates from a steady state.

Unit: Nile (100 niles is the reactivity corresponding to $k = 1$)

Dimension: There are no dimensions.

Note: 1. In chemistry, reactivity is defined as:

Reactivity is the tendency of a substance to undergo a chemical reaction, either by itself or with other materials, and to release energy.

Reactivity is dependent upon temperature. Increasing temperature increases the energy available for a chemical reaction, usually making it more likely.

2. Another definition of reactivity is that it is the scientific study of chemical reactions and their kinetics.

REDUCTION FACTOR, SOUND

Symbol: R

See *"transmission coefficient"* (note 4).

REFLECTANCE

See reflection coefficient (note 1)

REFLECTIVITY

Definition: In physics, reflectivity is a measure of the ability of a surface to reflect radiation, equal to the reflectance of a layer of material sufficiently thick for the reflectance not to depend on the thickness

Definition: The total reflection coefficient of a layer of the substance of such a thickness that the reflection coefficient does not change for an increase of thickness. Any conditions imposed will be the same as those for the reflection coefficient.

Unit: There are no units or dimensions.

Note: Also called reflectiveness, the quality or <u>capability</u> of being reflective

REFLECTION COEFFICIENT

Symbol: ρ sometimes r

Definition: Energy Er reflected by a surface divided by that incident on it E_o under identical conditions.

$$\rho = E_r / E_o.$$

Unit: There are no units or dimensions.

Note:

1. The quantity is also termed the *reflection factor or reflectance*, the use of the last name being deprecated.

2. The reflection coefficient is generally expressed as a percentage.

3. The reflection coefficient ρ is related to the scattering coefficient δ and the transmission coefficient τ by the relation: $\rho + \delta + \tau = I$

4. In sound, the reflection coefficient depends on the frequency of the sound.

5. In light, there are two reflection coefficients; the direct reflection coefficient is concerned with specular reflection, i.e., reflection in accordance with the usual laws of optics, where the angle of reflection is equal to the angle of incidence; the diffuse reflection coefficient is concerned with light reflected from every part of a surface in many directions. Both depend on the angle of incidence, the mode of illumination and the wavelength distribution of the light.

See also" *scattering coefficient" and "transmission coefficient* ".

REFLECTION DENSITY

Definition: The common logarithm of the ratio of the luminance L of a non-absorbing perfect diffuser to that of that of the surface under consideration L_o. both being illuminated at an angle of forty-five degrees to the normal, the direction of measurement being normal to the surface.

Reflection density = log (L/L_o).

Unit: There are no units or dimensions.

REFRACTIVE INDEX, ABSOLUTE

Symbol: n

Definition: Velocity of light in a vacuum c_o divided by the velocity of light in the medium concerned c.

$$n = c / c_0$$

Alternatively, the refractive index determines how much the path of light is bent or refracted when entering a material. This is described by Snell's law of refraction, $n_1 \sin\theta_1 = n_2 \sin\theta_2$, where θ_1 and θ_2 are the angles incidence and refraction, respectively, of a ray crossing the interface between two media with refractive indices n_1 and n_2. The refractive indices also determine the amount of light that is reflected when reaching the interface, as well as the critical angle for total internal reflection and Brewster's angle.

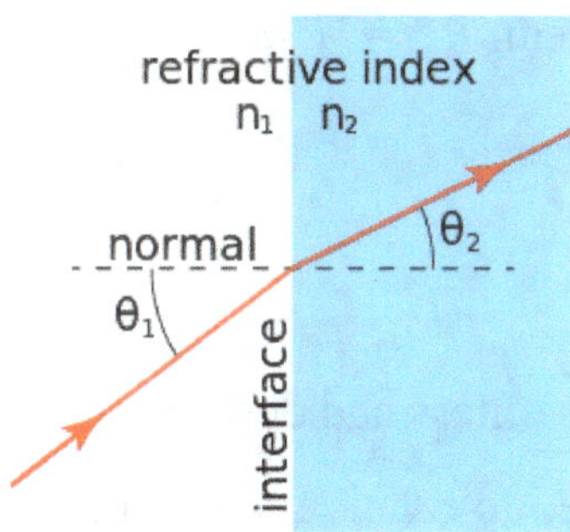

Unit: There are units or dimensions.

Note: 1. The refractive index n is defined as the ratio of the sine of the angle of incidence to the sine of the angle of refraction $n = \sin\theta_1 / \sin\theta_2$

2. The relative refractive index is defined in the same way but in respect of two media rather than

one medium and a vacuum.

RELATIVE BIOLOGICAL EFFECTIVENESS FACTOR

Definition: The ratio of the absorbed dose of standard ionizing radiation (usually hard-filtered 200 kV X-rays) that produces a particular biological effect to the absorbed dose of the radiation under consideration that produces the same effect under otherwise identical conditions.

Units: There are no units or dimensions.

Note: In 1968, the International Commission on Radiological Units recommended its use only in radiobiology.

RELUCTANCE

Symbol: R; sometimes R_m

Definition: The magnetomotive force U in a magnetic circuit divided by magnetic flux ϕ through any cross-section of the magnetic circuit.

$$R = U/\phi$$

Unit: Per Henry

Dimension: $L^{-2}\, M^{-1}\, T^2\, I^2$.

Note: For an unrationalized system, $R^* = U^*/\phi$

REYNOLD NUMBER

Symbol: Re

The Reynolds number is dimensionless and describes the ratio of inertial forces to viscous forces within a fluid, which is subjected to relative internal movement due to different fluid velocities, which is known as a boundary layer in the case of a bounding surface such as the interior of a pipe.

Definition: For fluid moving with velocity v and kinematic viscosity μ in tube of length l, the

The Reynolds number is defined as

$$\mathrm{Re} = \frac{uL}{\nu} = \frac{\rho u L}{\mu}$$

Where:

- ρ is the density of the fluid (SI units: kg/m³)

- u is the flow speed (m/s)

- L is a characteristic linear dimension (m) (see the below sections of this article for examples)

- μ is the dynamic viscosity of the fluid (Pa·s or N·s/m² or kg/(m·s))

- v is the kinematic viscosity of the fluid (m²/s).

In more detail, we can recognize the following equations for the Reynold number:

Fluid Flowing in Circular Pipes

The Reynolds number for fluid flowing in a circular pipe may be calculated as follows:

$$Re = \frac{\rho V D}{\mu}$$

A. Fluid Flowing in Non-Circular Pipe and Ducts

The Reynolds number for fluid flowing through a non-circular channel is calculated by substituting the hydraulic diameter of the flow path for the pipe diameter.

$$Re = \frac{\rho V D_h}{\mu}$$

B. Particle Moving Through Fluid

The Reynolds number for fluid flowing over a particle or a particle moving through fluid is calculated by substituting the diameter of the particle for the pipe diameter and the velocity of the particle for the fluid velocity.

$$Re = \frac{\rho V_p D_p}{\mu}$$

In the above equations:

D: Pipe Diameter

D_h: Hydraulic Diameter

D_p: Particle Diameter

Re: Reynolds number

V: Average velocity

V_P: Average particle velocity

P: Fluid density

M: Viscosity

Field of application: fluid mechanics (ratio of fluid inertial and viscous forces)

Units: There are no units or dimensions.

Note.

    1. The name is after O. Reynolds (1842-1912) 'who derived the expression in 1883.

    2. Low values of the number show that the viscous forces are predominant in controlling the flow, whereas higher values indicate that the inertial forces are more important.

RESILIENCE

Definition: Work done W in deforming a body to some predetermined limit (e.g., its elastic limit or breaking point) divided by the volume V of the body.

    Resilience = W/V

Unit: Joule per meter cubed.

Dimension: $L^{-1} M T^{-2}$

Note:

1. It is also the ability of a strained body, by virtue of high yield strength and low elastic modulus, to recover its size and form following deformation.

2. In material science, **resilience** is the ability of a material to absorb energy when it is deformed elastically and release that energy upon unloading. **Proof resilience** is defined as the maximum energy that can be absorbed up to the elastic limit without creating a permanent distortion. The **modulus of resilience** is defined as the maximum energy that can be absorbed per unit volume without creating a permanent distortion.

RESISTANTCE, ACOUSTICAL

Symbol: $R\alpha$

Definition: The real part of the acoustical impedance Za.

$Za = Ra + i\,Xa$ (Xa = acoustical reactance)

Unit: Pascal second per meter cubed.

Dimension: $L^{-4}\,M\,T^{-1}$

RESISTANCE, ELECTRICAL

Symbol: R

1. GENERAL

Definition: The resistance of an element, device, branch, network, or system is the factor by which the mean-square conduction current must be multiplied to give the corresponding power lost be dissipation as heat or as other permanent radiation or loss of electromagnetic energy from the circuit.

2. RESISTANCE TO A DIRECT CURRENT

Definition: Electric potential difference V divided by current I when there is no electromotive force in a conductor.

$R = V/I$

3. RESISTANCE TO AN ALTERNATING CURRENT

Definition: The real part of the electrical impedance Z.

$Z = R + i\,X$ (X= electric reactance).

Unit: Ohm.

Dimension: $L^2\,M\,T^{-3}\,I^{-2}$

RESISTANCE, MECHANICAL

Symbol: Rm.

Definition: The real part of the mechanical impedance Z_m.

$Z_m = R_m + i\,X_m$ (X_m = mechanical reactance).

Unit: Newton second per meter.

Dimension: $M\,T^{-1}$

Note. In damped harmonic motion, the mechanical resistance is the ratio of the frictional resistive force to the speed.

RESISTANCE, SPECIFIC ACOUSTICAL

Symbol: R_s.

Definition: The real part of the specific acoustical impedance Z_S.

$$Z_S = R_s + i\,X_s \ (X_S = \text{specific acoustical reactance}).$$

Unit: Pascal second per meter.

Dimension: $M\,L^{-2}\,T^{-1}$

Note: The quantity was formerly called the unit-area acoustical resistance.

RESISTANCE, THERMAL

Symbol: R

Definition 1: Generally, it is the reciprocal of any of the normally used heat transfer coefficient, but more particularly taken to be the reciprocal of thermal conductance C.

$$R = I/C.$$

Unit: Meter squared kelvin per watt.

Dimension: $L^2 M^{-1}\,T.$

Definition 2: The broad concept of thermal resistance is employed to ascertain temperature drop through any homogeneous or heterogeneous heat flow barrier since temperature gradient is proportional to thermal resistance. In this case, thermal resistance is the temperature difference T between two points divided by the mean rate of flow of entropy S with respect to time t.

$$R = T / (dS/dt)$$

Unit: Thermal ohm = kelvin squared per watt.

Dimension: $L^2\,M^{-1}\,T^{-1}$

Note: I. The fanner definition was: the temperature difference between two points divided by the rate of flow of heat energy Q with respect to time.

$$R = T / (dQ/dt)$$

2. In the case of a heterogeneous barrier, the overall thermal resistance is the sum of the individual resistance applicable to each component of the structure.

3. Also known as heat resistance.

Definition 3 (Of Semiconductor Device): The effective temperature rise per unit power dissipation of a designated junction above the temperature of a stated external reference point under conditions of thermal equilibrium.

Unit: Kelvin per watt.

Dimension: $M^{-1} T$

Note: Also known as *effective thermal resistance*.

RESISTIVITY

Symbol: ρ

Definition: Electric field strength E divided by current density J.

$$\rho = E/J$$

Alternatively, the resistivity is the product of the electrical resistance R and the cross-sectional area A, divided by the length l.

$$\rho = RA/l$$

Unit: ohm meter.

Dimension: $L^3 M T^{-3} I^{-2}$.

Note: 1.   The quantity is also termed the specific resistance.

2.   For pure metals at ordinary temperatures, the resistivity is of the order of 10^{-8} ohm meters, while for good insulators, it may exceed 10^{14} ohm meters.

3.   The reciprocal of resistivity is conductivity.

RESISTIVITY, MASS

Symbol: ρ_m.

Definition: The product of resistivity ρ and density d.

$$\rho_m = \rho\, d$$

Alternatively, the product of the electrical resistance R of a conductor and its mass m, divided by the square of its length l

$$\rho_m = R.\, m\,/\,l^2$$

Unit: Ohm kilogram per meter squared.

Dimension: $M^2\, T^{-3}\, I^{-2}$

RESPONSE TIME

Definition: The amount of elapsed time between the completion of a request and the receipt of the beginning of the reply.

RESISTIVITY, THERMAL

Symbol: ϕ

Definition: The reciprocal of the thermal conductivity λ.

$$\Phi = 1/\lambda$$

Unit: Meter per watt.

Dimension: $L\, T\, Q^{-1}\, \Theta$ or $M^{-1}\, L\, T$

Note: The quantity is also termed the thermal fluidity.

RESTITUTION COEFFICIENT (COEFFICIENT OF RESTITUTION (COR))

Symbol: e

Definition: Velocity v_2 of a body at the instant immediately following an impact divided by the velocity v_1 at the instant immediately preceding the impact.

$$e = v_2/\, v_1$$

The coefficient is related to (relative) kinetic energy KE by:

$$e = \sqrt{\frac{KE_{after\ collision}}{KE_{before\ collision}}}$$

Notes:

1. It normally ranges from 0 to 1, where 1 would be a perfectly elastic collision. A perfectly inelastic collision has a coefficient of 0, but a 0 value does not have to be perfectly inelastic.

2. The value is almost always less than one due to initial translational kinetic energy being lost to rotational kinetic energy, plastic deformation, and heat. It can be more than 1 if there is an energy gain during the collision from a chemical reaction, a reduction in rotational energy, or another internal energy decrease that contributes to the post-collision velocity.

Unit: There are no units or dimensions (scalar).

RICHARDSON NUMBER

Symbol: Ri

Definition: The **Richardson number (Ri)** is named after Lewis Fry Richardson (1881–1953). It is the dimensionless number that expresses the ratio of the buoyancy term to the flow shear term:

$$Ri = \frac{\text{buoyancy term}}{\text{flow shear term}} = \frac{g}{\rho} \frac{\partial\rho/\partial z}{(\partial u/\partial z)^2}$$

Where g is gravity, ρ is density, u is a representative flow speed, and z is depth.

The Richardson number, or one of several variants, is of practical importance in weather forecasting and in investigating density and turbidity currents in oceans, lakes, and reservoirs.

When considering flows in which density differences are small (the Boussinesq approximation), it is common to use the reduced gravity g', and the relevant parameter is the densimetric Richardson number.

$$Ri = \frac{g'}{\rho} \frac{\partial\rho/\partial z}{(\partial u/\partial z)^2}$$

Which is used frequently when considering atmospheric or oceanic flows.

If the Richardson number is much less than unity, buoyancy is unimportant in the flow. If it is much greater than unity, buoyancy is dominant (in the sense that there is insufficient kinetic energy to homogenize the fluids).

If the Richardson number is of order unity, then the flow is likely to be buoyancy-driven: the energy of the flow derives from the potential energy in the system originally.

Field of application: fluid dynamics (effect of buoyancy on flow stability; ratio of potential over kinetic energy)

Unit: Dimensionless

RIGIDITY, MAGNETIC

Definition: A measure of the momentum of a particle moving perpendicular to a magnetic field, equal to the magnetic induction B times the particle's radius of curvature r_c

Magnetic rigidity = $B. r_c$.

Note: It is defined also as the existence of restoring forces that resist displacements of a conducting fluid when a magnetic field is present.

RIGIDITY MODULUS

See elastic modulus (2)

ROCKWELL NUMBER

A hardness number.

ROLLING RESISTANCE

Symbol: C_{rr}

Definition: **Rolling resistance**, sometimes called **rolling friction** or **rolling drag**, is the force resisting the motion when a body (such as a ball, tire, or wheel) rolls on a surface. It is mainly caused by non-elastic effects; that is, not all the energy needed for deformation (or movement) of the wheel, roadbed, etc., is recovered when the pressure is removed. Two forms of this are hysteresis losses (see below) and permanent (plastic) deformation of the object or the surface (e.g., soil). Note that the slippage between the wheel and the surface also results in energy dissipation. Although some researchers have included this term in rolling resistance, some suggest that this dissipation term should be treated separately from rolling resistance because it is due to the applied torque to the wheel and the resultant slip between the wheel and ground, which is called **slip loss** or **slip resistance.** In addition, only the so-called slip resistance involves friction. Therefore, the name "rolling friction" is, to an extent, a misnomer.

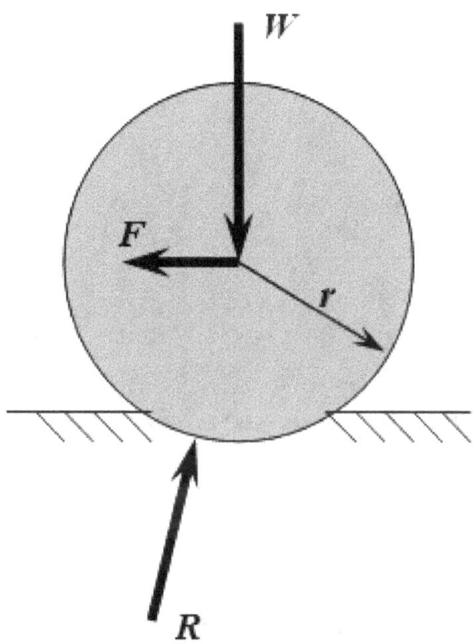

Figure: Hard wheel rolling on and deforming a soft surface, resulting in the reaction force R from the surface having a component that opposes the motion. (W is some vertical load on the axle, F is some towing force applied to the axle, r is the wheel radius, and both friction with the ground and friction at the axle are assumed to be negligible and so are not shown. The wheel is rolling to the left at a constant speed.) Note that R is the resultant force from non-uniform pressure at the wheel-roadbed contact surface. This pressure is greater towards the front of the wheel due to hysteresis.

In analogy with sliding friction, rolling resistance is often expressed as a coefficient times the normal force. This coefficient of rolling resistance is generally much smaller than the coefficient of sliding friction.

Any coasting wheeled vehicle will gradually slow down due to rolling resistance, including that of the bearings, but a train car with steel wheels running on steel rails will roll farther than a bus of the same mass with rubber tires running on tarmac. Factors that contribute to rolling resistance are the (amount of) deformation of the wheels, the deformation of the roadbed surface, and movement below the surface. Additional contributing factors include wheel diameter, load on the wheel, surface adhesion, sliding, and relative micro-sliding between the surfaces of contact. The losses due to hysteresis also depend strongly on the material properties of the wheel or tire and the surface. For example, a rubber tire will have higher rolling resistance on a paved road than a steel railroad wheel on a steel rail. Also, sand on the ground will give more rolling resistance than concrete. Sole rolling resistance factor is not dependent on speed.

The "rolling resistance coefficient" is defined by the following equation:

$$F = C_{rr}N$$

where

F is the rolling resistance force (shown as R in the above figure),

C_{rr} is the dimensionless **rolling resistance coefficient** or **coefficient of rolling friction (CRF)**, and N is the normal force, the force perpendicular to the surface on which the wheel is rolling.

C_{rr} is the force needed to push (or tow) a wheeled vehicle forward (at constant speed on a level surface, or zero grade, with zero air resistance) per unit force of weight.

Unit: Dimensionless

ROSHKO NUMBER

Symbol: **Ro**

Definition: In fluid mechanics, the **Roshko number (Ro)** is a dimensionless number describing oscillating flow mechanisms. It is named after the American Professor of Aeronautics, Anatol Roshko. It is defined as

$$Ro = \frac{fL^2}{\nu} = St\,Re$$

$$St = \frac{fL}{U},$$

$$Re = \frac{UL}{\nu}$$

where

- St is the dimensionless Strouhal number;

- Re is the Reynolds number;
- U is mean stream velocity;
- f is the frequency of vortex shedding;
- L is the characteristic length (for example, hydraulic diameter);
- v is the kinematic viscosity of the fluid.

Field of application: fluid dynamics (oscillating flow, vortex shedding)

Unit: Dimensionless

ROSSBY NUMBER

Symbol: Ro

Definition: The **Rossby number (Ro)**, named for Carl-Gustav Arvid Rossby, is a dimensionless number used in describing fluid flow. The Rossby number is the ratio of inertial force to Coriolis force terms.

$$|\mathbf{v} \cdot \nabla \mathbf{v}| \sim U^2/L$$

and

$$\Omega \times \mathbf{v} \sim U\Omega$$

in the Navier–Stokes equations, respectively. It is commonly used in geophysical phenomena in the oceans and atmosphere, where it characterizes the importance of Coriolis accelerations arising from planetary rotation. It is also known as the **Kibel number**.

The Rossby number (Ro, not R_o) is defined as

$$\mathrm{Ro} = \frac{U}{Lf}$$

where U and L are, respectively, characteristic velocity and length scales of the phenomenon, and $f=2\Omega\sin\phi$ is the Coriolis frequency, with Ω being the angular frequency of planetary rotation and ϕ the latitude.

A small Rossby number signifies a system strongly affected by Coriolis forces, and a large Rossby number signifies a system in which inertial and centrifugal forces dominate. For example, in tornadoes, the Rossby number is large ($\approx 10^3$), in low-pressure systems, it is low ($\approx 0.1–1$), and in oceanic systems, it is of the order of unity, but depending on the phenomena can range over several orders of magnitude ($\approx 10^{-2}–10^2$). As a result, the Coriolis force is negligible in tornadoes, and the balance is between pressure and centrifugal forces (called *cyclostrophic balance*). Cyclostrophic balance also commonly occurs in the inner core of a tropical cyclone. In low-pressure systems, centrifugal force is negligible, and balance is between Coriolis and pressure forces (called *geostrophic balance*). In the oceans, all three forces are comparable (called *cyclogeostrophic balance*). For a figure showing spatial and temporal scales of motions in the atmosphere and oceans, see Kantha and Clayson.

When the Rossby number is large (either because f is small, such as in the tropics and at lower latitudes, or because L is small, that is, for small-scale motions, such as flow in a bathtub, or for large speeds), the effects of planetary rotation are unimportant and can be neglected. When the Rossby number is small, then the effects of planetary rotation are large, and the net acceleration is comparably small, allowing the use of the geostrophic approximation.

Unit: Dimensionless

ROUGHNESS (or SURFACE FLATNESS)

Definition: [In optical industry] The distance between the highest and lowest parts of a surface measured in terms of the wavelength λ of the mercury green line (546 nanometers).

An optical flat is a glass surface worked to within λ /60 or 9 nanoseconds.

Definition: [In workshops] In workshop practice, there are two systems for expressing surface flatness: the M (mean line) and the E (envelope) systems. Flatness in both systems is expressed as the distance of some characteristic of the surface from a suitable datum line. The surface characteristic and datum line are rigorously defined in standards issued by the major countries.

Unit: Micrometer

Dimension: L

ROUSE NUMBER

Symbol: **P or Z**

Definition: The **Rouse number** (**P** or **Z**) is a non-dimensional number in fluid dynamics that is used to define a concentration profile of suspended sediment and which also determines how sediment will be transported in a flowing fluid. It is a ratio between the sediment fall velocity ws and the upwards velocity on the grain as a product of the von Kármán constant κ and the shear velocity u∗.

$$P = \frac{w_s}{\kappa u_*}$$

Occasionally, the factor β is included before the von Kármán constant in the equation, which is a constant that correlates eddy viscosity to eddy diffusivity. This is generally taken to be equal to 1 and, therefore, is ignored in actual calculation. However, it should not be ignored when considering the full equation.

$$P = \frac{w_s}{\beta \kappa u_*}$$

It is named after the *United States* fluid dynamicist Hunter Rouse. It is a characteristic scale parameter in the Rouse Profile of suspended sediment concentration with depth in a flowing fluid. The suspended sediment concentration with depth goes as the power of the negative Rouse number. It also is used to determine how the particles will move in the fluid. The required Rouse numbers for transport, as bed load, suspended load, and wash load, are given below.

Mode of Transport	Rouse Number
Bed load	>2.5
Suspended load: 50% Suspended	>1.2, <2.5
Suspended load: 100% Suspended	>0.8, <1.2
Wash load	<0.8

Unit: Dimensionless

S

SAE NUMBER (SAE number)

Symbol: SAE number

Definition: An arbitrary number based on viscosity used for the classification of lubricating oils.

The original viscosity grades were all mono-grades, e.g., a typical engine oil was a SAE 30. This is because all oils are thin when heated, therefore, to get the right film thickness at operating temperatures, manufacturers needed to start with a thick oil. This meant that in cold weather, it would be difficult to start the engine as the oil was too thick to crank. However, oil additive technology was introduced that allowed oils to thin more slowly (i.e., to retain a higher viscosity index); this allowed selection of a thinner oil to start with, e.g., "SAE 15W-30", a product that acts like an SAE 15 at cold temperatures (15W for winter) and like an SAE 30 at 100 °C (212 °F).

Therefore, one set measures cold temperature performance (0W, 5W, 10W, 15W and 20W). The second set of measurements is for high-temperature performance (8, 12, 16, 20, 30, 40, 50). The document SAE J300 defines the viscometrics related to these grades.

Notes: 1.   The numbers for crankcase lubricants range from 5 to 50; for transmission and axle lubricants, they range from 75 to 250; the lower the number, the more readily the oil flows.

2. The suffix W indicates that the oil is suitable for winter use. W oils are rated according to their flow rates at 0° F (-17.8° C); other types are tested at 210° F (99° C).

3. Multirated oils, such as 10W–30, contain additives that oppose the tendency to thicken at low temperatures, making the same oil satisfy both summer and winter requirements.

The next Table gives the relationship between SAE numbers and viscosity.

SAE Viscosity Grade	Max. Temperature for 150 000 cP [°C] (ASTM D 2983)	Min. Viscosity [mm²/s] at 100 °C (ASTM D445)	Max. Viscosity [mm²/s] at 100 °C (ASTM D445)
110	--	17.4	<24.0

SAE Viscosity Grade	Max. Temperature for 150 000 cP [°C] (ASTM D 2983)	Min. Viscosity [mm²/s] at 100 °C (ASTM D445)	Max. Viscosity [mm²/s] at 100 °C (ASTM D445)
140	--	23.74	<32.5
190	--	33.33	<41.0
250	--	48.49	--
70W	-55	3.72	--
75W	-40	4.4	--
80	--	8.02	<11.0
80W	-26	5.29	--
85	--	10.15	<13.5
85W	-12	6.46	--

Note: The unit was first introduced by the American Society of Automotive Engineering in 1923.

SATURATION RATIO

Symbol: Ψ

Definition: The ratio of the actual amount of water vapor m present in a given volume of air to the amount necessary to saturate the air m_0 at the same temperature.

$$\Psi = m/m_o$$

Equally defined as the actual specific humidity x divided by the specific humidity x_0 of saturated air at the same temperature

$$\Psi = x/x_o,$$

Unit: There are no units or dimensions.

Note: The saturation ratio and the relative humidity differ only slightly at temperature below about 40°C.

See "*humidity, specific*" and "*humidity, relative.*"

SCATTERING COEFFICIENT

Symbol: δ

Definition: Energy E_s scattered by a surface or medium divided by that incident at the point E_o under identical conditions.

$$\delta = E_s / E_o$$

Unit: There are no units or dimensions.

Note: 1. The quantity is also termed the *scattering factor* or, *dissipation coefficient*, or *dissipation factor*.

2. The scattering factor, the absorption coefficient α and the transmission coefficient τ are related by the relation:

$$\delta = \alpha - \tau$$

See also *"absorption coefficient"* and *"transmission coefficient "*.

SCHMIDT NUMBER

Symbol: Sc

Definition: The Schmidt number is a dimensionless number named after Ernst Heinrich Wilhelm Schmidt and describes the ratio of momentum diffusivity to mass diffusivity that is commonly used in analysis of mass transfer systems. It is used to characterize fluids in which simultaneous momentum and mass diffusion convection processes and occurs.

Quantitatively, the Schmidt number determines the thickness of the hydrodynamic layer relative to the mass transfer boundary layer and describes whether momentum or diffusion will dominate mass transfer. The Schmidt number is stated as follows:

$$Sc = \frac{\text{viscous diffusion rate}}{\text{mass diffusion rate}}$$
$$= \frac{\nu}{D}$$
$$= \frac{\mu}{\rho D}$$

Where

- v is the kinematic viscosity (m^2/s)

- D is the diffusion coefficient (mass diffusivity) (m^2/s)

- P is the density (kg/m^3)

- μ is the Dynamic viscosity ($N.s/m^2$)

Notes:

1. Where the Schmidt number is small, mass diffusion will dominate, whereas, for high Schmidt numbers, momentum diffusion will dominate. More specifically, changes in the three key properties will have the following effects on Schmidt number:

   - Increase in dynamic viscosity will increase Schmidt number

   - Increase in density will reduce Schmidt number

   - Increase in mass diffusivity will reduce Schmidt number

   For gas-gas diffusive systems at standard conditions, the Sc is typically in the range of 0.2 - 4, while for gas-liquid and liquid-liquid systems, values are typically 200-1500.

2. The Schmidt number is the mass transfer analogue of the Prandtl number and may be used with the <u>Reynolds number</u> to determine the <u>Sherwood number.</u>

See: "Prandtl number", "Reynolds number," "and Sherwood number."

(Reference: <u>Chemical Engineering Volume 1, Sixth Edition: Fluid Flow, Heat Transfer and Mass Transfer</u>)

Field of application: mass transfer (viscous over molecular diffusion rate)

Unit: There are no units or dimensions.

SECTION MODULUS

Section modulus is a geometric property for a given cross-section used in the design of beams or flexural members. Other geometric properties used in the design include area for tension and shear, radius of gyration for compression, and moment of inertia and polar moment of inertia for stiffness.

Any relationship between these properties is highly dependent on the shape in question. Equations for the section moduli of common shapes are given below.

There are two types of section moduli, the elastic section modulus and the plastic section modulus.

1. Elastic Section Modulus

Symbol: Z or W, also S

Definition: The elastic section modulus of a plane area about an axis in its plane is the ratio of the second moment of area I to the distance (or area moment of inertia, not to be confused with a moment of inertia) from the axis to the most area.

The elastic section modulus $S = I / y$

Note: Elastic section modulus is often used to determine the yield moment (M_y) such that

$$M_y = S \times \sigma_y,$$

where σ_y is the yield strength of the material.

Unit: Meter cubed. $(m^{3)}$

Dimension: L (scalar).

2. Plastic Section modulus

The plastic section modulus is used for materials where elastic yielding is acceptable and plastic behavior is assumed to be an acceptable limit. Designs generally strive to ultimately remain below the plastic limit to avoid permanent deformations, often comparing the plastic capacity against amplified forces or stresses.

The plastic section modulus depends on the location of the plastic neutral axis (PNA). The PNA is defined as the axis that splits the cross-section such that the compression force from the area in compression equals the tension force from the area in tension. So, for sections with constant yielding stress, the area above and below the PNA will be equal, but this is not necessarily the case for composite sections.

The plastic section modulus is the sum of the areas of the cross-section on each side of the PNA (which may or may not be equal) multiplied by the distance from the local centroids of the two areas to the PNA.

SEDIMENTATION COEFFICIENT

Symbol: *s*

Definition: Is the velocity of sedimentation of molecules per unit accelerating field. If v is the velocity of the boundary between the solution containing the molecules and the solvent, x is the distance of the boundary from the axis of rotation, and ω is the angular velocity in radian per second, then the sedimentation coefficient *s* is:

$$s = v/\omega^2\, x$$

Units: Second

Dimension: T

Note: 1. The Svedberg (S) (= 10^{-13} seconds) is used normally as a unit for the tile coefficient.

2. The value of the coefficient is in the range 0.025 x 10^{-12} to 50 x10^{-12},

SEEBECK COEFFICIENT

Symbol: a_s

Definition: Difference between the heat energy ΔE liberated at the cold junction of a thermocouple and that absorbed at the hot junction, divided by the charge Q flowing through the thermocouple.

$$a_s = \Delta E / Q$$

Unit: Joule per coulomb = volt $(kg.m^2.s^{-3}.A^{-1})$

Dimension: $M\,L^2\,T^{-3}\,I^{-1}$

SENSATION LEVEL

Symbol: L or L_p, sometimes S (O)

Definition: The common logarithm of the ratio of the intensity I or power P or energy E of a sound to the threshold level of aural sensation, I_o or P_o or E_o, respectively, the two being expressed in the same units

$$L = \log(I/I_o) = \log P/P_o = \log(E/E_o)$$

Unit: Bel; in practice, the decibel is always used.

Dimension: There are no dimensions (scalar).

Note: (1) The experimentally-determined values of the threshold level (for binaural hearing of the sinusoidally-varying plane progressive tone of frequency one thousand hertz) are $I_o =$ 2. 5 x 10^{-12} watts per meter squared, $P_o = 2.5$ x 10^{-12} watts, $E_o = 2.5$ x 10^{-12} joules.

(2) The sensation level is also equivalent to twice the common logarithm of the ratio of the root-mean-square pressure p to the threshold level of aural sensation p_o, each expressed in same units. $L = 2log(p/p_o)$ The experimentally-determined value of p_o is 3.16 x 10^{-5} pascals.

(3) See the entry intensity level. The intensity level of the threshold sensation level is experimentally determined as 3.98 decibels.

SHAPE FACTOR

Symbol: H

Definition: A shape factor is used in boundary layer flow to help to differentiate laminar and turbulent flow. It also shows up in various approximate treatments of the boundary layer, including the Thwaites method for laminar flows. The formal definition is given by:

$$H_{12}(x) = \frac{\delta_1(x)}{\delta_2(x)}$$

where H_{12} is the shape factor, δ_1 is the displacement thickness and δ_2 is the momentum thickness.

Conventionally, $H_{12} = 2.59$ (Blasius boundary layer) is typical of laminar flows, while $H_{12} = 1.3$ - 1.4 is typical of turbulent flows near the laminar-turbulent transition For turbulent flows near separation, $H_{12} \approx 2.7$. The dividing line defining laminar-transitional and transitional-turbulent H_{12} values is dependent on a number of factors, so it is not always a definitive parameter for differentiating laminar, transitional, or turbulent boundary layers.

Field of application: boundary layer flow (ratio of displacement thickness to momentum thickness)

Unit: Dimensionless

SHEAR, ANGLE OF

See strain (2) (note)

SHEAR MODULUS

See elastic modulus (2)

SHERWOOD NUMBER

Symbol: *Sh*

Definition 1: Using dimensionless analysis:

Using dimensional analysis, it is defined as a function of the Reynolds number R_e and Schmidt number *Sc*:

$$Sh = f(R_e, Sc)$$

For example, it can be expressed as:

$$Sh = j_m \, Re. \, (Sc)^{1/3}$$

where J_m is the mass transfer factor, *Re* is Reynold's number, and *Sc* is Schmidt's number.

A more specific correlation is the Froessling equation:

$$Sh = Sh_0 + 0.552 \, R^{1/2} \, Sc^{1/3}$$

This form is applicable to molecular diffusion from a single spherical particle. It is particularly valuable in situations where the Reynold number and Schmidt number are readily available.

Definition 2: The Sherwood number is a dimensionless number named in honor of Thomas Kilgore Sherwood and describes the ratio of convective mass transfer to the rate of diffusive mass transfer. It is the mass transfer equivalent of the Nusselt Number and is formulated as follows:

$$Sh = \frac{h}{D/L}$$

Where *h* is the convective mass transfer rate and *D/L* is the mass diffusion rate.

For gas systems, an alternative formulation utilizing the gas phase mass transfer coefficient k can be used:

$$\text{Sh} = \frac{kRT}{DP}$$

Field of application: boundary layer flow (ratio of displacement thickness to momentum thickness)

Unit: There are no units or dimensions.

Note: It is also known as "*Nusselt number for mass transfer*".

SOMMERFELD NUMBER

Symbol: S

Definition: In the design of fluid bearings, the **Sommerfeld number** (S) is a dimensionless quantity used extensively in hydrodynamic lubrication analysis. The Sommerfeld number is very important in lubrication analysis because it contains all the variables normally specified by the designer. The Sommerfeld number is named after Arnold Sommerfeld (1868–1951)

The Sommerfeld Number is typically defined by the following equation.

$$S = \left(\frac{r}{c}\right)^2 \frac{\mu N}{P}$$

Where:

S is the Sommerfeld Number or bearing characteristic number

r is the shaft radius

c is the radial clearance

μ is the absolute viscosity of the lubricant

N is the speed of the rotating shaft in rev/s

P is the load per unit of the projected bearing area

The second part of the equation is seen to be the Hersey number. However, an alternative definition for S is used in some texts based on angular velocity:

$$S = \left(\frac{r}{c}\right)^2 \frac{\mu N}{P} = \left(\frac{r}{c}\right)^2 \frac{\mu \omega L D}{W}$$

Where:

ω is the angular velocity of the shaft in rad/s.

W is the applied load.

L is the bearing length.

D is the bearing diameter.

It is, therefore, necessary to check which definition is being used when referring to design data or textbooks since the value of S will differ by a factor of 2π.

Field of application: hydrodynamic lubrication (boundary lubrication

Unit: Dimensionless

SPECIFIC

Definition: A qualifying word denoting the value of physical quantity per unit mass, area, volume, length, etc., according to circumstances, e.g., specific resistance etc.

It has been recommended by IUPAC that, for extensive quantities, the word should be restricted to the meaning "*divided by mass*".

SPECIFIC HEAT CAPACITY (MASS BASIS)

Symbol: c.

Under the conditions of constant pressure or of constant volume, the symbols are c_p and C_v, respectively.

Definition: The quantity of heat Q required to raise the temperature of one kilogram of substance one Kelvin, i.e. heat capacity dQ/dT divided by mass m.

$$c = (1/m)\,(dQ/dT),$$

where T = temperature.

Unit: Joule per kilogram Kelvin.

Dimension: There are no mechanical dimensions.

Note: 1. The older name of the quantity, specific heat, is deprecated.

2. The specific heat capacity at constant pressure c_p always exceeds that at constant volume c_v by the work done in expansion. For a solid:

$$c_p - c_v = A\, c_p^{\,2}\, T,$$

where A is a constant, and T is the thermodynamic temperature.

For an ideal gas in which the internal energy is independent of the volume, $c_p - c_v = n\,R$,

where n is the number of moles per kilogram, and R is the molar gas constant.

SPECIFIC HEAT CAPACITY (VOLUME BASIS)

Definition: The quantity of heat Q required to raise the temperature of unit volume of substance one Kelvin, i.e. heat capacity dQ/dT divided by volume V.

Specific heat capacity, volume basis $= (1/V)(dQ/dT)$

where T = temperature.

Unit: Joule per meter cubed Kelvin. (kg.m^{-3})

Dimension: M L^{-3}.

SPECIFIC LATENT HEAT OF FUSION

Symbol: l_f

Definition: The quantity of heat required to change the state of a unit mass of a substance from the solid to the liquid state at the melting point.

Unit: Joule per kilogram

Note: 1. Also called *enthalpy of melting*

2. According to statistical mechanics, the change in entropy on melting one mole of an ideal solid, in the absence of any other changes such as expansion, would be equal to the molar gas constant R. This gives:

$$l_f/T = nR \quad \text{or} \quad l_f = T\,(nR),$$

where n is the number of moles per kilogram.

By experiment, it is found that:

$$l_s / T = (1.35 \pm 0.4)\, nR$$

SPECIFIC LATENT HEAT OF SUBLIMATION

Symbol: l_s.

Definition: The quantity of heat required to change unit mass of a substance from the solid to the vapor state without a change of temperature.

Unit: Joule per kilogram.

Note: Also called *enthalpy of sublimation.*

SPECIFIC LATENT HEAT OF VAPORIZATION

Symbol: l_v

Definition: The quantity of heat required to change unit mass of a substance from the liquid to the vapor state at the boiling point.

Unit: Joule per kilogram ($J.kg^{-1}$ or $m^2.s^{-2}$)

Note: 1. Also called *enthalpy of evaporation.*

SPECTRAL EXITANCE

Symbol: $M_{e,v}$ and $M_{e,\lambda}$

Definition: Radiant exitance of a *surface* per unit frequency or wavelength. The latter is commonly measured in $W \cdot m^{-2} \cdot nm^{-1}$. "Spectral emittance" is an old term for this quantity. This is sometimes also confusingly called "spectral intensity."

1.   *Spectral exitance in frequency:*

Symbol: $M_{e,v}$

Spectral exitance in frequency of a *surface*, denoted $M_{e,v}$, is defined as

$$M_{e,v} = \frac{\partial M_e}{\partial v}$$

where v is the frequency.

Unit: watt per square meter per hertz ($W \cdot m^{-2} \cdot Hz^{-1}$)

Dimension: $M \cdot T^{-2}$

2. **Spectral exitance in wavelength:**

Symbol: $M_{e,\lambda}$

Spectral exitance in wavelength of a *surface*, denoted $M_{e,\lambda}$, is defined as

$$M_{e,\lambda} = \frac{\partial M_e}{\partial \lambda}$$

Where λ is the wavelength.

Unit: watt per square meter, per meter (W/m^3)

Dimension: $\mathbf{M \cdot L^{-1} \cdot T^{-3}}$

SPECTRAL EXPOSURE

Symbol: $H_{e,\nu}$ and $H_{e,\lambda}$ [

Definition: Radiant exposure of a *surface* per unit frequency or wavelength. The latter is commonly measured in $J \cdot m^{-2} \cdot nm^{-1}$. This is sometimes also called "spectral fluence."

Spectral exposure in frequency of a *surface*, denoted $H_{e,\nu}$, is defined as

$$H_{e,\nu} = \frac{\partial H_e}{\partial \nu}$$

Where ν is the frequency.

Unit: Joule per square meter per hertz ($J \cdot m^{-2} \cdot Hz^{-1}$)

Dimension: $\mathbf{M} \cdot \mathbf{T}^{-1}$

Spectral exposure in wavelength of a *surface*, denoted $H_{e,\lambda}$, is defined as

$$H_{e,\lambda} = \frac{\partial H_e}{\partial \lambda}$$

where λ is the wavelength.

Unit: joule per square meter, per meter ($J/m^{3)}$)

Dimension: $\mathbf{M} \cdot \mathbf{L}^{-1} \cdot \mathbf{T}^{-2}$

SPECTRAL FLUX

1. **Symbol:** $\Phi_{e,\nu}$

    Definition: Radiant flux per unit frequency

    Spectral flux in frequency, denoted $\Phi_{e,\nu}$, is defined as

    $$\Phi_{e,\nu} = \frac{\partial \Phi_e}{\partial \nu}.$$

    where ν is the frequency.

    Unit: watt per hertz – W/Hz

    Dimension: $\mathbf{M \cdot L^2 \cdot T^{-2}}$

2. *Symbol*: $\Phi_{e,\lambda}$

    Definition: Radiant flux per unit wavelength.

    Spectral flux in wavelength, denoted $\Phi_{e,\lambda}$, is defined as

    $$\Phi_{e,\lambda} = \frac{\partial \Phi_e}{\partial \lambda}$$

    where λ is the wavelength.

    Unit: watt per meter - W/m

    Is commonly measured in $W \cdot nm^{-1}$

    Dimension: $\mathbf{M \cdot L \cdot T^{-3}}$

SPECTRAL INTENSITY

3. *Symbol:*　　$I_{e,\,\Omega,\nu}$

    Definition: Radiant intensity per unit frequency. This is a *directional* quantity.

    Spectral intensity in frequency, denoted $I_{e,\Omega,\nu}$, is defined as

    $$I_{e,\Omega,\nu} = \frac{\partial I_{e,\Omega}}{\partial \nu}.$$

    where ν is the frequency.

Unit: watt per steradian per hertz ($W \cdot sr^{-1} \cdot Hz^{-1}$)

Dimension: $\mathbf{M \cdot L^2 \cdot T^{-2}}$

4. *Symbol: $I_{e,\,\Omega,\lambda}$*

Definition: Radiant intensity per unit wavelength. This is a *directional* quantity.

Spectral intensity in wavelength, denoted $I_{e,\Omega,\lambda}$, is defined as

$$I_{e,\Omega,\lambda} = \frac{\partial I_{e,\Omega}}{\partial \lambda}$$

where λ is the wavelength.

Unit: watt per steradian per meter ($W \cdot sr^{-1} \cdot m^{-1}$)

Is commonly measured in $W \cdot sr^{-1} \cdot nm^{-1}$.

Dimension: $\mathbf{M \cdot L \cdot T^{-3}}$.

SPECTRAL IRRADIANCE

Spectral irradiance is the irradiance of a surface per unit frequency or wavelength, depending on whether the spectrum is taken as a function of frequency or of wavelength. The two forms have different dimensions and units:

1. **Spectral irradiance of a frequency spectrum**

Unit: watts per square meter per hertz ($W \cdot m^{-2} \cdot Hz^{-1}$),

Dimension: $\mathbf{M \cdot T^{-2}}$

2. **spectral irradiance of a wavelength** spectrum

Unit: watts per square meter per meter ($W \cdot m^{-3}$), or more commonly, watts per square meter per nanometer ($W \cdot m^{-2} \cdot nm^{-1}$).

Dimension: $\mathbf{M \cdot L^{-1} \cdot T^{-3}}$

Note: Non-SI units of spectral flux density include jansky (1 Jy $= 10^{-26}$ $W \cdot m^{-2} \cdot Hz^{-1}$) and solar flux unit (1 sfu $= 10^{-22}$ $W \cdot m^{-2} \cdot Hz^{-1} = 10^4$ Jy)

See: "irradiance"

SPECTRAL RADIANCE (Specific intensity)

Spectral irradiance is the irradiance of a surface per unit frequency or wavelength, depending on whether the spectrum is taken as a function of frequency or of wavelength. The two forms have different dimensions and units:

1.   **spectral irradiance of a frequency spectrum**

Unit: watts per square meter per hertz ($W \cdot m^{-2} \cdot Hz^{-1}$),

Dimension: $\mathbf{M \cdot T^{-2}}$

2.   **spectral irradiance of a wavelength** spectrum

Unit: watts per square meter per meter ($W \cdot m^{-3}$), or more commonly, watts per square meter per nanometer ($W \cdot m^{-2} \cdot nm^{-1}$).

Dimension: $\mathbf{M \cdot L^{-1} \cdot T^{-3}}$

Note: Non-SI units of spectral flux density include jansky ($1\ Jy = 10^{-26}\ W \cdot m^{-2} \cdot Hz^{-1}$) and solar flux unit ($1\ sfu = 10^{-22}\ W \cdot m^{-2} \cdot Hz^{-1} = 10^4\ Jy$)

See: "irradiance"

SPEED

See velocity (note)

The magnitude of velocity without reference to direction.

SPEED, ROTATIONAL

See frequency, rotational (note)

STANTON NUMBER

Symbol: St

Definition: It is a dimensionless number that measures the ratio of heat transferred into a fluid to the thermal capacity of the fluid. It is used to characterize heat transfer in forced convection flows.

It is defined by:

$$St = h/\rho\, c_p\, v,$$

Where h is the heat transfer coefficient, ρ is the density of the fluid, c_p is the specific heat capacity, and v is the speed of flow.

It is equal to the Nusselt number divided (Nu) by the product of the Prandtl (Pr) and Reynolds numbers (Re), i.e.,

$$St = Nu\,/Re.\ Pr$$

Field of application: heat transfer and fluid dynamics (forced convection)

Unit: There are no units or dimensions.

Note: The name is after Sir Thomas Stanton (1865-1931)

See" Prandtl number" and "Reynolds number ".

STANTON NUMBER FOR MASS TRANSFER

Symbol: St^*

Definition: A dimensionless parameter used in mass transfer problems. It is given by:

$$St^* = m\,/(t\,A\,\rho\,v),$$

where m is the mass transferred across area A in time t, ρ is the density, and v is the speed of flow.

Unit: There are no units or dimensions.

See also" Stanton number."

STAUDINGER VALUE

Definition: A number which is sometimes used to give a value to the molecular weight of a polymer. The number is still used in sales literature, and charts that relate the number to the real molecular weight are available.

Units: There are no units or dimensions.

Note: 1. It is sometimes known as the Staudinger molecular weight but does not represent the actual molecular weight of the polymer, which is usually considerably higher.

2. The name is after the Nobel Prize winner H. Staudinger (1881-1965).

STEFAN NUMBER

Symbol: St or Ste

Definition: The **Stefan number** (**St** or **Ste**) is defined as the ratio of sensible heat to latent heat. It is given by the formula.

$$\text{Ste} = \frac{c_p \Delta T}{L}$$

where

- c_p is the specific heat,
  - c_p is the specific heat of the solid phase in the freezing process, while c_p is the specific heat of the liquid phase in the melting process.
- ΔT is the temperature difference between phases,
- L is the latent heat of melting.

It is a dimensionless parameter that is useful in analyzing a Stefan problem. The parameter was developed from Josef Stefan's calculations of the rate of phase change of water into ice on the polar ice caps and coined by G.S.H. Lock in 1969.

Unit: Dimensionless

STERADIANCY

See radiance (note)

STIFFNESS, ACOUSTICAL

Symbol: **Sa (BS)**

Definition: The product of the acoustical stiffness reactance Xa and the angular frequency ω .

$$S_a = X_a\, \omega$$

If the volume V of an enclosure has dimensions that are small in comparison with the wavelengths involved, the acoustical stiffness is the product of the density ρ of the medium and the square of the velocity c of the wave propagation divided by the volume.

$$S_a = \rho c^2 / V$$

Unit: Pascal per meter cubed. (kg.m^{-4}.s^{-2})

Dimension: M L^{-4} T^{-2}(vector).

STIFFNESS (MECHANICAL)

Symbol: s

Definition: The product of the mechanical stiffness reactance X_m and the angular frequency ω.

$$S = X_m\,\omega$$

Unit: Newton per meter.

Dimension: $M\,T^{-2}$ (vector)

STOKES NUMBER

Symbol: Stk

Definition: The **Stokes number (Stk)**, named after George Gabriel Stokes, is a dimensionless number characterizing the behavior of particles suspended in a fluid flow. The Stokes number is defined as the ratio of the characteristic time of a particle (or droplet) to a characteristic time of the flow or of an obstacle or

$$\mathrm{Stk} = \frac{t_0\,u_0}{l_0}$$

Where t_0 is the relaxation time of the particle (the time constant in the exponential decay of the particle velocity due to drag), u_0 is the fluid velocity of the flow well away from the obstacle and l_0 is the characteristic dimension of the obstacle (typically its diameter). A particle with a low Stokes number follows fluid streamlines (perfect advection), while a particle with a large Stokes number is dominated by its inertia and continues along its initial trajectory.

Field of application: particle suspensions (ratio of characteristic time of particle to time of flow)

Unit: Dimensionless

STRAIN

(1) TENSILE STRAIN

Symbol: e; sometimes ε

Definition: The fractional increase in length Δl from the length l_0 in a specified reference state.

$$e = \Delta l / l_0$$

Note: The quantity is also termed the linear strain or fractional (or relative) elongation.

(2) SHEAR STRAIN

Symbol: γ; sometimes ϕ (CBS)

Definition: The shear strain is given by the angle (in radians) through which twisting takes place.

Note: The quantity is also termed by the angle of shear (shear angle).

(3) BULK STRAIN

Symbol: θ

Definition: The fractional increase in volume ΔV from the volume V_o in a specified reference state.

$$\theta = \Delta V / V_0$$

Note: The quantity is also called the volume strain or hydrostatic strain.

Unit: There are no units or dimensions (except that shear strain may be measured in radians) (scalar).

STRENGTH (OF A SOURCE), SOUND

Symbol: A (BS)

Definition: Rate of volume V displacement of the surface which constitutes the source.

$$A = dV//dt \ (t = \text{time})$$

Unit: Meter cubed per second.

Dimension: $L^3 T^{-1}$(scalar)

STRESS

See pressure (note)

STROUHAL NUMBER

Symbol: *Sr*

Definition: A number involving the frequency of the vibrations produced in a taut wire by the passage of a current of fluid. The vibrations are called aeolian tones. For fluid of velocity v passing in wire of diameter d and the frequency of the note is f, the number is given by:

$$Sr = f\,d\,/v$$

Field of application: Vortex shedding (ratio of characteristic oscillatory velocity to ambient flow velocity)

Unit: There are no units or dimensions.

Note: 1. The name is after V. Strouhal (1850-1922), who derived the relation in 1878.

2. The number has a value between 0.185 and 0.2 or 5.4 and 5, according to the definition used.

3. The Strouhal number is sometimes called the **"Reduced frequency"** and is used extensively in work on fast moving fluids as, for example, the air in the vicinity of the tip of an aircraft propeller.

STUART NUMBER

Symbol: N

Definition: The **Stuart number** (**N**), also known as the magnetic interaction parameter, is a dimensionless number of fluids, i.e., gases or liquids. It is defined as the ratio of electromagnetic to inertial forces, which gives an estimate of the relative importance of a magnetic field on a flow. The Stuart number is relevant for flows of conducting fluids, e.g., in fusion reactors, steel casters or plasmas.

$$N = \frac{B^2 L_c \sigma}{\rho U} = \frac{\mathrm{Ha}^2}{\mathrm{Re}}$$

- B – magnetic field
- L_c – characteristic length
- σ – electric conductivity
- U – characteristic velocity scale
- ρ – density
- Ha – Hartmann number
- Re – Reynolds number

Field of application: magnetohydrodynamics (ratio of electromagnetic to inertial forces)

Unit: Dimensionless

SUNSPOT NUMBER (also called WOLF NUMBER)

Symbol: R

Definition: A number describes sunspot activity given by the relation:

$$R = k\,(10g + f),$$

Where k is a constant depending on the instrument used, g is the number of disturbed regions, and f is the total number of sunspots.

Units: There are no units or dimensions.

Note: The number is also called Wolf number, after R. Wolf, who proposed it in 1852.

SURFACE TENSION

Symbol: γ; sometimes σ

Definition: Force F across a line element in a surface divided by the length l of the line element.

$$\gamma = F / l\,\mathrm{I}$$

Alternatively, surface tension is the free (i.e., isothermal) surface energy E divided by the area A over which the energy is applied.

$$\gamma = E/A$$

Unit: Newton per meter (equivalent to the Joule per meter squared).

Dimension: $M\,T^{-2}$ (vector).

SUSCEPTANCE

Symbol: B

Definition: The magnitude of the imaginary part of admittance Y.

$$Y = G + i\,B \;(G = \text{electrical conductance}).$$

Unit: Siemens.

Dimension: $M^{-1}\,L^{-2}\,T^3\,I^2$

SUSCEPTIBILITY, ELECTRIC

Symbol: Xe

Definition: One less than the relative permittivity ε_r.

$$Xe = \varepsilon_r - 1$$

Unit: There are no units or dimensions (scalar).

Note: For unrationalized system of units, $X^*e = (\varepsilon_r - 1)\,/\,4\pi$

SUSCEPTIBILITY, MAGNETIC

Symbol: k

Definition: One less than the relative permeability μ_r.

$$k = \mu_r - 1$$

Unit: There are no units or dimensions (scalar).

Note: 1. The quantity is more correctly termed the magnetic volume susceptibility.

The magnetic mass susceptibility **x** (BS) is the volume susceptibility divided by the density.

$$\mathbf{x} = k\,/\,\rho$$

This latter quantity is also termed the specific susceptibility.

2. The magnetic susceptibility in the case of unrationalized system of unit is given by:

$$k^* = k\,/\,4\pi = (\mu_r - 1)\,/\,4\pi$$

3. Magnetic materials are classified according to the value of the magnetic susceptibility into three categories:

- *Diamagnetic*: The materials of this group have very small negative susceptibility (about 10^{-6}).

- *Paramagnetic:* The susceptibility of the material of this group is positive but small (between 10^{-3} and 10^{-6}).

- *Ferromagnetic*: The susceptibility of the material of this group is positive and much more than 10^{-3}.

T

TAYLOR NUMBER

Symbol: Ta

Definition: In fluid dynamics, the **Taylor number (Ta)** is a dimensionless quantity that characterizes the importance of centrifugal "forces" or so-called inertial forces due to rotation of a fluid about an axis relative to viscous forces.

In 1923, Geoffrey Ingram Taylor introduced this quantity in his article on the stability of flow.[2]

The typical context of the Taylor number is in the characterization of the Couette flow between rotating colinear cylinders or rotating concentric spheres. In the case of a system that is not rotating uniformly, such as the case of cylindrical Couette flow, where the outer cylinder is stationary, and the inner cylinder is rotating, inertial forces will often tend to destabilize a system, whereas viscous forces tend to stabilize a system and damp out perturbations and turbulence.

On the other hand, the effect of rotation can be stabilizing in other cases. For example, in the case of cylindrical Couette flow with positive Rayleigh discriminant, there are no axisymmetric instabilities. Another example is a bucket of water that is rotating uniformly (i.e., undergoing solid body rotation). Here, the fluid is subject to the Taylor-Proudman theorem, which says that small motions will tend to produce purely two-dimensional perturbations to the overall rotational flow. However, in this case, the effects of rotation and viscosity are usually characterized by the Ekman number and the Rossby number rather than by the Taylor number.

There are various definitions of the Taylor number, which are not all equivalent, but most commonly, it is given by

$$\mathrm{Ta} = \frac{4\Omega^2 R^4}{\nu^2}$$

Where Ω is a characteristic angular velocity, R is a characteristic linear dimension perpendicular to the rotation axis, and ν is the kinematic viscosity.

In the case of inertial instability such as Taylor–Couette flow, the Taylor number is mathematically analogous to the Grashof number, which characterizes the strength of buoyant forces relative to viscous forces in convection. When the former exceeds the latter by a critical ratio, convective instability sets in. Likewise, in various systems and geometries, when the Taylor number exceeds a critical value, inertial instabilities set in, sometimes known as Taylor instabilities, which may lead to Taylor vortices or cells.

A Taylor–Couette flow describes the fluid behavior between 2 concentric cylinders in rotation. A textbook definition of the Taylor number is

$$Ta = \frac{\Omega^2 R_1 (R_2 - R_1)^3}{\nu^2}$$

Where R_1 is the internal radius of the internal cylinder, and R_2 is the external radius of the external cylinder.

The critical Ta is about 1700.

Field of application: fluid dynamics (rotating fluid flows; inertial forces due to rotation of a fluid versus viscous forces)

Unit: Dimensionless

[Ref. HandWiki]

TELEPHONE TRAFFIC INTENSITY

Symbol: A also y and R

Definition: Is a measure of the density of the traffic. It is the product of the number of calls c_A made in a given period of time and the average length of the calls t_m (measured in the same time unit).

$A = c_A . t_m$

Unit: Many units are in use, e.g., Erlang (E or Erl), Traffic Unit (TU), Verkehrseinheit (VE), Cent Call Seconds (CCS), Hundred Call Seconds (HCS), Unit Call (UC), Appels reduits a' l'heure chargee (ARHC) and Equated Busy Hour call (EBHC)

Dimension: There are no dimensions.

TEMPERATURE

(1) ABSOLUTE, i.e. THERMODYNAMIC TEMPERATURE

Symbol: T; sometimes Θ

Definition: There is no formal definition of absolute temperature. It can only be explained in terms of an inadequate synonym, eg, degree of hotness.

Unit: Kelvin

Dimension: Θ, $L^2 T^{-2}$ (scalar)

(2) CUSTOMARY TEMPERATURE

Symbol: θ; sometimes t.

Definition: The difference between the absolute temperature T and a conventional constant T_0. $\theta = T - T_0$. (The value of T_0 is 273.15 kelvins).

Unit: Degree Celsius.

Dimension: Θ $L^2 T^{-2}$ (scalar)

(3) TEMPERATURE INTERVAL or DIFFERENCE

Symbol: θ; sometimes t. Also $\Delta\theta, \Delta T$ sometimes Δt , $\Delta\Theta$

Definition: The difference between two temperatures θ_1, θ_2 each measured in the same units. $\theta = \theta_1 - \theta_2$

Unit: Kelvin

Dimension: Θ $L^2 T^{-2}$ (scalar)

Note: The quantity is also termed the thermal potential difference, and the unit is then termed the thermal volt.

Note: (1) The several different kinds of temperature include the following examples.

(a) Color temperature (of a light source). The temperature of a full (i.e., Planckian) radiator that would emit radiation of substantially the same spectral distribution in the visible region as the radiation from the source and which would produce in the eye the same sensation of color as the given radiator. An alternative definition implies the same color as the given radiator. An alternative definition implies the same color sensation in the eye but not necessarily the same spectral distribution. This alternative definition is not preferred, and the temperature as defined by it is not identical with that in the first case.

(b) Luminance temperature (of a light source at a given wavelength). The temperature of full (i.e., Planckian) radiator, which has the same luminance as the radiator concerned at the given wavelength. This was formerly termed the brightness temperature.

(2) Because of the difficulty of measuring the absolute temperature of body, a practical scale has been devised such that temperatures on it agree as closely as possible with those of the thermodynamic scale (and certainly within the limits of experimental determination). The International Practical Temperature Scale of 1968 (IPTS-68) is based on the concept of assigning values to certain reproducible equilibrium states (fixed points) and on standard interpolation procedures. The defining fixed points are given in the following Table.

State	Assigned value on the IPTS – 68		Estimated uncertainty Kelvin
	Kelvin	^0C	
Equilibrium between the solid, liquid and vapor phases of equilibrium hydrogen (triple point hydrogen)[2]	13.81	-259.34	0.01
Equilibrium between hydrogen and its vapor at a pressure of 25/76 standard atmosphere	17.042	-256.108	0.01
Equilibrium between liquid equilibrium hydrogen[1] and its vapor (boiling point of equilibrium hydrogen)[3]	20.28	-256.87	0.01
Equilibrium between liquid neon and its vapor (boiling point of neon)[3]	27.102	-246.048	0.01
Equilibrium between the solid, liquid and vapor phases of oxygen (triple point of oxygen)[2]	54.361	-218.789	0.01
Equilibrium between liquid	90.188	-182.962	0.01

neon and vapor phases of water (triple point of oxygen)[3]			
Equilibrium between the solid, liquid and vapor phases of water (triple point of water)[2,4]	273.1[6]	0.01[5]	0[6]
Equilibrium between liquid water and its vapor (boiling point of water)[3,4] Or Equilibrium between solid and liquid tin (freezing point of tin)[3]	373.15 505.1181	100 231.9681	0.005 0.015
Equilibrium between solid and liquid zinc (freezing point of zinc)[3]	692.73	419.58	0.03
Equilibrium between solid and liquid silver (freezing point of silver)[3]	1234.08	961.93	0.2
Equilibrium between solid and liquid gold (freezing point of gold)[3]	1337.58	1064.43	0.2

Notes to the Table

The interpolation procedures employed are:

-259.35 °c to 630.74 DC, measurement of resistance using a platinum resistance thermometer; 630.74 °c to 1 064.43 DC, measurement of electromotive force using a platinum 10% platinum 90% rhodium thermocouple; above 1 064.43 DC, measurement of spectral concentration of radiation and the application of Planck's black-body law.

1 I.e. hydrogen having equilibrium ortho-para composition

2 At zero pressure

3 At standard atmospheric pressure (101 325 pascals)

4 With the isotopic composition of sea water

5 Values fixed by definition

6 By definition

TEMPERATURE COEFFICIENT

Symbol: a

Definition: Temperature coefficient is defined in connection with a quantity X that varies with temperature. Often, for quantities that vary linearly (or approximately so) with temperature, the coefficient is defined as the fractional increase in X divided by the increase in temperature under specified conditions.

$$\alpha = \frac{\Delta X}{X \Delta \theta} \approx \frac{1}{X} \frac{dX}{d\vartheta}$$

Unit: Per Kelvin.

Dimensions: $L^{-2} T^2$ (scalar)

Note: Expansion coefficient (qv) and pressure coefficient (qv) are examples of temperature coefficients.

TEMPERATURE GRADIENT

Definition: The rate of change of temperature θ with respect to distance x.

Temperature gradient $= d\theta / dx$

Unit: Kelvin per meter.

Dimension: $L^{-1}\,\Theta$; L T2 (scalar).

TENSION

See force (note 1)

TENSION, ELECTRIC

See potential difference, electric (note)

TENSION, MECHANICAL

See pressure (note)

THOMSON COEFFICIENT

Symbol: σ; sometimes αT

Definition: Heat energy E developed between two points in a wire as a result of a difference in temperatures divided by the product of the charge Q flowing and the difference in temperature ΔT between the two points.

$\sigma = E / Q\Delta T$

Unit: Joule per coulomb Kelvin = volt per Kelvin.

Note: 1. This coefficient measures the Thomson effect, and the definition assumes that the Joule effect (the heat developed in a conductor due to the flow of current) is zero.

2. The Thomson coefficient was called the specific heat of electricity by William Thomson.

THROUGHPUT

Definition: Net data transfer rate between an information source and an information sink. The American National Standards Institute (ANSI) recommended the use of the Transfer Rate of Information Bits (TRIB) as a measure for the net throughput. TRIB is defined as the number of information bits accepted by the sink divided by the total time required to get those bits accepted. For a block of length M characters of B bits per character which contains C noninformation characters, the TRIB is given by:

$$TRIB = \frac{B(M - C)(1 - p)}{t + (\frac{BM}{R})} \; bit/second$$

where, p = The probability of an error occurring in a block,

t = The time between blocks in seconds, and

R = The nominal data rate in bits per second.

Note: Throughput is rarely exceeding 80% of the nominal link data rate. However, data compression techniques can produce an effective data rate exceeding the nominal rate.

THRUST

See force (note 1)

TIME

Symbol: t

Definition: There is no formal definition of time. It can only be explained in terms of a synonym, e.g., duration.

Unit: Second.

Dimension: T (scalar).

Note: (1) The symbol T is used for periodic time (period), i.e., time taken to describe one complete cycle of operations.

(2) The symbol τ (occasionally T) is used for the time constant of an exponentially varying quantity f(t), and is defined as the time after which the quantity would reach a specified limit if it maintains its initial rate of variation. $f(t) = A + Be^{-t/}\tau$

(3) The symbol T is used in acoustics for reverberation time: this is the time required for the average sound energy density in an enclosure, initially in a steady state, to decrease to one millionth of its initial value after the sound has ceased.

This decrease represents a fall of 60 decibels in intensity level.

TRAFIC FACTOR

1.   FUEL CONSUMPTION

Symbol: F

Definition: Volume V of fuel used up in traveling a certain distance is divided by the distance.

$$F = V/s$$

Unit: Meter squared.

Dimension: L^2

2.   **MASS-DISTANCE**

Definition: Mass m carried multiplied by distance s traveled.

Mass-distance = $m\ s$.

Unit: Kilogram meter.

Dimension: M L.

3.   **MASS PER FUEL CONSUMPTION**

Definition: Mass m carried divided by fuel consumption F.

Mass per fuel consumption = m/F

Unit: Kilogram per meter squared.

Dimension: $M L^2$.

TRANSFER COEFFICIENT, HEAT

See conductance, thermal (note)

TRANSMISSION COEFFICIENT

Symbol: τ

Definition: Energy E, transmitted through and beyond a surface divided by that incident on it E_o under identical conditions.

$$\tau = E_t/E_o$$

Unit: There are no units or dimensions.

Note: 1. The quantity is also termed the transmission factor or trasmitance, the use of the last name being deprecated.

2. The transmission coefficient is generally expressed as a percentage.

3. The transmission coefficient, the reflection coefficient ρ and the scattering coefficient δ are related by the relation.

$\tau + \delta + \rho = 1$.

4. In sound, the transmission coefficient depends on the frequency of the sound. Also, $R = 10 \log(1/\tau)$, where R is the sound reduction/actor or sound reduction index.

5. In light, there are two transmission coefficients: the direct transmission coefficient is concerned with transmission without scatter; the diffuse transmission coefficient is concerned with light transmitted with scatter in many directions. Both depend on the angle of incidence, the mode of illumination and the wavelength distribution of the light.

See also" reflection coefficient" and "scattering coefficient"

TRANSMISSION DENSITY, INTERNAL

Symbol- Di

Definition: · A measure of the ability of a body to absorb radiation as expressed by the logarithm to base ten of the reciprocal of the internal transmittance

$Di = log_{10} (I / \tau_i)$

Unit: There are no units or dimensions.

Note: Also called absorbance.

See" transmittance. *Internal and "absorbance."*

TRANSMISSIVITY

Definition: The internal transmission coefficient of a unit thickness of a transmitting material under conditions in which the boundary of the material has no influence.

Unit: There are no units or dimensions (scalar)

TRANSMITTANCE

See transmission coefficient (note J); transmittancy (note)

TRANSMITTANCE, INTERNAL

Symbol: τ_i

Definition: A measure of the ability of a material to transmit radiation as expressed by the ratio of flux reaching Φ_r the exit surface of the body to the flux leaving Φ_l the entry surface.

$\tau_l = \Phi_r / \Phi_l$

Unit: There are no units or dimensions.

Note: 1. The internal transmittance only applies to regular transmission and not to substances that scatter light or to reflection at tile surfaces of the body (Compare with transmittance).

2. The internal transmittance is related to the internal absorptance α_i by the relation:

$\alpha_i + \tau_i = 1$

See "absorptance, internal ", "transmission density, internal" and "transmittance"

TRANSMITTANCE, THERMAL

See conductance thermal (note)

TRANSMITTANCY

Definition: transmission coefficient of a liquid or solid solution divided by that of the solvent of the same form and thickness.

Unit: There are no units or dimensions (scalar).

Note: The quantity has also been known by the deprecated name transmittance.

U

URSELL NUMBER

Symbol: U

Definition: In fluid dynamics, the **Ursell number** indicates the nonlinearity of long surface gravity waves on a fluid layer. This dimensionless parameter is named after Fritz Ursell, who discussed its significance in 1953.

The Ursell number is derived from the Stokes wave expansion, a perturbation series for nonlinear periodic waves, in the long-wave limit of shallow water – when the wavelength is much larger than the water depth. Then the Ursell number U is defined as:

$$U = \frac{H}{h}\left(\frac{\lambda}{h}\right)^2 = \frac{H\lambda^2}{h^3}$$

Which is, apart from a constant $3/(32\,\pi^2)$, the ratio of the amplitudes of the second-order to the first-order term in the free surface elevation. The used parameters are:

- H: the wave height, *i.e.,* the difference between the elevations of the wave crest and trough,
- h: The mean water depth and
- λ: the wavelength, which has to be large compared to the depth, $\lambda " h$.

So, the Ursell parameter U is the relative wave height H/h times the relative wavelength λ/h squared.

For long waves ($\lambda " h$) with small Ursell numbers, $U " 32\,\pi^2/3 \approx 100$, linear wave theory is applicable. Otherwise (and most often), a non-linear theory for fairly long waves ($\lambda > 7\,h$) – like the Korteweg–de Vries equation or Boussinesq equations – has to be used. The parameter, with different normalization, was already introduced by George Gabriel Stokes in his historical paper on surface gravity waves of 1847.

Field of application: wave mechanics (nonlinearity of surface gravity waves on a shallow fluid layer)

Unit: Dimensionless

V

VAPOUR CONCENTRATION

See humidity, absolute (note)

VAPOUR DENSITY

See density, relative (note 1)

VECTOR POTENTIAL, MAGNETIC

Symbol: A

Definition: The curl of the magnetic vector potential is equal to the magnetic flux density

B. $\nabla \times A = B$

Unit: Webber per meter.

Dimension: $M\,L\,T^{-2}\,I^{-2}$ (vector)

VELOCITY

Symbol: v.

The symbols u, v, *and* w are used for the vector components of velocity. The symbol c is used for the velocity of electromagnetic radiation in free space; Co is used if c must be kept for phase velocity in a medium. In problems on translational motion, u is used for the initial velocity.

Definition: Rate of change of displacement s with respect of time t. $v = ds/dt$

Unit: Meter per second.

Dimension: $L\,T^{-1}$ (vector)

Note: The term speed refers to the scalar form of velocity, i.e., linear or translational velocity.

VELOCITY, ANGULAR

Symbol: ω; sometimes Ω

Definition: The rate at which a body rotates about an axis, i.e., the rate of char of the rotation angle ϑ with respect to time t.

$\omega = d\vartheta / dt$

It is a vector quantity equal to the linear velocity divided by the radius.

(See also "Angular frequency" for an alternative definition.)

Unit: Radian per second, degree per second.

Dimension: T^{-1}

Note: (1) The term angular velocity implies a reference to an analytical angle; an alternative term, rotational velocity, implies a reference to a geometrical angle, although there is no practical distinction between the two. Other alternative terms are angular frequency, circular frequency, circular frequency and pulsitance, the use of the last-named being deprecated.

(2) This quantity must be distinguished from rotational frequency.

VELOCITY GRADIENT

See viscosity

VELOCITY POTENTIAL

Symbol: ϕ (BS)

Definition: The gradient of the velocity potential is equal to the particle velocity v with a reversed sign. $\nabla\phi = -v$

Unit: Per second.

Dimension T^{-1} (scalar)

VELOCITY RATIO

Symbol: V (O)

Definition: The velocity v_2 given to the effort (input force) of a machine divided by the velocity v_1 that the load (output force) acquires. $V = v^2/v_1$

Unit: There are no units or dimensions (scalar).

VISCOSITY

Symbol: η sometimes μ

Definition: Tangential stress t: in a liquid undergoing streamline (i.e., laminar) flow divided by the velocity gradient. (The velocity gradient is the rate of change of velocity v with distance z across the flow of liquid, *dv/dz*

$$\eta = \tau / (dv/dz)$$

Unit: Newton second per meter squared. $(kg.m^{-1}.s^{-1})$

Dimension: $M\ L^{-1}\ T^{-1}$ (scalar).

Note: The quantity is more correctly termed the dynamic or absolute viscosity.

VISCOSITY, KINEMATIC

Symbol: *v*

Definition: Dynamic viscosity η of fluid divided by its density ρ.

$$v = \eta / \rho$$

It measures the kinematic effect of the viscosity.

Unit: Meter squarer per second. $(m^2.s^{-1})$

Dimension: $L^2\ T^{-1}$

Note: Kinematic viscosity is used in modifying the equation of motion of a perfect fluid to include the terms due to a real fluid.

VISCOSITY, MAGNETIC

Definition: The existence of a time delay between a change in the magnetic field applied to a ferromagnetic material and the resulting change in magnetic induction, which is too great to be explained by the existence of an eddy current.

Also, is the effect possessed by a magnetic field in the absence of sizeable mechanical forces or electric fields, of damping motions of a conducting fluid perpendicular to the field similar to ordinary viscosity.

VISCOSITY, SPECIFIC

Definition: Viscosity η_1 of a substance divided by the viscosity η_2 of a reference substance under conditions specified for both substances (normally equal temperatures).

Specific viscosity = η_1 / η_2

Unit: There are no units or dimensions (scalar).

Note. In the case of liquids, the reference substance is usually water.

VOLTAGE

See potential difference.

VOLUME

Symbol: V; occasionally v.

Definition: The space contained by a closed area. The size of the volume will be expressed by a formula, the nature of which depends on the shape of the space.

Unit: Meter cubed. (m^3)

Dimension: L^3 (scalar).

Note: The term capacity is also used, often where the unit of measurement is not of the form cubic.

VOLUME, ATOMIC

Definition: The volume in the solid state of one mole of an element. Thus:

Atomic volume = (Atomic weight) / (Density of solid)

VOLUME FLOW RATE

Symbol: q_{vi}; sometimes U or q

Definition: Rate of change of volume V with respect to time t.

Unit: Meter cubed per second. ($m^3.s^{-1}$)

Dimension: $L^3 T^{-1}$ (scalar)

Note: The quantity is also termed the volume velocity

VOLUME, MOLAR

Definition: The **molar volume**, symbol V_m, of a substance is the ratio of the volume V occupied by a substance to the amount of substance n, usually given at a given temperature and pressure.

$$\text{Molar volume} = V/n$$

It is equal to the molar mass (M) divided by the mass density (ρ):

$$V_m = \frac{M}{\rho}$$

Unit: Meter cubed per mole ($m^3.mol^{-1}$)

Dimension: $L^3 N^{-1}$ (scalar)

Note: N is used as the dimensional symbol of molar value.

VOLUME, SPECIFIC

Symbol: v

Definition: Volume V divided by mass m, i.e., the reciprocal of density.

$$V = V/m$$

Unit: Meter cubed per kilogramme.

Dimension: $M^{-1} L^3$ (scalar)

WALLIS PARAMETER

Symbol: j*

Definition: **Nondimensional parameter defined as:**

$$j^* = R\left(\frac{\omega\rho}{\mu}\right)^{\frac{1}{2}}$$

It is used in multiphase flows (nondimensional superficial velocity)

WAVE LENGTH

See length (note)

WAVE NUMBER

Symbol: The symbol is used in spectroscopy

Definition: The reciprocal of length l, especially wavelength λ

$\omega = I / l$, especially $\bar{\upsilon} = I/\lambda$

Unit: Per meter

Dimension: L^{-1} (generally regarded as scalar).

Note: The term circular wave number is used for the quantity k defined by $k = 2\pi\sigma$

WEBER NUMBER

Symbol: *We*

Definition: A dimensionless parameter used in the study of the formation of bubbles. It is the ratio of inertia to surface tension forces and is given by:

$$We = \rho v^2 \, l \, / \, \gamma$$

Where ρ is the density of the liquid, v is the velocity of the wave, γ is the surface tension, and l represents some characteristic length.

Field of application: multiphase flow (strongly curved surfaces; ratio of inertia to surface tension)

Unit: There are no units or dimensions.

Note: Occasionally, the Weber number is defined as the square root of the above function.

WEIGHT

See force (note 2)

WEIGHT DENSITY

See weight, Specific (note 1)

WEIGHT, SPECIFIC

Symbol: γ

Definition: Weight W divided by Volume V. $\gamma = W / V$

Unit: Kilogramme-weight per meter cubed: kilogramme-force per meter cubed.

Dimension: $M\ L^{-2}\ T^{-2}$ (vector).

Note: (1)   The quantity is also termed the weight density

(2)   Because the specific weight of a body has a value that depends on the value of the local acceleration of free fall, it is here to measure it in practice with reference to the standard value of the better to measure it in practice with reference to the standard value of the acceleration of free fall, or (best of all) in terms of absolute force, i.e., in newton's per meter cubed.

WEISSENBERG NUMBER

Symbol: Wi

Definition: The **Weissenberg number (Wi)** is a dimensionless number used in the study of viscoelastic flows. It is named after Karl Weissenberg. The dimensionless number compares the elastic forces to the viscous forces. It can be variously defined, but it is usually given by the relation of stress relaxation time of the fluid and a specific process time. For instance, in simple steady shear, the Weissenberg number, often abbreviated as Wi or We, is defined as the shear rate $\gamma\dot{}$ times the relaxation time λ. Using the Maxwell Model and the Oldroyd Model, the elastic forces can be written as the first Normal force (N_1).

$$Wi = \frac{\text{elastic forces}}{\text{viscous forces}} = \frac{\tau_{xx} - \tau_{yy}}{\tau_{xy}} = \frac{\lambda\mu\dot{\gamma}^2}{\mu\dot{\gamma}} = \dot{\gamma}\lambda.$$

Since this number is obtained from scaling the evolution of the stress, it contains choices for the shear or elongation rate and the length scale. Therefore, the exact definition of all nondimensional numbers should be given, as well as the number itself.

While Wi is similar to the Deborah number and is often confused with it in technical literature, they have different physical interpretations. The Weissenberg number indicates the degree of anisotropy or orientation generated by the deformation and is appropriate to describe flows with a constant stretch history, such as simple shear. In contrast, the Deborah number should be used to describe flows with a non-constant stretch history and physically represent the rate at which elastic energy is stored or released.

Field of application: viscoelastic flows (shear rate times the relaxation time)

Unit: Dimensionless

WOMERSLEY NUMBER

Symbol: α or W_o

Definition: The **Womersley number** (α or W_o) is a dimensionless number in biofluid mechanics and biofluid dynamics. It is a dimensionless expression of the pulsatile flow frequency in relation to viscous effects. It is named after John R. Womersley (1907–1958) for his work with blood flow in arteries. The Womersley number is important in keeping dynamic similarity when scaling an experiment. An example of this is scaling up the vascular system for experimental study. The Womersley number is also important in determining the thickness of the boundary layer to see if entrance effects can be ignored.

The Womersley number, usually denoted α, is defined by the relation

$$\alpha^2 = \frac{\text{transient inertial force}}{\text{viscous force}} = \frac{\rho\omega U}{\mu U L^{-2}} = \frac{\omega L^2}{\mu\rho^{-1}} = \frac{\omega L^2}{\nu}$$

Where L is an appropriate length scale (for example the radius of a pipe), ω is the angular frequency of the oscillations, and $v,\ \mu,\ \rho$ are the kinematic viscosity, density, and dynamic viscosity of the fluid, respectively. The Womersley number is normally written in the powerless form

$$\alpha = L\left(\frac{\omega\rho}{\mu}\right)^{\frac{1}{2}}$$

This square root of this number is also referred to as **Stokes number**, due to the pioneering work done by Sir George Stokes on the Stokes second problem.

Below is a list of estimated Womersley numbers in different human blood vessels:

Vessel	Diameter (m)	
Aorta	0.025	13.83
Artery	0.004	2.21
Arteriole	3×10^{-5}	0.0166
Capillary	8×10^{-6}	4.43×10^{-3}
Venule	2×10^{-5}	0.011
Veins	0.005	2.77
Vena cava	0.03	16.6

Field of application: biofluid mechanics (continuous and pulsating flows; ratio of pulsatile flow frequency to viscous effects)

Unit: Dimensionless

WORK

See energy (note)

Y

YOUNG'S MODULUS

See elastic modulus (1)

Z

ZEL'DOVICH NUMBER

Symbol: β

Definition: The **Zel'dovich number** is a dimensionless number that provides a quantitative measure for the activation energy of a chemical reaction which appears in the Arrhenius exponent, named after the Russian scientist Yakov Borisovich Zel'dovich, who along with David A. Frank-Kamenetskii, first introduced in their paper in 1938. In the 1983 ICDERS meeting at Poitiers, it was decided to name it after Zel'dovich. It is defined as

$$\beta = \frac{E_a}{RT_b} \cdot \frac{T_b - T_u}{T_b}$$

where

- E_a is the activation energy of the reaction

- R is the universal gas constant

- T_b is the burnt gas temperature

- T_u is the unburnt mixture temperature.

In terms of heat release parameter α, it is given by

$$\beta = \frac{E_a}{RT_b}\alpha$$

For typical combustion phenomena, the value for Zel'dovich number lies in the range β≈8−20. Activation energy asymptotic use this number as the large parameter of expansion.

Field of application: fluid dynamics, Combustion (Measure of activation energy)

Unit: Dimensionless

Section 2

Tables of quantities

and

Physical & Mathematical Constants

(Main Source: From Wikipedia, the free encyclopedia)

Section 2

Tables of quantities

The above dictionary introduced and defined the known physical and engineering quantities. For each quantity, the dictionary gave the following: definition, symbol, units and dimensions. The next section of the dictionary gives in tabulated form a summary of: Name of the quantity, Symbol, Units, Dimension and field of application.

This summary is given in three tables:

- Table -1: Summary of Dimensionless quantities
- Table 2: SI dimensions of Physical Quantities in alphabetic order
- Table 3: SI Dimensions of Physical quantities listed by Category.

Beside these three tables, additional two tables are given:

- Table 4: Constant of Physics and Mathematics
- Table 5: Mathematical Constants and Sequences

Table -1   Dimensionless Quantities

In dimensional analysis , a **dimensionless quantity** is a <u>quantity</u> to which no physical dimension is assigned, also known as a **bare, pure,** or **scalar quantity** or **a quantity of dimension one,** with a corresponding unit of measurement in the <u>SI</u> of the unit **one** (or **1**), which is not explicitly shown. Dimensionless quantities are widely used in many fields, such as mathematics, physics, chemistry, engineering, and economics. Dimensionless quantities are distinct from quantities that have associated dimensions, such as Time (measured in seconds). However, the symbols rad and so are written explicitly where appropriate in order to emphasize that, for radians or steradians, the quantity being considered is or involves the plane angle or solid angle, respectively. For example, etendue is defined as having units of meters times steradians.

Table-1 gives a list of well-known dimensionless quantities illustrating their variety of forms and applications. The table does not include pure numbers, dimensionless ratios, or dimensionless physical constants. (Source: From Wikipedia, the free encyclopedia)

List of dimensionless quantities

Abbe number	V	$V = \dfrac{n_d - 1}{n_F - n_C}$	Optics (dispersion) in optical materials)
Activity coefficient	γ	$\gamma = \dfrac{a}{x}$	Chemistry (Proportion of "active" molecules or atoms)
Albedo	α	$\alpha = (1 - D)\bar{\alpha}(\theta_i) + D\bar{\bar{\alpha}}$	Climatology, astronomy (reflectivity of surfaces or bodies)
Archimedes number	Ar	$\mathrm{Ar} = \dfrac{gL^3 \rho_\ell (\rho - \rho_\ell)}{\mu^2}$	Fluid mechanics (motion of fluids due to density differences)
Arrhenius number	A	$\alpha = \dfrac{E_a}{RT}$	Chemistry (ratio of activation energy to thermal energy)
Atomic weight	M		Chemistry (mass of one atom divided by the atomic mass constant, 1 Da)
Atwood number	A	$A = \dfrac{\rho_1 - \rho_2}{\rho_1 + \rho_2}$	Fluid mechanics (onset of instabilities in fluid mixtures due to density differences)
Bagnold number	Ba	$\mathrm{Ba} = \dfrac{\rho d^2 \lambda^{1/2} \dot{\gamma}}{\mu}$	Fluid mechanics, geology (ratio of grain collision stresses to viscous fluid stresses in flow of a granular material such as grain and sand)
Basic reproduction	R_0		number of infections caused on average by an infectious individual

number			over entire infectious period
Bejan number (fluid mechanics)	Be	$Be = \dfrac{\Delta PL^2}{\mu\alpha}$	Fluid mechanics (dimensionless pressure drop along a channel)
Bejan number (thermodynamics)	Be	$Be = \dfrac{\dot{S}'_{gen,\,\Delta T}}{\dot{S}'_{gen,\,\Delta T} + \dot{S}'_{gen,\,\Delta p}}$	Thermodynamics (ratio of heat transfer irreversibility to total irreversibility due to heat transfer and fluid friction)[
Bingham number	Bm	$Bm = \dfrac{\tau_y L}{\mu V}$	Fluid mechanics, rheology (ratio of yield stress to viscous stress)
Biot number	Bi	$Bi = \dfrac{hL_C}{k_b}$	Heat transfer (surface vs. volume conductivity of solids)
Blake Number	Bl or B	$B = \dfrac{u\rho}{\mu(1-\epsilon)D}$	Geology, fluid mechanics, porous media (inertial over viscous forces in fluid flow through porous media)
Blondeau Number	B_λ	$B_\lambda = \dfrac{t_g v_f}{l_{mf}}$	Sport science, team sports
Bondestin Number	Bo or Bd	$Bo = vL/D = Re\,Sc$	Chemistry (residence-time distribution; similar to the axial mass transfer peclet number)
Bond Number	Bo	$Bo = \dfrac{\rho\alpha L^2}{\gamma}$	Geology, fluids, porous media (bo0uyant versus capillary forces, similar to Eötvös number
Brinkman Number	Br	$Br = \dfrac{\mu U^2}{k(T_\omega - T_0)}$	Heat transfers, fluid mechanics (conduction from a wall to a viscous fluid)

Brownwell-Katz Number	N_{BK}	$N_{BK} = \dfrac{u\mu}{k_{rw}\sigma}$	Fluids mechanics (combination of capillary number and Bond number)
Capillary Number	Ca	$Ca = \dfrac{\mu V}{\gamma}$	Porous media, fluid mechanics (viscous forces versus surface tension)
Chandrasekhar	Q	$Q = \dfrac{B_0^{\ 2}\, d^2}{\mu_0 \rho v \lambda}$	Magnetohydrodynamics (ratio of the Lorentz force to the viscosity in magnetic conversation)
Colbum J factors	J_M, J_H, J_D		Turbulence; heat, mass and momentum transfer (dimensionless transfer coefficients)
Coefficient of Kinetic Friction	μ_K		Mechanics (friction of solid bodies in translational motion)
Coefficient of Static Friction	μ_9		Mechanics (friction of solid bodies at rest)
Coefficient of Determination	R^2		Statistics (Proportion of variance explained by a statistical model)
Coefficient of Variation	$\dfrac{\sigma}{\mu}$	$\dfrac{\sigma}{\mu}$	Statistics (ratio of standard deviation to expectation)
Cohesion Number	Coh	$Coh = \dfrac{1}{\rho g}\left(\dfrac{\Gamma^5}{E^{*2} R^{*\delta}}\right)^{1/2}$	Chemical engineering, material science, mechanics (A scale to show the energy needed for detaching two solid particles)
Correlation	ρ or r	$\dfrac{E\left[(X - \mu X)(Y - \mu Y)\right]}{\sigma_X \sigma_Y}$	Statistics (measure of linear dependence)
Cost of Transport	COT	$COT = \dfrac{E}{mgd}$	Energy efficiency, economics (ratio of energy input to kinetic motion)
Courant-Friedrich-Levy Number	C or $\boldsymbol{v}$	$C = \dfrac{u\Delta t}{\Delta x}$	Mathematics (numerical solutions of hyperbolic PDEs)

Damkohler Number	Da	$Da = k_\tau$	Chemistry (reaction time scales vs. residence time)
Damping Ratio	Ç	$\acute{C} = \dfrac{c}{2\sqrt{km}}$	Mechanics, electrical engineering (the level of damping in a system)
Darcy friction factor	C_f or f_D		Fluids mechanics (fraction of pressure losses due to friction in a pipe; four times the Fanning friction factor)
Darcy Number	Da	$Da = \dfrac{K}{d^2}$	Porous media (ratio of permeability to cross-sectional area)
Dean Number	D	$D = \dfrac{\rho V d}{\mu}\left(\dfrac{d}{2R}\right)^{1/2}$	Turbulent flow (vortices in curved ducts)
Deborah Number	De	$De = \dfrac{t_c}{t_p}$	Rheology (viscoelastic fluids)
Decibel	dB		Acoustics, electronics, control theory (ratio of two intensities or powers of a wave)
Drag Coefficient	C_d	$c_d = \dfrac{2F_d}{\rho v^2 A}$	Aeronautics, fluid dynamics (resistance of fluid motion)
Dukhin Number	Du	$Du = \dfrac{k^\sigma}{K_m a}$	Colloid science (ratio of electric surface conductivity to the electric bulk conductivity in heterogeneous systems)
Eckert Number	Ec	$Ec = \dfrac{V^2}{C_p \Delta T}$	Convective heat transfer (characterizes dissipation of energy; ratio of kinetic energy to enthalpy)
Ekman Number	Ek	$Ek = \dfrac{v}{2D^2 \Omega \sin\varphi}$	Geophysics (viscous versus Coriolis forces)
Elasticity (economics)	E	$E_{z,y} = \dfrac{\partial \ln(x)}{\partial \ln(y)} = \dfrac{\partial x}{\partial y}\dfrac{y}{x}$	Economics (response of demand or supply to price changes)

Eötvös Number	Eo	$Eo = \dfrac{\Delta \rho g L^2}{\sigma}$	Fluid mechanics (shape of bubbles or drops)
Ericksen Number	Er	$Er = \dfrac{\mu v L}{K}$	Fluids dynamics (liquids crystal flow behavior, viscous over elastic forces)
Euler Number	Eu	$Eu = \dfrac{\Delta p}{\rho V^2}$	Hydrodynamics (stream pressure versus inertia forces)
Euler's Number	E	$e = \displaystyle\sum_{n=0}^{\infty} \dfrac{1}{n!} \approx 2.72828$	Mathematics (base of the natural logarithm)
Excess Temperature coefficient	$\theta \tau$	$\theta \tau = \dfrac{C_p(T - T_e)}{U_e^2/2}$	Heat transfer, fluid dynamics (change in internal energy versus kinetic energy)
Fanning friction constants	F		Fluid mechanics (fraction of pressure losses due to friction in a pipe; 1/4th the Darcy friction factor)
Feigenbaum Constants	α, δ	$\alpha \approx 2.50290,$ $\delta \approx 4.66920$	Chaos theory (period doubling)
Fine structure Constant	α	$\alpha = \dfrac{e^2}{4\pi\varepsilon_0 \hbar c}$	Quantum electrodynamics (QED) (coupling constant characterizing the strength of the electromagnetic interaction)
f-number	F	$f = \dfrac{\ell}{D}$	Optics, photography (ratio of focal length to diameter of aperture)
Föppl-von Kármán Number	γ	$\gamma = \dfrac{Y \tau^2}{k}$	Virology, solid mechanic (thin-shell buckling)
Fourier Number	Fo	$Fo = \dfrac{\alpha t}{L^2}$	Heat transfer, mass transfer (ratio of diffusive rate versus strong rate)
Fresnel Number	F	$F = \dfrac{\alpha^2}{L\lambda}$	Optics (slit diffraction)

Froude number	Fr	$$Fr = \frac{v}{\sqrt{g\ell}}$$	Fluids mechanics (wave and surface behavior; ratio of a body's inertia to gravitational forces)
Gain	-		Electronics (signal output to signal input)
Gain Ratio	-		Bicycling (system of representing gearing; length traveled over length pedaled)
Galilei Number	Ga	$$Ga = \frac{gL^3}{v^2}$$	Fluid mechanics (gravitational over viscous forces)
Goal average	-	$$Goal\ average = \frac{goals\ Scored}{goals\ conceded}$$	Association football
Golden ratio	φ	$$\varphi = \frac{1 + \sqrt{5}}{2} \approx 1.61803$$	Mathematics, aesthetics (long side length to self-similar rectangle)
Görtler number	G	$$G = \frac{U_e \theta}{v}\left(\frac{\theta}{R}\right)^{1/2}$$	Fluids dynamics (boundary layer flow along a concave wall)
Graetz number	Gz	$$Gz = \frac{D_H}{L} RePr$$	Heat transfer, fluid mechanics (laminar flow through a conduit; also used in mass transfer)
Grashof number	Gr	$$Gr_L = \frac{g\beta(T_e - T_\infty)L^3}{v^2}$$	Heat transfer, natural convection (ratio of the buoyancy to viscous force)
Hatta number	Ha	$$Ha = \frac{N_{A0}}{N_{A0}^{phys}}$$	Chemical engineering (adsorption enhancement due to chemical reaction)
Hagen number	Hg	$$Hg = -\frac{1}{\rho}\frac{dp}{dx}\frac{L^3}{v^2}$$	Heat transfer (ratio of the buoyancy to viscous force in forced convection)
Havnes Parameter	P$_H$	$$P_H = \frac{Z_d n_d}{n_i}$$	In dusty plasma physics, ratio of the total charge Z_d carried by the dust particles d to the charge carried by the ions i with n the number density of particles
Helmholtz	He	$$He = \frac{wa}{C_0} = k_0 a$$	The most important parameter in duct acoustics. If ω is dimensional frequency, the

number			k_0 is the corresponding free field wavenumber and H_e is corresponding dimensionless frequency
Hydraulic gradient	i	$i = \dfrac{dh}{dl} = \dfrac{h_2 - h_1}{length}$	Fluid mechanics, groundwater flow (pressure head over distance)
Iribarren Number	Ir	$Ir = \dfrac{\tan \alpha}{\sqrt{H/L_0}}$	Wave mechanics (breaking surface gravity waves on a slope)
Jakob number	Ja	$Ja = \dfrac{C_p(T_s - T_{aat})}{\Delta H_f}$	Chemistry (ratio of sensible to latent energy absorbed during liquid-vapor phase change)
Karlovitz number	Ka	$Ka = \dfrac{t_F}{t_\eta}$	Turbulent combustion (characteristic chemical time scale to Kolmogorov time scale)
Keulegan Carpenter number	Kc	$K_c = \dfrac{VT}{L}$	Fluid dynamics (ratio of drag force to inertia for a bluff object in oscillatory fluid flow)
Knudsen number	Kn	$Kn = \dfrac{\lambda}{L}$	Gas dynamics (ratio of drag force to inertia for a bluff object in oscillatory fluid flow)
Kt/V	Kt/V		Medicine (hemodialysis and peritoneal dialysis treatment dimensionless time)
Kutateladze	Ku	$Ku = \dfrac{U_h \rho_g^{1/2}}{\left(\sigma g(\rho l - \rho g)\right)^{1/4}}$	Fluid mechanics (counter-current two-phase flow)
Laplace number	La	$La = \dfrac{\sigma \rho L}{\mu^2}$	Fluid dynamics (free convection within immiscible fluids; ratio of surface tension to momentum-transport)
Lewis number	Le	$Le = \dfrac{\alpha}{D} = \dfrac{Sc}{Pr}$	Heat and mass transfer (ratio of thermal to mas diffusivity)
Lit Coefficient	C_L	$C_L = \dfrac{L}{qS}$	Aerodynamics (lift available from an airfoil at a given angle of attack)

Lockhart Matineli parameter	χ	$\chi = \dfrac{m_l}{m_g} \sqrt{\dfrac{\rho_g}{\rho_l}}$	Two-phase flow (flow of wet gases; liquid fraction)
Love numbers	h, k, l		Geophysics (solidity of earth and other planets)
Lundquist number	S	$S = \dfrac{\mu_0 L V_A}{\eta}$	Plasma physics (ratio of a resistive time to an Alfvén wave crossing time in a plasma)
Mach Number	M or Ma	$M = \dfrac{u}{u_{\text{sound}}}$	Gas dynamics (compressible flow; dimensionless velocity)
Magnetic Reynolds number	R_m	$R_m = \dfrac{UL}{\eta}$	Magnetohydrodynamics (ratio of magnetic advection to magnetic diffusion)
Manning roughness coefficient	N		Open channel flow (flow driven by gravity)
Marangoni number	Mg	$Mg = -\dfrac{d\sigma}{dT} \dfrac{L\Delta T}{\eta \propto}$	Fluids mechanics (Marangoni flow; thermal surface tension forces over viscous forces)
Markstein	M	$M = \dfrac{\mathcal{L}_b}{\delta_L}$	Fluid dynamics, combustion (turbulent combustion flames)
Morton Number	Mo	$Mo = \dfrac{g\mu_c^4 \Delta\rho}{\rho_c^2 \sigma^3}$	Fluid dynamics (determination of bubble/drop shape)
Nusselt Number	Nu	$Nu = \dfrac{hd}{k}$	Heat transfer (forced convection; ratio of convection to conductive heat transfer)
Ohnesorge number	Oh	$Oh = \dfrac{\mu}{\sqrt{\rho\sigma L}} = \dfrac{\sqrt{We}}{Re}$	Fluids dynamics (atomization of liquids, Marangoni flow)
Pecelt number	Pe	$Pe = \dfrac{duc_\rho}{k} = RePr$	Heat transfer (advection-diffusion problems; total momentum transfer to molecular heat transfer)

Peel Number	Np	$Np = \dfrac{\text{Restoring force}}{\text{Adhesive force}}$	Coating (adhesion of microstructure with substrate)
Perveance	K	$K = \dfrac{I}{I_0}\dfrac{2}{\beta^3\Upsilon^3}(1 - \gamma^2 fe)$	Charged particle transport (measure of the strength of space charge in charged particle beam)
pH	pH	$pH = \log_{10}(a_{H+})$	Chemistry (the measure of the acidity or basicity of an aqueous solution)
Pi	π	$\pi = \dfrac{C}{d} \approx 3.41459$	Mathematics (ratio of a circle's circumference to its diameter)
Pierce Parameter	C	$C^3 = \dfrac{Z_c I_K}{4V_K}$	Traveling wave blue
Pixel	Px		Digital imaging (smallest addressable unit)
Beta (Plasma Physics)	β	$\beta = \dfrac{nk_bT}{B^2/2\mu_0}$	Plasma and fusion power. Ratio of plasma thermal pressure to magnetic pressure, controlling the level of turbulence in magnetized plasma
Poisson's Ratio	ν	$\nu = -\dfrac{d\varepsilon_{trans}}{d\varepsilon_{arial}}$	Elasticity (strain in transverse and longitudinal directly)
Porosity	ϕ	$\phi = \dfrac{V_V}{V_T}$	Geology, porous media (void fraction of the medium)
Power factor	Pf	$Pf = \dfrac{P}{S}$	Electrical (real power to apparent power)
Power number	Np	$Np = \dfrac{P}{\rho n^3 d^5}$	Fluid mechanics, power consumption by rotary agitators; resistance force versus inertia force
Prandtl number	Pr	$Pr = \dfrac{\nu}{\alpha} = \dfrac{C_P\mu}{k}$	Heat transfer (ratio of viscous diffusion rate over thermal diffusion rate)

Prater number	β	$\beta = \dfrac{-\Delta H_\tau D^e_{TA} C_{AS}}{\lambda^e T_8}$	Reaction engineering (ratio of heat evolution to heat conduction within a catalyst pellet)
Pressure Coefficient	Cp	$Cp = \dfrac{P - P\infty}{\frac{1}{2}\rho_\infty V_\infty^2}$	Aerodynamics, hydrodynamics (pressure experienced at a point on an airfoil, dimensionless pressure variable)
Q factor	Q	$Q = 2\pi f_\tau \dfrac{Energey\ stored}{Power\ Loss}$	Physics, engineering (Damping ratio of oscillator or resonator; energy stored versus energy lost)
Radian Measure	Rad	$arch\ Length/radius$	Mathematics (measurement of planar angles, 1 radian=$180/\pi$ degrees)
Reyleigh number	Ra	$Ra_x = \dfrac{g\beta}{va}(T_e - T_\infty)x^3$	Heat transfer (buoyancy versus viscous forces in free convection)
Refractive index	N	$n = \dfrac{c}{v}$	Electromagnetism, optics (speed of light in a vacuum over speed of light in a material
Relative density	RD	$RD = \dfrac{\rho_{substance}}{\rho_{reference}}$	Hydrometer, material comparisons (ratio of density of a material to a refence material- usually water)
Relative permeability	$\mu\tau$	$\mu\tau = \dfrac{\mu}{\mu_0}$	Magnetostatics (ratio of the permeability of a specific medium to free space)
Relative Permittivity	ε_τ	$\varepsilon_\tau = \dfrac{C_Z}{C_0}$	Electrostatics (ratio of capacitance of test capacitor with dielectric material versus vacuum)
Reynold number	Re	$Re = \dfrac{vL\rho}{\mu}$	Fluid mechanics (ratio of fluid inertial and viscous forces)
Richardson number	Ri	$Ri = \dfrac{gh}{v^2} = \dfrac{1}{Fr^2}$	Fluid dynamics (effect buoyancy on flow stability; ratio of potential over kinetic energy)
Rockwell scale	-		Mechanical hardness (indentation hardness of

			a material)
Rolling resistance Coefficient	$C_{\tau\tau}$	$C_{\tau\tau} = \dfrac{F}{N_f}$	Vehicle dynamics (ratio of force needed for motion of a wheel over the normal force)
Roshok number	Ro	$Ro = \dfrac{fL^2}{\nu} = StRe$	Fluid dynamics (oscillating flow, vortex shedding)
Rossby number	Ro	$Ro = \dfrac{U}{Lf}$	Geophysics (ratio of inertial to Coriolis force)
Rouse number	P or Z	$P = \dfrac{w_e}{ku_2}$	Sediment transport (ratio of the sediment fall velocity and upwards velocity of grain)
Run per wicket ratio	RpW ratio	$RpW\ ratio =$ $= \dfrac{runs\ scored}{wicket\ lost} \div \dfrac{runs\ conceded}{wickets\ taken}$	Cricket
Schmidt number	Sc	$Sc = \dfrac{\nu}{D}$	Mass transfer (viscous over molecular diffusion rate)
Shape factor	H	$H = \dfrac{\delta^*}{\theta}$	Boundary layer flow (ratio of displacement thickness to momentum thickness)
Sherwood number	Sh	$Sh = \dfrac{KL}{D}$	Mass transfer (forced convention; ratio of convection to diffusive mass transport)
Shields Parameter	$\tau*$ or θ	$\tau_* = \dfrac{\tau}{(\rho_z - \rho)gD}$	Sediment transport (threshold of sediment movement due to fluid motion; dimension less shear stress)
Sommerfeld number	S	$S = \left(\dfrac{r}{c}\right)^2 \dfrac{\mu N}{P}$	Hydrodynamic lubrication (boundary lubrication)
Specific gravity	SG		(Same as Relative density)

Stanton number	St	$St = \dfrac{h}{c_p \rho V} = \dfrac{Nu}{RePr}$	Heat transfer and fluid dynamics (forced convection)
Stefan number	Ste	$Ste = \dfrac{c_p \Delta T}{L}$	Phase change, thermodynamics (ratio of sensible latent heat)
Stokes number	Stk or Sk	$Stk = \dfrac{\tau U_0}{d_c}$	Particles suspensions (ratio of characteristics time of particles to time of flow)
Strain	ϵ	$\epsilon = \dfrac{\partial F}{\partial X} - 1$	Material science, elasticity (displacement between particles in body relative to a reference length)
Strouhal number	St or Sr	$St = \dfrac{\omega L}{v}$	Fluids dynamics (continuous and pulsating flow; nondimensional frequency)
Stuart number	N	$N = \dfrac{B^2 L_c \sigma}{\rho U} = \dfrac{Ha^2}{Re}$	Magnetohydrodynamics (ratio of electromagnetic to inertial forces)
Taylor number	Ta	$Ta = \dfrac{4\Omega^2 R^4}{v^2}$	Fluid dynamics (rotating fluids flows; inertial forces due to rotation of a fluid versus viscous forces)
Transmittance	T	$T = \dfrac{I}{I_0}$	Optics, spectroscopy (the ratio of the intensities of radiation exiting through and incident on a sample)
Ursell number	U	$U = \dfrac{H\lambda^2}{h^3}$	Wave mechanics (nonlinearity of surface gravity waves on a shallow fluid layer)
Vadasz number	Va	$Va = \dfrac{\phi Pr}{Da}$	Porous media (governs the effects of porosity ϕ, the Prandtl number and the Darcy number on flow in a porous medium)
Van't Hoff factor	I	$i = 1 + a(n - 1)$	Quantitative analysis (k_f and k_b)
Wallis Parameter	j^*	$j^* = R\left(\dfrac{\omega \rho}{\mu}\right)^{\frac{1}{2}}$	Multiphase flows (nondimensional superficial velocity)

Wagner number	Wa	$Wa = \dfrac{k}{l}\dfrac{d\eta}{di}$	Electrochemistry (ratio of kinetic polarization resistance to solution ohmic resistance in an electrochemical cell)
Weaver Flame speed number	Wea	$Wea = \dfrac{w}{w_H}100$	Combustion (laminar burning velocity relative to hydrogen gas)
Weber number	We	$We = \dfrac{\rho v^2 l}{\sigma}$	Multiple flow (strongly curved surfaced; ratio of inertia of surface tension)
Weissenberg number	Wi	$Wi = \gamma\lambda$	Viscoelastic flows (shear rate times the relaxation time)
Winning Percentage	-	Various, e.g. $\dfrac{\text{Games won}}{\text{Games played}}$ or $\dfrac{\text{Points won}}{\text{Points contested}}$	Various sports
Womersley number	a	$a = R\left(\dfrac{\omega\rho}{\mu}\right)^{\frac{1}{2}}$	Biofluid mechanics (continuous and pulsating flows; ratio of pulsatile flow frequency to viscos effect)
Zel'dovich number	β	$\beta = \dfrac{E}{RT_j}\dfrac{T_j - T_0}{T_j}$	Fluid dynamics, combustion (Measure of activation energy)

References

1.   (See) "Table of Dimensionless Numbers".

2.   (See) Bagnold number

3.   Bhattacharjee S.; Grosshandler W.L. (1988). "The formation of wall jet near a high-temperature wall under microgravity environment". ASME MTD 96: 711–6.

4.   Paoletti S.; Rispoli F.; Sciubba E. (1989). "Calculation of exergetic losses in compact heat exchanger passager". ASME AES 10 (2): 21–9.

5.   Blondeau, J.. "The influence of field size, goal size and a number of players on the average number of goals scored per game in variants of football and hockey: the Pi-theorem applied to team sports". Journal of Quantitative Analysis in Sports.

6.   Becker, A.; Hüttinger, K. J. (1998). "Chemistry and kinetics of chemical vapor deposition of pyrocarbon—II hydrocarbon deposition from ethylene, acetylene and 1,3-butadiene in the low-temperature regime". Carbon 36 (3): 177. .

7.   (see) Bond number

8.   (See) "Home". OnePetro. 2015-05-04.

9.   Behjani, Mohammadreza Alizadeh; Rahmanian, Nejat; Ghani, Nur Fardina bt Abdul; Hassanpour, Ali (2017). "An investigation on the process of seeded granulation in a continuous drum granulator using DEM". Advanced Powder Technology 28 (10): 2456–2464.

10.   Alizadeh Behjani, Mohammadreza; Hassanpour, Ali; Ghadiri, Mojtaba; Bayly, Andrew (2017). "Numerical Analysis of the Effect of Particle Shape and Adhesion on the Segregation of Powder Mixtures" (in en). EPJ Web of Conferences 140:

11.   (see) Courant–Friedrich–Levy number

12.   Schetz, Joseph A. (1993). Boundary Layer Analysis. Englewood Cliffs, NJ: Prentice-Hall, Inc.. pp. 132–134. ISBN 0-13-086885-X.

13.   (see) "Fanning friction factor".

14.   (See) Feigenbaum constants

15.   (See) Fresnel number

16.   (See) Gain Ratio – Sheldon Brown

17.   (See) "goal average".

18.   SW RIENSTRA, 2015, Fundamentals of Duct Acoustics, Von Karman Institute Lecture Notes

19.   Incropera, Frank P. (2007). Fundamentals of heat and mass transfer. John Wiley & Sons, Inc. p. 376.

20.   ↑ Tan, R. B. H.; Sundar, R. (2001). "On the froth–spray transition at multiple orifices". Chemical Engineering Science 56 (21–22): 6337.

21.   (See) Lockhart–Martinelli parameter

22.   (See) "Manning coefficient".

23.   Van Spengen, W. M.; Puers, R.; De Wolf, I. (2003). "The prediction of stiction failures in MEMS". IEEE Transactions on Device and Materials Reliability 3 (4): 167.

24.   Davis, Mark E.; Davis, Robert J. (2012). Fundamentals of Chemical Reaction Engineering. Dover. p. 215. ISBN 978-0-486-48855-4.

25.   (See) Richardson number

26.   "World Test Championship Playing Conditions: What's different?".

27.   (See) Schmidt number

28.   (See) Sommerfeld number

29.   (See) Strouhal number,

30.   Straughan, B. (2001). "A sharp nonlinear stability threshold in rotating porous convection". Proceedings of the Royal Society A: Mathematical, Physical and Engineering Sciences 457 (2005): 87–88.

31.   Petritsch, G.; Mewes, D. (1999). "Experimental investigations of the flow patterns in the hot leg of a pressurized water reactor". Nuclear Engineering and Design 188: 75–84.

32.   Popov, Konstantin I.; Djokić, Stojan S.; Grgur, Branimir N. (2002). Fundamental Aspects of Electrometallurgy. Boston, MA: Springer. pp. 101–102. ISBN 978-0-306-47564-1.

33.   Kuneš, J. (2012). "Technology and Mechanical Engineering". Dimensionless Physical Quantities in Science and Engineering. pp. 353–390.

34.   (See) Weissenberg number

35.   (See) Womersley number

Table – 2

SI Dimensions of Physical Quantities: Alphabetic List

SI Dimensions of Physical Quantities: Alphabetic List

(The table is taken from Wikipedia, the free encyclopedia.)

Quantity	Dimension	Alternatives	Definition/Notes
A:			
Abbé number | Constringence | V-number	1	Dimensionless	$V_D = (n_D-1)/(n_F-n_C)$
Absorbed radiation dose	$m^2.s^{-2}$	$J.kg^{-1}$, **Gy** (gray)	[Energy]/[Mass]
Absorbed dose rate	$m^2.s^{-3}$	$Gy.s^{-1}$	[Absorbed dose]/Time]
Acceleration, angular	s^{-2}	$rad.s^{-2}$	[ΔAngular velocity]/[ΔTime]
Acceleration | Deceleration	$m.s^{-2}$		[ΔVelocity]/[ΔTime]
Acoustic impedance / resistance / reactance	$kg.m^{-4}.s^{-1}$	$Pa.s/m^3$, $reyl/m^2$	[Pressure]/[Volume flow rate]
Acoustic impedance, specific	$kg.m^{-2}.s^{-1}$	$Pa.s/m$, **reyl**	[ΔPressure]*[Velocity]. Also **s.acu. resistance / reactance**
Acoustic conductance, specific	$kg^{-1}.m^2.s$	$reyl^{-1}$	Inverse of s.acu. impedance. Also **s.acu. susceptance**
Action	$kg.m^2.s^{-1}$	J.s	[Energy]*[Time], [Moment of motion]*[Distance]
Activity of a radioactive source	s^{-1}	**Bq** (becquerel)	[Counts]/[Time]
Activity, katalytic	$mol.s^{-1}$	**katal**	[ΔQuantity]/[Time]. Same as **molar production rate**

Activity, transactions rate	s^{-1}	1/year	[Transactions]/[Time period]. Economy and finance
Admittance, inductive	$kg^{-1}.m^{-2}.s^3.A^2$	S (siemens)	1/[Inductive impedance]
Admittance, of a circuit	$kg^{-1}.m^{-2}.s^3.A^2$	S (siemens)	1/[Circuit impedance]
Advection velocity	$m.s^{-1}$	m/s	In **porous media**; actual progress along pressure gradient
Albedo, of a surface	1	Dimensionless	[Reflected elmag power]/[Incident elmag power]
Amplification | Attenuation (generic)	1	usually in dB	[Quantity(p)]/[Quantity(p')], with p being some parameter
Angular acceleration	s^{-2}	$rad.s^{-2}$	[ΔAngular velocity]/[ΔTime]
Angular moment of inertia	$kg.m^2$		[Mass]*[Distance^2]
Angular moment of motion	$kg.m^2.s^{-1}$	J.s	[Moment of motion]*[Distance]. Like [**action**]
Angular velocity	s^{-1}	$rad.s^{-1}$	[ΔPlane angle]/[ΔTime]
Annealing point	K		Temperature at which viscosity drops below 10^{12} Pa.s
Area	m^2		[Distance]*[Distance]
Area growth rate	$m^2.s^{-1}$		[ΔArea]/[Time]
Asset | Wealth	cur	currency	Economy and finance
Atomic number	1	Dimensionless	Number of protons in an atomic nucleus
Atomic weight | Relative atomic mass	au	atomic units	Average over a typical isotopic composition
Attenuation | Amplification	1	usually in dB	[Quantity(p)]/[Quantity(p')], with p being

(generic)			some parameter
Attenuation / amplification over a distance	m^{-1}	dB/m	[Attenuation]/[Distance]. Mostly in acoustic and electronics
Attenuation / amplification over a period	s^{-1}	dB/s	[Attenuation]/[Time]. Mostly in acoustic and electronics

B:

Bandwidth	s^{-1}	Hz	[ΔFrequency]
Baud rate | Information flux	bit.s^{-1}	**baud**	[Information]/[Time]
Bond duration	s	year	Economy and finance
Bulk modulus	kg.m^{-1}.s^{-2}	N.m^{-2}, Pa	([ΔVolume]/[Volume])/[Pressure]. Inverse of **compressibility**

C:

Capacitance, electric	kg^{-1}.m^{-2}.s^4.A^2	C.V^{-1}, **F** (farad)	[Charge]/[ΔPotential]
Capacitive reactance	kg.m^2.s^{-3}.A^{-2}	**Ω** (ohm)	1/(i[Angular frequency].[Capacitance])
Capacitive susceptance	kg^{-1}.m^{-2}.s^3.A^2	**S** (siemens)	1/[Capacitive reactance]
Cash flow	cur.s^{-1}	currency/year	[Value]/[ΔTime]. Economy and finance
Circulation	m^2.s^{-1}	J.s.kg^{-1}	[Angular moment]/[Mass], [Velocity]*[Loop length]
Characteristic impedance	kg.m^2.s^{-3}.A^{-2}	V.A^{-1}, Ω, ohm	√([Mag.Permeability]/[El.Permittivity])
Charge, electric	s .A	**C** (coulomb)	[Current]*[Time]
Charge, magnetic (bound)	m^{-2}.A		- ∇.[Magnetization] , -Divergence of **magnetization**

Charge, quantum	1	Dimensionless	[Charge]/[Elementary charge quantum]
Charge, molecular/ionic, quantum	1	Dimensionless	[Charge of a molecule or ion]/[Elementary charge quantum]
Charge density	$m^{-3}.s^A$	$C.m^{-3}$	[Charge]/[Volume]
Charge/mass ratio | Specific charge	$kg^{-1}.s.A$	$C.kg^{-1}$	[Charge]/[Mass]
Charge, molar	$s.A.mol^{-1}$	$C.mol^{-1}$	[Charge]/[Quantity]
Chemical potential, molar	$kg.m^2.s^{-2}.mol^{-1}$	$J.mol^{-1}$	[ΔInternalEnergy]/[ΔQuantity]
Circuit admittance	$kg^{-1}.m^{-2}.s^3.A^2$	**S** (siemens)	1/[Circuit impedance]
Circuit impedance	$kg.m^2.s^{-3}.A^{-2}$	**Ω** (ohm)	
Circulation / velocity of money	s^{-1}	1/year	[Transactions]/[Time period]. Economy and finance
Circumference | Perimeter	m		
Collision cross section | Cross section	m^2		[Distance]*[Distance]
Compressibility	$kg^{-1}.m.s^2$	Pa^{-1}	[Pressure]/([ΔVolume]/[Volume]). Inverse of **bulk modulus**
Compression	$kg.m^{-1}.s^{-2}$	$N.m^{-2}$, **Pa** (pascal)	[Force]/[Area]. Same as **pressure**
Compression factor of a real gas	1	Dimensionless	pV/(nRT). For ideal gas equals 1; temperature dependent
Compressive strength	$kg.m^{-1}.s^{-2}$	$N.m^{-2}$, Pa	[Force]/[Area]. Like **pressure**
Concentration, molar	$m^{-3}.mol$		[Quantity]/[Volume]. Same as **molar density**

Concentration gradient, molar	$m^{-4}.mol$		[Molarity]/[Distance]. Same as **molarity gradient**
Concentration ratio, molar	1	Dimensionless	[Partial quantity]/[Total quantity]
Concentration ratio, by mass	1	Dimensionless	[Partial mass]/[Total mass]
Concentration ratio, by volume	1	Dimensionless	[Partial volume]/[Total volume]. .
Concentration, by weight (obsolete)	1	Dimensionless	[Partial mass]/[Total mass]. Obsolete: use **by mass**
Conductance, electric	$kg^{-1}.m^{-2}.s^3.A^2$	$A.V^{-1}$, **S** (siemens)	1/[Resistance]
Conductivity, electric	$kg^{-1}.m^{-3}.s^3.A^2$	$S.m^{-1}$	1/[Resistivity]
Conductivity, hydraulic	$m.s^{-1}$	m/s	Used for **porous media**
Conductivity, molar	$kg^{-1}.s^3.A^2.mol^{-1}$	$S.m^2.mol^{-1}$	[El.conductivity]/[Concentration]
Conductivity, thermal	$kg.m.s^{-3}.K^{-1}$	$W.m^{-1}.K^{-1}$	[Heat flux]/([Distance]*[ΔTemperature])
Constringence | Abbé number | V-number	1	Dimensionless	$V_D = (n_D-1)/(n_F-n_C)$
Convergence	m^{-1}	**dioptry**	in optics, but not only
Cosmological constant Λ	m^{-2}		Present in Einstein's equation
Cosmological expansion rate	s^{-1}	km/s/Mpc	[Velocity]/[Distance]. Mpc stands for Megaparsec
Count of events/instances	1		This covers all kinds of **enumerations**
Count rate	s^{-1}		[Counts]/[Time]
Couple	$kg.m^2.s^{-2}$	N.m	2*[Force]*[Distance] for two non-aligned

			opposing forces
Critical angle of repose	rad	or degree	Steepest angle of a slope before a slide
Cross section	m^2		[Distance]*[Distance]
Cryoscopic constant	$kg.mol^{-1}.K$	K/(mol/kg)	[ΔTemperature]/[Molality]
Current, electric	A	**A** (ampere)	
Current density, electric	$m^{-2}.A$		[Current]/[Area]. Same as **current intensity**
Current intensity, electric	$m^{-2}.A$		[Current]/[Area]. Same as **current density**
Current noise, variance n_J^2	$s.A^2$	A^2/Hz	$[Current]^2$/[Bandwidth]
Curvature	m^{-1}		1/[Curvature radius]
Curvature radius	m		of a line in plane/space or surface in space

D:

D'Alembert operator | D'Alembertian	m^{-2}		$(1/c^2)\partial^2/\partial t^2 - \partial^2/\partial x^2 - \partial^2/\partial y^2 - \partial^2/\partial z^2$
Debt | Liability	cur	**currency**	Economy and finance
Debt/GDP ratio	s	year	[Debt]/[Earnings]. Economy and finance
Deceleration | Acceleration	$m.s^{-2}$		[ΔVelocity]/[ΔTime]
Deceleration, angular	s^{-2}	$rad.s^{-2}$	[ΔAngular velocity]/[ΔTime]
Density of electric charge	$m^{-3}.s.A$	$C.m^{-3}$	[Charge]/[Volume]
Density of electric current	$m^{-2}.A$		[Current]/[Area]. Same as **current**

			intensity
Density of energy	kg.m^{-1}.s^{-2}	J.m^{-3}	[Energy]/[Volume]
Density of mass	kg.m^{-3}		[Mass]/[Volume]. Same as **specific density**
Density of mass, gradient of	kg.m^{-4}		[Mass density]/[Distance]. Same as **specific density gradient**
Density of particles	m^{-3}		[Count]/[Volume]. Obsolete: **number density**
Density of substance	m^{-3}.mol		[Quantity]/[Volume]. Same as **molar concentration**
Derivative with respect to **Time**	s^{-1}		d/dt, ∂/∂t
Derivative with respect to a length	m^{-1}		d/dr, ∂/∂r, r = x	y	z
**Dielectric constant	Relative permittivity**	1	Dimensionless	[Permittivity]/[Permittivity of vacuum]
**Dielectric strength/rigidity	Electric strength**	kg.m.s^{-3}.A^{-1}	V.m^{-1}	[ΔPotential]/[Distance]
Diffusion coefficient	m^2.s^{-1}		[Distance]^2/[Time]
Diffusivity, thermal	m^2.s^{-1}		([∂Temperatute]/[∂Time])/[∇^2Temperature].
Dipole moment, electric	m.s.A	C.m	[Charge]*[Distance]
Dipole moment, magnetic	m^2.A	J.T^{-1}	[Current]*[Area]
Dispersive power	1	Dimensionless	Ratio of differences of refractive indices
Dispersivity quotient	m^{-1}		[ΔRefractive index]/[ΔWavelength]

Displacement, electric	$m^{-2}.s.A$	$C.m^{-2}$	[Charge]/[Area]. Same as **electric flux density**
Displacement four-tensor (relativistic $D^{\mu\nu}$)	$m^{-1}.A$		Like **magnetic intensity**
Distance	m		in all Euclidean n-dimensional spaces
Dose of absorbed radiation	$m^2.s^{-2}$	$J.kg^{-1}$, **Gy** (gray)	[Energy]/[Mass]
Dose rate	$m^2.s^{-3}$	$Gy.s^{-1}$	[Absorbed dose]/Time]
Drift speed	$m.s^{-1}$		Steady-state speed of an object. .
Duration	s	**s** (second)	
Dynamic viscosity	$kg.m^{-1}.s^{-1}$	$Pa.s$	([Force]/[Area])/[ΔVelocity]

E:

Earnings | Income rate	$cur.s^{-1}$	currency/year	[Value]/[Time period]. Economy and finance
Ebullioscopic constant	$kg.mol^{-1}.K$	$K/(mol/kg)$	[ΔTemperature]/[Molality]
Electric capacitance	$kg^{-1}.m^{-2}.s^4.A^2$	$C.V^{-1}$, **F** (farad)	[Charge]/[ΔPotential]
Electric charge	$s.A$	**C** (coulomb)	[Current]*[Time]
Electric conductance	$kg^{-1}.m^{-2}.s^3.A^2$	$A.V^{-1}$, **S** (siemens)	[Current]/[ΔPotential]. Inverse of **resistance**
Electric conductivity	$kg^{-1}.m^{-3}.s^3.A^2$	$S.m^{-1}$	1/[Resistivity]
Electric conductivity, molar	$kg^{-1}.s^3.A^2.mol^{-1}$	$S.m^2.mol^{-1}$	[El.conductivity]/[Concentration]
Electric current	A	**A** (ampere)	
Electric dipole moment	$m.s.A$	$C.m$	[Charge]*[Distance]

Electric displacement	m^{-2}.s.A	C.m^{-2}	[Charge]/[Area]. Same as **electric flux density**
Electric field strength | Electric intensity	kg.m.s^{-3}.A^{-1}	V.m^{-1}	[ΔPotential]/[Distance]
Electric field gradient	kg.s^{-3}.A^{-1}	V.m^{-2}	[ΔEl.field strength]/[Distance]
Electric flux density | Electric induction	m^{-2}.s.A	C.m^{-2}	[Charge]/[Area]
Electric inductance	kg.m^2.s^{-2}.A^{-2}	V.s.A^{-1}, **H** (henry)	[ΔPotential]/[dCurrent/dt]
Electric induction	m^{-2}.s.A	C.m^{-2}	[Charge]/[Area]. More properly **electric flux density**
Electric intensity	kg.m. s^{-3}.A^{-1}	V.m^{-1}	[ΔPotential]/[Distance]. More properly **electric field strength**
Electric permittivity	kg^{-1}.m^{-3}. s^4.A^2	F.m^{-1}	[El.flux density]/[El.field strength]
Electric permittivity, relative	1	Dimensionless	[Permittivity]/[Permittivity of vacuum]. Same as **dielectric constant**
Electric polarization	m^{-2}.s. A	C.m^{-2}	[Charge]/[Area]. Like **electric flux density**
Electric potential	kg.m^2.s^{-3}.A^{-1}	W.A^{-1}, J.C^{-1}, **V** (volt)	[Power]/[Current], [Energy]/[Charge]
Electric quadrupole moment	m^2.s.A	C.m^2	[Electric dipole]*[Distance], [Electric charge]*[Distance^2]
Electric resistance	kg.m^2. s^{-3}.A^{-2}	V.A^{-1}, **Ω** (ohm)	[ΔPotential]/[Current]
Electric resistivity	kg.m^3.s^{-3}.A^{-2}	Ω.m	([Resistance]*[Length])/[Area]
Electric strength | Dielectric strength	kg.m.s^{-3}.A^{-1}	V.m^{-1}	[ΔPotential]/[Distance]. .
Electromagnetic field tensor	kg.s^{-2}.A^{-1}	**T**	Like **magnetic flux density**

(relativistic $F^{\mu\nu}$)			
Electromagnetic displacement (relat. $D^{\mu\nu}$)	$m^{-1}.A$		Like **magnetic intensity**
Electromagnetic four-current (relativistic J^{α})	$m^{-2}.A$		Like **current density** and [Charge]*[c]
Electromagnetic four-potential (relativistic A^{α})	$kg.m.s^{-2}.A^{-1}$	$m^{-1}.s.V$, $m.T$	Like **magnetic vector potential** and [El.potential]/[c]
Electromotive force (emf)	$kg.m^2.s^{-3}.A^{-1}$	V	[ΔPotential]
Electron affinity (always molar)	$kg.m^2.s^{-2}.mol^{-1}$	$J.mol^{-1}$	Energy released binding an electron
Electronegativity, Pauling χ	1	Dimensionless	Relative tendency of an atom to attract electrons; $\chi(H)=2.20$.
Electrostriction coefficient	$kg^{-2}.m^{-2}.s^6.A^2$	$m^2.V^{-2}$	([ΔVolume]/[Volume])/[Electric field strength]^2
Emittance, luminous	$cd.sr.m^{-2}$	$lm.m^{-2}$, **lx** (lux)	[Luminous flux]/[Area]. Same as **luminous exitance**
Energy	$kg.m^2.s^{-2}$	N.m, **J** (joule)	[Force]*[Distance], [Power]*[Time]
Energy, molar	$kg.m^2.s^{-2}.mol^{-1}$	$J.mol^{-1}$	[Energy]/[Quantity]
Energy, specific	$m^2.s^{-2}$	$J.kg^{-1}$	[Energy]/[Mass]
Energy density	$kg.m^{-1}.s^{-2}$	$J.m^{-3}$	[Energy]/[Volume]
**Energy flux	Power**	$kg.m^2.s^{-3}$	$J.s^{-1}$, **W** (watt)	[ΔEnergy]/[ΔTime]
Enthalpy	$kg.m^2.s^{-2}$	J	Like **energy** and **heat**
Enthalpy, molar	$kg.m^2.s^{-2}.mol^{-1}$	$J.mol^{-1}$	[Enthalpy]/[Quantity]. Like **molar heat**
Enthalpy, specific	$m^2.s^{-2}$	$J.kg^{-1}$	[Enthalpy]/[Mass]. Like **specific heat**

Entropy	$kg.m^2.s^{-2}.K^{-1}$	$J.K^{-1}$	[ΔHeat]/[Temperature]
Entropy, molar	$kg.m^2.s^{-2}.K^{-1}.mol^{-1}$	$J.K^{-1}.mol^{-1}$	[Entropy]/[Quantity]
Entropy, specific	$m^2.s^{-2}.K^{-1}$	$J.K^{-1}.kg^{-1}$	[Entropy]/[Mass]
Evolution rate, log-scale	s^{-1}		$d\{ln(Q)\}/dt = (dQ/dt)/Q$. Same as **relative evolution rate**
Expansion coefficient, thermal	K^{-1}		([ΔLength]/[Length])/[Temperature]
Expansion rate, cosmological	s^{-1}	km/s/Mpc	[Velocity]/[Distance]. Mpc stands for Megaparsec
Expectation frequency	s^{-1}		[Counts]/[Time]. Like **count rate**
Exposure	$kg^{-1}.s.A$	$C.kg^{-1}$	[Charge]/[Mass]. Used for ionising radiations
Extinction coefficient	m^{-1}	dB/m	Ratio]/m. Used mostly for radiation
F:			
Field tensor, electromagnetic (relativistic $F^{\mu\nu}$)	$kg.s^{-2}.A^{-1}$	T	Like **magnetic flux density**
Fire point	K		Temperature at which ignited vapour keeps burning
Flash point	K		Temperature at which vapour can be kept burning
Flow	$cur.s^{-1}$	currency/year	[ΔValue]/[ΔTime]. Economy and finance: time derivative
Flow rate, of mass | Mass production rate	$kg.s^{-1}$		[ΔMass]/[Time]. For example, through a pipe
Flow rate, of volume	$m^3.s^{-1}$		[ΔVolume]/[Time]. For example, through

			a pipe
Force	kg.m.s^{-2}	**N** (newton)	[Mass]*[Acceleration]
Force, thermodynamic	kg.m.s^{-2}.mol^{-1}	N/mol	[ΔChemical potential]/[Distance]
Four-current (relativistic J^{α})	m^{-2}.A		Like **current density** and [Charge]*[c]
Four-potential (relativistic A^{α})	kg.m.s^{-2}.A^{-1}	m^{-1}.s.V, m.T	Like **magnetic vector potential** and [El.potential]/[c]
Four-tensor elmag displacement (relat. D^{μν})	m^{-1}.A		Like **magnetic intensity**
Four-tensor elmag field (relativistic F^{μν})	kg.s^{-2}.A^{-1}	**T**	Like **magnetic flux density**
Free energy	kg.m^{2}.s^{-2}	J	Also **Helmholtz function**. Like **energy**
Free energy, molar	kg.m^{2}.s^{-2}.mol^{-1}	J.mol^{-1}	[Free energy]/quantity]. Like **Helmholtz function**
Free energy, specific	m^{2}.s^{-2}	J.kg^{-1}	[Free energy]/[Mass]. Like **specific Helmholtz function**
Free enthalpy	kg.m^{2}.s^{-2}	J	Also **Gibbs function**. Like **energy**
Free enthalpy, molar	kg.m^{2}.s^{-2}.mol^{-1}	J.mol^{-1}	[Free enthalpy]/quantity]. Like **molar Gibbs function**
Free enthalpy, specific	m^{2}.s^{-2}	J.kg^{-1}	[Free enthalpy]/[Mass]. Like **specific Gibbs function**
Frequency of events	s^{-1}		[Counts]/[Time]
Frequency of waves	s^{-1}	Hz	hertz
Frequency drift rate	s^{-2}	Hz.s^{-1}	[ΔFrequency]/[Time]
Friction	kg.m.s^{-2}	**N**	Tangential force between two moving

			surfaces
Friction coefficient	1	Dimensionless	[Tangential force]/[Normal force]
Fugacity	$kg.m^{-1}.s^{-2}$	Pa	Effective pressure in real gases

G:

Gain of a device	1	Dimensionless	[Output]/[Input], like-quantities ratio. Often in dB
GDP Gross domestic product	$cur.s^{-1}$	currency/year	[Earnings]. Economy and financee: of an administrative region
g-factor of a particle	1	Dimensionless	[Magnetic moment]/([Spin].[Bohr magneton])
Gradient, of electric field	$kg.s^{-3}.A^{-1}$	$V.m^{-2}$	[ΔEl.field strength]/[Distance]
Gradient, of magnetic field	$kg.m^{-1}.s^{-2}.A^{-1}$	$T.m^{-1}$	[ΔMag.flux density]/[Distance]
Gradient, of mass density	$kg.m^{-4}$		[Mass density]/[Distance]. Same as **specific density gradient**
Gradient, of pressure	$kg.m^{-2}.s^{-2}$	$N.m^{-3}$, **Pa/m**	[Pressure]/[Distance]
Gradient, thermal	$K.m^{-1}$		[ΔTemperature]/[Distance]. Same as **temperature gradient**
Gravitational constant G	$kg^{-1}.m^{3}.s^{-2}$		[Force]*[Distance]^2/[Mass]^2. Appears in Newton's equation
Gravitational field intensity | Gravity	$m.s^{-2}$		[Force]/[Mass], [Acceleration]
Gravitational field potential	$m^{2}.s^{-2}$		[Energy]/[Mass].
Gravity | Gravitational field intensity	$m.s^{-2}$		[Force]/[Mass], [Acceleration]

Growth rate, relative	s^{-1}		[Relative variation]/[Time]
Growth rate, linear	m.s^{-1}		[ΔLength]/[Time]
Growth rate, of area/surface	m^2.s^{-1}		[ΔArea]/[Time]
Growth rate, of volume	m^3.s^{-1}		[ΔVolume]/[Time]
Gyromagnetic ratio	kg^{-1}.s.A	Hz.T^{-1}	[Mag.moment]/[Angular moment of motion]

H:

Half life	s		of a non-conservative / decaying quantity
Hamiltonian	kg.m^2.s^{-2}	J	[Force]*[Distance], [Power]*[Time]. Like **energy**
Hardness	kg.m^{-1}.s^{-2}	N.m^{-2}	[Force]/[Area]. Same as **pressure**
Heat	kg.m^2.s^{-2}	J	Like **energy**
Heat, molar	kg.m^2.s^{-2}.mol^{-1}	J.mol^{-1}	[Heat]/[Quantity]
Heat, specific	m^2.s^{-2}	J.kg^{-1}	[Heat]/[Mass]
Heat capacity	kg.m^2.s^{-2}.K^{-1}	J.K^{-1}	[ΔHeat]/[ΔTemperature]
Heat capacity, molar	kg.m^2.s^{-2}.K^{-1}.mol^{-1}	J.K^{-1}.mol^{-1}	[Heat capacity]/quantity]
Heat capacity, specific	m^2.s^{-2}.K^{-1}	J.K^{-1}.kg^{-1}	[Heat capacity]/[Mass]
Heat conductivity | Thermal conductivity	kg.m.s^{-3}.K^{-1}	W.m^{-1}.K^{-1}	[Heat flux]/([Distance]*[ΔTemperature])
Heat flux	kg.m^2.s^{-3}	J.s, W	[ΔHeat]/[ΔTime]. Like **power**
Heat flux density	kg.s^{-3}	W.m^{-2}	[Heat flux]/[Area]. Same as **irradiance**

Heat of fusion/evaporation, specific	$m^2.s^{-2}$	$J.kg^{-1}$	[Energy]/[Mass]
Heat of fusion | evaporation, molar	$kg.m^2.s^{-2}.mol^{-1}$	$J.mol^{-1}$	[Energy]/[Quantity]
Hydraulic conductivity	$m.s^{-1}$	m/s	Used for **porous media**
Hydraulic permeability	m^2	$1\ darcy = 10^{-12}\ m^2$	[Velocity]*[Viscosity]/[Pressure gradient], in **porous media**
I:			
Illuminance	$cd.sr.m^{-2}$	$lm.m^{-2}$, **lx** (lux)	[Luminous flux]/[Area]
Impact resistance	$kg.s^{-2}$	$J.m^{-2}$	[Energy]/[Area]
Impedance, acoustic	$kg.m^{-4}.s^{-1}$	$Pa.s/m^3$, $reyl/m^2$	[ΔPressure]/[Volume flow rate]. Also **acu. resistance / reactance**
Impedance, acoustic, specific	$kg.m^{-2}.s^{-1}$	$Pa.s/m$, **reyl**	[ΔPressure]*[Velocity]. Also **s.acu. resistance / reactance**
Impedance, characteristic, electric	$kg.m^2.s^{-3}.A^{-2}$	$V.A^{-1}$, Ω, ohm	√([Mag.Permeability]/[El.Permittivity])
Impedance, inductive	$kg.m^2.s^{-3}.A^{-2}$	Ω (ohm)	i[Angular frequency].[Inductance]
Impedance, of a circuit	$kg.m^2.s^{-3}.A^{-2}$	Ω (ohm)	
Impulse	$kg.m.s^{-1}$		[ΔMoment of motion], [Force]*[ΔTime], [Mass]*[ΔVelocity]
Income rate | Earnings	$cur.s^{-1}$	currency/year	[Value]/[Time period]. Economy and finance
Inductance	$kg.m^2.s^{-2}.A^{-2}$	$V.s.A^{-1}$, $Wb.A^{-1}$, **H** (henry)	[ΔPotential]/[dCurrent/dt], [Mag.flux]/[Current]

Quantity	SI base units	SI derived unit	Definition / Notes
Induction, electric	$m^{-2}.s.A$	$C.m^{-2}$	[Charge]/[Area]. Same as **electric flux density**
Inductive admittance	$kg^{-1}.m^{-2}.s^3.A^2$	**S** (siemens)	1/[Inductive impedance]
Inductive impedance	$kg.m^2.s^{-3}.A^{-2}$	**Ω** (ohm)	i[Angular frequency].[Inductance]
Information	bit^{-1}	**bit**	One bit is the elementary information quantum
Information flux | Baud rate	$bit.s^{-1}$	**baud**	[Information]/[Time]
Intensity of electric current	$m^{-2}.A$		[Current]/[Area]. Same as **current density**
Interest	1	%	[ΔWealth]/[Wealth]. Economy and finance
Interest rate	s^{-1}	%/year	[Interest]/[Time period]. Economy and finance
Internal energy	$kg.m^2.s^{-2}$	J	Like **energy** and **heat**
Internal energy, molar	$kg.m^2.s^{-2}.mol^{-1}$	$J.mol^{-1}$	[Internal energy]/quantity]. Like **molar heat**
Internal energy, specific	$m^2.s^{-2}$	$J.kg^{-1}$	[Internal energy]/[Mass]. Like **specific heat**
Ion mobility	$kg^{-1}.m^{-1}.s^2.A$	$m^2.s^{-1}.V^{-1}$	[Velocity]/[Electric field strength] .
Ionic force (strength)	$m^{-3}.mol$		Sum([Concentration]*[Ionic quantum charge]^2).
Ionic quantum charge	1	Dimensionless	[Ion charge]/[Elementary charge quantum]
Ionic strength (force)	$m^{-3}.mol$		Sum([Concentration]*[Ionic quantum charge]^2).

Ionization energy, molar	$kg.m^2.s^{-2}.mol^{-1}$	$J.mol^{-1}$	Energy to ionize a molecule/atom
Irradiance	$kg.s^{-3}$	$W.m^{-2}$	[Heat flux]/[Area]. Same as **heat flux density**
J:			
Joule-Thomson coefficient	$kg^{-1}.m.s^2.K$	$K.Pa^{-1}$	[ΔTemperature]/[ΔPressure]
K:			
Katalytic activity	$mol.s^{-1}$	**katal**	[ΔQuantity]/[Time]. Same as **molar production rate**
Kinematic viscosity	$m^2.s^{-1}$		[Dynamic viscosity]/density]
K-space vector | Reciprocal space position	m^{-1}		
L:			
Lagrangian	$kg.m^2.s^{-2}$	J	[Force]*[Distance], [Power]*[Time]. Like **energy**
Laplace operator | Laplacian	m^{-2}		$\nabla^2 = \partial^2/\partial\mathbf{x}^2 + \partial^2/\partial\mathbf{y}^2 + \partial^2/\partial\mathbf{z}^2$
Length	m	**m** (meter)	
Liability | Debt	cur	**currency**	Economy and finance
Linear stiffness	$kg.s^{-2}$	$N.m^{-1}$	[Force]/[Displacement]. ... of a structure
Logarithmic ratio $\log_b(A/A')$ in any base b	1		Applicable to any ratio of commensurable quantities
Logarithmic ratio $\ln(A/A')$	1	**Np**	Neper. Uses natural logarithm
Logarithmic ratio $\log(P/P')/10$	1	**dB** (decibel)	Uses base-10 logarithm. Aplies only to

			power P
Logarithmic ratio Log(X/X')/20	1	dB (decibel)	Aplies to voltages (X=V) and currents (X=I)
Logarithmic scale differential	1	Dimensionless	dQ/Q, d{ln(Q)}, for any quantity Q. Also relative differential
Logarithmic scale probability density	1	1/Np	[Probability]/[Natural-logarithmic ratio]
Loss of a device	1	Dimensionless	[Output]/[Input], like-quantities ratio. Often in dB
Luminance	$cd.m^{-2}$		[Luminosity]/[Area]
Luminosity	cd	cd (candle)	Same as luminous intensity
Luminous coefficient	1	Dimensionless	[Luminous efficacy]/[683 lm/W]. Same as luminous efficiency
Luminous efficacy	$cd.sr.kg^{-1}.m^{-1}.s^{3}$	lm/W	[Luminous flux]/[Power]
Luminous efficiency	1	Dimensionless	[Luminous efficacy]/[683 lm/W]. Same as luminous coefficient
Luminous emittance	$cd.sr.m^{-2}$	$lm.m^{-2}$, lx (lux)	[Luminous flux]/[Area]. Same as luminous exitance
Luminous energy	cd.sr.s	lm.s	[Luminous flux]*Time]. Known as talbot
Luminous flux	cd.sr	lm (lumen)	[Luminosity]*[Solid angle]. Same as luminous power
Luminous intensity	cd	cd (candle)	Same as luminosity
Luminous power	cd.sr	lm (lumen)	[Luminosity]*[Solid angle]. Same as luminous flux
M:			

Magnetic charge (bound)	$m^{-2}.A$		- ∇.[Magnetization] , -Divergence of **magnetization**
Magnetic dipole moment	$m^2.A$	$J.T^{-1}$	[Current]*[Area]. Same as **magnetic moment**
Magnetic field gradient	$kg.m^{-1}.s^{-2}.A^{-1}$	$T.m^{-1}$	[ΔMag.flux density]/[Distance]
Magnetic field strength | Magnetic intensity	$m^{-1}.A$		[Current]/[Distance]
Magnetic flux	$kg.m^2.s^{-2}.A^{-1}$	$V.s$, $W.s.A^{-1}$, **Wb** (weber)	[ΔPotential]*[Time], [Power]/[dCurrent/dt]
Magnetic flux density | Magnetic induction	$kg.s^{-2}.A^{-1}$	$Wb.m^{-2}$, **T** (tesla)	[Mag.flux]/[Area]
Magnetic induction	$kg.s^{-2}.A^{-1}$	$Wb.m^{-2}$, **T** (tesla)	[Mag.flux]/[Area]. More properly **magnetic flux density**
Magnetic intensity	$m^{-1}.A$		[Current]/[Distance]. More properly **magnetic field strength**
Magnetic moment	$m^2.A$	$J.T^{-1}$	[Current]*[Area]
Magnetic permeability	$kg.m.s^{-2}.A^{-2}$	$H.m^{-1}$	[Mag.flux density]/[Mag.field strength]
Magnetic permeability, relative	1	Dimensionless	[Permeability]/[Permeability of vacuum]
Magnetic quadrupole moment	$m^3.A$	$m.J.T^{-1}$	[Mag.dipole]*[Distance]
Magnetic susceptibility	1	Dimensionless	[Relative permeability]-1
Magnetic vector potential	$kg.m.s^{-2}.A^{-1}$	$m^{-1}.s.V$, $m.T$	[Mag.flux density]*[Distance], [El.field strength]*[Time]
Magnetization	$m^{-1}.A$		[Mag.moment]/[Volume]. Like **magnetic field strength**
Magnetogyric ratio	$kg.s^{-1}.A^{-1}$	$T.Hz^{-1}$	[Angular moment of motion]/[Mag.moment]

Magnetomotive force (mmf)	A		[Current]*[Number of turns]
Magnitude of a star	1	Dimensionless	m-m'=-10$^{0.4}$(S/S'), where S,S' are the luminous fluxes of two stars
Mass	kg	**kg** (kilogram)	
Mass density	kg.m^{-3}		[Mass]/[Volume]. Same as **specific density**
Mass density gradient | Specific density gradient	kg.m^{-4}		[Mass density]/[Distance]
Mass concentration	1	Dimensionless	[Partial mass]/[Total mass]
Mass flow (total)	kg.s^{-1}	kg	[ΔMass]/[Time]. For example, through a device
Mass production rate	kg.s^{-1}		[ΔMass]/[Time]. Same as **mass flow**
Mass, molar	kg.mol^{-1}		[Mass]/[Quantity]
Mass number of an isotope	1	Dimensionless	Number of protons+neutrons in the isotope nuclide
Mean anomaly	1	Dimensionless	Of a body on a Kepler orbit; t.sqrt(G(M$_1$+M$_2$)/r^3)
Mean motion	s^{-1}		Of a body on a Kepler orbit; sqrt(G(M$_1$+M$_2$)/r^3)
Modulus of compression	kg^{-1}.m.s^2	Pa^{-1}	[Pressure]/([ΔVolume]/[Volume]). Same as **compressibility**
Modulus of rigidity	kg.m^{-1}.s^{-2}	N.m^{-2}, Pa	[Stress]/[Strain]. Same as **shear modulus**
Mobility, ionic	kg^{-1}.m^{-1}.s^2.A	m^2.s^{-1}.V^{-1}	[Velocity]/[Electric field strength] .
Molality (intended as	kg^{-1}.mol	mol/kg	[Quantity]/[Mass]

concentration)			
Molar charge	s.A.mol^{-1}	C.mol^{-1}	[Charge]/[Quantity]
Molar concentration	m^{-3}.mol		[Quantity]/[Volume]. Same as **concentration** or **molarity**
Molar concentration gradient	m^{-4}.mol		[Molarity]/[Distance]. Same as **molarity gradient**
Molar concentration ratio	1	Dimensionless	[Partial quantity]/[Total quantity]
Molar conductivity, electric	kg^{-1}.m^{-3}.s^3.A^2.mol^{-1}	S.m^{-1}.mol^{-1}	[El.conductivity]/[Concentration]
Molar density	m^{-3}.mol		[Quantity]/[Volume]. Same as **concentration**
Molar energy	kg.m^2.s^{-2}.mol^{-1}	J.mol^{-1}	[Energy]/[Quantity]
Molar enthalpy	kg.m^2.s^{-2}.mol^{-1}	J.mol^{-1}	[Enthalpy]/[Quantity]. Like **molar heat**
Molar entropy	kg.m^2.s^{-2}.K^{-1}.mol^{-1}	J.K^{-1}.mol^{-1}	[Entropy]/[Quantity]
Molar free energy	kg.m^2.s^{-2}.mol^{-1}	J.mol^{-1}	[Free energy]/quantity]. Also **molar Helmholtz function**
Molar free enthalpy	kg.m^2.s^{-2}.mol^{-1}	J.mol^{-1}	[Free enthalpy]/quantity]. Also **molar Gibbs function**
Molar heat	kg.m^2.s^{-2}.mol^{-1}	J.mol^{-1}	[Heat]/[Quantity]
Molar heat capacity	kg.m^2.s^{-2}.K^{-1}.mol^{-1}	J.K^{-1}.mol^{-1}	[Heat capacity]/quantity]
Molar internal energy	kg.m^2.s^{-2}.mol^{-1}	J.mol^{-1}	[Internal energy]/quantity]. Like **molar heat**
Molar mass	kg.mol^{-1}		[Mass]/[Quantity]

Molar particle count	mol^{-1}		[Count]/[Mol]. For example, the Avogadro constant
Molar production rate	mol.s^{-1}		[ΔQuantity]/[Time].
Molar refractivity	m^3.mol^{-1}		[(r^2-1)/(r^2+2)]/[Concentration], where r is the refractive index
Molar relaxivity	s^{-1}.mol^{-1}		[Relaxation rate]/[Concentration]
Molar solubility	m^{-3}.mol		[Quantity]/[Volume]. Same as **concentration**
Molar volume	m^3.mol^{-1}		[Volume]/[Quantity]
Molarity	m^{-3}.mol		[Quantity]/[Volume]. Same as **concentration** or **molar density**
Molarity gradient	m^{-4}.mol		[Molarity]/[Distance]. Same as **concentration gradient**
Molecular quantum charge	1	Dimensionless	[Charge of a molecule]/[Elementary charge quantum]
Moment of force	kg.m^2.s^{-2}	N.m	[Force]*[Distance]
Moment of motion	kg.m.s^{-1}		[Mass]*[Velocity], [Mass flow]*[Distance]
Multiple derivatives with respect to Time	s^{-p}		d^p/dt^p, $\partial^p/\partial t^p$; for p = 1,2,3,..
Multiple derivatives with respect to a length	m^{-p}		d^p/dr^p, $\partial^p/\partial r^p$; for p = 1,2,3,..., r = x | y | z
Mutual inductance	kg.m^2.s^{-2}.A^{-2}	V.s.A^{-1}, Wb.A^{-1}, **H** (henry)	[ΔPotential]/[dCurrent/dt], [Mag.flux]/[Current]

N:

Nabla (∇) | div | grad | rot | curl	m^{-1}		Any derivative-like construct with respect to a distance
Notch resistance	$kg.s^{-2}$	$J.m^{-2}$	[Energy]/[Area]
Number of instances / events	1		This covers all kinds of **enumerations**
Number density	m^{-3}		[Particles]/[Volume]. Obsolete; see **particle density**
Number of turns	1		Often used in electric engineering
O:			
Osmotic pressure	$kg.m^{-1}.s^{-2}$	Pa	
P:			
Particle count, molar	mol^{-1}		[Count]/[Mol]. For example, the Avogadro constant
Particle density	m^{-3}		[Count]/[Volume]. Obsolete: **number density**
P/E Price/Earnings ratio	s	year	[Value]/[Earnings]. Economy and finance
Peltier coefficient	$kg.m^2.s^{-3}.A^{-1}$	$W.A^{-1}$, V	[Heat flux]/[Current]
Perimeter | Circumference	m		
Permeability, magnetic	$kg.m.s^{-2}.A^{-2}$	$H.m^{-1}$	[Mag.flux density]/[Mag.field strength]
Permeability, hydraulic	m^2	1 darcy = 10^{-12} m^2	[Velocity]*[Viscosity]/[Pressure gradient], in **porous media**
Permittivity, electric	$kg^{-1}.m^{-3}.s^4.A^2$	$F.m^{-1}$	[El.flux density]/[El.field strength]
Permittivity, relative	1	Dimensionless	[Permittivity]/[Permittivity of vacuum]. **Dielectric constant**

Phase | Phase angle	1	rad	φ typically in $\exp(i(\omega t+\varphi))$
Phase drift rate	s^{-1}	$rad.s^{-1}$	[Phase angle]/Time
Pi coefficient, molar	$kg.m^{-1}.s^{-2}.mol^{-1}$	$J.m^{-3}$	[ΔInternalEnergy]/[ΔVolume]
Piezzoelectric coefficient	$kg.m.s^{-3}.A^{-1}$	$V.m^{-1}$	[Electric field strength]/([ΔLength]/[Length])
Plane angle	1	**rad**	
Poisson's ratio	1	Dimensionless	[Transversal striction]/[Londitudinal elongation]
Polarization, electric	$m^{-2}.s.A$	$C.m^{-2}$	[Charge]/[Area]. Like **electric flux density**
Porosity, superficial	1	Dimensionless	[Void cross section]/[Total cross section], in **porous media**
Porosity, volume	1	Dimensionless	[Pores volume]/[Total volume], in **porous media**
Position vector	m		in all Euclidean n-dimensional spaces
Potential, electric	$kg.m^2.s^{-3}.A^{-1}$	$W.A^{-1}$, $J.C^{-1}$, **V** (volt)	[Power]/[Current], [Energy]/[Charge]
Power	$kg.m^2.s^{-3}$	$J.s^{-1}$, **W** (watt)	[ΔEnergy]/[ΔTime]. Equivalent to **energy flux**
Prandtl number	1	Dimensionless	[Kinematic viscosity]/[Thermal diffusivity]
Propagation loss	m^{-1}	dB/m	Ratio]/m. Generic, usable for any quantity
Poynting vector	$kg.s^{-3}$	$W.m^{-2}$	[El.field strength]/[Mag.field strength]. Like **irradiance**
Pressure	$kg.m^{-1}.s^{-2}$	$N.m^{-2}$, **Pa** (pascal)	[Force]/[Area]
Pressure gradient	$kg.m^{-2}.s^{-2}$	$N.m^{-3}$, **Pa/m**	[Pressure]/[Distance]

Price | Value	cur	currency	Economy and finance
Probability of an event	1		Real number in a dimensionless interval [0,1]
Probability density on log-scale	1	Np^{-1}	[Probability]/[Natural-logarithmic ratio]
Purchase | Transaction value	cur	currency	Economy and finance

Q:

Quadrupole moment, electric	$m^2.s.A$	$C.m^2$	[Electric dipole]*[Distance], [Electric charge]*[Distance^2]
Quadrupole moment, magnetic	$m^3.A$	$m.J.T^{-1}$	[Mag.dipole]*[Distance]
Quantity of substance	mol	**mol**	
Quantum charge	1	Dimensionless	[Charge]/[Elementary charge quantum]
Quantum charge, molecular or ionic	1	Dimensionless	[Molecule/ion charge]/[Charge quantum]
Quotient of dispersivity	m^{-1}		[ΔRefractive index]/[ΔWavelength]

R:

Radiance	$kg.s^{-3}.sr^{-1}$	$W.m^{-2}.sr^{-1}$	([Power]/[Area])/[Solid angle]
Radiation dose	$m^2.s^{-2}$	$J.kg^{-1}$, **Gy** (gray)	[Energy]/[Mass]
Radiation dose rate	$m^2.s^{-3}$	$Gy.s^{-1}$	[Absorbed dose]/[Time]
Radioactivity	s^{-1}	**Bq** (becquerel)	[Counts]/[Time]
Radius of curvature	m		of a line in plane/space or surface in space

Rotational stiffness	$kg.m^2.s^{-2}.rad^{-1}$	$N.m.rad^{-1}$	[Moment of force]/[Angle]. ... of a structure
Ratio of commensurable quantities	1	Dimensionless	Q1/Q2, with Q1 and Q2 having the same dimension
Reactance, acoustic	$kg.m^{-4}.s^{-1}$	$Pa.s/m^3$, $reyl/m^2$	[ΔPressure]/[Volume flow rate]. Also **acu. impedance / resistance**
Reactance, acoustic, specific	$kg.m^{-2}.s^{-1}$	Pa.s/m , **reyl**	[ΔPressure]*[Velocity]. Also **s.acu. impedance / resistance**
Reactance, capacitive	$kg.m^2.s^{-3}.A^{-2}$	**Ω** (ohm)	1/(i[Angular frequency].[Capacitance])
Reciprocal space position | K-space vector	m^{-1}		
Redox potential	$kg.m^2.s^{-3}.A^{-1}$	**V** (volt)	Same as **reduction potential**
Reduction potential	$kg.m^2.s^{-3}.A^{-1}$	**V** (volt)	Same as **redox potential**
Refractive index	1	Dimensionless	Light speeds ration (in a medium)/(in vacuum)
Refractivity, molar	$m^3.mol^{-1}$		$[(r^2-1)/(r^2+2)]$/[Concentration]
Refractivity, specific	$m^3.kg^{-1}$		$[(r^2-1)/(r^2+2)]$/[Specific density],
Relative atomic mass | Atomic weight	au	atomic units	Average over a typical isotopic composition
Relative differential	1	Dimensionless	dQ/Q, d{ln(Q)}, for any quantity Q. Also **log-scale differential**
Relative evolution rate	s^{-1}		d{ln(Q)}/dt = (dQ/dt)/Q. Also **log-scale evolution rate**
Relative permeability, magnetic	1	Dimensionless	[Permeability]/[Permeability of vacuum]

Relative permittivity, electric	1	Dimensionless	[Permittivity]/[Permittivity of vacuum]. **Dielectric constant**
Relative variation	1	Dimensionless	$\Delta Q/Q$, for any quantity Q
Relativistic displacement four-tensor ($D^{\mu\nu}$)	$m^{-1}.A$		Like **magnetic intensity**
Relativistic electromagnetic field tensor ($F^{\mu\nu}$)	$kg.s^{-2}.A^{-1}$	T	Like **magnetic flux density**
Relativistic four-current (J^{α})	$m^{-2}.A$		Like **current density** and [Charge]*[c]
Relativistic four-potential (A^{α})	$kg.m.s^{-2}.A^{-1}$	$m^{-1}.s.V$, m.T	Like **magnetic vector potential** and [El.potential]/[c]
Relaxation rate	s^{-1}		1/[Relaxation time]. Used for returns to equilibria
Relaxation time	s		Used for returns to equilibria
Relaxivity, molar	$s^{-1}.mol^{-1}$		[Relaxation rate]/[Concentration]
Reluctance, magnetic	$kg^{-1}.m^{-1}.s^{2}.A^{2}$	$m.H^{-1}$	1/[Permeability]
Resistance, acoustic	$kg.m^{-4}.s^{-1}$	$Pa.s/m^{3}$, $reyl/m^{2}$	[ΔPressure]/[Volume flow rate]. Also **acu. impedance / reactance**
Resistance, acoustic, specific	$kg.m^{-2}.s^{-1}$	Pa.s/m, reyl	[ΔPressure]*[Velocity]. Also **s.acu. impedance / reactance**
Resistance, electric	$kg.m^{2}.s^{-3}.A^{-2}$	$V.A^{-1}$, Ω (ohm)	[ΔPotential]/[Current]
Resistance, thermal	$kg^{-1}.m^{-2}.s^{3}K$	K/W	of a device. [ΔT]/[Power].
Resistance to impact	$kg.s^{-2}$	$J.m^{-2}$	[Energy]/[Area]. Like **notch resistance**
Resistivity, electric	$kg.m^{3}.s^{-3}.A^{-2}$	$\Omega.m$	([Resistance]*[Length])/[Area]
Return on asset / equity	s^{-1}	%/year	([ΔValue]/[Value])/[Time period].

			Economy and finance
Reynolds number	1	Dimensionless	[Velocity]*[length]/[Kinematic viscosity]
RF attenuation	m^{-1}	dB/m	Ratio]/m. Used mostly for radiation
S:			
Sale | Transaction value	cur	currency	Economy and finance
Sales flow | Transactions volume	$cur.s^{-1}$		[Value]/[Time period]. Economy and Finance
Seeback coefficient	$kg.m^2.s^{-3}.A^{-1}.K^{-1}$	$V.K^{-1}$	[ΔPotential]/[ΔTemperature]. Same as **thermoelectric power**
Self-diffusion coefficient	$m^2.s^{-1}$		[Distance^2]/[Time]
Settling rate	s^{-1}	typically dB/s	[Ratio]/[ΔTime]
Settling Time	s	typically dB/s	Used to describe transient phenomena
Shear modulus	$kg.m^{-1}.s^{-2}$	$N.m^{-2}$, Pa	[Stress]/[Strain]. Like **Young modulus**
Softening point	K		Temperature at which hardness drops below a level
Solid angle	1	**sr** (steradian)	
Solubility, molar	$m^{-3}.mol$		[Quantity]/[Volume]. Same as **concentration**
Sonic attenuation	m^{-1}	dB/m	[Power ratio]/m. Used in acoustics
Specific acoustic impedance	$kg.m^{-2}.s^{-1}$	Pa.s/m , **reyl**	[ΔPressure]*[Velocity]. Also **s.acu. resistance / reactance**
Specific acoustic conductance	$kg^{-1}.m^2.s$	$reyl^{-1}$	Also **specific acoustic susceptance**
Specific charge	$kg^{-1}.s.A$	$C.kg^{-1}$	[Charge]/[Mass]. **Charge/mass ratio**

Specific density	kg.m^{-3}		[Mass]/[Volume]. Same as **density of mass**
Specific density gradient	kg.m^{-4}		[Mass density]/[Distance]. Same as **mass density gradient**
Specific energy	m^2.s^{-2}	J.kg^{-1}	[Energy]/[Mass]
Specific enthalpy	m^2.s^{-2}	J.kg^{-1}	[Enthalpy]/[Mass]. Like **specific heat**
Specific entropy	m^2.s^{-2}.K^{-1}	J.K^{-1}.kg^{-1}	[Entropy]/[Mass]
Specific free energy	m^2.s^{-2}	J.kg^{-1}	[Free energy]/[Mass]. Also **specific Helmholtz function**
Specific free enthalpy	m^2.s^{-2}	J.kg^{-1}	[Free enthalpy]/[Mass]. Also **specific Gibbs function**
Specific heat	m^2.s^{-2}	J.kg^{-1}	[Heat]/[Mass]
Specific heat capacity	m^2.s^{-2}.K^{-1}	J.K^{-1}.kg^{-1}	[Heat capacity]/[Mass]
Specific internal energy	m^2.s^{-2}	J.kg^{-1}	[Internal energy]/[Mass]. Like **specific heat**
Specific refractivity	m^3.kg^{-1}		[(r^2-1)/(r^2+2)]/[Specific density]
Specific volume	m^3.kg^{-1}		[Volume]/[Mass]
Speed	m.s^{-1}		[Distance]/[Time]. Same as **velocity**
Spin	1	Dimensionless	of a quantum particle
Star magnitude	1	Dimensionless	m-m' = -10$^{0.4}$(S/S'), where S,S' are luminous fluxes of two stars
Stiffness, linear	kg.s^{-2}	N.m^{-1}	[Force]/[Displacement]. ... of a structure
Stiffness, rotational	kg.m^2.s^{-2}.rad^{-1}	N.m.rad^{-1}	[Moment of force]/[Angle]. ... of a structure

Strain (mechanical)	1	Dimensionless	[ΔLength]/[Length] Relative deformation
Strain point	K		Temperature at which viscosity drops below $10^{13.5}$ Pa.s
Strength, compressive	$kg.m^{-1}.s^{-2}$	$N.m^{-2}$, Pa	[Force]/[Area]. Like **pressure**
Strength, dielectric	$kg.m.s^{-3}.A^{-1}$	$V.m^{-1}$	[ΔPotential]/[Distance]. Same as **electric strength**
Strength, electric field │ Electric intensity	$kg.m.s^{-3}.A^{-1}$	$V.m^{-1}$	[ΔPotential]/[Distance]
Strength, ionic	$m^{-3}.mol$		Sum([Concentration]*[Ionic quantum charge]^2).
Strength, magnetic field │ Magnetic intensity	$m^{-1}.A$		[Current]/[Distance]
Strength, tensile	$kg.m^{-1}.s^{-2}$	$N.m^{-2}$, Pa	[Force]/[Area]. Same as **pressure**
Superficial porosity	1	Dimensionless	[Void cross section]/[Total cross section], in **porous media**
Superficial velocity	$m.s^{-1}$	m/s	In **porous media**; as if the space was filled only by the fluid
Surface area	m^2		[Distance]*[Distance]. Applicable to 3D bodies
Surface density of charge	$m^{-2}.s.A$	$C.m^{-2}$	[Charge]/[Area]
Surface element	m^2		[Distance]*[Distance]. Same as **area**
Surface energy	$kg.s^{-2}$	J/m^2	[Energy]/[Area]. Same as **surface tension**
Surface growth rate	$m^2.s^{-1}$		[ΔArea]/[Time]
Surface tension	$kg.s^{-2}$	N/m	[Force]/[Length]. Same as **surface**

			energy
Susceptance, acoustic, specific	$kg^{-1}.m^2.s$	$reyl^{-1}$	Also **specific acoustic conductance**
Susceptance, capacitive	$kg^{-1}.m^{-2}.s^3.A^2$	**S** (siemens)	1/[Reactance]
Susceptibility, magnetic	1	Dimensionless	[Relative permeability]-1
Stress	$kg.m^{-1}.s^{-2}$	Pa, $N.m^{-2}$	[Force]/[Area]. Same as **pressure**

T:

Temperature	K	**K** (kelvin)	
Temperature gradient	$K.m^{-1}$		[ΔTemperature]/[Distance]. Same as **thermal gradient**
Tensile strength	$kg.m^{-1}.s^{-2}$	$N.m^{-2}$, Pa	[Force]/[Area]. Same as **pressure**
Tension	$kg.m^{-1}.s^{-2}$	Pa, $N.m^{-2}$	[Force]/[Area]. Like **pressure**
Thermal conductivity	$kg.m.s^{-3}.K^{-1}$	$W.m^{-1}.K^{-1}$	[Heat flux]/([Distance]*[ΔTemperature]). Same as **heat conductivity**
Thermal diffusivity	$m^2.s^{-1}$		([∂Temperatute]/[∂Time])/[∇^2Temperature].
Thermal expansion coefficient	K^{-1}		([ΔLength]/[Length])/[Temperature]
Thermal gradient	$K.m^{-1}$		[ΔTemperature]/[Distance]. Same as **temperature gradient**
Thermal resistance	$kg^{-1}.m^{-2}.s^3K$	K/W	of a device. [ΔT]/[Power].
Thermodynamic force	$kg.m.s^{-2}.mol^{-1}$	N/mol	[ΔChemical potential]/[Distance]
Thermoelectric power | Thermopower	$kg.m^2.s^{-3}.A^{-1}.K^{-1}$	$V.K^{-1}$	[ΔPotential]/[ΔTemperature]. Same as **Seeback coefficient**

Thickness	m		usually referred to planar structures
Thomson coefficient	$kg.m^2.s^{-3}.A^{-1}.K^{-1}$	$W.K^{-1}.A^{-1}$	[Heat flux]/([ΔTemperature]*[Current])
Time	s	**s** (second)	
Torque | Moment of force	$kg.m^2.s^{-2}$	N.m	[Force]*[Distance]
Traction	$kg.m.s^{-2}$	**N** (newton)	Maximum tangential force before slipping
Traction coefficient	1	Dimensionless	[Traction]/[Weight]
Transaction value | Sale | Purchase	cur	currency	Economy and finance
Transactions count	1	Dimensionless	Economy and finance
Transactions rate | Activity	s^{-1}	1/year	[Transactions]/[Time period]. Economy and finance
Transactions volume | Sales flow	$cur.s^{-1}$		[Value]/[Time period]. Economy and Finance
Transmission loss	m^{-1}	dB/m	Ratio]/m. Generic, usable for any quantity
U:			
V:			
V-number | Abbé number | Constringence	1	Dimensionless	$V_D = (n_D-1)/(n_F-n_C)$
Value | Price	cur	currency	Economy and finance
van der Waals constant: a	$kg.m^5.s^{-2}.mol^{-2}$	$Pa.m^6$	a in $(p+a/V^2)(V-b)=RT$, where V is molar volume
van der Waals constant: b	$m^3.mol^{-1}$		b in $(p+a/V^2)(V-b)=RT$, where V is molar volume

Variance of current noise $n_J{}^2$	$s.A^2$	A^2/Hz	[Current]^2/[Bandwidth]
Variance of voltage noise $n_V{}^2$	$kg^2.m^4.s^{-5}.A^{-2}$	V^2/Hz	[Voltage]^2/[Bandwidth]
Vector potential, magnetic	$kg.m.s^{-2}.A^{-1}$	$m^{-1}.s.V$, $m.T$	[Mag.flux density]*[Distance], [El.field strength]*[Time]
Velocity	$m.s^{-1}$	m/s	[Distance]/[Time]. Same as **speed**
Velocity, advection	$m.s^{-1}$	m/s	In **porous media**; actual progress along pressure gradient
Velocity, of money (circulation)	s^{-1}	1/year	[Transactions]/[Time period]. Economy and finance
Velocity, superficial	$m.s^{-1}$	m/s	In **porous media**; as if the space was filled only by the fluid
Verdet constant	$kg^{-1}.m^{-1}.s^2.A^1$	$rad.m^{-1}.T^{-1}$	([Angle]/[Length])/[Magnetic flux density]
Virial coefficient: second	$m^3.mol^{-1}$		B in $pV/(nRT)=1+B(n/V)+C(n/V)^2+D(n/V)^3+...$
Virial coefficient: third	$m^6.mol^{-2}$		C in $pV/(nRT)=1+B(n/V)+C(n/V)^2+D(n/V)^3+...$
Virial coefficient: fourth	$m^9.mol^{-3}$		C in $pV/(nRT)=1+B(n/V)+C(n/V)^2+D(n/V)^3+...$
Viscosity, dynamic	$kg.m^{-1}.s^{-1}$	Pa.s	([Force]/[Area])/[ΔVelocity]
Viscosity, kinematic	$m^2.s^{-1}$		[Dynamic viscosity]/density]
Voltage | Electromotive force	$kg.m^2.s^{-3}.A^{-1}$	V	[ΔPotential]
Voltage noise, variance $n_V{}^2$	$kg^2.m^4.s^{-5}.A^{-2}$	V^2/Hz	[Voltage]^2/[Bandwidth]
Volume	m^3		[Area]*[Distance]
Volume concentration	1	Dimensionless	[Partial volume]/[Total volume]

Volume flow	$m^3.s^{-1}$		[Volume]/[Time]. For example, through a device
Volume growth rate	$m^3.s^{-1}$		[Volume]/[Time]. For example, of a crystal
Volume porosity	1	Dimensionless	[Pores volume]/[Total volume], in **porous media**
W:			
Wave function for N particles (quantum)	$m^{-3N/2}$	tentative	$\|\psi\|^2 d\tau^N$ is a dimensionless probability element.
Wavelength	m		[Wave velocity]Frequency]
Wavenumber	m^{-1}		[Number of waves]/[Distance]
Wealth | Asset	cur	currency	Economy and finance
Work function	$kg.m^2.s^{-2}$	J, eV	Energy] needed to remove an electron
X:			
Y:			
Young modulus	$kg.m^{-1}.s^{-2}$	$N.m^{-2}$, Pa	[Stress]/[Strain]. Like **shear modulus**
Z:			

References

1. Beaman Jr. Joseph J., Longoria Raul G.,
    Modeling of Physical Systems,
    Wiley 2016. ISBN 978-1119945048.

2. Zohuri Bahman,
    Dimensional Analysis and Self-Similarity Methods for Engineers and Scientists,
    Springer 2015. ISBN 978-3319134758.

3. Isakov Edmund,
    International System of Units (SI):
    How the world measures almost everything, and the people who made it possible,
    Industrial Press 2014. ISBN 978-0831102319. Also available as Multimedia CD.

4. Bridgman Percy W.,
    Dimensional Analysis,
    Reprint of the 1922 clasic. TheClassics.us 2013. ISBN 978-1230226214..

5. Crease Robert P.,
    World in the Balance: The Historic Quest for an Absolute System of Measurement,
    W.W.Norton & Company 2012. ISBN 978-0393343540..

6. Gibbings JC,
    Dimensional Analysis,
    Springer 2011. ISBN 978-1849963169..

7. Klein Herbert A.,
    The Science of Measurement: A Historical Survey,
    Dover Publications 2011. ISBN 978-0486258393..

8. Gupta S.V.,
    Units of Measurement: Past, Present and Future. International System of Units,
    Springer 2009. ISBN 978-3642007378..

9. Palmer Andrew C.,
    Dimensional Analysis and Intelligent Experimentation,
    World Scientific Publishing 2008. ISBN 978-9812708199..

10. Charalambos D. Aliprantis, Border Kim,
    Infinite Dimensional Analysis: A Hitchhiker's Guide,
    3rd Edition, Springer 2007. ISBN 978-3540326960..

11. Strothman J, Editor,
    ISA Handbook of Measurement Equations and Tables,
    2nd Edition, ISA (Instrumentation, Systems, and Automation) 2006.
    ISBN 978-1556179464..

12. Szirtes Thomas,
    Applied Dimensional Analysis and Modeling,
    2nd Edition, Butterworth-Heinemann 2006. ISBN 978-0123706201..

13. Jerrard H.G.,
    Dictionary of Scientific Units Including Dimensionless Numbers and Scales,
    Springer 1992. ISBN 978-0412467202..

Table -3: SI Dimensions of Physical Quantities listed by Category

(Source: From Wikipedia, the free encyclopedia)

Quantity	Dimension	Alternatives	Root definition and Notes
Basic SI quantities			
Length	m	m	meter
Mass	kg	**kg**	kilogram
Time	s	**s**	second
Current, electric	A	**A**	ampere
Temperature	K	**K**	kelvin
Quantity of substance	mol	**mol**	mole
Luminosity | Luminous intensity	cd	**cd**	candle
Pseudo-dimensional quantities:			
Plane angle	1	rad	radian
Solid angle	1	sr	steradian
Universal dimensionless quantities			
Count of events | Number of instances	1		This covers all kinds of enumerations

Probability of an event	1		Real number in a dimensionless interval [0,1]
Ratio of commensurable quantities	1		Q1/Q2, with Q1 and Q2 having the same dimension
Relative variation	1		ΔQ/Q, for any quantity Q
Logarithmic ratio log$_b$(A/A') in any base b	1		Applicable to any ratio of commensurable quantities
Logarithmic scale differential | Relative differential	1		d{ln(Q)} = dQ/Q, for any quantity Q
Pseudo-dimensional quantities:			
Phase | Phase angle	1	rad	φ typically in exp(i(ωt+φ))
Logarithmic ratio Log(P/P')/10	1	**dB**	**decibel**. Uses base-10 logarithm. Applies to power P
Logarithmic ratio Log(X/X')/20	1	**dB**	**decibel**. Uses base-10 logarithm. Applies to amplitudes X
Gain or Loss of a device	1	usually in **dB**	[Output]/[Input], provided they are commensurable quantities
Attenuation | Amplification (generic)	1	usually in **dB**	[Quantity(p)]/[Quantity(p')], with p being some parameter
Logarithmic ratio ln(A/A')	1	**Np**	Neper. Uses natural logarithm
Logarithmic scale probability density	1	1/Np	[Probability]/[Natural-logarithmic ratio]

Operators

Derivative with respect to **time**	s^{-1}		d/dt, $\partial/\partial t$
Derivative with respect to a **length**	m^{-1}		d/dr, $\partial/\partial r$, $r = x \mid y \mid z$
Nabla (∇) | div | grad | rot | curl	m^{-1}		Any derivative-like construct with respect to a distance
Laplace operator | **Laplacian**	m^{-2}		$\nabla^2 = \partial^2/\partial x^2 + \partial^2/\partial y^2 + \partial^2/\partial z^2$
D'Alembert operator | **D'Alembertian**	m^{-2}		$(1/c^2)\partial^2/\partial t^2 - \partial^2/\partial x^2 - \partial^2/\partial y^2 - \partial^2/\partial z^2$
Multiple derivatives with respect to **time**	s^{-p}		d^p/dt^p, $\partial^p/\partial t^p$; for p = 1,2,3,..
Multiple derivatives with respect to a **length**	m^{-p}		d^p/dr^p, $\partial^p/\partial r^p$; for p = 1,2,3,..., $r = x \mid y \mid z$

Quantities related only to time

Time | Duration	s	**s**	**second**
Half life	s		of a non-conservative / decaying quantity
Settling time	s	typically dB/s	Used to describe transient phenomena
Relaxation time	s		Used for returns to equilibria
Activity | Frequency of events	s^{-1}		[Counts]/[Time]
Count rate | Expectation frequency	s^{-1}		[Counts]/[Time]
Relative growth rate	s^{-1}		[Relative variation]/[Time]
Relative evolution rate | Log-scale evolution rate	s^{-1}		$d\{\ln(Q)\}/dt = (dQ/dt)/Q$
Settling rate	s^{-1}	typically dB/s	[Ratio]/[ΔTime]. Used for

			transient phenomena
Relaxation rate	s^{-1}		1/[Relaxation time]
Frequency of waves	s^{-1}	**Hz**	**hertz**
Phase drift rate	s^{-1}	$rad.s^{-1}$	[Phase angle]/[Time]
Angular velocity / speed	s^{-1}	$rad.s^{-1}$	[Plane angle]/[Time]
Frequency drift rate	s^{-2}	$Hz.s^{-1}$	[ΔFrequency]/[Time]. Applicable to waves
Angular acceleration / deceleration	s^{-2}	$rad.s^{-2}$	[ΔAngularVelocity]/[Time]

Quantities related only to space

Position vector	m		in all Euclidean n-dimensional spaces
Length | Distance	m	**m**	**meter**
Perimeter | Circumference | Radius	m		
Thickness	m		usually referred to planar structures
Wavelength	m		[Wave velocity]/[Frequency]
Wavenumber	m^{-1}		[Number of waves]/[Distance]
K-space vector | Reciprocal space position	m^{-1}		
Curvature radius	m		of a line in plane/space or surface in space
Curvature	m^{-1}		1/[Curvature radius]

Convergence	m^{-1}	**dioptry**	used in optics, but not only ..
Attenuation / amplification over a distance	m^{-1}	dB/m	[Attenuation]/[Distance]. Mostly in acoustic and electronics
Extinction coefficient	m^{-1}	dB/m	[Ratio]/m. Used mostly for radiation
Propagation / transmission loss	m^{-1}	dB/m	[Ratio]/m. Generic, usable for any quantity
Area | Cross section	m^2		[Distance]*[Distance]
Surface element | Surface area	m^2		[Distance]*[Distance]. Applicable to 3D bodies
Volume element | Volume	m^3		[Area]*[Distance]

Propagation through space and time

Velocity | Speed	$m.s^{-1}$		[Distance]/[Time]
Acceleration | Deceleration	$m.s^{-2}$		[ΔVelocity]/[ΔTime]
Drift speed	$m.s^{-1}$		Steady-state speed of an object
Surface / area growth rate	$m^2.s^{-1}$		[ΔArea]/[Time]
Volume growth rate	$m^3.s^{-1}$		[ΔVolume]/[Time]. For example, of a crystal
Volume flow	$m^3.s^{-1}$		[Volume]/[Time]. For example, through a device

Matter distribution and transport

Particle density	m^{-3}		[Count]/[Volume]. Obsolete:

			number density
Mass	kg	kg	kilogram
Mass production rate	$kg.s^{-1}$		[ΔMass]/[Time]
Mass density | Specific density	$kg.m^{-3}$		[Mass]/[Volume]
Mass density gradient | Specific density gradient	$kg.m^{-4}$		[Mass density]/[Distance]
Specific volume	$m^3.kg^{-1}$		[Volume]/[Mass]
Concentration ratio by volume	1	Dimensionless	[Partial volume]/[Total volume]
Concentration ratio by mass	1	Dimensionless	[Partial mass]/[Total mass]. Not *by weight*: obsolete)
Mass flow (total)	$kg.s^{-1}$		[ΔMass]/[Time]. For example, through a device
Diffusion coefficient	$m^2.s^{-1}$		[Distance^2]/[Time]
Molar distribution and transport quantities:			
Particle count, molar	mol^{-1}		[Count]/[Mol]. For example, the Avogadro constant
Molar production rate	$mol.s^{-1}$		[ΔQuantity]/[Time]
Molar mass	$kg.mol^{-1}$		[Mass]/[Quantity]
Molar volume	$m^3.mol^{-1}$		[Volume]/[Quantity]
Molar density | Density of substance	$m^{-3}.mol$		[Quantity]/[Volume]

Molarity | Concentration	$m^{-3}.mol$		[Quantity]/[Volume]. Same as **molar density**
Molarity gradient | Concentration gradient	$m^{-4}.mol$		[Molarity]/[Distance]
Molar concentration ratio	1	Dimensionless	[Partial quantity]/[Total quantity]
Molality (intended as concentration)	$kg^{-1}.mol$	mol/kg	[Quantity]/[Mass]. Obsolete
Katalytic activity	$mol.s^{-1}$	**katal**	[ΔQuantity]/[Time]

Mechanics and hydrodynamics

Force	$kg.m.s^{-2}$	**N**	**newton**. [Mass]*[Acceleration]
Moment of motion	$kg.m.s^{-1}$		[Mass]*[Velocity], [Mass flow]*[Distance]
Impulse	$kg.m.s^{-1}$		[ΔMoment of motion], [Force]*[ΔTime], [Mass]*[ΔVelocity]
Moment of force | Torque	$kg.m^2.s^{-2}$	N.m	[Force]*[Distance]. Like **energy**
Couple	$kg.m^2.s^{-2}$	N.m	2*[Force]*[Distance] for two non-aligned opposing forces
Pressure	$kg.m^{-1}.s^{-2}$	$N.m^{-2}$, **Pa**	**pascal**. [Force]/[Area]
Pressure gradient	$kg.m^{-2}.s^{-2}$	$N.m^{-3}$, **Pa/m**	[Pressure]/[Distance]
Energy | Lagrangian | Hamiltonian	$kg.m^2.s^{-2}$	N.m, **J**	**joule**. [Force]*[Distance], [Power]*[Time]

Specific energy	$m^2.s^{-2}$	$J.kg^{-1}$	[Energy]/[Mass]
Energy density	$kg.m^{-1}.s^{-2}$	$J.m^{-3}$	[Energy]/[Volume]
Power | Energy flux	$kg.m^2.s^{-3}$	$J.s^{-1}$, **W**	**watt**. [ΔEnergy]/[ΔTime]
Action	$kg.m^2.s^{-1}$	$J.s$	[Energy]*[Time], [Moment of motion]*[Distance]
Angular moment of inertia	$kg.m^2$		[Mass]*[Distance^2]
Angular moment of motion	$kg.m^2.s^{-1}$	$J.s$	[Moment of motion]*[Distance]
Circulation	$m^2.s^{-1}$	$J.s.kg^{-1}$	[Angular moment]/[Mass], [Velocity]*[Loop length]
Spin	1	Dimensionless	of a quantum particle
Stress | Tension | Compression	$kg.m^{-1}.s^{-2}$	$N.m^{-2}$, **Pa** (pascal)	[Force]/[Area]. ... same as pressure
Compressive strength	$kg.m^{-1}.s^{-2}$	$N.m^{-2}$, Pa	[Force]/[Area]. Like **pressure**
Strain (mechanical)	1	Dimensionless	[ΔLength]/[Length] Relative deformation
Friction	$kg.m.s^{-2}$	**N**	Tangential force between two moving surfaces
Traction	$kg.m.s^{-2}$	**N**	Maximum tangential force before slipping
Velocity, superficial	$m.s^{-1}$	m/s	In **porous media**; as if the space was filled only by the fluid
Velocity, advection	$m.s^{-1}$	m/s	In **porous media**; actual progress along pressure gradient
Wave function for N particles (quantum)	$m^{-3N/2}$	tentative	$|\psi|^2 d\tau^N$ is a dimensionless

			probability element.
Mechanical and hydrodynamic properties of matter			
Compressibility | Modulus of compression	$kg^{-1}.m.s^2$	Pa^{-1}	[Pressure]/([ΔVolume]/[Volume]). Inverse of bulk modulus
Bulk modulus	$kg.m^{-1}.s^{-2}$	$N.m^{-2}$, Pa	([ΔVolume]/[Volume])/[Pressure]. Inverse of compressibility
Young modulus	$kg.m^{-1}.s^{-2}$	$N.m^{-2}$, Pa	[Stress]/[Strain]. Like **shear modulus**
Shear modulus | Modulus of rigidity	$kg.m^{-1}.s^{-2}$	$N.m^{-2}$, Pa	[Stress]/[Strain]. Same dimension aas Young modulus
Poisson's ratio	1	Dimensionless	[Transversal striction]/[Londitudinal elongation]
Impact | Notch resistance	$kg.s^{-2}$	$J.m^{-2}$	[Energy]/[Area]
Hardness | Tensile strength	$kg.m^{-1}.s^{-2}$	$N.m^{-2}$, Pa	[Force]/[Area]. Like **pressure**
Stiffness (linear)	$kg.s^{-2}$	$N.m^{-1}$	[Force]/[Displacement]. ... of a structure
Stiffness (rotational)	$kg.m^2.s^{-2}.rad^{-1}$	$N.m.rad^{-1}$	[Moment of force]/[Angle]. ... of a structure
Friction coefficient	1	Dimensionless	[Tangential force]/[Normal force]
Traction coefficient	1	Dimensionless	[Traction]/[Weight]
Self-diffusion coefficient	$m^2.s^{-1}$		[Distance^2]/[Time]
Surface tension	$kg.s^{-2}$	N/m	[Force]/[Length]. Same as surface energy

Surface energy	kg.s^{-2}	J/m^2	[Energy]/[Area]. Same as surface tension
Viscosity, dynamic	kg.m^{-1}.s^{-1}	Pa.s	([Force]/[Area])/[ΔVelocity]
Viscosity, kinematic	m^2.s^{-1}		[Dynamic viscosity]/[Density]
Reynolds number	1	Dimensionless	[Velocity]*[length]/[Kinematic viscosity]
Critical angle of repose	rad	or degree	Steepest angle of a slope before a slide
Porosity, volume	1	Dimensionless	[Volume of pores]/[Total volume], in **porous media**
Porosity, superficial	1	Dimensionless	[Void cross section]/[Total cross section], in **porous media**
Permeability, hydraulic	m^2	1 darcy = 10^{-12} m^2	[Velocity]*[Viscosity]/[Pressure gradient], in **porous media**
Conductivity, hydraulic	m.s^{-1}	m/s	Used for **porous media**
Specific acoustic impedance / resistance / reactance	kg.m^{-2}.s^{-1}	Pa.s/m , **reyl**	[ΔPressure]*[Velocity], intensive property
Specific acoustic conductance / susceptance	kg^{-1}.m^2.s	reyl^{-1}	Inverse of specific acoustic impedance
Acoustic impedance / resistance / reactance	kg.m^{-4}.s^{-1}	Pa.s/m^3, reyl/m^2	[ΔPressure]/[Volume flow rate], extensive property

Thermodynamics

Temperature	K	**K**	**kelvin**
Temperature gradient | Thermal gradient	K.m^{-1}		[ΔTemperature]/[Distance]

Heat | Internal energy | Enthalpy	$kg.m^2.s^{-2}$	J	Same as **energy**
Specific heat | internal energy | enthalpy	$m^2.s^{-2}$	$J.kg^{-1}$	[Heat]/[Mass]
Heat capacity	$kg.m^2.s^{-2}.K^{-1}$	$J.K^{-1}$	[ΔHeat]/[ΔTemperature]
Heat flux	$kg.m^2.s^{-3}$	J.s, W	[ΔHeat]/[ΔTime]. Same as **power**
Heat flux density | Irradiance	$kg.s^{-3}$	$W.m^{-2}$	[Heat flux]/[Area]
Entropy	$kg.m^2.s^{-2}.K^{-1}$	$J.K^{-1}$	[ΔHeat]/[Temperature]
Specific entropy	$m^2.s^{-2}.K^{-1}$	$J.K^{-1}.kg^{-1}$	[Entropy]/[Mass]
Free energy | Free enthalpy	$kg.m^2.s^{-2}$	J	**Helmholtz | Gibbs functions**, respectively
Specific free energy | free enthalpy	$m^2.s^{-2}$	$J.kg^{-1}$	[Energy]/[Mass]. Also specific **Helmholtz | Gibbs functions**
Molar thermodynamical quantities:			
Molar heat | internal energy | enthalpy	$kg.m^2.s^{-2}.mol^{-1}$	$J.mol^{-1}$	[Heat]/[Quantity]
Molar energy	$kg.m^2.s^{-2}.mol^{-1}$	$J.mol^{-1}$	[Energy]/[Quantity]
Molar entropy	$kg.m^2.s^{-2}.K^{-1}.mol^{-1}$	$J.K^{-1}.mol^{-1}$	[Entropy]/[Quantity]
Molar free energy | free enthalpy	$kg.m^2.s^{-2}.mol^{-1}$	$J.mol^{-1}$	[Energy]/[Quantity]. Molar versions of the above

Thermodynamic and thermal properties of matter

Thermal expansion coefficient	K^{-1}		([ΔLength]/[Length])/[Temperature]
Heat capacity, specific	$m^2.s^{-2}.K^{-1}$	$J.K^{-1}.kg^{-1}$	[Heat capacity]/[Mass]

Heat capacity, molar	kg.m^2.s^{-2}.K^{-1}.mol^{-1}	J.K^{-1}.mol^{-1}	[Heat capacity]/[Quantity]
Heat of fusion | evaporation, specific	m^2.s^{-2}	J.kg^{-1}	[Energy]/[Mass]
Heat of fusion | evaporation, molar	kg.m^2.s^{-2}.mol^{-1}	J.mol^{-1}	[Energy]/[Quantity]
Heat conductivity	kg.m.s^{-3}.K^{-1}	W.m^{-1}.K^{-1}	[Heat flux]/([Distance]*[ΔTemperature])
Thermal diffusivity	m^2.s^{-1}		([∂Temp]/[∂Time])/[∇^{2}Temp].
Prandtl number	1	Dimensionless	[Kinematic viscosity]/[Thermal diffusivity]
Joule-Thomson coefficient	kg^{-1}.m.s^2.K	K.Pa^{-1}	[ΔTemperature]/[ΔPressure]
Pi coefficient, molar	kg.m^{-1}.s^{-2}.mol^{-1}	J.m^{-3}	[ΔInternalEnergy]/[ΔVolume]
Chemical potential, molar	kg.m^2.s^{-2}.mol^{-1}	J.mol^{-1}	[ΔInternalEnergy]/[ΔQuantity]
Softening point	K		Temperature at which hardness drops below a level
Annealing point	K		Temperature at which viscosity drops below 10^{12} Pa.s
Strain point	K		Temperature at which viscosity drops below 10$^{13.5}$ Pa.s
Flash point	K		Temperature at which vapour can be kept burning
Fire point	K		Temperature at which ignited vapour keeps burning

Thermal properties of devices

Thermal resistance	$kg^{-1}.m^{-2}.s^3K$	K/W	$[\Delta T]/[Power]$.
Electromagnetism			
Charge, electric	s.A	**C**	**coulomb**. [Current]*[Time]
Charge density	$m^{-3}.s.A$	$C.m^{-3}$	[Charge]/[Volume]
Current, electric	A	**A**	**ampere**. [Charge]/[Time]
Current density | Current intensity	$m^{-2}.A$		[Current]/[Area]
Specific charge | Charge/mass ratio	$kg^{-1}.s.A$	$C.kg^{-1}$	[Charge]/[Mass]
Molar charge	$s.A.mol^{-1}$	$C.mol^{-1}$	[Charge]/[Quantity]
Quantum charge	1	Dimensionless	[Charge]/[Elementary charge quantum]
Surface density of charge	$m^{-2}.s.A$	$C.m^{-2}$	[Charge]/[Area]
Potential, electric	$kg.m^2.s^{-3}.A^{-1}$	$W.A^{-1}$, $J.C^{-1}$, $C.F^{-1}$, **V**	**volt**. [Power]/[Current], [Energy]/[Charge]
Electric dipole moment	m.s.A	C.m	[Charge]*[Distance]
Electric quadrupole moment	$m^2.s.A$	$C.m^2$	[Electric dipole]*[Distance], [Electric charge]*[Distance^2]
Electric field strength | Electric intensity	$kg.m.s^{-3}.A^{-1}$	$V.m^{-1}$	[ΔPotential]/[Distance]
Electric field gradient	$kg.s^{-3}.A^{-1}$	$V.m^{-2}$	[ΔEl.field strength]/[Distance]
Electric flux density | Electric induction	$m^{-2}.s.A$	$C.m^{-2}$	[Charge]/[Area]
Electric polarization | Electric displacement	$m^{-2}.s.A$	$C.m^{-2}$	[Charge]/[Area]. Same as **electric flux density**

Magnetic field strength | Magnetic intensity	$m^{-1}.A$		[Current]/[Distance]
Magnetic flux	$kg.m^2.s^{-2}.A^{-1}$	$V.s$, $W.s.A^{-1}$, **Wb**	**weber**. [ΔPotential]*[Time], [Power]/[dCurrent/dt]
Magnetic flux density | Magnetic induction	$kg.s^{-2}.A^{-1}$	$Wb.m^{-2}$, **T**	**tesla**. [Mag.flux]/[Area]
Magnetic vector potential	$kg.m.s^{-2}.A^{-1}$	$m^{-1}.s.V$, $m.T$	[Mag.flux density]*[Distance], [El.field strength]*[Time]
Magnetization	$m^{-1}.A$		[Magnetic moment]/[Volume]. Like **magnetic field strength**
Magnetic charge (bound)	$m^{-2}.A$		- ∇.[Magnetization] , -Divergence of **magnetization**
Poynting vector	$kg.s^{-3}$	$W.m^{-2}$	[El.field strength]/[Mag.field strength]. Same as **irradiance**
Magnetic field gradient	$kg.m^{-1}.s^{-2}.A^{-1}$	$T.m^{-1}$	[ΔMagnetic flux density]/[Distance]
Magnetic dipole moment	$m^2.A$	$J.T^{-1}$	[Current]*[Area]. Same as **magnetic moment**
Magnetic quadrupole moment	$m^3.A$	$m.J.T^{-1}$	[Magnetic dipole]*[Distance]
Gyromagnetic ratio	$kg^{-1}.s.A$	$Hz.T^{-1}$	[Mag.moment]/[Angular moment of motion]
Magnetogyric ratio	$kg.s^{-1}.A^{-1}$	$T.Hz^{-1}$	[Angular moment of motion]/[Mag.moment]
Relativistic four-current (J^α)	$m^{-2}.A$		Like **current density** and [Charge]*[c]
Relativistic four-potential (A^α)	$kg.m.s^{-2}.A^{-1}$	$m^{-1}.s.V$, $m.T$	Like **magnetic vector potential** and [El.potential]/[c]

Relativistic electromagnetic field tensor ($F^{\mu\nu}$)	kg.s^{-2}.A^{-1}	T	Like **magnetic flux density**
Relativistic displacement four-tensor ($D^{\mu\nu}$)	m^{-1}.A		Like **magnetic intensity**

Electromagnetic properties of matter

Resistivity	kg.m^3.s^{-3}.A^{-2}	Ω.m	[Resistance]*[Length])/[Area]
Conductivity	kg^{-1}.m^{-3}.s^3.A^2	S.m^{-1}	1/[Resistivity]
Permittivity, electric	kg^{-1}.m^{-3}.s^4.A^2	F.m^{-1}	[El.flux density]/[El.field strength]
Dielectric constant | Relative permittivity	1	Dimensionless	[Permittivity]/[Permittivity of vacuum]
Permeability, magnetic	kg.m.s^{-2}.A^{-2}	N.A^{-2}, H.m^{-1}	[Mag.flux density]/[Mag.field strength]
Reluctance, magnetic	kg^{-1}.m^{-1}.s^2.A^2	m.H^{-1}	1/[Permeability]
Relative permeability, magnetic	1	Dimensionless	[Permeability]/[Permeability of vacuum]
Susceptibility, magnetic	1	Dimensionless	[Relative permeability] - 1
Characteristic impedance	kg.m^2.s^{-3}.A^{-2}	V.A^{-1}, Ω, ohm	√([Mag.Permeability]/[El.Permittivity])
Electric | Dielectric strength | rigidity	kg.m.s^{-3}.A^{-1}	V.m^{-1}	[ΔPotential]/[Distance]
Verdet constant	kg^{-1}.m^{-1}.s^2.A^1	rad.m^{-1}.T^{-1}	([Angle]/[Length])/[Magnetic flux density]
Work function	kg.m^2.s^{-2}	J, eV	[Energy] needed to remove an electron
Thermoelectric power | Thermopower	kg.m^2.s^{-3}.A^{-1}.K$^-$	V.K^{-1}	[ΔPotential]/[ΔTemperature]

	[1]		
Seeback coefficient	kg.m^2.s^{-3}.A^{-1}.K^{-1}	V.K^{-1}	[ΔPotential]/[ΔTemperature]
Thomson coefficient	kg.m^2.s^{-3}.A^{-1}.K^{-1}	W.K^{-1}.A^{-1}	[Heat flux]/([ΔTemperature]*[Current])
Peltier coefficient	kg.m^2.s^{-3}.A^{-1}	W.A^{-1}, V	[Heat flux]/[Current]
Piezzoelectric coefficient	kg.m.s^{-3}.A^{-1}	V.m^{-1}	[El.field strength]/([ΔLength]/[Length])
Electrostriction coefficient	kg^{-2}.m^{-2}.s^6.A^2	m^2.V^{-2}	([ΔVolume]/[Volume])/[El.field strength]^2
g-factor of a particle	1	Dimensionless	[Mag.moment]/([Spin].[Bohr magneton])

Properties of electric/magnetic devices and circuit components

Bandwidth	s^{-1}	Hz	[ΔFrequency]
Voltage | Electromotive force (emf)	kg.m^2.s^{-3}.A^{-1}	V	[ΔPotential]
Current, electric	A	**A**	**ampere**. [Charge]/[Time]
Magnetomotive force (mmf)	A		[Current]*[Number of turns]
Impedance, of a circuit	kg.m^2.s^{-3}.A^{-2}	**Ω**	**ohm**
Admittance, of a circuit	kg^{-1}.m^{-2}.s^3.A^2	**S**	**siemens**. 1/[Circuit impedance]
Resistance	kg.m^2.s^{-3}.A^{-2}	V.A^{-1}, Ω(ohm)	[ΔPotential]/[Current]
Conductance	kg^{-1}.m^{-2}.s^3.A^2	A.V^{-1}, **S** (siemens)	1/[Resistance]
Capacitance	kg^{-1}.m^{-2}.s^4.A^2	C.V^{-1}, **F**	**farad**. [Charge]/[ΔPotential]

Reactance, capacitive	$kg.m^2.s^{-3}.A^{-2}$	Ω (ohm)	1/(i[Angular frequency].[Capacitance])
Susceptance, capacitive	$kg^{-1}.m^{-2}.s^3.A^2$	**S** (siemens)	1/[Reactance]
Inductance | Mutual inductance	$kg.m^2.s^{-2}.A^{-2}$	$V.s.A^{-1}$, $Wb.A^{-1}$, **H**	**henry.** [ΔPotential]/[dCurrent/dt] or [Magnetic flux]/[Current]
Impedance, inductive	$kg.m^2.s^{-3}.A^{-2}$	Ω (ohm)	i[Angular frequency].[Inductance]
Admittance, inductive	$kg^{-1}.m^{-2}.s^3.A^2$	**S** (siemens)	1/[Inductive impedance]
Number of turns	1		Applicable to coils, transformers, etc
Current noise, variance $n_J{}^2$	$s.A^2$	A^2/Hz	[Current]^2/[Bandwidth]
Voltage noise, variance $n_V{}^2$	$kg^2.m^4.s^{-5}.A^{-2}$	V^2/Hz	[Voltage]^2/[Bandwidth]

Chemistry, physical chemistry, atomic and molecular physics

Concentration | Molar density | Molarity	$m^{-3}.mol$		[Quantity]/[Volume]. Same as **Density of substance**
Molality	$kg^{-1}.mol$	mol/kg	[Quantity]/[Mass]
Katalytic activity | Molar production rate	$mol.s^{-1}$	katal	[Quantity]/[Time]
Molar mass	$kg.mol^{-1}$		[Mass]/[Quantity]
Molar charge	$s.A.mol^{-1}$	$C.mol^{-1}$	[Charge]/[Quantity]
Molecular | ionic quantum charge	1	Dimensionless	[Charge of a molecule or ion]/[Elementary charge quantum]
Ionic strength | Ionic force	$m^{-3}.mol$		Sum([Conc.]*[Ionic quantum charge]^2)

Ion mobility	$kg^{-1}.m^{-1}.s^2.A$	$m^2.s^{-1}.V^{-1}$	[Velocity]/[Electric field strength] .
Drift speed	$m.s^{-1}$		Steady-state speed of ions in electric field .
Fugacity	$kg.m^{-1}.s^{-2}$	Pa	Effective pressure in real gases
Osmotic pressure	$kg.m^{-1}.s^{-2}$	Pa	
Thermodynamic force	$kg.m.s^{-2}.mol^{-1}$	N/mol	[ΔChemical potential]/[Distance]

Chemico-physical properties of elements

Atomic number	1	Dimensionless	Number of protons in an atomic nucleus
Atomic weight | Relative atomic mass	au	atomic units	Average over a typical isotopic composition
Mass number of an isotope	1	Dimensionless	Number of protons+neutrons in the isotope nuclide
Electronegativity, Pauling χ	1	Dimensionless	Relative tendency of an atom to attract electrons; $\chi(H)=2.20$.
Electron affinity (always molar)	$kg.m^2.s^{-2}.mol^{-1}$	$J.mol^{-1}$	Energy released when binding an electron

Chemico-physical properties of matter

Ionization energy, molar	$kg.m^2.s^{-2}.mol^{-1}$	$J.mol^{-1}$	Energy to ionize a molecule/atom
Volume, molar	$m^3.mol^{-1}$		[Volume]/[Quantity]
Heat of fusion | evaporation, molar	$kg.m^2.s^{-2}.mol^{-1}$	$J.mol^{-1}$	[Energy]/[Quantity]
Chemical potential, molar	$kg.m^2.s^{-2}.mol^{-1}$	$J.mol^{-1}$	[ΔInternalEnergy]/[ΔQuantity]

Solubility, molar	$m^{-3}.mol$		[Quantity]/[Volume]
Reduction | Redox potential	$kg.m^2.s^{-3}.A^{-1}$	**V** (volt)	
Conductivity, molar	$kg^{-1}.s^3.A^2.mol^{-1}$	$S.m^2.mol^{-1}$	[El.conductivity]/[Concentration]
Relaxivity, molar	$s^{-1}.mol^{-1}$		[Relaxation rate]/[Concentration]
Ebullioscopic constant	$kg.mol^{-1}.K$	K/(mol/kg)	[ΔTemperature]/[Molality]
Cryoscopic constant	$kg.mol^{-1}.K$	K/(mol/kg)	[ΔTemperature]/[Molality]
Compression factor of a real gas	1	Dimensionless	pV/(nRT). For ideal gas equals 1; temperature dependent
van der Waals constant: a	$kg.m^5.s^{-2}.mol^{-2}$	$Pa.m^6$	a in $(p+a/V^2)(V-b)=RT$, where V is molar volume
van der Waals constant: b	$m^3.mol^{-1}$		b in $(p+a/V^2)(V-b)=RT$, where V is molar volume
Virial coefficient: second	$m^3.mol^{-1}$		B in $pV/(nRT)=1+B(n/V)+C(n/V)^2+D(n/V)^3+...$
Virial coefficient: third	$m^6.mol^{-2}$		C in $pV/(nRT)=1+B(n/V)+C(n/V)^2+D(n/V)^3+...$
Virial coefficient: fourth	$m^9.mol^{-3}$		C in $pV/(nRT)=1+B(n/V)+C(n/V)^2+D(n/V)^3+...$

Gravitation, Astronomy, Cosmology

Gravitational field intensity | Gravity	$m.s^{-2}$		[Force]/[Mass], Same as acceleration

Gravitational field potential	$m^2.s^{-2}$		[Energy]/[Mass]
Gravitational constant G	$kg^{-1}.m^3.s^{-2}$		[Force]*[Distance]^2/[Mass]^2. Appears in Newton's equation
Mean motion	s^{-1}		Of a body on a Kepler orbit; sqrt(G(M$_1$+M$_2$)/r^3)
Mean anomaly	1	Dimensionless	Of a body on a Kepler orbit; t.sqrt(G(M$_1$+M$_2$)/r^3)
Star magnitude (astronomy)	1	Dimensionless	m-m'= -10$^{0.4}$(S/S'). S,S' are luminous fluxes of two stars
Cosmological constant Λ	m^{-2}		Appears in Einstein's equation
Cosmological expansion rate	s^{-1}	km/s/Mpc	[Velocity]/[Distance]. Mpc stands for Megaparsec

Optics

Albedo, of a surface	1	Dimensionless	[Reflected elmag power]/[Incident elmag power]
Convergence	m^{-1}	**dioptry**	**dioptry**
Luminosity | Luminous intensity	cd	**cd**	**candle** or **lumen/sr**
Luminous flux | Luminous power	cd.sr	**lm**	**lumen**. [Luminosity]*[Solid angle]
Luminance	cd.m^{-2}		[Luminosity]/[Area]
Luminous energy	cd.sr.s	lm.s	[Luminous flux]*[Time]. Also known as **talbot**
Illuminance	cd.sr.m^{-2}	lm.m^{-2}, **lx**	**lux**. [Luminous flux]/[Area]
Luminous emittance	cd.sr.m^{-2}	lm.m^{-2}, **lx**	**lux**. Same as **illuminance**, but for

			sources
Luminous efficacy	$cd.sr.kg^{-1}.m^{-1}.s^3$	lm/W	[Luminous flux]/[Power]
Luminous efficiency | Luminous coefficient	1	Dimensionless	[Luminous efficacy]/[683 lm/W]
Irradiance	$kg.s^{-3}$	$W.m^{-2}$	[Power]/[Area]. For all kinds of energy deposition
Radiance	$kg.s^{-3}.sr^{-1}$	$W.m^{-2}.sr^{-1}$	([Power]/[Area])/[Solid angle]
Optical properties of matter			
Extinction coefficient	m^{-1}		
Refractive index	1	Dimensionless	Light speeds ratio (in medium)/(in vacuum)
Specific refractivity	$m^3.kg^{-1}$		$[(r^2-1)/(r^2+2)]$/[Specific density], where r is refractive index
Molar refractivity	$m^3.mol^{-1}$		$[(r^2-1)/(r^2+2)]$/[Concentration]
Dispersivity quotient	m^{-1}		[ΔRefractive index]/[ΔWavelength]
Dispersive power	1	Dimensionless	Ratio of differences of refractive indices
Constringence | Abbé number | V-number	1	Dimensionless	$V_D = (n_D-1)/(n_F-n_C)$
Radiation and radioactivity			
Radioactivity | Activity	s^{-1}	**Bq**	**bequerel**. [Counts]/[Time]
Irradiance	$kg.s^{-3}$	$W.m^{-2}$	[Power]/[Area]. For all kinds of energy deposition

Absorbed dose	$m^2.s^{-2}$	$J.kg^{-1}$, **Gy**	**gray**. [Energy]/[Mass]
Absorbed dose rate	$m^2.s^{-3}$	$Gy.s^{-1}$	[Absorbed dose]/[Time]
Absorbed dose equivalent	$m^2.s^{-2}$	$J.kg^{-1}$, **Sv**	**sievert**. [const].[Energy]/[Mass]
Exposure	$kg^{-1}.s.A$	$C.kg^{-1}$	[Charge]/[Mass]. For ionising radiations

Radiation properties of matter

Half life	s		Of a radioisotope
Radiation power	$m^2.s^{-3}$	**W/kg**	[Power]/[Mass]. Heat generated by a radioisotope
Radiation power, molar	$kg.m^2.s^{-3}.mol^{-1}$	**W/mol**	[Power]/[Quantity]. Heat generated by a radioisotope

Informatics

Information	bit^{-1}	**bit**	**bit**; the elementary information quantum
Baud rate | Information flux	$bit.s^{-1}$	**Baud**	**baud**. [Information]/[Time]

Economy and finance

Transactions count	1	Dimensionless	All kinds of counts
Interest	1	%	[ΔWealth]/[Wealth]. Usually expressed as percentage
Wealth | Asset	cur	**currency**	Currencies like $, EUR, Yuan, ... are different units
Debt | Liability	cur	**currency**	Usually intended as negative

			wealth
**Value	Price**	cur	currency	Prefixes: **K**..thousands, **M**..millions, **B**..billions
**Transaction value	Sale	Purchase**	cur	currency	Often used: mean and total values
Time period	s	**year,quarter,month**	Abbrevs: **mrq**.. most recent quarter, **ttm**.. trailing twelve months
**Fiscal year	Calendar year**	s	year	Abbrevs: **lfy**.. last fiscal year, **yoy**.. year over year
**Transactions rate	Activity**	s^{-1}	1/year	[Transactions]/[Time period]
**Transactions volume	Sales flow**	$cur.s^{-1}$		[Value]/[Time period]. For example \$/day or Eur/year
Velocity / circulation of money	s^{-1}	1/year	[Transactions]/[Time period]
Interest rate	s^{-1}	%/year	[Interest]/[Time period]
Return on asset / equity	s^{-1}	%/year	([ΔValue]/[Value])/[Time period]
**Cash flow	Flow** (generic)	$cur.s^{-1}$	currency/year	[Value]/[ΔTime]. Mathematically, time derivative
**Earnings	Income rate**	$cur.s^{-1}$	currency/year	[Value]/[Time period]
GDP Gross domestic product	$cur.s^{-1}$	currency/year	[Earnings]. Usually refered to nations/states/admin.regions
Debt/GDP ratio	S	year	[Debt]/[Earnings]. Independent of currency / population size
P/E Price/Earnings ratio	S	year	[Value]/[Earnings]. Used to assess an asset/company

Bond duration	S	year	In general, the duration of a fixed cash flow

References

1. Beaman Jr. Joseph J., Longoria Raul G.,
    Modeling of Physical Systems,
    Wiley 2016. ISBN 978-1119945048.

2. Zohuri Bahman,
    Dimensional Analysis and Self-Similarity Methods for Engineers and Scientists,
    Springer 2015. ISBN 978-3319134758.

3. Isakov Edmund,
    International System of Units (SI):
    How the world measures almost everything, and the people who made it possible,
    Industrial Press 2014. ISBN 978-0831102319..

4. Bridgman Percy W.,
    Dimensional Analysis,
    Reprint of the 1922 clasic. TheClassics.us 2013. ISBN 978-1230226214.

5. Crease Robert P.,
    World in the Balance: The Historic Quest for an Absolute System of Measurement,
    W.W.Norton & Company 2012. ISBN 978-0393343540..

6. Gibbings J.C.,
    Dimensional Analysis,
    Springer 2011. ISBN 978-1849963169.

7. Klein Herbert A.,
    The Science of Measurement: A Historical Survey,
    Dover Publications 2011. ISBN 978-0486258393..

8. Gupta S.V.,
    Units of Measurement: Past, Present and Future. International System of Units,
    Springer 2009. ISBN 978-3642007378..

9. Palmer Andrew C.,
    Dimensional Analysis and Intelligent Experimentation,
    World Scientific Publishing 2008. ISBN 978-9812708199.

10. Charalambos D. Aliprantis, Border Kim,
    Infinite Dimensional Analysis: A Hitchhiker's Guide,
    3rd Edition, Springer 2007. ISBN 978-3540326960.

11. Strothman J, Editor,
    ISA Handbook of Measurement Equations and Tables,
    2nd Edition, ISA (Instrumentation, Systems, and Automation) 2006.
    ISBN 978-1556179464..

12. Szirtes Thomas,
Applied Dimensional Analysis and Modeling,
2nd Edition, Butterworth-Heinemann 2006. ISBN 978-0123706201.

13. Jerrard H.G.,
Dictionary of Scientific Units Including Dimensionless Numbers and Scales,
Springer 1992. ISBN 978-0412467202.

14. Sena L.A.,
Units of physical quantities and their dimensions,
Mir Publishers 1973..

Table -4: Constants of Physics and Mathematics

(Source: From Wikipedia, the free encyclopedia)

Constant	Value	Dimension	Alias	Definition & Notes
Universal constants used in too many categories to constrain their scope				
Speed of light c	**2.997 924 580 e+8**	$m.s^{-1}$	m/s	**Assigned** (see SI units)
Permeability of vacuum μ_0	**12.566 370 614 359 ... e-7**	$kg.m.s^{-2}.A^{-2}$	H/m	N/A^2	$= 4\pi.10^{-7}$. **Assigned.**
Permittivity of vacuum ε_0	**8.854 187 817 620 ... e-12**	$kg^{-1}.m^{-3}.s^4.A^2$	F/m	$= 1 / (c^2\ \mu_0)$. **Assigned.**
Gravitation constant G	**6.673 84[80] e-11**	$kg^{-1}.m^3.s^{-2}$		force $= G\ M_1 M_2 / r_{12}^2$
Planck constant h	**6.626 069 57[29] e-34**	$kg.m^2.s^{-1}$	J.s	= (energy transfer quantum)/(channel frequency)
Angular Planck constant	1.054 571 726[47] e-34	$kg.m^2.s^{-1}$	J.s	$= h/2\pi$, the **angular momentum quantum**
Charge/Quantum ratio	2.417 989 348[53] e+14	$kg^{-1}.m^{-2}.s^2.A$	A/J	$= e / h$
Elementary charge e	**1.602 176 565[35] e-19**	s.A	C	
Quantum/Charge ratio	4.135 667 52[10] e-15	$kg.m^2.s^{-2}.A^{-1}$	J/A	$= h / e$
Fine structure constant α	7.297 352 5698[24] e-3	**Dimensionless**		$= \mu_0\ c\ e^2 / 2h$.

Inverse of fine structure constant	137.035 999 074[45]	**Dimensionless**		$= 1/\alpha = 2h / (\mu_0 c e^2)$. See ref.[1].
Boltzmann constant k	**1.380 6488[13] e-23**	$kg.m^2.s^{-2}.K^{-1}$	J/K	Sets thermodynamic temperature
Planck mass m_p	2.176 51[13] e-8	kg		$m_p^2 = (h/2\pi) c / G$
Planck time t_p	5.391 06[32] e-44	s		$= (h/2\pi) / (m_p c^2)$
Planck length l_p	1.616 199[97] e-35	m		$= ct_p$
Planck temperature	1.416 833[85] e+32	K		$= m_p c^2 / k$

Electromagnetic constants other than those already listed

Impedance of vacuum Z_0	**376.730 313 461 ...**	$kg.m^2.s^{-3}.A^{-2}$	Ω	Derived from **assigned's**: $Z_0^2 = \mu_0/\varepsilon_0$.
Magnetic flux quantum Φ_0	2.067 833 758[46] e-15	$kg.m^2.s^{-2}.A^{-1}$	Wb	$= h / 2e$
Josephson constant K_J	4.835 978 70[11] e14	$kg^{-1}.m^{-2}.s^2.A$	Hz/V	$= 2e / h$. Conventional: **483597.9 GHz/V**
von Klitzing constant R_K	2.581 280 744 34[84] e+4	$kg.m^2.s^{-3}.A^{-2}$	Ω	$= h / e^2$. Conventional: **25812.807 Ω**
Conductance quantum G_0	7.748 091 7346[25] e-5	$kg^{-1}.m^{-2}.s^3.A^2$	S	$= 2e^2 / h = 2 / R_K$
Inverse of conductance quantum	1.290 640 372 17[42] e+4	$kg.m^2.s^{-3}.A^{-2}$	Ω	$= R_K / 2$

Electromagnetic radiation constants.

Stefan-Boltzmann const. σ	5.670 373[21] e-8	$kg.s^{-3}.K^{-4}$	$W/m^2.K^4$	$= 2\,\pi^5\,k^4\,/\,15\,h^3\,c^2$
1st radiation constant c_1	3.741 771 53[17] e-16	$kg.m^4.s^{-3}$	$W.m^2$	$= 2\,\pi\,h\,c^2$
2nd radiation constant c_2	1.438 7770[13] e-2	$m.K$		$= h\,c\,/\,k$
Wien λ displacement constant $\lambda_{max}T$	2.897 7721[26] e-3	$m.K$		$= c_2\,/\,4.9651423...$
Wien f displacement constant f/T	5.878 9254[53] e+10	$s^{-1}.K^{-1}$	Hz/K	
Max. luminous efficacy: absolute	683	$cd.sr.kg^{-1}.m^{-1}.s^3$	lm/W	100% efficient, ideal 555 nm light source.
Max. luminous efficacy: black-body	95	$cd.sr.kg^{-1}.m^{-1}.s^3$	lm/W	Achieved at 7000 °K
Solar luminous efficacy	93	$cd.sr.kg^{-1}.m^{-1}.s^3$	lm/W	see Wikipedia
Solar illuminance	1.280[10] e5	$cd.sr.m^{-2}$	lx	in the brightest sunlight, on Earth
Electron and atomic physics constants				
Rydberg constant $R\infty$	1.097 373 156 8539[55] e+7	m^{-1}	m^{-1}	$= c\,\alpha^2\,m_e\,/\,2h$
Hartree energy	4.359 744 34[19] e-18	$kg.m^2.s^{-2}$	J	$= \alpha^2\,m_e\,c^2 = 2h\,c\,R\infty$

E_H				
Bohr radius	5.291 772 1092[17] e-11	m	m	$= \alpha / (4\pi R_\infty)$
Bohr magneton μ_B	9.274 009 68[20] e-24	$m^2.A$	J/T	$= (1/2)(h/2\pi)(e/m_e)$
Bohr magneton in Hz/T	1.399624555[31] e+10	$kg^{-1}.s.A$	Hz/T	$= \mu_B/h$ = [Larmor frequency]/[g-factor]; ~ 14 GHz/T
Quantum of circulation	3.636 947 5520[24] e-4	$m^2.s^{-1}$	m^2/s	$= h / 2m_e$
Richardson constant	1.20173 e+6	$A.m^{-2}.K^{-2}$		$= 4\pi e m_e k^2 / h^3$; arises in <u>thermionic emission</u>
*Electron (stable lepton, charge -1, spin 1/2, fermion, its antiparticle **positron** has positive charge)*				
Electron rest mass m_e	**9.109 382 91[40] e-31**	kg		$= 5.485 799 0946[22]$ e-4 u
Electron rest energy ($m_e c^2$)	8.187 105 06[36] e-14	$kg.m^2.s^{-2}$	J	$= 0.510 998 928[11]$ MeV
Electron charge/mass ratio	- 1.758 820 088[39] e11	$kg^{-1}.s.A$	C/kg	$= e / m_e$
Compton wavelength of electron $\lambda_{C,e}$	2.426 310 2389[16] e-12	m		$= h / c m_e$
Classical electron radius r_e	2.817 940 3267[27] e-15	m		$= e^2 / (4\pi\varepsilon_0 m_e c^2)$
Thomson cross section σ_e	0.665 245 8734[13] e-28	m^2		$= (8\pi/3) r_e^2$

Electron magnetic moment μ_e	- 9.284 764 30[21] e-24	m^2.A	J/T	
Electron g-factor g_e	- 2.002 319 304 361 53[53]	**Dimensionless**		= (μ_e / μ_B) / S_e
Electron magnetic moment anomaly	1.159 652 180 76[27] e-3	Dimensionless		= (abs(g_e) - 2) / 2
Electron gyromagnetic ratio $\gamma_e/2\pi$	28.024 952 66[62] e+9	kg^{-1}.s.A	Hz/T	= μ_e / (hS_e); ~ 28 GHz/T
Electron/Proton mass ratio	5.446 170 2178[22] e-4	**Dimensionless**		
Electron/Proton magnetic moments ratio	- 658.210 6848[54]	**Dimensionless**		
Electron/Proton magnetic moments ratio	- 658.227 597 1[72]	Dimensionless		**Shielded** in water; standard conditions

Physico-chemical constants

Atomic mass constant u	**1.660 538 921[73] e-27**	kg		Mass of ^{12}C nuclide / 12
Molar mass of ^{12}C	**12 e-3**	kg		**Assigned**
Molar mass constant	**1.0 e-3**	kg.mol^{-1}	kg/mol	**Assigned**

Boltzmann constant k	**1.380 6488[13] e-23**	$kg.m^2.s^{-2}.K^{-1}$	J/K	Sets thermodynamic temperature
Boltzmann constant in eV/K	8.617 3324[78] e-5	$kg.m^2.s^{-3}.A^{-1}.K^{-1}$	V/K	= k/e. Electrochemical potential ~ (k/e)T ln(c1/c2)
Avogadro's number N_A	**6.022 141 29[27] e+23**	mol^{-1}	count/mol	~ 602 **Z** *(Zetta)* particles in a mole of substance
Molar Planck constant	3.990 312 7176[28] e-10	$kg.m^2.s^{-1}.mol^{-1}$	J.s/mol	= h N_A
Molar Planck constant by c	0.119 626 565 779[84]	$kg.m^3.s^{-2}.mol^{-1}$	J.m/mol	= h c N_A
Electron molar mass	5.485 799 0946[22] e-7	$kg.mol^{-1}$	kg/mol	= m_e N_A
Electron molar charge	- 9.648 533 65[21] e+4	$s.A.mol^{-1}$	C/mol	= e N_A.
Faraday constant F	+9.648 533 65[21] e+4	$s.A.mol^{-1}$	C/mol	= |electron molar charge|.
Molar gas constant R	8.314 4621[75]	$kg.m^2.s^{-2}.K^{-1}.mol^{-1}$	J/K.mol	= k N_A
Molar volume of ideal gas V_m	22.413 968[20] e-3	$m^3.mol^{-1}$	m^3/mol	= (RT/p) at T=273.15 K, p=101325 Pa
Loschmidt constant n_0	2.686 7805[24] e+25	m^{-3}	count/m^3	= N_A / V_m at T=273.15 K, p=101325 Pa
Sackur-Tetrode constant S_0/R	- 1.164 8708[23]	**Dimensionless**		(5/2)+ln[(2πm_u kT/h^2)(kT/p)] at T=1K, p=101325 Pa.
Basic nuclear physics data (those listed in CODATA)				

Fermi coupling $G_F/(hc/2\pi)^3$	**3.670 336[31] e+48**	kg^{-2}		= (1.026 8365[88] e-5) / m_p^2
Fermi coupling in eV^{-2}	1.166 364[5] e+4	eV^{-2}		
Weak mixing angle $\sin^2\theta_W$	**0.2223[21]**	**Dimensionless**		= 1- $(m_W/m_Z)^2$
Nuclear magneton μ_N	5.050 783 53[11] e-27	m^2.A	J/T	= (1/2)(h/2π)(e/m_p)
Nuclear magneton in Hz/T	7.622 593 57[17] e+6	kg^{-1}.s.A	Hz/T	= μ_N/h = [Larmor frequency]/[g-factor]; ~ 7.6 MHz/T
Proton (stable baryon, nucleon, hadron, charge +1, spin 1/2, fermion, parity +, isospin 1/2, its anti-particle antiproton has opposite charge)				
Proton rest mass m_p	**1.672 621 777[74] e-27**	kg		1.007 276 466 812[90] u
Proton rest energy (mc^2)	1.503 277 484[66] e-10	kg.m^2.s^{-2}	J	938.272 046[21] MeV; quarks composition: **uud**
Proton / electron mass ratio	1836.15267245[75]	**Dimensionless**		inverse: 5.4461702178[22]e-4
Compton wavelength of proton $\lambda_{C,p}$	1.321 409 856 23[94] e-15	m		$\lambda_{C,p}$ = h / c m_p
Proton rms charge radius	**0.8775[51] e-15**	m		
Proton magnetic moment	**1.410 606 743[33] e-26**	m^2.A	J/T	μ_p

Proton g-factor	5.585 694 713[46]	Dimensionless		$= \mu_p / (S_p \mu_N)$
Proton gyromagnetic ratio	42.577 4806[10] e+6	kg^{-1}.s.A	Hz/T	$\gamma_p = \mu_p / h\, S_p.$
Proton gyromagnetic ratio shielded	42.576 388 1[12] e+6	kg^{-1}.s.A	Hz/T	In H_2O, standard conditions
Proton magnetic shielding	**25.694[14] e-6**	Dimensionless		Relative value for pure water at 25 °C
Electric dipole moment	< 8.7 e-45	m.s.A	C.m	< 5.4 e-24 e.cm; existence not confirmed
Electric polarizibility	**1.20[6] e-48**	m^3		
Magnetic polarizibility	**1.9[5] e-49**	m^3		
Neutron (baryon, nucleon, hadron, charge 0, spin 1/2, fermion, parity +, isospin 1/2, its anti-particle is ***antineutron***)				
Neutron rest mass m_n	**1.674 927 351[74] e-27**	kg		1.008 664 916 00[43] u
Neutron rest energy (mc^2)	1.505 349 631[66] e-10	kg.m^2.s^{-2}	J	939.565 379[21] MeV; quarks composition **udd**
Compton wavelength of neutron $\lambda_{C,n}$	1.319 590 9068[11] e-15	m		$\lambda_{C,n} = h / c\, m_n$
Neutron half-life time	**881.5[15]**	s		Beta-decay into proton + e$^-$ + ν_e

Neutron magnetic moment	**- 0.966 236 47[23] e-26**	m^2.A	J/T	μ_n
Neutron g-factor	- 3.826 085 45[90]	Dimensionless		= μ_n / (S$_n$ μ_N)
Neutron gyromagnetic ratio	29.164 6943[69] e+6	kg^{-1}.s.A	Hz/T	γ_n = μ_n / h S$_n$
Electric dipole moment	< 4.6 e-47	m.s.A	C.m	< 2.9 e-26 e.cm; existence not confirmed
Electric polarizibility	**1.16[15] e-48**	m^3		
Magnetic polarizibility	**3.7[20] e-49**	m^3		

Deuteron (stable nuclide, protons 1, neutrons 1, charge +1, spin 1, boson)

Deuteron rest mass	**3.343 583 48[15] e-27**	kg		2.013 553 212 712[77] u
Deuteron rest energy (mc^2)	3.005 062 97[13] e-10	kg.m^2.s^{-2}	J	1875.612 859[41] MeV
Deuteron rms charge radius	2.1424[21] e-15	m		
Deuteron magnetic moment	**0.433 073 489[10] e-26**	m^2.A	J/T	
Deuteron g-factor	0.857 438 2308[72]	Dimensionless		
Deuteron	6.535 903 381 41 e+6	kg^{-1}.s.A	Hz/T	

gyromagnetic ratio			
Deuteron quadrupole moment	4.581 e-50	$m^2.s.A$	$C.m^2$	0.2859 $e(fm)^2$

Triton (stable nuclide, protons 1, neutrons 2, charge +1, spin 1/2, fermion)			
Triton rest mass	**5.007 356 30[22] e-27**	kg		3.015 500 7134[25] u
Triton rest energy (mc^2)	4.500 387 41[20] e-10	$kg.m^2.s^{-2}$	J	2808.921 005[62] MeV
Triton half-life time	**3.888[70] e+8**	s		= 12.32 years; beta-decay into ^{3}He + e^- + ν_e
Triton magnetic moment	**1.504 609 447[38] e-26**	$m^2.A$	J/T	
Triton g-factor	5.957 924 896[76]	Dimensionless		
Triton gyromagnetic ratio	45.413 674 6[13] e+6	$kg^{-1}.s.A$	Hz/T	

Helion (stable nuclide, protons 2, neutrons 1, charge +2, spin 1/2, fermion, nuclide)			
Helion rest mass	**5.006 412 34[22] e-27**	kg		3.014 932 2468[25] u
Helion rest energy (mc^2)	4.499 539 02[20] e-10	$kg.m^2.s^{-2}$	J	2808.391 482[62] MeV
Helion magnetic moment	**- 1.074 617 486[27] e-26**	$m^2.A$	J/T	Shielded

Helion g-factor	- 4.255 250 613[50]	Dimensionless		
Helion gyromagnetic ratio	32.434 101 98[90] e+6	kg^{-1}.s.A	Hz/T	Shielded

Alpha particle *(stable nuclide, protons 2, neutrons 2, charge +2, spin 0, magnetic moment 0, boson)*				
α-particle rest mass	**6.644 656 75[29] e-27**	kg		4.001 506 179 125[62] u
α-particle rest energy (mc^2)	5.971 919 67[26] e-10	kg.m^2.s^{-2}	J	3727.379 240[82] MeV

Particle physics data (source: Particle Data Group)

Neutrinos ν (stable leptons, charge 0, exist in e,μ,τ flavors, each has matter / anti-matter version with opposite chirality, spin 1/2, fermions)				
Electron neutrino ν_e **rest energy** (mc^2)	max 3.5 e-13	kg.m^2.s^{-2}	J	**0 to 2.2** eV
Muon neutrino ν_μ **rest energy** (mc^2)	max 0.27 e-13	kg.m^2.s^{-2}	J	**0 to 0.17** MeV
Tau neutrino ν_τ **rest energy** (mc^2)	max 24.8 e-13	kg.m^2.s^{-2}	J	**0 to 15.5** MeV

Muon μ$^\pm$ (lepton, charge ±1, matter μ$^-$, antimatter μ$^+$, spin 1/2, fermion)				
Muon rest energy (mc^2)	1.692 833 667[86] e-11	kg.m^2.s^{-2}	J	**105.658 3715[35]** MeV

Muon rest mass	1.883 531 475[96] e-28	kg		0.113 428 9267[29] u
Muon magnetic moment	**- 4.490 448 07[15] e-26**	m^2.A	J/T	
Muon g-factor g_μ	- 2.002 331 8418[13]	Dimensionless		$(\mu / \mu_B) * (m / m_e) / spin$
Muon magnetic moment anomaly	1.165 920 91[63] e-3	Dimensionless		$(abs(g_\mu) - 2) / 2$
Muon gyromagnetic ratio	135.538 817[12] e+6	kg^{-1}.s.A	Hz/T	$= \mu_n / h\ S_n$
Muon half-life time	**1.52 e-6**	s		

Tau $\tau^\pm$ (lepton, charge ±1, matter τ, antimatter τ^+, spin 1/2, fermion)

Tau rest energy (mc^2)	2.846 78[26] e-10	$kg.m^2.s^{-2}$	J	**1776.82[16]** MeV
Tau rest mass	3.167 47[29] e-27	kg		1.907 49[17] u
Tau half-life time	**2.9 e-13**	s		

Quarks with charge +2/3 (baryon number 1/3, exist in u,c,t flavors, each has matter / anti-matter versions with some property flipped, spin 1/2, fermions)

u (up) quark rest energy (mc^2)	3.8 e-13	$kg.m^2.s^{-2}$	J	**2.4** MeV, **stable**

c (charm) quark rest energy (mc^2)	2.03 e-10	kg.m^2.s^{-2}	J	**1.27** GeV, unstable
t (top) quark rest energy (mc^2)	2.743 e-8	kg.m^2.s^{-2}	J	**171.2** GeV, terribly unstable
Quarks with charge -1/3 (baryon number 1/3, exist in d,s,b flavors, each has matter / anti-matter versions with some property flipped, spin 1/2, fermions)				
d (down) quark rest energy (mc^2)	7.7 e-13	kg.m^2.s^{-2}	J	**4.8** MeV, **stable**
s (strange) quark rest energy (mc^2)	1.67 e-11	kg.m^2.s^{-2}	J	**104** MeV, unstable
b (bottom) quark rest energy (mc^2)	6.7 e-10	kg.m^2.s^{-2}	J	**4.2** GeV, unstable
Pions π$^\pm$ (mesons, hadrons, charge ±1, anti-particles of each other, spin 0, boson, parity -, isospin 1)				
Pions π$^\pm$ rest energy (mc^2)	2.236 1607[56] e-11	kg.m^2.s^{-2}	J	**139.570 18[35]** MeV
Pions π$^\pm$ rest mass	2.488 0643[62] e-28	kg		0.149 834 75[37] u
Pions π$^\pm$ half-life time	**2.6 e-8**	s		quarks composition: π$^+$: **ud'**, π$^-$: **du'**
Pion π^0 (meson, hadron, charge 0, its own antiparticle, spin 0, boson, parity -,C-parity +, isospin 1)				
Pion π^0 rest energy (mc^2)	2.162 5634[96] e-11	kg.m^2.s^{-2}	J	**134.976 60[60]** MeV

Pion π^0 rest mass	2.406 176[11] e-28	kg		0.144 903 34[64] u
Pion π^0 half-life time	**8.4 e-17**	s		quarks composition: **(uu'-dd')/&radiv;2**
Kaons K$^\pm$ *('strange' mesons, hadrons, charge ±1, anti-particles of each other, spin 0, boson, parity -, isospin 1/2)*				
Kaons K$^\pm$ rest energy (mc^2)	7.909 58[26] e-11	kg.m^2.s^{-2}	J	**493.677[16]** MeV
Kaons K$^\pm$ rest mass	8.800 591[29] e-28	kg		0.529 984[17] u
Kaons K$^\pm$ half-life time	**1.2380[21] e-8**	s		quarks composition: K$^+$: **us'**, K$^-$: **su'**
Kaon K^0 *('strange' meson, hadron, charge 0, self-antiparticle, spin 0, boson, isospin 1/2, parity -)*				
Kaon K^0 rest energy (mc^2)	7.972 65[38] e-11	kg.m^2.s^{-2}	J	**497.614[24]** MeV; quarks: see below
Kaon K^0 rest mass	8.870 77[42] e-28	kg		0.534 211[26] u
Kaon K^0_L half-life time (long)	**5.116[20] e-8**	s		quarks composition: **(ds'+sd')/√2**
Kaon K^0_S half-life time (short)	**8.953[5] e-11**	s		quarks composition: **(ds'-sd')/√2**
Eta mesons *η and η' (hadrons, charge 0, antiparticles of each other, spin integer, bosons,*				
η rest energy (mc^2)	8.777 57[38] e-11	kg.m^2.s^{-2}	J	**547.853[24]** MeV
η rest mass	9.766 36[42] e-28	kg		0.588 144[25] u

η half-life time	**5.0[3] e-19**	s		quarks composition: **(uu'+dd'-2ss')/√6**
η' rest energy (mc²)	1.53434[38] e-10	kg.m².s⁻²	J	**957.66[24] MeV**
η' rest mass	1.70718[43] e-27	kg		1.02809[26] u
η' half-life time	**3.2[2] e-21**	s		quarks composition: **(uu'+dd'+ss')/√3**
<td colspan="5">Lambda hyperons (baryons, charge 0 or +1, spin 1/2, fermions, parity +; predicted only: top Λ_t⁺, quarks udt, but t-quark decays before it hadronizes)</td>				
Λ⁰ rest energy (mc²)	1.7875211[96] e-10	kg.m².s⁻²	J	**1.1156830[60] GeV; charge 0**
Λ⁰ rest mass	1.988885[11] e-27	kg		1.1977349[64] u
Λ⁰ half-life time	**2.631[20] e-10**	s		quarks composition: **uds**
Bottom Λ⁰_b rest energy (mc²)	9.0046[26] e-10	kg.m².s⁻²	J	**5.6202[16] GeV; charge 0**
Bottom Λ⁰_b rest mass	1.00189[29] e-26	kg		6.0335[17] u
Bottom Λ⁰_b half-life time	**1.409[55] e-12**	s		quarks composition: **udb**
Charmed Λ⁺_c rest energy (mc²)	3.66331[22] e-10	kg.m².s⁻²	J	**2.28646[14] GeV; charge +1**
Charmed Λ⁺_c rest mass	4.07599[25] e-27	kg		2.45462[15] u

Charmed Λ^+_c half-life time	**2.000[60] e-13**	s		quarks composition: **udc**
Sigma hyperons with spin 1/2 (barions, charge -1, 0, +1 or +2, fermions, parity +; predicted only: **udb**, **uut**, **udt**, **ddt**)				
Σ^+ **rest energy** (mc^2)	1.90558[11] e-10	$kg.m^2.s^{-2}$	J	**1.189370[70]** GeV; charge +1
Σ^+ rest mass	2.12024[12] e-27	kg		1.276841[75] u
Σ^+ half-life time	**8.018[26] e-11**	s		quarks composition: **uus**
Σ^0 **rest energy** (mc^2)	1.910823[38] e-10	$kg.m^2.s^{-2}$	J	**1.192642[24]** GeV; charge 0
Σ^0 rest mass	2.126077[43] e-27	kg		1.280353[26] u
Σ^0 half-life time	**7.40[70] e-20**	s		quarks composition: **uds**
Σ^- **rest energy** (mc^2)	1.918525[48] e-10	$kg.m^2.s^{-2}$	J	**1.197449[30]** GeV; charge -1
Σ^- rest mass	2.13465[53] e-27	kg		1.285514[32] u
Σ^- half-life time	**1.479[11] e-10**	s		quarks composition: **dds**
Charmed Σ_c^{++} **rest energy** (mc^2)	3.93177[29] e-10	$kg.m^2.s^{-2}$	J	**2.45402[18]** GeV; charge +2
Charmed Σ_c^{++} rest mass	4.37469[32] e-27	kg		2.63450[19] u
Charmed Σ_c^{++} half-life	**3.00[40] e-22**	s		quarks composition: **uuc**

time				
Charmed Σ_c^+ rest energy (mc^2)	3.92998[64] e-10	kg.m^2.s^{-2}	J	**2.45290[40]** GeV; charge +1
Charmed Σ_c^+ rest mass	4.37269[71] e-27	kg		2.63330[43] u
Charmed Σ_c^+ half-life time	**>1.4 e-22**	s		quarks composition: **udc**
Charmed Σ_c^0 rest energy (mc^2)	3.93136[29] e-10	kg.m^2.s^{-2}	J	**2.45376[18]** GeV; charge 0
Charmed Σ_c^0 rest mass	4.37422[32] e-27	kg		2.63422[19] u
Charmed Σ_c^0 half-life time	**3.0 e-22**	s		quarks composition: **ddc**
Bottom Σ_b^+ rest energy (mc^2)	9.3051[62] e-10	kg.m^2.s^{-2}	J	**5.8078[39]** GeV; charge +1
Bottom Σ_b^+ rest mass	1.03533[69] e-26	kg		6.2349[42] u
Bottom Σ_b^+ half-life time	?	s		quarks composition: **uub**
Bottom Σ_b^- rest energy (mc^2)	9.3170[43] e-10	kg.m^2.s^{-2}	J	**5.8152[27]** GeV; charge -1
Bottom Σ_b^- rest mass	1.03665[48] e-26	kg		6.2429[30] u
Bottom Σ_b^-	?	s		quarks composition: **ddb**

half-life time				
Sigma hyperons with spin 3/2 (barions, charge -1, 0, +1 or +2, fermions, parity +; predicted only: **uub**, **udb**, **ddb**, **uut**, **udt**, **ddt**)				
Σ^{*+} **rest energy** (mc^2)	2.21549[64] e-10	kg.m^2.s^{-2}	J	**1.38280[40]** GeV; charge +1
Σ^{*+} rest mass	2.46506[71] e-27	kg		1.48450[43] u
Σ^{*+} half-life time	**1.840[40] e-23**	s		quarks composition: **uus**
Σ^{*0} **rest energy** (mc^2)	2.21693[16] e-10	kg.m^2.s^{-2}	J	**1.38370[10]** GeV; charge 0
Σ^{*0} rest mass	2.46667[18] e-27	kg		1.48546[11] u
Σ^{*0} half-life time	**1.80[30] e-23**	s		quarks composition: **uds**
Σ^{*-} **rest energy** (mc^2)	2.22254[80] e-10	kg.m^2.s^{-2}	J	**1.38720[50]** GeV; charge -1
Σ^{*-} rest mass	2.47291[89] e-27	kg		1.48922[54] u
Σ^{*-} half-life time	**1.670[90] e-23**	s		quarks composition: **dds**
Charmed Σ^{*++}_c **rest energy** (mc^2)	4.03492[96] e-10	kg.m^2.s^{-2}	J	**2.51840[60]** GeV; charge +2
Charmed Σ^{*++}_c rest mass	4.4894[11] e-27	kg		2.70361[64] u

Charmed Σ^{*++}_c half-life time	**4.40[60] e-23**	s		quarks composition: **uuc**
Charmed Σ^{*+}_c rest energy (mc^2)	4.0335[37] e-10	kg.m^2.s^{-2}	J	**2.5175[23]** GeV; charge +1
Charmed Σ^{*+}_c rest mass	4.4879[41] e-27	kg		2.7026[25] u
Charmed Σ^{*+}_c half-life time	**> 3.9 e-23**	s		quarks composition: **udc**
Charmed Σ^{*0}_c rest energy (mc^2)	4.03428[80] e-10	kg.m^2.s^{-2}	J	**2.518** GeV; charge 0
Charmed Σ^{*0}_c rest mass	4.48874[89] e-27	kg		2.70318[54] u
Charmed Σ^{*0}_c half-life time	**4.10[50] e-23**	s		quarks composition: **ddc**
Xi hyperons (barions, charge -1, 0, +1, spin 1/2, fermions, parity +; predicted only: **ucc, ubb, dbb, ucb, dcb**)				
Ξ^0 **rest energy** (mc^2)	2.106638[32] e-10	kg.m^2.s^{-2}	J	**1.31486[20]** GeV; charge 0
Ξ^0 rest mass	2.34395[35] e-27	kg		1.41156[21] u
Ξ^0 half-life time	**2.900[90] e-10**	s		quarks composition: **uss**
Ξ^- **rest energy**	2.11697[21] e-10	kg.m^2.s^{-2}	J	**1.32131[13]** GeV; charge -1

(mc^2)				
Ξ^- rest mass	2.35544[23] e-27	kg		1.41848[14] u
Ξ^- half-life time	**1.639[15] e-10**	s		quarks composition: **dss**
Charmed Ξ_c^+ rest energy (mc^2)	3.95401[64] e-10	kg.m^2.s^{-2}	J	**2.46790[40]** GeV; charge +1
Charmed Ξ_c^+ rest mass	4.39943[71] e-27	kg		2.64940[43] u
Charmed Ξ_c^+ half-life time	**4.42[26] e-13**	s		quarks composition: **usc**
Charmed Ξ_c^0 rest energy (mc^2)	3.95898[64] e-10	kg.m^2.s^{-2}	J	**2.47100[40]** GeV; charge 0
Charmed Ξ_c^0 rest mass	4.40496[71] e-27	kg		2.65273[43] u
Charmed Ξ_c^0 half-life time	**1.12[13] e-13**	s		quarks composition: **dsc**
Double charmed Ξ_{cc}^+ rest energy (mc^2)	5.6379[14] e-10	kg.m^2.s^{-2}	J	**3.51890[90]** GeV; charge +1
Double charmed Ξ_{cc}^+ rest mass	6.2730[16] e-27	kg		3.77769[97] u
Double charmed Ξ_{cc}^+ half-life	**< 3.3 e-14**	s		quarks composition: **dcc**

time				
Bottom Ξ_b^0 rest energy (mc^2)	9.2798[48] e-10	kg.m^2.s^{-2}	J	**5.7920[30]** GeV; charge 0
Bottom Ξ_b^0 rest mass	1.0325[53] e-26	kg		6.2180[32] u
Bottom Ξ_b^0 half-life time	**1.42[28] e-12**	s		quarks composition: **usb**
Bottom Ξ_b^- rest energy (mc^2)	9.2815[48] e-10	kg.m^2.s^{-2}	J	**5.7929[30]** GeV; charge -1
Bottom Ξ_b^- rest mass	1.0335[53] e-26	kg		6.2191[32] u
Bottom Ξ_b^- half-life time	**1.42[28] e-12**	s		quarks composition: **dsb**
Ξ resonances: {**uss**, S=3/2, 1.53180[32] GeV}, {**dss**, S=3/2, 1.53500[60] GeV}, {**usc**, S=1/2, 2.57570[31] GeV}, {**dsc**, S=1/2, 2.57800[29] GeV, 1.1e-13 s},				

Ω^- rest energy (mc^2)	2.67956[46] e-10	kg.m^2.s^{-2}	J	**1.67245[29]** GeV; charge -1, spin 3/2
Ω^- rest mass	2.98141[52] e-27	kg		1.79544[31] u
Ω^- half-life time	**8.21[11] e-11**	s		quarks composition: **sss**
Charmed Ω_c^0 rest energy (mc^2)	4.3219[41] e-10	kg.m^2.s^{-2}	J	**2.6975[26]** GeV; charge 0, spin 1/2

Charmed Ω^0_c rest mass	4.8087[28] e-27	kg		2.8959[28] u
Charmed Ω^0_c half-life time	**6.9[12] e-14**	s		quarks composition: **ssc**
Bottom Ω^-_b rest energy (mc^2)	9.700[11] e-10	kg.m^2.s^{-2}	J	**6.0544[68]** GeV; charge -1, spin 1/2
Bottom Ω^-_b rest mass	1.0793[12] e-26	kg		6.49967[73] u
Bottom Ω^-_b half-life time	**1.13[53] e-12**	s		quarks composition: **ssb**
W$^\pm$ gauge boson (charge ±1, matter W$^-$, antimatter W$^+$, spin 1)				
W boson rest energy (mc^2)	1.28791[24] e-8	kg.m^2.s^{-2}	J	**80.385[15]** GeV
W boson rest mass	1.432993[25] e-25	kg		86.296[16] u
Z gauge boson (charge 0, spin 1)				
Z boson rest energy (mc^2)	1.460986[33] e-8	kg.m^2.s^{-2}	J	**91.1876[21]** GeV
Z boson rest mass	1.625566[37] e-25	kg		97.8939[23] u
Higgs boson H^0 (charge 0, spin 0, **predicted only**, **not found**)				
H^0 rest energy (mc^2)	2.0042[34] e-8	kg.m^2.s^{-2}	J	**125.09[21]** GeV; ATLAS/CMS 26 Mar 2015
H^0 rest mass	2.2299[37] e-25	kg		134.29[23] u

H^0 half-life time	1.56 e-22	s		$h/(2\pi\Gamma)$, predicted $\Gamma = 4.21$ MeV
Cosmic microwave background (CMB)				
Mean apparent CMB **temperature**	2.72548[57]	K	Kelvin	From CMB black-body radiation spectrum
rms variations of CMB temperature	1.8 e-7	K		18 µK; deviations from perfect isotropy
Peak frequency density v_{max}	1.6023 e+11	Hz		160.23 GHz, corresponding to λ = 1.871 mm
Peak wavelength density λ_{max}	1.063 e-3	m		1.063 mm, corresponding to 318.7 GHz
Metrics of the known Universe (for the prefixes **M** (Mega), **G** (Giga), **Z** (Zetta), and **Y** (Yocto), <u>click here</u>)				
Diameter visible by Hubble telescope	8.80[10] e+26	m		~ 93 **G** light-years
Volume of the visible sphere	3.60[10] e+80	m^3		~ 420 **MY** light-years^3 *(Mega-Yocta)*
Mass contained therein	3.56[10] e+54	kg		~ 3.56 **MYY** kg; mostly dark energy & matter
Mean density	9.90[20] e-27	kg.m^{-1}	kg/m	~ 9.9 e-30 g/ml
Age, assuming Big Bang theory	4.366[54] e+17	s		~ 13.75±0.17 **G** years
<u>Mean expansion rate</u>	2.29[13] e-18	s^{-1}		~ 70.8±4.0 (km/s)/**M**pc *(km/s per Megaparsec)*

Number of stars	**3.0[10] e+23**	Dimensionless		~ 300 **Z** , or 0.5 mols of stars
Number of galaxies	**1.25[20] e+11**	Dimensionless		~ 125 **G**, or 0.2 pico-mols of galaxies
Number of fundamental particles	1.00[25] e+80	Dimensionless		~ 100 **MYYY** *(Mega-Yocto-Yocto-Yocto)*
Mean concentration of particles	0.28[10]	m^{-3}	counts/m^3	~ 4.5e-28 molar "solution"

Milky Way galaxy. Type **BSc** (barred spiral), lentil-shaped, 9 arms, center in the direction of Sagittarius constellation

Diameter	1.04[10] e+21	m		100000 - 120000 light-years (30 - 37 Kpc)
Thickness	1.00[10] e+19	m		~1000 light-years (~300 pc)
Mass	2.50[50] e+42	kg		1.25[25] e+12 solar masses
Number of stars	3.0[10] e+11	Dimensionless	count	~300 e+9
Oldest known star	4.156[50] e+17	s		13.2 e+9 years
Speed with respect to CMB	5.520[60] e+5	m.s^{-1}		552 ± 6 km/s; the absolute galaxy motion
Angle between **galactic plane** and the <u>ecliptic</u>	1.05[10]	rad		~60 degrees

***Milky Way arms** look like logarithmic-spirals; galaxy is a kind of vortex and its apparent features keep changing faster than the motions of its stars*

Arms pattern rotation	1.58[15] e+15	s		~50 million years; move like ripple

(apparent)				patterns
Milky Way central bar				
Bar pattern rotation period (apparent)	5.20[47] e+14	s		15-18 million years; moves like a ripple pattern
Solar system data; see also <u>NASA Planetary Fact Sheets</u>				
Distance to Milky Way galaxy center	2.57[10] e+20	m		27200 ±1100 light-years
Rotation around galaxy center: period	7.49[39] e+15	s		225 - 250 million years
Rotation around galaxy center: orbital speed	2.20 e+5	m.s^{-1}	m/s	approximately opposed to absolute galaxy motion
Absolute speed with respect to CMB	3.7 e+5	m.s^{-1}	m/s	370 km/s; 0.123% of the speed of light
Extension (max.aphelion of a minor planet)	1.598 e+14	m		over 1068 au; planetoid <u>(87269) 2000 OO67</u>
Distance to nearest-neighbour system	3.970[50] e+16	m		4.2 light-years; <u>Proxima Centauri</u>
The Sun spectral class G2V, main sequence (V) yellow dearf (G2). Composition: 73.46% H, 24.85% He, 0.77% O, 0.29 C, 0.16% Fe, 0.12% Ne, 0.09% N				
Mass	1.98910[20] e+30	kg		330'000 times that of Earth

Mean radius	6.9550[50] e+8	m		109.2 times that of Earth
Flattening	9 e-6	Dimensionless		(equatorial - polar)/equatorial radii
Volume	1.41226[50] e+27	m^3		1'304'000 times that of Earth
Mean density	1.408 e+3	$kg.m^{-3}$	kg/m^3	0.255 times that of Earth
Surface gravity on equator	2.74 e+2	$m.s^{-2}$	m/s^2	27.94 g
Escape velocity	6.176 e+2	$m.s^{-1}$	m/s	55.2 times that of Earth
Photosphere temperature	5778	K		In the layer emitting the light we see
Absolute visual magnitude	+4.83	Dimensionless		see stellar magnitudes (Conventional constants)
Radiance I_{sol}	2.009 e+7	$W.m^2.sr^{-1}$		total from the layer emitting the light we see
Luminose efficacy	98	$lm.kg^{-1}.m^{-2}.s^3$	lm/W	see "Electromagnetic radiation constants"
Luminosity L_{sol}	3.841[14] e+26	$kg.m^2.s^{-3}$	W	~3.75 e+28 lm
Loss of mass due to elmag radiation	4.273[16] e+9	$kg.s^{-1}$	kg/s	<electromagnetic power output> / c^2
Total neutrino emissions	1.830[50] e+38	s^{-1}	count/s	Mean value (very variable)
Age	1.4420[14] e+17	s		4.57 e+9 years

Planet Earth in relation to the *Sun* and the *Solar system*. The orbit of Earth defines the **ecliptic plane**.

Earth aphelion, largest distance from Sun	1.52098232 e+11	m		1.01671388 au
Earth perihelion, smallest distance from Sun	1.47098290 e+11	m		0.98329134 au
Longitude of ascending node	6.08665006	rad		348.73936 degrees
Argument of perihelion	1.9933026	rad		114.20783 degrees
Semi-major orbital axis	1.49598261 e+11	m		1.00000261 au
Earth orbit inclination to Sun equator	0.1249	rad		7.155 degrees
Earth orbit inclination to invariable plane	0.0275533	rad		1.57869 degrees
Earth orbital excentricity	0.01671123	Dimensionless		will be about 0.015 after 5000 years
Mean anomaly of Earth orbit	3.5751716 e+2	Dimensionless		
Earth mean orbital velocity	2.9780 e+4	$m.s^{-1}$	m/s	107200 km/h
Sun visual brightess from	-26.74	Dimensionless		see stellar magnitudes (Conventional constants)

the Earth				
Sun angular diameter seen from the Earth	0.00919 - 0.00951	rad		Varies between 0.527 and 0.545 degrees
Solar constant (mean value for Earth)	1.36594[48] e3	kg.s^{-3}	W/m^2	Elmag irradiation from Sun at 1 AU distance
Solar neutrinos flux on Earth surface	6.50[10] e+14	m^{-2}.s^{-1}		Mean count per m^2 per second; very variable
Satellites count	1 natural	Dimesionless		994 artificial (December 2011)

Planets: see the PDF document <u>*SOLAR SYSTEM PLANETS AT A GLANCE*</u> *and the* <u>*NASA Planetary Fact Sheets*</u>

Number of planets	8	Dimensionless	count	<u>Planetary data table</u>

Minor planets see also **NASA Facts Sheets**: <u>*Pluto,*</u> <u>*Chiron,*</u> <u>*Asteroids,*</u> <u>*Comets*</u>

Registered, with known orbits	583'767	Dimensionless	count	Apr 2012; ~3000 are added every month
Numbered minor planets	326'266	Dimensionless	count	Apr 2012
Named minor planets	17'055	Dimensionless	count	Apr 2012

<u>*Planet Earth*</u> *(****Terra****) data, other than those listed above; see also* <u>*NASA Earth Fact Sheet*</u>

Age	1.4327[14] e+17	s		4.54 e+9 years
Global composition in	Fe 32.1, O 30.1, Si 15.1, Mg 13.9, S 2.9, Ni 1.8, Ca 1.5, Al 1.4, the rest: 1.2			

weight %				
Atmospheric composition in weight %	N_2 78.08, O_2 20.95, Ar 0.93, CO_2 0.038, the rest: 0.002; extra: 1% of H_2O wapor (variable)			
Mass	5.9736 e+24	kg		
Volume	1.08321 e+21	m^3		108.321 km^3
Mean density	5.515 e+3	$kg.m^{-3}$	kg/m^3	5.515 g/cm^3
Mean radius	6.3710 e+6	m		this is volumetric mean
Equatorial radius	6.3781 e+6	m		6378.1 km; circumpherence 40075.017 km
Polar radius	6.3568 e+6	m		6356.8 km; circumpherence 40007.860 km
<u>Flattening</u>	0.00335	Dimensionless		f = (a-b)/a; a = equatorial, b = polar radius
Surface area	5.100720 e+14	m^2		5.100720 e+8 km^2
Dry land surface area	1.48940 e+14	m^2		1.48940 e+8 km (29.200 %)^2
Surface temperature, mean	287.2	K		14.0 °C; range 184 to 331 K (-90 to 58 °C))
Surface pressure, mean	1.01325 e+5	$kg.m^{-1}.s^{-2}$	Pa	1 atm = 101325 Pa
Equatorial surface gravity	9.780327	$m.s^{-2}$	m/s^2	0.99732 g

Escape velocity	1.1186 e+4	m.s^{-1}	m/s	11.186 km/s
<u>Albedo, geometric</u>	0.367	Dimensionless		
<u>Albedo, Bond</u>	0.306	Dimensionless		
Sidereal rotation period	8.616410 e+4	s		0.99726968 days, or 23 h 56 m 4.100 s
Equatorial rotation speed	465.1	m.s^{-1}	m/s	0.4651 km/s (4.1579 % of escape volocity))
Axial tilt	0.40763819	rad		23.355948 °, or 23 ° 26' 21".4119
Radius of the core	3.485 e+6	m		3485 km
Average lunar month	2.5514430[5] e+6	s		29 days+ 12 hours+ 44 minutes+ 3 seconds
Conventional constants				
Molar mass constant	**0.001**	kg.mol^{-1}	kg/mol	**Assigned** (exact)
Molar mass of ^{12}C	**0.012**	kg		**Assigned** (exact)
Standard gravity acceleration	**9.806 65**	m.s^{-2}	m/s^2	**Assigned**. Called **1 g** (gee).
Standard atmosphere	**101 325**	Pa		**Assigned**. Called **1 atm** .

Stellar magnitudes. Reference points: **Apparent** brightness: bolometric, initially Vega was 0 (now it is +0.03). **Absolute**: the Sun is 4.83 (used to be 4.75)

<u>Stellar apparent</u> <u>magnitude</u> unit	**2.511 886 431 509 580 ...**	Dimensionless	a ratio	$100^{1/5} = 10^{0.4}$; also stellar **brightness**
<u>Stellar absolute</u> <u>magnitude</u> unit	**2.511 886 431 509 580 ...**	Dimensionless	a ratio	Brightness of a star when distant 10 parsecs

Conventional engineering constants. See also <u>Math constants pertinent to Engineering definitions</u>

dBm

0 dBm power	**0.001**	$kg.m^2.s^{-3}$	Watts	**1 mW; assigned**
0 dBm potential	0.774 596 669 241 483 ...	$kg.m^2.s^{-3}.A^{-1}$	Volts	1 mW into **600 Ohm** load
0 dBm current	0.001 290 994 448 736 ...	A	Amperes	1 mW into **600 Ohm** load

dBW

0 dBW power	**1.0**	$kg.m^2.s^{-3}$	Watts	**1 W; assigned**
0 dBW potential	7.071 067 811 865 475 ...	$kg.m^2.s^{-3}.A^{-1}$	Volts	$sqrt(Z_0)$; 1 W into **50 Ohm** load Z_0
0 dBW current	0.141 421 356 237 310 ...	A	Amperes	$sqrt(1/Z_0)$; 1 W into **50 Ohm** load Z_0
Conversion of dBW into dBm (additive)	+30	Dimensionless	dB	In terms of power

Relative luminance Y of RGB color primaries: $Y = 0.2126.R + 0.7152.G + 0.0722.B$. <u>More info ...</u>

Relative luminance of Red/RGB	0.2126	Dimensionless	a ratio	
Relative luminance of Green/RGB	0.7152	Dimensionless	a ratio	Human eye is most sensitive to green

Relative luminance of Blue/RGB	**0.0722**	Dimensionless	a ratio	
Music and acoustics				
Frequency of the A4 reference note	**440.0**	s^{-1}	Hz	ISO 16
Full-octave frequency ratio	**2.0** exact	Dimensionless	Ratio	C,C#,D,D#,E,F,F#,G,G#,A,A#,B,...next C
Half-tone frequency ratio $2^{1/12}$	**1.059 463 094 359 295 ...**	Dimensionless	Ratio	12 half-tones per octave, each worth 100 cents
Conversion factors for entities tolerated by SI, as well as some others				
Energy & its equivalents				
Electron volt	1.602 176 565[35] e-19	$kg.m^2.s^{-2}$	J	Basic eV-to-SI conversion
Electron volt to mass	1.782 661 845[39] e-36	kg		mass = energy/c^2
Electron volt to atomic units u	1.073 544 150[24] e-9	-	u	a mass equivalent
Electron volt to frequency	2.417 989 348[53] e+14	s^{-1}	Hz	frequency = energy/h
Electron volt to half-life time	6.582 119 28[22] e-16	s		Inverse relationship: $\tau = h/(2\pi\Gamma)$
Joul to eV	6.241 509 34[14] e+18	-	eV	Basic SI-to-eV conversion
Mass to eV	5.609 588 85[12] e+35	-	eV	energy = mass.c^2

Atomic unit u to eV	931.494 061[21] e+6	-	eV	a bit less than 1 GeV/atomic_unit
Frequency (1 Hz) to eV	4.135 667 516[91] e-15	-	eV	energy = frequency*h
Atomic mass constant u, m_u	1.660 538 921[73] e-27	kg		Mass of ^{12}C nuclide / 12
Atomic mass energy (uc^2)	1.492 417 954[66] e-10	$kg.m^2.s^{-2}$	J	931.494 061[21] MeV
Length / Distance				
Astronomical unit ua, au	1.49597870[30] e+11	m	~150 Gm	Mean Earth-to-Sun distance
Light-year **ly**	**9.4607304725808 e+15**	m	~9.5 Pm	Exact: light covers it in one Julian year
Parsec **pc** (~ 32.6 ly)	3.08567757[60] e+16	m	~30 Pm	Corresponds to au parallax of 1 second
Time				
Hour	**3.600 e+3**	s		Exact: 3600 seconds
Day	**8.6400 e+4**	s		Exact: 24 hours
Julian year	**3.1557600 e+7**	s		Exact: 365.25 days
Gregorian year (mean)	**3.1556952 e+7**	s		Exact: 365.2425 days
Tropical year (drops ~0.53 s/century)	3.155692518747072 e+7	s		365.2421896698 days in year 2000
Plane and solid angles				

1 radian in degrees	5.729577951308232... e+1	Dimensionless	°, degree	180/π; planar angle; 57° 17' 44.806247..."
1° degree in radians	1.745329251994330... e-2	Dimensionless	rad	π/180; planar angle
1' minute in radians	2.908882086657215 ... e-4	Dimensionless	rad	π/180/60; planar angle
1" second in radians	4.848136811095359 ... e-6	Dimensionless	rad	π/180/60/60; planar angle
1 steradian in degree^2	3.282806350011744... e+3	Dimensionless	degree^2	$(180/\pi)^2$; for solid angle infinitesimals
1 degree^2 in steradians	3.046174197867086... e-4	Dimensionless	sr	$(\pi/180)^2$; for solid angle infinitesimals

References:

Constants of Physics,

sorted by year and by the first author

((Source: From Wikipedia, the free encyclopedia)

1. Newcomb Simon,
   The Elements Of The Four Inner Planets And The Fundamental Constants Of Astronomy,
   Nabu Press 2011. ISBN 978-1178952315.

2. Karshenboim Savely G., Peik Ekkehard,
   Astrophysics, Clocks and Fundamental Constants,
   Springer 2010. ISBN 978-3642060250.

3. Nakamura K. et al (Particle Data Group),
   Review of Particle Physics,
   J.Phys.G: Nucl.Part.Phys. **37** 075021 (2010).

4. Fritzsch Harald,
   The Fundamental Constants: A Mystery of Physics,
   World Scientific Publishing Company 2009. ISBN 978-9812834324.

5. Mohr Peter J.,Taylor Barry N., Newell David B.
    CODATA recommended values of the fundamental physical constants: 2006,
    Rev.Mod.Phys. **80**,633-730 (2008).

6. Haensch T., Leschiutta S., Wallard A.J.,
    Metrology and Fundamental Constants,
    IOS Press 2007. ISBN 978-1586037840.

7. Hatch E.,
    A Few Simple Facts: From the Electron through the Fundamental Constants,
    Lulu.com 2007. ISBN 978-1430307907.

8. Gabrielse G., Hanneke D., Kinoshita T., Nio M., Odom B.,
    New Determination of the Fine Structure Constant from the Electron g Value and QED,
    Phys.Rev.Letters **97**, 030802 (2006).

9. Odom B., Hanneke D., D'Urso B., Gabrielse G.,
    New Measurement of the Electron Magnetic Moment Using a One-Electron Quantum Cyclotron,
    Phys.Rev.Letters **97**, 030801 (2006).

10. Barrow John,
    The Constants of Nature:
    The Numbers That Encode the Deepest Secrets of the Universe,
    Vintage 2004. ISBN 978-1400032259..

11. Benz S.P., Hamilton C.A.,
    Application of the Josephson Effect to Voltage Metrology,
    Proc.IEEE **92**(10),1617-1629 (2004).

12. Frölich C., Lean J.,
    Solar Radiative Output and its Variability: Evidence and Mechanisms,
    Astron.Astrophys.Rev. **12**,273-320 (2004).

13. Karshenboim S.G., Peik E., Editors,
    Astrophysics, Clocks and Fundamental Constants,
    Springer Verlag 2004. ISBN 978-3540219675.

14. Pap J.M., Fox P.A., Frölich C., Editors,
    Solar Variability and its Effect on Climate,
    in *Geophysical Monograph Series*, No.141,
    American Geophysical Union 2004. ISBN 978-0875904061.

15. Landwehr G.,
    25 Years of quantum Hall effect: how it all came about,
    Physica E **20**(1-2), 1-13 (2003).

16. Bachmair H. et al,
    The von Klitzing resistance standard,
    Physica E **20**(1-2), 14-23 (2003).

17. Conroy R.S.,

    Frequency standards, metrology and fundamental constants,

    Contemp.Phys. **44**44(2), 99-135 (2003).

18. Finch S.,

    Mathematical Constants,

    Cambridge University Press 2003. ISBN 0-521-81805-2.

19. Hall J.L.,Ye J.,

    Optical Frequency Standards and Measurement,

    IEEE Trans.Instrum.Meas. **52**(2), 227-231 (2003).

20. Hatch E.,

    Common Factors of The Fundamental Constants of Particle Physics,

    BookSurge Publishing 2003. ISBN 978-1594571749.

21. Kragh H.,

    Magic Number: A Partial History of the Fine-Structure Constant.

    Arch. Hist. Exact. Sci. **57**(5),395-431 (2003).

22. Uzan J.P.,

    The fundamental constants and their variation: observational and theoretical status,

    Rev.Mod.Phys. **75**(2), 403-455 (2003).

23. Marciano W.J.,

    Precision measurements and New Physics,

    J.Phys. G **29**(1), 225-234 (2003).

24. Martins , Editor,

    The Cosmology of Extra Dimensions and Varying Fundamental Constants,

    Springer Verlag 2003. ISBN 978-1402011382.

25. Faller J.E.,

    Thirty years of progress in absolute gravimetry:
    a scientific capability implemented by technological advances,

    Metrologia **39**(5), 425-428 (2002).

26. Hagiwara K. et al,

    Review of Particle Physics,

    Phys.Rev. D **66**, 010001, 974 p. (2002).

27. Fritzsch H.,

    Fundamental Constants at High Energy,

    Fortschr.Phys. **50**50(5-7), 518-524 (2002).

28. Becker P.,

    History and progress in the accurate determination of the Avogadro constant,

    Rep.Prog.Phys. **64**(12), 1945-2008 (2001).

29. Quinn T.J.,
Recent Advance in Metrology and Fundamental Constants,
Ios Press 2001. ISBN 978-1586031671.

30. Varshalovich D.A., Potekhin A.Y., Ivanchik A.V.,
Puzzle Of the Constancy Of Fundamental Constants,
Comments.At.Mol.Phys. **2**(5), D223-232 (2001).

31. Varshalovich D.A., Potekhin A.Y., Ivanchik A.V.,
Problems of Cosmological Variability of Fundamental Physical Constants,
Phys. Scr. T95, 76-80 (2001).

32. Taylor B.N,
The International System of Units (SI),
NIST Special Publication 330, 2001 Edition (supersedes the 1991 Edition).

33. Mohr P.J.,Taylor B.N.,
CODATA recommended values of the fundamental physical constants: 1998,
Rev.Mod.Phys. **72**,351-495 (2000).

34. Mohr P.J.,Taylor B.N.,
CODATA Recommended Values of the Fundamental Constants,
in *Atomic and Molecular Data and Their Applications*, Berrington K.A., Bell K.L., Editors, Vol.543,
Melville, New York: American Institute of Physics, 3-16 (2000).

35. Basov N.G., Gubin A.,
Quantum Frequency Standards,
IEEE J.Quantum Electron. **6**(6), 857-868 (2000).

36. Luo J., Hu Z.K.,
Status of measurement of the Newtonian gravitational constant G,
Class.Quantum Grav. **17**(12), 2351-2363 (2000).

37. Groom D.E. et al.,
Review of particle physics,
Eur.Phys.J. C **15**(1-4), 1-878 (2000).

38. *CODATA Recommended Values of the Fundamental Physical Constants: 1998*,
J.Phys.Chem.Ref.Data, **28**, No.6, 1999.

39. Quinn T.J.,
Practical realization of the definition of the meter (1997),
Metrologia **36**(3), 211-244 (1999).

40. Johnstone W.D.,
For Good Measure:
The Most Complete Guide to Weights and Measures and Their Metric Equivalents,
NTC Pub.Group 1998. ISBN 0-844-20851-5.

41. *The International System of Units (SI)*,
Bureau International des Poids et Measures (**BIPM**), 7th Edition, 1998.

42. Johnson P.,

    The Constants of Nature: A Realist Account,

    Ashgate Publishing 1997. ISBN 978-1840141023.

43. Cohen E.R.,Taylor B.N.,

    The Fundamental Physical Constants,

    Phys.Today, Aug. 1996, bg9.

44. Cowie, Songaila,

    Astrophysical Limits on the Evolution of Dimensionless Physical Constants over Cosmological Time,

    Astrophysical Journal **453**, 596 (1995).

Table -5: Mathematical Constants and Sequences

(Source: From Wikipedia, the free encyclopedia)

Basic mathematical constants		
Zero, **One**, and **i**	0, 1, $\sqrt{(-1)}$, respectively	Can anything be more basic than these two? (Oops, three!)
π, <u>Archimedes</u> constant	3.141 592 653 589 793 238 462 643 ••• #t	Circumference of a disk with unit diameter.
e, <u>Euler</u> number, <u>Napier's</u> constant	2.718 281 828 459 045 235 360 287 ••• #t	Base of natural logarithms.
γ, <u>Euler-Mascheroni</u> constant	0.577 215 664 901 532 860 606 512 •••	$L_{n\to\infty}\{(1+1/2+1/3+...1/n) - \log(n)\}$
$\sqrt{2}$, <u>Pythagora</u>'s constant	1.414 213 562 373 095 048 801 688 •••	Diagonal of a square with unit side.
Φ, <u>Golden ratio</u>	1.618 033 988 749 894 848 204 586 •••	$\Phi = (1+\sqrt{5})/2 = 2.\cos(\pi/5)$. Diagonal of a unit-side pentagon.
φ, **inverse golden ratio** $1/\Phi = \Phi -1 =(1-\varphi)/\varphi$	0.618 033 988 749 894 848 204 586 •••	Also $\varphi = (\sqrt{5} - 1)/2 = \sqrt{(2-\sqrt{(2+\sqrt{(2-\sqrt{(2+ ...)}}}})}$
δ_s, <u>Silver ratio</u> | <u>Silver mean</u>	2.414 213 562 373 095 048 801 688 •••	δ_s = $1+\sqrt{2}$. One of the **silver means** $(n+\text{sqrt}(n^2+1))/2$
<u>Plastic number</u> ρ (or **silver constant**)	1.324 717 957 244 746 025 960 908 •••	Real root of $x^3 = x + 1$. Attractor of $M(\#)=(1+\#)^{1/3}$.

Transfinite numbers, infinity cardinalities:

<u>Aleph$_0$</u> ≡ <u>Beth$_0$</u>, often denoted as ∞	$\aleph_0 \equiv \beth_0$	Cardinality of the set of <u>natural numbers</u>.
<u>Beth$_1$</u>, $\beth_1$ ≡ c, <u>cardinality of continuum</u>	$c = 2\char`^\beth_0 > \beth_0$	Cardinality of the set of <u>real numbers</u>.
<u>Beth$_2$</u>, $\beth_2$	In general, $\beth_{k+1} = 2\char`^\beth_k > \beth_k$;	Cardinality of the <u>power set</u> of real numbers.
<u>Aleph$_1$</u>	$\aleph_1 \leq \beth_1$, depending on axioms	The smallest cardinal number sharply greater than $\aleph_0$.

Constants derived from the basic ones

*Spin-offs of **zero**. $0^0 = 1$ is the number of mappings of an empty set into itself (the identity). Hence, "1" might be viewed as a spin-off of "0". **There is only one zero!***

*Spin-offs of **one**. The best known are the **natural numbers** (iterated sums of 1's) and the **golden ratio**, via its continued fraction $\Phi = 1+1/(1+1/(1+1/(\dots)))$*

$\Phi = \sqrt{(1+\sqrt{(1+\sqrt{(1+\sqrt{(1+\dots}}}})))}$; golden ratio again!	1.618 033 988 749 894 848 204 586 $\bullet\bullet\bullet$	Attractor of the mapping M1(#)=$\sqrt{(1+\#)}$ in C
$\sqrt{(1+\sqrt{(0+\sqrt{(1+\sqrt{(0+\dots}}}})))} \equiv \sqrt{(1+\sqrt{}\sqrt{(1+\sqrt{}\sqrt{(1+\sqrt{}\dots}}}))$	1.490 216 120 099 953 648 116 386 ...	Attractor of the mapping M10(#)=$\sqrt{(1+\sqrt{(\#)})}$ in C
$\sqrt{(1+\sqrt{}\sqrt{}\sqrt{(1+\sqrt{}\sqrt{}\sqrt{(1+\sqrt{}\sqrt{}\dots}}}))$	1.448 095 838 609 641 132 583 869 ...	Attractor of the mapping M100(#)=$\sqrt{(1+\sqrt{(\sqrt{(\#)})})}$ in C
$\sqrt{(-1+\sqrt{(1+\sqrt{(-1+\sqrt{(1+\dots}}}})))}$	0.453 397 651 516 403 767 644 746 $\bullet\bullet\bullet$	Attractor of the mapping M(#)=$\sqrt{(-1+\sqrt{(1+\#)})}$ in C
$\sqrt{(1+\sqrt{(-1+\sqrt{(1+\sqrt{(-1+\dots}}}})))}$	1.205 569 430 400 590 311 702 028 $\bullet\bullet\bullet$	Attractor of the mapping M(#)=$\sqrt{(1+\sqrt{(-1+\#)})}$ in C

*Spin-offs of the **imaginary unit i**. Formally, i is a solution of $z^2 = -1$ and of $z = e^{z\pi/2}$. Hence, for any integer k, $i^{2k} = (-1)^k$*

and, for any z, $i^{4k+z} = i^{z}$		
$i^{i} = e^{-\pi/2}$	0.207 879 576 350 761 908 546 955 ••• #t	the imaginary unit elevated to itself ... is real
$i^{-i} = (-1)^{-i/2} = e^{\pi/2}$	4.810 477 380 965 351 655 473 035 ••• #t	Inverse of the above. Square root of **Gelfond's constant**.
$\log(i) / i = \pi/2$	1.570 796 326 794 896 619 231 321 ••• #t	Imaginary part of log(log(-1))
$i! = \Gamma(1+i) = i*\Gamma(i)$ (see Gamma function)	0.498 015 668 118 356 042 713 691 •••	- i 0.154 949 828 301 810 685 124 955 •••
| i! |, absolute value of the above	0.521 564 046 864 939 841 158 180 •••	arg(i!) = - 0.301 640 320 467 533 197 887 531 ••• rad
i^i^i^... infinite power tower of i; solution of $z = i^{z}$	0.438 282 936 727 032 111 626 975 •••	+i 0.360 592 471 871 385 485 952 940 •••
| i^i^i^... |, absolute value of the above	0.567 555 163 306 957 825 384 613 •••	arg(i^i^i^...) = 0.688 453 227 107 702 130 498 767 ••• rad
Continued fraction c(i) = i/(i+i/(i+i/(...)))	0.624 810 533 843 826 586 879 804 •••	+i 0.300 242 590 220 120 419 158 909 ••• attractor of i/(i+#)
Continued fraction f(i) = i/(1+i/(1+i/(...)))	0.300 242 590 220 120 419 158 909 •••	+i 0.624 810 533 843 826 586 879 804 ••• attractor of i/(1+#)
Shared modulus |c(i)| = |f(i)|	0.693 205 464 623 797 320 434 363 •••	Note that i/(1+i/(1+i/(...))) = i*conjugate[i/(i+i/(i+i/(...)))]
Infinite nested radical r(i) = √(i+√(i+√(i+ ...)))	1.300 242 590 220 120 419 158 909 •••	+i 0.624 810 533 843 826 586 879 804 ••• (note: r(i) = 1+f(i))
Modulus |√(i+√(i+√(i+ ...)))| of r(i)	1.442 573 740 446 059 678 174 681 ...	r(i) is an attractor of the mapping M(#) = sqrt(i+#)
Infinite nested power p⁺(i)	0.269 293 437 169 311 227 190 868	+i 0.012 576 454 573 863 832 381 561 •••

$= (i+(i+(i+ \ldots)^i)^i)^i$	$\bullet\bullet\bullet$	
Modulus $\|(i+(i+(i+ \ldots)^i)^i)^i\|$ of $p^+(i)$	0.269 586 947 963 194 676 106 659 $\ldots$	$p^+(i)$ is an attractor of the mapping $M(\#) = (i+\#)^i$
Infinite nested power $p^-(i) = (i+(i+(i+ \ldots)^{-i})^{-i})^{-i}$	1.339 209 168 529 111 968 359 269 $\bullet\bullet\bullet$	$-i$ 0.5 (exact) $\ldots$ $p^-(i)$ is the invariant point of $M(\#)=(i+\#)^{-i}$
Modulus $\|(i+(i+(i+ \ldots)^{-i})^{-i})^{-i}\|$ of $p^-(i)$	1.429 503 828 981 383 114 270 109 $\ldots$	$p^-(i)$ is also an attractor of the mapping $M'(\#) = (\# + (i+\#)^{-i})/2$
<u>De Moivre</u> numbers $e^{i2\pi k/n}$	$\cos(2\pi k/n) + i.\sin(2\pi k/n)$	for any integer k and $n\neq 0$.

Roots of i, up to a term of 4k in the exponent (like $i^{4k+1/4} = i^{1/4}$, with any integer k):

$i^{1/2} = \sqrt{i} = (1 + i)/\sqrt{2} = \cos(\pi/4) + i.\sin(\pi/4)$	0.707 106 781 186 547 524 400 844 $\bullet\bullet\bullet$	$+i$ 0.707 106 781 186 547 524 400 844 $\bullet\bullet\bullet$
$i^{1/3} = (\sqrt{3} + i)/2 = \cos(\pi/6) + i.\sin(\pi/6)$	0.866 025 403 784 438 646 763 723 $\bullet\bullet\bullet$	$+i$ 0.5
$i^{1/4} = \cos(\pi/8) + i.\sin(\pi/8)$	0.923 879 532 511 286 756 128 183 $\bullet\bullet\bullet$	$+i$ 0.382 683 432 365 089 771 728 459 $\bullet\bullet\bullet$
$i^{1/5} = \cos(\pi/10) + i.\sin(\pi/10)$	0.951 056 516 295 153 572 116 439 $\bullet\bullet\bullet$	$+i$ 0.309 016 994 374 947 424 102 293 $\bullet\bullet\bullet$
$i^{1/6} = \cos(\pi/12) + i.\sin(\pi/12)$	0.965 925 826 289 068 2867 497 431 $\bullet\bullet\bullet$	$+i$ 0.258 819 045 102 520 762 348 898 $\bullet\bullet\bullet$
$i^{1/7} = \cos(\pi/14) + i.\sin(\pi/14)$	0.974 927 912 181 823 607 018 131 $\bullet\bullet\bullet$	$+i$ 0.222 520 933 956 314 404 288 902 $\bullet\bullet\bullet$
$i^{1/8} = \cos(\pi/16) + i.\sin(\pi/16)$	0.980 785 280 403 230 449 126 182 $\bullet\bullet\bullet$	$+i$ 0.195 090 322 016 128 267 848 284 $\bullet\bullet$
$i^{1/9} = \cos(\pi/18) + i.\sin(\pi/18)$	0.984 807 753 012 208 059 366 743 $\bullet\bullet\bullet$	$+i$ 0.173 648 177 666 930 348 851 716 $\bullet\bullet\bullet$

$i^{1/10}$ = cos(π/20) + i.sin(π/20)	0.987 688 340 595 137 726 190 040 •••	+i 0.156 434 465 040 230 869 010 105 <u>•••</u>
One and i spin-offs		
(1+(1+(1+...)^i)^i)^i, attractor, in **C**, of $M(\#)=(1+\#)^i$	0.673 881 331 107 875 515 780 231 •••	+i 0.407 563 930 545 621 844 739 663 <u>•••</u>
| (1+(1+(1+...)^i)^i)^i |	0.787 543 272 396 837 010 967 660 •••	Absolute value of the above complex number
Means of 1 and **i**: Harmonic HM(1,**i**)=1+**i**, Geometric GM(1,**i**)=(1+**i**)/√2, Arithmetic AM(1,**i**)=(1+**i**)/2, Quadratic RMS(1,**i**)=0, Lehmer L_2(1,**i**)=0		
AGM(1,**i**)/(1+**i**) = second Lemniscate constant	0.599 070 117 367 796 103 337 484 •••	where AGM is the <u>Arithmetic-Geometric Mean</u>
π spin-offs. *log(-1) = π.i, log(log(-1)) = log(π)+(π/2).i*		
2π	6.283 185 307 179 586 476 925 286 <u>•••</u> #t	1/π = 0.318 309 886 183 790 671 537 767 <u>•••</u> #t
2/π, <u>Buffon's</u> constant	0.636 619 772 367 581 343 075 535 <u>•••</u> #t	π^2*(π/2-1) = 5.633 533 939 060 551 468 903 666 <u>•••</u>
π^2	9.869 604 401 089 358 618 834 490 <u>•••</u> #t	$1/\pi^2$ = 0.101 321 183 642 337 771 443 879 <u>•••</u> #t
√π = Geometric mean GM(1,π)	1.772 453 850 905 516 027 298 167 <u>•••</u> #t	1/√π = 0.564 189 583 547 756 286 948 079 <u>•••</u> #t
log(2π)/2 = ζ'(0)	0.918 938 533 204 672 741 780 329 <u>•••</u>	= $I_{x=a,a+1}$\{log(Γ(x)\} + a - a.log(a). **Raabe** formula.
log(π) = real part of log(log(-1))	1.144 729 885 849 400 174 143 427 <u>•••</u>	Log_{10}(π) = 0.497 149 872 694 133 854 351 268 <u>•••</u>

$\log(\pi) \cdot \pi$	3.596 274 999 729 158 198 086 001 •••	$\log(\pi)/\pi$ = 0.364 378 839 675 906 257 049 587 •••
π^{π}	36.462 159 607 207 911 770 990 826 •••	$\pi^{-\pi}$ = 0.027 425 693 123 298 106 119 556 •••
$\pi^{1/\pi}$	1.439 619 495 847 590 688 336 490 •••	$\pi^{-1/\pi}$ = 0.694 627 992 246 826 153 124 383 •••
Infinite power tower of $1/\pi$	0.539 343 498 862 301 208 060 795 •••	$(1/\pi)^\wedge(1/\pi)^\wedge(1/\pi)^\wedge$...; also solution of $x = \pi^{-x}$
Infinite nested radical $\sqrt{(\pi+\sqrt{(\pi+\sqrt{(\pi+ ...)))}}}$	2.341 627 718 511 478 431 766 586 •••	= (1+sqrt(1+4π))/2
Means of 1 and π (for Geometric GM(1,π) = $\sqrt{\pi}$, see above)		
Harmonic HM(1,π)	1.517 093 985 989 552 290 688 861 •••	2*π/(1+π)
Arithmetic-Geometric AGM(1,π)	1.918 724 665 977 634 529 660 378 •••	
Arithmetic AM(1,π)	2.070 796 326 794 896 619 231 321 •••	(1+π)/2
Quadratic RMS(1,π)	2.331 266 222 580 484 116 215 253 •••	sqrt((1+π^2)/2), the root-mean-square.
Lehmer mean $L_2(1,\pi)$	2.624 498 667 600 240 947 773 782 ...	(1+π^2)/(1+π)
Complex valued spin-offs, with the imaginary part in the last column:		
$\pi^{\pm i}$ = cos(log(π)) $\pm$ i.sin(log(π))	0.413 292 116 101 594 336 626 628 •••	$\pm i$ 0.910 598 499 212 614 707 060 044 •••
i^{π} = cos(π^2/2) + i.sin(π^2/2)	0.220 584 040 749 698 088 668 945 •••	- i 0.975 367 972 083 631 385 157 482 •••

$\pi^{\pm i\pi}$ = cos(π.log(π)) ± i.sin(π.log(π))	-0.898 400 579 757 743 645 668 580 •••	±i -0.439 176 955 555 445 894 369 454 •••
$\pi^{\pm i/\pi}$ = cos(log(π)/π) ± i.sin(log(π)/π)	0.934 345 303 678 637 694 262 240 •••	±i 0.356 368 985 033 313 899 907 691 •••
Continued fraction i/(π+i/(π+i/(...)))	0.030 725 404 776 448 575 790 859 •••	+i 0.312 203 069 208 072 004 947 893 •••
e spin-offs. *Note that e = $S_{k=0,\infty}${1/k!} = $L_{k\&arr;\infty}${(1+1/k)^k} = (e$^{1/e}$)^(e$^{1/e}$)^(e$^{1/e}$)^... (power tower of e$^{1/e}$)*		
2e	5.436 563 656 918 090 470 720 574 ••• #t	1/**e** = 0.367 879 441 171 442 321 595 523 ••• #t
e^2, <u>conic constant</u>, <u>Schwarzschild constant</u>	7.389 056 098 930 650 227 230 427 ••• #t	e^{-2} = 0.135 335 283 236 612 691 893 999 ••• #t
$\sqrt{e}$	1.648 721 270 700 128 146 848 650 ••• #t	1/$\sqrt{e}$ = 0.606 530 659 712 633 423 603 799 ••• #t
e^e	15.154 262 241 479 264 189 760 430 •••	e^{-e} = 0.065 988 035 845 312 537 0767 901 •••
$e^{1/e}$	1.444 667 861 009 766 133 658 339 ••• #t	$e^{-1/e}$ = 0.692 200 627 555 346 353 865 421 ••• #t
Infinite power tower of 1/e (**Omega constant**)	0.567 143 290 409 783 872 999 968 •••	(1/e)^(1/e)^(1/e)^... Also solution of x = e^{-x} and Lambert $W_0(1)$
Infinite nested radical $\sqrt{(e+\sqrt{(e+\sqrt{(e+ ...)}})}$	2.222 870 229 721 044 670 695 387 •••	= (1+sqrt(1+4e))/2
<u>Ramanujan number</u>: 262537412640 768743 +	0.999 999 999 999 250 072 597 198 •••	exp($\pi\sqrt{163}$). Closest approach of exp($\pi\sqrt{n}$) to an integer.
<u>Means</u> of 1 and **e** (for Geometric GM(1,**e**) = $\sqrt{e}$, see above)		
Harmonic HM(1,**e**)	1.462 117 157 260 009 758 502 318	2***e**/(1+**e**)

	...	
Arithmetic-Geometric AGM(1,**e**)	1.752 351 558 081 080 826 714 086 •••	
Arithmetic AM(1,**e**)	1.859 140 914 229 522 617 680 143 ...	(1+**e**)/2
Quadratic RMS(1,**e**)	2.048 054 698 846 035 487 304 997 ...	sqrt((1+**e**^{2})/2), the root-mean-square
Lehmer mean L$_2$(1,**e**)	2.256 164 671 199 035 476 857 968 ...	(1+**e**^{2})/(1+**e**)

Complex valued, with the imaginary part in the last column:

e$^{\pm i e}$ = cos(**e**) ± i.sin(**e**)	- 0.911 733 914 786 965 097 893 717 •••	±i 0.410 781 290 502 908 695 476 009 •••
i^{e} = cos(eπ/2) ± i.sin(eπ/2)	-0.428 219 773 413 827 753 760 262 •••	±i -0.903 674 623 776 395 536 600 853 •••
e$^{\pm i/e}$ = cos(1/**e**) ± i.sin(1/**e**)	0.933 092 075 598 208 563 540 410 •••	±i 0.359 637 565 412 495 577 0382 503 •••
Continued fraction i/(**e**+i/(**e**+i/(...)))	0.045 820 234 137 835 028 060 158 •••	+i 0.355 881 727 107 562 782 631 319 •••

e and π combinations, *except trivial ones like, for any integer k, e$^{i\pi k}$ = (-1)^k, cosh(iπk) = (-1)^k, sinh(iπk) = 0*

eπ	8.539 734 222 673 567 065 463 550 •••	√(**eπ**) = 2.922 282 365 322 277 864 541 623 •••
e/π	0.865 255 979 432 265 087 217 774 •••	**π/e** = 1.155 727 349 790 921 717 910 093 •••
√(**π/e**)	1.075 047 603 499 920 238 722 755 •••	$I_{-\infty,+\infty}${exp(-x^2)*cos(x√2)}

$\sqrt{(\pi/\sqrt{e})}$	1.380 388 447 043 142 974 773 415 •••	$I_{-\infty,+\infty}\{exp(-x^2)*cos(x)\}$
$e^{\pi} = (-1)^{-i}$, <u>Gelfond's constant</u>	23.140 692 632 779 269 005 729 086 ••• #t	$e^{-\pi}$ = 0.043 213 918 263 772 249 774 417 ••• #t
π^e	22.459 157 718 361 045 473 427 152 ••• #t	π^{-e} = 0.044 525 267 266 922 906 151 352 ••• #t
$e^{1/\pi}$	1.374 802 227 439 358 631 782 821 •••	$e^{-1/\pi}$ = 0.727 377 349 295 216 469 724 148 ...
$\pi^{1/e}$	1.523 671 054 858 931 718 386 285 •••	$\pi^{-1/e}$ = 0.656 309 639 020 204 707 493 834 •••
$\sinh(\pi)/\pi = (e^{\pi}-e^{-\pi})/2\pi$	3.676 077 910 374 977 720 695 697 •••	$P_{n>0}\{1+1/n^2)\}$
Infinite power tower of e/π	0.880 367 778 981 734 621 826 749 •••	Solution of $x = (e/\pi)^x$
Infinite power tower of π/e	1.187 523 635 359 249 905 438 407 •••	Solution of $x = (\pi/e)^x$
Continued fraction $e/(\pi+e/(\pi+e/(...)))$	0.706 413 134 087 300 069 274 143 •••	Solution of $x(x+\pi)=e$;. Attractor of the mapping $M(\#)=e/(\pi+\#)$
Continued fraction $\pi/(e+\pi/(e+\pi/(...)))$	0.874 433 950 941 209 866 417 966 •••	Solution of $x(x+e)=\pi$. Attractor of the mapping $M(\#)=\pi/(e+\#)$
Arithmetic-Geometric mean AGM(e,π)	2.926 108 551 572 304 696 665 895 •••	
$e^{\pm i/\pi} = \cos(1/\pi) \pm i.\sin(1/\pi)$	0.949 765 715 381 638 659 994 406 •••	$\pm i$ 0.312 961 796 207 786 590 745 276 •••
γ spin-offs and some e and γ combinations		
2γ	1.154 431 329 803 065 721 213 024	1/γ = 1.732 454 714 600 633 473 583 025 •••

	...	
$\log(\gamma)$	-0.549 539 312 981 644 822 337 661 •••	$\text{Log}(\gamma)$ = -0.238 661 891 216 832 389 460 288 ...
$\gamma+\log(\pi)$	1.721 945 550 750 933 034 749 939 ...	= $\text{Ci}(\pi z)+\text{Cin}(\pi z)-\log(z)$; Ci, Cin being cosine integrals
$e\gamma$	1.569 034 853 003 742 285 079 907 •••	e/γ = 4.709 300 169 327 103 330 744 143 •••
e^{γ}	1.781 072 417 990 197 985 236 504 •••	$L_{n\to\infty}\{P_{k=1,n}\{(1-1/\text{prime}(k))^{-1}\}/\log(\text{prime}(n))\}$
$e^{-\gamma}$	0.561 459 483 566 885 169 824 143 •••	$L_{n\to\infty}\{\varphi(n)*\log(\log(n))/n\}$, $\varphi(n)$ being the Euler totient
Infinite power tower of γ	0.685 947 035 167 428 481 875 735 •••	$\gamma^{\wedge}\gamma^{\wedge}\gamma^{\wedge}...$; solution of x = γ^x
Infinite nested radical $\sqrt{(\gamma+\sqrt{(\gamma+\sqrt{(\gamma+...)}})}$	1.409 513 971 801 166 373 157 694 ...	= (1+sqrt(1+4γ))/2
Arithmetic-Geometric mean AGM(1,γ)	0.774 110 217 793 039 338 108 461 ...	
$\zeta(2)/e^{\gamma} = \pi^2/(6*e^{\gamma})$	0.923 563 831 674 181 382 323 509 •••	$L_{n\to\infty}\{\log(\text{prime}(n))*P_{k=1,n}\{(1+1/\text{prime}(k))^{-1}\}\}$
$e^{\pm i\gamma} = \cos(\gamma) \pm i\sin(\gamma)$	0.837 985 287 880 196 539 954 992 •••	$\pm i$ 0.545 692 823 203 992 788 157 356 •••
Golden ratio spin-offs and combinations. Note that Φ = 1+1/(1+1/(1+1/(1+ ...))) = $\sqrt{(1+\sqrt{(1+\sqrt{(1+...)}})}$ can be viewed as a spin-off of 1.		
Complex golden ratio Φ_c = $2.e^{i\pi/5}$	1.618 033 988 749 894 848 204 586 •••	+i 1.175 570 504 584 946 258 337 411 •••
Associate of Φ =	1.175 570 504 584 946 258 337 411	2.sin(π/5), while Φ = 2.cos(π/5) = real part of Φ_c

imaginary part of Φ_c	•••	
Square root of Φ	1.272 019 649 514 068 964 252 422 •••	$\sqrt{\Phi}$; ratio of the sides of squares with golden-ratio areas.
Square root of the inverse φ	0.786 151 377 757 423 286 069 559 •••	$1/\sqrt{\Phi}$
Cubic root of Φ	1.173 984 996 705 328 509 966 683 •••	$\Phi^{1/3}$, ratio of edges of cubes with golden-ratio volumes.
Cubic root of the inverse φ	0.851 799 642 079 242 917 055 213 ...	$1/\Phi^{1/3}$
$\pi/\Phi = \pi.\varphi$	1.941 611 038 725 466 577 346 865 •••	Area of **golden ellipse** with semi_axes $\{1,\varphi\}$
$\log(\Phi) = - \log(\varphi) = \mathrm{acosh}((\sqrt{5})/2) = -i\ \mathrm{acos}((\sqrt{5})/2)$	0.481 211 825 059 603 447 497 758 •••	Natural logarithm of Φ
$\Phi^{2/\pi}$, such as in the <u>golden spiral</u>	1.358 456 274 182 988 435 206 180 •••	$(2/\pi)$ **log**$(\Phi) = 0.306\ 348\ 962\ 530\ 033\ 122\ 115\ 675$ •••
Infinite power tower of the inverse φ	0.710 439 287 156 503 188 669 345 •••	$\varphi^{\wedge}\varphi^{\wedge}\varphi^{\wedge}...$; also solution of $x = \varphi^x = \Phi^{-x}$
Infinite nested radical $\sqrt{(\Phi+\sqrt{(\Phi+\sqrt{(\Phi+ ...)}})}$	1.866 760 399 173 862 092 990 872 ...	$= (1+\mathrm{sqrt}(1+4\Phi))/2$
Arithmetic-Geometric mean AGM$(1,\Phi)$	1.290 452 026 322 977 466 179 732 ...	
Named real math constants. Hint: See a <u>list of many </u>**corresponding continued fractions** on Wikipedia.		
<u>Alladi-Grinstead constant</u>	0.809 394 020 540 639 130 717 931 •••	$\exp(\boldsymbol{S}_{n>0}\{(\mathrm{zeta}(n+1)-1)/n\}-1)$. Re: factorizations of n!
<u>Apéry's constant</u> $\zeta(3)$	1.202 056 903 159 594 285 399 738	Special value of the <u>Riemann zeta function</u> $\zeta(x)$

	••• #t	
Artin's constant	0.373 955 813 619 202 288 054 728 •••	$P_{\text{prime } p}\{1-1/(p(p-1))\}$
Backhouse constant B = $L_{k\to\infty}|q_{k+1}/q_k|$ =	1.456 074 948 582 689 671 399 595 •••	when $Q(x)=S_{k\geq0}\{q_k\,x^k\} = 1/P(x)$, with $P(x)$ defined below
Inverse of Backhouse constant 1/B	0.686 777 834 460 634 954 426 540 •••	-1/B is the only real root of $P(x)=1+S_{k\geq1}\{\text{prime}(k)\,x^p\}$
Barban's constant	2.596 536 290 450 542 073 632 740 •••	$P_{\text{prime } p}\{1+(3p^2-1)/[p(p+1)(p^2-1)]\}$
Bernstein's constant β	0.280 169 499 023 869 133 036 436 •••	Re: theory of function approximations by polynomials
Besicovitch constant (a 10-normal number)	0.149 162 536 496 481 100 121 144 •••	String concatenation of squares in base 10
Blazys constant	2.566 543 832 171 388 844 467 529 •••	Its Blazys' expansion generates prime numbers
Boling's constant	1.805 917 418 986 691 013 997 505 •••	$S_{n\geq1}\{(n(n+1)/2)/P_{k\geq0}\{n!/k!\}\}$
Brun's constan B_2 for twin primes	1.902 160 583 104 •••	Sum of reciprocals of prime pairs (p,p+2)
Brun's constant B_4 for cousin primes	1.197 044 9 •••	Sum of reciprocals of prime pairs (p,p+4)
Brun's constant B'_4 for prime quadruples	0.870 588 380 •••	Sum of reciprocals of prime quadruplets (p,p+2,p+6,p+8)
Buffon's constant	0.636 619 772 367 581 343 075 535 ••• #t	2/π. Solution of a 1733 *needle-throwing problem*
Cahen's constant C	0.643 410 546 288 338 026 182 254	$C = S_{k\geq0}\{(-1)^k/(s_k-1)\}$, where s_k is the **Sylvester's**

	•••	sequence
Catalan's constant C	0.915 965 594 177 219 015 054 603 •••	$C = \boldsymbol{S}_{k \geq 0}\{(-1)^k 2\}$
Champernowne constant C_{10} (10-norma)	0.123 456 789 101 112 131 415 161 ••• #t	String concatenation of natural numbers in base 10
Copeland-Erdös constant (10-normal number)	0.235 711 131 719 232 931 374 143 •••	String concatenation of prime numbers in base 10
Conway's constant $\lambda(3)$	1.303 577 269 034 296 391 257 099 •••	Growth rate of derived look-and-say strings
Delian constant	1.259 921 049 894 873 164 767 210 •••	$2^{1/3}$. The name refers to the Oracle on island Delos.
Dottie number	0.739 085 133 215 160 641 655 312 ••• #t	The only real solution of $x = \cos(x)$
Efimov's scaling constant in quantum physics	22.694 382 595 366 695 192 860 217 •••	$= \exp(\pi/r)$, r being the root of $x.\cosh(x\pi/2)=8.\sinh(x\pi/6)/\sqrt{3}$.
Embree - Trefethen constant β	0.70258 •••	Theory of 2nd order recurrences with random add/subtract
Erdös - Borwein constant	1.606 695 152 415 291 763 783 301 •••	$\boldsymbol{S}_{n>0}\{1/(2^n -1)\}$
Favard constants $K_r = \pi^r R$	$R = {}^1/_1, {}^1/_2, {}^1/_8, {}^1/_{24}, {}^5/_{384}, {}^1/_{240}, {}^{61}/_{46080},$ •••	$K_r = (4/\pi)\boldsymbol{S}_{k \geq 0}\{[(-1)^k/(2k+1)]^{r+1}\}$. Also Akhiezer - Krein - Favard cons.
Feigenbaum reduction parameter α	-2.502 907 875 095 892 822 283 902 •••	Appears in the theory of chaos
Feller - Tornier constant F	0.661 317 049 469 622 335 289 765 •••	$F = (1+\boldsymbol{P}_{\text{prime p}}\{1-2/p^2\})/2$.

Often (mis)labeled as Feller - Tornier's	0.322 634 098 939 244 670 579 531 •••	$P_{\text{prime } p}\{1-2/p^2\}$.
Feigenbaum bifurcation velocity δ	4.669 201 609 102 990 671 853 203 ••• #t	Appears in the theory of chaos
Flajolet-Odlyzko constant	0.757 823 011 268 492 837 742 175 •••	$2\,I_{t=0,\infty}\{1-\exp(\text{Ei}(-t)/2)\}$
Foias constant α	1.187 452 351 126 501 054 595 480 •••	$x_{n+1}=(1+1/x_n)^n$ converges for all $x_1>0$ except $x_1 = \alpha$
Foias-Ewing constant β	2.293 166 287 411 861 031 508 028 •••	Attractor of $f(\#)=(1+1/\#)^\#$; converges for any starting $x>0$
Fransén-Robinson constant	2.807 770 242 028 519 365 221 501 •••	$I_{x=0,\infty}\{1/\Gamma(x)\}$; see Gamma function
Gauss' constant G	0.834 626 841 674 073 186 814 297 •••	$1/\text{AGM}(1,\sqrt{2})$; AGM is the Arithmetic-Geometric mean
Gauss-Kuzmin-Wirsing constant λ_1	0.303 663 002 898 732 658 597 448 •••	2nd eigenvalue of GKW functional operator (first is 1)
Gelfond's constant	23.140 692 632 779 269 005 729 086 ••• #t	$e^\pi = (-1)^{-i}$
Gelfond-Schneider constant	2.665 144 142 690 225 188 650 297 ••• #t	$2^{\wedge}\sqrt{2}$
The last two constants are sometimes called	Hilbert's:	he named them in his 1900 Mathematical Problems address
Gerver's moving sofa constant	2.219 531 668 871 97 (? largest so far)	A sofa that can turn unit-width hallway corner
Hammersley's lower bound on Gerver's const.	2.207 416 099 162 477 962 306 856 •••	$\pi/2 + 2/\pi$. Also the **mean angle of a random rotation**.

Gibbs constant G	1.851 937 051 982 466 170 361 053 •••	Si(π), $I_{x=0,pi;}$ {sin(x)/x}.
Wilbraham-Gibbs constant G'	1.178 979 744 472 167 270 232 028 •••	2G/π. Quantifies Gibbs effect in Fourier Transform.
Gieseking's constant G	1.014 941 606 409 653 625 021 202 •••	Integral of log(2.cos(x/2)) from 0 to 2π/3.
Glaisher-Kinkelin constant A	1.282 427 129 100 622 636 875 342 •••	exp(1/12 -ζ'(-1)). Appears often in number theory
Kinkelin constant	-0.165 421 143 700 450 929 213 919 •••	1/12-log(A) = ζ'(-1). Unstable nomenclature.
Golomb-Dickman constant λ	0.624 329 988 543 550 870 992 936 •••	Average longest cycle length in random permutations
Gompertz constant G	0.596 347 362 323 194 074 341 078 •••	G = -e.Ei(-1), Ei(x) being the *exponential integral*
Graham's constant G(3)	0.783 591 464 262 726 575 401 950 •••	Digits of 3^^k, read backwards, for k->infinity
Grossmann's constant	0.737 338 303 369 29 •••	The only x for which {a_0=1; a_1=x; a_{n+2}=a_n/(1+a_{n+1})} converges
Heat - Brown - Moroz constant	0.001 317 641 154 853 178 109 817 •••	$P_{prime\ p}$ {(1-1/p)^7(1+(7p+1)/p^2)}
Kempner-Mahler number κ	0.816 421 509 021 893 143 708 079 ••• #t	$S_{k\geq0}$ {1/2^(2^k)}
Khinchin's constant K_0	2.685 452 001 065 306 445 309 714 •••	$P_{n\geq1}$ {(1+1/(n(n+2)))$^{\log_2(n)}$}. Limit geom.mean of cont.fract. terms
Khinchin-Lévy constant β	1.186 569 110 415 625 452 821 722 •••	β = π^2/(12.ln2) = $S_{k\geq1}$ {(-1)$^{k+1}$/k^2}/$S_{k\geq1}$ {(-1)$^{k+1}$/k} = η(2)/η(1)

Lévy constant γ	3.275 822 918 721 811 159 787 681 •••	$\gamma = e^\beta = \exp(\pi^2/(12.\ln 2))$. <u>Unstable nomenclature</u>
Knuth's random-generators constant	0.211 324 865 405 187 117 745 425 •••	$(1-1/\sqrt{3})/2$
Kolakoski constant γ	0.794 507 192 779 479 276 240 362 •••	Related to <u>Kolakoski sequence</u>
Komornik-Loreti constant q	1.787 231 650 182 965 933 013 274 ••• #t	Least x such that $S_{k>0}\{a_k/x^k\}=1$ for a unique sequence $\{a_k\}$
Landau-Ramanujan constant	0.764 223 653 589 220 662 990 698 •••	Related to the density of sums of two integer squares
Lagrange numbers $L_1=\sqrt{5}$, $L_2=\sqrt{8}$, $L_3=(\sqrt{221})/5=$	2.973 213 749 463 701 104 522 401 •••	$L_n = \mathrm{sqrt}(9-4/M(n)^2)$, M(n) being n-th **Markov** number
Laplace limit constant λ	0.662 743 419 349 181 580 974 742 •••	Let $\eta = \sqrt{(1+\lambda^2)}$; then $\lambda e^\eta = 1+\eta$
Lieb's square ice constant	1.539 600 717 839 002 038 691 063 •••	$(8/9)\sqrt{3}$. Counting directed graphs. Related to <u>ice lattice</u>
Twenty-Vertex entropy constant	2.598 076 211 353 315 940 291 169 •••	$(3/2)\sqrt{3}$. As above, but for triangular lattices
Linnik's constant L	$1 \le L \le 11/2$,	Regards primes in integer arithmetic progressions
Liouville's constant	0.110 001 000 000 000 000 000 001 ••• #t	$S_{n>0}\{10^{\wedge}(-n!)\}$
Loch's constant	0.970 270 114 392 033 925 740 256 •••	$6.\log(2).\log(10)/\pi^2$; convergence rate of continued fractions
Madelung's constant M_3	-1.747 564 594 633 182 190 636 212 •••	$M3 = S_{i,j,k}\{(-1)^{i+j+k}/\mathrm{sqrt}(i^2+j^2+k^2)\}$

Meissel - Mertens constant B_1	0.261 497 212 847 642 783 755 426 •••	$L_{n\to\infty}\{S_{prime\ p\leq n}\{1/p\}-\log(\log(n))\}$
Meissel - Mertens constant is also known as	**Kronecker constant**, and as	**Hadamard - de la Vallee-Poussin constant**
Mills' constant θ	1.306 377 883 863 080 690 468 614 •••	Smallest θ such that floor(θ^3^n) is prime for any n
Minkowski-Bower constant b	0.420 372 339 423 223 075 640 993 •••	For Minkowski question-mark function, a solution of ?x = x
MRB constant (after Marvin R. Burns)	0.187 859 642 462 067 120 248 517 •••	$S_{k>0}\{(-1)^k\ (k^{1/k} - 1)\}$
Oscillatory-integral MRB constant, modulus	0.687 652 368 927 694 369 809 312 •••	abs($L_{n\to\infty}\{I_{x=1,2n}\{e^{i\pi x}\ x^{1/x}\}\}$). Note: $e^{i\pi x} \equiv (-1)^x$
Oscillatory-integral MRB constant, real part	0.070 776 039 311 528 803 539 528 •••	real($L_{n\to\infty}\{I_{x=1,2n}\{e^{i\pi x}\ x^{1/x}\}\}$), also called MKB constant
Oscillatory-integral MRB constant, imag part	-0.684 000 389 437 932 129 182 744 •••	imag($L_{n\to\infty}\{I_{x=1,2n}\{e^{i\pi x}\ x^{1/x}\}\}$)
Murata's constant	2.826 419 997 067 591 575 546 391 •••	$P_{prime\ p}\{1+1/(p-1)^2\}$
Niven's constant C	1.705 211 140 105 367 764 288 551 •••	Mean maximal exponent in prime factorization
Norton's constant B for Euclid's GCD algorithm	0.065 351 425 923 037 321 378 782 •••	for $1\leq n,m\leq n$, GCD(n,m) takes av. $(12.\log(2)/\pi^2)\log(n)$+B steps.
Odlyzko-Wilf constant K	1.622 270 502 884 767 315 956 950 •••	When $x_0=1$, x_{n+1}=ceil($3x_n/2$), then x_n=floor($K.(3/2)^n$)

<u>Omega</u> <u>constant</u> = Lambert $W_0(1)$	0.567 143 290 409 783 872 999 968 •••	Root of $(x-e^{-x})$ or $(x+\log(x))$..
<u>Otter's constant</u> α	2.955 765 285 651 994 974 714 817 •••	Appears in enumeration of rooted and unrooted trees:
Otter's asymptotic constant β_u	0.534 949 606 1(?) •••	for unrooted trees: $UT(n) \sim \beta_u \, \alpha^n \, n^{-5/2}$
Otter's asymptotic constant β_r	0.439 924 012 571 (?) •••	for rooted trees: $RT(n) \sim \beta_r \, \alpha^n \, n^{-3/2}$ (V. Kotesovec)
<u>Plouffe's constant</u>	0.147 583 617 650 433 274 175 401 ••• #t	= $\operatorname{atan}(1/2)/\pi$
<u>Pogson's ratio</u>	2.511 886 431 509 580 111 085 032 •••	$100^{1/5}$; in astronomy 1 stellar magnitude brightness ratio
<u>Polya's</u> <u>random-walk</u> <u>constant</u> p_3	0.340 537 329 550 999 142 826 273 •••	Probability a 3D-lattice random walk returns back.
<u>Porter's constant</u> C	1.467 078 079 433 975 472 897 798 •••	Arises analyzing efficiency of Euclid's GCD algorithm
<u>Prévost's</u> <u>constant</u> (reciprocal Fibonacci)	3.359 885 666 243 177 553 172 011 •••	Sum of reciprocals of Fibonacci numbers
<u>Reciprocal</u> <u>even</u> <u>Fibonacci constant</u>	1.535 370 508 836 252 985 029 852 •••	Sum of reciprocals of even-indexed Fibonacci numbers
<u>Reciprocal</u> <u>odd</u> <u>Fibonacci constant</u>	1.824 515 157 406 924 568 142 158 •••	Sum of reciprocals of odd-indexed Fibonacci numbers
<u>Prince</u> <u>Rupert's</u> <u>cube</u> constant	1.060 660 171 779 821 286 601 266 •••	$(3\sqrt{2})/4$. Side of largest cube passing through a unit cube
<u>Rényi's parking constant</u> m	0.747 597 920 253 411 435 178 730 •••	Linear space occupied by randomly parked cars

Robbins, or **cube line picking constant** $\Delta(3)$	0.661 707 182 267 176 235 155 831 •••	Average length of a random line inside a unit 3D cube
Salem number σ_1	1.176 280 818 259 917 506 544 070 •••	Related to the structure of the set of algebraic integers
Sarnak's constant	0.723 648 402 298 200 009 408 849 •••	$P_{\text{prime } p\geq3}\{1-(p+2)/p^3\}$
Schwarzschild constant or conic constant	7.389 056 098 930 650 227 230 427 ••• #t	e^2
Shall-Wilson or twin primes constant Π_2	0.660 161 815 846 869 573 927 812 •••	$P_{\text{primes } p\geq3}\{1-1/(p-1)^2\}$
Sierpinski constant S	0.822 825 249 678 847 032 995 328 •••	$S = \log(4*\pi^3 e^{2\gamma}/\Gamma^4(1/4))$
and Sierpinski constant $K = \pi S$	2.584 981 759 579 253 217 065 893 •••	Related to decompositions of n into k squares
Soldner's constant (or **Ramanujan-Soldner's**) μ	1.451 369 234 883 381 050 283 968 •••	Positive real root of logarithmic integral li(x).
Somos' quadratic recurrence constant σ	1.661 687 949 633 594 121 295 818 •••	$\sigma=\sqrt{(1\sqrt{(2\sqrt{(3\ \ldots)}})})$. Somos's sequence tends to $\sigma^{(2^n)}/(n+2)$
Taniguchi's constant	0.678 234 491 917 391 978 035 538 •••	$P_{\text{prime } p}\{1-3/p^3+2/p^4+1/p^5-1/p^6\}$
Theodorus' constant	1.732 050 807 568 877 293 527 446 •••	$\sqrt{3}$.
Thue-Morse constant	0.412 454 033 640 107 597 783 361 ••• #t	**Thue-Morse sequence** as a binary number .0110 ...
Viswanath's constant	1.131 988 248 794 3 •••	Growth of Fibonacci-like sequence with random +/-

Wallis' constant	2.094 551 481 542 326 591 482 386 •••	Root of x^3-2x-5. A kind of historic curiosity.
Weierstrass constant $\sigma(1\|1,\mathbf{i})$	0.474 949 379 987 920 650 332 504 •••	$2^{5/4}\pi^{1/2}e^{\pi/8}/\Gamma^2(1/4)$. σ is the Weierstrass σ function
Wyler's constant	0.007 297 348 130 031 832 128 956 •••	$(9/(16*\pi^3))(\pi/5!)^{1/4}$. Approximation to fine structure constant
Zagier's constant	0.180 717 104 711 806 478 057 792 •••	Limit of [Count of Markoff numbers < x]/log(3x)^2
Zolotarev-Schur constant σ	0.311 078 866 704 819 209 027 546 •••	σ = (1-E(c)/K(c))/c^2, ... see the link for more details

Other notable real-valued math constants. Note: OGF stands for Ordinary Generating Function.

Continued fractions constant	1.030 640 834 100 712 935 881 776 •••	$(1/6)\pi^2/(\log(2)\log(10))$. Mean c.f.terms per decimal digit
Evil numbers:	π, Φ, $2^{1/3}$, $3^{1/2}$, π^{666}, $\sqrt{6}$, ... and many more:	Running sum of their fractional-part digits hits 666
Probability that a random real number is evil	0.2 - 2.16622268371352394472 0••• e-64	starts with "0.1", followed by 62 "9"s, and then "783..."
FoxTrot series sum	0.239 560 747 340 741 949 878 153 •••	$= \mathbf{S}_{k\geq1}\{(-1)^{n+1} n^2/(1+n^3)\}$
Hard square entropy constant $\mathbf{L}_{n\to\infty}\{F_n{}^\wedge(1/n^2)\}\}$	1.503 048 082 475 332 264 322 066 •••	F_n = number of nXn binary matrices with no adjacent 1's
$\sqrt{(1+\sqrt{(2+\sqrt{(3+\sqrt{(4+\sqrt{(5+}}}}}$ ...)))))	1.757 932 756 618 004 532 708 819 •••	Infinite nested radical of natural numbers
$\sqrt{(2+\sqrt{(3+\sqrt{(5+\sqrt{(7+\sqrt{(11+}}}}}$ ...)))))	2.103 597 496 339 897 262 619 939 •••	Infinite nested radical of primes

$(1+(1+(1+(1+$ ... $)^{1/4})^{1/3})^{1/2})^{1/1}$	2.517 600 167 877 718 891 370 658 ...	An infinite nested power on one's
$(1!+(2!+(3!+(4!+$ ... $)^{1/4})^{1/3})^{1/2})^{1/1}$	3.005 583 659 206 261 169 270 945	An infinite nested power on factorials
$(1/2)^{\wedge}((1/2)^{\wedge}((1^{\wedge}2)^{\wedge}$ ... $))$	0.641 185 744 504 985 984 486 200 •••	Infinite power tower of 1/2; solution of $x = 2^{-x}$
Lemniscate constant L	2.622 057 554 292 119 810 464 839 •••	$L = \pi G$, where G is the **Gauss'** constant
First lemniscate constant L_A	1.311 028 777 146 059 905 232 419 •••	$L_A = L/2 = \pi G/2$
Second lemniscate constant L_B	0.599 070 117 367 796 103 337 484 •••	$L_B = 1/(2G) = AGM(1,i)/(1+i)$
Mandelbrot set area	1.506 591 •••	Hard to estimate
$(1-1/2)(1-1/4)(1-1/8)(1-1/16)$ ...	0.288 788 095 086 602 421 278 899 •••	Infinite product $P_{k=1,\infty}\{1-x^k\}$, for $x=1/2$
Quadratic Class Number constant	0.881 513 839 725 170 776 928 391 •••	$P_{\text{prime } p}\{1-1/(p^2(p+1))\}$
Rabbit constant	0.709 803 442 861 291 314 641 787 •••	See the binary rabbit sequence and numbe
Real root of $P(x) \equiv$ <OGF for primes>	-0.686 777 834 460 634 954 426 540 •••	$P(x)=1+S_{k>0}\{prime(k).x^k\}$. The real root is unique.
Square root of Gelfond - Schneider constant	1.632 526 919 438 152 844 773 495 ••• #t	$\sqrt{2}^{\wedge}\sqrt{2} = 2^{\wedge}(1/\sqrt{2})$. Notable because proved transcendental
Sum $1+1/2^2+1/3^3+1/4^4+$ ..	1.291 285 997 062 663 540 407 282 •••	$S_{k>0}\{1/k^k\}$
Sum of reciprocals of	1.611 114 925 808 376 736 111 111,	Search this doc for "exponential factorials"

exponential factorials	••• #t	
Sum of reciprocals of distinct powers	0.874 464 368 404 944 866 694 351 •••	See also the perfect powers without repetitions
Tribonacci constant	1.839 286 755 214 161 132 551 852 •••	Asymptotic growth rate of tribonacci numbers.
Tetranacci constant	1.927 561 975 482 925 304 261 905 •••	Asymptotic growth rate of tetranacci numbers.
Z-numbers ξ: for any k>1, $0 \leq \text{frac}(\xi(3/2)^k) < 1/2$	**No Z-number is known**	There exists at most one in each (n,n+1) interval, n>0
Constants related to harmonic numbers $H_n = \mathbf{S}_{k=1,2,\dots,n}\{1/k\}$		
$\mathbf{S}_{n\geq1}\{(-1)^n H_n/n!\}$	-0.484 829 106 995 687 646 310 401 ...	
$\mathbf{S}_{n\geq1}\{H_n/n!\}$	2.165 382 215 326 936 359 420 986 ...	
$\mathbf{S}_{n\geq1}\{(-1)^n H_n/n!^2\}$	-0.672 462 966 936 363 624 928 336 ...	$= \gamma.J_0(2) - (\pi/2).Y_0(2)$. See Bessel functions for J_0 and Y_0
$\mathbf{S}_{n\geq1}\{H_n/n!^2\}$	1.429 706 218 737 208 313 186 746 ...	$= (\log(i)+\gamma).J_0(2i) - (\pi/2).Y_0(2i)$
Hausdorff dimensions for selected fractal sets		
Feigenbaum attractor-repeller	0.538 045 143 580 549 911 671 415 •••	No explicit formula
Cantor set removing 2nd third	0.630 929 753 571 457 437 099 527 ••• #t	$\log_3(2) = \log(2)/\log(3)$. See also Devil's staircase function
Asymmetric **Cantor set**, removing 2nd quarter	0.694 241 913 630 617 301 738 790 •••	$\log_2(\Phi) = \log(\Phi)/\log(2)$, related to the golden ratio Φ

<u>Real numbers with no even decimal digit</u>	0.698 970 004 336 018 804 786 261 •••	Log(5) = log(5)/log(10)
Rauzy fractal boundary r	1.093 364 164 282 306 639 922 447 •••	Let $z^3-z^2-z-1 = (z-c)(z-a)(z-a^{\cdot})$. Then $2|a|^{3r}+|a|^{4r}=1$
<u>2D Cantor dust</u>, **Koch snowflake**, plus more	1.261 859 507 142 914 874 199 054 ••• #t	$\log_3(4) = 2.\log(2)/\log(3)$. A case of **Liedenmayer's systems**
Apollonian gasket (triples of circles in 2D plane)	1.305 686 729 (?) •••	No explicit formula
Heighway-Harter dragon curve boundary	1.523 627 086 202 492 106 277 683 •••	$\log_2((1+(73-6\sqrt{87})^{1/3}+(73+6\sqrt{87})^{1/3})/3)$
Sierpinsky triangle	1.584 962 500 721 156 181 453 738 ••• #t	$\log_2(3) = \log(3)/\log(2)$
<u>3D Cantor dust</u>, **Sierpinski carpet**	1.892 789 260 714 372 311 298 581 ••• #t	$\log_3(8) = 3.\log(2)/\log(3)$
**Lévy C curve	Lévy fractal / dragon**	1.934 007 182 988 290 978 (?) •••	No explicit formula
Menger sponge	2.726 833 027 860 842 041 396 094 •••	$\log_3(20) = \log(20)/\log(3)$
<u>Simple continued fractions</u> CF{a} of the form $a_0+1/(a_1+1/(a_2+1/(a_3+(...))))$ for integer sequences a = {$a_0,a_1,a_2,a_3,...$}. See also a <u>list of CF's for various constants</u>.		
a_k = 1, k=0,1,2,3,...	1.618 033 988 749 894 848 204 586 •••	<u>golden rati</u> Φ
a_k = k, nonnegative integers	0.697 774 657 964 007 982 006 790 •••	
a_k = prime(k+1), primes	2.313 036 736 433 582 906 383 951 •••	

$a_k = k^2$, perfect squares	0.804 318 561 117 157 950 767 680 •••	
$a_k = 2^k$, powers of 2	1.445 934 640 512 202 668 119 554 •••	See also OEIS A096641
$a_k = k!$, factorials	1.684 095 900 106 622 500 339 633 •••	

<table>
<tr><td colspan="3" style="background:#ffffcc"><u>Special continued fractions</u> of the form $a_1+a_1/(a_2+a_3/(a_3+(...)))$ for integer sequences a = {a1,a2,a3,...}.</td></tr>
<tr><td>$a_n = n$, natural numbers</td><td>1.392 211 191 177 332 814 376 552 •••</td><td>= 1/(e-2)</td></tr>
<tr><td>$a_n = prime(n)$, primes</td><td>2.566 543 832 171 388 844 467 529 •••</td><td>Blazys constant</td></tr>
<tr><td>$a_n = n^2$, squares > 0</td><td>1.226 284 024 182 690 274 814 937 •••</td><td></td></tr>
<tr><td>$a_n = 2^{n-1}$, powers of 2</td><td>1.408 615 979 735 005 205 132 362 •••</td><td></td></tr>
<tr><td>$a_n = (n-1)!$, factorials</td><td>1.698 804 767 670 007 211 952 690 •••</td><td></td></tr>
<tr><td colspan="3" style="background:#ffffcc">Alternating sums of inverse powers of prime numbers, $sip(x) = -S_{k>0}\{(-1)^k/p^x(k)\}$, where p(n) is the n-th prime number</td></tr>
<tr><td>sip(1/2)</td><td>0.347 835 4 ...</td><td>$1/\sqrt{2}$ -$1/\sqrt{3}$ +$1/\sqrt{5}$ -$1/\sqrt{7}$ +$1/\sqrt{11}$ -$1/\sqrt{13}$ +$1/\sqrt{17}$ -...</td></tr>
<tr><td>sip(1)</td><td>0.269 606 351 916 7 •••</td><td>1/2 -1/3 +1/5 -1/7 +1/11 -1/13 +1/17 -...</td></tr>
<tr><td>sip(2)</td><td>0.162 816 246 663 601 41 •••</td><td>1/2^2 -1/3^2 +1/5^2 -1/7^2 +1/11^2 -1/13^2 +...</td></tr>
<tr><td>sip(3)</td><td>0.093 463 631 399 649 889 112 4 •••</td><td>1/2^3 -1/3^3 +1/5^3 -1/7^3 +1/11^3 -1/13^3 +...</td></tr>
<tr><td>sip(4)</td><td>0.051 378 305 166 748 282 575 200 •••</td><td>1/2^4 -1/3^4 +1/5^4 -1/7^4 +1/11^4 -1/13^4 +...</td></tr>
</table>

sip(5)	0.027 399 222 614 542 740 586 273 •••	1/2^5 -1/3^5 +1/5^5 -1/7^5 +1/11^5 -1/13^5 +...

Some notable natural and integer numbers

Large integers

Bernay's number	67^257^729	Originally an example of a hardly ever used number
Googol	10^{100} = 10^100	A large integer ...
Googolplex	10 ^{googol} = 10^10^100	... a larger integer ...
Googolplexplex	10 ^{googolplex} = 10^10^10^100	... and a still larger one.
Graham's number (last 30 digits)	••• 5186439059104575627262464195387	3^^...^^3, 64 times (3^^64); see **Graham's constant**
Shannon number, lower bound estimate:	10^120	The game-tree complexity of chess
Skewes' numbers	10^14 < n < e^e^e^79	Bounds on the first integer n for which π(n) < li(n)

Notable | interesting integers

Ishango bone prime quadruplet	11, 13, 17, 19	Crafted in the paleolithic Ishango bone
Hardy-Ramanujan number	$1729 = 1^3+12^3 = 9^3+10^3$	Smallest cubefree taxicab number T(2); see below
Heegner numbers h (full set)	1,2,3,7,11,19,43,67,163	The quadratic ring Q($\sqrt{-h}$) has class number 1
Vojta's number	15170835645 (see	Smallest cubefree T(3) taxicab number (see the link)

Gascoigne-Moore number	1801049058342701083	Smallest cubefree T(4) taxicab number (see the link)
Tanaka's numbe	906150257	Smallest number violating Polya conjecture that $L(n>1)\leq0$
Related to **Lie groups** ...		
Orders of **Weyl** groups of type E_n, n=6,7,8	51840, 2903040, 696729600	$2^7 3^4 5^1$, $2^{10} 3^4 5^1 7^1$, $2^{14} 3^5 5^2 7^1$, respectively.
Largest of ...		
Narcissistic numbers	There are only 88 of them (A005188	max = 115132219018763992565095597973971522401
Not composed of two abundants	20161	Exactly 1456 integers are the sum of two abundants
Consecutive 19-smooth numbers	11859210, 11859211	In case you wonder: this pair was singled-out on MathWorld
Factorions in base 10	40585	Equals the sum of factorials of its dec digits
Factorions in base 16	2615428934649	Equals the sum of factorials of its hex digits
Right-truncatable prime in base 10	73939133	Truncate any digits on the right and it's still a prime.
Right-truncatable primes in base 16	hex 3B9BF319BD51FF (	Truncate any hex digits on the right and it's still a prime.
Left-truncatable prime with no 0 digit	357686312646216567629137	Each suffix is prime. Admitting "0", such primes never end.
Primes slicing only into primes	739397 (	Prime whose decimal prefixes and postfixes are all prime.

Composites slicing only into primes	73313	All its decimal prefixes and postfixes are prime.
Smallest of ...		
<u>Sierpinsky numbers</u>	78557	m is a Sierpinsky number if $m*2^k+1$ is not prime for any k>0.
<u>Riesel numbers</u> (conjectured!)	509203	m is a Riesel number if $m*2^k-1$ is not prime for any k>0.
Known <u>Brier numbers</u>	3316923598096294713661	Numbers that are both **Riesel** and **Sierpinski**
Non-unique sums of two 4th powers	635318657	$= 133^4 + 134^4 = 59^4 + 158^4$
Odd abundant numbers	945	Odd number whose sum of proper divisors exceeds it
<u>Sociable numbers</u>	12496	Its aliquot sequence terminates with a 5-member cycle
Number of The Beast (Revelation 13:18), **etc...**	666; also the 6x6-th <u>triangular number</u>	and the largest left- and <u>right-truncatable triangular number</u>
<u>Evil numbers</u> (real) and <u>evil integers</u>	are two <u>distinct categories</u>	which must not be confused!
Belphegor numbers B(n)	16661, 1066601, 100666001, •••	prime for n=0, 13, 42, 506, 608, 2472, 2623, 28291, •••
<u>Belphegor prime</u> B(13).	1000000000000066600000000000001	Belphegor: one of the seven princes of Hell.
Smallest <u>apocalyptic number</u>	2^{157}, a power of 2 containing digits 666	182687704666362864775460604089535377456991567872
Other <u>Apocalyptic number</u> exponents	157, 192, 218, 220, 222, 224, 226, 243, •••	m such that 2^m contains the sequence of digits "666"

Legion's number of the first kind L_1	666^{666}	It has 1881 decimal digits
Legion's number of the second kind L_2	$666!^{666!}$	It has approximately 1.609941...e1596 digits

Named / notable functions of natural numbers. Each is also an integer sequence. Their domain {n=1,2,3,...} can be often extended.

Aliquot sum function $s(n)$	0, 1, 1, 3, 1, 6, 1, 7, 4, 8, 1, 16, 1, 10, 9, •••	$s(n) = \sigma(n)-n$. Sum of *proper* divisors of n.
Divisor function $d(n) \equiv \sigma_0(n)$	1, 2, 2, 3, 2, 4, 2, 4, 3, 4, 2, 6, 2, 4, 4, 5, •••	Number of *all* divisors of n. Also $S_{d|n}\{d^0\}$
Euler's totient function $\varphi(n)$	1, 1, 2, 2, 4, 2, 6, 4, 6, 4, 10, 4, 12, 6, 8, •••	Number of k's smaller than n and relatively prime to it
Iterated Euler's totient function $\varphi(\varphi(n))$	1, 1, 1, 1, 2, 1, 2, 2, 2, 2, 4, 2, 4, 2, 4, 4, 8, •••	Pops up in counting the primitive roots of n
Factorial function n! = 1*2*3...*n, but 0!=1	1, 1, 2, 6, 24, 120, 720, 5040, 40320, •••	Also: **permutations of ordered sets** of n labeled elements
Hamming weight function $Hw(n)$	1, 1, 2, 1, 2, 2, 3, 1, 2, 2, 3, 2, 3, 3, 4, 1, 2, •••	Number of 1's in the binary expansion of n
Liouville function $\lambda(n)$	1, -1, -1, 1, -1, 1, -1, -1, 1, 1, -1, -1, -1, 1, •••	$\mu(n)=(-1)^{\wedge}\Omega(n)$. For the *bigomega* function, see below.
Partial sums of **Liouville function** $L(n)$	0, 1, 0, -1, 0, -1, 0, -1, -2, -1, 0, -1, -2, -3, •••	The **Polya conjecture**, L(n>1)≤0, breaks at **Tanaka's number**
Möbius function $\mu(n)$	1, -1, -1, 0, -1, 1, -1, 0, 0, 1, -1, 0, -1, 1, 1, •••	$\mu(n)=(-1)^{\wedge}\omega(n)$ if n is *squarefree*; else $\mu(n)=0$
omega function $\omega(n)$	0, 1, 1, 1, 1, 2, 1, 1, 1, 2, 1, 2, 1, 2, 2, 1, 1, •••	Number of *distinct* prime factors of n.

Omega (or bigomega) function $\Omega(n)$	0, 1, 1, 2, 1, 2, 1, 3, 2, 2, 1, 3, 1, 2, 2, 4, 1, •••	Number of **all** prime factors of n, with multiplicity.
Primes sequence function prime(n)	2, 3, 5, 7, 11, 13, 17, 19, 23, 29, 31, 37, •••	A prime number is divisible only by 1 and itself; excluding 1
Primes counting function $\pi(n)$	0, 1, 2, 2, 3, 3, 4, 4, 4, 4, 5, 5, 6, 6, 6, 6, 7, •••	$\pi(x)$ is the number of primes not exceeding x..
Primorial function n#	1, 1, 2, 6, 6, 30, 30, 210, 210, 210, 210, •••	Product of all primes not exceeding n
Sigma function $\sigma(n) \equiv \sigma_1(n)$	1, 3, 4, 7, 6, 12, 8, 15, 13, 18, 12, 28, 14, •••	Sum of **all** divisors of n. Also $S_{d\mid n}\{d^1\}$.
Sigma-2 function $\sigma_2(n)$	1, 5, 10, 21, 26, 50, 50, 85, 91, 130, 122, •••	$S_{d\mid n}\{d^2\}$. Sum of squares of all divisors.
Sigma-3 function $\sigma_3(n)$	1, 9, 28, 73, 126, 252, 344, 585, 757, •••	In general, for $k \geq 0$, $\sigma_k(n) = S_{d\mid n}\{d^k\}$
Sum of distinct prime factors sopf(n)	0, 2, 3, 2, 5, 5, 7, 2, 3, 7, 11, 5, 13, 9, 8, •••	Example: sopf(12) = sopf(2^2.3) = 2+3 = 5.
Sum of prime factors with repetition sopfr(n)	0, 2, 3, 4, 5, 5, 7, 6, 6, 7, 11, 7, 13, 9, 8, •••	Also said with *multiplicity*. Example: sopfr(12) = 2+2+3 = 7.

Notable integer sequences (each of them is also an integer-valued function). Here n = 0, 1, 2, ..., unless specified otherwise.

Named sequences

Catalan numbers C(n)	1, 1, 2, 5, 14, 42, 132, 429, 1430, 4862, •••	C(n) = C(2n,n)/(n+1); ubiquitous in number theory
Cullen numbers C_n	1, 3, 9, 25, 65, 161, 385, 897, 2049, •••	$C_n = n.2^n+1$. Very few are prime.

Cullen primes subset of C_n, for n =	1, 141, 4713, 5795, 6611, 18496, 32292, •••	Largest known (Feb 2016): n = 6679881
Euclid numbers 1+prime(n)#	2, 3, 7, 31, 211, 2311, 30031, 510511, •••	1 + (product of first n primes) = 1 + $P_{k=1,n}\{prime(k)\}$
Euler numbers E(n) for n = 0, 2, 4, ...	1, -1, 5, -61, 1385, -50521, 2702765, •••	E.g.f: 1/cosh(z) (even terms only)
Fermat numbers F(n)	3, 5, 17, 257, 655337, 4294967297, •••	$F(n) = 2^{\wedge}(2^n)+1$. Very few are primes.
Fermat primes subset of Fermat numbers F(n)	3, 5, 17, 257, 655337, ••• (? Feb 2016)	F(n) for n=0,1,2,3,4. Also prime(n) for n=2,3,7,55,6543,•••.
Fibonacci numbers F(n)	0, 1, 1, 2, 3, 5, 8, 13, 21, 34, 55, 89, 144, •••	$F_n = F_{n-1}+F_{n-2}$; F_0=0, F_1=1
<u>Tribonacci numbers</u> T(n)	0, 0, 1, 1, 2, 4, 7, 13, 24, 44, 81, 149, 274, •••	$T_n = T_{n-1}+T_{n-2}+T_{n-3}$; T_0=T_1=0, T_2=1
<u>Tetranacci numbers</u> T(n)	0, 0, 0, 1, 1, 2, 4, 8, 15, 29, 56, 108, 208, •••	$T_n = T_{n-1}+T_{n-2}+T_{n-3}+T_{n-4}$; T_0=T_1=T_2=0, T_3=1
Golomb's | Silverman's sequence, n = 1, 2, ...	1, 2,2, 3,3, 4,4,4, 5,5,5, 6,6,6,6, 7,7,7,7, 8, •••	a(1)=1, a(n)= least number of times n occurs if a(n)≤a(n+1)
Jordan-Polya numbers	1, 2, 4, 6, 8, 12, 16, 24, 32, 36, 48, 64, 72,•••	Can be written as products of factorials
Kolakoski sequence	1, 2, 2, 1, 1, 2, 1, 2, 2, 1, 2, 2, 1, 1, 2, 1, 1, •••	1's and 2's only. Run-lengths match the sequence
Lucas numbers L(n)	2, 1, 3, 4, 7, 11, 18, 29, 47, 76, 123, 199,•••	$L_n = L_{n-1} + L_{n-2}$; L_0 = 2, L_1 = 1
Markov numbers, n = 1, 2, ...	1, 2, 5, 13, 29, 34, 89, 169, 194, 233, 433, •••	Members of a Markoff triple (x,y,z): $x^2 + y^2 + z^2 = 3xyz$

Mersenne numbers, n = 1, 2, ...	3, 7, 31, 127, 2047, 8191, 131071, •••	$2^{prime(n)}$-1;
Ore's harmonic divisor numbers, n = 1, 2, ...	1, 6, 28, 140, 270, 496, 672, 1638, •••	The harmonic mean of their divisors is integer
Pell numbers P(n)	0, 1, 2, 5, 12, 29, 70, 169, 408, 985, •••	$P_n = 2 \cdot P_{n-1} + P_{n-2}$; $P_0 = 0$, $P_1 = 1$
Pell-Lucas (or **companion** Pell) **numbers** Q(n)	2, 2, 6, 14, 34, 82, 198, 478, 1154, 2786, •••	$Q_n = 2 \cdot Q_{n-1} + Q_{n-2}$; $Q_0 = 2$, $Q_1 = 2$
Proth numbers	3, 5, 9, 13, 17, 25, 33, 41, 49, 57, 65, •••	They have the form $k.2^m+1$ for some m and some $k < 2^m$.
Proth primes subset of Proth numbers	3, 5, 13, 17, 41, 97, 113, 193, 241, 257, •••	Largest known (Feb 2016): $19249.2^{13018586}+1$
Riesel numbers	509203 •••	Numbers m such that $m.2^k-1$ is not prime for any k>0.
Sierpinsky numbers	78557, 271129, 271577, 322523, •••	Numbers m such that $m.2^k+1$ is not prime for any k>0.
Somos's quadratic recurrence s(n)	1, 1, 2, 12, 576, 1658880, •••	s(0)=1,s(n)=n.s²(n-1). See **Somos**'s constant
Sylvester's sequence	2, 3, 7, 43, 1807, 3263443, •••	$s_{n+1} = s_n^2 - s_n + 1$, with $s_0 = 2$. $S_{k≥0}\{1/s_k\} = 1$.
Thabit numbers T_n	2, 5, 11, 23, 47, 95, 191, 383, 767, 1535, •••	3.2^n-1.
Thabit primes subset of Thabit numbers for n =	0, 1, 2, 3, 4, 6, 7, 11, 18, 34, 38, 43, 55, •••	As of Feb 2016, only 62 are known, up to n = 11895718.
Wolstenholme numbers	1, 5, 49, 205, 5269, 5369, 266681, •••	Numerators of the reduced rationals $S_{k=1,n}\{1/k\text{^}2\}$
Woodall numbers	1, 7, 23, 63, 159, 383, 895, 2047,	$W_n = n.2^n$-1, n = 1, 2, 3, ... Very few are prime

(**Cullen** of 2nd kind), W_n	4607, •••	
Other notable integer sequences (unclassified)		
<u>Hungry numbers</u> (they want to eat the π)	5, 17, 74, 144, 144, 2003, 2003, 37929, •••	Smallest m such that 2^m contains first m digits of π
*Sequences **related to Factorials** (maybe just in some vague conceptual way)*		
<u>Double factorials</u> n!!	1, 1, 2, 3, 8, 15, 48, 105, 384, 945, 3840, •••	0!!=1; for n > 0, n!! = n*(n-2)*(n-4)*...*m, where m ≤ 2
<u>Triple factorials</u> n!!! or $n!^3$, n = 1,2,3,...	1, 1, 2, 3, 4, 10, 18, 28, 80, 162, 280, 880, •••	0!!!=1; for n > 0, n!!! = n*(n-3)*(n-6)*...*m, where m ≤ 3
<u>Exponential factorials</u> a(n)	1, 1, 2, 9, 262144, •••	a(0)=1; for n > 0, $a(n) = n^{a(n-1)}$. Next term has 183231 digits
<u>Factorions</u> in base 10	1, 2, 145, 40585 (that's all)	Equal to the sum of factorials of their dec digits
<u>Factorions</u> in base 16	1, 2, 2615428934649 (that's all)	Equal to the sum of factorials of their hex digits
<u>Hyperfactorials</u> H(n) = $P_{k=1,n}\{k^k\}$	1, 1, 4, 108, 27648, 86400000, •••	H(0) is conventional
<u>Quadruple</u> factorials (2n)!/n!	1, 2, 12, 120, 1680, 30240, 665280, •••	Equals (n+1)!C(n), C(n) being the *Catalan number*
Pickover's tetration superfactorials (n!^^n!)/n!	1, 1, 4, (incredible number of digits), ...	Here the term 'superfactorial' is deprecated
<u>Subfactorials</u> !n = $n!*S_{k=0,n}\{(-1)^k/k!\}$	1, 0, 1, 2, 9, 44, 265, 1854, 14833, •••	Also called *derangements* or *rencontres* numbers
<u>Superfactorials</u> n\$ = $P_{k=0,n}\{k!\}$	1, 1, 2, 12, 288, 34560, 24883200, •••	Prevailing definition (see below another one by Pickover)
*Sequences **related to the Hamming weight** function*		

Evil integers	0, 3, 5, 6, 9, 10, 12, 15, 17, 18, 20, 23, 24, •••	Have even Hamming weight Hw(n)
Odious numbers	1, 2, 4, 7, 8, 11, 13, 14, 16, 19, 21, 22, 25, •••	Have odd Hamming weight Hw(n)
Primitive odious numbers	1, 7, 11, 13, 19, 21, 25, 31, 35, 37, 41, 47, •••	They are both odd and odious
Pernicious numbers	3, 5, 6, 7, 9, 10, 11, 12, 13, 14, 17, 18, 19, •••	Their Hamming weights Hw(n) are prime.
Sequences _related to powers_		
Narcissistic | **Armstrong** | Plus perfect numbers	1,2,3,4,5,6,7,8,9, 153, 370, 371, 470, •••	n-digit numbers equal to the sum of n-th powers of their digits
Powers of 2	1, 2, 4, 8, 16, 32, 64, 128, 256, 512, 1024, •••	Also 2-smooth numbers
Perfect powers without duplications	4, 8, 9, 16, 25, 27, 32, 36, 49, 64, 81, 100, •••	Includes any number of the form a^b with a,b > 1
Perfect powers with duplications	4, 8, 9, 16, 16, 25, 27, 32, 36, 49, 64, 64, •••	Repeated entries can be obtained in different ways
Perfect squares	0, 1, 4, 9, 16, 25, 36, 49, 64, 81, 100, 121, •••	Same as _figurate polygonal square numbers_
Perfect cubes	0, 1, 8, 27, 64, 125, 216, 343, 512, 729, •••	Same as _figurate polyhedral cubic numbers_
Taxicab numbers Ta(n); only six are known	2, 1729, 87539319, 6963472309248, •••	Smallest number equal to a^3+b^3 for n distinct pairs (a,b).
Sequences _related to divisors_. For functions like σ(n) and s(n) = σ(n)-n, see above.		
Abundant numbers	12, 18, 20, 24, 30, 36, 40, 42, 48, 54, 56, •••	Sum of proper divisors of n exceeds n: s(n) > n

Primitive abundant numbers	20, 70, 88, 104, 272, 304, 368, 464, 550, •••	All their proper divisors are deficient
odd abundant numbers	945, 1575, 2205, 2835, 3465, 4095, •••	Funny that the smallest one is so large
odd abundant numbers not divisible by 3	5391411025, 26957055125, •••	
Composite numbers	4, 8, 9, 10, 14, 15, 16, 18, 20, 21, 22, 24, •••	Have a proper divisor d > 1
highly composite numbers	1, 2, 4, 6, 12, 24, 36, 48, 60, 120, 180, •••	n has more divisors than any smaller number
Cubefree numbers	1, 2, 3, 4, 5, 6, 7, 9, 10, 11, 12, 13, 14, 15, •••	Not divisible by any *perfect cube*.
Deficient numbers	1, 2, 3, 4, 5, 7, 8, 9, 10, 11, 13, 14, 15, 16, •••	Sum of proper divisors of n is smaller than n: $s(n) < n$
Even numbers	0, 2, 4, 6, 8, 10, 12, 14, 16, 18, 20, 22, 24, •••	Divisible by 2
Odd numbers	1, 3, 5, 7, 9, 11, 13, 15, 17, 19, 21, 23, 25, •••	Not divisible by 2
Perfect numbers	6, 28, 496, 8128, 33550336, 8589869056, •••	Solutions of $s(n) = n$
semiperfect / pseudoperfect numbers	6, 12, 18, 20, 24, 28, 30, 36, 40, 42, 48, •••	n equals the sum of a subset of its divisors
primitive / irreducible semiperfect numbers	6, 20, 28, 88, 104, 272, 304, 350, 368, •••	Semiperfect with no proper semiperfect divisor
quasiperfect numbers	Not a single one was found so far!	Such that $s(n) = n+1$ or, equivalently, $\sigma(n) = 2n+1$
superperfect numbers	2, 4, 16, 64, 4096, 65536, 262144, •••	Solutions of $n = \sigma(\sigma(n)) - n$

Practical numbers	1, 2, 4, 6, 8, 12, 16, 18, 20, 24, 28, 30, 32, •••	Any smaller number is a sum of distinct divisors of n
Squarefree numbers	1, 2, 3, 5, 6, 7, 10, 11, 13, 14, 15, 17, 19, •••	Not divisible by any *perfect square*. Equivalent to $\mu(n) \neq 0$
Untouchable numbers	2, 5, 52, 88, 96, 120, 124, 146, 162, 188, •••	They are not the sum of proper divisors of ANY number
Weird numbers	70, 836, 4030, 5830, 7192, 7912, 9272, •••	Abundant, but not semiperfect

Sequences **related to the** <u>aliquot sequence</u> **As**(n), $As_0 = n$, $As_{k+1} = s(As_k)$, *other than **perfect numbers** whose aliquot sequence repeats the number itself:*

Amicable number pairs (n,m)	(220,284); (1184,1210); (2620,2924); •••	m = s(n), n = s(m); As(n) is a cycle of two elements
Aspiring numbers	25, 95, 119, 143, (276? *maybe!*), •••	n is not perfect, but As(n) eventually reaches a perfect number.
Lehmer five numbers	276, 552, 564, 660, 966	First five n whose As(n) **might** be totally a-periodic.
Sociable numbers	12496, 14316, 1264460, 2115324, •••	As(n) is a cycle of C > 2 elements;

Sequences **related to prime numbers** and **prime factorizations**

Achilles numbers	72, 108, 200, 288, 392, 432, 500, 648, •••	Powerful, but not perfect.
Carmichael's pseudoprimes (or **Knödel** C_1)	561, 1105, 1729, 2465, 2821, 6601, •••	Composite n such that $a^{n-1}=1 \pmod n$ for any coprime a<n
D-numbers (**Knödel numbers** C_k for k=3)	9, 15, 21, 33, 39, 51, 57, 63, 69, 87, 93, •••	Composite n such that $a^{n-k}=1 \pmod n$ for any coprime a<n
Euler's pseudoprimes in	341, 561, 1105, 1729, 1905, 2047,	Composite odd n such that $2^{(n-1)/2} = \pm 1 \pmod n$

base 2	2465, •••	
Isolated (single) numbers	2, 4, 6, 12, 18, 23, 30, 37, 42, 47, 53, 60, •••	Either an isolated prime or the mean of twin primes.
Mersenne primes (p = 2,3,5,7,13,17,19,...)	3, 7, 31, 127, 8191, 131071, 524287, •••	Some $M(p) = 2^p-1$; p prime; <u>Largest known</u> M(74207281)
<u>Powerful numbers</u> (also **squareful** or **2-full**)	1, 4, 8, 9, 16, 25, 27, 32, 36, 49, 64, 72, •••	Divisible by the squares of all their prime factors.
<u>3-full numbers</u> (also **cubeful**)	1, 8, 16, 27, 32, 64, 81, 125, 128, 216, •••	Divisible by the cubes of all their prime factors.
<u>Prime twins</u> (starting element)	3, 5, 11, 17, 29, 41, 59, 71, 101, 107, •••	For each prime p in this list, p+2 is also a prime
<u>Prime cousins</u> (starting element)	3, 7, 13, 19, 37, 43, 67, 79, 97, 103, 109, •••	For each prime p in this list, p+4 is also a prime
<u>Prime triples</u> (starting element)	5, 11, 17, 41, 101, 107, 191, 227, 311, •••	For each prime p in this list, p+2 and p+6 are also primes
<u>Prime quadruples</u> (starting element)	5, 11, 101, 191, 821, 1481, 1871, 2081, •••	For each prime p in this list, p+2, p+6, p+8 are also primes
<u>Primorial</u> numbers prime(n)#	1, 2, 6, 30, 210, 2310, 30030, 510510, •••	Product of first n primes
<u>Pseudoprimes</u> to base 2 (**Sarrus numbers**)	341, 561, 645, 1105, 1387, 1729, 1905, •••	Composite odd n such that $2^{n-1} = 1 \pmod n$
<u>Pseudoprimes</u> to base 3	91, 121, 286, 671, 703, 949, 1105, 1541, •••	Composite odd n such that $3^{n-1} = 1 \pmod n$
<u>Semiprimes</u> (also **biprimes**	4, 6, 9, 10, 14, 15, 21, 22, 25, 26, 33, 34, ••	Products of two primes.
<u>3-smooth number</u>	1, 2, 3, 4, 6, 8, 9, 12, 16, 18, 24, 27,	b-smooth numbers: not divisible by any prime p

	32, ••	> b
Pierpont primes	2, 3, 5, 7, 13, 17, 19, 37, 73, 97, 109, 163, •••	Primes p such that p-1 is 3-smooth
Thabit primes (so far, 62 are known)	2, 5, 11, 23, 47, 95, 191, 383, 6143, •••	Thabit number 3.2^n-1 which are also prime
Wieferich primes	1093, 3511, ••• (next, if any, is > 4.9e17)	Primes p such that $2^{(p-1)}-1$ is divisible by p^2
Wilson primes	5, 13, 563, ••• (next, if any, is > 2e13)	Primes p such that ((p-1)!+1)/p is divisible by p
Wolstenholme primes	16843, 2124679, ••• (next, if any, is > 1e9)	Primes p such that C(2p,p)-2 is divisible by p^4
*Sequences **related to partitions** and **compositions***		
<u>Polite numbers</u> | *staircase* numbers	3, 5, 6, 7, 9, 10, 11, 12, 13, 14, 15, 17, 18, •••	Can be written as sum of two or more consecutive numbers.
<u>Politeness of a number</u>	0, 0, 1, 0, 1, 1, 1, 0, 2, 1, 1, 1, 1, 1, 3, 0, •••	Number of ways to write n as a sum of consecutive numbers.
Some named | notable binary sequences of "digits" {0,1} or {-1,+1}. An important case is defined by the **Liouville function.**		
Baum - Sweet sequence	1,1,0,1,1,0,0,1,0,1,0,0,1,0,0,1,1,0,0 •••	1 if binary(n) contains no block of 0's of odd length
Fredholm-Rueppel sequence	1,1,0,1,0,0,0,1,0,0,0,0,0,0,0,1,0,0,0, •••	1 at positions 2^k. Binary exp. of **Kempner-Mahler** number
Fibonacci words; binary:	0, 01, 01 0, 010 01, 01001 010, ...	Like Fibonacci recurrence, using string concatenation
<u>Infinite **Fibonacci** word</u>	0100101001001010010010 •••	Infinite continuation of the above
<u>Rabbit sequence;</u>	1, 10, 10 1, 101 10, 10110 101, •••	Similar, but with different starting strings

binary:		
Rabbit number; binary:	.1101011011010110101 •••	Converted to decimal, gives the rabbit constant
Jeffrey's sequence	10110000111111110000000000000 •••	Does not have any limit mean density of 1's
Golay - Rudin - Shapiro sequence	+1,+1,+1,-1,+1,+1,-1,+1,+1,+1,+1,-1 •••	$b(n)=(-1)^{\wedge}S_k\{n_k n_{k+1}\}$, with n_i denoting the i-th binary digit of n
Thue - Morse sequence t_n	0,1,1,0,1,0,0,1,1,0,0,1,0,1,1,0,1,0,0 •••	$t_n = 1$ if binary(n) has odd parity (number of ones)

Combinatorial numbers such as Pascal-Tartaglia triangle binomials, Stirling, Lah and Franel numbers

Binomial coefficients $C(n,m) = n!/(m!(n-m)!)$ (ways to pick m among n labeled elements); C(n,m)=0 if m<0 or m>n; C(n,0)=1; C(n,1)=n; C(n,m)=C(n,n-m):

m = 2, n = 4,5,6,...	6, 10, 15, 21, 28, 36, 45, 55, 66, 78, 91, •••	n(n-1)/2; shifted triangular numbers
m = 3, n = 6,7,8,...	20, 35, 56, 84, 120, 165, 220, 286, 364, •••	n(n-1)(n-2)/3!; shifted tetrahedral numbers
m = 4, n = 8,9,10,...	70, 126, 210, 330, 495, 715, 1001, 1365, •••	n(n-1)(n-2)(n-3)/4!; for n < 2m, use C(n,n-m)
m = 5, n = 10,11,12...	252, 462, 792, 1287, 2002, 3003, 4368, •••	n(n-1)(n-2)(n-3)(n-4)/5!
m = 6, n = 12,13,14,...	924, 1716, 3003, 5005, 8008, 12376, •••	$n(n-1)(n-2)(n-3)(n-4)(n-5)/6! = n^{(6)}/6!$
m = 7, n = 14,15,16...	3432, 6435, 11440, 19448, 31824, •••	$n^{(7)}/7!$ Use C(n,m)=C(n,n-m) to cover all cases up to n=14
Central binomial coefficients $C(2n,n) = (2n)!/n!^2$	1, 2, 6, 20, 70, 252, 924, 3432, 12870, •••	$C(2n,n) = S_{k=0,n}\{C^2(n,k)\}$: **Franel** number of order 2

Entringer numbers E(n,k), k = 0,1,...,n (triangle)	1; 0,1; 0,1,1; 0,1,2,2; 0,2,4,5,5; •••	Counts of particular types of permutations
Euler zig-zag numbers A(n)	1, 1, 1, 2, 5, 16, 61, 272, 1385, 7936, •••	$\equiv$ alternating permutation numbers. E.g.f: $\tan(z/2+\pi/4)$
Franel numbers of order 3	1, 2, 10, 56, 346, 2252, 15184, 104960, •••	$S_{k=0,n}\{C^3(n,k)\}$
Lah numbers L(n,m) (unsigned); signed $L(n,m) = (-1)^n L(n,m)$; They expand rising factorials in terms of falling factorials and vice versa. L(n,1) = n!		
m = 2, n = 2,3,4,...	1, 6, 36, 240, 1800, 15120, 141120, •••	
m = 3, n = 3,4,5,...	1, 12, 120, 1200, 12600, 141120, •••	General formula: L(n,m)=C(n,m)(n-1)!/(m-1)!
m = 4, n = 4,5,6,...	1, 20, 300, 4200, 58800, 846720, •••	
Stirling numbers of the first kind c(n,m), unsigned; signed $s(n,m) = (-1)^{n-m}c(n,m)$; number of permutations of n distinct elements with m cycles. s(n,0) = 1.		
m = 1, n = 1,2,3,...	1, 1, 2, 6, 24, 120, 720, 5040, 40320, •••	(n-1)!
m = 2, n = 2,3,4,...	1, 3, 11, 50, 274, 1764, 13068, 109584, •••	a(n+1)=n*a(n)+(n-1)!
m = 3, n = 3,4,5,...	1, 6, 35, 225, 1624, 13132, 118124, •••	
m = 4, n = 4,5,6,...	1, 10, 85, 735, 6769, 67284, 723680, •••	A definition of s(n,m):
m = 5, n = 5,6,7,...	1, 15, 175, 1960, 22449, 269325, •••	$x^{(n)} = x(x-1)(x-2)...(x-(n-1)) = S_{m=0,n}\{s(n,m).x^m\}$
m = 6, n = 6,7,8,...	1, 21, 322, 4536, 63273, 902055, •••	See also OEIS

m = 7, n = 7,8,9,...	1, 28, 546, 9450, 157773, 2637558, •••	
m = 8, n = 8,9,10,...	1, 36, 870, 18150, 357423, 6926634, •••	
m = 9, n = 9,10,11,...	1, 45, 1320, 32670, 749463, 16669653, •••	

Stirling numbers of the second kind $S(n,m)$; number of partitions of n distinct elements into m non-empty subsets. $S(n,1) = 1$. By convention, $S(0,0) = 1$.

m = 2, n = 2,3,4,...	1, 3, 7, 15, 31, 63, 127, 255, 511, 1023, •••	$2^{(n-1)}-1$
m = 3, n = 3,4,5,...	1, 6, 25, 90, 301, 966, 3025, 9330, •••	
m = 4, n = 4,5,6,...	1, 10, 65, 350, 1701, 7770, 34105, •••	A definition of $S(n,m)$:
m = 5, n = 5,6,7,...	1, 15, 140, 1050, 6951, 42525, 246730, •••	$x^n = \mathbf{S}_{m=0,n}\{S(n,m).x^{(m)}\}$
m = 6, n = 6,7,8,...	1, 21, 266, 2646, 22827, 179487, •••	
m = 7, n = 7,8,9,...	1, 28, 462, 5880, 63987, 627396, •••	
m = 8, n = 8,9,10,...	1, 36, 750, 11880, 159027, 1899612, •••	
m = 9, n = 9,10,11,...	1, 45, 1155, 22275, 359502, 5135130, •••	

Counting (enumeration) sequences relevant to finite sets

| Subsets (cardinality of the | 1, 2, 4, 8, 16, 32, 64, 128, 256, 512, | 2^n; also mappings into a binary set |

power set)	1024, •••	
Derangements (subfactorials) !n	1, 0, 1, 2, 9, 44, 265, 1854, 14833, •••	$n!*S_{k=0,n}\{(-1)^k/k!\}$ Permutations leaving no element in-place
Endomorphisms	1, 1, 4, 27, 256, 3125, 46656, 823543, •••	n^n. Operators, mappings (functions) of a set into itself
Binary relations | Digraphs with self-loops	1, 2, 16, 512, 65536, 33554432, •••	$2^{\wedge}(n^2)$. This counts also *no relation*
Reflexive relations | Irreflexive relations	1, 1, 4, 64, 4096, 1048576, 1073741824, •••	$2^{\wedge}(n*(n-1))$. The two types have the same count
Symmetric relations	1, 2, 8, 64, 1024, 32768, 2097152, •••	$2^{\wedge}(n*(n+1)/2)$. Any self loop is optional
Symmetric & Reflexive relations	1, 1, 2, 8, 64, 1024, 32768, 2097152, •••	$2^{\wedge}(n*(n-1)/2)$. Also Symmetric & Irreflexive
Transitive relations	1, 2, 13, 171, 3994, 154303, 9415189, •••	
Preorder relations (quasi-orderings)	1, 1, 4, 29, 355, 6942, 209527, 9535241, •••	Transitive & Reflexive
Partial-order relations (posets)	1, 1, 3, 19, 219, 4231, 130023, 6129859, •••	
Total-preorder rels | Weakly ordered partitions	1, 1, 3, 13, 75, 541, 4683,47293,545835, •••	**Ordered Bell numbers**, or **Fubini numbers**
Total-order relations | Bijections	1, 1, 2, 6, 24, 120, 720, 5040, 40320, •••	n! Also **permutations** | *orders of symmetry groups* S_n
Equivalence relations | Set partitions	1, 1, 2, 5, 15, 52, 203, 877, 4140, 21147, •••	**Bell numbers** B(n)
Groupoids | Closed Binary	1, 1, 16, 19683, 4294967296, •••	$n^{\wedge}n^2 = (n^{\wedge}n)^n$

Operations (CBOs)		
Abelian groupoids	1, 1, 8, 729, 1048576, 30517578125, •••	Commutative CBOs. n^(n(n+1)/2)
Non-associative Abelian groupoids	0, 0, 2 , 666, 1047436, •••	Commutative but non-associative CBOs.
Non-associative non-Abelian groupoids	0, 0, 6, 18904, 4293916368, •••	Non-commutative & non-associative CBOs.
Semigroups	1, 1, 8, 113, 3492, 183732, 17061118, •••	Associative CBOs
Non-Abelian semigroups	0, 0, 2, 50, 2352, 153002, 15876046, •••	Associative but non-commutative CBOs
Abelian semigroups	1, 1, 6, 63, 1140, 30730, 1185072, •••	Associative and commutative CBOs
Monoids	0, 1, 4, 33, 624, 20610, 1252032, •••	Associative CBOs with an identity element
Non-Abelian monoids	0, 0, 0, 6, 248, 13180, 1018692, ...	Associative but non-commutative CBOs with identity
Abelian monoids	0, 1, 4, 27, 376, 7430, 233340, •••	Associative & commutative CBOs with identity element
Groups	0, 1, 2, 3, 16, 30, 480, 840, 22080, 68040, •••	Associative CBOs with identity and invertible elements
Abelian groups (commutative)	0, 1, 2, 3, 16, 30, 360, 840, 15360, 68040, •••	
Non-Abelian groups	0, 0, 0, 0, 0, 0, 120, 0, 6720, 0, 181440, 0, ...	Difference of the previous two
The following items in this section count the **isomorphism classes** of the specified objects on n labeled nodes		
Binary relations	1, 2, 10, 104, 3044, 291968,	This counts also *no relation*

	96928992, •••	

*Enumerations of **set-related** objects, assuming **unlabeled elements** (counting **types of objects**). Set size | order is n=0,1,2,..., unless specified otherwise.*

Compositions c(n)	1, 1, 2, 4, 8, 16, 32, 64, 128, 256, 512, •••	For n>0, c(n)=2^(n-1)
Partitions p(n)	1, 1, 2, 3, 5, 7, 11, 15, 22, 30, 42, 56, 77, •••	
Partitions into distinct parts (strict partitions)	1, 1, 1, 2, 2, 3, 4, 5, 6, 8, 10, 12, 15, 18, •••	Also *Partitions into odd parts*

The following items in this section count the **isomorphism classes** of the specified objects on n unlabeled nodes

Binary relations	1, 1, 5, 52, 1522, 145984, 48464496, •••	This counts also *'no relation'*
Groupoids (more data are needed!)	1, 1, 10, 3330, 178981952, •••	Closed Binary Operations (CBOs)
Abelian groupoids	1, 1, 4, 129, 43968, 254429900, •••	Commutative CBOs
Non-associative Abelian groupoids	0, 0, 1, 117, 43910, •••	Commutative but non-associative CBOs
Non-associative non-Abelian groupoids	0, 0, 4, 3189, 178937854, •••	Non-commutative non-associative CBOs
Semigroups	1, 1, 5, 24, 188, 1915, 28634, 1627672, •••	Associative CBOs
Non-Abelian semigroups	0, 0, 2, 12, 130, 1590, 26491, 1610381, •••	Associative but non-commutative CBOs
Abelian semigroups	1, 1, 3, 12, 58, 325, 2143, 17291, 221805, •••	Associative & commutative CBOs

Monoids	0, 1, 2, 7, 35, 228, 2237, 31559, 1668997 •••	Associative CBOs with identity element
Non-Abelian monoids	0, 0, 0, 2, 16, 150, 1816, 28922, ...	Associative but non-commutative CBOs with identity
Abelian monoids	0, 1, 2, 5, 19, 78, 421, 2637, •••	Associative & commutative CBOs with identity
Groups	0, 1, 1, 1, 2, 1, 2, 1, 5, 2, 2, 1, 5, 1, 2, 1, 14, •••	Associative CBOs with identity and inverses
Abelian groups (commutative)	0, 1, 1, 1, 2, 1, 1, 1, 3, 2, 1, 1, 2, 1, 1, 1, 5, 1, •••	Factorizations of n into prime powers
Non-Abelian groups	0, 0, 0, 0, 0, 0, 1, 0, 2, 0, 1, 0, 3, 0, 1, 0, 9, •••	

Counting (enumeration) sequences relevant to finite graphs

*Enumerations of **graph-related** objects, assuming **labeled vertices**. Number of vertices is n=1,2,3,..., unless specified otherwise.*

Simple graphs with n vertices	1, 2, 8, 64, 1024, 32768, 2097152, •••	$2^{n(n-1)/2}$
Free trees with n vertices	1, 1, 3, 16, 125, 1296, 16807, 262144, •••	n^{n-2} (Cayley formula)
Rooted trees with n vertices	1, 2, 9, 64, 625, 7776, 117649, 2097152, •••	n^{n-1}

*Enumerations of **graph-related** objects, assuming **unlabeled vertices** (i.e., counting **types of objects**). Number of vertices is n=1,2,3,..., unless specified otherwise.*

Simple connected graphs with n vertices	1, 1, 2, 6, 21, 112, 853, 11117, 261080, •••	isomorphism classes
Free trees with n vertices	1, 1, 1, 2, 3, 6, 11, 23, 47, 106, 235,	isomorphism classes

	551, •••	
Rooted trees with n vertices	1, 2, 4, 9, 20, 48, 115, 286, 719, 1842, •••	isomorphism classes

Selected sequences of rational numbers

Bernoulli *numbers* $B_0 = 1$, $B_1 = -1/2$, $B_{2k+1} = 0$ for $k>1$, $B_n = \delta_{n,0} - S_{k=0,(n-1)}\{C(n,k)B_k/(n-k+1)\}$; $x/(e^x-1) = S_{k\geq0}\{B_n x^n/n!\}$; *Example:* $B_{10} = 5/66$

$B_n = N/D$; $n = 2,4,6,...$	N: 1, -1, 1, -1, 5, -691, 7, -3617, 43867, •••	D: 6, 30, 42, 30, 66, 2730, 6, 510, 798, •••

Harmonic *numbers* $H_n = S_{k=1,n}\{1/k\}$, *in reduced form. Example:* $H_5 = 137/60$.

$H_n = N/D$; $n = 1,2,3,...$	N: 1, 3, 11, 25, 137, 49, 363, 761, 7129, •••	D: 1, 2, 6, 12, 60, 20, 140, 280, 2520, •••

Other:

Rationals ≤1, sorted by denominator/numerator	$^1/_1$, $^1/_2$, $^1/_3$, $^2/_3$, $^1/_4$, $^3/_4$, $^1/_5$, $^2/_5$, $^3/_5$, $^4/_5$, $^1/_6$, •••	Take the inverse values for rationals ≥ 1
Farey fractions F_n (example for order n=5)	$^0/_1$, $^1/_5$, $^1/_4$, $^1/_3$, $^2/_5$, $^1/_2$, $^3/_5$, $^2/_3$, $^3/_4$, $^4/_5$, $^1/_1$, ...	$F_1=\{ ^0/_1, ^1/_1 \}$; higher n: interpolate ($^a/_c, ^b/_d$) → $^{a+b}/_{c+d}$
Stern - Brocot sequence (example n=4)	$^1/_1$, $^1/_2$, $^2/_1$, $^1/_3$, $^2/_3$, $^3/_2$, $^3/_1$, $^1/_4$, $^2/_5$, $^3/_5$, $^3/_4$, ...	Wraps up the binary **Stern - Brocot tree**

Some Diophantine solutions and their sequences, such as those related to compositions of powers

Pythagorean triples (a,b,c), $a^2 + b^2 = c^2$	(3,4,5) (5,12,13) (7,24,25) (8,15,17)	(9,40,41) (11,60,61) (12,35,37) (13,84,85) (16,63,65) •••
Pythagorean quadruples, $a^2 + b^2 + c^2 = d^2$	(1,2,2,3) (2,3,6,7) (4,4,7,9) (1,4,8,9)	(6,6,7,11) (2,6,9,11) (10,10,23,27) (7,14,22,23) ...

Pythagorean quintuples	(1,2,4,10,11) (1,2,8,10,13) ...	etc; there is an infinity of them in each category
Markov triples, $x^2 + y^2 + z^2 = 3xyz$	(1,1,1) (1,1,2) (1,2,5) (1,5,13) (2,5,29)	(1,13,34) (1,34,89) (2,29,169) (5,13,194) (1,89,233) ...
Brown number pairs (m,n), $n!+1 = m^2$	(5, 4) (11, 5) (71, 7)	Erdös conjectured that there are no others

Selected sequences of Figurate Numbers (formulas are adjusted so that n=1 gives always 1)

<table>
<tr><td colspan="3" style="background:#fbfbdf">Polygonal (2D). See also <u>A090466</u> (numbers which are polygonal) and <u>A090467</u> (numbers which are not).</td></tr>
<tr><td><u>Triangular numbers</u> T_n</td><td>1, 3, 6, 10, 15, 21, 28, 36, 45, 55, 66, •••</td><td>n(n+1)/2</td></tr>
<tr><td><u>Square numbers</u>, squares</td><td>1, 4, 9, 16, 25, 36, 49, 64, 81, 100, 121, •••</td><td>n*n</td></tr>
<tr><td><u>Pentagonal numbers</u></td><td>1, 5, 12, 22, 35, 51, 70, 92, 117, 145, •••</td><td>n(3n-1)/2</td></tr>
<tr><td><u>Hexagonal numbers</u></td><td>1, 6, 15, 28, 45, 66, 91, 120, 153, 190, •••</td><td>n(2n-1); also cornered hexagonal numbers</td></tr>
<tr><td><u>Heptagonal numbers</u></td><td>1, 7, 18, 34, 55, 81, 112, 148, 189, 235, •••</td><td>n(5n-3)/2</td></tr>
<tr><td><u>Octagonal numbers</u></td><td>1, 8, 21, 40, 65, 96, 133, 176, 225, 280, •••</td><td>n(3n-2)</td></tr>
<tr><td><u>Square-triangular numbers</u></td><td>1,   36,   1225, 41616,1413721,48024900, •••</td><td>$[[(3+2\sqrt2)^n-(3-2\sqrt2)^n]/(4\sqrt2)]^2$; both triangular and square</td></tr>
</table>

<table>
<tr><td colspan="3" style="background:#fbfbdf">Pyramidal (2D). $P_n^{(r)} = n(n+1)[n(r-2)+(5-r)]/6$ for r-gonal base = partial sum of r-gonal numbers. For r=3, see tetrahedral numbers Te_n (below)</td></tr>
<tr><td><u>Square</u>   pyramidal</td><td>1, 5, 14, 30, 55, 91, 140, 204, 285,</td><td>n(n+1)(2n+1)/6. The only ones that are squares:</td></tr>
</table>

numbers, r=4	385, •••	1, 4900
Pentagonal pyramidal numbers, r=5	1, 6, 18, 40, 75, 126, 196, 288, 405, 550, •••	$n^2(n+1)/2$
Hexagonal pyramidal numbers, r=6	1, 7, 22, 50, 95, 161, 252, 372, 525, 715, •••	$n(n+1)(4n-1)/6$. Also called **greengrocer's numbers**
Heptagonal pyramidal numbers, r=7	1, 8, 26, 60, 115, 196, 308, 456, 645, 880, •••	$n(n+1)(5n-2)/6$
Octagonal pyramidal numbers r=8	1, 9, 30, 70, 135, 231, 364, 540, 765, 1045, •••	$n(n+1)(5n-2)/6$
Polyhedral *(3D)*		
Tetrahedral numbers Te_n (pyramidal with r=3)	1, 4, 10, 20, 35, 56, 84, 120, 165, 220, •••	$n(n+1)(n+2)/6$. The only Te_n squares: 1, 4, 19600
C++ubic numbers, cubes	1, 8, 27, 64, 125, 216, 343, 512, 729, •••	n^3
Octahedral numbers	1, 6, 19, 44, 85, 146, 231, 344, 489, 670, •••	$n(2n^2+1)/3$.
Icosahedral numbers	1, 12, 48, 124, 255, 456, 742, 1128, •••	$n(5n^2-5n+2)/2$.
Dodecahedral numbers	1, 20, 84, 220, 455, 816, 1330, 2024, •••	$n(3n-1)(3n-2)/2$.
Platonic numbers	1, 4, 6, 8, 10, 12, 19, 20, 27, 35, 44, 48, •••	Union of the above sequences.
Pentatopic (or pentachoron) numbers	1, 5, 15, 35, 70, 126, 210, 330, 495, •••	$n(n+1)(n+2)(n+3)/24$
Centered polygonal *(2D)*		

Centered triangular numbers	1, 4, 10, 19, 31, 46, 64, 85, 109, 136, •••	$(3n^2-3n+2)/2$. Click for the primes subset: •••
Centered square numbers	1, 5, 13, 25, 41, 61, 85, 113, 145, 181, •••	$2n^2-2n+1$. Click for the primes subset: •••
Centered pentagonal numbers	1, 6, 16, 31, 51, 76, 106, 141, 181, 226, •••	$(5n^2-5n+2)/2$. Click for the primes subset: •••
Centered hexagonal numbers	1, 7, 19, 37, 61, 91, 127, 169, 217, 271, •••	$n^3 - (n-1)^3 = 3n(n-1)+1$; also **hex numbers**
Centered heptagonal numbers	1, 8, 22, 43, 71, 106, 148, 197, 253, •••	$(7n^2-7n+2)/2$
Centered octagonal numbers	1, 9, 25, 49, 81, 121, 169, 225, 289, •••	$(2n-1)^2$; squares of odd numbers

***Centered polyhedral** (3D)*

Centered tetrahedral numbers	1, 5, 15, 35, 69, 121, 195, 295, 425, 589, •••	$(2n+1)(n^2-n+3)/3$
Centered cube numbers	1, 9, 35, 91, 189, 341, 559, 855, 1241, •••	$(2n-1)(n^2-n+1)$
Centered octahedral numbers	1, 7, 25, 63, 129, 231, 377, 575, 833, •••	$(2n-1)(2n^2-2n+3)/3$

Selected geometry constants

Named and various notable geometry constants

Area doubling (Pythagora's) constant	1.414 213 562 373 095 048 801 688 •••	$\sqrt{2}$. Area-doubling **scale factor**
Area tripling (Theodorus's) constant	1.732 050 807 568 877 293 527 446 •••	$\sqrt{3}$. Area-tripling **scale factor**

Volume doubling (Delos) constant	1.259 921 049 894 873 164 767 210 •••	$2^{1/3}$. Volume-doubling **scale factor**
Volume tripling constant	1.442 249 570 307 408 382 321 638 •••	$3^{1/3}$. Volume-tripling **scale factor**
Minimum area of a constant-width figure	0.704 770 923 010 457 972 467 598 •••	(pi - sqrt(3))/2 for width = 1. See Reuleaux triangle
Moser's worm constant	0.232 239 210 ••• ?	Area of smallest region accomodating any curve of length 1
Square-drill constant	0.987 700 390 736 053 460 131 999 •••	Portion of square area covered by a *Reuleaux drill*
Universal parabolic constant, log(1+√2)+√2	2.295 587 149 392 638 074 034 298 ••• #t	= asinh(1)+√2. Arc-to-latus_rectum ratio in any parabola.
Gravitoid constant	1.240 806 478 802 799 465 254 958 •••	$2\sqrt{(2/(3\sqrt{3}))}$. Width/Depth of **gravitoid curve** or **gravidome**
Notable plane angles *in radians and degrees*		
Magic angle φ = acos(1/√3) = atan(√2)$_m$	0.955 316 618 124 509 278 163 857 •••	Degrees: 54.735 610 317 245 345 684 622 999 •••
Complementary magic angle φ'$_m$ = π/2 - φ$_m$	0.615 479 708 670 387 341 067 464 •••	Degrees: 35.264 389 682 754 654 315 377 000 ...
Tetrahedral angle θ$_m$ = 2φ = π - acos(1/3)$_m$	1.910 633 236 249 018 556 327 714 •••	Degrees: 109.471 220 634 490 691 369 245 999 •••
Complemetary tetrahedral angle θ'$_m$ = π - θ$_m$	1.230 959 417 340 774 682 134 929 •••	Degrees: 70.528 779 365 509 308 630 754 000 ...
Notable solid angles *in steradians*		
Square on a sphere with	0.927 689 475 322 313 640 795 613	4*asin(sin(1/2)^2)

sides of 1 radian	•••	
Square on a sphere with sides of 1 degree	3.046 096 875 119 366 637 825 ••• e-4	$\underline{4\,\text{asin}(\sin(\alpha/2)\sin(\beta/2))}$; $\alpha = \beta = 1$ degree $= \pi/180$
Spherical triangle with sides of 1 radian	0.495 594 895 733 964 750 698 857 •••	See Huilier's formula
Spherical triangle with sides of 1 degree	1.319 082 346 912 923 487 761 ... e-4	See Huilier's formula

Sphere and hyper-spheres in n = 2, 3, 4, ..., 10 Euclidean dimensions

2D-Disk | Circle.

Area / Radius^2 = V(2) = π	3.141 592 653 589 793 238 462 643 ••• #t	Area of a disk with unit radius
Radius / Area$^{1/2}$ = Rv(2) = $1/\sqrt{\pi}$	0.564 189 583 547 756 286 948 079 •••	Radius of a sphere with unit area
Circumference / Radius^2 = S(2) = 2π	6.283 185 307 179 586 476 925 286 •••	
Radius / Circumference = Rs(2) = $1/(2\pi)$	0.159 154 943 091 895 335 768 883 •••	Radius of a disk with unit circumference

3D-Sphere, the Queen of all bodies.

Volume / Radius^3 = V(3) = $4\pi/3$	4.188 790 204 786 390 984 616 857 •••	Volume of a sphere with unit radius
Radius / Volume$^{1/3}$ = Rv(3) = $(3/(4\pi))^{1/3}$	0.620 350 490 899 400 016 668 006 •••	Radius of a sphere with unit volume
Surface / Radius^2 = S(3) = 4π	12.566 370 614 359 172 953 850 573 •••	See also surface indices.
Radius / Surface$^{1/2}$ =	0.282 094 791 773 878 143 474 039	Radius of a sphere with unit surface

$Rs(3) = 1/(4\pi)^{1/2}$	•••	

nD-<u>Hyperspheres</u> in n>3 dimensions (see disk and sphere for n≤3): $V(n) = $ <u>Volume</u>$/Radius^n$ and $Rv(n) = Radius/Volume^{1/n} = 1/ V(n)^{1/n}$.

$V(4) = \pi^2/2$	4.934 802 200 544 679 309 417 245 •••	$Rv(4) = 0.670\ 938\ 266\ 965\ 413\ 916\ 222\ 789\ ...$
$V(5) = 8\pi^2/15$, the largest of them all	5.263 789 013 914 324 596 711 728 •••	$Rv(5) = 0.717\ 365\ 200\ 794\ 964\ 260\ 816\ 144\ ...$
$V(6) = \pi^3/6$	5.167 712 780 049 970 029 246 052 •••	$Rv(6) = 0.760\ 531\ 030\ 982\ 050\ 466\ 116\ 446\ ...$
$V(7) = 16\pi^3/105$	4.724 765 970 331 401 169 596 390 •••	$Rv(7) = 0.801\ 050\ 612\ 642\ 752\ 206\ 249\ 327\ ...$
$V(8) = \pi^4/24$	4.058 712 126 416 768 218 185 013 •••	$Rv(8) = 0.839\ 366\ 184\ 571\ 988\ 024\ 335\ 065\ ...$
$V(9) = 32\pi^4/945$	3.298 508 902 738 706 869 382 106 ...	$Rv(9) = 0.875\ 808\ 485\ 845\ 386\ 610\ 603\ 654\ ...$
$V(10) = \pi^5/120$	2.550 164 039 877 345 443 856 177 ...	$Rv(10) = 0.910\ 632\ 588\ 621\ 402\ 549\ 723\ 631\ ...$

nD-<u>Hyperspheres</u> in n>3 dimensions (see disk and sphere for n≤3): $S(n) = $ <u>Surface</u>$/Radius^{(n-1)}$ and $Rs(n) = Radius/Surface^{1/(n-1)} = 1/S(n)^{1/(n-1)}$.

$S(4) = 2\pi^2$	19.739 208 802 178 717 237 668 981 •••	$Rs(4) = 0.370\ 018\ 484\ 153\ 678\ 110\ 702\ 808\ ...$
$S(5) = 8\pi^2/3$	26.318 945 069 571 622 983 558 642 •••	$Rs(5) = 0.441\ 502\ 208\ 724\ 281\ 499\ 461\ 813\ ...$
$S(6) = \pi^3$	31.006 276 680 299 820 175 476 315 •••	$Rs(6) = 0.503\ 164\ 597\ 143\ 259\ 315\ 750\ 866\ ...$
$S(7) = 16\pi^3/15$, the	33.073 361 792 319 808 187 174 736	$Rs(7) = 0.558\ 153\ 445\ 139\ 655\ 576\ 810\ 770\ ...$

largest of all of them	•••	
$S(8) = \pi^4/3$	32.469 697 011 334 145 745 480 110 •••	Rs(8) = 0.608 239 384 088 163 635 224 747 ...
$S(9) = 32\pi^4/105$	29.686 580 124 648 361 824 438 958 ...	Rs(9) = 0.654 530 635 654 477 183 429 699 ...
$S(10) = \pi^5/12$	25.501 640 398 773 454 438 561 775 ...	Rs(10) = 0.697 773 792 101 567 380 147 922 ...

Cones: *a cone has a polar angle and subtends a solid angle which is a fraction of the full solid angle of 4π*

Solid angle fractions f cut-out by cones with a given polar angle θ, f = (1 - cosθ)/2. The subtended solid angle in steradians is therefore **4π*f**

$\theta = \theta'_m$, the complementary tetrahedral angle	0.333 333 333 333 333 333 333 333 •••	1/3 exact
$\theta = 60$ degrees	0.25	1/4 exact
$\theta = 1$ radian	0.229 848 847 065 930 141 299 531 •••	(1-cos(1))/2
$\theta = \varphi_m$, the magic angle	0.211 324 865 405 187 117 745 425 •••	(1-√(1/3))/2; also the Knuth's constant
$\theta = 45$ degrees	0.146 446 609 406 726 237 799 577 ...	(1-√(1/2))/2
$\theta = \varphi'_m$, the complementary magic angle	0.091 751 709 536 136 983 633 785 ...	(1-√(2/3))/2
$\theta = 30$ degrees	0.066 987 298 107 780 676 618 138 ...	(1-√(3/4))/2
$\theta = 15$ degrees	0.017 037 086 855 465 856 625 128 ...	(1-sqrt((1+√(3/4))/2))/2

θ = 0.5 degrees (base disk of 1 degree diameter)	1.903 846 791 435 563 132 241 ...e-5	Steradians: 2.392 444 437 413 785 769 530 ...e-4
Polar angles θ of cones cutting a given fraction f of the full solid angle, θ = acos(1-2f)		
f = (Φ-1)/Φ, where Φ is the golden-ratio	1.332 478 864 985 030 510 208 009 •••	Degrees: 76.345 415 254 024 494 986 936 602 •••
f = 1/3	1.230 959 417 340 774 682 134 929 •••	The complemetary tetrahedral angle. Degrees: 70.528 779 •••
f = 1/4	1.047 197 551 196 597 746 154 214 •••	$\pi/3$. Degrees: 60
f = 0.1 (10%)	0.643 501 108 793 284 386 802 809 •••	Degrees: 36.869 897 645 844 021 296 855 612 ...
f = 0.01 (1%)	0.200 334 842 323 119 592 691 046 ...	Degrees: 11.478 340 954 533 572 625 029 817 ...
f = 1e-6 (1 ppm)	0.002 000 000 333 333 483 333 422 ...	Degrees: 0.114 591 578 124 766 407 153 079 ...
Perimeters of ellipses with major semi-axis 1, and minor semi-axis b (area = πab). Special cases: b=0 ... **flat ellipse**, b = 1 ... **circle**.		
b = 1/Φ, where Φ is the golden-ratio	5.154 273 178 025 879 962 492 835 ...	**Golden ellipse**
b = 0.613 372 647 073 913 744 075 540 ...	π+2 = mean of flat ellipse and circle	**Mid-girth ellipse** differs from golden ellipse by < 1%
b = 1/√2	5.402 575 524 190 702 010 080 698 ...	**Balanced ellipse** (interfocal_distance = minor_axis)
b = 1/2, the **midway ellipse**	4.844 224 110 273 838 099 214 251 ...	b = 1/3: 4.454 964 406 851 752 743 376 500 ...
b = 3/4	5.525 873 040 177 376 261 321 396	b = 2/3: 5.288 479 863 096 863 263 777 221 ...

	...	
b = 1/4	4.289 210 887 578 417 111 478 604 ...	b = 1/5: 4.202 008 907 937 800 188 939 832 ...
b = 1/6	4.150 013 265 005 047 157 825 880 ...	b = 1/7: 4.116 311 284 366 438 220 003 847 ...
b = 1/8	4.093 119 575 024 437 585 615 711 ...	b = 1/9: 4.076 424 191 956 689 482 335 178 ...
b = 1/10	4.063 974 180 100 895 742 557 793 ...	b = 0.01: 4.001 098 329 722 651 860 747 464 ...
b = 0.001	4.000 015 588 104 688 244 610 756 ...	b = 0.0001: 4.000 000 201 932 695 375 419 076 ...

For **CLOSED 3D bodies**, sorted by surface index value:

Sphere	4.835 975 862 049 408 922 150 900 •••	$(36\pi)^{1/3}$; **the absolute minimum** for closed bodies
Icosahedron, regular	5.148 348 556 199 515 646 330 812 •••	$(5\sqrt{3})/[5(3+\sqrt{5})/12]^{2/3}$; a Platonic solid
Dodecahedron, regular	5.311 613 997 069 083 669 796 666 •••	$(3\sqrt{(25+10\sqrt{5})})/[(15+7\sqrt{5})/4]^{2/3}$; a Platonic solid
Closed cylinder with smallest σ_3	5.535 810 445 932 085 257 290 411 •••	$3*(2\pi)^{1/3}$; Height = Diameter. **Cannery constant**.
Octahedron, regular	5.719 105 757 981 619 442 544 453 •••	$(2\sqrt{3})/[(\sqrt{2})/3]^{2/3}$; a Platonic solid
Cube	6.000 exact	A Platonic solid
Cone (closed) with	6.092 947 785 379 555 603 436 316	$6*(\pi/3)^{1/3}$; Height=BaseDiameter*$\sqrt{2}$. **Frozon**

smallest σ_3	...	cone constant.
Tetrahedron, regular	7.205 621 731 056 016 360 052 792 ...	$(\sqrt{3})/[(\sqrt{2})/12]^{2/3}$; a Platonic solid

For **OPEN 3D bodies**, sorted by surface index value:

Open cylinder (tube)	3.690 540 297 288 056 838 193 607 ...	$2*(2\pi)^{1/3}$, to be multiplied by $(Length/Diameter)^{1/3}$
Open cone with smallest σ_3	4.188 077 948 623 138 128 725 597 ...	$3*\sqrt{3}*(\pi/6)^{1/3}$; Height = BaseRadius*$\sqrt{2}$. **TeePee constant**.
Half-closed cylinder (cup/pot) with smallest σ_3	4.393 775 662 684 569 789 060 427 ...	$3\pi^{1/3}$; Height = Radius. **Cooking pot constant.**

*Perimeter-to-Area indices for **CLOSED 2D figures**, $\sigma_2 = Perimeter/Area^{1/2}$ (i.e., perimeter per unit area), sorted by value:*

Disk	3.544 907 701 811 032 054 596 334 ...	$2\sqrt{\pi}$; this is *the absolute minimum* for all figures
Regular heptagon	3.672 068 807 445 035 069 314 605 ...	Regular n-gon: $\sigma_2 = 2*sqrt(n*tan(\pi/n))$ = *minimum* for all n-gons
Regular hexagon	3.722 419 436 408 398 395 764 874 ...	$2*sqrt(6*tan(\pi/6))$; *the minimum* for all hexagons.
Regular pentagon	3.811 935 277 533 869 372 492 013 ...	$2*sqrt(5*tan(\pi/5))$; *the minimum* for all pentagons.
Square	4.000 exact	Also the minimum for disk wedges, attained for angle of 2 rad.
Equilateral triangle	4.559 014 113 909 555 283 987 126 ...	$6/\sqrt{(\sqrt{3})}$; *the minimum* for all triangles

Packing ratios (monodispersed)

Densest packing ratios Δ_n in the n-dimensional Euclidean space by (n-1)-dimensional spheres. $\Delta_1 = 1$. Values for n>3 are [very likely] conjectures. Also listed are the powers $h(n) = (\gamma_n)^n$ of Hermite constants $\gamma_n = 4(\Delta_n / V(n))^{2/n}$, where $V(n)$ is the unit hypersphere volume.

$\Delta_2 = \pi/(2\sqrt{3})$, **Kepler constant** for disks	0.906 899 682 117 089 252 970 392 •••	$h(n) = 4/3$. See <u>Disks-packing</u>
$\Delta_3 = \pi/(3\sqrt{2})$, **Kepler constant** for spheres	0.740 480 489 693 061 041 169 313 •••	hcp / fcc lattices (see below). $h(n) = 2$. See <u>Spheres-packing</u>
$\Delta_4 = \pi^2/16$, **Korkin-Zolotarev** constant	0.616 850 275 068 084 913 677 155 •••	$h(n) = 4$.
$\Delta_5 = (\pi^2\sqrt{2})/30$, **Korkin-Zolotarev** constant	0.465 257 613 309 258 635 610 504 •••	$h(n) = 8$.
$\Delta_6 = \pi^3(\sqrt{3})/144$	0.372 947 545 582 064 939 563 477 •••	$h(n) = 64/3$.
$\Delta_7 = \pi^3/105$	0.295 297 873 145 712 573 099 774 •••	$h(n) = 64$.
$\Delta_8 = \pi^4/384$	0.253 669 507 901 048 013 636 563 •••	$h(n) = 256$.

Densest random packing ratios in the n-dimensional Euclidean space by (n-1)-dimensional spheres. Known only approximately.

2D disks, densest random	0.772 ± 0.002	<u>Empirical & theoretical</u>
3D spheres, densest random	0.634 ± 0.007	<u>Empirical & theoretical</u>

Atomic packing factors (**APF**) of crystal lattices (3D).

Hexagonal close packed (hcp)	0.740 480 489 693 061 041 169 313 •••	and face-centered cubic (fcc). $\pi/(3\sqrt{2})$.

Body-centered cubic (bcc) •••	0.680 174 761 587 831 693 972 779	$(\pi\sqrt{3})/8$.
Simple cubic •••	0.523 598 775 598 298 873 077 107	$\pi/6$. In practice found only in polonium.
Diamond cubic •••	0.340 087 380 793 915 846 986 389	$(\pi\sqrt{3})/16$. This is the smallest possible APF.

Platonic solids data, except those already listed above, such as surface-to-volume indices

***Platonic solids: Tetrahedron**, regular, 4 vertices, 6 edges, 4 faces, 3 edges/vertex, 3 edges/face, 3 faces/vertex, 0 diagonals.*

Volume / edge^3 •••	0.117 851 130 197 757 920 733 474	$(\sqrt{2})/12$
Surface / edge^2 •••	1.732 050 807 568 877 293 527 446	$\sqrt{3}$; see also <u>surface indices</u>.
Height / edge •••	0.816 496 580 927 726 032 732 428	$(\sqrt{6})/3$
Angle between an edge and a face •••	0.955 316 618 124 509 278 163 857	**magic angle** φ_m (see above)
Dihedral angle (between adjacent faces) •••	1.230 959 417 340 774 682 134 929	**complementary tetrahedral angle** θ'_m (see above)
Tetrahedral angle (vertex-center-vertex) •••	1.910 633 236 249 018 556 327 714	θ_m (see above)
Circumscribed sphere radius / edge •••	0.612 372 435 695 794 524 549 321	Circumradius = $(\sqrt{6})/4$, congruent with vertices
Midsphere radius / edge •••	0.353 553 390 593 273 762 200 422	Midradius = $1/\sqrt{8}$, tangent to edges
Inscribed sphere radius /	0.204 124 145 231 931 508 183 107	Inradius = $(\sqrt{6})/12$, tangent to faces;

edge	•••	Circumradius/Inradius = 3
Vertex solid angle	0.551 285 598 432 530 807 942 144 •••	acos(23/27) steradians
Polar angle of circumscribed cone	0.615 479 708 670 387 341 067 464 •••	**complementary magic angle** φ'_m (see above)
Solid angle of circumscribed cone	1.152 985 986 532 130 094 749 141 ...	2π(1-sqrt(2/3)) steradians
Hamiltonian cycles	3	Acyclic Hamiltonian paths: 0

Platonic solids: Octahedron, *regular, 6 vertices, 12 edges, 8 faces, 4 edges/vertex, 3 edges/face, 4 faces/vertex, 3 diagonals of length √2.*

Volume / edge³	0.471 404 520 791 031 682 933 896 •••	(√2)/3
Surface / edge²	3.464 101 615 137 754 587 054 892 •••	2√3; see also <u>surface indices</u>.
Dihedral angle (between adjacent faces)	1.910 633 236 249 018 556 327 714 •••	**tetrahedral angle** (see above)
Circumscribed sphere radius / edge	0.707 106 781 186 547 524 400 844 •••	Circumradius = 1/√2, congruent with vertices
Midsphere radius / edge	0.5 exact	Midradius, tangent to edges
Inscribed sphere radius / edge	0.408 248 290 463 863 016 366 214 •••	1/√6; Tangent to faces. Circumradius/Inradius = √3
Vertex solid angle	1.359 347 637 816 487 748 385 570 •••	4 asin(1/3) steradians
Polar angle of circumscribed cone	0.785 398 163 397 448 309 615 660 •••	π/4 = atan(1); Degrees: 45 exact

Solid angle of circumscribed cone	1.840 302 369 021 220 229 909 405 ...	2π(1-sqrt(1/2)) steradians
Hamiltonian cycles	16	Acyclic Hamiltonian paths: 24 (8 span each body diagonal)

Platonic solids: Cube, *or Hexahedron, 8 vertices, 12 edges, 6 faces, 3 edges/vertex, 4 edges/face, 3 faces/vertex, 4 diagonals of length* √3.

Body diagonal / edge	1.732 050 807 568 877 293 527 446 •••	√3. Diagonal of a cube with unit side
Body diagonal / Face diagonal	1.224 744 871 391 589 049 098 642 •••	sqrt(3/2)
Angle between body diagonal and an edge	0.955 316 618 124 509 278 163 857 •••	**magic angle** φ_m (see above)
Angle between body and face diagonals	0.615 479 708 670 387 341 067 464 •••	**complementary magic angle** φ'_m (see above)
Circumscribed sphere radius / edge	0.866 025 403 784 438 646 763 723 •••	Circumradius = (√3)/2, congruent with vertices
Midsphere radius / edge	0.707 106 781 186 547 524 400 844 •••	Midradius = 1/√2, tangent to edges
Inscribed sphere radius / edge	0.5 exact	Circumradius/Inradius = √3
Vertex solid angle	1.570 796 326 794 896 619 231 321 •••	π/2 steradians
Polar angle of circumscribed cone	0.955 316 618 124 509 278 163 857 •••	**magic angle** φ_m (see above)
Solid angle of circumscribed cone	2.655 586 578 711 150 775 737 130 •••	2π(1-sqrt(1/3)) steradians

Hamiltonian cycles	6	Acyclic Hamiltonian paths: 24 (6 span each body diagonal)

Platonic solids: Icosahedron, *regular, 12 vertices, 30 edges, 20 faces, 5 edges/vertex, 3 edges/face, 5 faces/vertex, 6 main diagonals, 30 short diagonals.*

Volume / edge^3	2.181 694 990 624 912 373 503 822 •••	$5\Phi^2/6 = 5(3 + \sqrt{5})/12$, where Φ is the **golden ratio**
Surface / edge^2	8.660 254 037 844 386 467 637 231 •••	$5\sqrt{3} = 10*$A010527. See also surface indices.
Dihedral angle (between adjacent faces)	2.411 864 997 362 826 875 007 846 •••	$2.\text{atan}(\Phi^2)$; Degrees: 138.189 685 104 221 401 934 142 083 ...
Main diagonal / edge	1.902 113 032 590 307 144 232 878 •••	$2*$Circumradius $= \xi\Phi = \text{sqrt}(2+\Phi)$, ξ being the **associate of** Φ.
Circumscribed sphere radius / edge	0.951 056 516 295 153 572 116 439 •••	Circumradius $= \xi\Phi/2 = \text{sqrt}((5+\text{sqrt}(5))/8)$, ξ as above.
Midsphere radius / edge	0.809 016 994 374 947 424 102 293 •••	Midradius $= \Phi/2$, tangent to edges
Inscribed sphere radius / edge	0.755 761 314 076 170 730 480 133 •••	Inradius $= \Phi^2/(2\sqrt{3}) = \text{sqrt}(42+18\sqrt{5})/12$
Vertex solid angle	2.634 547 026 044 754 659 651 303 •••	$2\pi - 5\text{asin}(2/3)$ steradians
Polar angle of circumscribed cone	1.017 221 967 897 851 367 722 788 •••	$\text{atan}(\Phi)$; Degrees: 58.282 525 588 538 994 675 ...
Solid angle of circumscribed cone	2.979 919 307 985 462 371 739 387 ...	$2\pi(1-\text{sqrt}((5-\sqrt{5})/10))$ steradians
Hamiltonian cycles	1280	Acyclic Hamiltonian paths: 22560 (6*720 + 30*608)

Platonic solids: Dodecahedron, regular, 20 vertices, 30 edges, 12 faces, 3 edges/vertex, 5 edges/face, 3 faces/vertex; 10 main, 30 secondary, and 60 short diagonals.		
Volume / edge^3	7.663 118 960 624 631 968 716 053 •••	$(5\Phi^3)/(2\xi^2)$ = (15+7√5)/4, ξ being the **associate of** Φ
Surface / edge^2	20.645 728 807 067 603 073 108 143 •••	$15\Phi/\xi$ = 3.sqrt(25+10√5); see also <u>surface indices</u>.
Dihedral angle (between adjacent faces)	2.034 443 935 795 702 735 445 577 •••	2atan(Φ); Degrees: 116.565 051 177 077 989 351 572 193 ...
Main diagonal / edge	2.080 251 707 688 814 708 935 335 ...	2*Circumradius = Φ√3
Circumscribed sphere radius / edge	1.401 258 538 444 073 544 676 677 •••	Circumradius = Φ (√3)/2 = (sqrt(15)+sqrt(3))/4
Midsphere radius / edge	1.309 016 994 374 947 424 102 293 •••	Midradius = $\Phi^2/2$, tangent to edges
Inscribed sphere radius / edge	1.113 516 364 411 606 735 194 375 •••	Inradius = $\Phi^2/(2\xi)$ = sqrt(250+110√5)/20
Vertex solid angle	2.961 739 153 797 314 967 874 090 •••	π - atan(2/11) steradians
Polar angle of circumscribed cone	1.205 932 498 681 413 437 503 923 •••	acos(1/(Φ√3)); Degrees: 69.094 842 552 110 700 967 ...
Solid angle of circumscribed cone	4.041 205 995 440 192 430 566 404 ...	2π(1-1/(Φ√3)) steradians
Hamiltonian cycles	30	Acyclic Hamiltonian paths: ? coming soon
Selected geometry sequences		
Constructible regular	1, 2, <u>3</u>, <u>4</u>, <u>5</u>, 6, <u>8</u>, <u>10</u>, <u>12</u>, <u>15</u>, <u>16</u>, <u>17</u>,	2^m*k, where k is any product of distinct Fermat

polygons	<u>20</u>, •••	primes.
Non-constructible regular polygons	<u>7</u>, <u>9</u>, <u>11</u>, <u>13</u>, <u>14</u>, <u>18</u>, <u>19</u>, 21, 22, 23, 25, 26, •••	Complement of the above sequence.

Constants related to number-theoretical functions

<u>*Riemann zeta function*</u> $\zeta(s) = \mathbf{S}_{k \geq 0}\{k^{-s}\} = (1/\Gamma(s)).\mathbf{I}_{x=0,\infty}\{(x^{s-1})/(e^x-1)\} = \mathbf{P}_{prime\,p}\{1/(1-p^{-s})\}$. *It has a single pole at s = 1 (simple, with residue 1).* $\mathbf{L}_{s\to\infty}\{\eta(s)\} = 1$

Exact values & trivial zeros (n is integer >0)	$\zeta(0)$ = -0.5, $\zeta(-1) = \zeta(-13)$ = -1/12	$\zeta(-2n) = 0$, $\zeta(-n) = -B_{n+1}/(n+1)$. B_n are **Bernoulli** numbers
$\zeta(-1/2) = -\zeta(3/2)/(4\pi)$	-0.207 886 224 977 354 566 017 306 •••	$\zeta(-3/2)$ = -0.025 485 201 889 833 035 949 542 •••
$\zeta(+1/2)$	-1.460 354 508 809 586 812 889 499 •••	$\zeta(+3/2)$ = 2.612 375 348 685 488 343 348 567 <u>•••</u>
$\zeta(2)$ = π^2 /6. $\zeta(2n) = |B_{2n}|(2\pi)^{2n}/(2(2n)!)$	1.644 934 066 848 226 436 472 415 ••• #t	$\zeta(3)$ = 1.202 056 903 159 594 285 399 738 <u>•••</u> #t (**Apéry's**)
$\zeta(4)$ = π^4 /90	1.082 323 233 711 138 191 516 003 ••• #t	$\zeta(5)$ = 1.036 927 755 143 369 926 331 365 <u>•••</u>
$\zeta(6)$ = π^6 /945	1.017 343 061 984 449 139 714 517 ••• #t	$\zeta(7)$ = 1.008 349 277 381 922 826 839 797 <u>•••</u>
$\zeta(8)$ = π^8 /9450	1.004 077 356 197 944 339 378 685 ••• #t	$\zeta(9)$ = 1.002 008 392 826 082 214 417 852 <u>•••</u>
$\zeta(10)$ = π^{10} /93555	1.000 994 575 127 818 085 337 145 ••• #t	$\zeta(11)$ = 1.000 494 188 604 119 464 558 702 <u>•••</u>
$\zeta(12)$ = π^{12} (691/638512875)	1.000 246 086 553 308 048 298 637 ••• #t	$\zeta(13)$ = 1.000 122 713 347 578 489 146 751 <u>•••</u>
$\zeta(\,i\,)$, real and imaginary parts:	0.003 300 223 685 324 102 874 217 •••	- i 0.418 155 449 141 321 676 689 274 <u>•••</u>

Local extrema along the negative real axis (location in central column, value in last column). Remember that $\zeta(-2n) = 0$ for any integer $n > 0$		
1-st Maximum	-2.717 262 829 204 574 101 570 580 •••	0.009 159 890 119 903 461 840 056 •••
1-st minimum	-4.936 762 108 594 947 868 879 358 ...	-0.003 986 441 663 670 750 431 710 ...
2-nd Maximum	-7.074 597 145 007 145 734 335 798 ...	0.004 194 001 958 045 626 474 146 ...
2-nd minimum	-9.170 493 162 785 828 005 353 111 ...	-0.007 850 880 657 688 685 582 151 ...
3-rd Maximum	-11.241 212 325 375 343 510 874 637 ...	0.022 730 748 149 745 047 522 814 ...
3-rd minimum	-13.295 574 569 032 520 384 733 960 ...	-0.093 717 308 522 682 935 623 713 ...
4-th Maximum	-15.338 729 073 648 281 821 158 316 ...	0.520 589 682 236 209 120 459 027 ...
4-th minimum	-17.373 883 342 909 485 264 559 273 ...	-3.743 566 823 481 814 727 724 234 ...
5-th Maximum	-19.403 133 257 176 569 932 332 310 ...	33.808 303 595 651 664 653 888 821 ...
5-th minimum	-21.427 902 249 083 563 532 039 024 ...	-374.418 851 865 762 246 500 180 ...
Imaginary parts of first **nontrivial roots** (for more, see OEIS Wiki). Note: they all have real parts +0.5. Trivial roots are the even negative integers		
1st root	14.134 725 141 734 693 790 457 251 •••	2nd root: 21.022 039 638 771 554 992 628 479 •••

3rd root	25.010 857 580 145 688 763 213 790 •••	4th root: 30.424 876 125 859 513 210 311 897 •••
5th root:	32.935 061 587 739 189 690 662 368 •••	6th root: 37.586 178 158 825 671 257 217 763 ...
7th root:	40.918 719 012 147 495 187 398 126 ...	8th root: 43.327 073 280 914 999 519 496 122 ...
9th root:	48.005 150 881 167 159 727 942 472 ...	10th root: 49.773 832 477 672 302 181 916 784 ...

Expansion about the pole at s = 1: $\zeta(s) = 1/(s-1) + \boldsymbol{S}_{n=0,\infty}\{(-1)^n\gamma_n(s-1)^n/n!\}$, where $\gamma_0 \equiv \gamma$ is the **Euler-Mascheroni constant**, and γ_n, n > 0, are the Stieltjes constants

Stieltjes constant γ_1	-0.072 815 845 483 676 724 860 586 •••	In general: $\gamma_n = \boldsymbol{L}_{m\to\infty}\{\boldsymbol{S}_{k=1,m}\{\log^n(k)/k\} - \ln^{n+1}(m)/(n+1)\}$
γ_2	-0.009 690 363 192 872 318 484 530 •••	$\gamma_3 = $ -0.002 053 834 420 303 345 866 160 •••
γ_4	0.002 325 370 065 467 300 057 468 •••	$\gamma_5 = $ -0.000 793 323 817 301 062 701 753 •••
γ_6	-0.000 238 769 345 430 199 609 872 •••	$\gamma_7 = $ -0.000 527 289 567 057 751 046 074 •••

Derivative: $\zeta'(s) \equiv d\,\zeta(s)/ds = \boldsymbol{S}_{n=1,\infty}\{\log(n)/n^s\}$. In what follows, A is the **Glaisher-Kinkelin** constant and γ the **Euler** constant

$\zeta'(-1)$	-0.165 421 143 700 450 929 213 919 •••	1/12 - log(A); called sometimes **Kinkelin constant**
$\zeta'(-1/2)$	-0.360 854 339 599 947 607 347 420 •••	
$\zeta'(0)$	-0.918 938 533 204 672 741 780 329 •••	-log(2π)/2

$\zeta'(+1/2)$	-3.922 646 139 209 151 727 471 531 •••	$\zeta(1/2)(\pi+2.\gamma+6.\log(2)+2.\log(\pi))/4$
$\zeta'(2)$	-0.937 548 254 315 843 753 702 574 •••	$\pi^2(\gamma + \log(2\pi) - 12.A)/6$
$\zeta'(\ i)$, real and imaginary parts:	0.083 406 157 339 240 564 143 845 •••	- i 0.506 847 017 167 569 081 923 677 •••

Dirichlet eta function $\eta(s) = -S_{k>0}\{(-1)^k\,k^{-s}\} = (1 - 2^{1-s})\zeta(s) = (1/\Gamma(s)).I_{x=0,\infty}\{(x^{s-1})/(e^x+1)\}.$ $L_{s\to\infty}\{\eta(s)\} = 1$. Below, B_n are **Bernoulli** numbers.

Exact values & trivial zeros (n is integer >0)	$\eta(0) = 1/2$, $\eta(-1) = 1/4$, $\eta(1) = \log(2)$	$\eta(-2n) = 0$, $\eta(-n) = (2^{n+1}-1)B_{n+1}/(n+1)$
$\eta(1) = \log(2)$	0.693 147 180 559 945 309 417 232 ••• #t	Note that at s=1, $\zeta(s)$ is not defined, while $\eta(s)$ is smooth
$\eta(2) = \pi^2/12$	0.822 467 033 424 113 218 236 207 ••• #t	$\eta(2n) = \pi^{2n}[(2^{2n-1}-1)/(2n)!].|B_{2n}|$
$\eta(3) = 3.\zeta(3)/4$	0.901 542 677 369 695 714 049 803 ••• #t	Note that $\zeta(3)$ is the **Apéry**'s constant
$\eta(4) = \pi^4 (7/720)$	0.947 032 829 497 245 917 576 503 ••• #t	$\eta(6) = \pi^6 (31/30240)$, $\eta(8) = \pi^8 (127/1209600)$, etc
$\eta(\ i)$, real and imaginary parts:	0.532 593 181 763 096 166 570 965 •••	i 0.229 384 857 728 525 892 457 886 •••

Derivative: $\eta' \equiv d\,\eta(s)/ds = S_{k=1,\infty}\{(-1)^k \log(k).k^{-s}\} = 2^{1-s}\log(2)\zeta(s)+(1-2^{1-s})\zeta'(s)$

$\eta'(-1)$	0.265 214 370 914 704 351 169 348 •••	$3.\log(A) - \log(2)/3 - 1/4$
$\eta'(0)$	0.225 791 352 644 727 432 363 097 •••	$\log(\text{sqrt}(\pi/2))$
$\eta'(1)$	0.159 868 903 742 430 971 756 947	$\log(2)(\gamma - \log(\sqrt{2}))$

	•••	
$\eta'(2)$	0.101 316 578 163 504 501 886 002 •••	$\pi^2(\gamma + \log(\pi) + \log(4) - 12.\log(A))/12$
$\eta'(\ i\ )$, real and imaginary parts:	0.235 920 948 050 440 923 634 079 •••	- i 0.069 328 260 390 357 410 164 243 •••

Dedekind eta function $\eta(\tau) = q^{\wedge}(1/24)*P_{n>0}\{(1-q^{\wedge}n)\}$, where $q=exp(2\ \pi\ \tau\ i)$ is the 'nome'. This function is a *modular form*.

$\eta(x\ i)$ maximum: Location x_{max}	0.523 521 700 017 999 266 800 534 •••	For real $x>0$, $\eta(x\ i)>0$ is real, $\eta(0)=0$, and $\lim_{x\to\infty}\eta(x\ i)=0$
$\eta(x\ i)$ maximum: Value at x_{max}	0.838 206 031 992 920 559 691 418 •••	In this complex-plane cut, the maximum is unique
$\eta(\ i\ )$	0.768 225 422 326 056 659 002 594 •••	$\Gamma(1/4)\ /(\ 2\ \pi^{3/4})$; one of four values found by Ramanujan:
$\eta(\ i\ /2) = 2^{1/8}\ \eta(\ i)$	0.837 755 763 476 598 057 912 365 •••	$\Gamma(1/4)\ /\ (2^{7/8}\ \pi^{3/4})$
$\eta(2\ i) = \eta(\ i)\ /\ 2^{3/8}$	0.592 382 781 332 415 885 290 363 •••	$\Gamma(1/4)\ /\ (2^{11/8}\ \pi^{3/4})$
$\eta(4\ i) = (\sqrt{2}\ -1)^{1/4}\ \eta(\ i)\ /\ 2^{13/16}$	0.350 919 807 174 143 236 430 229 •••	$(\sqrt{2}\ -1)^{1/4}\ \Gamma(1/4)\ /\ (2^{29/16}\ \pi^{3/4})$

Constants related to selected complex functions. Notes: y(z) is a stand-in for the function. *Integral* is a stand-in for anti-derivative, up to a constant.

Exponential $exp(z) = S_{k\geq0}\{z^k/k!\}$; $exp(y+z) = exp(y)exp(z)$; integer n: $exp(n.z) = exp^{\ n}(z)$; $exp(n.z.i) = cos(n.z)+sin(n.z).i = (cos(z)+sin(z).i)^n$.

More: exp(z) equals its own derivative. Right-inverse funtions $Log(z,K)=log(z)+2\pi Ki$; left-inverse function $log(z)$. Diff.eq. $y' = y$.

exp(1) = e, the <u>Euler number</u>	2.718 281 828 459 045 235 360 287 ••• #t	Other: $exp(\pi k\ i)=(-1)^k$ for any integer k, etc.; see <u>e spin-offs</u>.

atan(e)	1.218 282 905 017 277 621 760 461 •••	For real x>0, y=atan(e).x is tangent to exp(x), kissing it at x=1
exp(±i) = cos(1) ± i sin(1) = cosh(i) ± sinh(i)	0.540 302 305 868 139 717 400 936 •••	±i 0.841 470 984 807 896 506 652 502 ••• #t
Some <u>fixed points</u> of exp(z): exp(z) = z, or z = log(z)+2πK i. They form a denumerable set, but none is real-valued.		
$z_{\pm 1}$, relative to K=0. Lambert $W_0(-1)$	0.318 131 505 204 764 135 312 654 •••	±i 1.337 235 701 430 689 408 901 162 •••
$z_{\pm 3}$, relative to K=±1. Equals $W_{\pm 1}(-1)$	2.062 277 729 598 283 884 978 486 •••	±i 7.588 631 178 472 512 622 568 923 •••
$z_{\pm 5}$, relative to K=±2. Equals $W_{\pm 2}(-1)$	2.653 191 974 038 697 286 601 106 •••	±i 13.949 208 334 533 214 455 288 918 •••
Some <u>fixed points</u> of -exp(z): -exp(z) = z, or z = log(-z)+2πK i. They form a denumerable set, but only one is real-valued.		
z_0, real, relative to K=0. Equals $-W_0(1)$	-0.567 143 290 409 783 872 999 968 •••	-z(0) is a solution of exp(-x) = x in **R**; **Omega constant**
$z_{\pm 2}$, relative to K=±1. Equals $-W_{\pm 1}(1)$	1.533 913 319 793 574 507 919 741 •••	±i 4.375 185 153 061 898 385 470 906 •••
$z_{\pm 4}$, relative to K=±2. Equals $-W_{\pm 2}(1)$	2.401 585 104 868 002 884 174 139 •••	±i 10.776 299 516 115 070 898 497 103 •••
Natural logarithm log(z)≡Log(z,0). For integer K, Log(z,K)=log(z)+2πK i is a multivalued right inverse of exp(z). Conventional cut is along negative real axis.		
More: log(1/z)=-log(z); log(1) = 0, log(± i) = (π/2)i, log(e) = 1. Derivative = 1/z. Integral = z(log(z)-1). Inverse = exp(z). Diff.eqs: y'z = 1, y'exp(y) = 1, y"+(y')² = 0.		
atan(1/e) = π/2 - atan(e)	0.352 513 421 777 618 997 470 859 •••	For real x, y=c.x kisses exp(x) at [1,e] when c=atan(1/e).
Trigonometric (or circular) functions trig(z): sin(z)=(e^{iz}-e^{-iz})/2, cos(z)=(e^{iz}+e^{-iz})/2, tan(z)=sin(z)/cos(z), csc(z)=1/sin(z),		

sec(z)=1/cos(z), cot(z)=1/tan(z).		

More: sin(z),cos(z) are **entire**. *trig* functions are periodic with period 2π: trig(z+2πK)=trig(z), but tan(z),cot(z) have a period of π. *Identity*: $\cos^2(z)+\sin^2(z) = 1$.

sin(±1); sine	± 0.841 470 984 807 896 506 652 502 ••• #t	sin(0)=0, sin(π/2)=1, sin(π)=0, sin(3π/2)=-1.
sin(±i)	±i 1.175 201 193 643 801 456 882 381 ••• #t	In general: sin(-z)=-sin(z), sin(z+π)=-sin(z), sin(iz) = i.sinh(z).
csc(±1); cosecant	± 1.188 395 105 778 121 216 261 599 •••	csc(π/2)=1, csc(3π/2)=-1.
csc(±i)	-(±i) 0.850 918 128 239 321 545 133 842 •••	In general: csc(-z)=-csc(z), csc(z+π)=-csc(z), csc(iz) = -i.csch(z).
cos(±1); cosine	0.540 302 305 868 139 717 400 936 •••	cos(0)=1, cos(π/2)=0, cos(π)=-1, cos(3π/2)=0.
cos(±i)	1.543 080 634 815 243 778 477 905 ••• #t	In general: cos(-z)=cos(z), cos(z+π)=-cos(z), cos(iz)=cosh(z).
tan(±1); tangent	± 1.557 407 724 654 902 230 506 974 •••	tan(0)=0, tan(±π/2)=±∞, tan(π)=0, tan(3π/2)=-(±∞).
tan(± i)	± i 0.761 594 155 955 764 888 119 458 •••	In general: tan(-z)=-tan(z), tan(z+π)=tan(z), tan(iz)=i.tanh(z).

<u>*Inverse trigonometric functions*</u> asin(z), acos(z), atan(z), acsc(z), asec(z), acot(z). *In general: atrig(z) = Atrig(z,0).*		

More: *Atrig*(z,K) are multivalued right inverses of *trig*(z), integer K being the branch index. *Atrig*(z,K) = *atrig*(z)+πK for *trig* ≡ tan, cot; otherwise *Atrig*(z,K) = *atrig*(z)+2πK.

asin(±i) = ±i.log(1+sqrt(2))	± i 0.881 373 587 019 543 025 232 609 ••• #t	asin(0) = 0, asin(±1) = ±π/2.
acos(±i) = π/2 - asin(±i)	In general, acos(z) = π/2 - asin(z)	acos(0) = π/2, acos(1) = 0, acos(-1) = π.

atan(±1) = ±π/4	± 0.785 398 163 397 448 309 615 660 •••	atan(0) = 0, atan(±i) = ±∞, atan(z) = -i.atanh(iz).

Hyperbolic functions trigh(z): sinh(z)=(e^z-e^{-z})/2, cosh(z)=(e^z+e^{-z})/2, tanh(z)=sinh(z)/cosh(z), csch(z)=1/sinh(z), sech(z)=1/cosh(z), coth(z)=1/tanh(z).

More: sinh(z),cosh(z) are **entire**. *trigh* functions are periodic with period 2πi: trigh(z+2πiK)=trig(z), but tanh(z),coth(z) have a period of π. *Identity*: $\cosh^2(z)-\sinh^2(z) = 1$.

sinh(±1) = (e - e^{-1})/2	±1.175 201 193 643 801 456 882 381 ••• #t	sinh(0)=0
sinh(±i) = ±i.sin(1)	±i 0.841 470 984 807 896 506 652 502 ••• #t	In general: sinh(-z)=-sinh(z), sinh(iz)=i.sin(z)
cosh(±1) = (e + e^{-1})/2	1.543 080 634 815 243 778 477 905 ••• #t	cosh(0)=1
cosh(±i) = cos(1)	0.540 302 305 868 139 717 400 936 •••	In general: cosh(-z)=cos(z), cosh(iz)=cos(z)
tanh(±1)	± 0.761 594 155 955 764 888 119 458 •••	tanh(0)=0. $L_{x\to\pm\infty}\{tanh(x)\}=\pm1$.
tanh(± i)	± i 1.557 407 724 654 902 230 506 974 •••	In general: tanh(-z)=-tanh(z), tanh(iz) = i.tan(z)

Inverse hyperbolic functions asinh(z), acosh(z), atanh(z), acsch(z), asech(z), acoth(z). In general: atrigh(z) = Atrigh(z,0).

More: *Atrigh*(z,K) are multivalued right inverses of *trigh*(z), K being the branch index. *Atrigh*(z,K) = atrigh(z)+πiK for *trigh* ≡ tanh, coth; otherwise *Atrigh*(z,K) = atrigh(z)+2πiK.

asinh(±1) = ±log(1+sqrt(2))	±0.881 373 587 019 543 025 232 609 •••	asinh(0) = 0, asinh(± i) = ± i π/2.
acosh(± i) = asinh(1) ± i π/2	acosh(0) = (π/2) i	acosh(1) = 0, acosh(-1) = π.
atanh(±i) = ± i.π/4 =	± i 0.785 398 163 397 448 309 615	atanh(0) = 0, atanh(±1) = ±∞, atanh(z) = -

$\pm\log((1+i)/(1-i))/2$	660 •••	$i.\mathrm{atan}(iz)$.

Logarithmic integral $li(z) = I_{t=0,z}\{1/\log(t)\}$, $x \geq 0$; $Li(x) = li(x)-li(2) = I_{t=2,x}\{1/\log(t)\}$; $L_{x\rightarrow+\infty}(li(x)/(x/\log(x))) = 1$. For $li(e)$, see $Ei(1)$.	

li(2); for real x>0, Imag(li(x))=0	1.045 163 780 117 492 784 844 588 •••	More: li(0)=0, li(1)=-∞, li(+∞)=+∞, Re(li(-∞))=-∞
li(-1); upper sign applies just above the real axis	0.073 667 912 046 425 485 990 100 •••	± i 3.422 733 378 777 362 789 592 375 •••
li(±i)	0.472 000 651 439 568 650 777 606 •••	± i 2.941 558 494 949 385 099 300 999 •••
Unique positive real root of li(z), z = μ	1.451 369 234 883 381 050 283 968 •••	**Ramanujan-Soldner's constant** (or just **Soldner's**)
Derivative of li(z) at its root z = μ	2.684 510 350 820 707 652 502 382 •••	Equals 1.0/log(μ)
Unique negative real root of Real(li(z))	-2.466 408 262 412 678 075 197 103 •••	Real(li(z)) has three real roots: μ, 0, and this one
Imaginary value of li(z) at the above point	± i 3.874 501 049 312 873 622 370 969 •••	Upper/lower sign applies just above/below the real axis
Solution of x*li(x) = 1 for real x	1.715 597 325 769 518 883 130 074 ...	

Fixed points of li(z): solutions li(z) = z other than z_0=0.	

$z_{\pm1}$, main-branch attractors of li(z)	1.878 881 747 908 123 091 969 486 ...	±i 2.065 922 202 370 662 188 988 104 ...

Fixed points of -li(z): solutions li(z) = -z.	

Solution of x+li(x) = 0 for real x>1	1.162 128 219 976 088 745 102 790 ...	This is a repulsor of the li(z) mapping!
Solution of x+real(li(x)) = 0	0.647 382 347 652 898 263 175 288	For real x<1, y=0, li(x+iy) is regular in x but

for real x<1, x≠0	...	discontinuous in y
Complex main-branch attractors of -li(z)	1.584 995 337 729 709 022 596 984 ...	±i 4.285 613 025 032 867 139 156 436 ...

Exponential integral $E_1(z) = I_{t=1,\infty}\{exp(-zt)/t\}$*; multivalued, has a cut along the negative real axis.* $E_1((0+)+i(0\pm))=\infty$*,* $E_1((0-)+i.(0\pm))=\infty$ *-(±).π,* $E_1(\infty)=0$

$E_1(1)$	0.219 383 934 395 520 273 677 163 •••	Equals (Gompertz constant)/e
$E_1(\pm i)$	-0.337 403 922 900 968 134 662 646 •••	-(±) i 0.624 713 256 427 713 604 289 968 •••
$E_1(-1+i.0\pm)$	-1.895 117 816 355 936 755 466 520 •••	-(±) π.i
Unique **real root** r of real($E_1(x)$)	-0.372 507 410 781 366 634 461 991 •••	imag($E_1(r+i.(0\pm))$) = -(±)π

Exponential integral $Ei(z) = -I_{t=-z,\infty}\{exp(-t)/t\}$*; multivalued, has a cut along the negative real axis.* $Ei(0+)=-\infty$*,* $Ei(0-)=-\infty$ *-π.i,* $Ei(-\infty)=0$*,* $Ei(+\infty)=+\infty$*,* $Ei(\pm\infty.i)=\pm\pi$

$Ei(1) = -real(E_1(-1))$	1.895 117 816 355 936 755 466 520 •••	Equals li(e)
$Ei(\pm i)$	0.337 403 922 900 968 134 662 646 •••	(±) i 2.516 879 397 162 079 634 172 675 ...
$Ei(-1+i.0\pm)$	-0.219 383 934 395 520 273 677 163 •••	±π.i
Unique **real root** of Ei(x)	0.372 507 410 781 366 634 461 991 •••	Equals log(μ); μ being the **Ramanujan-Soldner's constant**

Sine integral $Si(z) = I_{t=0,z}\{sin(t)/t\}$*;* $Si(-z)=-Si(z)$*;* $Si(conj(z))=conj(Si(z))$*;* $Si(0)=0$*; For real x>0: maxima at* $x=(2k-1)\pi$*, minima at* $x=2k\pi$*, k=1,2,3,...*

More: This covers also the hyperbolic sine integral Shi(z) = Si(i*z). Si(z) and Shi(z) are both entire complex functions.

Si(1) ≡ Shi(-i)	0.946 083 070 367 183 014 941 353 •••	$S_{k≥0}\{(-1)^k/((2k+1)!(2k+1))\}$ = 1/(1!1)-1/(3!3)+1/(5!5)-1/(7!7)+
Si(i) ≡ Shi(1)	i 1.057 250 875 375 728 514 571 842 •••	$S_{k≥0}\{1/((2k+1)!(2k+1))\}$ = 1/(1!1)+1/(3!3)+1/(5!5)+...
Si(π), absolute maximum for real z	1.851 937 051 982 466 170 361 053 •••	The **Gibbs constant**, equal to $I_{x=0,pi}\{sin(x)/x\}$.
Si(2π), first local minimum for real z	1.418 151 576 132 628 450 245 780 •••	With growing real x, Si(x) exhibits ripples converging to π/2.
Solutions of Si(z) = π/2 for real z:	1st: 1.926 447 660 317 370 582 022 944 ...	2nd: 4.893 835 952 616 601 801 621 684 ..., etc.

Cosine integral Ci(z) = γ+log(z)+$I_{t=0,z}\{(cos(t)-1)/t\}$; Ci(conj(z))=conj(Ci(z)); For real x>0: maxima at x=(2k-1/2)π, minima at x=(2k+1/2)π, k=1,2,3,...

More: This covers also the related <u>entire cosine integral</u> function Cin(z) = $I_{t=0,z}\{(1-cos(t))/t\}$. Identity: Cin(z)+Ci(z) = γ+log(z).

Ci(1) = real(Ci(-1))	0.337 403 922 900 968 134 662 646 •••	γ+$S_{k>0}\{(-1)^k/((2k)!(2k))\}$ = γ-1/(2!2)+1/(4!4)-1/(6!6)+1/(8!8)+...
Ci(±i)	0.837 866 940 980 208 240 894 678 •••	±i π/2
Ci(π/2), absolute maximum for real z	0.472 000 651 439 568 650 777 606 •••	= real(li(i)), li being the logarithmic integral
Ci(3π/2), first local minimum for real z	-0.198 407 560 692 358 042 506 401 ...	With growing real x, Ci(x) exhibits ripples converging to 0.
Solutions of Ci(x) = 0 for real x:	1st: 0.616 505 485 620 716 233 797 110 ...	2nd: 3.384 180 422 551 186 426 397 851 ..., etc.
Real solution of x+Ci(x) = 0	0.393 625 563 408 040 091 457 836 ...	The unique real-valued fixed point of -Ci(z)

Location of $\Gamma(x)$ minimum for $x \geq 0$	1.461 632 144 968 362 341 262 659 •••	Also the positive root of **digamma function** $\psi(x)$
Value of $\Gamma(x)$ minimum for $x \geq 0$	0.885 603 194 410 888 700 278 815 •••	For $x > 0$, the Gamma function minimum is unique
$I_{x=a,a+1}(\log(\Gamma(x)) + a - a.\log(a)$	0.918 938 533 204 672 741 780 329 •••	$= \log(2\pi)/2$, for any $a \geq 0$ (the **Raabe** formula)
Location and value of $\Gamma(x)$ maximum in (-1,-0)	x= -0.504 083 008 264 455 409 258 269 •••	$\Gamma(x)$= -3.544 643 611 155 005 089 121 963 •••
Location and value of $\Gamma(x)$ minimum in (-2,-1)	x= -1.573 498 473 162 390 458 778 286 •••	$\Gamma(x)$= +2.302 407 258 339 680 135 823 582 •••
$\Gamma(1/2)$	1.772 453 850 905 516 027 298 167 •••	$\sqrt{\pi}$, this crops up very often
$\Gamma(1/3)$	2.678 938 534 707 747 633 655 692 ••• #t	$\Gamma(2/3)$ = 1.354 117 939 426 400 416 945 288 •••
$\Gamma(1/4)$	3.625 609 908 221 908 311 930 685 ••• #t	$\Gamma(3/4)$ = 1.225 416 702 465 177 645 129 098 •••
$I_{x=0,\infty}\{1/\Gamma(x)\}$	2.807 770 242 028 519 365 221 501 •••	Fransén-Robinson constant
$\Gamma(\ i)$ (real and imaginary parts)	-0.154 949 828 301 810 685 124 955 •••	- i 0.498 015 668 118 356 042 713 691 •••
$1/\Gamma(\pm\ i)$ (real and imaginary parts)	-0.569 607 641 036 681 806 028 615 ...	$\pm$ i 1.830 744 396 590 524 694 236 582 ...

More: Recurrence: $\psi_n(z+1) = \psi_n(z)+(-1)^n n! / z^{n+1}$. Reflection: $\psi_n(1-z)+(-1)^{n+1}\psi_n(z) = \pi \, (d/dz)^n\cot(\pi z)$. For integer $k\leq 0$, $L_{x\to k\pm}\{\psi_n(x)\} = (-(\pm 1))^{n+1}\infty$.

Digamma $\psi(z) = d \log(\Gamma(z)) / dz$. $\psi(z+1) = \psi(z) + 1/z$. $\psi(1-z) = \psi(z) + \pi.\cot(\pi z)$. $\psi(2z) = (\psi(z)+\psi(z+1/2))/2 + \log(2)$. For positive real root, see above. <u>See also</u>.

$\psi(1) = -\gamma$	- 0.577 215 664 901 532 860 606 512 •••	$\psi(2) = 1-\gamma = +0.422\ 784\ 335\ 098\ 467\ 139\ 393\ 488$ •••
$\psi(\pm i)$	0.094 650 320 622 476 977 271 878 •••	$\pm i\ 2.076\ 674\ 047\ 468\ 581\ 174\ 134\ 050$ •••
$\psi(1/2) = -\gamma\ -2.\log(2)$	- 1.963 510 026 021 423 479 440 976 •••	$\psi(-1/2) = 2+psi(1/2) = 0.036\ 489\ 973\ 978\ 576\ 520\ 559\ 024$ •••

Trigamma $\psi_1(z) = d\ \psi(z) / dz$. $\psi_1(z+1) = \psi_1(z) - 1/z^2$. <u>See also</u>.

$\psi_1(1)$	1.644 934 066 848 226 436 472 415 ••• #t	$= \zeta(2) = \pi^2/6$, ζ being the Riemann zeta function.
$\psi_1(\pm i)$	-0.536 999 903 377 236 213 701 673 ...	$-\pm i\ 0.794\ 233\ 542\ 759\ 318\ 865\ 583\ 013$ ...
$\psi_1(1/2) = \pi^2/2$	4.934 802 200 544 679 309 417 245 •••	$\psi_1(-1/2) = 4+\psi_1(1/2) = 4+\pi^2/2$

<u>Bessel functions</u> (**BF**) $B_v(z) \equiv y(z)$ are solutions of the differential equation $z^2.y''+z.y'+(z^2\pm v^2).y = 0$ (lower sign is for modified Bessel functions)

<u>BF of the first kind</u> (regular at z=0): $J_v(z) = (1/\pi)\ I_{t=0,\pi}\{\cos(vt-z.\sin(t))\}$, and the <u>modified BF of the first kind</u>: $I_v(z) = (1/\pi)\ I_{t=0,\pi}\{\exp(z.\cos(t)).\cos(vt)\} = i^{-v}\ J_v(iz)$

General properties: For integer k, $J_k(-z) = (-1)^k\ J_k(z)$ and $I_k(-z) = (-1)^k\ I_k(z)$. For k=0, $J_0(0) = I_0(0) = 1$, otherwise $J_k(0) = I_k(0) = 0$.

$J_0(\pm 1) = I_0(\pm i)$	0.765 197 686 557 966 551 449 717 ...	In general, $I_0(z) = J_0(-i.z)$
$J_0(\pm i) = I_0(\pm 1)$	1.266 065 877 752 008 335 598 244 •••	For real r, $J_0(r)$ and $J_0(r.i)$ are real
$J_0(\pm 2) = I_0(\pm 2i)$	0.223 890 779 141 235 668 051 827	$= S_{k\geq 0}\{(-1)^k/k!^2\}$

	•••	
$J_0(\pm 2i) = I_0(\pm 2)$	2.279 585 302 336 067 267 437 204 •••	$= S_{k\geq 0}\{1/k!^2\}$
1st root of $J_0(x)$	$\pm$2.404 825 557 695 772 768 621 631 •••	2nd: $\pm$5.520 078 110 286 310 649 596 604 ...
3rd root of $J_0(x)$	$\pm$8.653 727 912 911 012 216 954 198 ...	4th: $\pm$11.791 534 439 014 281 613 743 044 ...
$J_1(\pm 1) = -i.I_1(\pm i)$	$\pm$0.440 050 585 744 933 515 959 682 ...	In general, $I_1(z) = -i.J_1(\pm i\, z)$
$J_1(\pm i) = -i.I_1(-(\pm)1)$	At real x, $J_1(\pm ix)$ is imaginary, $I_1(\pm ix)$ is real	$\pm i$ 0.565 159 103 992 485 027 207 696 •••
1st root of $J_1(x)$, other than x = 0.0	$\pm$3.831 705 970 207 512 315 614 435 •••	2nd: $\pm$7.015 586 669 815 618 753 537 049 ...
3rd root of $J_1(x)$	$\pm$ 10.173 468 135 062 722 077 185 711 ...	4th: $\pm$ 13.323 691 936 314 223 032 393 684 ...
Imaginary order:		
$J_{\pm i}(\pm 1) = \exp(\pm\pi/2).I_{\pm i}(i)$	1.641 024 179 495 082 261 264 869 ...	$-(\pm)\, i$ 0.437 075 010 213 683 064 502 605 ...
$J_{\pm i}(\pm i) = \exp(\pm\pi/2).I_{\pm i}(-(\pm) 1)$	0.395 137 431 337 007 718 800 172 ...	$-(\pm)\, i$ 0.221 175 556 871 848 055 937 508 ...
$J_{\pm i}(-(\pm)\, i) = \exp(\pm\pi/2).I_{\pm i}(\pm 1)$	9.143 753 846 275 618 780 610 618 ...	$-(\pm)\, i$ 5.118 155 579 455 226 532 551 733 ...

BF of the second kind: $Y_v(z) = (J_v(z)\cos(v\pi)-J_{-v}(z))/\sin(v\pi)$, and the modified BF of the second kind $K_v(z) = (\pi/2)(I_{-v}-I_v)/\sin(v\pi)$; for integer v, apply limit (continuity in v)

Notes: These are all singular (divergent) at z=0. The Y-functions are sometimes denoted as **Bessel N-functions**.

$Y_0(+1)$	0.088 256 964 215 676 957 982 926 ...	For positive real arguments, $Y_n(z)$ is real
$Y_0(-1)$; its real part equals $Y_0(+1)$	0.088 256 964 215 676 957 982 926 ...	+i 1.530 395 373 115 933 102 899 435 ...
$Y_0(\pm\ i)$; its imaginary part equals $J_0(\pm\ i)$	-0.268 032 482 033 988 548 762 769 ...	$\pm$ i 1.266 065 877 752 008 335 598 244 •••
1st root of $Y_0(x)$	±0.893 576 966 279 167 521 584 887 ...	2nd: ±3.957 678 419 314 857 868 375 677 ...
3rd root of $Y_0(x)$	±7.086 051 060 301 772 697 623 624 ...	4th: ±10.222 345 043 496 417 018 992 042 ...
$K_0(+1)$	0.421 024 438 240 708 333 335 627 ...	For positive real arguments, $K_n(z)$ is real
$K_0(-1)$; its real part equals $K_0(+1)$	0.421 024 438 240 708 333 335 627 ...	-i 3.977 463 260 506 422 637 256 609 ...
$K_0(\pm\ i)$	-0.138 633 715 204 053 999 681 099 ...	-(±) i 1.201 969 715 317 206 499 136 662 ...
$Y_1(+1)$	-0.781 212 821 300 288 716 547 150 ...	For positive real arguments, $Y_n(z)$ is real
$Y_1(-1)$; its real part equals $-Y_1(+1)$	0.781 212 821 300 288 716 547 150 ...	-i 0.880 101 171 489 867 031 919 364 ...
$Y_1(\pm\ i)$; its real part equals $imag(J_1(-i))$	-0.565 159 103 992 485 027 207 696 •••	$\pm$ i 0.383 186 043 874 564 858 082 704 ...
1st root of $Y_1(x)$	±2.197 141 326 031 017 035 149 033 ...	2nd: ±5.429 681 040 794 135 132 772 005 ...
3rd root of $Y_1(x)$	± 8.596 005 868 331 168 926 429 606 ...	4th: ± 11.749 154 830 839 881 243 399 421 ...

Hankel functions, alias **Bessel functions of the third kind**

HF of the first kind $H1_v(z) = J_v(z)+i.Y_v(z) = (J_{-v}(z) -e^{-iv\pi}J_v(z))/(i.\sin(v\pi))$, and HF of the second kind $H2_v(z) = J_v(z)-i.Y_v(z) = (J_{-v}(z) -e^{iv\pi}J_v(z))/(-i.\sin(v\pi))$

$H1_0(\pm 1)$	$\pm 0.765\ 197\ 686\ 557\ 966\ 551\ 449\ 717$ ...	$+i\ 0.088\ 256\ 964\ 215\ 676\ 957\ 982\ 926$ ...
$H1_0(+i)$	0.0	$-i\ 0.268\ 032\ 482\ 033\ 988\ 548\ 762\ 769$ ...
$H1_0(-i)$	$2.532\ 131\ 755\ 504\ 016\ 671\ 196\ 489$	$-i\ 0.268\ 032\ 482\ 033\ 988\ 548\ 762\ 769$ ...
$H2_0(+1)$	$0.765\ 197\ 686\ 557\ 966\ 551\ 449\ 717$ ...	$-i\ 0.088\ 256\ 964\ 215\ 676\ 957\ 982\ 926$ ...
$H2_0(-1)$	$2.295\ 593\ 059\ 673\ 899\ 654\ 349\ 152$ ...	$-i\ 0.088\ 256\ 964\ 215\ 676\ 957\ 982\ 926$ ...
$H2_0(i)$	$2.532\ 131\ 755\ 504\ 016\ 671\ 196\ 489$ ...	$-i\ 0.268\ 032\ 482\ 033\ 988\ 548\ 762\ 769$ ...
$H2_0(-i)$	0.0	$-i\ 0.268\ 032\ 482\ 033\ 988\ 548\ 762\ 769$ ...

Spherical Bessel functions $b_v(z) \equiv y$ *are solutions of the* ___differential equation___ $z^2.y''+2z.y'+[z^2-v(v+1)].y = 0.$

Spherical BF of the first kind (regular at z=0): $j_v(z) = \sqrt{\pi/(2z)}\ J_{v+1/2}(z)$, where J is the Bessel J-function. $j_v(-z) = (-1)^v j_v(z)$. Using Kroneker δ, $j_v(0) = \delta_{v,0}$.

$j_0(\pm 1) = \sin(1) = \sinh(i)/i$	$0.841\ 470\ 984\ 807\ 896\ 506\ 652\ 502$ ••• #t	$j_0(z) = $ sinc$(z) = \sin(z)/z$ is an entire functtion. Note: $j_0(0) = 1$.
$j_0(\pm i) = \sinh(1) = \sin(i)/i$	$1.175\ 201\ 193\ 643\ 801\ 456\ 882\ 381$ ••• #t	$j_0(z) = S_{k\geq 0}\{(-1)^k z^{2k}/(2k+1)!\}$.
$j_1(\pm 1) = \pm(\sin(1)-\cos(1))$	$\pm 0.301\ 168\ 678\ 939\ 756\ 789\ 251\ 565$ •••	$j_1(z) = (\sin(z)-z*\cos(z))/z^2$ is an entire function. Note: $j_1(0) = 0$.
$j_1(\pm i)$	$\pm i\ 0.367\ 879\ 441\ 171\ 442\ 321\ 595$	$j_1(\pm i) = \pm i / e$.

	523 ••• #t	

Spherical BF of the second kind: $y_v(z)$ = sqrt(π/(2z)) $Y_{v+1/2}(z)$, where Y is the Bessel Y-function. Often denoted also as $n_v(z)$. $L_{x \to 0\pm}$ = -($\pm$)∞.

$y_0(\pm 1)$ = -($\pm$)cos(1) = -($\pm$)cosh(i)	-($\pm$) 0.540 302 305 868 139 717 400 936 •••	$y_0(z)$ = -cos(z)/z.
$y_0(\pm$ i) = $\pm$ i.cos(i) = $\pm$ i.cosh(1)	$\pm$ i 1.543 080 634 815 243 778 477 905 ••• #t	$y_0(z)$ = -(1/z)$S_{k\geq0}\{(-1)^k z^{2k}/(2k)!\}$.
$y_1(\pm 1)$ = -(sin(1)+cos(1))	-1.381 773 290 676 036 224 053 438 ...	$y_1(z)$ = -(z*sin(z)+cos(z))/z^2. Note: $y_1(0)$ = -∞.
$y_1(\pm$ i)	0.367 879 441 171 442 321 595 523 ••• #t	= 1/ e = j_1(i) / i.

Dawson integral $F(x)$ = e^{-x^2} $I_{t=0,x}\{e^{t^2}\}$

Maximum: Location x_{max}	0.924 138 873 004 591 767 012 823 •••	F(x) being an odd function; there is a minimum at -x_{max}
Maximum: Value at x_{max}	0.541 044 224 635 181 698 472 759 •••	$F(x_{max})$ = 1/(2x_{max}). The value of -$F''(x_{max})$ is twice this one.
Inflection: Location x_i	1.501 975 268 268 611 498 860 348 •••	Dawson integral: see above.
Inflection: Value at x_i	0.427 686 616 017 928 797 406 755 •••	$F(x_i)$ = $x_i/(2x_i^2-1)$.
F(x) inflection: Derivative at x_i	-0.284 749 439 656 846 482 522 031 •••	$F(x_i)$ = $x_i/(2x_i^2-1)$.

Lambert W-function $W_K(z)$: *multi-valued left inverse of the mapping z*exp(z). $W_0(x)$ is real for x $\in$ [-1/e,+∞). $W_{-1}(x)$ is real for x $\in$ [-1/e,0).*

$W_0(1)$ ≡ **omega constant**	0.567 143 290 409 783 872 999 968 •••	W_0(-1/e) = -1, W_0(0) = 0, $L_{x\to\infty}\{W_0(x)\}$ = ∞

$W_0(\pm i)$	0.374 699 020 737 117 493 605 978 ...	$\pm i$ 0.576 412 723 031 435 283 148 289 ...
$W_0(-1)$ = conjugate of $W_{-1}(-1)$	-0.318 131 505 204 764 135 312 654 •••	$\pm i$ 1.337 235 701 430 689 408 901 162 •••
Inflection location x_i of $W_{-1}(x)$ for real x	-0.270 670 566 473 225 383 787 998 ...	= $-2/e^2$ so that $W_{-1}(x_i)$ = -2. $W_{-1}(-1/e)$ = -1, $L_{x \to 0-}\{W_{-1}(x)\} = -\infty$
$W_{-1}(+i)$ = conjugate of $W_1(-i)$	-1.089 648 913 877 781 029 302 988 ...	$-i$ -2.766 362 603 273 869 178 517 538 ...
$W_{-1}(-i)$ = conjugate of $W_1(i)$	-1.834 271 700 407 880 400 923 088 ...	$-i$ -5.985 834 988 966 545 709 364 109 ...

Function $f(z) = z^z$ = exp(z*log(z)). *This is an entire function. f(0)=f(1)=1, f(-1)=-1.*

$f(i) = f(-i) = i^i$	0.207 879 576 350 761 908 546 955 ••• #t	= $e^{-\pi/2}$ (real value!)
Location of minimum (on real axis)	0.367 879 441 171 442 321 595 523 •••	x_{min} = 1/e. The minimum is unique.
Location of minimum (on real axis)	0.367 879 441 171 442 321 595 523 •••	x_{min} = 1/e. The minimum is unique.
Value at minimum	0.692 200 627 555 346 353 865 421 •••	$e^{-1/e}$.

Mathematical constants useful in Sciences

Planck's radiation law **on frequency scale: Prl**$(x) = x^3/(e^x - 1)$, *or wavelength scale:* **Prl**$(\lambda) = \lambda^{-5}(e^{1/\lambda} - 1)^{-1}$

Integral $I_{x=0,\infty}\{x^3/(e^x - 1)\}$	6.493 939 402 266 829 149 096 022 •••	$\pi^4/15$.
Related: the roots of x = $K*(1 - e^{-x})$	K=5: 4.965 114 231 744 276 303 698 759 •••	K=4: 3.920 690 394 872 886 343 560 891 •••

See Calculation of blackbody radiation, App.C	K=3: 2.821 439 372 122 078 893 403 191 •••	K=2: 1.593 624 260 040 040 092 323 041 •••

$\underline{sinc}(z) = \sin(z)/z = j_0(z)$ (the spherical Bessel function). $sinc(-z) = sinc(z)$, $sinc(0) = 1$, $sinc(\pm i) = \cosh(1)$, $sinc(\pm 1) = imag(\exp(\mathbf{i}))$.

Half-height argument	1.895 494 267 033 980 947 144 035 •••	Solution of $sinc(x) = 1/2$
First minimum location	4.493 409 457 909 064 175 307 880 •••	First positive solution of $\tan(x) = x$
First minimum value	-0.217 233 628 211 221 657 408 279 •••	

$\mathbf{hsinc}(z) = (1-\cos(z))/z$, appearing in spectral theory (transient data truncation artifacts). $hsinc(-z) = -hsinc(z)$.

First maximum location	2.331 122 370 414 422 613 667 835 •••	Also first positive solution of $\mathbf{x.\sin(x) = 1-\cos(x)}$
First maximum value	0.724 611 353 776 708 475 738 990 •••	

First roots ξ_n and definitions of $sinc(n,x)$ in terms of Bessel functions

ξ_0	2.404 825 557 695 772 768 621 631 ••• #t	$\underline{sinc}(0,x) = J_0(x)$, the Bessel function
$\xi_1 = \pi$	3.141 592 653 589 793 238 462 643 ••• #t	$\underline{sinc}(1,x) = \sin(x)/x = sinc(x) = j_0(x)$, 1st kind spherical Bessel
ξ_2	3.831 705 970 207 512 315 614 435 •••	$\underline{sinc}(2,x) = 2J_1(x)/x$

ξ_3 , also location of 1st negative lobe of sinc(1,x)	4.493 409 457 909 064 175 307 880 •••	$\underline{sinc}(3,x) = 3[\sin(x)/x - \cos(x)]/x^2 = 3j_1(x)/x$
ξ_4	5.135 622 301 840 682 556 301 401 •••	$\underline{sinc}(4,x) = 8J_2(x)/x^3$
Ideal gas statistics *with n randomly distributed particles per unit volume*		
1st **Chandrasekhar** constant c = $\Gamma(4/3)/(4\pi/3)^{1/3}$	0.553 960 278 365 090 204 701 121 •••	Mean distance to nearest neighbor = $c/n^{1/3}$
2nd **Chandrasekhar constant** C = $(2\pi)^{-1/3}$	0.541 926 070 139 289 008 744 561 •••	Most probable distance to nearest neighbor = $C/n^{1/3}$
Spectral peaks *(lines) of height H and half-height width W:*		
Area of a Lorentzian peak / HW	1.570 796 326 794 896 619 231 321 •••	$\pi / 2$
Area of a Gaussian peak / HW	1.064 467 019 431 226 179 315 267 •••	sqrt($\pi /(4\ln 2)$)
Area of a Sinc peak / HW	0.828 700 120 129 003 061 896 869 •••	$\pi/(2\eta)$, η being defined by **sinc**(η) = 1/2 (see **sinc** function)
Bloembergen-Purcell-Pound function bpp(x) = $x/(1+x^2) + 4x/(1+4x^2)$, *ubiquitous in the theory of 2nd rank relaxation processes*		
bpp(x) maximum: Location x_{max}	0.615 795 146 961 756 244 755 982 ...	bpp(x) being an odd function; there is a minimum at -x_{max}
bpp(x) maximum: Value at x_{max}	1.425 175 719 086 501 535 329 674 ...	For first term only: $bpp_{1,max}(y)$ = 0.5, for y = 1
Exponential settling *(relaxation) to an equilibrium of a physical system with a characteristic settling time T*		
Settling time to 10%, in units of T	2.302 585 092 994 045 684 017 991 •••	log(10). Settling level equals initial_deviation/final_deviation

... to 1% (10^{-2})	4.605 170 185 988 091 368 035 982 •••	log(100)
... to 0.1% (10^{-3})	6.907 755 278 982 137 052 053 974 ...	log(1000)
... to 100 ppm (10^{-4}, 1000 ppm)	9.210 340 371 976 182 736 071 965 ...	log(10^4)
... to 10 ppm (10^{-5})	11.512 925 464 970 228 420 089 957 ...	log(10^5)
... to 1 ppm (10^{-6})	13.815 510 557 964 274 104 107 948 ...	log(10^6)
... to 1 ppb (10^{-9})	20.723 265 836 946 411 156 161 923 ...	log(10^9)
Settling level after 1 T	0.367 879 441 171 442 321 595 523 •••	After time t = n*T exp(-1), the settling level equals exp(-n).
... 2 T	0.135 335 283 236 612 691 893 999 •••	3 T: 0.049 787 068 367 863 942 979 342 •••
... 4 T	0.018 315 638 888 734 180 293 718 •••	5 T: 0.006 737 946 999 085 467 096 636 •••
... 6 T	0.002 478 752 176 666 358 423 045 •••	7 T: 0.000 911 881 965 554 516 208 003 ...

Statistics and probability constants

Normal probability distribution *with mean μ and variance σ. Density N(x,σ,μ) = exp(-((x-μ)/σ)^2 /2) / (σ√(2π)):*

Density maximum * σ	0.398 942 280 401 432 677 939 946 •••	1/√(2π), attained at x = 0
$E[x^{2n}]$ /$σ^{2n}$, for μ=0, n =	1, 1, 3, 15, 105, 945, 10395, 135135,	= (2*n-1)!!. Note: $E[x^n]$ is zero for odd n.

0,1,2,...	•••	
$E[\|x\|^{2n-1}] * \sqrt{2*\pi} / \sigma^{2*n-1}$, for $\mu=0$, $n = 1,2,3,...$	2, 4, 16, 96, 768, 7680, 92160, 1290240, •••	= $(n-1)! * 2^n$. Note: $E[\|x\|^{2n}]$ values match the entry above.
Entropy - $\log(\sigma)$	1.418 938 533 204 672 741 780 329 •••	= $(1+\log(2\pi))/2$, independent of μ.
Percentiles: x/σ for which $I_{t=-\infty,x}\{N(t,\sigma)\} = P$, $I_{t=-x,x}\{N(t,\sigma)\} = 2P-1$		
75%	0.674 489 750 196 081 743 202 227 •••	Probable error: x/σ for which $I_{t=-x,x}\{N(t,\sigma)\} = 0.5$
80%	0.841 621 233 572 914 205 178 706 ...	85% ... 1.036 433 389 493 789 579 713 244 ...
90%	1.281 551 565 544 600 466 965 103 ...	95% ... 1.644 853 626 951 472 714 863 848 ...
98%	2.053 748 910 631 823 052 937 351 ...	99% ... 2.326 347 874 040 841 100 885 606 ...
99.9%	3.090 232 306 167 813 541 540 399 ...	99.99% ... 3.719 016 485 455 680 564 393 660 ...
99.999%	4.264 890 793 922 824 628 498 524 ...	99.9999% ... 4.753 424 308 822 898 948 193 988 ...
Probability that a random value superates n standard deviations, $p_n = 0.5 * \mathrm{erfc}(n/\sqrt{2})$. Equals $P\{x/\sigma > n\}$ or $P\{x/\sigma < -n\}$, which is half of $P\{\|x/\sigma\| > n\}$:		
$n = 1$	0.158 655 253 931 457 051 414 767 •••	$n = 2$ ... 0.022 750 131 948 179 207 200 282 •••
$n = 3$	0.001 349 898 031 630 094 526 651 •••	$n = 4$ ... 0.000 031 671 241 833 119 921 253 •••
$n = 5$	0.000 000 286 651 571 879 193 911 •••	$n = 6$ ... 0.000 000 000 986 587 645 037 698 •••

Engineering constants;

Amplitude / Effective_ Amplitude	1.414 213 562 373 095 048 801 688 •••	$\sqrt{2}$, holds only for harmonic functions
Power factor of 2 (or 0.5) in dB	±3.010 299 956 639 811 952 137 388 •••	$\pm 10.\text{Log}(2)$; corresponding amplitudes ratio is $\sqrt{2}$: 1
Amplitude factor of 2 (or 0.5) in dB	±6.020 599 913 279 623 904 274 777 •••	$\pm 20.\text{Log}(2)$

±1 dB ratios:

Power	1.258 925 411 794 167 210 423 954 •••	$10^{+1/10}$
Inverse power	0.794 328 234 724 281 502 065 918 ...	$10^{-1/10}$
Amplitude	1.122 018 454 301 963 435 591 038 •••	$10^{+1/20}$
Inverse amplitude	0.891 250 938 133 745 529 953 108 ...	$10^{-1/20}$

±3 dB ratios:

Power	1.995 262 314 968 879 601 352 455 ...	$10^{+3/10}$ +3 dB in power or +6 dB in amplitude
Inverse power	0.501 187 233 627 272 285 001 554 ...	$10^{-3/10}$ -3 dB in power or -6 dB in amplitude
Amplitude	1.412 537 544 622 754 302 155 607 ...	$10^{+3/20}$
Inverse amplitude	0.707 945 784 384 137 910 802 214 ...	$10^{-3/20}$

Music and acoustics:		
Half-note frequency ratio	1.059 463 094 359 295 264 561 825 •••	$2^{1/12}$
Perfect fifth ratio	3/2, exact	also 2/3
Pythagorean comma	1.013 643 264 770 507 8125	$(3/2)^{12}/2^7$, frequency ratio of 12 perfect fifth to 7 octaves
Rumors constant	0.203 187 869 979 979 953 838 479 •••	Solution of $x.e^2 = e^{2x}$. Appears in the statistical theory of noise.
Software and computer engineering constants		
Decadic-to-binary precision/capacity factor	3.321 928 094 887 362 347 870 319 •••	$\log_2(10)$; Example: 7 decadic digits require 23+ binary bits
Binary-to-decadic precision/capacity factor	0.301 029 995 663 981 195 213 738 •••	$\text{Log}(2)$; Example: 31 binary bits require 9+ decimal digits
Unsigned integer data types *maximum values (for* **signed integers** *see the 3rd column)*		
byte (8 bits) 2^8-1	255	signed max = 2^7-1 = +127
word (16 bits) 2^16-1	65'535	signed max = 2^15-1 = +32'767
dword (double word, 32 bits) 2^32-1	4'294'967'295	signed max = 2^31-1 = +2'147'483'647
qword (quad word, 64 bits) 2^64-1	18'446'744'073'709'551'615	signed max = 2^63-1 = +9'223'372'036'854'775'807
Bit configurations which **can't be used as signed integers** *since, though formally negative, aritmetic negation returns the same value (***weird numbers***)*		
8 bits	hex 0x80	signed -2^7 = -128

16 bits	hex 0x8000	signed -2^15 = -32'768
32 bits	hex 0x80000000	signed -2^31 = -2'147'483'648
64 bits	hex 0x8000000000000000	signed -2^63 = -9'223'372'036'854'775'808
Floating point data types. *The epsilon value is the precision limit, such that, for $x < \varepsilon$, $1+\varepsilon$ returns 1*		
float (1+8+23 bits): **Maximum** value	3.40282366920938463463746...e+38	2^(2^(8-1)); IEEE 754; bits are for: sign, exponent, mantissa
float (1+8+23 bits): **minimum** value	1.40129846432481707092372 9...e-45	2*2^(-2^(8-1))*2^(-(23-1))
float (1+8+23 bits): **epsilon** value	1.1920928955078125 e-7	2^(-23)
double (1+11+52 bits): **Maximum** value	1.79769313486231590772930...e+308	2^(2^(11-1)); IEEE 754; bits are for: sign, exponent, mantissa
double (1+11+52 bits): **minimum** value	4.94065645841246544176568...e-324	2*2^(-2^(11-1))*2^(-(52-1))
double (1+11+52 bits): **epsilon** value	2.22044604925031308084726 3...e-16	2^(-52)
long double (1+15+64 bits): **Maximum** value	1.18973149535723176508575 9...e+4932	2^(2^(15-1)); internal 10-byte format of Intel "coprocessor"
long double (1+15+64 bits): **minimum** value	1.82259976594123730126420 2...e-4951	2*2^(-2^(15-1))*2^(-(64-1))
long double (1+15+64 bits): **epsilon** value	5.42101008624275221700372 6...e-20	2^(-64)
Conversion constants		
Conversions between logarithms in bases **e** *(natural), 10 (decadic), and 2 (binary).*		

log(2), Natural logarithm of 2	0.693 147 180 559 945 309 417 232 ••• #t	Solution of $e^x = 2$
Log(2), Decadic logarithm of 2	0.301 029 995 663 981 195 213 738 •••	Solution of $10^x = 2$
log(10), Natural logarithm of 10	2.302 585 092 994 045 684 017 991 •••	Solution of $e^x = 10$
$\log_2(10)$, Binary logarithm of 10	3.321 928 094 887 362 347 870 319 •••	Solution of $2^x = 10$
Log(e), Decadic logarithm of e	0.434 294 481 903 251 827 651 128 •••	Solution of $10^x = e$
$\log_2(e)$, Binary logarithm of e	1.442 695 040 888 963 407 359 924 •••	Solution of $2^x = e$

Plane angles. *Radians (rad) and degrees (deg) are* **plane angles**

1 rad in **degs**	57.295 779 513 082 320 876 798 15 •••	$180/\pi$ = 57° 17' 44.80624709635515647335 7330..."
1 deg in **rads**	0.017 453 292 519 943 295 769 237 •••	$\pi/180$
1 rad in **arcmin**	3437,746 770 784 939 252 607 889 ...	$60*(180/\pi)$
1 arcmin in **rads**	2.908 882 086 657 215 961 539... e-4	$(\pi/180)/60$
1 rad in **arcsec**	206264,806 247 096 355 156 473 357 •••	$60*60*(180/\pi)$
1 arcsec in **rads**	4.848 136 811 095 359 935 899 ••• e-6	$(\pi/180)/60/60$

Solid angles. *Steradians (sr), square radians (rad^2), and square degrees (deg^2) are* **areas on a unit sphere**.

Full solid angle of 4π steradians in deg^2	41252.961 249 419 271 031 294 671 •••	$4\pi/(\pi/180)^2 = 360^2/\pi$
1 sr in deg^2	3282.806 350 011 743 794 781 694 •••	$(180/\pi)^2$; exact for infinitesimal areas
1 deg^2 in **sr**	0.000 304 617 419 786 708 599 346 •••	$(\pi/180)^2$; exact for infinitesimal areas; inverse of the above
1 sr in rad^2	1.041 191 803 606 873 340 234 607 •••	$2*asin(\sqrt{(sin(1/4))})$

References

1. Andreescu Titu, Andrica Dorin,
    Number Theory: Structures, Examples, and Problems,
    Birkhauser 2009. ISBN 978-0817632458.
2. Caldwell Chris K., Honaker Jr. G.L.,
    Prime Curios! The Dictionary of Prime Number Trivia,
    CreateSpace Independent 2009. ISBN 978-1448651702.
3. Clawson Calvin C., ***Mathematical Mysteries: The Beauty and Magic of Numbers***,
    Basic Books 1999. ISBN 978-0738202594.
4. Das Abhijit,
    Computational Number Theory,
    Chapman and Hall/CRC 2013. ISBN 978-1439866153.
5. Finch S.R., ***Mathematical Constants***,
    Cambridge University Press 2003. ISBN 978-0521818056..
6. Hardy G.H, Wright E.M., ***An Introduction to the Theory of Numbers***,
    6th Edition, Oxford University Press 2009. ISBN 978-0199219865.
7. Knuth D.E., ***The Art of Computer Programming***
    Volume 1: Fundamental Algorithms. ISBN 978-0201896831.
    Volume 2: Seminumerical Algorithms, ISBN 978-0201896848.. See Section 3.3.3, Eq.41, for *Knuth's constant*.
    Volume 3: Sorting and Searching, ISBN 978-0201896855.
    Addison-Wesley 1997 (Vol.3, 1998).

8. Mazur Berry, Stein William,
    Prime Numbers and the Riemann Hypothesis,
    Cambridge University Press 2015. ISBN 978-1107499430.

9. Muller Jean-Michel, Brisebarre Nicolas, de Dinechin Florent, Jeannerod Claude-Pierre, Lefèvre Vincent, Melquiond Guillaume,
    Handbook of Floating-Point Arithmetic,
    Birkhäuser Boston 2009. ISBN 978-0817647049.

10. Murty M. Ram, Rath Purusottam,
    Transcendental Numbers,
    Springer 2014. ISBN 978-1493908318..

11. Pickover Clifford A.,
    The Mathematics Devotional: Celebrating the Wisdom and Beauty of Mathematics,
    Sterling 2014. ISBN 978-1454913221..

12. Pickover Clifford A.,
    A Passion for Mathematics: Numbers, Puzzles, Madness, Religion, and the Quest for Reality,
    Wiley 2005. ISBN 978-0471690986..

13. Pickover Clifford A.,
    Wonders of Numbers: Adventures in Mathematics, Mind, and Meaning,
    Oxford University Press 2002. ISBN 978-0195157994.

14. Vazzana Anthony, Garth David,
    Introduction to Number Theory,
    Chapman and Hall/CRC 2015. ISBN 978-1498717496.